C

FATAL
TERRAIN

DALE BROWN

FATAL

TERRAIN

HarperCollins*Publishers*

HarperCollins*Publishers*
77–85 Fulham Palace Road,
Hammersmith, London W6 8JB

Published by HarperCollins*Publishers* 1997
1 3 5 7 9 8 6 4 2

First published in the USA by
G. P. Putnam's Sons 1997

A catalogue record for this book
is available from the British Library

ISBN 0 00 225452 2
ISBN 0 00 225575 8 (Special Trade Paperback)

Set in Simoncini Garamond

Printed and bound in Great Britain by
Caledonian International Book Manufacturing Ltd, Glasgow

···· ACKNOWLEDGMENTS

Thanks to Harold J. Hough, military technology journalist and author of *Satellite Surveillance,* for his help in researching modern Chinese military capabilities and strategies.

A valuable resource on ancient Chinese military thought from which some of the quotations in this book were taken is *The Seven Military Classics of Ancient China,* translated by Ralph D. Sawyer (Boulder, CO: Westview Press, 1993).

To Diane: Thanks for starting the adventure with me.

Please leave your comments and suggestions for me at:

ReaderMail@Megafortress.com

or visit my Web site at: http://www.Megafortress.com.

I promise to read everyone's comments, but due to the tremendous number of messages I receive, it may take a while to reply. Thanks!

JANE'S INTELLIGENCE REVIEW, SPECIAL REPORT #7, "Territorial Disputes," 1995—There is one particular instance of an island dispute which could certainly prove very dangerous—the island of Taiwan. There is no doubt that China is very sensitive to any possibility that Taiwan may drift into complete independence from the mainland . . .

Should Taiwan be seen to embark on the course of independence, China would almost certainly use force to stop it, and full-scale war could easily result . . .

. . . Many analysts believe this to be the most serious long-term threat to Asia's security . . .

"PRESCRIPTION FOR PEACE AND PROSPERITY"–speech by former British Prime Minister Margaret Thatcher, 17 January 1996, Taipei, Taiwan—The principle of the balance of power, in which several weaker forces combine to counterbalance a stronger one, is often underrated. In fact it makes for stability. But there also has to be one global power, a military power of last resort, to ensure that regional disputes do not escalate to uncontainable levels. That power is and can only be the United States. It is in all our interests to keep her committed to upholding international order, which means remaining a Pacific and indeed a European power.

That requires encouragement and support from America's allies and those who benefit from America's presence. It would have been a rash person who would have predicted at the end of the Vietnam War that America would still have substantial forces in Asia two decades later. But thank goodness America has had the stamina and resolve to stay because its presence is the critical element in the Asian security equation . . .

BEIJING WARNS U.S. IT'S READY TO ATTACK TAIWAN–01/24/96–New York—Reuters—China has warned the United States it has completed plans for a limited attack on Taiwan that could be launched in the weeks after Taiwan's president wins an election in March, the *New York Times* reported on Wednesday.

However, a senior U. S. official was quoted by the *New York Times* as saying the Clinton administration had "no independent confirmation or even credible evidence" that Beijing was considering an attack.

The *New York Times* report from Beijing said the most direct warning was conveyed through former U.S. Assistant Secretary of Defense Chas Freeman, who held discussions this winter with senior Chinese officials.

Freeman told National Security Advisor Anthony Lake that the Chinese army had prepared plans for a missile attack against Taiwan at one strike a day for 30 days, the newspaper said.

BEIJING REAFFIRMS CLAIM TO ROC AS "PART OF CHINA" (JAN 30/DPA)–Beijing—DPA—Taiwan is an "inalienable part" of China, Chinese Prime Minister Li Peng said Tuesday on the anniversary marking the reunification initiative of state and party head Jiang Zemin.

"There is only one China in the world and Taiwan is an inalienable part of it," Li said. "Whatever changes might occur in the way in which the leadership in Taiwan is chosen, they cannot change the fact that Taiwan is a part of China and its leaders are only leaders of a region." Li warned, however, against using a change of government leaders in Taiwan as an excuse to put their separatist activities in legal guise.

PERRY DECLINES TO SAY THAT U.S. WOULD DEFEND TAIWAN (Feb 7/Blmbrg)—Washington (Feb 6)—Bloomberg—U.S. Defense Secretary William Perry declined today to say the U.S. would definitely defend Taiwan if that country is attacked by China.

How the U.S. would respond to such an attack "depends very much on the circumstances" that prompted the incident, Perry said during a speech at the Washington Institute here today. His speech was broadcast throughout the Pentagon.

Perry said the Taiwan Relations Act continues to guide U.S. policy. That 1979 U.S. law doesn't require the U.S. to defend Taiwan if Taiwan is attacked. The act does say the U.S. would consider an attack on Taiwan "a threat to the peace and security of the Western Pacific area and of grave concern to the United States."

JANE'S INTELLIGENCE REVIEW, "China's View of Strategic Weapons," March 1996—Since its first nuclear detonation in 1964, China has maintained a declaratory policy not to use nuclear weapons first . . . But should the threat of defeat become real, all bets are off. Presumably since nuclear strikes [against Taiwan] would be taking place "within China's borders," this is considered to be technically a non-violation of nuclear declaratory policy.

DEFENSE & FOREIGN AFFAIRS HANDBOOK (London: International Media Corp. Ltd., 1996)—It became clear, however, as the elections in the ROC [Republic of China] approached, that the PRC [People's Republic of China] was not, in reality, ready for a conventional invasion of Taiwan . . . The only option open to the PRC to achieve its objective would be a full missile bombardment of Taiwan, using nuclear weapons. The PRC made it clear that this was not ruled out; and, if the U.S. interfered in this "domestic" matter, then a nuclear strike by PRC ICBMs on U.S. cities, such as Los Angeles, could not be discounted . . .

B-52 MISSION SHOWS GLOBAL REACH, AIR FORCE SAYS, by Bryan Bender, 09/05/96, Phillips Business Information, Inc. (used with permission)—The effective use of two Air Force B-52 bombers that fired 13 of the 27 cruise missiles in the first attack on Iraqi air defenses Tuesday demonstrated the viability of the service's post–Cold War strategy of striking anywhere at any time, according to the mission commander.

The bombers from the 96th Bomb Squadron left Barksdale AFB, La., Monday for Andersen AFB, Guam, where they then launched the Operation Desert Strike mission.

The 34-hour, 13,600-mile mission—which included four midair refuelings—"proved the concept" of global reach and global power, or being able to launch assets on short notice—in this case from the United States—at targets across the world, Lt. Col. Floyd Carpenter, also commander of the 96th Bomb Squadron, told reporters late Tuesday after returning with his crew to Guam.

"We can reach out and touch people if we need to," he said in a telephone interview. . . .

. . . Carpenter added that he and his crew would be ready to launch another mission—if directed—just 12 hours after completion of the first mission . . .

"**Where if your enemy
fights with intensity he will
survive but if not he will
perish, it is called
'fatal terrain.'
On fatal terrain,
always engage in battle.**"

—SUN-TZU,
Chinese military theoretician,
from his essays
The Art of War

PROLOGUE

NATIONAL ASSEMBLY HALL, GOVERNMENT HOUSE,
TAIPEI, REPUBLIC OF CHINA
SUNDAY, 18 MAY 1997, 1900 HOURS LOCAL
(17 MAY, 0700 HOURS ET)

The fistfight broke out as suddenly as a thunderclap. Several men and women leaped over seats to clutch at those who dared disagree with them or support another side over theirs. Railings and seats were used as ladders to try to get at one another, and the entire crowd seemed to surge forward like a pack of wolves on the attack.

The scene resembled an unruly crowd at a World Cup soccer match, or a riot in South Central—but this was a special session of the National Assembly of the government of the Republic of China on Taiwan.

The president *pro tem* of the National Assembly hammered his gavel, trying to restore order. He glanced over at the national guard troops peeking through the window in the back of the chamber, ready to burst in if necessary. He heard breaking glass and almost hit the panic button, but stayed calm and watched nervously as the noisy politicians surged forward. It took nearly thirty minutes to restore some level of calm, and another ten minutes for the legislators to clear the aisles enough so the

National Police could escort the president of the Republic of China, Lee Teng-hui, to the podium.

"My fellow citizens, your attention, please. I am pleased to announce the results of the ratification vote of the Legislative Branch, which was taken just a few hours ago," President Lee began. "By a vote of two hundred seventy-one for, thirty against, three abstaining, Mr. Huang Chouming is hereby approved by the people of the Republic of Taiwan to serve as vice president and premier. Mr. Huang, step forward, please."

Amid renewed cheering and yelling, mostly from the left side of the hall, the new premier of the Republic of China stepped up to the dais and accepted the green-and-gold sash of office. Huang was a major figure in the Democratic Progressive Party (DPP), and his election to the number-two position in the Taiwanese government was significant—it was the first major advance of a non–Kuomintang (KMT) Party member in the country's short history. Although the Kuomintang still held a solid majority in all branches of the Taiwanese government, the advancement of the DPP was a major shift from nearly fifty years of KMT philosophy and control.

The shouting, cheering, celebrations, and accusations suddenly and violently turned into another brawl on the floor of the National Assembly. While bodyguards surrounded the president and vice president, members of Taiwan's National Assembly ran up and down the aisles, stood on desks, and screamed at each other; several members were up on the dais near the president, fighting with one another to decide who would speak with the president first. Members of the National Police Administration, charged with the protection of government buildings and property and who acted as security guards in the National Assembly chamber, had moved into the chamber itself and stood stock-still along the outer aisles of the Assembly chamber, long cane batons nearly invisible at their sides and tear-gas canisters safely tucked away inside their tunics. They did nothing but watch with stone-expressionless faces while the fights and bedlam raged all around them.

"My fellow citizens," President Lee tried. His voice, even amplified, was barely heard. He waited patiently for any sign that the near-riot was subsiding. He heard clothing rip just a few paces away from him—the fight had somehow moved up to the dais, where police were trying to keep Assembly members from reaching the president and new premier— and decided that he needed to wait a few moments longer. He had a pistol tucked away in a holster inside his pants at the small of his back, and Lee considered firing a shot in the air to get everyone's attention, but quickly decided that a gunshot might just make this place explode.

The Taiwanese National Assembly was composed of members elected for life. Since most of the membership had been elected to their post in 1948, prior to the Communist overthrow of the Nationalist Party on the mainland, there were some very old gentlemen here in the Assembly Hall. But the old goats, Lee noticed, were arguing and fighting just as hard as the more newly elected members—they just had less endurance. The hall was splitting into two distinct sections, a normal and common occurrence here in the National Assembly. The largest group was the Kuomintang, along with their nominal allies the New Party, the Young China Party, and the Chinese Democratic Socialist Party. On the other side were the members of the Democratic Progressive Party, a more liberal and modern-thinking political party filled with young, energetic, rather idealistic members. Although the right side of the hall, filled with KMT members and supporters, was much larger, both sides were equally boisterous.

"My fellow citizens, please," Lee tried again. When he realized there was no response to his pleas, Lee finally ordered the police to step in. Order was quickly restored. "Thank you. We will now proceed with the main piece of business on tonight's agenda." Huang respectfully stepped behind and to Lee's right; this simple action got the Assembly's attention right away, and the chamber quieted. Lee quickly continued: "This election also signals a unity of purpose and policy within our government, my friends, a union between rival patriotic groups that has been much too long in the making. Our newfound coalition between the KMT and DPP forms the basis of our pride in our accomplishments and our standing in the world community. It is time for our unity, our pride, to be brought forth upon the world for all to see."

President Lee let the loud applause continue for a few long moments; then: "With humble pride and great joy, Premier Huang and I hereby bring to the floor of the National Assembly a bill, drafted by the Central Standing Committee of the Kuomintang, amended by the Legislative Yuan Major Constitutional Committee, and passed this date unanimously by the Legislative Branch, to amend the constitution of the Republic of China. It is now up to us to ratify this constitutional amendment.

"The bill amends the constitution by proclaiming that the Republic of China, including the island archipelagoes of Formosa, Quemoy, Matsu, Makung, Taiping, and Tiaoyutai, is now and forever shall be a separate, sovereign, and independent nation, subordinate or component to none. The people of the Republic of China hereby renounce all allegiance and ties to land, title, property, legal claims, and jurisdiction to the mainland. Our prayers will always be that we are someday reunited with our motherland, but until that day comes, we hereby proclaim that the Republic of China is a separate nation, with all the rights and responsibilities of free and sovereign nations anywhere in the world. The bill is hereby submitted for a vote. May I please have a second?"

"I proudly second the motion," the new premier, Huang Chou-ming, shouted, which lifted the applause to a new, outrageous level. Huang and the DPP had been fighting for such a declaration of independence for many years, and their victory in getting this legislation passed and onto the Assembly floor was the most significant event in the history of the Nationalist Chinese.

The introduction of this bill meant that the Kuomintang's basic philosophy of one China, introduced by Dr. Sun Yat-sen as he and Nationalist General Chiang Kai-shek fought to liberate China from the grasp of the Japanese empire after World Wars I and II, and proclaimed ever since the Nationalists were pushed off the mainland to the island of Taiwan by the Communists in 1949, was effectively dead. There had always been a hope that the Nationalists could somehow liberate the mainland from the dark clutches of communism, now the government and the people were saying that hope was moot. Mainland China could someday join in the prosperity and power of the Republic of China—but until then, Taiwan was in control of its own destiny.

The cheering in the Assembly hall was deafening; the applause and demonstrations in the aisles lasted for nearly ten minutes. There was still a small group of KMT members opposed to the amendment, and they tried to start another fight on the Assembly floor, but their anger and outrage could not undo years of Lee's gentle persuasiveness and coalition-building efforts.

But it was more than releasing an improbable dream. It was an assertion, a declaration to the world, and especially to the gargantuan presence known as the People's Republic of China, that the Republic of China on Taiwan was taking its rightful place on the world stage. Taiwan was no longer a breakaway republic of China; the ROC was no longer a rebel government. It had the strongest economy in Asia, the ninth-largest economy on the planet, and the largest deposits of foreign currencies in the world. Now it was a sovereign nation. No one was going to take any of that away from them.

It took an entire hour for the votes to be cast, but the results were finally tallied and the announcement was made, soon for all the world to hear: independence.

SOUTHBEACH, OREGON
SATURDAY, 17 MAY 1997, 0415 HOURS PT
(0715 HOURS ET)

As he had done for the past thirty-two years of his life, the retired U.S. Air Force general was up at four A.M., without the assistance of an aide, an operator, or even an alarm clock. He was a man who had always *set* the agenda, not followed those of others. He was accustomed to having everyone else get moving on *his* timetable.

But now no one in a base command center was waiting for him, there were no "dawn patrol" missions to fly, no world crisis that had to be analyzed so a response could be planned. His uniform now was not a green Nomex flight suit or freshly pressed blue wool class A's, but a flannel shirt, thermal underwear—one of innumerable pairs he had used in his flying days, in aircraft where keeping the electronics warm was more important than keeping the humans warm—hunting socks, hip waders, an old olive-drab nylon flying jacket, and an old Vietnam-era camouflage floppy "boonie hat" with spinners and lures stuck in it. He didn't know that all those things in his hat had nothing to do with open-sea fishing, but it didn't matter—it was part of the "uniform."

By force of habit, he put the hardened polycarbonate Timex aviator's watch on his left wrist, although his own internal body clock was all he needed now; and he plucked the cellular phone from its recharging cradle, turned it on, and stuck it in his fanny pack, although no one ever called him and he had no one to call. For a long, long time, since assuming his first command more than twenty years before, leaving his quarters without a portable radio or a cell phone and pager had been unthinkable, and such habits die hard. The cell phone was something of a link to his old life, his old base of power. The old life had been stripped away from him, but he would not let it go completely.

The weather in Oregon's central coast matched the man's mood—gray, cloudy, and a little depressing. The man had spent many years in the Southwest, especially southern Nevada, where they had more than three hundred clear, sunny days a year. Many times he cursed the sun and the oppressive heat it brought—one-hundred-degree days in April, lots of ninety-degree midnights, terrible jet performance especially in the high deserts—but right now a little sun and warmth would be very welcome. It was not looking good—typical low overcast, drizzle with occasional light rain, winds out of the southwest fairly light at ten knots but threatening to increase, as they usually did, to thirty to forty knots by afternoon.

Not ideal fishing weather, but what the hell—nothing else to do except sit around and look at the mountain of unpacked boxes still cluttering his little mobile home in Southbeach, an isolated vacation and retirement village on Oregon's central coast, about eighty miles southwest of Portland. The Air Force–contracted movers had delivered his household goods seven months before, but there they sat, virtually untouched. He saw a small hole the size of a pencil in the corner of one box marked "Memorabilia" and wondered if the mice were enjoying nibbling on the plaques, awards, photos, and mementos he had stuffed in there. At least someone was enjoying them.

The man decided just to get the hell out and do what he had planned to do, and to hell with the bad memories and bitterness. Concentrating on his boat, the sea, and staying alive on the cold waters of coastal Oregon in freshening breezes would take his mind off the neglected remnants of the life that had been taken away from him. The prospect of catching a glimpse of a migrating pod of whales filled him with a sense of excitement, and soon he was speeding down the long gravel driveway, eagerly looking forward to getting on the water.

It was a short drive north on Highway 101 to the marina, just south of the Yaquina Bay bridge. The marina's general store had just opened, so he had his thermos filled with coffee, his cooler packed full of orange juice, fresh and dried fruit, and some live sardines for bait—he didn't have the money to buy live mackerel or squid, which would really improve his chances. What he knew about fishing would embarrass himself if he tried to talk about it, but it didn't matter—if he caught anything, which was unlikely these days in the fished-out waters of central Oregon, he would probably let it go. He filled out a slip of paper that explained where he was headed and how long he was going to be out—somewhat akin to filing a flight plan before a sortie—stuck the paper in the "Gone Fishin'" box near the door on his way out, and headed for the piers.

His boat was a thirty-year-old thirty-two-foot Grand Banks Sedan, bought with most of his savings and the sixty days' worth of unused accumulated leave time he had sold back to the United States Air Force. Made of Philippine mahogany instead of fiberglass, the heavy little trawler was easy enough to handle solo, and stable in seas up to about five feet. It had a single Lehman diesel engine, covered flybridge, a good-size fishing cockpit aft, a large salon with lower helm station, settee, and galley, and a forward cabin with a head/shower and a V-berth with decent but fish-smelling foam cushions. He turned on the marine band radio and got the weather and sea states from WX1, the Newport Coast Guard weather band, while he pulled off the canvas covers, checked his equipment and made ready to get under way—he still called it "preflighting" his ship, although the fastest he'd fly would be ten knots—then motored over to the pumps, filled the fuel and water tanks, and headed out of the marina into Yaquina Bay and then to the open ocean.

There was a very light drizzle and a fresh breeze blowing, but the man did make his way up to the flybridge to get a better feel for the sea. Visibility was about three to five miles offshore, but the Otter Rock light was visible nine miles north. The waves were maybe a foot, short and choppy, with the first hint of whitecaps, and it was cool and damp—again, typical weather in Oregon for early summer. He headed northwest, using an eyeball bearing off the lighthouse to sail into the fishing area. When he'd first started sailing, he'd brought an entire bag full of electronic satellite navigation gear, backup radios, and charts for almost the entire West Coast with him, because that's how he had prepared for a flying mission. After ten trips, he'd learned to navigate by compass and speedometer and left the GPS satellite navigation gear at home; after fifteen trips, by compass and tachometer and currents; after twenty trips, by compass alone; after twenty-five, by bearings off landmarks; just off feel and birds and whale sightings thereafter. Now, he could sail just about anywhere with confidence and skill.

The man thought that perhaps flying could also be just as uncomplicated and carefree as this, the way pilot-authors Richard Bach and Stephen Coonts wrote about it, but in his ten thousand–plus hours of flying he had never done it that way. Every sortie needed a flight plan, a precise schedule of each and every event and a precise route to follow. Every sortie needed a weather briefing, target study, and a crew briefing, even if the crew had flown that sortie a hundred times before. Hop in and go? Navigate by watching birds and listening for horns? That was for kids, for irresponsible captains. Plan the flight, then fly the plan—that had been the man's motto for decades. Now he followed birds and looked for whales.

Almost an hour later, just as the eastern sky began to show signs of sunrise, the man shut down his engine, threw a sea anchor out by the bow to keep pointed into the wind, poured a cup of coffee, stuck a granola bar in his shirt pocket, and got his gear ready for fishing. Halibut and salmon were running now, and he might get lucky with live sardines on a big hook with one-hundred-pound test and a little weight. He cast out about a hundred feet, couched the pole, set the reel clutch, sat out on deck surveying the horizon . . .

. . . and said aloud, "What in hell am I doing out here? I don't belong here. I hate fishing, I've never caught a damned thing, and I don't know what the hell I'm doing. I like boats, but I've been out here an hour and I'm bored. I'm wet, I'm cold, I'm miserable, and I feel like tying the fucking anchor around my neck and seeing exactly how long I can hold my breath underwater. I feel like shit. I feel like—"

And then the cell phone rang.

At first he was surprised at the sudden, unexpected noise. Then he was angry at the intrusion. Then he was curious—who knew his number? He'd left his home number on the little slip of paper at the general store, not the cell phone number. He was even outside max range of the Newport cell site—he didn't think he could get calls way out here. Puzzled and still a bit peeved, he retrieved the phone from his fanny pack, flipped it open, and growled, "Who the hell is this?"

"Good morning, General. How are you, sir?"

He recognized the voice immediately, of course, and it was as if the sun had just popped out and the skies had turned clear and blue, even though it was still gray and cold and wet out here. The man opened his mouth to ask a question, answered it himself—dumb question; he *knew* they could find his number easily enough if they wanted—so remained silent.

"How are you doing, sir?" the voice repeated.

Always friendly, always disarming, always at ease, the man thought.

This was obviously some kind of business call, but with this guy there was always time for business later. Always so damned polite, too. You work with a guy for, what, almost ten years, and even though there's an age and rank difference you expect to be on a first-name basis and can the "sir" stuff. Not this guy, at least most of the time. "Fine . . . good," Brad replied. "I'm doing . . . okay."

"Any luck out there?"

He knew I was out fishing? That was odd. It was no state secret or anything, but he hadn't told anybody he was fishing, or given out his phone numbers, or even told anyone he was living in a little trailer in Nowhere, Oregon. "No," Brad replied.

"Too bad," the voice on the phone said, "but I got an idea. Want to do some flying?"

The sun that had come out in his heart a few moments before was now setting his soul on fire, and Brad fairly leapt to his feet. The waders suddenly felt as if they weighed a thousand pounds. "What's going on?" Brad asked excitedly. "What are you up to now?"

"Look to the south and find out."

Brad did—and saw nothing. He had a brief, sinking feeling that this was all a hoax, some complicated and brutal joke . . .

. . . but then he felt it, that sound, that feeling. It was a change in the atmosphere, an electricity flowing through the air stirring and ionizing the moist sea breeze. It felt like an electric current flowing through nearby high-tension power lines, a snap of unseen force that made little hairs stand up on your skin. Then you feel the air pressure rising, of a thin column of air being pushed ahead like air streaming out of a giant hypodermic needle aimed right at you, the plunger being pushed by what could very well be God's thumb, but was, Brad knew, a very human construct . . .

. . . and then the overcast parted and the clouds disgorged a huge black aircraft. It was low, pointed, and very deadly-looking. Brad expected it to roar past him, but instead it hissed by like a giant ebony viper on the move across a jungle floor. Only when the monstrous vehicle had zoomed past him, barely a hundred feet above the Pacific and almost directly overhead, could he hear the thunder of its eight turbofan engines . . . no, Brad realized with faint shock, not eight, only *four* engines, but four *huge* engines. The aircraft banked hard to the left, showing its long, thin fuselage, its long, low, swept-back V-tail ruddervators, its wide wings tipped with pointed tip tanks—and yes, it carried weapon fairings on its wings, stealthy pods that enclosed externally-carried weapons. It was not only flying, but the damned beautiful creature was *armed*.

"What do you think, Brad?" retired Air Force Lieutenant Colonel Patrick McLanahan asked on the cell phone. "You like it?"

"Like it?" retired Air Force Lieutenant General Bradley James Elliott gasped. "*Like it?* It's the . . ." He had to be careful—last he knew, the EB-52 Megafortress defense-suppression and attack bomber was still highly classified. ". . . it's flying again!"

"It may be the only model flying in a few months, Brad," McLanahan said. "The Air Force let us play with a couple. We need crews to fly them and commanders to organize a new unit. If you're interested, climb aboard the Gulfstream that'll be waiting for you at Newport Municipal in two hours."

"I'll be there!" Elliott shouted as the Megafortress climbed back into the overcast and disappeared from view. "I'll be there! Don't you dare leave without me!" Bradley James Elliott dropped the phone onto the deck, quickly stepped forward to the bow, began reeling in the sea anchor, swore because it wasn't coming in fast enough, then simply detached it from the bow cleat and dropped it overboard. He did the same with the fishing rod. The cold diesel engine was cranky and wouldn't start on the third try, but thankfully it started on the fourth, because Elliott was ready to jump out and run all the way back to Newport. After seeing the Megafortress again, a *new* Megafortress, he felt light and happy enough to give walking on water a try.

It was back. It was really back . . . and so, with the grace of God, was he.

OVER THE SOUTH CHINA SEA, TWO HUNDRED MILES
SOUTHWEST OF PRATAS ISLAND
SUNDAY, 18 MAY 1997, 2200 HOURS LOCAL
(17 MAY, 1300 HOURS ET)

"Doors coming open! Stand by! All hands, secure loose items and prepare for exposure!"

The rear cargo doors of the Yunshuji-8C cargo plane motored open at one hundred and twenty seconds time-to-go in the countdown. Admiral Sun Ji Guoming, deputy chief of staff of the People's Liberation

Army of the People's Republic of China, was standing in the forward section of the cargo plane as the temperature of the cargo hold, already below freezing, suddenly dropped nearly fifty degrees almost in the blink of an eye. The ice-cold wind swirled around the huge cargo hold, tugging at legs and arms as if trying to pull the humans out into the frigid sky. Yes, it was mid-May over the generally warm, relaxing South China Sea, but at 30,000 feet just before midnight, the air, rushing into the plane at over a hundred miles an hour, was still bone-snapping cold. The roar of the Y-8C's four Wojiang-6 turboprops, at 4,250 horsepower per engine, was deafening even in the thin air.

The senior naval officer, like the other engineers and technicians in the cargo bay, was dressed in a sub-Arctic snowsuit, layered over an oceangoing exposure suit that was required to be worn anytime they were flying outside safe gliding range of land. Sun also wore a fur-lined aviation helmet with an oxygen mask and cold-weather anti-fog goggles. Sun marveled at some of the soldiers working on the cargo inside the plane—they wore parkas and boots but no gloves, and they took only occasional gulps of 100-percent oxygen from the masks dangling down on the sides of their faces as they worked. These men, obviously born in the punishing cold and high altitudes of Xizang and Xinjiang Provinces of western China, were very accustomed to working in cold, thin air.

Sun Ji Guoming was one of a rare breed in the People's Liberation Army—a young, intelligent officer with vision. At the age of only fifty-three, Admiral Sun, known as the "Black Tiger" because of his noticeably darker, almost Indian-like complexion, was by far the youngest full flag officer in the history of the People's Republic of China. He was at least fifteen years younger than any other member of the Central Military Commission and thirty years younger than his superior officer, General Chin Po Zihong, the chief of staff. Sun's family were high Party officials—his father, Sun Jian, was minister of the State Science and Technology Commission, in charge of restructuring and modernizing China's vastly outdated telecommunications infrastructure.

But Sun had not earned his post merely by his family's powerful Party connections, but by his utter devotion to the Party and to its leadership, first as commander of the South China Sea Fleet, then as former hard-line premier Li Peng's military advisor, then as chief of staff of the People's Liberation Army Navy (PLAN), and now as first deputy chief of the general staff and certainly its next chief, possibly even the next minister of defense. The Black Tiger was truly one of the fiercest officers in the huge Chinese military.

As deputy chief of staff, Sun's main goal was to modernize the huge People's Liberation Army, to drive it into the twenty-first century. He had been executive officer several years earlier aboard China's most ambitious blue-water naval project, code-named EF5, the destroyer *Hong Lung,* or Red Dragon. The *Hong Lung* was an amazing warship, equal to any other warship owned by any nation on earth. The ship had been the spearhead of an ambitious plan by the chief of staff, High General Chin Po Zihong, to occupy several of the Philippine islands, and had been destroyed in fierce attacks by the United States Air Force and Navy, including bombardment from outer space. But until the final crushing blow, the *Hong Lung* had controlled the sea and airspace in the southern Philippines for hundreds of miles.

That was the kind of military power China needed to succeed in the twenty-first century—and Admiral Sun Ji Guoming was going to make it his career to see to it that China developed the technology to meet the challenges of the future.

"Sixty seconds to release! Navigation data transfer in progress. Pilots, maintain constant heading and airspeed and conform to prelaunch axis limits."

The soldiers backed away from the cargo as the countdown neared an end. Sun did a count of the men in the cargo bay—six had gone in, and he counted six, plus himself. Accidents were easy and common in this kind of work, but it would not look good for an accident to occur with the deputy chief of staff aboard.

"Stand by for release! All hands, prepare for cargo release! Five . . . four . . . three . . . two . . . one . . . zero. Release!" Sun heard several loud *snap!* sounds and a slight burble through the fuselage; then, slowly, the cargo began to roll backward through the cargo bay and out through the open clamshell doors.

The "cargo" was a Chinese M-9 rocket, an intermediate-range ballistic missile. Admiral Sun Ji Guoming, as chief of development for the People's Liberation Army, was conducting yet another experiment on the possible future deployment of the M-series tactical ballistic missiles on nonconventional platforms. For years, other countries had experimented with alternative methods for deploying missiles to make them less vulnerable to counterattack. The most common was rail-garrison or road-mobile launchers, and China relied heavily on these. But although the missiles were transportable, they still needed presurveyed launch points to ensure an accurate position fix for their inertial guidance units, which meant that the launch points could be known and attacked.

The advent of satellite-based positioning and navigation greatly increased the accuracy of military weapons—at any moment, even while moving in an aircraft, it was possible to capture position, speed, and time from the satellites, dump the information to a missile or rocket, and be assured of previously unbelievable accuracy. If the weapon could get position updates from the satellites while in flight—and the M-9 missile Sun had just launched could do just that—the weapon's accuracy could be improved even more. And if the missile contained a TV camera with a datalink back to the launch aircraft so an operator could lock onto a particular target and steer it right to impact, pinpoint accuracy was possible.

Sun stepped back through the cargo bay, waving away several soldiers who cautioned him not to go back there, and walked right to within a few feet of the edge of the open mouth of the cargo bay. What he saw was absolutely spectacular.

The M-9 missile was suspended vertically below three sixty-foot parachutes, fitted with strobe lights so he could see where they were in the darkness. He knew that as the 14,000-pound missile fell, it was receiving yet another position update from the American Global Positioning System satellite navigation constellation, and gyros were compensating for winds and missile movement, and were aligning the missile as vertically as possible. Sun's cargo plane was about two miles away now—the missile could just barely be seen under the three chutes—when suddenly a long white tongue of fire and smoke appeared from under the parachutes. The three chutes deflated as the weight was taken off the risers, then they cut away completely as the M-9 rose up through the sky.

A perfect launch! Sun had proven—again, for this was his seventh or eighth successful air launch—that it was possible to launch a ballistic missile from a cargo plane. No special aircraft was necessary. Any cargo plane—military or civilian—could do it, with the right modifications. All of the avionics needed to transfer satellite navigation data to the missile was in a "strap-down" container that could be transported with ease and installed in less than an hour.

Sun signaled that he was clear of the opening and that it was safe to close the cargo doors, hurried forward, and entered the air lock leading to the crew cabin. Ignoring the biting cold, he stripped off his gloves and snowsuit as the air lock pressurized, then removed his oxygen mask and helmet, opened the forward air lock door, and entered the launch-control compartment. "Status!" he called out excitedly.

"M-9 is running hot and true," the launch officer replied. "Altitude eighty thousand feet, twenty-nine miles downrange. Datalink active." The officer handed Sun a messageform. "This came in for you while you were aft, sir. Message from headquarters."

Sun took the messageform but did not bother to look at it—he was too excited about the launch. He watched in childlike fascination as the tracking numbers changed, moving his finger along a chart following its position as the missile zoomed northeastward. It was running perfectly.

Minutes later, the M-9 was approaching its target—Tung Ying Dao, what the rebel Nationalist government on the Chinese island province of Formosa called Tungsha Tao. Tung Ying Dao was a large archipelago of islands and reefs in the South China Sea, claimed by Taiwan, about midway between the southern tip of Formosa and Hainan Island, almost two hundred miles east-southeast of Hong Kong. The rebel Taiwanese government had erected several military sites on the largest island, Pratas Island, including U.S.-made Hawk and Taiwanese-made Tien-Kung antiaircraft and Hsiung Feng anti-ship missile sites. The defenses on the island were a great threat to Chinese ships passing between the mainland and the South China Sea, especially ships bound for the Spratly Islands, the archipelago of islands, reefs, and atolls claimed by many western Asian nations.

"M-9 reaching apogee," the technicians reported. "Altitude one hundred fifteen thousand feet, seventy-one miles downrange."

Admiral Sun touched the sensor control, and in a few seconds several white dots appeared on a dark black and green background. This was an infrared image of the scene below from the nose cone of the M-9 missile, beamed to the launch aircraft via radio datalink. Sun magnified the image to maximum and could just barely make out the outline of Pratas Island. Several other large, hot targets, far more intense on the heat-sensitive sensor than the island, showed as well—these were target barges with large diesel heaters set up on them, arrayed around Pratas Island to act as targets for the M-9 missile.

But Sun ignored the target barges. Instead, he locked the targeting bug of the M-9 missile on the northwest section of Pratas Island, where he knew the missile installations were located. The senior technician noted this at once: "Excuse me, Comrade Admiral, but you have locked the missile on the landmass. . . ."

"Yes, I know," Sun replied with a sly smile. "Continue the test."

"Our telemetry systems won't record the impact if it strays more than twenty miles off course," the tech reminded him.

"How long will we have datalink contact before impact?"

"It should hold lock all the way to impact," the tech replied, "although terrain or cultural obstructions may block the signal within approximately eight seconds to impact."

"How far will the missile drift off course in eight seconds?"

"If it stays locked on, it will not drift off course," the tech replied. "If it breaks lock when we lose the datalink . . . it will miss perhaps by not more than a few dozen meters."

"Then I think we will get all the telemetry we need," Sun said. "Continue the test."

The closer the M-9 got to its target, the more detail they could see. Through occasional spats of static and one short nine-second datalink break as the warhead separated from the booster section, Sun could start to make out large buildings, then piers and wharves, then finally individual buildings. Through long hours of study, Sun knew exactly what he was looking at, and as soon as the system allowed him to do so, he locked the warhead on the main barracks building, a two-story wooden frame structure just a few hundred meters from the northwestern shoreline of Pratas Island. Sun knew that approximately a thousand rebel Nationalist soldiers were stationed on Pratas Island, manning and servicing the antiair and -ship sites—and he knew that about one hundred Taiwanese soldiers would be asleep right now in those barracks.

"Twenty seconds to impact," the tech reported. "Uh . . . sir, should we lock on one of the target barges now?"

"Captain, if you dare question my actions ever again, you will be commanding a garbage detail in Inner Mongolia province by tomorrow night," Sun Ji Guoming said in a low voice. "As far as you are aware, I locked the missile warhead's targeting sensor on the primary target barge, and you saw it lock on perfectly as expected. Is that clear, Captain?"

"Yes, *sir,*" the technician responded. He watched in horror as the warhead careened down out of the sky, faster and faster, never wavering—it had held lock all the way until it passed below datalink coverage. The last thing they saw on the TV monitor was the broad, flat roofline of the barracks building. Even if the warhead started to drift, which it didn't, the warhead would not have missed that building full of sleeping soldiers. The warhead had no explosive charge on board, only concrete ballast to simulate a 300-pound high-explosive warhead, but such a large object smashing home at over 900 miles an hour was going to do major damage even without a major explosion. The devastation would be catastrophic—and the rebel Nationalists would never know what hit them.

"Excellent test, comrades, excellent," Admiral Sun announced. "Secure all stations." He remembered the urgent message from Beijing just then, and fished the messageform out of his flight suit pocket and read as he continued, "Section leaders, I expect full reports on any difficulties to me before we land. Pilot, let us head back to base and—"

He stopped, dumbfounded, as he read. No, *no,* this was impossible!

"Cancel that last order, pilot," Sun shouted. "All available speed to Juidongshan naval base. What is our time en route?"

"Stand by, sir," the pilot responded. Sun was in a daze as the pilot, copilot, and flight engineer pulled out charts and started computing the new flight planning information. The three officers looked at each other nervously; then the pilot turned to the navy admiral lower class and said, "Sir, the naval base at Juidongshan does not have a runway long enough to accommodate this aircraft. The closest base that can safely accommodate us is Shantou, ETE, five-zero minutes. We can have a helicopter standing by to take you to Juidongshan, ETE—"

"Pilot, I did not ask you to fly to Shantou," Sun said angrily. "Are the runways and taxiways at Juidongshan stressed to take this aircraft?"

The copilot looked up the information in the airman's flight supplement manual and replied, "Yes, sir, the runways can handle us at minimum gross weight. The taxiways and ramp areas are limited to thirty thousand pounds, so—"

"That is all I need," Sun said. "I do not need you to park this plane— I only require that you drop me off. You can dump fuel as you begin your approach to get down to emergency-landing fuel weight."

"But, sir, the runway is made for only liaison aircraft and helicopters," the flight engineer said. "It is only five thousand feet long! Even with only minimum fuel to reach Shantou, our safe takeoff roll will exceed the runway available by—"

"Lieutenant, I do not care if this plane becomes a permanent fixture at Juidongshan—I want to be on the ground at Juidongshan in less than a hour. If I am not in a car and on my way to headquarters in that time, the next destination you will be landing at will be a security ice cave in Tibet. Now, *go!*"

PEOPLE'S LIBERATION ARMY NAVY EASTERN FLEET
(TAIWAN OPERATIONS) HEADQUARTERS,
JUIDONGSHAN NAVAL BASE, FUJIAN PROVINCE,
PEOPLE'S REPUBLIC OF CHINA
SUNDAY, 18 MAY 1997, 2316 HOURS LOCAL
(17 MAY, 1416 HOURS ET)

"Greetings to you, Comrade Admiral Sun Ji Guoming," General Major Qian Shugeng, the elderly deputy commander for plans of the Military Command Headquarters Targeting Taiwan, said in a low, gravelly voice. "It is a pleasure to present our operational plans to you on behalf of the general staff. I will now turn the briefing over to my young deputy, Colonel Lieutenant Ai Peijian. Colonel Peijian has been most helpful in preparing this briefing for you. He is one of our hardest workers and a true and loyal son of the Party."

The nearly eighty-year-old general officer waved a withered hand to tonight's briefer, Colonel Lieutenant Ai Peijian—"young" in his case meant about age fifty-five—who moved to his feet and bowed respectfully. "Welcome, comrade, to our status briefing regarding our standing war plans for the glorious pacification and reunification with the rebel Nationalist Chinese on the island of Taiwan. Before I begin in detail, I am happy to report that our plans are in perfect order and await only the command from our Paramount Leader to execute the war plan. In less than one week, we can destroy the Nationalists' defenses, capture the Nationalist president and his key advisors and Kuomintang leadership, and start the process of reunification under the Communist Party of China."

"That will be for me and Comrade General Chin to decide, Colonel," Sun said, impatiently waving a hand for the briefing to begin.

Just two minutes into the briefing, Sun knew that not much had been changed—this was the same briefing he had been given every two weeks for the past year now. This military committee—the Operations and Plans Committee, part of the Military Command Headquarters Targeting Taiwan, or MCHTT, based here in Juidongshan—was in charge of continually revising the war plans drawn up by the Central Military Commission, China's main military command body, for the initial attack, invasion, occupation, and subjugation of the rebel Chinese Nationalist government on the island of Formosa. Every two weeks, the MCHTT was required to brief the Central Military Commission or its designated representative—that had been Admiral Sun Ji Guoming for quite some time now—on any changes to the war plan made because of force or command changes on either side.

But it was a farce, typical of the huge, bloated People's Liberation Army bureaucracy, Sun thought. No member of the lowly MCHTT would dare make any substantive changes in the war plans drawn up by the Central Military Commission—that would be an act tantamount to treason. Colonel Ai was the commanding officer of the planning division of the MCHTT, but he was such a junior officer that if he worked in Sun's office of the chief of staff, his day would be spent mostly making tea and emptying wastebaskets for all the middle- and upper-class flag officers there. If the Central Military Committee wanted any changes made as to how Taiwan was to be "reunited" with the mainland, the CMC would tell the chief of staff, who would tell Sun, who would tell the MCHTT to make the changes. That process might take six months—six months spent by each bureaucrat in order to make sure that his superior wasn't trying to screw him, each bureaucrat making sure that the orders made him look good if it worked and made someone else look bad if it didn't work.

The initial thrust of the attack on the island of Formosa was to destroy the island's thick air and coastal security units from long range. Seven fixed bases and ten mobile presurveyed launch points in east-central China were programmed to launch up to twenty Dong Feng-15 intermediate- and short-range missiles each on Taiwanese targets per day, that was one hundred and fifty to three hundred missiles per day, an incredible bombardment. The attacks were programmed to last as long as a month, but of course would be halted right before the amphibious invasion began, or upon the rebel's unconditional surrender. The high-explosive missile attacks would be followed by tactical air strikes to mop up any surviving targets, escorted by waves of fighters to ensure air superiority and to fight off an expected counterattack by Taiwanese air forces. An amphibious invasion was deemed unnecessary—the thought being that loyal Communists on Taiwan would rise up, throw off their Nationalist oppressors, and welcome the People's Liberation Army ashore peacefully—but the aircraft carrier *Mao Zedong,* formerly the Russian carrier *Varyag* and for a short time the Iranian carrier *Ayatollah Ruhollah Khomeini,* and its battle group would be used to ferry troops and supplies ashore if necessary, while providing air cover against any resistance.

"Hold please, Colonel," Sun finally said. "You show the employment of seventy-five DF-15 missiles on Longtian to launch against Taoyuan and Hsinchu Air Bases on Taiwan."

"Yes, sir . . . ?"

"Yet I was briefed two days ago that there has been extensive flooding on Longtian peninsula and that the base and city are not fully repaired," Sun went on angrily. "The undamaged missiles were removed and sent to Fuzhou. What forces are covering Longtian's targets while their missiles are evacuated?"

Colonel Ai seemed stunned at Sun's question. "The evacuation was merely precautionary, sir," he responded. "We expect the missiles to be back at their presurveyed launch points in just a few days. . . ."

"But then you are in fact telling me that Taoyuan and Hsinchu are not really at risk right *now*," Sun insisted. "You are saying—"

"Comrade Admiral, Longtian covers the initial bombardment of Taoyuan and Hsinchu," General Lieutenant Qian said in a loud, irritated voice. "Colonel Ai, continue the briefing—"

"But, sir, I just said there are no missiles at Longtian," Sun interrupted. Although Qian was senior to Sun, they were both of equal rank and authority, and it was certainly within Sun's purview to question anything in this briefing. He turned to Colonel Ai and asked, "Did you bother to move any bombers from the interior or from the north to cover those targets? Zeguo Air Base can perhaps handle twenty or thirty B-6 bombers; Hangzhou and Fuzhou might be able to handle thirty each as well. One hundred bombers might be able to cover those two Nationalist cities until the DF-15s can be replaced at Longtian. You might be able to get a number of Q-5s to cover the targets, but it might take a hundred and fifty or more, depending on the status of Taiwan's Tien Kung-2 antiaircraft missile deployment that was scheduled for this month at

Hsinchu. But the weather is getting a bit better, so the Q-5s might have a good chance." Sun paused, regarding Ai. He still looked absolutely petrified with confusion, his eyes shifting back and forth from Sun to Qian. "Are you getting any of this, Comrade Colonel?"

"Yes, sir," Ai said, his Adam's apple bobbing up and down as if he were choking on his own tongue. But a warning glare from General Qian got his attention, and he pressed on: "Ah . . . yes, as I was saying, Longtian's DF-15 missiles will destroy the air defense bases at Taoyuan and Hsinchu, with secondary targets at Taipei and Lung Tan available when intelligence reports the destruction of these two air facilities—"

"Comrade Colonel, are you listening to what I am saying?" Sun interjected angrily. "You cannot destroy any air bases with weapons you do not have. Now, I have told you that there are no missiles at Longtian, and I have suggested using bombers or attack planes to cover Taoyuan and Hsinchu until the missiles are operational again. Why do you continue to brief outdated information?"

"I . . . because, Comrade Admiral, the plan calls for Longtian to attack and destroy those two Nationalist bases," Ai said. "It is all in the plan, sir. . . ."

"Yes, I know, but the plan is *wrong*," Sun said. This caused a gasp from Ai and from most of the officers attending the briefing—and an absolutely explosive grimace from Qian. "It is wrong because . . . Damn you, Colonel, you can *see* it is wrong. *Change* it. We could be called upon at any moment to execute this attack plan, and I want to be sure it is *perfect*."

"It is not wise to change the war plans," General Qian said. "Yes, yes, some missiles are not in place right now, but they will be soon. If we are ordered to execute our war plans, we can move additional forces eastward to cover those two Nationalist air bases. Does that alleviate your concern, Comrade Admiral?"

"Comrade General, the purpose of this planning committee is to continually modify the existing war plans to reflect current circumstances and conditions," Sun Ji Guoming said. "This is done so we do not have to wait until the moment we execute the war order to learn that we do not have the forces in place to accomplish the mission. When you were notified that Longtian was flooded and missiles were being relocated, you should have immediately moved additional forces to cover those targets."

"You mean, fly hundreds of aircraft and thousands of troops all over China just for a few days until some mud is swept away?" General Qian asked. "Do you realize how much that would cost? And what of other war plans for which those aircraft and personnel are committed? That means coordinating with dozens of other headquarters all over China."

"But, sir, that is the *purpose* of this planning group—to respond immediately to changes that might affect this war plan," Sun argued. "If it becomes necessary to move men and equipment to a new location, then so be it. We should—"

"We should look at the solution in a different way, a way that will not be as complicated or as costly," Qian interjected, obviously impatient to get this briefing over with. "Perhaps in the future we can brief possible replacement units that could be utilized to fill in, in situations such as have occurred in Longtian. We do not actually *move* any forces, but we earmark them for possible action in case the war plan is activated. How does that sound to you, Comrade Sun?"

Sun opened his mouth to respond, but thought better of it. It was a bad idea. The war plan for the invasion of Taiwan was supposed to be a rapid reaction plan—the invasion was supposed to begin within twenty-four hours of the execution order. The world, especially Taiwan and its de facto ally, the United States of America, would immediately detect any massive troop or equipment movements; the element of surprise would be lost, and China no doubt would be forced to stand down its forces. If there were huge gaps in the reaction time of forces key to the plan—especially the Dong Feng-15 missile bombardment units, which were supposed to destroy key air defense and coastal defense sites in western Taiwan—the entire invasion plan was in jeopardy.

But now was not the time to argue this point. "Very well, Comrade General," Sun acquiesced. "As long as the chief of staff is aware of the degradation, and immediately advised as to the steps being taken to correct the deficiency, a briefing note such as you suggest could be acceptable. But it is certainly *not* acceptable to brief that a certain element in the attack plan is mission-capable if it is in fact not so. The war plans are not carved in stone—they must be continually modified or they are useless. Please do not commit that error again, Comrade Colonel."

"Yes, Comrade Admiral," Colonel Ai responded, nodding contritely. Ai took a moment to take a sip of water, collect his thoughts, and find his place again—and immediately proceeded to give his briefing exactly as prepared, errors and all. There were at least two more instances that Sun knew of where attack units were not in place—in one case, an attack unit that Ai briefed was key to the destruction of a radar site on the Pescadores Islands in the Formosa Strait did not even *exist* any longer! The planning committee had done virtually nothing to the original Central Military Commission war plans drafted several years earlier.

"Another question, Comrade Colonel," Sun interjected, swallowing his exasperation. "You seem quite content to sail the carrier *Mao* and her escorts right up to Kaohsiung, supported by air forces from Pingtan and naval air units from Quanzhou. But that means our J-6s will be up against the Nationalists' F-16s from T'ainan. . . ."

"We enjoy a six to one superiority in fighters, Comrade Admiral," Ai responded. "Also, the DF-15 bombardment is guaranteed to destroy all of the runways that might possibly be used by the F-16s. Even if we do not destroy many F-16s on the ground, they will be trapped either aloft running out of fuel and weapons, or on the ground unable to launch."

"Your estimates of the amount of damage our rockets might do to the Nationalists' bases is arguable, since they have a great quantity of ballistic missile defense systems and much of their warfighting infrastructure is belowground, where our rockets would have little effect," Sun said. "But even if our rocket attack is *twice* as effective as you say, our numerical fighter aircraft superiority can be completely erased if our air attack is at night."

"Sir . . . ?"

"Our J-5 and J-6 fighters and most of our J-7 fighters are not capable of night operations—I see that seventy-five percent of the air cover for the carrier is composed of J-6s," Sun explained. "Only about ten percent are J-7s and J-8s. Where are the Sukhoi-27s? Those are our most capable fighters."

"The Su-27s are based at Haikou Airfield, on Hainan Dao, Comrade Admiral," Ai replied.

"I know where they are based, comrade—my question is, why are they not part of this offensive?" Sun asked. "Our fifty best fighters against their fifty best fighters—it would be an excellent battle, one that we could very well win. Such a battle could be decisive."

"There you go again, comrade," General Qian interjected, with a chuckle that sounded as if he were losing a lung. "The Sukhoi-27s have been deployed to Hainan Island to patrol the Nansha Dao. Their base facilities are specially made just for them. Do you now suggest we spend billions of *yuan* more to move them north to Pingtan or Fuzhou?"

"For this offensive—of course we should, sir," Sun replied. "We need our best equipment and best pilots to blunt the rebel's superior technological advantage, and the Sukhoi-27s are just as capable and perhaps superior to the F-16 Fighting Falcon. The teaming of J-8s with Su-27s is easily superior to a matchup between Taiwan's F-16s and F-5 Freedom Fighters. The key, obviously, is the Sukhoi-27s."

"We also have the advantage of superior command and control," Ai interjected, "namely, the Ilyushin-76 radar surveillance planes. Two of our Il-76s operating in the region during the conflict greatly increase the flexibility of the J-7s and J-6s."

"Our radar plane crews are just now being certified for combat duties," Sun responded. "I feel it is not wise to trust them to carry the air battle for us, especially if we are top-heavy with fighters that require constant airborne intercept and even weapon-control information right down to 'knife-fighting' range. That could overload the radar operators and cause confusion."

"Every commander wants the best, especially the young ones like yourself," Qian argued, his voice very grandfatherly, almost jovial. "The J-6s and J-7 fighters, along with the Ilyushin-76 radar planes, will perform well beyond all expectations."

"But the Su-27s will give us an edge—"

"The Sukhoi-27s were based on Hainan Dao to protect our interests in the South China Sea, in case of attack by Vietnamese or Philippine forces on our holdings in the Spratly Islands," Qian said. He raised a suspicious eyebrow and asked Sun, "You are not suggesting we abandon our rights to the South China Sea, Comrade Admiral?"

"Of . . . course . . . not, sir," Sun Ji Guoming replied, stunned by the question. "Sir, I am not trying to discredit the war plan or impose my own views over that of the Party or the Central Military Commission. My intention is to suggest improvements on the plan to ensure a safe and successful outcome. The Formosa invasion—"

"Is well planned and ready for execution, without the added complication of the Sukhoi-27 fighters," Qian said confidently. "They can always be brought north in case they are needed, but with a six-to-one numerical advantage in fighters now, along with the carrier *Mao*'s fleet of Sukhoi-33 fighters, we feel the carrier is well-protected and we can destroy any opposition from Kaohsiung. A little danger is to be expected, my young friend—you cannot summon every rifle or every jet you wish. The plan has been formulated to concentrate necessary strength on defeating the rebels without sacrificing security or strategic balance in other areas of our vast nation. Please continue, comrade. . . ."

"Perhaps you do not understand, Comrade General," Sun said. "The National Assembly of the rebel Nationalist government on Taiwan has just voted to amend their constitution to declare themselves independent and sovereign from the mainland."

Colonel Lieutenant Ai Peijian appeared to be a bit confused. Since no one else was speaking, he said, "Permit me to speak, sir, but why is this such shocking news? The rebels have been thinking they can be independent from us for a long time."

"But now they've declared it to the world!" Sun shouted. "They have put it in their constitution! They have dared to declare that there are *two* Chinas, separate and equal! *Equal!* To *us?* How dare they! *How dare they* do such a thing!"

"It is meaningless, sir," Colonel Ai said, still unsure as to why Sun was so angry. "The world knows it is not true. It is like a bug declaring it is equal to the elephant. The world knows that eventually the rebel government will be overthrown and the province of Taiwan will return to the People's—"

"The world knows, does it? The world knows?" Sun interrupted, suddenly stopping his furious pacing. "You did not hear the rest of the news, then, Comrade Colonel: It is expected that the governments of the United States, Great Britain, France, Germany, Russia, South Africa, Saudi Arabia, and many others will formally recognize the new Republic of China within the coming days. Intelligence reports that a new American embassy will open in Taipei within the week. It is also estimated that the United States will petition for permanent membership for the Nationalists in the United Nations. It will be a simple majority vote—our country cannot block membership with a veto."

"No . . . it cannot be," General Qian muttered. He got to his feet, his hands still shaking. "This demands an immediate response. This cannot be!"

"We shall establish contact with the general staff immediately," Sun said. "Comrade General, you must convene your operations staff and be prepared to execute the war orders immediately."

"Execute . . . the . . . war . . . orders!" Colonel Ai sputtered. "You mean, we are at *war* with the Nationalists?"

"You thought all this was a joke, Colonel?" Sun shouted angrily. "You thought none of this could really happen, that you would be somewhere else, doing something else? I am going to recommend that this plan be put into operation *immediately!* Within forty-eight hours, Colonel, I expect to be standing on the remains of the rebels' capital, walking over the bodies of the rebels' so-called 'sovereign' legislature.

"But first, I must figure out a way to fix your incompetence in amending the war plans so our attack will be successful," Sun Ji Guoming thundered. "What do you think of the plan now, Colonel? What if I put *you* on the first landing craft that rolls across the beachhead at Kaohsiung? Would you brief the plan the same, knowing that it was *your* ass that would be the first to face the remnants of the Nationalist forces that were *supposed* to be destroyed? Tell me, Colonel!" He suddenly swung on the aged general. "Tell me, General! How is the plan shaping up now? Perhaps I should nominate you to lead the invasion force!"

"Have a care, Comrade Admiral," Qian said, but in a panicked, squeaky voice. "You are on the verge of insubordination."

"And what about the Americans, Colonel?" Sun Ji Guoming said, his voice rising in absolute frustration. "Your time line extends out to thirty days—but it will not take the Americans more than one day to respond. Their fighters from Okinawa have the range to engage our fighters in the northern sector; their fighters with their air refueling can protect their sub hunters and anti-ship attack planes. And that is *before* one of their carriers arrives to begin a counteroffensive. What forces do you propose to use when that begins?"

"The Americans would not risk a carrier during the initial thrust against the rebels," Ai Peijian argued. "The Military Intelligence Department reports that if the Americans do decide to engage, it will be well after the initial thrust."

"I am referring to the land-based forces on Okinawa, comrade," Sun said. "American navy, marines, air forces—it seems the Americans have as many planes on Okinawa as Taiwan has in their entire fleet! If they commit those forces, all our forces arrayed against the northern half of Taiwan could be in jeopardy. If they get control of the skies and bring in their P-3 sub-chasers, all of our submarine fleet in the Formosa Strait and East China Sea could be in jeopardy. What will you do if—?"

"Comrade Admiral," General Qian interjected wearily, "you are raving. Be silent."

"Why not just destroy Okinawa, Comrade Colonel?" Sun Ji Guoming said, ignoring the general's admonition. "That would eliminate one of the biggest threats to our forces committed to the Taiwan battle. Destroy Okinawa, destroy Kunsan, South Korea, and we push the Americans back to the 135th meridian, out of range of their medium attack planes. If the Japanese refuse to allow American forces to stage attacks against us from their bases, we can then push the Americans back to Guam. Destroy Guam—one DF-5 long-range ballistic missile fired from Changsha, or one sea-launched ballistic missile fired from the *Xia,* our nuclear submarine—and we push the Americans back to the other side of the International Date Line. They would not even be fighting on the same *day* as us! We could then—"

"You . . . you are talking about using *nuclear weapons,* Admiral?" General Qian gasped. "You know that the Chinese Communist Party has officially stated that the People's Liberation Army will not use nuclear weapons first in any conflict?"

"Using nuclear weapons would be much better than relying on false and misleading war plans such as *these* to retake what is rightfully ours!" Admiral Sun shouted, sweeping his copy of the war plans onto the floor. "We are doomed to failure unless we commit ourselves to using every weapon in our arsenal."

"That is quite *enough*, Comrade Admiral," Qian interjected sternly. "The war plans do not call for the use of nuclear weapons against our own province—may I remind you that the island of Formosa *is* our territory, our twenty-third province—and it does not call for using nuclear weapons against the Americans, South Koreans, Japanese, or anyone else. I think this news has unsettled you. You appear to be on the verge of a mental breakdown." And that was the end of the discussion.

This was a travesty, Sun Ji Guoming thought, as the others filed out of the conference room—for all he cared, the war plans didn't exist. China was completely unprepared for what had just happened and what was about to happen.

Sun Ji Guoming had his own plans, and they had nothing to do with missile and air bombardments or massive naval engagements. Taiwan could be taken, without prompting war with the United States or hatred from the other Asian nations. It would be simple to isolate Taiwan, even from its staunchest supporters.

But capturing Taiwan and making it part of Zhongguo again was not the most important mission facing them right now—the biggest threat was the domination of the United States in every aspect of life in the Far East. The Americans' ability to project its military power throughout this region was crushing China's struggle to take its place as the most important power in Asia. Yes, the Americans' military might was awesome, its technological superiority enormous. But Asia was far away, mysterious; its military had been greatly downsized, its economy was unsteady, its leadership tenuous. America's influence on its Asian allies was not as strong as it once was.

Sun believed that he had a way to topple the great United States of America off its perch—and now was the time to do it.

> "One who speaks
> deferentially but increases his
> preparations will advance;
> one who speaks belligerently
> and advances hastily
> will retreat."
>
> —SUN-TZU,
> *The Art of War*

CHAPTER
ONE

ATTENTION, DATALINK BOGEY, ELEVEN O'CLOCK LOW, "Sharon" reported.

U.S. Air Force Major Scott Mauer saw the flashing diamond floating before his eyes even before the computer-synthesized female voice they had named "Sharon"—after actress Sharon Stone, whose voice could have been an exact duplicate of the computer's—issued its advisory. Mauer immediately jammed his back and butt deeper into the ejection seat of his F-22 Lightning fighter and locked the inertial reel, securing himself tightly in his seat. The action was about to start.

Mauer moved his head until a circular target designator symbol centered on the diamond symbol, then toggled the radio transmit button on his right throttle quadrant down to the "intercom" position and said, "Lock bogey." "Sharon" was much more than a verbal warning system as the first-generation "Bitchin' Bettys" had been in earlier fighters—Sharon had a five-thousand-word vocabulary, could respond to questions with a surprisingly human voice, and could activate almost all of the F-22's subsystems. It was more akin to a human copilot than a computer.

BOGEY LOCKED, Sharon replied, and instantly a box surrounded the white diamond symbol and the bogey's flight information—speed, altitude, heading—displayed in midair. Mauer's F-22 Lightning, the Air Force's newest air-superiority fighter and attack plane, was equipped with the new "supercockpit" system, which included a helmet-mounted virtual display (VD), replacing the standard heads-up display mounted atop the instrument panel with symbols and information that could be seen no matter where the pilot looked—left, right, straight down, or even backward, the pilot could always "see" his flight and target readouts. Most of the heads-down cockpit dials, gauges, and multifunction displays in the F-22 fighter had also been replaced with three seamless color computer monitors that could be configured to display anything the pilot wished to see—radar, infrared, digital map, satellite photos, text, or flight instruments—called up and displayed by asking the computer or by touching the screen.

"Interrogate the bogey," Mauer ordered.

INTERROGATING . . . Sharon the computer replied; then, after a short pause: NEGATIVE REPLY. Sharon had sent out an IFF (Identification Friend or Foe) signal, to which only friendly aircraft would reply. The white diamond in Mauer's VD changed to red—it was no longer just a "bogey," an unidentified aircraft. It was now a "bandit," a hostile aircraft.

Mauer was a ten-year Air Force fighter veteran and knew how to close in and kill a hostile aerial target from any direction, speed, or attitude, but the attack computer system was new and he wanted to put it through its paces. He keyed the intercom button: "Give me an intercept vector on the bandit."

SAY AGAIN, PLEASE, Sharon replied in a surprisingly seductive voice.

Mauer took a deep breath, containing his frustration and forcing himself to relax. "Say again, please" was Sharon's favorite phrase. The computer system did not need voice coaching for individual pilots, but if a pilot started to get excited or hurried, the computer would not understand his voice commands. Mauer touched the supercockpit screen to call up the weapons status display and moved it with his finger to the upper right corner of the supercockpit display—in case his voice commands wouldn't take, he was ready to finish the intercept without it. "I said, display intercept vector on the bandit."

She understood that time, and a twin-tiered 3-D ribbonlike path appeared in thin air. Naturally distrustful of computers to do their thinking for them, pilots called the computer's attack recommendation the "primrose path." Despite its name, however, it was not a bad recommendation, Mauer thought—high, left rear quarter, the westbound bandit's pilot would be looking into the rising sun trying to find him—so he decided to follow it. Mauer maneuvered the F-22 so he was flying in between the two parallel ribbons, then ordered, "Engage the autopilot on the intercept course."

AUTOPILOT ENGAGED, Sharon verified. The autopilot would now automatically fly the entire intercept. Mauer was a good stick and he loved flying, but unlike most of his fighter-jock colleagues, he wasn't afraid to let the ultrasophisticated computers relieve some of the workload. The "primrose path" pulled Mauer's F-22 into a steep descent, and Mauer kept the throttles at just below mil power and let the airspeed build up toward the Mach. With all of its weapons and fuel stored internally, the F-22 had few speed restrictions—it could go to its max speed of Mach 1.5 at any time in clean configuration, and the Lightning liked to go fast. Its weapons bay doors opened inwardly as well, so there was no speed restriction on missile launch either.

The intercept was working out perfectly. So far the bandit was cruising along fat, dumb, and happy, still subsonic and mostly traveling in a straight, uncomplicated course, flying low but not doing any real aggressive terrain masking. The radar lock was intermittent, but that was understandable, because Mauer's F-22 was not tracking the bandit. One hundred miles away, an Air Force E-3C Sentry AWACS (Airborne Warning and Control System) radar plane had picked up the bandit and had datalinked the target information via the JTIDS (Joint Target Information Distribution System) to Mauer's F-22, which processed and displayed the data as if the F-22's own radar were tracking the target. The bandit's threat radar warning receiver would pick up only the AWACS, not the F-22. Even better, Mauer could launch the F-22's AIM-120 AMRAAMs (Advanced Medium-Range Air To Air Missiles) using JTIDS information until the missile's own active radar picked up the target—he didn't even need the fighter's radar to launch his radar-guided missiles.

"Recommend a weapon for the attack," Mauer asked on interphone. As before, he didn't need Sharon to tell him which missile to fire, but it was fun and educational to play with the new system. He purposely did not ask only for missiles but for any weapon, just to see if the computer would select the correct one.

RECOMMEND AIM-120, Sharon replied, and both of the F-22's AM-RAAM missiles depicted on the weapon status page blinked green. Mauer's Lightning was lightly loaded on this mission, and carried only two AIM-120s and two AIM-9P Sidewinder missiles in the weapons bay, plus five hundred rounds of ammunition for the 20-millimeter cannon.

"Arm AIM-120."

ROGER, AIM-120 ARMED, WARNING, MISSILE ARMED, Sharon responded, and the left AMRAAM missile changed from green to yellow, indicating it was powered up and receiving target and flight information from the attack computer.

"Time to launch?"

TEN SECONDS TO LAUNCH, Sharon responded, with only a hint of hesitation.

They were still screaming earthward at 3,000 feet per minute, and the hills below were starting to become a factor. Mauer knew that he was getting a little target-fixated, so he expanded his look-down supercockpit display to a God's-eye view of the surrounding area. Only one other plane within fifty miles, and that was a friendly, another F-22. The "primrose path" was steering him around some high terrain—the navigation computer had all of the terrain elevations programmed—but he was still flying close to those hills. The computer-generated flight path was too gentle and not aggressive enough for Mauer's taste, so he laid his hands on the control stick and throttles and said, "Autopilot heading nav mode off, autopilot altitude nav mode off, fail-safe terrain avoidance mode on."

ROGER, HEADING NAV OFF, ALTITUDE NAV OFF, WARNING, CHECK AUTOPILOT MODES, ROGER, TERRAIN AVOIDANCE MODE ENGAGED, Sharon replied. The F-22's terrain-avoidance mode would provide a last-second emergency fly-up in case he strayed too close to the ground or the hills.

"Time to launch?"

SAY AGAIN, PLEASE, Sharon replied. Mauer was getting excited again—his voice was getting clipped, more high-pitched, and therefore harder for Sharon to understand. No matter—he saw the time-to-launch countdown on his virtual display and didn't ask again. He was breathing faster and shallower. *Relax,* dammit, *relax!* he told himself. You've got this intercept nailed. Even without Sharon's help, he had it wired.

Mauer now knew what the bandit's target was: the industrial site, the fifty-acre military weapons and research facility. It was imperative that this plant be protected. The Air Force had assigned two F-22 Lightning fighters, their most modern and high-tech warplane, to the industrial site's defense. A Patriot air defense missile site was active in the area, but with the F-22s operating in the area at the same time, the Patriot would be kept in reserve until the air defense fighters ran out of missiles.

"Tell me when to shoot," Mauer said.

MAX RANGE IN FIVE SECONDS . . . MAX RANGE IN THREE SECONDS . . . TWO SECONDS . . . ONE SECOND . . . MAX IN RANGE . . . OPTIMAL IN RANGE, Sharon said.

Mauer keyed the intercom button: "AIM-120 shoot," he ordered.

ROGER, AIM-120 SHOOT, AIM-120 SHOOT . . . WARNING, WEAPONS DOOR OPENING . . . AIM-120 AWAY. Mauer felt the rumble of the weapons doors sliding inwardly, felt the *slap!* of the gas ejectors forcing the left AM-RAAM missile into the supersonic slipstream, then saw a streak of white smoke arc across the sky from the belly of his Lightning fighter. The VD display showed an estimated "time to die" countdown: nine seconds . . . eight . . . seven . . . six . . . at five seconds, the AMRAAM's own active radar seeker head activated, which would guide the missile in the last few seconds of its kill. . . .

The bandit suddenly dipped from 1,000 feet above the terrain to fifty feet—literally in the blink of an eye!—then made an impossible left turn behind a tall butte. The AMRAAM, just seconds from impact, lost sight of its target. The missile's seeker head was only a ten-degree cone and its turn rate was about seven Gs—the bandit had turned *ninety* degrees and pulled fifteen, maybe *twenty* Gs. There was no way, *no way,* any bomber could turn like that. The AMRAAM missile was lost, smoothly and completely faked out by a move that would make Jerry Rice hang up his cleats.

Mauer yanked the Lightning fighter left. "Radar on, lock on bandit . . ." But before the ship's radar could lock on and send new steering signals to the missile, it had plowed into the ground. Clean miss! That was the first time Mauer had ever seen an AMRAAM missile miss its intended target. What kind of bomber was this? The F-15E Strike Eagle was not this fast or agile with weapons aboard . . . was it a foreign job, like the Japanese FS-X or a Messerschmidt X-31? Maybe an F-16XL cranked arrow . . . ?

Just then, Mauer glanced off to his right and saw it—a cloud of black smoke over the industrial site. Mauer had been hoping to reacquire the bandit on this southbound jog before it turned westbound again toward the industrial site, but he was too late. The industrial site was hit. Dammit, looked like a direct fucking hit—wait, no, not quite. The bad guy's intel was obviously poor—the hit was on the center of the big building, mostly crating and shipping stuff and empty space. The bandit got a hit, but it didn't do much harm!

Westbound again, radar on in wide-area look-down search—got him! BANDIT ONE O'CLOCK LOW, TWELVE MILES, Sharon advised.

"Lock bandit, arm AIM-120, AIM-120 shoot," Mauer ordered immediately.

BANDIT LOCKED . . . ROGER, AIM-120 ARMED, WARNING, WEAPONS ARMED . . . AIM-120 SHOOT, AIM-120 SHOOT, WARNING, WEAPONS DOORS OPENING . . . AIM-120 AWAY, Sharon responded in rapid-fire succession, and his last AMRAAM missile was flying. But almost as soon as it launched, Mauer could see its white smoke trail wobbling, then breaking first hard to the left, then in a wide sharply arcing curve to the right, then again to the left in an even wider arc. He knew it was going to miss well before the "time to die" meter ran down to zero. That bandit had made two high-G jinks that again beat the hell out of the highly maneuverable AIM-120 missile.

Another cloud of black smoke—*another* hit on the industrial site, and this time it was on the smaller building southeast of the large building, where a lot of finished munitions and products were stored awaiting transportation. That son of a bitch had actually gone all the way around and *reattacked,* with a fighter on his tail! He had balls, that's for sure—any mud-mover worth his wings would hit, then get out of the defended area as fast as he could.

Enough of this super-automated datalink shit, Mauer thought—time to call in some help. They were supposed to stay off the voice radios and use the datalink as much as possible, but he was in deep shit and his first priority was to defend his territory. He rocked the radio switch on the throttles up to the UHF position: "Saber One-Two, this is One-One on Red."

"One-Two," replied his fellow hunter, Captain Andrea Mills. She had a slight twinge of sarcasm already in her voice, and Mauer almost regretted calling her—he knew she knew he was having trouble.

"Come give me a hand with this bandit," Mauer said.

"Roger, I'm on my way," Mills replied, the sarcasm gone. Mills looked for every opportunity to rub her fellow fighter jocks' noses in the macho hunter-killer game they all relished, but when it came time to get down to business, she was serious, focused, and as deadly as any swinging dick.

Mauer switched his heads-down supercockpit screen to a God's-eye view and expanded it until Mills's fighter symbol appeared—good, she was off to the north, racing southwestbound to cut off the bandit from the other major ground target in the area, the fighter base and Patriot missile emplacements. Mills was staying high, establishing a high patrol, so Mauer pushed his stick forward and zoomed down lower, closer to the bandit's altitude. He had two missiles left, both heat-seekers with a max range of only seven miles, and he had to make them count. If the bomber got the airfield and the Patriot site, their forces would be left wide open to attack, the airborne fighters would have to find someplace else to land, and the fighters on the ground were sitting ducks and wouldn't be able to depart.

At 3,000 feet above the ground, the hills and buttes looked close enough to scrape the bottom of Mauer's fighter. He kept the power up at full military power, speeding westbound at Mach 1.5, searching for the bomber . . . but Mills's radar locked on first. The JTIDS datalink transferred the bandit's position to Mauer's attack computer, and he again locked onto the bomber and began his pursuit—twelve o'clock, nine miles . . . eight . . .

HIGH TERRAIN, HIGH TERRAIN! Sharon cried into the intercom. Mauer yanked back on the stick to crest a sharply rising razorback ridgeline directly ahead. Jesus, this was *nuts*—trying to concentrate on the pursuit while dodging hills and ridges was going to get him killed. But as soon as he lowered the nose again, the bandit was dead in his sights, straight ahead.

"Arm Sidewinder," Mauer ordered. "Open weapon doors."

ROGER, AIM-9 ARMED, WARNING, MISSILE ARMED . . . WARNING, WEAPON DOORS OPENING. As soon as the door opened, the AIM-9 Sidewinder missile's seeker head slaved to the attack computer's steering signal, saw the hot dot from the bandit's exhaust, and locked onto it, matching its seeker azimuth exactly with the attack computer's target bearing. AIM-9 LOCKED ON, Sharon reported.

"AIM-9 shoot," Mauer ordered.

AIM-9 SHOOT, AIM-9 SHOOT, AIM-9 AWAY. The smaller, faster Sidewinder fired from the weapons bay in a flash, wobbled a bit as it stabilized itself in the air, then homed straight and true. . . .

Flares! Mauer saw them immediately—a line of white dots hanging in the sky, hot and very bright even over six miles away. The radar-lock square jutted sharply left as the bandit made its customary first left break, but the decoy flares hung in the sky straight ahead for several seconds before winking out. The Sidewinder wobbled as if it were trying to decide between locking onto the decoys or turning to chase the bomber. It decided on the decoys, then changed its mind as the decoys began to extinguish. But just as it made a sharp left turn to pursue, the bomber ejected more flares and jinked right, and the Sidewinder locked solidly on the new, brighter, closer decoys and would not let go. The Sidewinder exploded harmlessly a full five miles behind the bomber.

One missile to go, Mauer reminded himself, as he turned to pursue. He had closed to within four miles of the bandit, and now he was straining hard to see what in hell it was. The virtual display made it easy to focus on where the target was, no matter which way it jinked. It was small, probably an F-16, judging by its size and its maneuverability, or maybe some experimental job. . . .

A cruise missile! Mauer got a good look at it as it made another hard right turn, heading right for the airfield—a goddamn cruise missile! No wonder it was so maneuverable—there was no pilot on board to get knocked unconscious by hard G turns. It was the first cruise missile he had ever heard of that ejected decoy flares, could obviously detect enemy fighters' and missiles' radars, and could attack multiple targets and even reattack targets it missed the first time around! It was a little bit bigger than a Tomahawk or standard Air-Launched Cruise Missile, but it had no wings—it was almost like a big fat flying surfboard. When it was straight and level, it was almost impossible to see.

"One-One, bogeydope," Mills radioed.

"One-One has a single cruise missile, and it's haulin' ass," Mauer said, grunting against the G-forces as he turned hard left again to stay behind the missile. "I got one heater left. C'mon in and nail this bastard if my last shot misses." The time for being macho was over, Mauer thought—this cruise missile had beat him pretty good, and it looked as if it was going to take both of the F-22s working together to nail it.

"One-Two has a judy."

"Take the shot," Mauer said. "I'll try to nail it in the ass while you shoot it in the face."

Mills didn't reply—she let her AMRAAMs do the talking. The JTIDS datalink showed Mills launching her first AIM-120, followed by her second AMRAAM five seconds later. The cruise missile made its usual left break—Mauer was close enough now to see that it was ejecting chaff decoys, trying to get the radar-guided missile to lock onto the tinsel-like chaff! But Mauer anticipated that left break, and at the exact right moment, Mauer launched his last Sidewinder, then began a right turning climb to clear the area. The Sidewinder would get a good, solid look at the missile's entire profile, and it couldn't miss.

But as he turned, he looked to the west and saw three bright explosions and another cloud of smoke—the airfield was hit, this time with some kind of binary weapon, a fuel-air explosive or a chemical weapon. No one was going to be landing or taking off from that airfield for a long, long time.

Mauer got visual contact on Mills's F-22 high and heading in the opposite direction. Just as he began his climbing left turn to join up, he heard Mills report, "Splash one bandit—but I think he got the Patriot site and the airfield first."

Good job, Scottie, Mauer told himself angrily—the F-22 Lightning, the best fighter ever to leave the ground, beat out by a robot plane. Shit, shit, *shit!*

He saw Mills wag her F-22's tail back and forth, clearing him into right fingertip formation. Might as well let Andrea lead for a while until he got his composure back, he was too angry right now to make any decisions as flight lead.

Just then, Mauer's heads-down display blinked—another inbound bandit had been detected by the AWACS. Mills rocked her wings up and down, the signal to move out to combat spread formation to get set up for the intercept, then started a thirty-degree bank turn to the left toward the new bandit. She was the only one with missiles now, Mauer thought forlornly, so he slid out to wide-line-abreast formation and got ready to back up his leader on this intercept. He was backup now, he thought, just backup. The bad guys were three for fucking three. . . .

•••• "Three for three, General," Patrick McLanahan said matter-of-factly. "The Wolverine autonomously located four preprogrammed targets, attacked three, reattacked one, and was on its way to nail the fourth one before the F-22s got it. Pretty good hunting, I'd say."

"Unbelievable," Samson finally muttered. "I don't believe what I just saw." Even in the EB-52B Megafortress bomber's wide cockpit, Lieutenant General Terrill Samson's big frame barely seemed to fit—his shoulders were slightly slumped, his knees high up on the instrument panel. Terrill "Earthmover" Samson, a former B-52 and B-1B bomber pilot and wing commander, was commander of U.S. Air Force's Eighth Air Force, in charge of training and equipping all of the Air Force's heavy and medium bomber units. The Air Force general was in the modified B-52's left seat, piloting the experimental bomber. Copiloting the EB-52 Megafortress was Air Force Colonel Kelvin Carter, a veteran bomber pilot and a former EB-52 test pilot at HAWC, the High Technology Aerospace Weapons Center. Retired Air Force Colonel Patrick McLanahan was seated behind and to the right of Samson in the aft section of the upper crew compartment in the OSO, or offensive systems officer's, console, and to McLanahan's left in the DSO's, or defensive systems officer's, seat was Dr. Jon Masters, president of a small high-tech satellite and weapons contractor from Arkansas.

The EB-52B Megafortress was a radically modified B-52 bomber, changed so extensively from tip to tail that now its size was the only sure point of comparison. It had a long, pointed, streamlined nose that smoothly melded into sharply raked cockpit windows and a thin, glass-smooth fuselage. Unlike a line B-52, the Megafortress's wingtips did not curl upward while in flight—the plane's all-composite fibersteel skeleton and skin, as strong as steel but many times lighter, maintained an aerodynamically perfect airfoil no matter how heavily it was loaded or what flight condition it was in. A long, low, canoe-shaped fairing sat atop the fuselage, housing long-range surveillance radars for scanning the sea, land, or skies for enemy targets in all directions, as well as active laser anti-missile countermeasures equipment and communications antennae. The large vertical and horizontal stabilizers on the tail were replaced by low, curving V-shaped ruddervators. A large aft-facing radar mounted between the ruddervators searched and tracked enemy targets in the rear quadrant; and instead of a 20-millimeter Gatling tail gun, the Megafortress had a single long cannon muzzle that looked far more sinister, far more deadly, than any machine gun. The cannon fired small guided missiles, called "airmines," that would fly toward an oncoming enemy fighter, then explode and scatter thousands of BB-like titanium projectiles directly in the fighter's flight path, shelling jet engines and piercing thin aircraft skin or cockpit canopies.

The most striking changes in the Megafortress were under its long, thin wings. Instead of eight Pratt & Whitney T33 turbofan engines, the EB-52 Megafortress sported just four airliner-style General Electric CF6 fanjet engines, modified for use on this experimental aircraft. The CF6 engines were quieter, less smoky, and gave the Megafortress over 60 percent more thrust than did the old turbofans, but with 30 percent *greater* fuel economy. At nearly a half-million pounds gross weight, the Megafortress could fly nearly halfway around the world at altitudes of over 50,000 feet—unrefueled!

The Megafortress was so highly computerized that the normal B-52 crew complement of six had been reduced down to four—a pilot and copilot; a defensive systems officer, who was in charge of bomber defense; and an offensive systems officer, who was in charge of employing the ground and anti-radar attack weapons and who also acted as the reconnaissance, surveillance, and air intelligence officer. The OSO's and DSO's stations were now on the upper deck of the EB-52, facing forward; the lower deck was now configured as an expanded avionics bay and also included a galley, lavatory, and seats and bunk area for extra crew members who might be taken aboard for long missions.

"Jon's only intervention was to redesignate the first target again so the Wolverine could reattack," McLanahan pointed out. McLanahan was not nearly as tall as Terrill Samson, but he, too, was broad-shouldered and powerfully built—he just seemed to fit perfectly in the EB-52 bomber's OSO's seat, as if that's where he always belonged. It was as if McLanahan had been born to fly in that seat, or as if the controls and displays had been sized and positioned precisely to fit him and him alone—which, in fact, they had. "The upgraded missile has a rearward sensor capability for autonomous bomb damage assessment. With a satellite datalink, an operator—either on the carrier aircraft, on any other JTIDS-equipped aircraft in the area, or eventually from a ground command station thousands of miles away—could command the Wolverine to reattack."

"That twenty-G turn, evading the AMRAAM," Samson remarked, his voice still quivering with excitement, ". . . it was breathtaking. It looked like a cartoon, some kind of science-fiction-movie thing."

"Not science fiction—science *fact,*" McLanahan said. "The Wolverine has thrust-vectored control jets instead of conventional wings and tail surfaces, and a mission-adaptive fuselage controlled by microhydraulics—the entire body of the missile changes shape, allowing it to use lifting-body aerodynamics to turn faster. In fact, the faster it goes, the tighter it can turn—just the opposite of most aircraft. All moving parts on the missile are driven by microhydraulic devices, so a simple five-hundred-psi pump the size of my wristwatch can power three hundred actuators at over ten thousand psi—theoretically we can maintain control at up to thirty Gs, but at that speed the missile would probably snap in half or the pressure might cook off the explosives in the warheads. But no fighter or missile yet built can keep up with the Wolverine."

Samson fell silent again in amazement. McLanahan turned to his left and looked at the man seated beside him and added, "Good job, Jon. I think you watered his eyes."

"Of course we did," Masters said. "What did you expect?" He tried to say it as casually and as coolly as McLanahan, but the excitement bubbling in his voice could not be disguised. Unlike the other two men in the cockpit with him, Jon Masters shared only their dancing, energetic eyes and boundless enthusiasm—he was as thin as they were broad, with a boyish, almost goofy-looking face. Jon Masters, the designer of the incredible AGM-177 Wolverine cruise missile along with dozens of other high-tech military weapons and satellites, was aboard to watch his missile do its stuff; in case anything went wrong, he could also abort the missile's flight, if necessary. That was also a Jon Masters hallmark—rarely, if ever, did the first operational test of one of his missiles or satellites work properly. This test appeared to be a welcome exception.

McLanahan commanded the EB-52 bomber into a right turn back toward the exit point to the RED FLAG range. "A little professional modesty might help sell a few Wolverines to the Air Force, Jon," McLanahan pointed out. McLanahan, retired as a colonel from the Air Force after sixteen years in service, was now a paid consultant to Sky Masters, for which he performed a number of tasks, from test-pilot duties to product design.

"Trust me on this one, Patrick," Masters said, slouching in his ejection seat and taking a big swig out of his ever-present squeeze bottle of Pepsi. "When it comes to the military, you've got to yell it to sell it. Talk to Helen in marketing—her budget is almost as big as the research-and-development budget."

"Dr. Masters has a right to be proud," General Samson said, "and I'm proud to back him and the Wolverine project. With a fleet of Wolverine missiles in the inventory, we can locate and kill targets with zero-zero precision from standoff range and at the same time virtually eliminate the risk of sending a human pilot over a heavily defended target area, and eliminate having to send in special forces troops on the ground to search for enemy missile or radar sites."

"It also breathes new life into the heavy-bomber program," McLanahan added. "I know there's been a lot of congressional pressure to do away with all of the 'heavies,' especially the B-52s, in favor of newer fighter-bombers. Well, load up one B-52 with twenty-six Wolverine missiles, and it's like launching a squadron of F-16 or F/A-18 fighter-bombers, except it cuts costs by nine-tenths and doesn't put as many pilots at risk." ·

A tone in all their headsets stopped the conversation. Two bat-wing fighter symbols had appeared at the bottom of McLanahan's super-cockpit display, and they were closing fast. "Fighters—probably the two F-22s, gunning for *us*," McLanahan said. "I'll bet they're pissed after missing the Wolverines."

"Let 'em come," Masters said. "We won—we already blasted the places they were assigned to protect."

"The exercise isn't over as long as we're inside the range, Doctor," Kelvin Carter said in a loud, excited voice, pulling his straps tighter and refastening his oxygen mask in place with a quick thrust. "We accomplished the mission—all we gotta do now is *survive*."

· Masters literally gulped on interphone. "You mean . . . you mean we're going to try to *outrun* those fighters? *Now*?"

"We didn't brief an air-to-air engagement," Samson pointed out. "We shouldn't be doing this."

"Well, go ahead and get us clearance for air-to-air," McLanahan suggested. "We own this airspace. Got it, Kel?"

"Rog, Patrick." Carter clicked open the range safety channel. "Saber One-One flight, this is Sandusky. Wanna play?"

"Sandusky, this is Saber leader. Roger, we're in and we're in. Payback time for the bomber pukes. Phase One ROE?"

"Affirmative, Phase One, we're ready," Carter replied. "Phase One" ROE, or Rules of Engagement, were the safest of three standard aerial-combat exercise levels with which all aircrews entering the RED FLAG ranges were familiar: no closer than two miles between aircraft, no closure rates greater than three hundred knots, no bank angles greater than forty-five degrees, no altitudes below two thousand feet above the ground.

"Roger, Sandusky, this is Saber One-One flight of two, Phase One, fight's on."

"I don't believe this, I don't believe this," Masters said excitedly. "Two Lightning fighters are gunning for *us*."

"It's all part of the tactics of standoff attack defense, Jon," McLanahan said. "If you can destroy the missile's carrier aircraft, you've destroyed the enemy's ability to launch more cruise missiles. Tighten your straps, everybody. General Samson, get out of here, please."

Carter's fingers flew over his instrument panel, and seconds later the electronic command bars on Samson's center multifunction display snapped downward. "Terrain-avoidance mode selected, command bars are active, pilot," he said to Samson. "Let's go, General!"

Masters suddenly became very light in his seat, as Samson engaged the EB-52 bomber's autopilot and the big bomber nosed over toward the earth. The sudden negative Gs made the young scientist's head spin and his stomach churn, but he was able to keep from blowing lunch all over his console as he tightened his straps and finally managed to focus over his console toward the cockpit—and when he did, all he could see out the front cockpit windows was brown desert. Masters could feel his helmet dangling upward as the negative Gs threatened to float the helmet right off his head, and he hurriedly fastened his chin strap and oxygen mask.

"Thirty miles and closing," McLanahan reported.

"They can't see us on radar, right?" Masters squeaked on intercom in his high, tinny voice. "Not this far out, right?"

"It's daytime, Jon—we're sitting ducks," McLanahan said. "Stealth doesn't help much if they can see you without radar. We've probably been leaving contrails, too—might as well have been towing a lighted banner. We've still got fifteen thousand feet to lose before they get in missile range. Clear right. Ready for COMBAT mode." Samson heeled the EB-52 bomber into a steep right bank, spilling lift from the bomber's huge wings and increasing their descent rate. He kept the bank in for about twenty seconds.

"Wings level now," Carter said. "Five thousand to level . . . command bars moving . . . four thousand . . . three thousand . . . two thousand to go . . . command bars coming to level pitch . . . one thousand . . . command bars indicating climb . . . descent rate to zero . . . command bars are terrain-active. Take it around that butte, then come left and center up."

"Take it to max power, General," McLanahan urged. "We're not going to make it to the butte before they're in missile range." Samson pushed the throttles to maximum power and saw the warning lights illuminate on his cockpit warning indicators—max power was only supposed to be used for takeoff or go-arounds, usually with the landing gear down. "Get your finger off the paddle switch, sir—let the terrain-avoidance system do its job."

"Jesus, McLanahan," Samson gasped, as they sped toward the rocky mountains. He found he had been unconsciously "paddling off" the terrain-avoidance autopilot with his right little finger, flying higher than the autopilot wanted—the command bars were a full five degrees below the horizon. "No one said anything about flying TA on this flight."

"We can't let those fighter jocks get us, sir," McLanahan said. "Let the TA system take it. Get the nose down."

They heard a slow-pitched *deedle deedle deedle!* warning tone. "Radar lock!" McLanahan shouted. "Simulate MAWS activated!" The MAWS, or Missile Active Warning System, used a laser emitter tied to the threat receivers to blind incoming enemy missiles—MAWS could also blind a pilot. "Left turn, take them around that butte!" Samson released the paddle switch, letting the bomber tuck down to an even lower altitude, then pushed the stick left and aimed for the north side of the butte. "Tighter, General," McLanahan shouted. "We've got to make them overshoot!"

"I'm as far as I can go." But he felt the bomber heel even more sharply to the left, as Carter pushed the stick over even more, pulling to tighten the turn. It seemed as if the entire left side of the cockpit windscreen was filled with the towering gray slab of rock, although they were not yet at forty-five degrees of bank. "McLanahan . . . dammit, *enough*!"

"They're overshooting—they're breaking off!" McLanahan said. "Hard right, center up!" On the supercockpit display, the two F-22 fighters had broken off the pursuit, climbed, and arced west to get away from the butte. Samson hauled the control stick to the right, a brief thrill of fear shooting through his brain as he felt the bomber mush slightly at the cross-control point—the stick was full right, the bomber was still turning left, and he was out of control until the bomber started to respond—

but a few moments later the autopilot was back in control and they were wings-level, flying 2,000 feet above ground down a wide valley.

"Sandusky, this is Saber flight," the pilot of the lead F-22 radioed. "No fair. We can't chase you guys down that low without busting the ROE. How about one pass at Phase Three?" Phase Three was the most realistic, most dangerous level of combat exercise: 1,000 feet between aircraft, no lower than 200 feet above the ground, max closure rate of 1,000 knots, unlimited bank angles. Samson said nothing; Carter considered that silence as permission and agreement from the aircraft commander.

McLanahan didn't ask if Samson wanted to play, didn't wait for any comments from anyone else. "Saber flight, this is Sandusky, acknowledged, Phase Three, we're in."

"Saber flight's in, Phase Three, fight's on."

"They're coming around again," McLanahan said. "I've got a sliver valley off to the left. Take it right in between those ridges. I'll dial it down to COLA—they'll lose us for sure." COLA stood for Computer-generated Lowest Altitude, where the terrain-avoidance computer would sacrifice safety to choose the lowest possible altitude—it could be as low as just a few dozen feet above ground, even in this rocky, hilly terrain. "We'll pop up through that saddle to the south before the valley ends and swing all the way around behind them. They won't know what the hell happened." But instead of turning right, McLanahan felt the EB-52 start a climb. "Hey, get the nose down, sir, and give me a right turn, there's your track."

"I said enough, Patrick," Samson said. He punched off the attack computer from the autopilot and started a slow climb, straight ahead down the wide valley. It did not take long for the kill—the F-22 fighters roared on them at supersonic speed, radars locked on, and passed less than 600 feet overhead. The sonic boom sent a dull shudder and a loud thunderclap through the bomber. Samson switched his number one radio to the range safety frequency and keyed the mike: "All players, knock it off, knock it off, knock it off. Sandusky is RTB." The F-22s could be seen rocking their wings in acknowledgment as they climbed out of sight.

Patrick McLanahan punched in commands to give Samson steering cues to the range exit point, then stripped off his oxygen mask in exasperation. "What in hell was that, General?" he asked. "You don't give up during a chase like that!"

"Hey, McLanahan, you may be a civilian, but you watch your mouth and your attitude," Samson said angrily, his head jerking to the right. "It wasn't a chase, McLanahan, it was showboating. We weren't scheduled to go low, and we sure as hell weren't fragged to do terrain avoidance or do lazy eights around mountains like that!"

"I know we weren't," McLanahan said, "but we got the gas, the TA system was up, we got the fighters, and they wanted to play."

"We didn't brief it, we didn't plan it, and I've got two civilians on board," Samson interjected angrily. "Yes, you're a civilian, McLanahan. I know you can do the job, I know you're every bit as capable as an active-duty crew member, but you're still just a civilian observer. Hell, McLanahan, I'm *not* qualified in this contraption, and I haven't flown terrain-avoidance missions in ten years, let alone been chased by Lightnings at five hundred AGL! It was dangerous."

"It's nothing you haven't done before, General," McLanahan said. "I know you've gone over the Mach at one hundred AGL in the B-1B, and you've shook off fighters in a B-52 down low before, too."

"That's enough, McLanahan," Samson said. "The test is over. Sit back and enjoy the ride back to Edwards." He turned to look over his right shoulder at Masters. "You okay, Dr. Masters?"

"Sure . . . fine." He looked right at the edge of losing control of his stomach's contents, but he wore a concerned expression. "I hope you didn't stop all that yanking and banking pilot stuff because of me. Actually, I was starting to get into it."

"Why *did* you stop, Terrill?" McLanahan asked. "Why did you let those guys get us?"

"What's the point, Patrick?" Samson asked in an angry tone. "Like you said, it was daylight, they had us visually. They got us. We didn't have a chance. We were just rolling around down close to the ground, waiting for them to kill us. We couldn't escape. It was inevitable."

"*Nothing* is inevitable, sir," McLanahan said. "We can beat even the F-22 Lightning down low. I've seen the best fighters in the world lose a B-52 when it's down in the rocks—the more high-tech a fighter gets, the less capable it'll be in a visual chase down low."

"I know that, Patrick. I've done it myself."

"But we can't show the powers that be how good we are if we keep on calling 'knock it off' the minute we're bombs-away, sir. We've got to prove that we can survive in this day and age of superfighters and high-tech air defense systems."

"You're preaching to the choir, Patrick," Samson said, "but unfortunately I think the heavy bomber is going to become a thing of the past with or without the Wolverine missile. The Pentagon understands the concept of employing squadrons of fighters and fighter-bombers overseas or aboard carriers—they don't understand, or refuse to accept, the idea that we might not be able to send a carrier into a certain part of the world, or we might not be able to establish a forward operating base close enough to the enemy to use a fighter-bomber."

"So . . . what are you saying, sir?"

"I'm saying, as of October first, Eighth Air Force goes away—and with it, most of the heavies."

"*What?*" McLanahan interjected. "The Air Force is doing away with the long-range bombers?"

"Not entirely," Samson replied. "Twelfth Air Force gets one B-2 wing, twenty planes by the year 2000—hopefully with ten or twenty more, if Congress gets their act together, by 2010—and three B-1B wings, two Reserve wings, and one Air National Guard group."

"No B-1Bs in the active duty force—and *all* the BUFFs and Aardvarks go to the boneyard?" McLanahan exclaimed, referring to the B-52s and F-111s by their crewdog-given nicknames. "Unbelievable. It doesn't seem *real*."

"Fiscal realities," Samson said. "You can fill the sky with F-15E fighter-bombers for the same price as a single B-2 squadron. The President looks at Mountain Home with a huge ramp full of a hundred F-15s, F-16s, and tankers, and he knows he can precision-bomb the shit out of North Korea with just that one wing for three hundred million per year; or he looks at Barksdale or Ellsworth with just twenty heavies and virtually no precision-guided stuff for the same money. Which one does he pick? Which one looks worse to the bad guys?"

"But the heavies drop more ordnance, cause more damage, inflict more psychological confusion—"

"That's arguable, and besides, it doesn't matter," Samson interjected. "I can tell you that European or Central Command planners much prefer to hear that a hundred Eagles or Falcons are on their way rather than twenty B-52s or even thirty B-1s, even though a B-1 can beat an F-16 any day in conventional radar bombing. Pacific Command—well, forget it. They won't even ask for an Air Force bomber wing unless every carrier is on the bottom of the ocean—for them, almost nothing except tankers and an occasional AWACS radar plane exist outside Navy or Marine Corps fighter."

"I just hope, sir," McLanahan said, "that you don't let the Pentagon kill off the heavy bombers as easily as you just let those fighters kill *us.*"

"Hey, McLanahan, that's out of line," Samson said bitterly. "You listen to me—I believe in the heavy bombers just as much as you, probably more. I fight to keep the heavies in the arsenal every fucking *day.*"

"I didn't mean to accuse or insult you, sir," McLanahan said, iron still in his voice, "but I'm not ready to give up on the heavy-bomber program. We'd be committing national defense suicide."

"You might want to loosen up a bit, Patrick," Samson interjected, with a wry smile. "Those decisions are made far, far above our pay grade. Besides, it was the *success* of the heavy bomber that helped kill it off more than anything else."

"What do you mean?"

"After your overflying of China with a B-2 everyone thought had been destroyed, the world is scared shitless," Samson explained. "Any talk of using strategic bombers in a conflict, especially with China, looks like a return to the Cold War days, and it has lawmakers on both sides nervous. The President has ordered all the Beaks back to Whiteman, and he's lying low, waiting for the 'lynch mobs' to quiet down."

"Lynch mobs? Someone's upset that we struck back at the Iranians?"

"Don't you read the papers, Patrick?" Samson asked with surprise. "Half of Congress, mostly the left side of the aisle, is howling mad at the President for authorizing those bombing missions against Iran. There's talk of an investigation, an independent counsel, even impeachment. Nothing will come of it, of course—it's all political mudslinging, and few outside the Pentagon or the closed-door congressional military committees know what we did over Iran—but the President's neck is stretched way out there."

"We proved today that the B-52 is still a first-class weapon system," McLanahan said resolutely. "We've got five more EB-52s sitting in storage right now, and Sky Masters can arm them all with Wolverine attack missiles and Tacit Rainbow anti-radar missiles. The mission has changed, General, but we still need the B-52s."

"The B-52s have already been fragged for the boneyard, Patrick, including the Megafortresses," Samson said. "The money's already been spent to get rid of them. Minot and Barksdale go civilian by the end of next year—hell, my desk will be auctioned off by Christmas. Give it up, Patrick. I'll recommend that Air Force buy Wolverines, but not to equip B-52s—that's a losing proposition. Mate Wolverines with Beaks and Bones"—Samson used the crewdog nicknames for the B-2A and B-1B bombers—"and I think we'll have a deal."

But McLanahan wasn't listening—he was lost in thought, his eyes locked in the "thousand-yard stare" that he seemed to lapse into from time to time. Even though he ran checklists and did his duties as a B-2 bomber mission commander, he seemed to think about a hundred different things all at once. Just like Brad Elliott, Samson thought. Thinking about how he was going to twist the game to his advantage, turning over each and every possibility, no matter how weird or outlandish, until the solution presented itself. Elliott was famous . . . no, *infamous* . . . for that.

"Twenty B-2s and sixty B-1s to cover all of the long-range strike contingencies around the world?" McLanahan muttered. "You can't do it, sir. Deploy the force to Diego Garcia for a Middle East conflict, then swing them to Guam for an Asia conflict? Maybe for a few days, but not for more than that. Who leads the way for the little guys?"

"That's why we got the Navy and the F-117," Samson said. "Bombers aren't the only answer, MC, you know that. You're forgetting the other twenty-five Air Force, Reserve, and Guard combat strike wings, the thirteen Navy air wings, the four Marine air wings . . ."

"Tactical bombers need forward airstrips, lots of tankers, and lots of ground support," McLanahan reminded the general, "and naval bombers need carriers that can sail safely within range of the target. A conflict in Asia, for example, could do away with all of these."

"But a B-52 can't stand up to modern-day air defenses, Patrick," Samson said. "All of the reports and studies prove this. Even with two-hundred mile standoff weapons, a B-52 can't survive. Put it in a low- or zero-threat environment and it could chew up a lot of earth, but it's not worth the money to support a bomber that can only be used once the war's almost won."

"General, the Megafortress will cream anything the Air Force, Navy, or Marines can put up against it," Jon Masters. "All by itself, it'll go up against a squadron of whatever you want to put up and 'destroy' every strategic target in the RED FLAG range—and it'll come out alive, ready to fight again."

"Spoken like a true salesman, Doc," Samson said over his shoulder, with a broad smile. To McLanahan he said, "I'm not promising that anything will come of this, you two, remember that. I did this flight test as a favor to you and Dr. Masters. You and Jon might not get a contract from the Air Force after all this is over, no matter how well your gear works or how much of your own money you spend."

"When the Air Force sees what we can do, they'll make a deal," Masters said confidently. "They won't be able to resist."

"General, Jon's business is making money—we all understand that," McLanahan said earnestly. "But my objective is to build the best long-range rapid-deployment attack fleet possible with our shrinking defense budget, and I believe part of that objective is the EB-52B Megafortress, combined with smart standoff attack and defense-suppression weapons. Jon and his company are backing my ideas. All I want is a chance to show the brass what we can do, and we need your help. We're the best, General. We need the chance to prove it."

Samson smiled and shook his head in amusement. "You better watch yourself, Colonel—you're starting to sound an awful lot like that old warhorse friend of yours, Brad Elliott." McLanahan smiled at the mention of his mentor. "He's a good buddy and one fine man, but he sure got stung by the hornets from all the nests he stirred up. A friendly word of caution: don't be like him."

Judging by the silence, Samson guessed that McLanahan hadn't heard a word he said.

CENTRAL MILITARY COMMISSION CONFERENCE
ROOM, GOVERNMENT HOUSE, BEIJING,
PEOPLE'S REPUBLIC OF CHINA
TUESDAY, 27 MAY 1997, 2341 HOURS LOCAL
(MONDAY, 26 MAY, 1041 HOURS ET)

"Loyal fathers of the Party, stand and pay respect to our Paramount Leader!"

The assembled general officers and ministers of the People's Liberation Army stood and bowed deeply as the president of the People's Republic of China, Paramount Leader Jiang Zemin, entered the conference chamber, bowed slightly to the others, and took his place at the head of the table. They remained standing, all bowing at the waist except Jiang, until the Chinese anthem, "Xiang Yang Hong," or "East Is Red," was played. They stood at attention until after the Intonation of Strength and Solidarity was read; then the ministers applauded the Paramount Leader as he took his seat. The Intonation was a solemn promise to support and defend the Communist Party, Zhongguo Renmin Gongheguo, the People's Republic of China, and the people; but unlike the American Pledge of Allegiance, the Intonation contained a threat of the particular punishment one might expect if he or she did not sacrifice one's life for the Party and for the people—disgrace, humiliation, death, and public dishonor of self and one's ancestors.

Jiang Zemin carefully watched the faces of the assembled ministers and generals as the Intonation was read, looking to see if anyone's eyes glanced over toward his or to anyone else's—the threat of death and humiliation in the Intonation was sometimes enough to make a guilty or conspiratorial man fidgety. It was of course possible to bury any outward signs of treason, but Jiang knew that a man bent on betrayal sometimes looked for reassurance from coconspirators or for evidence that he was under suspicion. Jiang was an expert in detecting such subtle, outward signs of a man's innermost fears.

Paramount Leader and President Jiang Zemin was seventy-one years old, in excellent health and looking far younger than his years. He had a square, tough-looking face with a high forehead and thick dyed black hair combed straight back. He wore a simple olive short-sleeved open-collar rough-cotton tunic shirt belted at the waist, with matching pants. His horn-rim spectacles were plain; he wore no jewelry except a wristwatch. Educated as an engineer but trained in Communist Party doctrine and theory in Moscow, formerly the mayor and Communist Party chief of China's second-largest city, Shanghai, Jiang was a master at power politics in China, a man well-suited to run his nation's large and complicated Party mechanism.

Today, Jiang Zemin was president of the world's most populous nation and, as such, arguably the most powerful man on planet Earth. Among his many responsibilities and duties, the engineer from Jiangsu Province was general secretary of the six-member Chinese Communist Party Secretariat, the genesis for all political thought in China; chairman of the Politburo, the group of twenty-one senior Party leaders who determined all Chinese political ideology and direction; chairman of the Standing Committee, the highest policy-making body in China and the body who actually wrote legislation (the 3,500-member National People's Congress always rubber-stamped their approval of all legislation drafted by the Standing Committee and Politburo); chairman of the powerful Military Commission of the Chinese Communist Party, who determined Party policy in military affairs; chairman of the Central Military Commission, responsible for implementing Party military policy in the People's Liberation Army; and commander in chief of the People's Liberation Army—a force of two hundred million regular, reserve, paramilitary, and militia troops.

Jiang not only had the power to enforce laws, but also made laws and even created the philosophy and ideas behind the laws, the ideals that formed the very basis of Communist Chinese thought. He was not only leader and chief executive of the most populous nation on earth, but was also commander in chief of the largest military force on the planet—and now he was planning to set that huge machine in motion.

Jiang was presiding over a crucial late-night meeting of the Central Military Commission, made up of civilian and military members in charge of the key divisions of the military infrastructure: the Minister of National Defense, Chi Haotian; High General Chin Po Zihong, chief of the general staff of the Chinese People's Liberation Army (PLA); General Yu Yongpo, chief of General Political Affairs of the PLA; General Fu Qanyou, chief of the PLA General Logistics Department; the chiefs of staff of the army, air force, navy, and the East China Sea Fleet; and the chiefs of China's ten military and civilian intelligence agencies and institutes.

"Comrades, loyal ministers and generals, there is a saying in the ancient military philosophy of Zhongguo that the government must evaluate not only the enemy, but evaluate itself before pondering the beginning of hostilities," Paramount Leader Jiang Zemin said. "I am here to inform you that the Party and the government have looked deep within ourselves, at the state of our nation and of the people and our way of life, and we have seen that our nation is being pulled apart piece by piece by the encroachment of the Western world. It is time to end the rape upon our nation, our people, and our way of life. In China, as it should be through-

out the world, the government must govern, and that is the will and the task of the Party.

"The disintegration of the state is seen in the usurpation of several regions on the periphery of our nation," Jiang went on, "including India, Kyrgyzstan, Vietnam, Mongolia, and threats against our Communist brothers in North Korea; and three critical regions belonging to China since the dawn of recorded history: Senkaku Dao, taken from us by Japan in World War Two; Nansha Dao, taken from us by European imperialists and by Asian anarchists and dictators using Western governments as their puppets; and Formosa Dao, taken from us by the Nationalists and now protected by the United States. The Party's stated goal is simple, comrades: The twenty-third Chinese province of Taiwan will be ours once again. The Party demands that our attack plan against Taiwan be activated."

The ministers and generals nodded dutifully, but Jiang was surprised to hear applause from the commission! Rising to his feet while continuing to applaud his president's words was Admiral Sun Ji Guoming, the first deputy chief of the general staff and General Chin's expected successor. Moments later, other generals followed Sun's lead, rising and applauding, and even some of the aged ministers clapped, their soft, withered hands making virtually no sound. It was unheard of, totally out of character for a Chinese to express himself so openly, especially a military officer.

"You dishonor yourself by such a pretentious and disrespectful display, Comrade Sun," General Chin, the chief of staff, said in a low, croaking voice. "Be seated."

Sun bowed to both Chin and Jiang. "Forgive me, comrades," Sun said, without being given permission to speak. "But I welcome the Paramount Leader's words with great joy. I meant no disrespect." He quickly dropped back into his seat and apologetically averted his eyes—but only for a moment.

"Comrade Sun's enthusiasm is shared by us all, Comrade Jiang," General Chin said, after giving Sun a deadly stern warning glance. "Implementing the Party's wishes will be a challenging but ultimately victorious task. I urge the Central Military Commission to order the aircraft carrier *Mao Zedong* and its new battle group into position to take Quemoy immediately, so the Taiwanese Nationalists cannot use them as staging or observation bases against us," Chin said. Quemoy was a large Taiwanese-occupied island just a mile from the Chinese mainland, used as an observation outpost and tourist destination. "We can blockade the island with ease with our task force, cut off their supplies, and starve them into submission. The task force can land five thousand troops on Quemoy right away, and we can eventually move three thousand troops a day onto the island. In two weeks, we can retake the island and claim it."

Jiang was surprised at Chin's comments—he expected resistance from the People's Liberation Army. Bloated, gargantuan, hopelessly encrusted and weighed down with decades' worth of nameless bureaucrats, the military seemed to require a full ten years of preparation before embarking on the simplest program or operation. Under Deng Xiaoping, Jiang's predecessor, the People's Liberation Army had been reduced in size by one-fourth and the militias reduced by almost half, but there were still over three million active-duty troops in China and over *two hundred million* men and women that could be mobilized for military service.

The centuries-old "sea of humanity" concept of warfighting was being replaced by modern ideas, but it would take several generations to eliminate the old ways—and the old inertia. Chin Po Zihong was a daring leader who truly believed China was destined to rule Asia, but he was not the best tactician. It was Chin who had tried to form an alliance with a socialist government faction in the Philippines; it was Chin who had devised the current alliance among China, North Korea, and the Islamic Republic of Iran. Although both programs had ended in disaster, thanks to the United States Air Force, the political ties still held firm, and there was no doubt that China was becoming a major economic, political, and military force in Asia.

"A very positive attitude, Comrade General," Jiang said. "But what about the Americans? What will their response be? In the past, they have threatened nuclear war with Zhongguo to protect the Nationalists. Only the threat of nuclear war kept us from reoccupying Quemoy in 1958."

"The Americans have no interest in the region, and they certainly have no stomach for nuclear war," Chin said confidently. "We have historical and legal rights to Taiwan, a fact that has never been disputed by the Americans. Even after the Philippines conflict, America has no presence in the area. Private American companies assisted us in exploiting the wealth of the region—that is the extent of American presence. As always, their government's policy is dictated by the capitalist overlords, and for now the capitalists demand that they help us exploit the oil deposits, so they dictate that their government step aside. But now it is our time to enjoy what is rightfully and legally ours.

"The United States will complain of our actions, but the deed will be done, and after time the conflict will be forgotten," Chin went on in a loud, demonstrative voice. "China invests twenty-seven billion dollars a year in the United States; we are responsible for creating ten million jobs in that country alone. They dare not start a war that might result in our country withdrawing all that economic support. Their carriers are not in position to oppose us. Why? Because they fear our economic power, and they fear an unpopular and costly war for a province they do not care about—Taiwan. The United States wants China united again. They do not want a divided China because they have suffered defeat in every other such conflict in Asia—Korea and Vietnam. They fight for a nation that cares nothing about the United States, and they are defeated. They will not fight for Taiwan."

There was a general nodding of heads in the commission chamber, Jiang observed—all except Admiral Sun. The Black Tiger had been the most enthusiastic and vocal supporter of the idea of asserting dominance in Asia, now, when the actual framework of a plan was introduced, he was silent. Sun was not brooding or resentful because he had been slapped down by General Chin.

. . . and then Jiang realized that Admiral Sun actually dared to *disagree* with his superior officer, in the middle of a Central Military Commission meeting! Sun was still sitting on his hands, not averting his eyes but not meeting Chin's murderous gaze either. To everyone's surprise, Jiang turned to the youngest of all his generals and asked, "Comrade Sun, do you agree with General Chin's assessment?"

Sun moved slowly to his feet, riveting the attention of all. He stood and bowed to Jiang, then said, "Sir, Sun-tzu advises us that being unconquerable lies within oneself, and that being conquerable lies within the enemy. In that regard, I agree with General Chin—we must quickly retake Taiwan, capture and imprison all Kuomintang officials, and heavily fortify it with our best naval, air, and air defense forces. But with all due respect, I do not agree with General Chin regarding an attack on Quemoy, or about the Americans."

"Oh? Explain yourself, Admiral."

"Comrade General Chin is quite correct: the American capitalists and special interests determine the law and direction of government in the United States," Sun went on. "The American government does not interfere in the South China Sea because the American oil companies profit by operating the drilling platforms; they do not side with the Nationalists because it is in their economic interests to side with us. But if we bombard Taiwan or Quemoy and imprison or kill the Nationalist leadership, they will seek retribution from the American government and its military forces. And as mighty as the People's Liberation Army is, we cannot long stand against a strong, determined, organized American military. It would be a complete failure. My former commander of the South China Sea Fleet, Admiral Yin Po L'un, acting on orders from General Chin, proved this.

"In my opinion, the Nationalist forces on Quemoy can easily withstand a blockade, bombardment, and even a full-scale invasion long enough for the United States to organize a counterattack," Sun went on. "Meanwhile, our country would suffer the anger of world opinion. We would be twice defeated."

General Chin looked as if he were about to explode; the other generals shifted restlessly, offended but interested enough to want to hear more before they tore off this insolent pup's stars. *What nerve!* Jiang thought. *What courage!* Sun could be dead in four hours—Chin could never allow Sun to remain on his general staff after this blatant show of disrespect, and Jiang knew of Chin's henchmen that would work secretly and effectively to cause Sun to have an untimely, unexplained "accident"—but Jiang admired him his youthful strength and audacity. Chin thundered, "I order you to leave this chamber and report to—!"

Jiang raised a hand. "I wish for the young admiral to continue," he said, then turned his hand palm upward, a signal to continue. Chin looked as if he had been slapped—he even rubbed his face, as if still feeling the blow. Jiang said, "So, Comrade Admiral, you think we cannot prevail against the Americans?"

"Not in a direct engagement with an organized, determined, and bloodthirsty American military force, sir," Sun replied. "The American military—any large military force, including our own—is like a large, heavy sledgehammer. It is unwieldy and takes great strength to employ, but once in action, it is highly effective. Hammer against hammer, army against army, the American military is clearly superior, and Sun-tzu teaches us to evade a superior opponent.

"But the buzzing of a single mosquito, the hot rays of the sun, or a single bead of sweat in the eyes can disrupt he who wields the hammer enough so that his blows are less effective, or can even prevent him from swinging the hammer altogether. Even more important, if the target of the hammer's blow is small, irregular, or moves too quickly, even the best smith can miss his mark. After several ineffective blows, the strongest smith will tire, lose patience, make mistakes, and eventually cease. He has lost. He has been defeated by a vastly inferior force—and he has been defeated by *himself*.

"Sir, I have studied the *tao* of the American military, and I have examined our *tao,* and my studies conclude that the Americans have no desire for prolonged battle in Asia. Asia in general and China in particular have an aura of deadly mystery and foreboding for Westerners—they fear China's massive population, its history of violence and warfare, our homogeneous society, and the knowledge we have gained over centuries of civilization. Americans in particular are reluctant to have anything to do with us, fearing to be drawn into another protracted Vietnam-like battle—they fear traveling far from home, of being drawn into a dark tunnel of mystery and killed by punji sticks and knives carried by billions of tiny yellow hands. And they are far weaker than they appear. The American navy is three-fourths the size it was in 1991 after the Persian Gulf War; the American air force is almost half the size. American forces in Japan, including Okinawa, have been cut in half since 1992. And for all their bluster about safeguarding Taiwan, the United States still has not recognized the Nationalist government and still has no embassy, consulate, bases, soldiers, advisors, or equipment there. During the Olympic games last year, the Americans even referred to the rebel government as 'Chinese Taipei,' not as 'Taiwan' or the 'Republic of China.'

"But even so, Comrade General Chin is wrong—the American president Martindale will send in his carriers," Sun went on. "Two of them are within four days' steaming time to Taiwan, and within two weeks a third will join them. The U.S. government claims that the three carriers will rendezvous somewhere in the Philippine Sea for what they term a 'photo opportunity,' because one of the carriers supposedly will be decommissioned, but we all know that these carriers are rendezvousing to set up an attack on our homeland. They will set up east of Taiwan so they can take advantage of air defense protection from Taiwan and appear not to be concerned about events in China, but close enough so they can conduct air attacks on our ships and land bases if war breaks out. We must not blindly cruise within range of the Americans' carrier-based attack planes. Instead, we must draw the carriers toward *us*.

"The key to victory over the Americans is contained in the words of Sun-tzu: we must draw their carriers away from the protection of the Nationalists' air defense forces and into 'fatal terrain'—that is, a battleground where they must be unconquerable, where they must fight with reckless abandon and complete disregard for any protest against the campaign, or face total defeat. In order to draw them into fatal terrain, we must force them to come to the rescue or force them to intervene with the thought of preventing a conflict. That conflict is Taiwan, comrades. In the confines of the Strait, we can destroy the carriers. At the same time, we strike at the most likely resupply and air staging base in the area: Okinawa. Once Okinawa is destroyed, American forces will be forced to stage out of the heart of Japan, and so the threat to Japan becomes clear—"

"You speak in double-talk, Sun," General Chin shouted. "You talk about dancing around the American carriers, but then talk about a full frontal assault on Okinawa. How do you expect to destroy one of the Americans' strongest bases, comrade?"

Without one change in his expression or voice, Admiral Sun said matter-of-factly, "We should by all means use our nuclear arsenal."

The reaction was swift and powerful—and all of it against Sun. President Jiang called for order, and his command was echoed by the sergeant-at-arms and his officers. Jiang said crossly, "Admiral Sun, you are to be reprimanded once again for your impertinence and ignorance. It is obvious you are not familiar with the Party's policy on the use of nuclear, chemical, or biological weapons."

"If I may speak, sir—I am very familiar with the Communist Party's policy," Sun said. "The government of China and the Chinese Communist Party officially rejects the first use of nuclear, chemical, or biological weapons because it conflicts with the ideals of peaceful unification of all the peoples of the world under socialism. I studied the policy towards the use of special weapons in both the National Academy and the College of War, and advised the office of the premier on its implementation."

"Then you should know that no one on this Commission or the Communist Party is suggesting or even contemplating the use of nuclear weapons against the Americans, Admiral."

"On the contrary, sir, I know their use is contemplated quite often," Sun said, calmly but firmly. "I know exactly at what bases they are kept, how many, and which missiles and ships carry them—including the carrier *Mao Zedong*."

General Chin looked as if he was ready to murder Sun with his bare hands. "Sit down, damn you, Sun!" he ordered from between clenched teeth. "Be *silent*!"

"I will *not* be silent!" Admiral Sun said. His voice rang like a shot through the Commission chamber, and it had the same effect as if a real gun had been fired in that room. "We seem content to have our foreign policy dictated by the Americans, even though the Americans have no cohesive policy with regards to Asia except the furtherance of fair trade—fair only to themselves, of course. The threat of American military intervention paralyzes this commission, even though we have it in our power to reduce or perhaps eliminate the force of American intervention, or even whether or not they will choose to intervene."

"I order you, *be silent,* Sun!" Chin shouted. "Be seated!"

"Wait, General," Jiang said. He motioned to Sun. "Speak, Admiral, but be warned—your fitness for your post will be determined by what you say here to this commission."

"I will accept that, sir," Sun said resolutely. "Comrade President, members of this commission, the Party and our government has said that it wishes our country first to reunify with the pieces lost to us by foreign conquests—namely, Senkaku Dao, Formosa Dao, and Nansha Dao—and second to make China the preeminent power in Asia for all time. These are worthy goals. I believe we have the support of the people, which Sun-tzu says is necessary before the ruler may charge the generals with preparations for war, and so we should carry out this mandate immediately.

"But it is obvious to me, as I am sure it is to you, that the United States, by its foreign policy and tremendous military might, is the dominant force in Asia now. We do not retake Formosa, Quemoy, or Matsu from the Nationalists because we fear American intervention. We do not retake the Senkaku Islands, taken from us by Japan, again for fear of retaliation from the Americans. But we have retaken the Nansha Dao, what the West calls the Spratly Islands, and America has done nothing—

in fact, American companies *help* us pump oil and natural gas out of fields *we* took from other countries. America does not care about what happens in Asia, as long as it does not affect their bottom line—their ability to make money.

"But our very political and social framework is under attack by America. They try to influence our laws, tell us not to limit how many children our families can have, or tell us to buy more automobiles, televisions, and blue jeans or else they will not permit our goods to be sold anywhere in the world. This evil influence is strangling our very souls, comrades, and I see no solution except one: remove the Americans from Asia, permanently. This means destroy the American aircraft carriers and destroy the main American military staging base on the island of Okinawa. We have no choice, comrades."

"You are advocating nuclear war with the Americans?" General Chin retorted. "Are you insane, Sun? It will spell certain annihilation!"

"Nuclear war with America is not inevitable, Comrade General," Sun said. "America has almost completely eliminated its ability to wage nuclear war—they believe it is unthinkable and unnecessary, given their perceived conventional weapons technological superiority. In a war that does not threaten American lives or territory, my studies conclude that America, even led by a hawk such as their president Kevin Martindale, will not launch a nuclear strike against us. But if we are determined to win, then we must acknowledge that we shall use nuclear weapons against the Americans. We can be secure in the knowledge that America will not retaliate with nuclear weapons unless their homeland is attacked, and that even if they do employ nuclear weapons against us, we can withstand the attack as a nation.

"We can use our subatomic arsenal, our neutron bombs, to eradicate the Nationalist forces on Quemoy and Matsu—quickly, before the Americans can react," Sun said. "We can hide the attack behind a blockade and bombardment, but the truth will be known soon enough anyway. But the Nationalists cannot hide from the effects of a neutron bomb in their bunkers and tunnels. Before the American carriers arrive, we will have retaken Quemoy."

President Jiang was startled, even a bit intimidated, by Sun's ideas and by the strength of his convictions—but he was also intrigued by them. Here was a military man who was not afraid to lead, Jiang thought. Here was an officer who studied Chinese military history and ancient Chinese military teachings, then employed those time-honored and time-tested ideas to solve modern-day problems. Here was a man of action, a man willing to lead a struggle of liberation against the most technologically powerful military force ever known—the United States of America.

And he was not afraid to use the most terrible weapons known to man: atomic weapons, especially the neutron bomb. The neutron bomb, developed from stolen U.S. plans ten years earlier, was a small, "dirty" nuclear device that killed by saturating the target area with radiation. The nuclear yield was small enough that blast damage was confined to a few hundred meters from "ground zero," but the effects on human beings of the neutron radiation released by the weapon was devastating. Any living creature within two miles of the blast would die of radiation poisoning within forty-eight hours, no matter how deep underground they were; unprotected humans within five miles of the blast would die within seventy-two hours. Further, all significant traces of radiation would be gone within a week, leaving structures and machines virtually untouched and unaffected. The People's Liberation Army could march in and take Quemoy without firing a shot.

"You speak of not conducting a direct engagement against American air or naval forces," Jiang asked, "but you speak of destroying American carriers and bases. Can you explain how this can be done, Admiral Sun? Do you plan on exploding nuclear weapons all over the Pacific now?"

The confident smile that spread across Ji Guoming's face was filled with energy and enthusiasm—two emotions so alien in this old Commission chamber. "Comrade President," Sun said, "Sun-tzu teaches us that the army goes to war in the orthodox, but is victorious in the unorthodox. That is the key to victory against the Americans."

As Jiang Zemin and the other members of the Military Commission listened, it soon became obvious that Admiral Sun had carefully thought this plan out, and that he was highly intelligent and his staff highly competent. In just a few minutes, President Jiang actually believed that this man, this Black Tiger, could pull off the impossible.

"The admiral should be congratulated for the attention to detail and daring of his plan," General Chin said, after Sun had finished. "But it is also a reckless and dangerous plan, one that could spell disaster to the republic if a full-scale confrontation breaks out. I feel that Admiral Sun wants vengeance, and that in his thirst for revenge he is not thinking of the people nor of the fatherland. Your ideas have much merit, Comrade Admiral, and may withstand serious scrutiny by the Plans and Operations bureau of the Military Commission. But I believe the president wishes us to formulate a strategy that will achieve the Party's objectives quickly and effectively. The carrier *Mao* and the task force will accomplish those objectives."

"Comrade President, I must say again, we must not send the *Mao Zedong* aircraft carrier battle group anywhere near Taiwan," Sun said earnestly. "It would be seen as a large-scale provocation. I have a plan to draw the American carriers well within range of our shore-based attack planes. We would have the upper hand then. We must—"

"I said be silent, Admiral," Chin said angrily. "That is your final warning."

Admiral Sun looked as if he was going to continue the argument— but a reassuring glance from the president himself, Jiang Zemin, caused him to relent. He bowed, folded his hands, kept his head lowered, and did not raise his eyes again for most of the rest of the meeting. He'd taken the chance to get his ideas presented in front of the Commission, and he'd failed, and he'd dishonored himself in doing so.

"We will begin preparations for the invasion of Quemoy immediately," President Jiang announced. "The carrier battle group will be diverted north with its invasion force to blockade the island. Within thirty days, comrades, victory will be ours!"

BARKSDALE AIR FORCE BASE, NEAR SHREVEPORT, LOUISIANA FRIDAY, 30 MAY 1997, 0845 HOURS LOCAL (0945 HOURS ET)

"Like most transitions, my friends," Air Force Lieutenant General Terrill Samson, commander of Eighth Air Force, began in a deep, emotional voice, "today we are witnesses to both an end and a beginning. Although you might have a tough task believing this is a happy occasion, I believe it truly is." Samson was standing before a crowd of about two hundred out on the flight line in front of Base Operations at Barksdale Air Force Base, Louisiana. It was still early in the morning, and the event was scheduled early to avoid the inevitable summer heat and humidity common this time of year.

Flanking Samson was the wing commander of Air Combat Command's Second Bomb Wing, Brigadier General George Vidriano, along with members of the staff of Eighth Air Force, the major Air Force operational command that for years had organized, trained, and equipped America's bomber forces, and Colonel Joseph Maxwell, commander of the 917th Wing of the Air Force Reserves based at Barksdale. Standing at parade rest next to him was a detail of officers and NCOs, carrying small blue-and-gold squadron guidons, representing the various squadrons based at Barksdale. Behind Samson were three Air Force aircraft, washed, waxed, and polished as brilliantly as if they had just rolled off the assembly line: a T-38 Talon jet trainer used for copilot proficiency training, an A-10 Thunderbolt II close-air support attack jet, and a huge, light gray B-52H Stratofortress strategic bomber, with cruise missiles hanging off its wing pylons.

"We are here today," General Samson continued, "to stand down one of the world's premier bomber units, the Second Bomb Wing, and to retire the last of this nation's most successful aerial war machines, the B-52 Stratofortress bomber. In the sixty-four year history of Barksdale Air Force Base, the men and women assigned here have stood at the forefront of our nation's peace and security. They have proved this by an impressive string of awards and achievements: the Fairchild Trophy for the best bomber wing in bombing and navigation competition; twelve Air Force Outstanding Unit citations; and sixteen Eighth Air Force Outstanding Unit Awards.

"But what makes me proudest of this base's legacy is its commitment to its community. The people of Bossier City and Shreveport, and the soldiers of Barksdale, have been tightly linked, supporting one another through good times and bad, through triumphs and tragedies. I was privileged to serve as a wing commander of the Second Bomb Wing during my career—the year we missed the Fairchild Trophy by missing one time-over-target by eleven seconds, I hasten to add—and so I know firsthand the link that has always existed between the uniformed and civilian members of the Bossier City and Shreveport community. It is a tradition that has set the standard for the rest of the United States' armed services.

"I am pleased to tell you that the Air Force is giving back to this great community a great deal of the support that we have received over the decades. Barksdale Air Force Base will become Barksdale Jetport, with a variety of aviation and non-aviation businesses relocating here with state and federal assistance, including an aviation-career campus of Louisiana State University; the base hospital will become a joint Veterans Administration and community hospital; and the other buildings, housing units, and dormitories on base will be used for a variety of programs and industries, including job retraining and agricultural research.

"In addition, the men and women of the 917th Wing of the Air Force Reserves under Brigadier General selectee Maxwell will still be here with the A-10 Thunderbolt II, but will eventually transition from the B-52H to the B-1B Lancer bomber when all of the B-1s go to the Guard and Reserves; and the beautiful Eighth Air Force Museum will still be here, open to the public, mostly because of the generous support from our friends in western Louisiana and eastern Texas. The Air Force is committed to easing the impact of the loss of a one-hundred-and-sixty-million-dollar federal payroll to the citizens of the cities of Shreveport and Bossier City."

Samson paused, fidgeted with his notes for a moment, then added solemnly, "I can also tell you that it has been announced by the Pentagon that Eighth Air Force will stand down, as of October first of this year."

There was a plainly shocked expression from most of the audience and even from most of the staff—this was news to almost everybody. "For sixty years, Eighth Air Force has been synonymous with the heavy bomber," Samson went on, sticking to his prepared remarks, even though he, like many in the audience, was obviously emotionally affected by the surprise announcement. "From northern Africa to Europe to Korea to Vietnam to the Kremlin to the Middle East, warplanes bearing the 'Mighty Eighth' seal have struck terror into the hearts of the enemy as they hunkered down against the relentless bombardment of our planes.

"Our planes were rarely pretty—the B-17, B-29, B-36, even the B-52H behind me could hardly be called sexy except by a few romantic ex-crewdogs like myself. Our missions were certainly never very glamorous—Dresden, Hiroshima and Nagasaki, Inchon Harbor, Linebacker Two, the Iraqi Second Corps and Republican Guards, and the nightmarish concept of MAD, or 'mutually assured destruction.' But the men, women, and machines of Eighth Air Force have always been victorious by the use of the world's deadliest war machines, the heavy bomber. As the old saying goes, 'fighters are fun, but bombers win wars,' and that has been true ever since Lieutenant Eugene M. Barksdale of the Eighth Aero Group, Army Air Corps, the pioneer for whom this base was named, first carried a seven-pound mortar shell aloft in his Curtis-Wright Aero to test out the then-outlandish idea of dropping bombs from an airplane."

Finally, the emotions welling to the surface could be contained no more. Ignoring the reporters and cameras—CNN was here, carrying this ceremony internationally, as were a number of local stations, but still the big three-star general ignored the warning lights flashing in his brain—Samson put aside his notes and affixed his audience with a deep, sincere stare, as he continued:

"As commander of Eighth Air Force, the major operational command in charge of Air Combat Command's heavy and medium bomber forces, I can tell you that I'm not in agreement with my superiors on their decision to drastically reduce the size of the bomber force by retiring all the B-52H and F-111F bombers and to turn all of the sixty operational B-1B Lancer bombers over to the Air National Guard and Air Force Reserves, with the other thirty B-1 bombers going into flyable storage. This decision will leave Air Combat Command with only twenty active-duty long-range bombers, the B-2A Spirit stealth bombers, by the year 2000—yes, twenty bombers, twenty planes." The audience, which was made up of community leaders and military dependents, all very knowledgeable of the Air Force's plans for the heavy bomber force and how their plans affected their lives, shook their heads in sympathetic amazement.

"The argument is of course that the B-2 stealth bomber is that much more capable, that the threat has changed, and the B-52s and B-1s are too costly to maintain and don't have enough precision-guided weapon capability. The newer planes, the F-15s and F-16s and F-22s and the Navy birds with their laser-guided weapons, can perform surgical strikes on any target, while the 'heavies' lack a similar precision-kill capability and it would be far too costly to retrofit them to give them the same capability. I can't argue with the fact that the B-2 is an incredible warplane and it is redefining strategic warfare almost every time it flies. I will also not argue that the threats facing the United States and its military have changed: we are no longer using nuclear deterrence to threaten any nation, a strategy that the people of Barksdale and the other warriors of the U.S. Air Force exemplified but whose time is now past. We now foresee numbers of low-intensity non-nuclear conflicts similar to Desert Storm, rather than a major intercontinental war between superpowers with the possible use of nuclear weapons.

"But I will continue to argue the fact that when a crisis of any size erupts anywhere in the world, there is only one weapon system in existence, short of nuclear weapons—which in my mind are totally obsolete, except for the very small numbers that should be kept in case of a totally unforeseen political occurrence—that can quickly and effectively reduce or even eliminate an enemy's ability to wage war, and that is the heavy bomber," Samson went on, gripping the sides of the podium, as if he had to restrain himself from pounding on it or rushing into the audience to punctuate his points. "With or without forward bases, with or without sea access, with or without warning, with or without cooperation from allies or other nations, only the long-range bombers, along with the tanker force and with the latest in standoff and near-precision guided-weapon technology, can destroy the enemy's will to fight. In the opening days of a conflict, the intercontinental-range bombers would make the difference between stabilizing or even eliminating the crisis, and losing control of it.

"Twenty B-2 bombers plus the ready Reserve B-1s might be able to affect the course of a conflict in one region of the world for a few days, perhaps even a few weeks, until other land- or sea-based forces could arrive. My concern is, what if no other forces are available? What if the seas are denied us, unlikely as that scenario may be? We were lucky in Desert Storm because we had a great and powerful ally, Saudi Arabia, with large bases close to the action and plenty of fuel and with two major bodies of water under Coalition control to operate carriers and submarines. We were also very lucky because Saddam Hussein chose not to sweep into northern Saudi Arabia and destroy Riyadh, the Saudi oil fields, or the numerous Saudi military bases there, and instead allowed the Coalition a full six months to prepare for war. We should not rely on any of those advantages in the next conflict.

"And what if another even more serious conflict breaks out somewhere else in the world, so we are faced with two major low-intensity conflicts? In my opinion, eighty bombers, or whatever number of them that survive the first crisis, would be hard-pressed to respond to a second crisis elsewhere in the world with the speed and power necessary to make a difference."

The audience was very quiet; a few nodding heads could be seen, a few surprised expressions at Samson speaking his mind so plainly. This was not an uplifting good-bye speech by the bomber forces commander—this was an ominous warning message. Samson paused to get his emotions under control; then he took a deep breath and continued: "I want to thank the men and women of Second Bomb Wing for your service, and also add a personal thank-you to the men and women of Eighth Air Force for your hard work and dedication to duty to the command, to our nation, and to me.

"And I know it seems silly to do so, but indulge me: I want to thank the B-52 bomber, and all the men and women who have taken them into battle and who have sat with them on nuclear alert, defending our homes, our freedom, our way of life, and protecting our allies. You're only a big hunk of metal, ten thousand random parts flying in formation, but God bless you anyway." The applause was unexpectedly loud and long, which greatly pleased General Samson, who took a long look at the B-52H behind him and gave it a thumbs-up. He then turned back to the audience, snapped to attention, and said in a loud voice, "Attention to orders from the commander in chief."

"Wing, ten-*hut!*" General Vidriano shouted. The uniformed men and women came to attention, and the audience respectfully stood.

Samson was passed a blue binder, and he opened it and read, "By order of the commander in chief of the armed forces of the United States of America, the Second Bombardment Wing, Heavy, and its component squadrons, Barksdale Air Force Base, Louisiana, are hereby relieved of all combat and support duties and ordered to stand down this date." The tears flowed again, from the big man at the podium to the combat veterans to the tough young security policemen guarding the line. "Your success in long-range bombardment missions, as well as in maintaining a strategic combat-ready posture over the years, has ensured the peace and security of the United States and of the free world, and reflects great credit upon yourselves and the United States Air Force. I am pleased to express the heartfelt thanks of a grateful nation. Mission accomplished. Job well done. Signed, The Honorable Arthur S. Chastain, Secretary of Defense; The Honorable Sheila F. Hewlett, Secretary of the Air Force; General Victor A. Hayes, Chief of Staff, United States Air Force. General Vidriano, carry out the orders."

Vidriano saluted, then said in a loud voice, "Wing, present your colors!" Samson closed the binder, then left the podium and walked in front of the group of officers and their guidon-bearers. One by one, the individual squadrons were called out. As the squadron commander's and senior NCOIC's names, along with a little of each squadron's history and major accomplishments, were read aloud to the audience, the officers and guidon-bearers stepped forward, and the guidon was rolled up on its staff, covered, and presented to the Second Bomb Wing commander, who gave it to his wing NCOIC.

After all of the squadron guidons were furled and covered, General Vidriano then took the wing flag, the tip of its flag's staff festooned with dozens of campaign ribbons won from more than fifty years of combat service, from his wing's senior noncommissioned officer and, holding it in two hands, held it out stiffly with both arms fully extended and presented it to General Samson. "Sir, I present to you the Second Bomb Wing, Heavy, the best heavy bombardment wing in the world. The wing has stood down, as ordered."

Samson saluted. "Thank you, General. Please personally thank your men and women for their outstanding service to the nation."

At precisely the moment that General Samson took the wing flag in his hands, a loud rumbling was heard in the distance. The audience members looked up and saw an incredible sight: flanked by three T-38 Talon jet trainers that looked insectlike in comparison, a massive formation of twenty B-52 bombers passed slowly only 5,000 feet overhead, forming a gigantic number 2 in the sky. The sound of those huge planes passing overhead sounded as if a magnitude ten earthquake were in progress—metal folding chairs rattled, bits of dirt on the ground jumped like giant fleas, a thin cloud of dust began to rise over the ground stirred up by the vibration, car alarms in the nearby parking lot went off, and somewhere behind the audience a window shattered in the Base Operations building.

Soldiers yelled and screamed in delight, civilians put their hands to their ears and made comments to people beside them that couldn't be heard, and children clutched their parents' legs and cried in abject fear—and combat veteran and (at least until October 1) Eighth Air Force commander Lieutenant General Terrill Samson felt a lump of awe lodge in his throat, dredged up by a wellspring of pride from his heart. The sounds of cracking glass in the Base Ops building finally caused his emotions to bubble forth, and the big three-star general laughed until he cried, clapping as hard as a young kid at a circus. The audience happily joined in.

Even without dropping any iron, Samson thought gleefully, the damn BUFFs—the Big Ugly Fat Fuckers—could still do what they had done best for the past thirty-five years: they could still break things on the ground with power and ease.

●●●● As General Samson's C-21A Learjet transport plane pulled up to the VIP parking area in front of Base Ops a few hours after the stand-down ceremony ended, General Samson shook hands with Barksdale's senior officers and enlisted men and women, returned their salutes, picked up his briefcase, and headed to the jet's airstair. Normally Samson would insist on taking the pilot's seat, but this time he had business to attend to, so he headed back to the cabin and strapped in at the commander's seat at the small desk. The copilot ensured that the general was comfortable, gave a short safety briefing to the general and the other three passengers already aboard, and hurried back to the cockpit. The plane taxied back to the runway and was airborne again within minutes.

"Forgot how emotional these damn stand-down ceremonies can be," Samson said to his three fellow passengers. "I've been presiding over too damn many of them."

"Some pretty cool flying, though," said Dr. Jon Masters, as he sipped from a can of Pepsi. Jon Masters, barely thirty years old, drank several such cans of sugar-laden beverages every day, but somehow was still as skinny as a pole, still had all his teeth, and still had no detectable chemical imbalances or vitamin deficiencies. "They must've been practicing that formation for days."

"Weeks, Dr. Masters," Samson said. "That's all the flying they've been doing lately." He looked over at passenger number two, paused as if considering whether or not he should do it, then stuck out a hand. "How the hell are you, Brad?"

Retired Air Force Lieutenant General Bradley James Elliott smiled, noticing Samson's discomfort at his presence with undisguised amusement. "Peachy, Earthmover, just peachy," he replied, and took Samson's hand in his.

There it was again, Samson thought grimly—that irritating cocksure attitude. Samson was not sure exactly how old Elliott was, probably in his early sixties, but he had the demeanor and attitude of a young, spoiled brat, of a guy who just knew he was going to get his way. Medium height, medium build, still as healthy-looking in a business suit as ever—even with the leg. Samson's eyes wandered down to Elliott's right leg, barely visible behind the desk. It looked normal under the nicely tailored suit, but Samson knew it was not normal—it was artificial. Very high-tech, fully articulating, it had been good enough to get Elliott re-cleared for flying duties back when he was in the Air Force—but it was still very artificial.

Elliott saw Samson checking out his leg. He smiled that irritatingly smug grin and said, "Yep, still have the appliance onboard, Earthmover." He flexed his foot around in a circle, an incredible feat for a prosthetic device—it truly did look real. "It only hurts when I think about what's happening to my Air Force." Samson chuckled, but the joke was DOA—no one, not even Elliott, was smiling.

Elliott had always been this way, Samson remembered—grim, demanding, headstrong to the point of being reactionary. A former Strategic Air Command bomb wing commander, Pentagon staffer, and expert in strategic bombing and weapons, Brad Elliott had been living the dream that Terrill Samson had harbored for many years—to be universally acknowledged as the expert, the one that everyone, from the line crewdogs to the President of the United States, called on for answers to difficult questions and problems. Elliott was a protégé of strategic nuclear aerial warfare visionaries such as Curtis E. LeMay and Russell Dougherty, and a contemporary of modern conventional strategic airpower leaders such as Mike Loh and Don Aldridge, the true proponents of long-range airpower. It was Elliott who had engineered the hasty but ultimately successful rebirth of the B-1 bomber, developed new cruise missile technology for the B-52, and kept the B-2 stealth bomber on track through its long and expensive trek through the halls of Congress when it had been a deep "black" program that could be canceled in the blink of an eye.

Rising quickly through the ranks, Brad Elliott had become director of Air Force plans and programs at the Pentagon, then deputy commander of the Strategic Air Command. He had been well on his way to a fourth star and command of SAC, and possibly back to the Pentagon as Air Force chief of staff, when . . . he'd suddenly dropped almost completely out of sight. He'd surfaced only once, as a military advisor to the abortive U.S. Border Security Force, but he'd been suddenly so far under cover, wrapped in an airtight cocoon of secrecy of which Samson had never seen the like, then, now, or ever since.

Elliott's name was linked to dozens of dramatic, highly classified military operations and programs supposedly originating from the High Technology Aerospace Weapons Center, or HAWC, the top-secret research and testing facility in the deserts of south-central Nevada known as "Dreamland." Many risky, bold military operations all over the world had Brad Elliott's signature style on them: small, powerful, high-tech air attacks aimed directly into the heart of the enemy, usually involving heavily modified bombers. Although he didn't know for certain, Samson was sure that Brad Elliott and the crewdogs at HAWC had been behind unbelievable military successes from central America to Lithuania to the Philippines.

Well, here he was again. Brad Elliott was now a civilian, working on classified Air Force programs as a senior vice president of Sky Masters, Inc. Elliott had been shit-canned, forced to retire, after a major spy scandal had shut down HAWC and shoved military research programs back at least a decade. But, as always, Brad Elliott had landed on his feet, cocky as ever. No one in Washington liked him, not even his advocates—like the President of the United States, for example. But he had this mystique, this air of complete command, of prescience. He was known as the man to turn to, plain and simple. You didn't have to like him, but you had better get him working on your problem.

Samson decided to ignore him for the moment, and he turned and shook hands warmly with the third passenger. "Patrick, good to see you again," he said to retired Air Force Colonel Patrick McLanahan.

"Same here, sir," McLanahan said in return. Now, here was a kid he could get to like, Samson thought. McLanahan was, pure and simple, the best pilot-trained navigator-bombardier in the United States, probably the best in the world. He had been an engineer, designer, and team chief at HAWC, working as one of Brad Elliott's supersecret whiz kids, designing aircraft and weapons that would someday be used in wars. Like Elliott, McLanahan had been forced to accept an early retirement in 1996 in the wake of the Kenneth Francis James spy scandal and the HAWC closing. Even though McLanahan had risked his life to bring the Soviet deep-cover agent Maraklov back from Central America before he had a chance to escape to Russia with a stolen secret Air Force experimental aircraft, he'd been sacrificed for the good of the service. McLanahan and Elliott had been close friends for many years.

But unlike Brad Elliott, Patrick McLanahan got the job done without pissing the leadership off, without copping an attitude. When the

President had wanted someone to head up a secret aerial strike unit under the Intelligence Support Agency to counter Iranian aggression in the Persian Gulf, he hadn't turned to Brad Elliott, the acknowledged expert in long-range bomber tactics—he specifically had *not* wanted Elliott involved in the secret project, although Elliott had planned and executed many such operations. The President's staff instead had turned to Elliott's protégé, McLanahan. And the young Californian, who looked more like a young college professor or corporate lawyer than an aerial assassin, had come through brilliantly, taking a modified B-2 Spirit stealth bomber halfway around the world to nearly single-handedly shut down the newly rebuilt Iranian war machine. Now McLanahan was getting a reputation as the "go-to" guy when the shooting started, even over well-qualified active-duty crewdogs.

"So, what do you have for us, Earthmover?" Brad Elliott asked, rubbing his hands in exaggerated anticipation. "Are we going after the North Korean chemical weapons plants? We going to polish up in Iran? Someone tried to whack the Iranian military chief of staff Buzhazi and missed— let *us* take a shot at him. And that ex–Russian carrier is in the South China Sea, on its way to Hong Kong—we should sink that thing before it gets within striking range of Taiwan. Rumor has it that it's fully operational and carrying."

Samson ignored Elliott for the moment—hard to do, since they were sitting right across from each other—and turned to Jon Masters instead. "I take it that Brad here is part of your team, Dr. Masters? I wasn't made aware of that."

"We've got five of the eight Megafortresses flying now, General," Masters said. "We need experienced crews."

"The Air Combat Command guys you sent need at least six months of training time," McLanahan interjected. "They're good sticks, and they can certainly handle the beast, but the systems are unlike anything they've experienced before. And we're changing the systems, too, so we put them to work as engineers and test pilots while they're getting checked out on the plane." He paused, searching Terrill Samson's face for any signs of difficulty. "Brad Elliott *is* the Megafortress. He's the creator, the progenitor." Samson was silent, his mouth a hard line on his face. "Problem, Terrill?"

"Terrill thinks the President's going to have a cow when he sees me," Elliott answered for the big three-star general. He turned to McLanahan.

"We're going to meet the President—didn't you know that? I called the White House communications office and confirmed the meeting. That cute V.P. Whiting, Chastain, Freeman, Hartman, Collier from NSA I think, and George Balboa, that old Navy squid sack of—"

"Brad . . ."

"We go way back, me and Martindale, so don't worry about it, big guy," Elliott interrupted, watching Samson's face turn puffy with anger. "We'll have a good meeting, and we'll have all the right answers."

"The President *specifically* didn't want you for the Iran operation," Samson said coldly, "because you have this knack for stepping on toes, for sticking your face in where it doesn't belong. Apparently, retirement hasn't mellowed you one bit." He paused, then shook his head. "The President asked only for Jon and Patrick. Sorry, Brad—I'm not going to bring you into the meeting. I'll mention to General Freeman that you're on board—he can notify the President."

"Sheesh, you make it sound like Jon hired Saddam Hussein to fly for him," Elliott said sarcastically. "I'm not trying to take over this operation, Earthmover. I advise the kid here on how to design, build, and fly the Megafortress. That's all."

Samson ignored Elliott again and said to Masters and McLanahan, "Jon, Patrick, he's your man, so you deal with him. I'll back you all the way, but it's still my opinion that Brad's presence in the White House or the Pentagon will only hurt your chances of getting this operation approved."

"You still haven't told us what operation we're being considered for, General," Jon Masters said. "What is it?"

"You'll be conducting a maritime reconnaissance operation in the Formosa Straits," Samson replied. "I'll run it down."

"Shit, you don't mean we'll be working for Admiral 'Tight-Ass' Allen at Pacific Command?" Elliott interjected wearily. "Man, I was glad to get out of the service just so I didn't have to listen to him bitch about the Philippines conflict. Now we've got to listen to him *again*? And with Balboa on as chairman of the Joint Chiefs, we'll spend half our time arguing over who's got the bigger cruise missiles."

"You still get your orders from me," Samson said. "I report directly to Philip Freeman at the White House, who will report to the NCA."

"You just make sure Allen or Balboa don't try to snatch this mission," Elliott said, admonishing Samson with that cocksure grin again. "If they get control, they'll screw it up for sure. We've got to have maximum autonomy out there, and you know the squids aren't going to allow us to have it."

"I'll take your *suggestion* under advisement, Brad," Samson said, his lips taut. Dammit, the guy was a real pain, but he sure knew the score in Washington—Elliott had correctly guessed who would probably be in the *real* chain of command in this operation. "I signed for the Megafortresses when I took them out of mothballs to let you characters play with them, and I picked Eighth Air Force crews to fly them, so I think I'll keep operational command. But if you're harboring any thoughts about maybe making the EB-52 an operational weapon system, play nice with the rest of the kids in the pool. Follow me? Any problem with that, Brad? Is that enough full disclosure for you?"

"No problem, Earthmover, none whatsoever," Elliott said. "Actually, I'm happy to have you in the loop—even though you *are* responsible for eliminating all the BUFFs from the Air Force inventory. One of the greatest aerial attack platforms ever devised, and you, of all people, allowed it to be retired on your watch."

"Let's not get into a discussion about who's responsible for any good—or any *bad*—stuff happening in the Air Force or the bomber world in recent history," Samson growled, trying hard to control the sudden flush of anger rising up from his chest. He knew his comment had hit Elliott, but the bastard did not show it. Samson knew that Elliott knew that the downfall of HAWC had put air weapon research and development back several years and may have even ensured the downfall of the heavy bomber. So there was plenty of blame to go around.

"The bottom line is, boys, you got your chance to show what a modified B-52 bomber can do," Samson said. "Let me deal with Washington—I want you to loudly kick some ass out there, then bring yourselves home in one piece."

"Mr. President, may I present Ambassador Kuo Han-min, the new representative of the *independent* Republic of China," U.S. Secretary of State Jeffrey Hartman announced, as he was ushered into the Oval Office. Already in the room with the President of the United States, Kevin Martindale, were Vice President Ellen Christine Whiting, National Security Advisor Philip Freeman, Secretary of Defense Arthur Chastain, and White House Chief of Staff Jerrod Hale. "Ambassador Kuo, the President of the United States, Mr. Kevin Martindale."

The two shook hands, Ambassador Kuo bowing deeply, then presenting his blue leather credentials folder directly to the President. Kuo appeared a bit older than the President, with thick dark hair, thick wire-rimmed glasses, and a thin frame. "This is an honor for my country and for myself, Mr. President," he said.

"Good to see you again, Ambassador," the President said, as he handed the folder to Hartman. The two had met during a Republican Party fund-raiser in Washington a year earlier; Kuo Han-min had been a Taiwanese high-tech aerospace industry trade lobbyist at the time, whose organization had made several very large contributions to the Party to help with Martindale's election campaign. The President steered Kuo around, where several White House photographers recorded the historic handshake—the arrival of the first Taiwanese ambassador in Washington since the United States had broken diplomatic ties with the exiled Nationalist Chinese government on Formosa in 1979 in favor of the Communist regime on the mainland.

The President made introductions to his other advisors in the room as the photographers departed, then offered him a seat. "Unfortunately," the President began after everyone took seats, "our first meeting here has to be a working one. We feel your country is in serious danger, and we'd like to fill you in as quickly as possible as to what we know, and discuss what we should do about it. Jeffrey, you spoke with China's foreign minister just a few moments ago. Bring us up to date."

Hartman stood behind one of the sofas surrounding the coffee table and said, "Foreign Minister Qian of the PRC says that the movement of ships along the Chinese coast is normal, preplanned activity. As far as any threats towards Taiwan, Qian says, in effect, 'Mind your own business.' Any activities between the People's Republic and Chinese Taipei, as he continues to refer to the ROC, is a quote-unquote 'internal matter.' "

"You told them to keep their hands off the ROC until we can meet and talk about this?" the President asked. "We just recognized the Republic of China's independence, for Christ's sake! Attacking them now would be a slap in the face towards us."

"In no uncertain terms, sir," Hartman replied. "I sent him your letter, which he had received, and explained that the United States would consider any military action against Taiwan as a seriously destabilizing and overtly hostile act, and would respond with any means at our disposal, including military means, to help bring stability back to the region. I plan on meeting with Foreign Minister Qian in Beijing in three days; hopefully I can get in to see President Jiang as well."

"Good," the President said. He stayed at his desk, quietly contemplating something, then rose to his feet and started pacing the floor. "Ambassador Kuo, any thoughts?"

"Sir, President Lee Teng-hui of the Republic of China believes as you do—that an invasion of Quemoy, the Pescadores, Matsu, or even Formosa Tao is imminent," Ambassador Kuo said. "He has ordered the mobilization of reserves and arming the militia. He is standing firm—he is not withdrawing any troops from Quemoy or Matsu. In fact, he is increasing them—he is flying in a thousand additional troops a day to both islands, and is shipping in additional air defense units. He has ordered the entire navy at sea to counter the Communist fleet's movements."

"You're going to stand up to the Chinese army?" Secretary of Defense Chastain asked incredulously. "Even if the PRC doesn't invade, your army could suffer substantial losses."

"We have made the decision to fight and die to the very last man, woman, and child to maintain our independence," Kuo said resolutely. "We must stand and fight, or die as a country. We have chosen our way." He paused for a moment, then looked the President square in the eyes and said, "Our concern is not with the Communists, but with the United States. You have declared your support for the Republic of China, but we understand that there is much to be done before you may legally recognize my country."

"That's being taken care of, Mr. Ambassador," the President said. "The bill we sponsored repealing the 1979 Taiwan Relations Act comes up for a vote next week, and we expect to be successful. Our support for the Republic of China is firm and unwavering."

"Yet we understand that you risk much politically by such action," Kuo said. "Your country's trade with the mainland could be in jeopardy— if the Communists shut the United States out, it will cost you at least thirty billion dollars a year. But worse than a trade war is the prospect of military action, of a large Pacific conflict."

"Ambassador, everyone wants trade with China, so they all look the other way when China does something to one of its neighbors," the President said angrily. "My father died fighting the Chinese in North Korea when I was a kid—everyone forgets that war and China's involvement. Everyone also forgets that we almost went to war—*nuclear* war—with Red China in 1955 over their bombardment of Taiwan. I was a kid, just getting over the death of my father in North Korea, when mainland China started shelling Quemoy—Jesus, I thought World War Three was going to start any day, that the Communists were going to sweep across the planet just like we saw that red stain sweep across the globe in the propaganda films. Throughout the sixties, Red China was just as much a threat as the Soviet Union—I remember China supporting North Vietnam and China imprisoning American POWs. The Soviet Union and China were both our hated enemies.

"The death of Stalin and Mao's break with the Soviets changed our strategy," the President went on. "In the rush to counterbalance the Soviet threat, we embraced the Chinese Communist government and turned our backs on democratic, capitalist governments like yours. No more. The United States is not going to wait patiently a hundred years for mainland China to adopt a free-market society, and in the meantime sit idly by while they destroy the Republic of China, gobble up oil fields in the South China Sea, refuse to enforce international copyright laws, and threaten free trade with the rest of Asia. America can't put off the decision any longer: we're either for an independent, democratic Republic of China, or we're for the *hope* that mainland China will keep Taiwan capitalist and free while they absorb you, like they're absorbing Hong Kong."

"I thank you, Mr. President," Kuo said, bowing sincerely, "for your words and for sharing your thoughts with me. But I must still ask about the political realities of your decision; I apologize if I am too forward . . ."

"Ask anything, Ambassador," the President urged.

"Thank you, sir. My government is aware of the opposition party's inquiries as to your actions against the Islamic Republic of Iran, about the rumors that you sent a stealth bomber over China. Since that incident, you have withdrawn all of your carrier battle groups from Chinese waters, despite the threat of a Communist invasion of my country. Is there a threat of a no-confidence vote in your congress or of any legal action that might preclude you from helping in the defense of my country?"

"I appreciate your concern, Ambassador," the President replied, "but I think I can handle the opposition party. Fortunately, it takes a lot more than a no-confidence vote to get me out of office. Now I've got a couple blunt questions for you, Han-min."

"Of course, sir," Kuo responded. "Please."

"We are very concerned about the protests in your country over the Senkaku Islands," Secretary of State Hartman said. The Senkaku Islands were a series of small, uninhabited islands in the East China Sea between Okinawa and Taiwan, which were claimed by China, Japan, and Taiwan; Japan had taken the islands from China in 1894 and had not relinquished possession after World War II, as it had with Formosa. Taiwan claimed the Senkakus as part of its archipelago. Diplomatic relations between the three countries had been strained for years because of overlapping fishing and oil-drilling rights in the area. "Japanese nationals have been attacked by protesters in Taipei, and no arrests have been made. It will be difficult to support the ROC if we get in the middle of a Japan-Taiwan conflict."

Ambassador Kuo thought for a moment; then: "Many in my country feel strongly that the Tiaoyutai, what Japan calls the Senkaku Islands, be returned to us, that they are spoils of war taken from us by imperial Japan."

"We understand the source of the disagreement, Ambassador, but a Japanese woman is dead and seven more are injured, in the middle of a riot with over a thousand protesters and two hundred police and army units, and no one saw anything? No evidence? No suspects?" Vice President Whiting interjected incredulously. "It looks like a huge cover-up, Mr. Ambassador. The Japanese government is hopping mad, and they want us to set up an arms and technology embargo against your country. We need definitive action immediately, or our Asian coalition will be broken before it has a chance to solidify."

"What do you suggest, Madame Vice President?" Kuo asked.

"We suggest your government ask for assistance from the American Federal Bureau of Investigation," Whiting replied, "and I also strongly suggest that you—and this is totally off the record—round up some suspects and publicly arraign them, and *fast*. Let's not be losing friends over some small, uninhabited piles of rocks while you lose friendly neighbors and your home island is in danger of being overrun."

Kuo lowered his eyes for a moment, then raised them and nodded. "We feel that the Tiaoyutai is much more than a 'pile of rocks,' Madame

Vice President," Kuo said solemnly. "But you are correct—I understand that our inability to solve the murder appears as if we condone it. I shall recommend that my government request immediate assistance from your government in the investigation, and I assure you that there will be swift action."

"We also need a statement from you on exactly when your country will discontinue nuclear weapons development and begin dismantling your nuclear weapon stockpiles," Secretary of Defense Chastain cut in.

Kuo swung toward Chastain, then to the President, with a look of horror in his face. "Nuclear weapons?" he sputtered. "Sir, the Republic of China possesses no nuclear weapons."

"Our intelligence information tells us otherwise, Ambassador," National Security Advisor Philip Freeman said. "According to our data, over the past fifteen years you have been involved in a nuclear weapons co-production effort with the Republic of South Africa, and our information suggests you may have developed a warhead small enough to be used on a gravity bomb or cruise missile."

"I most strenuously deny—!"

"Don't bother responding, Ambassador—denials will only embarrass you," Freeman went on bitterly. "More recently, we've received information that you are sharing nuclear-weapons information with Israel, and that you have a nuclear warhead on some license-built versions of the Gabriel anti-ship cruise missile. Finally, we received information from the JIO of the Australian Ministry of Defense that you have been sharing nuclear and chemical weapons technology with Indonesia. Australia is so sure of its information that it has considered a preemptive air strike on Indonesian weapons plants—and some attacks on certain Taiwanese vessels suspected of carrying weapon-making equipment into Indonesia." Kuo's eyes bulged at that news—he was completely unable to contain his surprise. "If any of this news ever leaked out, Mr. Ambassador, it would be a political disaster for the Republic of China and a great embarrassment for the United States of America."

"We *trust* you'll do the right thing," Secretary of State Hartman said, "and eliminate any sharing of nuclear weapons technology, with an eye on completely eliminating your nuclear weapons programs in the *very* near future. It would be extremely difficult for the United States to support any country secretly violating American nuclear weapons antiproliferation regulations. *Very* difficult."

The President hadn't said a word, but when Ambassador Kuo looked into his eyes, he saw disappointment and distrust conveyed to him as surely as if Martindale had screamed it in his face. The Taiwanese ambassador had noted with amusement the American people's preoccupation with their new President's hair, but now he saw what they all fixated on—the two silver-gray curls that had drooped across his forehead and eyes, making him look sinister, like a gray wolf ready to attack. "I . . . I will convey your message and request an immediate response," Kuo stammered, averting his eyes apologetically. "I assure you all, the Republic of China will obey international law and honor our treaty obligations, and, most importantly, we would not knowingly do anything to harm our strong and steadfast relationship with the United States of America."

"Then our commitment will remain equally strong to the Republic of China," the President said, in a light voice that seemed to clear the room of a dense choking haze. Magically, without a touch, the silver curls were now gone from the President's forehead. It is true, Kuo thought—this man certainly *is* bewitched!

Kuo looked very wobbly in the knees as he got to his feet when the President stood, signaling an end to the meeting. He extended a hand to Kuo, who accepted it and added a deep bow. "We'll set up a hot-line system with President Lee's office as soon as possible," the President said. "Until then, we'll be in contact with you, and you may contact my office or Secretary Hartman's office twenty-four hours a day, for any reason whatsoever. It was a pleasure to see you again. Please convey my best wishes and support to President Lee and Premier Huang. Good day." Kuo looked pale and a little sweaty as he was shown out of the Oval Office.

"God bless it," the President muttered, after Kuo had departed. "I'm getting ready to put our political necks on the chopping block for Taiwan, and the whole time Taiwan is handing over the ax to use on us. I'd like to talk with President Lee first thing in the morning—set it up," he told his chief of staff. Jerrod Hale nodded and picked up a phone to relay the order.

In the reception area down the hall from the Oval Office, Ambassador Kuo was on his way to the staircase down to the West Wing driveway when several men walking toward the reception area from the National Security Advisor's office caught his attention. Kuo stopped, then turned and walked over to them. "Forgive me, sir," Kuo said to the youngest of the men walking by, "but do I have the pleasure of addressing Dr. Jonathan Colin Masters?"

Jon Masters was surprised to hear his name. "You got it," he replied. "And who are you?"

"My name is Kuo Han-min, Ambassador to the United States from the Republic of China, at your service, sir," Kuo replied, bowing and then extending a hand. "It is a great pleasure to meet you. We met many years ago at the Singapore Air Show. Your company's exhibit was most impressive."

"Thanks, Mr. Min," Masters said, shaking hands with him, not realizing he had mixed up his surname and given name. When Kuo's eyes wandered over to the other men, who had walked on past them, Masters, feeling obligated to make introductions, pointed to them and said, "Mr. Ambassador, that's Brad Elliott, Patrick Mc—"

"No you don't, Dr. Masters," Patrick McLanahan said. Jon Masters didn't know, or had forgotten, about the extremely high security classification under which they were working, a classification definitely off-limits to foreign nationals. "Let's *go*."

"Elliott . . . General Bradley Elliott?" Kuo said, with a knowing twinkle in his eye. "And so you, sir, must be Colonel Patrick McLanahan of the United States Air Force. May I ask . . . ?"

Just then, two Secret Service agents stepped in front of Kuo, blocking his view, and said in a stern voice, "I'm sorry, sir. Please move along." Masters, Elliott, McLanahan, and the big black general Kuo recognized as Terrill Samson, commander of all the heavy bomber forces in the United States, were quickly hustled away into the Cabinet Room to wait for their meeting with the National Security Council, and Kuo was politely but firmly escorted outside.

So! Kuo thought. The President was meeting with the three-star general in charge of all the long-range bomber forces, and also with Elliott, Masters, and McLanahan. Those three had an international reputation for developing very high-tech attack weapons that were reportedly put to effective use in conflicts from Russia to eastern Europe to the Philippines. Now that he saw them all together, it made very good sense that such forces were used recently against the Islamic Republic of Iran—to extraordinarily great effectiveness. Now, with a probable conflict between China and Taiwan brewing, the President was conferring with them once again? Could the President be considering the use of stealth attack bombers in the defense of the Republic of China?

Kuo Han-min filed that brief but extremely interesting chance encounter away in his head—the information might be vital someday very soon.

• • • • "Okay. We're getting ready to side with Taiwan against China, which is bound to stir up some shit in the Pacific for sure," the President said. "What about Japan and South Korea? I hope they're not reacting."

"I've spoken with Japanese deputy prime minister Kubo and President Kim of South Korea, and they're watching events closely but not reacting, except for a few South Korean reinforcements along the DMZ," Hartman replied. "North Korea is blasting Taiwan and saying they're provoking war in Asia, but they don't seem to be exacerbating any conflicts—at least, not more than usual."

Hartman looked a little uneasy, and the President picked up on it. "What else? Did Nagai have a comment?" Kazumi Nagai was the new prime minister of Japan, an ultra-left-wing politician of the new Kaishin Party, a coalition of left-wing political parties including the Japan Communist Party. Nagai was staunchly but carefully anti-West and anti–United States; he'd won the recent elections by opposing continued U.S. military bases in Japan, by extending a two-hundred-mile Japanese economic exclusion zone around islands also claimed by South Korea, Taiwan, and China, and by calling for gradual increases in Japan's military expenditures and total Japanese nuclear self-reliance. Few of his more radical programs and propositions had been passed, but the favorable attention he was receiving in Japan was cause for concern in Washington.

"Exactly what you might expect," Hartman replied with a sigh. "Kubo told me the Prime Minister is going to give a speech tomorrow, calling for the U.S. to end its support of Taiwan as long as they claim ownership of the Senkaku Islands. The buzz is that Nagai will call for the Diet to withdraw basing rights for U.S. warships if we continue support for Taiwan."

"Christ almighty," the President muttered. "Jerrod . . ."

"I'm ahead of you, sir," Hale shot back, getting on the phone to order the staff to schedule a call to the Japanese prime minister's office. From his years as vice president, Martindale had learned that a simple phone call to a foreign leader was worth a dozen communiqués and State Department visits, and he spent quite a bit of time on the phone.

"Okay, so Japan and South Korea aren't saying anything about Chinese military moves," the President summarized. "It seems no one would really shed a tear—except Taiwan, of course—if China took back Quemoy, Matsu, or even Formosa."

"That's because Taiwan has a fairly balanced trading ledger and is a stiff trading competitor with everyone else in Asia—except the U.S. and China," Hartman explained. "Taiwan is the ninth-largest economy in the world and competes as an equal with Japan, Indonesia, South Korea, and Singapore. But Taiwan has a ten-billion-dollar trade surplus with the United States and holds two billion dollars' worth of U.S. currency and bonds. Its balance of trade is even more one-sided with China—all in Taiwan's favor. Most Asian nations see the Taiwanese Nationalists as rabble-rousers supported by the United States, similar to Israel. They feel that China should absorb Taiwan as it is absorbing Hong Kong—as long as the Communists allow them to keep making money."

"What's the balance of trade between Japan and South Korea and China?" Vice President Ellen Christine Whiting asked. A former governor of Delaware, Ellen Whiting's expertise was economic matters, whether on a local, national, or international arena—she believed the world revolved around money, and she was most often correct. "China's total economy has got to be, what? Ten times larger than Taiwan's?"

"Something like that," Hartman admitted.

"China is the trading partner everyone wants. Over a billion potential customers—that's why almost every nation in the world, officially including the United States, has abandoned Taiwan in favor of mainland China," Whiting maintained. "If China wants Taiwan back, who says the other Asian countries would stand in their way? Why would they make an enemy of China in favor of Taiwan?"

"So we shouldn't expect too much help from our allies in Asia, should Taiwan come under attack," National Security Advisor Freeman summarized.

"Privately, even secretly, I think we can count on Japan's and South Korea's support of any actions we undertake against China," Hartman said. "Both countries still rely on us for their security and for general stability throughout Asia. If we want to support Taiwan against China, I feel Japan and South Korea will support us."

"So we're it," the President said. "If the Chinese are going after Taiwan, we're the only ones who seem to give a shit." He paused, and the Oval Office turned quiet—everyone knew that the President was absolutely right. "And the bottom line is, I *do* give a shit. I don't want war with mainland China, but I also don't want mainland China taking Taiwan by force. They got Hong Kong back peacefully. If Taiwan and the mainland are going to be reunited, it should be done peacefully too. It would hurt our country if Taiwan was taken back by force."

"No question," Vice President Whiting joined in. "Trade, financial markets, multinational business, our national debt structure, our standing in Asia would all suffer if Taiwan was attacked and absorbed by Communist China."

"Agreed," the President said. "Question is, if the Chinese are moving against Taiwan, what do we have to stop them?"

"Ordinarily, I'd recommend instituting economic sanctions, pulling China's most-favored-nation trading status, setting up another embargo of high-tech and military goods," Hartman said. "But with China amassing this naval task force, I think it's beyond economic warfare. We should hear some military options—low-key, quiet, not too bombastic."

"We've got two briefings set up for you, sir," Freeman said. "Admiral Balboa will brief the first recommendation, and Lieutenant General Terrill Samson from Eighth Air Force will brief the second."

"Okay, let's get to it," the President said. "Where's Admiral Balboa?"

Jerrod Hale was on the phone instantly to the White House Communications Center; he got his answer a few seconds later. "En route, Mr. President," he replied, and motioned for the Secret Service to show the others in.

The President got to his feet as Terrill Samson, Patrick McLanahan, and Jon Masters were escorted into the Oval Office. "Damn, it's good to see you again, Patrick," the President of the United States said warmly, as he greeted each of them. "How the hell are you?"

"I'm fine, Mr. President," McLanahan said, shaking hands and receiving a brotherly clasp on the shoulder. "I'm glad to see you, and *very* glad to see you here, where you belong."

"Sometimes I wish I was back in the Vice President's office, working with troops like you—lots of power but no responsibility," Martindale said, rather wearily. "How's your wife? Wendy, right? Doing well, I hope."

"She's well, thanks."

"Shit hot. It's a miracle, after her accident. Congrats." Martindale knew all about the aerial duel between Wendy McLanahan in the original EB-52 Megafortress and the thought-controlled fighter that had been piloted by the Russian deep-cover spy Kenneth Francis James. "And thank you for what you and Tiger Jamieson did over Iran and the Persian Gulf. You averted a major world oil crisis, and possibly another Desert Storm. Job well done."

"I hope we get a chance to talk about the recent cuts in the bomber force, sir," McLanahan said. "Speaking as a concerned and knowledgeable individual and not just as a defense contractor, I have some ideas about the bomber force structure that you should know."

"You will get a chance to talk about it, I promise," the President said. "You've earned that right. Just keep in mind, the cuts were made long before I came into office, and the money has already been spent on the back end. But we'll talk about all this later. I've heard some good things about what you and this young man here have been doing." The President shook hands with Jon Masters. "Good to see you too, Dr. Masters. I'm looking forward to you naming a satellite after me soon. Make it a good one, okay?"

"The new space-based surveillance and targeting satellite needs a name," Masters said with a boyish grin. "At the risk of being accused of out-and-out brown-nosing the President of the United States, I wonder if I should skip Taylor and Clinton and go right to Martindale?" They all laughed—the answer to that one was obvious.

"General, good to see you again," the President said as he shook hands with the big three-star general. "I know I haven't had time to thank you for all the hard work you did getting Colonel McLanahan here back in the air for that Iranian mission. Your work was instrumental in averting a certain disaster in the Persian Gulf. We were very impressed with the proposal you wrote concerning this Taiwan reconnaissance/strike mission."

"Thank you, sir," Samson responded. "I understand you're getting a lot of political heat for the things we did. You don't have to take the fall for this alone, sir."

"I do, I will, and I'll survive, Terrill," the President said. "Unless the opposition wants to suspend the Constitution, I'm on solid ground. You worry about the mission we're thinking about sending your boys on, I'll worry about the Democrats." His weak smile told Samson that he was more than just a little concerned about the political pressure he was under.

"Jerrod's going to call me to go to that American Bar Association dinner thing in about thirty minutes, so let's get to it." The President steered the three newcomers over to places around the coffee table in front of the big Resolute desk in the Oval Office. "Ellen, gents, I think you all know Air Force Lieutenant General Terrill Samson, commander of Eighth Air Force and bomber guru. Let me introduce Dr. Jonathan Colin Masters, boy genius, defense contractor, and reportedly the smarter younger brother of Merlin the Magician. And this is ace bombardier Patrick McLanahan. He and I have some stories that will curl your toes, if they ever declassify them. You'll never guess how close to the brink we've been together, and how often we've been there." The Presidential advisors, except Philip Freeman, mumbled hellos and little else.

"Here's what's going on, boys," the President began, taking his seat at the head of the circle, with Vice President Whiting beside him. "A few weeks ago, the intelligence wonks said the PRC is massing a naval task force at Juidongshan, of about forty ships, mostly small combatants but a few large destroyers and frigates. The press reported it as minor ship movements associated with Reunification Day celebrations. We believe the ships have some other purpose. Meanwhile, the aircraft carrier *Mao Zedong* moved into Hong Kong Harbor, supposedly also participating in the Reunification Day stuff—but then we learned it lifted anchor. Phil, bring us up to speed."

"In a nutshell, sir: that task force is getting bigger, and the carrier's on the way to join them," Philip Freeman began. "Estimated size of the PRC task force right now is fifty-seven ships, including six Luda-class guided-missile destroyers and twelve Jianghu-class frigates. Lots of support ships for surface forces and submarines. The carrier *Mao* has departed Hong Kong and is heading north along the coast, apparently to join the Juidongshan task force. The *Mao* is being escorted by four Luda-class destroyers, among others, so the PLAN has almost all of their operational destroyers involved in this task force.

"Along with the naval task force, we've noted increased activity at eleven army bases and ten air force and naval air bases within six hundred miles of Taipei, Taiwan. We're watching a gradual activation of rocket artillery units at the army bases, with M-9 and M-11 ballistic missiles. We're estimating at least two hundred attack planes, one hundred fighters, and fifty long-range bombers on line, each capable of carrying one or two large anti-ship cruise missiles . . . or nuclear weapons."

There was a muted "Oh, shit" from someone in the Oval Office. "Run down the nuclear-capable forces for us, Phil," the President asked somberly.

"China's main nuclear threat comes from land-based mobile missiles," Freeman said, reciting data completely from memory. "The Chinese have approximately one hundred mobile medium-range nuclear missiles, each of which can carry multiple reentry warheads, plus approximately one hundred mobile short-range single-warhead nuclear missiles similar to Scuds, and a total of twelve intercontinental-range missiles. A few of these units have been moved east arrayed against forces in the Pacific, although most are still set against Russian and Indian forces in the southwest or north. Only two nuclear-capable subs in the Chinese fleet; the Navy keeps very good track of both of them when they put to sea, which is not very often. The H-6 bombers are all nuclear capable, but with gravity bombs only—so far, the Chinese seem to have no nuclear-capable air-launched cruise missiles. The bombers are not considered a threat against a full-up American carrier or surface action group.

"With the addition of the *Mao* carrier, however, we can expect the addition of nuclear-capable anti-ship missiles, particularly the SS-N-12 Granit," Freeman concluded. "Supersonic, over two-hundred-mile range, big warhead, radar-guided—a real threat if it gets past the outer and middle ring of air defense in the carrier battle group. The Sukhoi-27 or -33 fighters deployed on the carrier can presumably deliver nuclear gravity bombs, too."

"Chance of the Chinese using nukes for whatever they got in mind?"

"Until the Philippine conflict in 1994, it was considered low," Freeman replied. "The Chinese have always disavowed first use of special weapons—nuclear, chemical, and biological. But China used a tactical nuclear weapon against Philippine naval forces in 1994, and threatened to use them again in March of 1996 if Taiwan held their presidential elections and declared independence from the mainland. They even mentioned military retaliation against the United States if we should interfere, and refused to deny that they were in essence threatening to use nuclear weapons against the United States.

"The attacks of course never materialized. We always thought it was mere rhetoric, but . . . I think it would be irresponsible to dismiss any country threatening to use nuclear weapons. China has an advanced nuclear development program, including neutron, fractional orbital bombardment systems, tactical, battlefield, man-portable, and multi-megaton weapons."

"Good ol' Admiral Yin Po L'un, firing nukes around the South China Sea and Celebes Sea from that huge-ass destroyer *Hong Lung* like spitballs in a third-grade classroom," the President reminded everyone wryly. "We're *very* lucky World War Three didn't break out. Thanks to Patrick and Jon here, we put a hole in that destroyer of his big enough to drop a house through."

"Well, General Chin Po Zihong is still chief of staff of the People's Liberation Army; Yin's former second in command, Admiral Sun, is now a deputy chief of staff; and China has an apparently fully operational aircraft carrier that our sources say may be carrying nuclear ballistic missiles and anti-ship cruise missiles," Freeman summarized. "Chin might be out for revenge for what we did to his navy, and Sun might want revenge for what we did to his brand-new destroyer. A nuclear weapon might be the only way China can dig the Nationalists out of the tunnels and mountain fortresses of Quemoy." Two groups of islands just off the coast of mainland China were claimed and occupied by Taiwan: the Matsu Islands northwest of Taiwan, no more than eleven miles off the coast; and Quemoy, a large island directly west of the island of Formosa and no more than two miles off the Chinese coast. Both Taiwanese islands had been heavily bombarded by Chinese artillery and naval forces in the past, but they had held firm—capturing them would be a major moral as well as a tactical victory for the Chinese Communists.

"So you're saying we're looking at the possibility of a nuclear war over Taiwan?" the President asked. "Any chance they're just going to sail all these ships down to Hong Kong to celebrate Reunification Day?"

"Always a chance of that, sir," Freeman responded, "but a better bet would be an invasion force or a covering force against one of the Taiwanese island formations near the PRC coastline. The lack of landing craft in the task force suggests it's not an amphibious invasion, although the aircraft carrier itself makes a very formidable troop carrier and it does have the capability to launch amphibious assault ships. The task force could set up a blockade while their invasion forces go ashore. Quemoy would be the most logical target. Taiwan garrisons approximately fifty-five to sixty thousand Taiwanese troops there, along with antiaircraft and coast defense missile sites, but they're nothing but a political trip wire, designed to inflame the world against the Communists if they attack. The attack would be over quickly, probably well before we could do anything to assist.

"The Communists will probably conduct an amphibious assault soon after the missile or bomber attacks—they won't make the same mistake they did in 1958," Freeman went on. "Then, the Communists bombarded the island for six straight *weeks*—it's estimated that every square mile of the island was hit by *two thousand* artillery shells. Even after the offensive stopped, the Communists continued to bombard the island every other day for *eighteen years*. But the Nationalists dug in, using a complex of underground fire bases and supply tunnels. The Communists never were able to dig out the Nationalists, so the invasion plans were shelved.

"That won't happen again. A neutron-bomb attack would destroy the island's defenses, and the People's Liberation Army would simply march right in after the radiation levels subside in a few months. Target date: right around July first. Chinese Reunification Day. Maybe earlier, so victory could be won by Reunification Day."

The President seemed to swallow hard at that bit of news. "You think they'd start a *nuclear war* over Taiwan, even though Taiwan declared its independence and the whole world will be watching?"

"I think the Chinese military machine began gearing up for this offensive several months ago," Freeman replied, "and it's too late to stop it. In fact, Taiwan declaring independence probably *guaranteed* they were going to go ahead with an invasion."

"Damn," the President muttered. "The elephant is getting ready to squash the flea." He paused for a moment, then asked, "Where are the carriers right now?"

"Admiral Balboa should be here in a few minutes to brief you, sir," Freeman said, glancing at his watch, "but I'll summarize. We have no carriers within striking range of the Chinese task force or their missile bases, but that can be remedied in about three days. The *Independence* battle group is closest, getting ready to depart Yokosuka on patrol. It's on its last cruise before retirement, carrying a standard package air wing. *Indy*'s replacement is the *George Washington,* getting ready to depart Pearl, carrying an attack-heavy wing. ETE five days."

"Any other air units in the area?"

"We fly daily P-3 Orion anti-submarine patrols up and down the Formosa Strait," Freeman responded. "We also have Air Force reconnaissance planes flying nearby, RC-135 Rivet Joint intelligence-gathering planes. Daily satellite passes as well."

"I meant strike or defense-suppression air," the President said.

Freeman nodded. "We've got Marine F/A-18 Hornets and A-6 Intruders on Okinawa, but they need heavy aerial refueling tanker support," he replied. "The Orions can carry torpedoes and Harpoon missiles in a strike configuration. We made the decision not to load up the region so as to avoid provoking China during their Reunification Day celebrations."

"But it seems to have had a reverse effect," Secretary of Defense Chastain cut in. "President Jiang sees an opportunity. He has the people whipped up by all this reunification talk and solidly behind him, he got the Politburo and military behind him, and it looks like they're going for it."

The President had little reaction except to ask, "Submarines?"

"We have two Los Angeles–class attack subs, *Springfield* and *Pasadena*, assigned to shadow the Chinese task force," Freeman replied. "Two more Sturgeon-class subs are patrolling the Formosa Strait itself, and the *Honolulu* is shadowing the Chinese nuclear sub *Xia*. Two more subs are on patrol in the South China Sea. All seven subs have relief on the way."

"Two subs versus a fifty-ship task force is a bit skimpy," Secretary of Defense Chastain interjected.

"We can have two more subs on station in five to six days," Freeman said. "But Taiwan has two, maybe three subs between the task force and Formosa, and so the Chinese are aggressively hunting subs."

"All the more reason to put a few more in," Chastain argued. They all looked at the President, waiting for guidance.

The conversation fascinated Patrick McLanahan. This was the White House Oval Office, the center of world power—but thorny questions were discussed and massaged and examined as if they were all sitting around in a farmhouse kitchen in Iowa, discussing the weather and the markets and the crops and trying to decide whether to begin the harvest now or wait another couple days. McLanahan was also surprised at Martindale's hesitancy. Kevin Martindale had never been shy about committing U.S. military forces anywhere, anytime—but the political fallout from the conflict with Iran, and especially the decision to fly a B-2 bomber secretly across Chinese airspace to get at Iran from the "back door," was murderous. Impeachment had been mentioned more than once in interviews with the opposition party, and the media seemed to be fanning those flames. Martindale's presidency was less than six months old, and it was already seriously in hot water.

"Send them," the President ordered. "Two more subs, specifically against the task force, plus two reinforcements. Right away." Arthur Chastain made a note to himself to cut orders. The President paused for a moment, then said, "We need more firepower out there, gents, but we don't have the time. The Navy is our best bet this time, but they'll take a few days to get set up." He paused, then said in a contrite, almost embarrassed voice, "And I want this done quietly. I'm getting hammered by the Democrats and the press on the use of the B-2 bomber against Iran. I can't use the active duty or Reserve bombers. I don't even like the idea of sending in aircraft carriers, because to me it forces the conflict to a new, deadly level—and it gives the media and the Democrats more ammunition to use against me."

The President looked at McLanahan and Masters. "General Samson and Air Force chief of staff General Hayes briefed me on the new Megafortress project—of course, I'm well familiar with the previous Megafortress missions," the President said. "I understand you have eight planes altogether, but crews and weapons for only five. Correct?" Masters nodded. "We need all you can muster for an armed patrol over the Formosa Strait."

"You got it," Masters replied immediately. "When and where do you need them?"

"This isn't a sales meeting, Dr. Masters," Philip Freeman interjected sternly. "The President is asking you to provide flight crews and experimental strike aircraft for a secret armed patrol mission. The crews could be in serious danger. You could lose the crews, all the aircraft, and your entire investment, and you'd have no recourse or legal redress to recoup your losses. If your crews are captured, they will be tried as terrorists, spies, or armed aggressors, subject to all Chinese criminal laws, without any support or protection from the U.S. government. Think about it first."

"Okay," Masters responded. He fell silent for about two heartbeats, smiled, then said, "When and where do you need them?"

"We thought about it already," Patrick McLanahan said resolutely, by way of explaining his boss's weird reply. "I speak for the aircrews, Mr. President, and we are ready to fly. The planes are fueled, armed, and ready to go. We even have our own aerial refueling tanker fleet, and they've been sent to Sky Masters, Inc.'s, facilities in Hawaii. We just need secure basing at Andersen Air Force Base on Guam."

"We can do that," Freeman said. He turned to the President and said, "There's one option ready to execute, Mr. President."

"How would you be able to help out there, Patrick?" the President asked.

"The Megafortresses carry four different standoff weapons: jammers, antiradar, antiair, and anti-ship," McLanahan explained. "Nothing is activated until there is some sign of hostilities, and then the response is graduated, depending on what the Chinese do. Our plan is to match, never exceed, the PLAN's level of hostility. We defend ourselves with every weapon we have, but our primary purpose is to defend the assigned area."

"How would they be employed?" the President asked.

"Two groups of two, plus one ground spare, for the armed surveillance role," McLanahan replied. "One plane just outside Chinese long-range radar coverage, the other over the assigned defense area. From the refueling track near Okinawa, it's one hour to the southern tip of Taiwan, near Quemoy Island, so each bomber can stay about four hours on station. Just before the first bomber is scheduled to depart the station to refuel, the other bomber takes its place. The teams rotate every sixteen hours, so the second team gets a full eight hours of crew rest on the ground. If fighting breaks out, we switch into surge mode—we recover, rearm, refuel, and relaunch bombers as fast as we can, at least two at a time."

"And how long can you possibly keep that up?" Secretary of Defense Chastain asked. "Aren't you afraid of exhausting your crews?"

"The limiting factor is the planes, not the crews," McLanahan answered. "On patrol, it's all high-altitude cruising time. All combat flying is stressful, but the high-altitude cruise legs will give the crews a little opportunity to decompress. During a combat surge, the crews will only be in actual hostile territory anywhere from ten to twenty minutes maximum—that's the power we have with standoff weapons. In a combat surge, we anticipate running out of weapons before running out of combat-ready aircraft. Of course, we're just a covering force, sir—we'd expect support from the Navy and Air Force within three to four days."

"Pretty optimistic," Chastain sniffed. "I haven't heard you give any estimates for combat attrition."

"Attrition? You mean, how many Megafortresses will we lose?" Masters retorted. "I'll answer that one, Art—zero. Zip. Nada. The EB-52s will be grounded because of systems failures before China even gets a shot off at one."

"That's pretty arrogant of you, Dr. Masters," Chastain said. "If I'm not mistaken, the PRC got a couple of your EB-52s in the Philippines conflict."

"The planes we're using now are a generation more advanced than the ones we used three years ago—the weapons are, too," Masters said resolutely. "The bad guys won't *touch* us. We're a lot safer than those subs you got shadowing that battle group, I guarantee *that*."

"All we ask is that you let us act with a great degree of autonomy, once you send us into the area defense 'basket,' " General Samson said. "We can set up real-time datalinks to provide the task force commander with a look at everything we're looking at, but we're vulnerable and weak if we can't act right away."

"That can't be helped, General," Chastain said. "A B-52 bomber loaded to the gills with cruise missiles, taking on a Chinese naval battle group—we're going to *insist* on absolute control."

"Although we're using strategic bombers, sir, we're actually flying a close-air-support–type mission," Samson explained. "We're flying close to the enemy, staying out of sight but zooming into lethal range when it's time to strike, then bugging out of lethal range again. We must be given authority to shoot when it comes time to do so—we can't loiter within lethal range *hoping* to be given the order. As Patrick explained, sir, our objective is to match, and never exceed, the level of force used by the enemy—but we need absolute real-time authority to shift our level of response. As good as Dr. Masters's surveillance and communications gear is, it's not perfect nor one hundred percent reliable. Our guys *must* be given authority when to shoot. That's why we're here, sir."

President Martindale shook his head and gave them a weary smile. "Can't believe we're considering using a *private company* to fight our battles for us," he said. "I feel like I'm hiring mercenaries."

"Then make us part of the military, sir," Patrick McLanahan said.

Several mouths dropped open in surprise—the President's, Freeman's, Samson's, even Masters's. "What did you say, Patrick?" Samson finally asked.

"Make us part of the military again," McLanahan explained. "Recommission the B-52 bombers—but make it a fleet of EB-52 Megafortresses instead. Right now, you have a fleet of eight converted bombers. Dr. Masters and I have identified thirty H-model B-52s in the fleet that are suitable for the conversion. Within two years, maybe less, we can have a wing, two squadrons, of EB-52 Megafortresses flying. They can do any mission you can think of: reconnaissance, drone control, defense suppression, minelaying, strategic or tactical precision attack, heavy bombardment, even air defense and space launch. Reactivate Dyess Air Force Base in Texas as the initial base, or colocate the unit with Jon's facilities in Arkansas."

"I think we've got plenty on our plate right now without having to digest that idea," Chief of Staff Jerrod Hale interjected. He made it obvious he didn't think much of the idea—but Freeman, Samson, Masters, and even Secretary of Defense Arthur Chastain suddenly wore thoughtful expressions as Hale continued, "You've got ten minutes before you need to be on the road for that speech, Mr. President. I suggest—"

Just then, there was a knock on the Oval Office door, and before the Secret Service agent could fully open it, Admiral George Balboa, chairman of the Joint Chiefs of Staff, stormed into the room. "I'm sorry, Mr. President," he thundered, "but my aide was given a message by someone in the communications center that the meeting had been postponed an hour. But there's no record of any such message. Then, as if by some weird *coincidence*, I find Brad Elliott outside in the reception area. *Brad Elliott*. Would somebody tell me what he's doing?" And then Balboa noticed General Samson, Patrick McLanahan, and Jon Masters in the Oval Office, seated with the President and his military advisors. "Would somebody mind telling me what's going on?"

"Brad Elliott?" the President asked in a suddenly squeaky voice. "He's *here*?" And then everyone understood why Balboa was late for this meeting with the President. He smiled mischievously and shook his head, saying, "Nooo . . . no, Elliott wouldn't *dare*."

"Wouldn't dare leave a phony message with my aide so he or his cronies can talk with the President of the United States alone about some cockamamie secret stealth bomber attack plan?" Balboa asked in a breathlessly sarcastic tone. "Hell, sir, I'm surprised he didn't try to ambush my car with one of his robot drone missiles. But it worked, didn't it? You've been talking about some covert air patrol of the Formosa Strait against the PLAN."

"We're discussing what China's next move might be," Freeman said, "and what we should do about it."

"Do . . . what we should *do*?" Balboa asked, with considerable restraint evident in his voice. Balboa was a hot-tempered but dynamic and well-respected Navy veteran, strong-willed and intelligent, just the way Martindale liked his advisors. "Oh, yeah, the Air Force's scheme to put those experimental 'stealth' B-52s out there." Balboa said "B-52" as if it were the punch line to a very bad joke. "Mr. President, I'm prepared to brief you on the Joint Chiefs' recommendation."

"The carriers," the President guessed. "Full-court press."

"It's the best response—maximum firepower if we need it, maximum visibility otherwise," Balboa said. "Send both *Independence* and *Washington* into the Formosa Strait right away. When *Vinson* replaces *Lincoln* in the Arabian Sea, we send *Lincoln* into the theater until things calm down, then rotate it with *Indy* and send her home for her decommissioning party."

"I'm reminding the President that there are powerful elements of the Japanese parliament that see this administration as more hawkish when it comes to Asia in general and China in particular, and they're fearful of us using military force if it means threatening trade and instigating military and economic conflict," Freeman said. "The carriers are a powerful weapon—maybe *too* big a stick. The bombers could keep an eye on things without stirring up too much hostility."

"He's right, Admiral," the President said. "Two, three carriers in the Formosa Strait—that's an awful lot of firepower, almost Desert Storm–sized. It's bound to make China nervous."

"It's *supposed* to make 'em nervous," Balboa said with a loud laugh.

"Mr. President, we're totally exposed right now. If the Chinese try an attack against Quemoy, Matsu, or any of Taiwan's islands, we pound on 'em. My guess is, they'll back off with two flattops parked in their front yards.

"Mr. President, the Chinese wouldn't dare try an invasion of Taiwan," Balboa went on with a confident tone, punctuated with an exasperated glance at Freeman, "but if they're contemplating following up their attacks on Quemoy with a play on the island of Formosa itself, we can have the carriers standing by ready to respond. The carriers'll discourage the Taiwanese from getting too frisky too. We'll see to that."

"The carriers aren't in position, Admiral," Freeman argued.

"We've got four frigates in the area ready to assist Taiwan, sir, plus land-based attack planes out of Okinawa," Balboa said. "Plus the Taiwanese are no slouches when it comes to defending their islands. *Indy* will be on station in two days, and *George* will be on in five, tops. Just the *news* that two American carriers are on the way will scare that PLAN task force right back to base. They'll back off, just like they did last March."

"Admiral, we're marching towards a huge naval confrontation by racing to put two aircraft carrier battle groups in the Formosa Strait to oppose China's task force," Freeman said. "Yes, it might scare them into retreating—or it might provoke them into firing first. Putting a couple of our EB-52 Megafortress stealth bombers in the area will keep things quiet and give us plenty of firepower in case the Chinese task force tries something. No one will know we ever had the Megafortress bombers on station."

"Is that what you said about the B-2 attacks against Iran, General?" Balboa retorted. The conflict in the Persian Gulf region between Iran and the United States was still classified top secret, but the rumors and the heated debate over the mysterious attacks on Iran's secret military bases and warships in the Gulf of Oman were just beginning. " 'No one would find out?' Then why is it that half of Congress is calling for an investigation into an alleged illegal overflight of several Asian countries, including China, by a B-2 stealth bomber? Why is it that some loudmouth congresspersons are calling for the President's *impeachment*?"

Jerrod Hale's head jerked up angrily at that word, but before he could react, the President said, "Hold on, now, Admiral, but no one's going to impeach me, and sure as hell no one's going to intimidate me into responding or not responding." That sentence was aimed as much at Balboa as it was at the few opposition party legislators who'd actually suggested an independent prosecutor investigate the President for his actions during the Iranian conflict. "The bottom line is, the B-2 stealth bomber attacks over Iran and the Persian Gulf forced the Iranians to stop their attacks and back off. If China, Afghanistan, and Congress are upset about us flying one lousy stealth bomber around to do the job, that's tough."

"Mr. President, the American people are upset because you conducted a secret, covert war," Balboa said. He saw Hale's face flush, but ignored him. "The American people don't like secret wars, sir—the fallout from our escapades in Central America prove that." Everyone realized that Balboa's remark was aimed directly at the President, who, as the ex–vice president, had engineered many of those secret military missions in Central America in the aftermath of the James spy incident. Martindale had been severely criticized for initiating so many "dirty" skirmishes in Central America.

But Martindale could dish it out as well as take it. "You wouldn't happen to be upset, Admiral," the President said, "because I chose to keep the *Abraham Lincoln* carrier group out of the Persian Gulf but sent in a B-2 bomber to bust Iran's chops; that I allowed the *Lincoln* to get shot at by the Iranians but didn't give them a chance to retaliate?" It was no secret that many in the Navy were upset at precisely that point: Iran had attacked the USS *Abraham Lincoln* with long-range cruise missiles and shot down one of its E-3C Hawkeye radar planes, but the President had not allowed the *Lincoln* to spearhead a retaliatory strike.

"Don't be ridiculous, sir," Balboa said, his voice showing the slightest hint of irritation toward his commander in chief. "We're all on the same side. True, the *Lincoln* was ready to conduct their counterattacks, destroy the Iranian bomber bases, sink the Iranian carrier, and rescue those CIA operatives long before the stealth guys got on the scene. True, we were cut out of the game unfairly and unnecessarily. But I'm not going to prefer the Navy over any other service just because I wear a Navy uniform." Eyes turned away from Balboa at that instant, and the reply "Bullshit" came to many of their minds. "But this Taiwan operation is totally different. The Navy is in a much better position to assist Taiwan than these . . . *things* the general wants to send in."

"We need to make our involvement deniable and perfectly black," Freeman said, "or we risk starting a war on the high seas in the entire region. That's the advantage of using the aircraft we suggest."

"Does the Joint Chiefs have a problem using Air Force assets in the Pacific?" the President asked.

"Sir, I apologize if I sounded too . . . argumentative to General Freeman, and of course CINCPAC will use any and all assets available in his theater if needed, including the Air Force," Admiral Balboa responded, saying the words as if they were part of a well-rehearsed boilerplate speech—very little sincerity in those words at all. "But I think we've already seen the harmful result of using renegade, secretive units in military operations. The B-2 bomber operation the general put together against Iran could have been a complete disaster and a major embarrassment for the United States."

"Instead, it was a major victory and completely stopped all further aggression," Freeman said. "We proved that."

"All you proved, General Freeman, was that *terrorism* works," Balboa said acidly.

"What in *hell* did you say, Balboa?" Jerrod Hale exploded. Hale was a tall, very large man in his early fifties, a former Los Angeles district attorney who, as the Martindale for President campaign director, had engineered Martindale's stunning comeback from a defeated, divorced former vice president to a powerful, awe-inspiring, and rather fearsome President of the United States. More than almost any other person in Washington besides the President, Hale commanded a lot of power because he controlled access to the man in the White House—and Hale was not shy about wielding the forces under his control. "Who the *fuck* do you think you're talking to? General Freeman is an advisor to the President of the United States. You're right on the verge of getting yourself shit-canned!"

The President's eyes narrowed and his lips tightened, but he raised a hand to silence Hale. "All right, Admiral," he said, carefully controlling his surprised anger, "it's obvious you've got something to say, so say it. It sounded like you're accusing me of terrorism. Did I hear you correctly?"

"With all due respect, Mr. President—yes, I believe the B-2 bomber attacks were tantamount to acts of terrorism," Balboa said. "Under advisement from General Freeman, you ordered a stealth bomber to overfly China and bomb Iran without warning. In my book, in anyone's book, that's terrorism, and it ought to be eliminated in this administration." He paused for a few breaths, then added, "The Chiefs recommend that this latest operation, this Megafortress support mission, be canceled and more conventional means be used to support Taiwan's naval forces. What in hell is this thing? You call it a modified B-52, but it's sure as hell not like any B-52 I've ever seen! Where is it now, Mr. President? I want to see it and give my evaluation."

"Excuse me, Admiral," Chief of Staff Hale interjected, much more forcibly than before, "but the *President* will issue *his* instructions to *you,* not the other way around. If you have any further questions, submit them to me and I'll see that he gets them."

Although Hale towered over the Navy four-star, Balboa wasn't going to be intimidated by a civilian staffer, even if he was the chief of staff and, arguably, the second-most-powerful man in Washington. His gaze encompassed McLanahan and Masters as well as Freeman as he said, "I think it might be better if you dismissed your *civilian* staffers, sir, so we could discuss this operation."

Hale's eyes blazed, and even the old veteran sailor Balboa took notice. "That's *it,* Balboa!"

The President tried to defuse the tension by grasping Balboa's arm as they headed for the door. "Look, gents, I've got a function to attend, and if I'm late, the press will have me for breakfast," the President said. "Admiral, I'm going with the Megafortresses. I'm augmenting the sub fleet and keeping the frigates on patrol, but I don't want the carriers in the Formosa Strait right now."

"But, sir, the Chiefs—"

"Admiral, there's a time for shooting, a time for gunboat diplomacy, and a time for negotiations. We made the decision to keep the carriers out of the Strait during China's Reunification Day celebrations, and I think it was a good decision even though China now seems to be taking advantage of it. I agree, we're on the back side of the power curve now, and if China makes a move against Taiwan, there won't be a hell of a lot we can do. As you recall, Admiral, one reason to keep the carriers out of the Strait was because of our concern that China might use nuclear or subatomic weapons against Taiwan, and I think that fear is all but a certainty now.

"But I think we've got a new option: we use our technological advantage and make our enemies *think* we're right on their ass ready to blow their shit away," the President went on. "The ability to make the Iranians or the North Koreans or even the Chinese think that we can freely, effortlessly fly an armed warplane right over their damned heads without them knowing about it is an awesome capability, powerful enough to stop a war dead in its tracks, and I want to take maximum advantage of it."

"Yes, sir, I understand," Balboa said in a low voice, not masking the intense disappointment in his face, "but at least change the pecking order a little. We've got civilian spooks—intelligence agents, mercenaries, defense contractors, I'm not even sure exactly what to call them!—flying Air Force planes asking for Navy support. It's too confusing. Even the Air Force hates this plan. At least put the flyboys under CINCPAC, Admiral Bill Allen at Pacific Command. He's got to be informed of any military assets entering his operational theater anyway, sir—let's use him and his staff at Pearl to keep track of things. If things go to hell, he'll see it coming and can jump in immediately to contain the damage. All the chiefs will sign on in support for this mission, if you make this change."

The President thought for a moment, then nodded. "Okay, I'll buy that idea, Admiral." He turned over his shoulder and said to Freeman, "Phil, brief CINCPAC on the ROC support mission, and turn operational control over to him. Include Admiral Allen on progress updates and video conferences. Draft up the execution order and have it ready for me to sign in one hour."

The President paused and turned toward Freeman and Balboa. "Make no mistake, gents, I *am* getting a lot of heat for flying that B-2 over Asia, so the press has parked themselves at the front gate of every bomber base in the country counting to make sure they're all there. I've been presented with a new option, a plane that's not on the books and can't be counted, so I'm taking it. I expect full support from all of the service chiefs.

"If it fails, I take full responsibility, and then I expect advice and assistance in formulating a new plan, with no *lip* and no *attitude* from *anyone*. Interservice rivalry is a reality, and I know I've got to deal with it, but I don't want it to interfere with my wishes, is that clear?" Those last two sentences were aimed squarely at Balboa, who nodded slightly. "The Taiwan support operation will be executed as planned; the Navy will assume operational command. Anything else for me?"

But Jerrod Hale didn't give anyone the opportunity to respond. He gave Freeman a silent urging not to ask anything else, then blasted Admiral Balboa with a warning glare that threatened to cause a sunburn. He hustled the President expertly out of reach and covered all sides from anyone else trying to get his attention as they made their way toward the stairs to the President's private quarters.

     National Security Advisor Philip Freeman led Balboa, Samson, Masters, and McLanahan down the hall past the Roosevelt Room, past the Vice President's office, and into his office in the northwest corner of the West Wing; Brad Elliott was waiting for them inside, chatting with a Secret Service agent assigned to accompany him.

Admiral Balboa ignored everyone in the office that he outranked, which meant he planted himself right in front of Freeman's desk. "Things are getting a little out of control here, Philip," he said in a low voice. "The President looks like he's under considerable pressure these days. How's he doing? How's he holding up?"

"The President is doing just fine, George," Freeman said. "Let me give you a piece of friendly advice, my friend: stop leading with your mouth. You could find yourself out on the street if you keep on equating the President's decisions with acts of terrorism. I think you had a chance to dissuade him from approving the bomber operation, but you blew it by copping this do-what-I-want-or-kiss-my-ass attitude. And I also suggest you don't get on the bad side of Jerrod Hale. You talk with the President maybe an hour a day—but Jerrod Hale talks to him *sixteen* hours a day, maybe more. And as you know, no one is closer to the boss than Hale, not even his actress-*du-jour* Monica Scheherazade. So back off."

Balboa waved that suggestion away like an irritating fly. "If the President wanted a yes-man as his Joint Chiefs chairman, he should've hired someone else."

"You called the President a terrorist, George?" Brad Elliott remarked. "Shit, someone better check your medication."

"Button it, Elliott," Balboa retorted, turning and pointing a warning finger at the retired Air Force three-star general. He studied Elliott for a moment, his eyes turning from white-hot angry to disapproving and pitying. "You're looking kinda thin, Brad. Maybe we need to schedule you for another flight physical, maybe check that fancy peg-leg of yours.

I frankly don't think you'd pass. Wonder what would happen to your project if you were grounded?"

"I'll compare my blood pressure and prostate size with yours any day, you old fart."

"That *will be* the last of that shit I will ever hear from either one of you in my presence, or else the next sound you will hear is the door to your cell in Leavenworth slamming behind you," Freeman angrily interjected. "No judge, no jury, no court-martial. Is that clear? If you don't think I have the juice to do it, try me." Balboa and Elliott simply glared at each other—Balboa with a dark scowl, Elliott with his sly, maddening grin. "Our mission is to keep an eye on the Chinese navy and back each other up if a shooting war starts. Anything that interferes with that mission is nothing but background noise, and I will squelch background noise immediately and permanently.

"George, you're responsible for notifying Admiral Allen that the Megafortresses are en route and will be in his theater. He will have full operational command of the bombers . . ." Admiral Balboa smiled at that, until: ". . . through General Samson."

"What?" Balboa asked. "What does Samson have to do with this mission? This is Pacific Command's theater. COMNAVAIRPAC has the staff and experience to—"

"The boss wants Samson in the loop," Freeman said. "No one knows bombers better than he does. General Samson is hereby temporarily assigned the billet as CINCPAC's deputy, effective today. Make it happen, George."

"And what about Elliott?" Balboa asked. "What are you going to make him—chief of naval operations?"

"Elliott is an employee of Sky Masters, Inc., a military retiree and a private citizen," Philip Freeman said, ignoring Balboa's sarcasm. "He has no rights or responsibilities except those given to him by Dr. Jon Masters and his company as defense contractors."

"But if I know Elliott, he'll be piloting one of these Megafortresses you're sending to Pacific Command," Balboa said. "He'll have his finger on the trigger. Who gives him the order to cease fire? I ask that because Mr. Elliott here usually decides for *himself* when to *open* fire—it doesn't matter to him what his superior officers or his commander in chief thinks."

"Admiral, fair warning—button it," Freeman said. "You get Admiral Allen up to speed on the mission, and let me worry about the civilians. Anything else for me?"

"I'd like to make an appointment with the President to talk about this so-called plan," Balboa said sternly. "The sooner the better. There might still be time to convince him of what a stupid idea this is."

"Of course, Admiral," Freeman replied. "Just go over to Jerrod Hale's office. I'm sure he'll be glad to help you any way he can. Out the door, turn right, end of the hall, straight ahead." He picked up his desk phone and added, "Shall I phone the chief of staff's office and tell him to expect you?" Balboa scowled again, spun on a heel, and left the National Security Advisor's office without another word, slamming the door behind him with just enough force to rattle a few pictures but not enough to inflame Freeman's anger any more.

"Well, Brad, I expected the President to hit the roof when he heard you were involved in this project—it wasn't so bad coming from the chairman of the Joint Chiefs," Freeman said wryly. "We might still get an earful from the boss." Despite all this, however, Freeman had to smile at seeing Brad Elliott again, looking pretty damned good regardless of his recent travails. He was a big pain in the butt, but, Katy bar the doors, he made things *happen*! To Patrick McLanahan, he asked, "So when can you get your flying circus in-theater, Patrick?"

"We can be on-station in twenty-four hours," McLanahan replied. "Give us your choice of weapon load, and we'll have it uploaded by the time we arrive back at Blytheville. Crew rest, briefing, preflight, and fourteen hours' flight time."

"Good," Freeman said. "We won't need you to go right on-station, so you'll recover at Andersen. You can change your weapon load at Andersen if necessary?"

"We can refuel and rearm hot if you need it," Jon Masters said. "Hot" reloading meant reloading weapons and fuel with engines running, trying to get the plane in the air and into the fight as quickly as possible. "We've got enough weapons available for two weeks of combat operations. First-line stuff."

"Shouldn't be necessary—but we'll keep that capability in mind," Freeman said. He nodded and smiled at McLanahan. "A whole wing of Megafortresses, huh? Pretty good idea. There's no money in the budget for another wing of paper airplanes, let alone high-tech B-52s, but it's a cute idea. Any idea who we might pick as commander of the first wing of EB-52 Megafortresses, *Colonel* McLanahan?" The young navigator-bombardier had no reply, just a smile. Freeman stood and shook hands with each of them. "Yeah, right. Get out of here, flyboys. Good luck and good hunting."

• • • • Heading down the Grant Staircase next to the Vice President's office to the visitors' entrance to the West Wing, McLanahan said in a low voice, "You really irritated Admiral Balboa back there, Brad."

"Irritated him? You gave him a verbal wedgie back there," Masters remarked with a laugh.

"Don't worry about Balboa, Patrick," Elliott said. "He's worried that we'll steal his thunder, just like we did when he was CINCPAC and we brought the Air Battle Force in to nail the Chinese invasion fleet near the Philippines."

"I just think it's not a good idea to twist his tail, Brad," McLanahan urged. "Back then, we had General Curtis as chairman of the Joint Chiefs, and he ran a lot of interference for us in the White House and Pentagon so we could employ the bomber fleet. We don't have Wilbur or the bombers anymore. If we want to get a chance to show what our upgraded Megafortresses can do, we've got to work with Balboa and Allen, not fight them."

"They should be happy for *our* assistance, Patrick," Elliott said. "They're the ones out of position. *We're* the ones who can bail them out until they get back in the game. You don't want to make us look like a naval air support unit or something."

"I'd be more than satisfied to be flying in support of the Navy, Brad," McLanahan said. Elliott looked at him in surprise, but McLanahan continued. "Sir, I know that the bombers are a powerful frontline weapon system, and the Megafortress is the best all-around attack aircraft ever flown. We can deliver more firepower than any one of those frigates the Navy has in the Formosa Strait. But we're not the frontline force anymore. Let the Navy take care of the Strait—let's prove to the brass and the White House that we can hold the line."

Elliott stopped in the staircase, looked at his young protégé, sniffed, and worriedly shook his head. "C'mon, Muck, don't tell me you've bought this 'jointness' crap, all this bullshit about how the U.S. military can't do anything unless every branch of the service does it together?"

he asked derisively. "The service chiefs, especially the Navy, whine about the lack of 'jointness' whenever any of the other services, especially the Air Force, shows 'em up. The Navy was aced out in Desert Storm and they whined because we weren't sharing the target load. The Navy was embarrassed in the Celebes Sea against China, and Balboa whined because we supposedly weren't cooperating. Now Balboa almost loses the *Lincoln* in the Arabian Sea to an Iranian cruise missile, and he whines because a stealth bomber takes out the Iranian bomber base. Balboa doesn't want us to support the naval forces, Patrick. He wants us to step aside and let him and Allen and the Navy take on China single-handedly. He doesn't want 'joint' anything."

"Brad, you may be right, but I'm not in it, so I can thumb my nose at the Navy or wave the Air Force banner over the burning hulks of Red Chinese warships," McLanahan said. "I want to prove how good the Sky Masters's Megafortress conversion is to the Air Force."

"Good answer, Patrick," Jon Masters interjected. "I knew you had the proper point of view."

"And I'm interested in showing what the heavy bomber can do, no matter who's in charge," McLanahan went on. "If we get into the game as support forces, good—at least we're still in the game. But your goal seems to be to rub Balboa's nose in our bomber's jet exhaust. We don't need to do that."

"Hey, Colonel, I'm trying to do the same as you—get our bombers into the fight where we can do the most good," Elliott retorted testily. "But you're not paying attention to the politics. Balboa and Allen and all the brass squids at the five-sided puzzle palace don't care about jointness and cooperation—they care about *funding*.

"Look. We're trying to get a six-hundred-million-dollar contract from Congress and the Pentagon to convert thirty B-52s to EB-52 Megafortresses. That's one-third the cost of a new Arleigh Burke–class destroyer. Destroyers are good on the open seas, frigates are good in the littoral regions—shallower water, within a nation's territorial waters—but we know in today's tactical environment that a long-range stealth bomber with precision-guided standoff weapons is *the* most effective weapon in the arsenal, in any combat area, with lower costs and much greater mobility. Balboa knows all that, but he doesn't care—he just wants that new destroyer, so maybe they'll stick his name on it someday. Is that 'joint' thinking? Hell no. He doesn't care about joint anything. Neither should we. Maybe if we started naming bombers after Joint Chiefs of Staff chairmen, he'd want more of them."

"I disagree," McLanahan insisted. "I think we should—"

"Patrick, I've got a lot more experience dealing with the Gold Chamber and White House types than you, so how about letting me handle Balboa and Pacific Command, and you handle the hardware and the crews?" Elliott said in a light but definitive voice. "We'll show the brass who can do the job. Trust me."

It was good to see the old fire and fighting spirit in his old boss, McLanahan thought, as they made their way to the waiting limo that would take them to Andrews Air Force Base to catch the flight back to Sky Masters, Inc.'s, headquarters in Blytheville, Arkansas. But the old fighting spirit also meant the old antagonisms, the old competitiveness, the old victory-at-any-cost attitude.

They were back in the fight—but could they prove to the brass that they deserved to stay?

ARKANSAS INTERNATIONAL AIRPORT,
BLYTHEVILLE, ARKANSAS
LATER THAT EVENING

The Sky Masters, Inc., team was whisked by limousine from the White House to the Washington Navy Yard, helicoptered to Andrews Air Force Base, then flown by military jet transport directly to its headquarters in northeastern Arkansas. Arkansas International Airport was the civilianized Eaker Air Force Base, where B-52 Stratofortress bombers and KC-135 Stratotankers of the old Strategic Air Command had once pulled round-the-clock strategic nuclear alert for many years. Despite its grandiose name, Arkansas International Airport had had no aviation facilities on the field after the Air Force had departed until Jon Masters built his new high-tech aerospace development center here shortly after the base closed. Now it was a thriving regional airport, which acted as a reliever facility for passenger flights and overnight shipping companies from nearby Memphis. The civilian and commercial operations were on the east side of the field; Sky Masters, Inc., occupied brand-new buildings and hangars on the west side of the 11,600-foot-long concrete runway.

While everyone else slept on the flight back from Washington, Jon Masters was on the phone; and, still bouncing with boyish energy, he was the first one off the plane after it taxied to a stop in front of the corporate headquarters. Patrick McLanahan's wife, Wendy, was just pulling off her ear protectors as Masters lowered the C-21's airstair door. "Wendy! Nice to see you!" Masters shouted over the gradually diminishing turbine noise. "I need you to get me the latest—"

Wendy McLanahan held up a hand, then slapped a blue-covered binder into her boss's hands. "Latest faxes from Guam—both our DC-10 tanker and DC-10 booster aircraft arrived code one. One NIRTSat booster had an overtemp warning when they did a test. They need a call from you ASAP. Munitions are being off-loaded."

"Good," Masters said excitedly. "Great. Now, I need to see—"

She slapped five more binders in his hands—and she had a dozen more binders ready. "Airframe reports for your review. Better take a look at –030 and –040—I don't think they're going to make it, but you might be able to work your magic on them. Everyone else is ready to fly." She piled the rest of the binders into his arms. "Revised flight plans, engineering requests, prelaunch reports, invoices you need to initial, and things I think you need to think about before we get the flying circus in the air. Look 'em over."

"But I need—"

"Jon, you got what you need—here's what *I* need," Wendy said, as her husband stepped off the plane. She gave him a long, deep kiss as Patrick pulled his wife into his arms. Jon was going to ask her for something else, but the kiss lasted longer than his level of patience, so he ran off yelling for someone to get him a phone.

Masters did not see Patrick pat his wife's tummy after their kiss parted. "How's our new crewdog?" he asked in a low voice.

"Fine, Daddy, just fine," Wendy replied, punctuated with another kiss. "A little stretch now and then—"

"Stretch? You mean cramps? Are you in pain?"

"No, worrywart," she said with a reassuring smile. "Just enough to let me know that things are happening down there."

"You feeling all right?"

"A little indigestion in the evening, and a sudden rush of sleepiness about every other hour," Wendy replied. "I close the office door and take a nap."

"I think about you all the time, sweetie," Patrick said. "Working around jet fuel and rocket chemicals and transmitters, pulling long hours, on your feet all day."

"I stay away from manufacturing and the labs, I take lots of naps, and I find working on the couch with my feet up just as effective as working at my desk," Wendy said. "Don't worry, lover. I'll take good care of your child."

"*Our* child."

"Our what?" Brad Elliott said, as he met up with the couple.

"Old married couple talk, Brad," Wendy said, giving her ex-boss a peck on the cheek. With Wendy between both men, they walked arm in arm into the admin building. "How was the meeting at the White House?"

"Good," Patrick said.

"Shit, Muck, it went *great*—we're a go!" Elliott said excitedly. "The President approved our plan. They want us to get ready to fly out in the next couple days—and they want us armed. Fully operational, offensive and defensive. We watered their eyes but *good*! The only lousy part is we gotta play nice-nice with the squids."

"Oh, God, no!" Wendy said with mock horror and plenty of sarcasm. "Now, that's just totally *unacceptable*. Why would we ever want to be backed up by five thousand highly trained sailors and seventy aircraft? Nothing bad ever happens in our missions."

" 'Old married couple' is right—you're sounding more like your old man every day," Elliott said. "We don't need the Navy, and we sure as hell don't need 'em telling us what to do."

"Well, that's the way it's going to be," Patrick said, rubbing his eyes wearily. "We've got to rechannelize the planes to new Navy fleet frequencies—Admiral William Allen, commander in chief of U.S. Pacific Command, is taking charge of the mission, with Terrill Samson as his number two."

"That's good news, isn't it, Brad?" Wendy asked. "General Samson is one of us."

"Hey, the Earthmover might speak bombers, but he's just feathering his nest and looking for a soft place to land—he's got his eyes on a fourth star and a cushy job at the Pentagon," Elliott said with a sneer. "He's afraid to go toe-to-toe with the suits. Because of him, we won't be able to clear off for relief without calling CINCPAC first."

"Brad, you've been bitching ever since we left the Oval Office,"

Patrick said wearily. The exhaustion in his voice was obvious. "The only thing the Navy's asked us to do is rechannelize our radios."

"And they want to have a remote 'check fire' datalink to our attack computers, don't forget *that,*" Elliott interjected. "They not only want to tell us when, where, and how to fly our missions, but they want to be able to electronically inhibit any weapon releases, even for defensive weapons."

"Can we do that—*should* we do that?" Wendy asked.

"We already told them we can't tie into the computers, and wouldn't even if we could," Patrick said. "We're going to put the datalink in, but it's simply a communications link, not a remote control. That was the end of the discussion. Brad wants us to tell the Chief of Naval Operations where to stick his datalink."

"I just wish we had someone a little stronger than Samson out there sitting with Allen in that command post, someone not interested in playing politics," Elliott scoffed.

"Terrill Samson is *precisely* the guy we should have in the command center," Patrick said. "Now, can we please terminate this discussion? The Navy's on board and running the show, period. You're going to get the avionics shop going on the rechannelization and the datalink, right, Brad?"

"Yeah, yeah," Elliott said resignedly. "But I tell ya, Muck, you've gotta get tougher with those Navy bastards. They're not interested in seeing us succeed. They're only—"

"Okay, Brad, okay, I hear you loud and clear, so just drop it. Enough."

Wendy grasped both men's arms and steered them toward the stairs leading up to the second-floor executive offices. "Both you guys are suffering from hypoglycemia—I'll bet you haven't had anything except coffee since this morning. I've got hot soup and sandwiches set up in the little conference room. Let's go."

Both men let Wendy lead them upstairs, but outside the conference room, Elliott said, "I think I'll pass on the midnight snack, Wendy. Wrap up a couple sandwiches for me and leave 'em in the fridge, and I'll have them in the morning. I want to brief the day shift on the prelaunch checklist."

"Okay, Brad," Wendy said. "I figured you were going to be up early, so I made up the sleeper sofa in your office. Flight suit's cleaned and pressed, too."

Elliott gave Wendy a kiss on the forehead and gave Patrick a friendly punch in the shoulder. "You are one lucky son of a bitch, Muck. Thanks, lady. See you in the morning. You going to go running with me at five A.M., Colonel, or do I go by myself again?" Elliott laughed—he already knew the answer to *that* one.

"Good night, General," Patrick said with mock irritation. He found a seat in the conference room, while Wendy poured him a cup of chicken noodle soup and fixed a turkey and tomato sandwich. Patrick remained stiff and uneasy until he heard the door to Elliott's office close down the quiet hallway. "Christ, it's like trying to handle a hyperactive three year-old sometimes."

"Don't tell me—Brad Elliott on the warpath in the halls of the White House."

Patrick downed the soup in hungry bites and began to attack the sandwich. "I think he's out to prove that the government made a huge mistake by forcing him to retire and closing his research facility," he said. "Everybody is a target—Samson, the Navy, the President, even me. He's got a chip the size of the *Spruce Goose* on his shoulder. The more people resent his arrogant attitude, the more it delights him, because it proves how right he is. And you know what the biggest problem is?"

"Sure," Wendy Tork McLanahan replied, sitting beside her man and giving him a kiss. "He's your friend, your mentor—and you need him."

• • • • Brad Elliott simply left his suit, shirt, shoes, and underwear on a chair in the outer office—here in the corporate world, someone took care of cleaning and pressing and stuff like that. He usually took the time to hang up his suit neatly, bag his underwear, and spit-shine his shoes before hitting the rack, but why waste the time?—someone would do all that for him in the morning no matter how neatly it was all put away. He said "someone." He assumed it would be his "assistant"—they didn't use the term "secretary" anymore, and the more military titles "clerk" and "aide" were usually met with round eyes full of shock. It didn't matter anyway, because he spent little time in the office, preferring to be in the labs or on the flightline, and he didn't even know his "assistant's" name. He didn't even know that the sofa in his office was a sleeper, because he never sat in the damn thing.

The sofa bed had stiff fresh sheets and an old thick green wool blanket, and Wendy had left an apple and a glass of milk on the table next to the sofa. What a sweetheart she was, Elliott thought. Years ago, back when she was a civilian contractor working on new high-tech defensive electronic countermeasures systems for heavy bomber aircraft, she had been such a serious, technoid cold fish. But then she'd met Patrick McLanahan at the Strategic Air Command Bomb Competition Symposium at Barksdale Air Force Base, and she'd come back an entirely new woman. Now, as a wife—and a mother, Elliott guessed, although neither McLanahan had announced anything yet, and Wendy tried her best to hide it—she had been transformed into a caring, loving woman as well as a brilliant electronics engineer.

Unfortunately, Elliott thought, now her husband Patrick was the technoid cold fish. He showed no life, no spark, no drive. Sure, he'd been brilliant as ever on the secret B-2 stealth bomber project. Sure, he'd worked hard to get Sky Masters's new B-52 modification program signed and funded. But he seemed to have lost a lot of his killer instinct since his voluntary early retirement last year. His appetite for decisive, raw, raging combat, to do whatever it took to achieve victory, the urge to drive your enemies before you and take command, was gone. He was a technoid now, almost reaching full "suit" status. Elliott couldn't imagine it, but Patrick might actually prefer flying a desk now instead of flying a bomber. The old "Muck" McLanahan, bombardier extraordinaire, would never allow a squid to get between him and control of the skies, the earth, or the seas anywhere in the—

Brad Elliott was just starting to ease his artificial leg under the stiff, clean white sheets when the phone on the table near the window rang. Swearing aloud, he got up to answer it. "What?"

It was an Asian voice on the other end: "Do I have the pleasure of speaking with Lieutenant General Bradley James Elliott?"

"Who the hell is this?"

"My name is Kuo Han-min, General. I am the ambassador to the United States of America from the Republic of China, calling from New York. I am very pleased to speak to you."

"You were in the White House, meeting with the President."

"Yes, General. I am pleased that the President has pledged his support for my country, and I hope he successfully convinces your parliament and the American people that my country should remain independent from the Communists."

"How did you find my number?"

"I am well familiar with Dr. Jon Masters and his company," Kuo explained. "Once I saw you and Colonel Patrick McLanahan with Dr. Masters, I logically assumed you were working with him. After that, it was easy to trace your office number."

"I'm not listed," Elliott said, in an angry tone. "Not here, not anywhere."

"I must give credit to my eager staff," Kuo said, in a light tone, "and admit I do not know how I came to get your number, only that I have it—as well as your Oregon address and your travel itinerary for today."

"What do you want?"

"General, sir, I have called to ask a great boon," Kuo said. "I deduce by your conversation with President Martindale and your hasty return to Dr. Masters's facility in your charming southern American state of Arkansas that you are preparing to launch a great mission to support my people and my country against the threat we now face by the Chinese Communists."

"You deduce wrong," Elliott said. "Good-bye."

"Let us coordinate our attacks, General," Kuo went on quickly. "Together, we can destroy the Communist fleet once and for all. The power of your incredible bomber fleet, matched with my country's naval power, will mean certain death for any who threaten my country or any democratic society in Asia."

"I don't know what you're talking about," Elliott said. "What we're doing is none of your business. What you're doing is none of ours."

"The Communist carrier battle group is carrying nuclear weapons," Ambassador Kuo said. "The carrier is carrying three nuclear-tipped M-11 land attack missiles, and the two destroyers each carry four nuclear-tipped SS-N-12 anti-ship missiles."

Elliott's jaw dropped open in surprise. "You're *shitting* me . . . you know this for a fact? Are you sure?"

"We are positive of our information, General," Ku said. "We believe their target is Quemoy Tao. My country is sending our newest frigate, the *Kin Men,* out to intercept and destroy these vessels before they can get within range and launch their missiles. I am begging you to help us. Use the power of your Megafortress bombers to help defend our warship until it can successfully destroy the three nuclear-armed Communist warships."

"How in hell do you know . . . ?"

"General Elliott, I assure you, many friends as well as many enemies know or can logically assume much about your special bomber fleet," Kuo said. "Believe me, sir, the Republic of China is a friend. You are our best hope for survival until President Martindale can defeat his opponents in your Congress and commit the full force of American military strength against the Chinese Communists. You are the new Flying Tigers, the new American Volunteer Group, the band of brave Americans who seek to save your friends the Chinese Nationalists from being destroyed by powerful imperialist invaders. Please help us. Let us fight together."

Brad Elliott knew he should put the phone down and ignore this man. He knew he should report this foreign contact to the Air Force Office of Special Investigations and to Sky Masters, Inc.'s, security department right away. The Megafortress mission to Asia was in jeopardy, and it hadn't even begun. This man, whoever he was, knew far too much about the Megafortress project.

But instead, Brad Elliott said, "Don't tell me where you are—I'll track you down."

"Thank you, General Elliott," the Asian voice said, and hung up.

Elliott retrieved his electronic address book and found the name of a friend in the Military Liaison Office of the U.S. State Department. He would tell him how to contact the new Taiwan embassy in Washington, who would tell him how to contact the ROC ambassador. If they gave him a number and it connected him to Kuo, he would hang up, call the ROC embassy again, and ask to be patched in to Kuo. If that worked, he would then redo the embassy patch, this time through the Pentagon's National Military Command Center communications room, which could detect and defeat any blind phone drops, shorts, or secret outside switches.

If the third call was successful—then they'd talk about stopping the damned Chinese.

"... Evaluating the enemy,
causing the enemy's *ch'i* to be
lost and his forces to scatter
so that even if his disposition
is complete he will not be
able to employ it, this is
victory through the Tao."

—WEI LIAO-TZU
Chinese military theoretician
and advisor, fourth century B.C

CHAPTER
TWO

**IN THE FORMOSA STRAIT, NEAR QUEMOY ISLAND,
JUST OFF THE PEOPLE'S REPUBLIC
OF CHINA COAST
WEDNESDAY, 4 JUNE 1997, 0631 HOURS LOCAL
(TUESDAY, 3 JUNE, 1831 HOURS ET)**

"Who in blazes is it?" Admiral Yi Kyu-pin asked of no one in particular, peering nervously through his high-power binoculars. The ship he was watching was moving slowly toward them on an intercept bearing. It had not been spotted on radar until it was only twenty kilometers away from the lead escort ship, practically within visual range; now it was no more than ten kilometers from the lead escort. The challenge was obvious. The sixty-seven-year-old admiral had already launched a Zhi-9 light shipboard helicopter to investigate and was waiting for the pilot's report.

Yi was not too concerned about the vessel, though, because he dwarfed it and easily outgunned it. Yi was in command of the *Mao Zedong,* a 64,000-ton aircraft carrier of the People's Republic of China's Liberation Army Navy. Although the carrier did not have its entire fixed-wing air group of more than twenty Russian-made Sukhoi-33 fighters on board—an agreement between China and Taiwan prohibited the

Mao Zedong from carrying attack planes until after passing Matsu Island during its transit of the Formosa Strait—it did carry four Su-33 fighters, configured only for air defense, plus three times its normal complement of attack and anti-submarine helicopters. Accompanying the *Mao* were two 4,000-ton Luda-class destroyers, *Kang* and *Changsha*, the 14,600-ton replenishment oiler *Fuqing*, and the repair and support vessel *Hudong*, which acted as a floating repair shop. Flanking the *Mao* battle group was an armada of more than forty smaller vessels, everything from Huangfeng-class coastal patrol boats to Fushun-class minesweepers to Huchuan semi-hydrofoil missile boats—anything that could keep up with the nuclear-powered carrier and its escorts.

While he waited, Admiral Yi took a few moments to think about— no, to *savor*—the immense power at his command as the skipper of this vessel. Even though this warship, the first aircraft carrier owned by an Asian nation since World War II, had had a very checkered existence, it was now at the absolute pinnacle of its fighting capability.

Its keel had been laid down in June of 1985 at the Nikolayev ship-yards near the Black Sea in the Ukrainian Soviet Socialist Republic, and it had been launched in April of 1988 as the second true Soviet fixed-wing aircraft carrier, much larger and more capable than its Kiev- or Moskva-class anti-submarine helicopter carrier cousins. It had first been dedicated as the "defensive aviation cruiser" *Riga*; it had been called a "cruiser" because the Republic of Turkey, which guards the approaches in and out of the Black Sea, forbids any aircraft carriers to sail through the Bosporus and so would never have allowed it to leave the Black Sea. Because of severe budget cuts and technological difficulties, it had never fully completed its fitting-out and never joined its sister ship *Tbilisi* in the Northern Fleet of the Soviet Navy. It had been renamed *Varyag* when the Latvian Soviet Socialist Republic, whose capital the ship had been named for and where the ship was to be based once it entered Soviet fleet service, had become the independent Republic of Latvia in 1991.

The *Varyag*, which means "Viking" or "dread lord," had been sold to the People's Republic of China in 1991 for the paltry sum of thirty mil-lion U.S. dollars in cash, completely stripped of all electronic and weapon systems; the world military press believed that it had been sold as scrap for cash to line the pockets of ex–Soviet admirals and bureaucrats, forced out of service without pensions when the Soviet Union collapsed. Because of an international embargo on any military sales to China, and because most of Asia feared what China might do with a nuclear-powered aircraft carrier—the Tiananmen Square massacre had been only two years earlier—the carrier had been sent to Chah Bahar Naval Base in the Islamic Republic of Iran, where it had been used as a floating prison and barracks. But in 1994, it had undergone a $2 billion crash rearming and refit program, and Iran and China had jointly made it operational in 1996— the first aircraft carrier and the greatest warship ever owned by a Middle East or Islamic nation.

In early 1997, Iran's military leaders had immediately put the carrier, now called the *Ayatollah Ruhollah Khomeini,* to use against its enemies in the Persian Gulf region, attacking several pro-American states with the carrier as the spearhead. They had been turned away by the American air force, using stealth bombers and high-tech cruise missiles to attack the carrier. The stealth bomber attack had caused one of the *Khomeini*'s Sukhoi-33 fighter-bombers to crash on deck, causing a huge fire that had cooked off a P-500 Granit anti-ship missile—the ship had been one more explosion away from heading to the bottom of the sea. Iran, beaten and humiliated by the unseen American attackers, had been forced to sue for peace before its prized possession was completely lost.

The United States had been ready, willing, and happy to make the carrier into an instant artificial reef in the Arabian Sea by putting a few torpedoes or cruise missiles into it, but Iran had quickly surrendered the carrier to its real owners, the People's Republic of China, and the United States had not wanted to anger that superpower by sinking its property. The carrier, now renamed the *Mao Zedong* after the People's Republic of China's Communist leader, had been taken in tow by the Chinese destroyer *Zhanjiang* and sent back to China, carefully watched during its transit by every country with long-range maritime surveillance capability. Most Asian nations were still fearful of China sailing a carrier through the politically turbulent east Asian seas, but the carrier was little more than floating scrap now—wasn't it?

The twice-orphaned carrier was not yet ready to be cut up into razor blades. In a few short weeks, repairs had been completed, and now the little ski-jump carrier *Mao* was once again operational. Only a few of its complete wing of twenty-four ex–Russian Sukhoi-33 supersonic fighter-bombers were on board, but it carried a full complement of anti-submarine helicopters, as well as antiaircraft and land attack weapons. Six of the P-500 Granit anti-ship missiles in the forward launch tubes had been replaced with a navalized version of the M-11 ballistic land attack missile, each with a range of over sixty kilometers. Despite its armament, however, the carrier was considered little more than an expensive Chinese plaything—perhaps something to impress the neighbors—and not a grave military threat.

That idea, Admiral Yi thought gleefully, was going to be known as one of the biggest errors of judgment made in recent history.

After what seemed like hours, the first officer approached his captain with a copy of an intelligence report, complete with radar, optronic, and visual profiles, several weeks old but hopefully still useful. "Received the patrol's report, sir. It is flying a Taiwanese flag," the first officer reported. "The vessel is a French-designed, indigenously built Kwang Hwa III–class frigate. One of the Nationalists' new toys, launched just last year."

"Armament?"

"Has a thirty-six-round vertical launch system with twelve Harpoon anti-ship cruise missiles, ten ASROC rocket-boosted torpedoes, and fourteen Standard antiair missiles—the Standard missiles can be used for surface attack as well. Four side-firing torpedo tubes. Sea Sparrow close-in antiaircraft and anti-missile system, 40-millimeter bow-mounted dual-purpose gun, Phalanx close-in air defense cannons fore and aft, and several 12.7-millimeter machine gun mounts."

"Very impressive," Yi mused. "Strange our patrols have not detected it before. Where is it based?"

"Unknown, sir," the first officer replied. "Perhaps in the Nationalists' secret underground naval base?"

Yi did not share in the joke. The first officer referenced the current intelligence estimate—if the term "intelligence" could even be loosely applied—that the Nationalists were spending trillions of *yuan* on constructing huge underground military facilities so they could withstand an expected nuclear attack by the People's Republic of China's Liberation Army. Supposedly they had built an underground base large enough to barrack an entire division and store hundreds of tanks and armored vehicles—and had even constructed an underground *airfield* in the eastern mountains on Formosa big enough to launch and recover two squadrons of F-16 Fighting Falcon jet fighters. Of course, years of espionage work had uncovered no evidence of any secret underground bases. "What about its aviation fit?"

"Large helicopter hangar, can carry two small helicopters," the first officer continued. "Typically carries one S-70 helicopter, armed with AS-30L laser-guided attack missiles, torpedoes, or Harpoon anti-ship missiles. The superstructure is built of composite materials and aluminum covered in radar-absorbent materials. The slanted foredeck, angled superstructure, and folding antenna arrays are supposed to be stealth devices to reduce radar signature."

"I would say it worked—we did not spot him until he was less than twenty kilometers out," Yi said. He was not familiar with this class of warship, but he knew that Taiwan, one of the richest and fastest-growing nations in the world, could afford the best military hardware. Well, it may be a modern, high-tech boat, but it was no match for the *Mao* and its escorts. "Have Communications transmit a Flash priority message to Taiwan Operations headquarters, advising them that we are in contact with a rebel warship. Have the patrol helicopter maintain visual contact and report if—"

Just then, the officer of the deck interrupted: "Captain, message from the Nationalist frigate *Kim Men*. They are ordering that we not approach Quemoy Island any farther or we will be fired upon!"

"They *what*?" Yi exploded, nearly rising out of his seat in total surprise. "They are trying to tell us where we can sail? Are they crazy?" The idea was laughable—the smallest ship in Admiral Yi's carrier battle group was twice as big and four times more heavily armed than this Nationalist toy boat! This was obviously some kind of publicity stunt. "Put them on the phone. This is ludicrous! What . . . ?" The officer of the deck nodded, and Yi picked up the ship-to-ship radio handset and keyed the mike button: "Nationalist vessel *Kim*, this is Admiral Yi Kyu-pin, captain of the People's Republic of China People's Liberation Army Navy aircraft carrier *Mao Zedong* and commander of this task force," he said in Mandarin Chinese. "Repeat your last message, please."

"Carrier *Mao Zedong*, this is Captain Sung Kun-hui, captain of the Republic of China Navy Quemoy Flotilla frigate *Kin Men*," a voice responded in Mandarin. "You are approaching territorial waters of the Republic of China, and we demand that you remain clear."

"We are peaceful vessels in *Chinese* waters, not Nationalist waters," Yi responded angrily, "and we will pass through this area as we please. Do not approach this task force. This is your last warning." Yi turned to his first officer in surprise and muttered, "This is some kind of trap. I want a full long-range sweep of the area, all sensors. Look for any other ships or subs in the area. Maintain formation speed and heading." He keyed the mike again: "Captain Sung, this is Admiral Yi. We intend to continue on to our destination, which is classified and which I am not permitted to reveal. Do not approach this task force. Over."

"Admiral Yi, you and your escorts are then hereby *ordered* to heave-to immediately," Sung replied. "If it is necessary, we will use deadly force to stop your ships and force you to comply. Heave-to immediately. Maintaining this course towards Quemoy Tao will be seen as a hostile act."

Yi shot out of his chair, nearly dropping the ship-to-ship phone in total shock and surprise. "This bastard . . . he is threatening *us* with *force*? I will blast his puny little toy boat straight to *hell*." He picked up the phone and keyed the mike: "Your request is utterly foolhardy and without cause, rebel captain!" Yi sputtered into the ship-to-ship phone. "I warn you, Captain, that if I see any of your guns traverse in my direction, if I see your helicopters leave your deck or even spin up their rotors, or if you approach my task force any closer, I will order my escorts to attack without further warning. How *dare* you threaten warships of the People's Republic of China on the high seas like this?"

"And how dare *you*, Admiral," Sung responded, "bring nuclear warheads into our waters?"

Yi looked puzzled, his eyes darting back and forth across his bridge. "What did you say?" he replied. "I am not carrying any such weapons!"

"With all due respect, sir, you are a liar, Admiral Yi," Sung radioed. "You and your ships are carrying at least six thermonuclear warheads on your M-11 ballistic missiles and SS-N-19 anti-ship missiles. You loaded the warheads while at sea via submarine and commercial traders, in violation of the United Nations Missile Technology Control Regime Treaty. The Republic of China strictly prohibits the transportation of nuclear warheads or nuclear-capable missiles into our waters. You will be detained until the warheads and missiles are confiscated. I now order you to heave-to immediately. This is your last warning."

Admiral Yi was virtually beside himself, his eyes spinning—not from anger or confusion this time, but in utter disbelief, because the rebel captain's information was maddeningly accurate: the Chinese warships were indeed carrying nuclear warheads. Three of the six M-11 land attack missiles and three of the P-500 Granit missiles, what the West called SS-N-19 "Shipwreck," carried in the forward vertical launch tubes were armed with NK-55 thermonuclear warheads, small selectable-yield warheads powerful enough to destroy an aircraft carrier or a small city. It was impossible to tell how in hell Taiwan had found out. Security and secrecy had been painstakingly maintained throughout the transfers, and the ships never docked at any port after on-loading the warheads, so access to the ship could be carefully controlled. A spy on the ship? Improbable, but it was the only . . .

"Admiral Yi, this is Captain Sung. You will be considered a hostile target if you do not stop. What is your response?"

Get a hold of yourself, Yi, the captain told himself. This could be part of some elaborate ruse, some sort of propaganda ploy to embarrass the People's Liberation Army Navy—perhaps they were only guessing about the missiles and warheads. If the media showed pictures of a lone, lightly armed Taiwanese frigate challenging the Chinese carrier battle group, it would be a monumental propaganda coup for Taiwan and its Western partners. Perhaps he only wanted a photo opportunity? Perhaps this was all a big show, some sort of act of bravado. Sung and his crew faced certain death if Yi's escort ships unleashed even one of their missiles, and even the escort *Kang*'s twin-barreled 130-millimeter guns could shred that aluminum-hulled Nationalist toy boat in a few minutes.

But Yi had a bad feeling about this: this was no photo opportunity or publicity ploy. The rebel warship was serious—it meant to board and search a foreign warship nearly twenty times its size! "Sound general quarters, all ships, all hands at battle stations, not an exercise," Yi shouted. "Get the fighters up on deck and ready to launch, full air defense weapon load. Comrade Chong, report to the Combat Information Center, prepare to take charge of the engagement if they get a lucky shot off and hit the bridge. I will take the battle helm from here."

"They cannot be serious!" the first officer, Chong, shouted as the quartermaster sounded the general quarters bell. "They mean to engage us?"

"If they try, it will be the shortest naval engagement in history," Yi said angrily. "Officer of the deck, signal the task force to shift to combat formation. Bring the formation to thirty knots, give me twenty degrees to port to put our guns on the starboard side. Get Helicopter Group One on deck armed for anti-submarine warfare, and Helicopter Groups Two and Three ready for rescue duties." Yi knew that Taiwan had a small force of F-16 and F-5 fighter-bombers and, although they were very far away, they could do some damage if they got through the *Kang*'s Crotale Modulaire surface-to-air missile screen—they could easily overwhelm Yi's small fleet of Sukhoi-33 fighters and close-in weapon systems.

"All stations report manned and ready," the officer of the deck reported a few minutes later. "The group also reports all stations manned and ready for combat. Estimate five minutes before the group is in combat formation. Interceptor flight one is up on deck, ready to launch in about ten minutes."

"Very well," Yi responded. "Combat, range to the rebel frigate?"

"Range fifteen thousand meters."

Well within range of the frigate's Harpoon missiles, Yi thought, but if the rebels were going to use them, they would've done it long ago. "Cowards," Yi said to the captain of the Taiwanese frigate acidly. "You should have taken the shot when you had the chance—now you have *no* chance." To his officer of the deck, Yi ordered, "I want a lookout to watch that frigate—if it tries to launch its helicopter or traverse that gun, I want to know about it immediately. Send a Flash priority signal to fleet headquarters; notify them that we are being threatened by an armed Taiwanese frigate that is ordering us to stop and be boarded. Advise them that we are proceeding at best speed and ask for instructions—and I want permission to engage and destroy that patrol boat if necessary."

THIRTY MILES NORTHWEST OF THE CHINESE CARRIER *MAO ZEDONG* THAT SAME TIME

"That PLAN battle group's got everything lit up, crew," defensive systems officer (DSO) Air Force First Lieutenant Emil "Emitter" Vikram reported, referring to the Chinese People's Liberation Army Navy vessels. "Rice Screen Golf–band air search, Crotale antiair, Square Tie Type 331 anti-ship targeting, India-band Sun Visor fire control, Great Leader satellite communications, jammers across the entire spectrum—he's broadcasting everything but AM and FM golden oldies. He's leaking so much power out his side lobes that I can feel it in my fillings."

"We get the message, DSO," retired Lieutenant General Brad Elliott, the pilot, replied. Vikram had been the youngest and one of the brightest engineers at the now-closed High Technology Aerospace Weapons Center, but he had the least amount of flight experience, so he still hadn't learned to completely control his excitement when using the interphone. "Just give us the important news and record the rest. Co, you should be double-checking the 'combat' checklist. If you're just sitting there with nothing to do, with a Chinese battle group ready to attack just twenty miles away, you're probably missing something."

"Hey, I was born ready, General," the copilot retorted, causing an exasperated scowl from the pilot. "My checklist's complete—I'm just waiting for the fur to start flying." Sitting across from Elliott, monitoring the four large color multifunction displays on the forward instrument panel, was his copilot, Air Force Major Nancy Cheshire. A longtime test pilot and engineer, Cheshire had spent several years at HAWC as one of Elliott's most talented pilots and flight test engineers; she had already flown two secret strike missions in the EB-52 as part of Brad Elliott's classified stealth raiders. When HAWC had closed, she had been assigned as one of the first female B-2 Spirit stealth bomber pilots in the U.S. Air Force—but she had readily given up that choice assignment when McLanahan and Elliott had asked to "borrow" her to fly one of Jon Masters's Megafortress strategic escort "flying battleships."

This Megafortress was loaded for bear with both offensive and defensive weapons. Instead of a standard weapon pylon, each wing held a large teardrop-shaped stealthy fibersteel fairing that contained the external weapons on ejector racks. Each wing weapons fairing held six AGM-177 Wolverine stealth turbojet cruise missiles, which were targetable rocket-powered cruise missiles with a range of up to fifty miles, fitted with three small internal bomb bays that could carry a variety of weapons or other payloads. The Wolverine missiles on this mission carried a mix of payloads—half were configured as area jammer/decoys that could simulate a massive bomber or fighter attack and completely shut down radar screens and disrupt enemy air defense systems for miles in all directions; the other half carried cluster bomb packages so each missile could attack three targets, then dive into a fourth. Each pylon also carried four radar-guided AIM-120C AMRAAMs for bomber defense—in total, the same number of missiles as on a F-15 Eagle fighter—that could be fired at enemy targets up to thirty miles away, even *behind* the bomber.

Internally, the EB-52 Megafortress was armed with twelve AGM-136 Tacit Rainbow anti-radar cruise missiles in the forward part of the bomb bay, which were small turbojet-powered missiles that would loiter over an area and automatically attack an enemy radar that activated nearby which transmitted specific threat frequencies—the missiles could orbit for up to an hour over a twenty-five-square-mile area. The aft section of the fifty-foot long bomb bay contained the bomber's maximum offensive punch that would hopefully not be needed on this mission—a rotary launcher with eight AGM-142B Striker missiles. The Strikers were rocket-powered, supersonic bombs with a 1,000-pound high-explosive warhead that carried a satellite navigation system and TV and imaging infrared terminal guidance packages that gave them precision-kill capability; wings that unfolded after release from the bomb bay gave the Striker missile a ballistic cruising range of nearly fifty miles.

"I show us in COMBAT mode and ready to fight," retired Lieutenant Colonel Patrick McLanahan, the offensive systems officer, said. McLanahan could sense the tension in the voices of everyone on board, even Brad Elliott. It had been over two years since Elliott had flown in combat, and almost a year since losing command of HAWC, and his nervousness and hyperalertness were obvious. McLanahan checked the mission status readout on his weapons display. The mission status readout was a direct satellite link with U.S. Pacific Command headquarters at Pearl Harbor, which indicated their orders continuously. Although McLanahan could override PACCOM's orders, the active datalink was the same as a direct verbal order from U.S. Pacific Command. "Datalink mission status is CHECK FIRE, and my nose is cold. Everyone stand by."

McLanahan's offensive systems suite was dominated by the SMFD, or Super Multi Function Display, a two-by-three foot screen on the forward instrument panel, from which McLanahan controlled all of his systems and weapons. Using a Macintosh-like interface, McLanahan could display any combination of flight, navigation, weapons, systems, or sensor information on that screen, and resize, stack, or move any of the windows around with ease. McLanahan controlled the SMFD in three ways: he could touch the screen with a finger to manipulate windows; he could use a trackball and pointer like a mouse; or he could issue commands to the computer by hitting a switch near his right foot and speaking to the computer. Using all three methods together allowed McLanahan to operate his systems with incredible speed and accuracy.

Part of McLanahan's air intelligence suite was the "God's-eye" view of the area supplied by Jon Masters's satellite reconnaissance systems. A string of small low-orbiting satellites developed by Sky Masters, Inc., nicknamed NIRTSats (Need It Right This Second Satellite), scanned the

Formosa Strait with powerful synthetic aperture radars, then downlinked the information to the EB-52 Megafortress via satellite relays. This produced an overhead image of the area depicting all of the ships, aircraft, and landmasses on the SMFD computer monitor. McLanahan could manipulate the image in thousands of ways, zooming in and out to individual targets or back to get the "big picture" tactical situation, and he could use the real-time image to pick targets to attack.

"The PRC vessels are redeploying their ships," McLanahan reported. "They're turning west, trying to get out of Taiwanese waters. Speed up to twenty knots and increasing. Smaller ships are heading forward to take the point, but that big destroyer is still in the lead."

"They're not trying to avoid that Taiwanese boat—they're turning to get ready to open fire," Elliott observed. "What in hell does Sung think he's doing? Those carrier escorts will chew him to pieces."

The secure UHF radio transceiver channel clicked to life, as the encryption-decryption algorithms instantly synchronized the two parties; then, in English with a thick Chinese accent, they heard: "American bomber, American bomber, this is Captain Sung aboard the *Kin Men,* how do you read?"

"Who in the world is that?" Nancy Cheshire shouted. "The captain of *what?*"

"He said he was the captain of the *Kin Men*—that's the name of that Taiwanese frigate that's cruising near the Chinese fleet," Elliott said.

"How in hell did he get our secure UHF frequency?" McLanahan asked. "And how does he know we're a bomber?"

"So much for communications security," Elliott groused on interphone. "Typical Navy COMSEC procedures—as leaky as a wet paper bag. Or else this frigate is part of the Navy's surveillance of that Chinese fleet. Good thing we're on secure frequencies." He keyed the mike, waited for the transceivers to synchronize, then responded, "Loud and clear, *Kin Men.* This is Headbanger."

"Jesus, Brad!" McLanahan interjected. "You're going to *talk* to him? We don't know who the hell he is! It could be a PRC tap."

"There is no way the PRC or anybody else could have broken the encryption logarithm and channelized with us—we only decided on it six hours ago, before we launched from Guam," Elliott said. In fact it was relatively easy to do with the right equipment. The secure radio system they used simply changed frequencies in random intervals. The timing and direction of the hop was controlled by a predetermined code that only the mission participants used. It was possible to scan the entire radio band and pick up the conversation, but an eavesdropper might only hear a snippet of conversation before another hop occurred. "The only way that Taiwanese captain can be talking to us is if he got the codes from the Navy. Obviously, we're all working together here."

McLanahan was not convinced, but Elliott's argument made some sense. "Tell him to authenticate," McLanahan suggested. Everyone involved in this surveillance operation, from the Navy and Air Force crews in Asia to radio operators half a world away to the President's communications staff, used a standard challenge-and-response code system to verify that the other party in the conversation was who they were supposed to be and not an eavesdropper or faker. The challenge-and-response was supposed to be used even over secure frequencies. Either party could initiate a challenge, or ask for multiple challenges, but for maximum security the *calling* party initiated the challenge. Once both sides were properly authenticated and satisfied of the other's identity, any instructions or changes to standing orders were followed by a lookup code system, using the current UTC date-time group followed by a letter. McLanahan punched up the current decode document on his computer terminal: "Give him bravo-India—response should be 'bravo.' "

"Look, Muck, we're on a secure satellite link," Elliott argued. "We don't have time for alphabet soup right now." Before McLanahan could argue further, Elliott switched radios: "*Kin Men*, we're picking up major radar emissions from the Chinese carrier group. It appears you are closing on the carrier group, and the *Mao* looks like it's getting ready to attack. What is your status?"

"Headbanger, we are moving to intercept the Communist battle group," Sung replied. "We will not stand by while the Communists close in and attack our territory. We ask that you stand by and assist us if the Communists should attack."

"He's *what*?" McLanahan retorted.

"*Kin Men,* we think that is a very unwise decision, repeat, that's a very bad idea," Elliott radioed. "Recommend you reverse course and avoid direct contact. We can give you position and status reports. Do not engage that group."

"Negative, Headbanger," Sung responded. "My headquarters has recommended that I attempt to keep the group out of missile bombardment range. Our intelligence has revealed that the Communists are carrying nuclear land attack and anti-ship missiles. We are counting on you to provide heavy attack cover if necessary. Stand by. We are launching our helicopter now."

"Shit," Elliott swore, "the Chinese ships are carrying *nukes*." Elliott and McLanahan had both been involved in the China-Philippines conflict three years earlier, when China had set off one low-yield thermonuclear device against some Filipino warships and later threatened to launch another; he had no doubt that China would try it again against the Taiwanese navy. "I'll contact Samson. Jesus, Taiwan could be in serious trouble here." Elliott switched to his number two radio, which was a secure satellite patch to General Samson, who was in charge of the bomber mission as a staff member of the U.S. Navy's Pacific Command headquarters, reporting to Admiral William Allen. "Buster, this is Headbanger."

"Go ahead, Headbanger, this is Buster," Samson himself responded. "Authenticate delta-delta."

McLanahan looked up the response and read it off to Elliott: "Headbanger has Mike."

"Good copy," Samson replied. "Go ahead, Headbanger."

"Buster, we got problems out here, and I just wanted you to know I had nothing to do with it," Elliott said, with just a trace of amusement in his voice. "We were just contacted by a Taiwanese frigate named the *Kin Men*. Its captain is named Sung. He is about to lock horns with Pig One. He claims the Pigs have nukes and they're getting ready to use them. Sung is launching his fling-wing and is getting ready to start pumping 'em out. Better notify the squids and the dolphins to come give us a hand. We need permission to engage the Pigs if necessary."

"Repeat that last, Headbanger?" Samson responded, the surprise and shock evident in his voice even over the secure satellite link. "You've been in contact with a Taiwanese warship over the secure radio link?"

"Hey, he contacted me, he knew we were an American bomber, he knew exactly where we were, and he's locked on to our comm algorithm," Elliott said. "I figured either the squids gave all this information to him, or someone leaked it to the ROC. In any case, he says the Liberation Army Navy battle group is carrying nuclear weapons that they're going to use on Quemoy, and he's going out to stop them right now. We need permission to set up a protective electronic screen around his ships and engage as necessary. Over."

"Headbanger, this is Buster. Keep your nose cold until I get the straight word from Atlas," Samson replied, telling Elliott to hold his fire until he notified Admiral Allen directly. "Stand by."

"Confirmed," McLanahan said, checking his weapons status. "I've still got a CHECK FIRE data message from PACCOM. My nose is cold. Someone better get on the horn to Taiwan Navy headquarters. One of their naval units is about to start a war with China!"

ABOARD THE CHINESE CARRIER *MAO ZEDONG*
THAT SAME TIME

"Sir, port lookout reports that the S-70 helicopter on the Nationalist ship's platform is turning rotors!" the officer of the deck shouted. Admiral Yi swung around and scanned the ship with his binoculars. Although the Taiwanese ship was still facing its bow directly toward the Chinese ships, it was possible to see the S-70's turning main rotor behind the large aircraft hangar. The 40-millimeter gun's barrel was now lowered and aimed directly at the *Mao*. "Radar reports a second vessel coming over the horizon heading right for us, possibly another Nationalist warship."

Dammit, Yi shouted at himself, *this is accelerating too fast!* He was only minutes away from starting a shooting war with the Nationalists! He yanked the phone off its cradle, keyed the mike, and said in Mandarin, "Frigate *Kin Men,* frigate *Kin Men,* this is the carrier *Mao Zedong.* I warn you, if you attempt to launch your helicopter now, I will open fire on it. We do not wish a war with you, but you must not provoke us further!"

"Carrier *Mao,* you will reverse course immediately, or *you* will be fired upon without further warning!" the skipper of the Taiwanese frigate responded. "You and your entire fleet are in danger of anti-ship cruise missile attack at this very moment. I warn you, shut down your radars or they will be destroyed by anti-radar weapons that have been launched against you."

"Prepare to lock radars on enemy aircraft, traverse the Crotale launcher and prepare to open fire," Yi shouted to the officer of the deck. "Clear to load the AK-130s." The two 130-millimeter gun mounts began to turn toward the Taiwanese frigate; at the same time, the large octuple French-made Crotale Modulaire launcher swiveled port and down, aiming its eight Crotale antiaircraft missiles directly at the frigate.

"Crotale launcher elevated, hot birds on the rail, sir!" the officer of the deck reported. "Hong-Yang-2 anti-ship missiles on *Kang* and *Chang-sha* aligned and ready for targets. P-500s spinning up and ready in two minutes."

"Where are my fighters?" Yi shouted.

"Interceptor One flight of two is on deck; first aircraft should be ready to launch in five minutes. Interceptor Two flight of two will be on deck in three minutes."

"Acknowledged," Yi replied. "Lock fire control and targeting radars on the Taiwanese frigate. Notify me immediately if the helicopter lifts off." Then, aloud, to the rebel commander, he muttered, "Very well, Captain, you wanted to play tough guy. What will you do now?"

ABOARD THE EB-52 MEGAFORTRESS

"Target-tracking radars locked onto the Taiwanese frigate," Vikram shouted excitedly on interphone. "They got him nailed. Crotale target-tracking radar is up. They're tracking the helicopter even while it's still on deck. Square Tie anti-ship missile-targeting radar locked on, bearing to the *Kin Men* and a second bearing on the newcomer to the southeast. They can attack at any time."

Elliott swore aloud and keyed the mike again: "Buster, this is Head-banger, the Pigs are getting ready to start breakfast. What do you want us to do?"

"Stand by, Headbanger," Samson replied a few long, agonizing moments later. "We're waiting for word from Wrangler." That was Admiral Balboa, chairman of the Joint Chiefs of Staff—this decision was going right to Washington.

"Screw Balboa, Earthmover," Elliott shouted on the radio, forgetting all communications security procedures. "That Taiwanese frigate is going to be blown out of the water in about sixty seconds if we don't do anything."

"Check your fire—and your mouth, Headbanger!" Samson responded angrily. "If no one has opened fire yet, you don't open fire. And maintain proper COMSEC procedures!"

Suddenly, McLanahan's God's-eye view on his large supercockpit display picked up a new flying target. "I got missile launch detection—and it's from the Taiwanese frigate!" he shouted. "Subsonic, low-flying, probably a Harpoon anti-ship missile . . . Taiwanese helicopter lifting off . . .

now picking up several more missile launches from the *Kin Men* . . . I've got missile launch detection from the newcomer as well, subsonic missile launch, probably Harpoons."

"Dammit, the Taiwanese frigate attacked," Elliott said. "Why in the hell didn't he wait?"

McLanahan heard that comment, but he was too busy to ask about it: "I've got six missiles in the air, all aiming for the Chinese carrier and destroyer," he reported. "Lead PLAN destroyer now opening fire with missiles now, subsonic, probably HY-2 anti-ship missiles."

"Commit all countermeasures!" Elliott shouted. "Clear for wing pylon weapon release!"

"We don't have authorization yet, Brad," McLanahan shouted.

"Patrick, that Taiwanese frigate is going to be Swiss cheese unless we do something," Elliott retorted. "Get on it right now! DSO, stand by on the Wolverines."

"Brad, wait. . . ."

"We're only launching decoys, Patrick," Elliott said. "What in hell are you waiting for? You're clear for wing pylon release."

Vikram looked over at McLanahan, his finger poised over the launch commit button. McLanahan hesitated for a moment; Vikram considered that approval and pressed the buttons on his keyboard. "Roger. Stand by for pylon launch, crew," Vikram announced. He launched two defensive Wolverine missiles, one from each wing pylon pod. McLanahan knew he should halt the launch, but decided not to interfere.

The turbojet-powered Wolverine cruise missiles set up a protective orbit around the Taiwanese frigate and activated its powerful electronic jammers, creating an intense blanket of jamming and decoy signals. When the Chinese Hong Yang-2 Sea Eagle anti-ship missiles activated their terminal homing radars in the preprogrammed target "basket" area, they suddenly found not one, but hundreds of radar targets. The seeker heads merely picked out the electronically largest radar target and aimed right for it, descending from two hundred feet above the water to twenty feet to make it harder for anti-missile weapons to stop it.

But every Chinese Sea Eagle missile had locked onto a false target created by the Wolverine missile's jammers. When it lost radar contact, it immediately turned and locked onto the next largest radar target. Every time the Sea Eagle missile turned, it slowed down, making it easier for the *Kin Men*'s guns and Standard missiles to hunt them down; the ones that were not destroyed by the Taiwanese frigate were detoured farther and farther away until they simply ran out of fuel and crashed into the sea.

"All right, everyone, check fire," McLanahan shouted on interphone after both Wolverine cruise missiles were on their way. "Brad, turn us away from the Chinese battle group before they backtrack those Wolverine missiles."

"We can't stop now, Patrick," Elliott shouted. "Get the Rainbows and Strikers out! That Taiwanese frigate is still unprotected!"

"Negative, pilot," McLanahan responded. "Everyone stand by." He switched his radio to the scrambled satellite channel: "Buster, this is Headbanger, we've got Screamers in the air, repeat, Screamers in the air. Advise if you want seconds."

"Say again, Headbanger?" Samson responded. "You launched? On whose orders?"

"Let's get with the program, Earthmover," Elliott cut in. "We're the only thing standing between that carrier battle group and the Taiwanese navy. Let's send the Tacit Rainbows and Strikers and end this right *now*."

"Headbanger, you check your fire until we get word from the boss," Samson said. "Stay nose cold. You hear me, pilot? Noses *cold*. If you're still in contact with the Taiwanese frigate, tell him to disengage and get out of the area. I'm getting permission for you to cover his withdrawal."

"What if he attacks again?" Elliott asked, but Samson had no reply. He swore loudly into his oxygen mask and switched to the secondary secure radio channel: "*Kin Men,* this is Headbanger," Elliott radioed to the Taiwanese frigate. "We showed PLAN missile launches on your position. We recommend you get the hell out of there. Do you copy?"

There was no response, but, seconds later, McLanahan shouted, "I've got missiles in the air, high-speed, high-altitude ballistic, from the *Kin Men* again. Multiple high-speed missiles, probably Standard missiles programmed for anti-ship attack. Targeting the lead destroyer and the carrier . . . looks like the destroyer took a couple hits . . . can't tell if the carrier got hit. It might've taken one hit or a near miss . . . frigate *Kin Men* launching missiles again, subsonic sea-skimmers, probably Harpoons, a couple at the destroyer and the rest at the carrier . . . the Taiwanese frigate is reversing course, looks like he's heading back to Quemoy . . . about sixty seconds to Harpoon missile impact . . ."

"PLAN destroyer launching antiair missiles," Vikram announced. "Targeting the Harpoon missiles, not the Taiwanese frigate."

"Anything still tracking the *Kin Men*?" Cheshire asked.

"They've got everything up and transmitting," Vikram said. "The PLAN fleet is still alive and probably mad as hell. Sung's never going to get out of there."

ABOARD THE AIRCRAFT CARRIER *MAO ZEDONG*

"Launch commit on all battle group anti-ship missiles!" Admiral Yi ordered after the report of inbound Taiwanese missiles was relayed to the bridge. "Sink both those ships! *Now!* Radio South Sea fleet headquarters, request air support for possible follow-on surface and submarine attacks. Full countermeasures! I want—"

"Bridge, combat, radar contact aircraft, *close aboard*, bearing three-zero-zero, range three-five kilometers and closing, altitude two thousand meters, speed four hundred knots, turning!" the first officer shouted, relaying the message from the Combat Information Center.

Suddenly, the reports stopped. Yi fairly lunged for the intercom mike. "Combat, continue report! Where is that plane?"

"Bridge . . . bridge, combat, we have lost contact!" the first officer reported in a high, squeaky, panicked voice. "No contacts. Attempting optical and thermal contact, still negative. Heavy jamming on search and uplink frequencies, all bearings."

Just then, the unit-to-unit radiophone buzzed, and Yi picked it up himself: "Speak."

"This is the *Kang*," came the reply. It was the captain of one of the destroyers, Commander Xiao Rongji. This was Xiao's first major command, and he was known in the Chinese navy as a bold, even rash, young boat commander; it was no surprise to Yi that he was the first to break tactical radio procedures. "We have detected a small aircraft just over the horizon, bearing two-three-four, range ten kilometers, altitude approximately five hundred meters." Xiao had detected one of the Wolverine "Screamer" decoy missiles that had strayed within range of the frigate's sensors. "Are we cleared to engage?"

"You will protect your ship and this carrier with everything you have got—including your life!" Yi shouted in reply. "Full air defense screen. Stand by to launch another missile salvo on my command. And keep this channel clear!" Yi hung up the radiophone in disgust.

"Carrier *Mao,* this is the *Kin Men*," the rebel skipper radioed again.

"All of your weapons missed their targets. The bomber is now targeting you and your capital warships. If you do not reverse course, they will attack."

"Bomber?" Yi shouted. "Did he say 'bomber'? Combat, any contact on that aircraft?"

"No, sir," the first officer replied. "Lookouts report occasional contact with dark contrails low on the horizon, possibly from a formation of small aircraft or a few large aircraft, but we have no visual or electronic contact."

"Check your systems, make sure everything's working properly. Find whatever's out there *now*!" Yi swore loudly, then fell silent once again.

It had to be an American stealth bomber, he thought. The American stealth bombers almost destroyed the *Mao,* then known as the *Khomeini,* in the Gulf of Oman just a few weeks earlier. It stood to reason that the Americans would track the carrier with the same stealth bomber so it could strike. If so, there was nothing he could do. His radars couldn't detect it—the intermittent contacts were probably when the bomber was releasing attack missiles.

"Bridge, Combat!" the intercom buzzed to life, "the *Kang* locking fire control radars on unidentified aircraft!" Yi swung around to starboard and raised his binoculars to his eyes—just as the frigate opened fire with its 100-millimeter dual-purpose guns.

"Sequence the fighter launch and get Interceptor One off the deck before the P-500 or M-11 missile launches," Yi shouted. "Find that American bomber!"

ABOARD THE EB-52 MEGAFORTRESS

"Drum Tilt fire-control radar up from the northwest destroyer," the EB-52 Megafortress's DSO, Emil Vikram, called out on interphone. "Drum Tilt radar . . . radar locked on, looks like he's tracking one of our Wolverines . . . or he could be tracking *us*!"

"He can match bearings back to us—we've got to turn!" McLanahan shouted on interphone.

At that same instant, they heard on the secure radio channel, "Headbanger, Headbanger, this is *Kin Men,* northwest Communist destroyer just opened fire!"

"Emitter, what do you got?" Elliott shouted.

"Just the Drum Tilt fire control," Vikram responded. "Constantly changing bearings—I don't think they have a lock-on, or they're locking on false targets and have to manually break lock to try to reacquire a real target."

"Good enough, DSO," Elliott said. "Don't fire up our jammers unless we become an item of interest. Patrick!"

"We don't have authorization to launch Striker missiles," McLanahan said immediately, anticipating Brad Elliott's order. "Besides, we're not an item of interest. My nose is cold."

"What else do you need, Muck—you want to see how fast that frigate can go down with a Granit missile in its gut? We've got to launch an attack *before* the Chinese carrier or that destroyer can take a shot."

"Brad, I've got the missiles ready to fly—as soon as we get the order," McLanahan insisted. "We're not going to attack unless we're given permission or we come under attack ourselves, and then it'll just be to defend ourselves. Nose is *cold*."

The redeploying Chinese patrol boats looked like little ants crawling forward around their queen, McLanahan thought as he watched his God's-eye tactical display being beamed to him by the NIRTSat reconnaissance satellites. "I'm showing eight small, fast patrol boats moving north, overtaking the lead destroyer," he reported. "Looks like they're getting into missile-firing position. I've got six . . . no, eight more going after the southeast Taiwanese vessel."

"Checks," Vikram said, watching the new threats as well. "India-band targeting radars up. The northern group is in maximum missile-firing range now; they'll be in optimal missile-firing range in about ten minutes. The southeast group is closing fast and will be in optimal firing range in two minutes."

Elliott was already on the satellite transceiver: "Hey, Buster, do you see what the hell's happening? Give us permission to launch before it's too late! How do you copy?"

COMMAND CENTER, U.S. PACIFIC COMMAND
HEADQUARTERS, HONOLULU, HAWAII
THAT SAME TIME

"Hey, Buster, how do you copy?" Elliott repeated. "That Taiwanese frigate and its buddy are going to be blasted to hell any minute now. Give us permission to take them out!"

"Why in hell doesn't Elliott shut up?" Admiral William Allen, the dual-hatted commander in chief of U.S. Pacific Command and the U.S. Navy's Pacific Fleet, asked of no one in particular. He, along with General Terrill Samson and a group of aides and technicians, were studying a large three-by-four-foot computer monitor that showed the tactical situation near the Taiwanese island of Quemoy, downloaded by Sky Masters, Inc.'s, NIRTSat "Martindale" synthetic aperture radar-imaging satellites. Allen called out, "Range from the closest Chinese patrol boat to the northern Taiwanese frigate."

Before one of the Navy technicians could answer, Masters's voice-recognition computer replied in a curiously seductive female voice, TWENTY-TWO KILOMETERS AND CLOSING AT FIVE HUNDRED METERS PER MINUTE.

"Goddamn gadgets," Allen muttered, afraid to raise his voice lest the computer make a snide comment in return. "Shut that computer voice thing off. Combat, sing out with all further reports."

"Aye, sir."

"Range from PLAN patrol boats to southeast frigate."

"Eight miles and steady."

"Well, serves him right for not bugging out sooner," Allen muttered. "Elliott doesn't know squat about PLAN missile attack tactics. He'd better shut up and stay off the radio or I'll recall his ass. Any word from Washington?"

"No, sir," the tactical action officer (TAO), the senior officer in charge of the combat response teams in the command center, responded. "Repeating your priority request."

"Where did those Taiwanese ships come from, anyway?" Allen asked rhetorically again—the Navy veteran was fond of thinking out loud, which he thought encouraged the officers around him to speak up. "My mission was not to baby-sit a Taiwanese warship while it launches a suicide attack on a Chinese carrier battle group. And I did *not* order Elliott to launch anything! I'm going to see to it that he's thrown in jail for what he's done!"

"He was responding to an attack by the PLAN destroyers," Samson offered.

"That *Taiwan* precipitated!" Allen interjected. "My orders were to monitor the situation and *prepare* for the *eventuality* of hostile contact, not dog-pile on when some asshole wants to play hero to Mother Taiwan.

We are not at war with the People's Republic of China, General Samson. But the Taiwanese frigate fired first, and Elliott launched right afterwards without getting permission. This is exactly what George Balboa warned me about: Elliott popping off and pulling the trigger before receiving proper authorization." He slumped in his command chair and carefully studied the tactical display. "What in hell is the PLAN going to do now? Chase that frigate all the way to Formosa?"

Samson couldn't argue with CINCPAC—but now wasn't the time to just sit and fume over Elliott. "Sir, it looks like the northern Taiwanese frigate is bugging out," Samson observed. "He can probably outrun the big ships and hold his distance against the smaller patrol boats, and the 'Screamer' decoy cruise missiles will be orbiting for another few minutes unless the PLAN manages a lucky shot and shoots them down."

"So what?"

"The Megafortress crew needs to know if they have authority to counterattack if the PLAN starts to launch more missiles against the frigate," Samson said. "They can help defend the frigate."

"More decoys?"

"Yes, the Megafortress is carrying four more Screamer cruise missiles—"

"Who in hell came up with these comic-book names?" Allen interrupted. "Megafortress? Screamers? Sounds like Elliott's warped mind at work."

"—but they're also carrying anti-radar cruise missiles," Samson went on, "that can shut down a dozen emitters in use on the PLAN warships. They can also use their antiaircraft missiles to—"

"That B-52 is carrying antiaircraft missiles?" Allen exclaimed incredulously. "Sidewinders?"

"Scorpions, sir," Samson responded. He had briefed all this information to Allen and his staff as recently as yesterday—and he was just as surprised then as he was now—but it didn't hurt to tell it all again. "Advanced Medium-Range Air-to-Air Missiles, about thirty miles' range, radar-guided, total of eight. They have to move in closer to the PLAN fleet, but the AMRAAMs are capable against ballistic missiles and anti-ship sea-skimmers too. The anti-radar cruise missiles will home in on radar transmissions; if the radar shuts down, it'll orbit over the area for up to fifteen minutes until the radar comes back on. Also, the offensive Wolverine missiles can drop cluster munitions on three targets, then impact a fourth—the Megafortress carries six. If the smaller patrol boats try to attack the Taiwanese frigate, those'll be the best weapons to use on them. The larger warships can be attacked by the Striker missiles—they're small, supersonic, and lethal. If we can shut down the PLAN's radars with the Tacit Rainbow missiles, the Striker missiles will have an excellent chance of hitting their targets."

Allen shook his head in exasperation. "You got more toys than Santa Claus, General," he muttered. He studied the Gods-eye display carefully and fell silent.

"The helicopter that launched from the Taiwanese frigate has been shot down by antiaircraft fire," one of the combat technicians reported. "Three guided-missile patrol boats closing quickly on the northern Taiwanese frigate. Should be in missile launch position in three minutes. Five more in pursuit, but they are not closing and remain at estimated max launch range. The lead PLAN destroyer has slowed to five knots; the carrier is overtaking."

"Looks like Taiwan got one," Allen said. "My guess is that the carrier will rendezvous with the destroyer." He fell silent once again; then: "No, I don't want that B-52—Megaplane, Megabomber, whatever you call it—launching any more missiles. Tell them to—"

"PLAN missile boats launching against the southeast Taiwanese vessel," the combat technician reported. "Numerous missiles . . . two salvos . . . direct hit. The southeast Taiwanese vessel is dead in the water . . . direct hit by second salvo . . . lost contact with southeast Taiwanese vessel."

The ferocity of that attack stunned even Allen, who watched the scene played out on the God's-eye view in silence. "Jesus Christ," Terrill Samson breathed. "That boat went down in less than a minute . . . it must've been hit by a dozen missiles."

"Overkill," Allen said. "The PLAN wasted a lot of missiles, and those little guided missile patrol boats don't have reloads. They're out of the fight."

"Admiral, for God's sake, you've got to make a decision about the northern Taiwanese frigate," Samson said, not quite believing that Allen could be so detached and unemotional about the loss of the Taiwanese frigate and the apparent deaths of hundreds of Taiwanese sailors. "Or do you want to see the PLAN chase down and sink another Taiwanese frigate?"

"This is not my damned fight, General," Allen shouted. "I was only supposed to observe and report. Taiwan threw the first punch, and Elliott only helped aggravate the situation."

"So you're going to let the PLAN sink that frigate?" Samson asked incredulously. "You're going to sit back and watch and do nothing?"

"If it happens, it'll be his own damned fault," Allen said. "Anyway, the score's even now—one PLAN destroyer for one ROC frigate and helicopter. Good time for everybody to break it up and go back to their corners." He was handed a telephone just then. "Trident. Go."

"This is Wrangler," Admiral Frederick Cowen, the Chief of Naval Operations, said, using his call sign. "JCS and NSC got your message; NSC asked me to give you a buzz. What's happening?"

"Shit's hitting the fan, sir," Allen replied. "Two Taiwanese frigates closed on the PLAN carrier battle group and attacked. One PLAN destroyer damaged. One of the ROC frigates has been sunk, and the PLAN's getting ready to deep-six the other."

"Too bad," Cowen replied with obvious disinterest in his voice. "I'll pass the word along. Any of our guys in the area?"

"Just that Thunder Pig," Allen replied derisively, smiling when Terrill Samson turned toward him when he heard Allen's name for the Megafortress.

"Just make sure Headbanger doesn't pop off any of his flying wet dreams until we get a look at the situation."

"Too late, sir," Allen said. "Headbanger's already launched—without permission. A couple decoy cruise missiles that suckered a bunch of PLAN anti-ship cruise missiles pretty good."

"Dammit, Crusher *knew* he'd do that," Admiral Cowen swore across the secure satellite hookup. "Crusher" was Admiral George Balboa's call sign—and it fit his personality and management style too, both he and Allen knew. "Recall that contraption. Get it on the ground. Elliott is *history*!"

"Aye, sir," Allen responded. To the TAO, he shouted, "Issue recall instructions to Headbanger. Disengage and RTB, right now."

Samson hit a button on his communications panel. "Excuse me, Wrangler. This is Buster—"

"You give Elliott the order to launch those missiles?" Cowen snapped.

"No, sir," Samson replied. "Headbanger reacted to protect the Taiwanese frigate when the PLAN launched an anti-ship missile and gun barrage. One Taiwanese warship's been sunk, and the other is in imminent danger. We need permission to launch anti-radar and anti-missile weapons and, if necessary, attack the PLAN guided-missile boats with attack cruise missiles."

"Denied," Cowen said immediately. "Terminate the mission, recall all aircraft, and get them on the ground immediately."

"Sir, the captain of the Taiwanese frigate, Captain Sung, reports that the PLAN carrier battle group is carrying nuclear land attack and anti-ship missiles," Samson said. "We should stop the task force from—"

"What do you mean, the captain of the Taiwanese frigate *reports?*" Cowen exploded. "You mean, you're in *contact* with the Taiwanese vessels? How—?"

"The skipper of the lead Taiwanese frigate contacted Headbanger," Samson said. "I don't know how—there must've been a security breakdown."

"Or else Elliott gave them the UHF synchronizer codes!" Cowen retorted. "I'll bet *he's* the damned security breakdown! This mission is *supposed* to be secret, General! That was your damn idea from the beginning—it was supposed to be secret even from the ROC. I want those planes recalled and that bastard Elliott . . ." he stopped, realizing he was breaking communications security, which made him even madder, ". . . put on house arrest!"

"Sir, if Headbanger is recalled, that second Taiwanese frigate will be a sitting duck," Samson argued. "At least authorize Headbanger to release their defensive weapons—the remaining Wolverines and the Tacit Rainbow cruise missiles. These weapons will stay in the area protecting the frigate while they withdraw."

"I'm giving you a direct order, Buster—recall Headbanger *now!*" Cowen shouted. "They are not to release any weapons except to protect themselves while they clear the area and recover. Is that clear?"

"Perfectly clear, sir," Admiral Allen, who had been listening in, replied. "I'll see to it myself immediately." And the line went dead. Allen hung up the phone, then said, "TAO, issue a recall order to the bomber force, and have the order authenticated—by Elliott personally. The mission is terminated, and he's on report."

"Terminated?" Elliott retorted. "They can't do this to us *now*!" He keyed the mike on the secure satellite link: "Hey, Earthmover, tell the squids to go to hell! We're going to cover that frigate's withdrawal!"

"Negative, Headbanger," Admiral Allen replied. "This is Trident, and it's a direct order from Wrangler. Your orders are to terminate and withdraw. You are authorized to expend weapons only to defend yourself as you withdraw and RTB. Time now, zero-three-two-two-four-eight, authentication tango. Do you copy?"

"Hey, Billy, authenticate this: *fuck you*!" Elliott shot back angrily, and he switched the secure satellite transceiver off his comm panel. "I knew they'd do this," he said hotly. "First chance they got, they recalled us."

"We've done everything we could," Nancy Cheshire said. "If we try to defend that Taiwanese frigate any more, we risk getting sucked closer and closer in toward that Chinese fleet—and that might not be as bad as the ass-kicking we'd get by CINCPAC or Balboa once we got back home. You got a heading to the refueling anchor point, Patrick?"

"Heading indicator is good back to the air refueling anchor point," McLanahan said, calling up the coordinates on his computer and entering them into his navigation system.

"Hey, we can't bug out of here now," Elliott said angrily, as he connected the autopilot to the navigation computers and monitored the turn to the east. "We haven't done squat, and we're about to watch the PLAN sink a Taiwanese frigate and kill hundreds more sailors. Doesn't that mean anything to you guys?"

"Sir, we were given an order to withdraw," Cheshire said. "I know you don't like it, but we've got to follow those orders." She hesitated for a moment, then added, "Don't we?"

"Patrick, you're the mission commander—it's up to you," Elliott said. "But you know as well as I do that if Allen or Balboa had their fingers on the triggers, they'd shoot."

"Maybe, maybe not—that's not our problem," McLanahan said. "We were ordered to withdraw, so we withdraw. We'll follow orders." The interphone got very quiet. He called up a repeater of Emil Vikram's large threat display, superimposing it over his God's-eye view so he could map out exactly which ships were transmitting. "Emitter, I see that carrier, the northern destroyer, and those seven northern patrol boats all hitting us with target-tracking radar. We're under attack."

"Why, you sly devil," Cheshire said, turning and grinning at her OSO over her shoulder.

"I believe you're right, Muck," Elliott said. "The PLAN is attacking us!"

"The signal thresholds are too low," Vikram said, still confused. "Call up my sigma-echo screen and look for yourselves. They can't possibly have a lock."

"I say we're an item of interest, and we're allowed to use all weapons to defend ourselves," McLanahan said emphatically. "We need to shut down those radars. Stand by for bomb bay missile launch, crew, twelve Rainbows." McLanahan designated the targets for the anti-radar cruise missiles: the carrier, the northern destroyer, and four of the seven guided-missile patrol boats that were transmitting anti-ship missile-targeting radar energy. "Doors coming open, crew." He hit the command button and spoke: "Launch commit Rainbow missiles."

WARNING, LAUNCH COMMIT TWELVE BOMB BAY TACIT RAINBOW MISSILES, the computer reported, then entered a launch hold.

"Launch," McLanahan commanded. The launch hold was cleared, and the crew felt the rumble of the fibersteel bomb doors retracting inside the bomb bay; a few seconds later, the noise was gone. "All Tacit Rainbows away," McLanahan reported.

As they dropped clear of the bomb bay, the AGM-136 Tacit Rainbow cruise missiles, each about six feet long, a little more than a foot in diameter, and weighing less than a thousand pounds, deployed short stubby wings and horizontal and vertical stabilizers and descended toward the sea. As they got closer to the surface, they activated their turbojet engines, increasing their speed to over 300 miles an hour, and leveled off at 500 feet above the sea. One missile's engine failed to light off despite dozens of automatic relights, and it glided for another nine miles before hitting the ocean and breaking into pieces. Another missile, performing its automatic self-test, determined that its navigational and sensor accuracy was not within its standards; it performed a systems reset, still found its systems faulty, then automatically performed a suicide dive straight down into the rock-hard sea.

One by one, the missiles took up five-mile-long figure-eight orbits at its assigned patrol point, took a GPS satellite fix to nail down its navigational accuracy, and activated its passive electronic sensors. The frequency and pulse rate of every signal received was instantly compared to signatures in their computer memories, and if it matched, the missile immediately began homing in on the signal. Each missile would then instantly report back to McLanahan by datalink that it was locked on.

"All surviving Rainbows tracking," McLanahan reported. "I'm sending a couple back into their orbits." Several Rainbows had locked onto the same radar, so McLanahan had to divert a couple of them back into patrol racetracks so he didn't waste any missiles. "Looking good, guys."

ABOARD THE CHINESE CARRIER *MAO ZEDONG*

"Interceptor Group One ready for launch, sir," the officer of the deck reported.

"Very well," Admiral Yi responded. "Have Interceptor One establish a high combat patrol at the last known—"

Just then, they heard a loud *booom!* roll across the sea. Yi ran over to the port rail and saw a cloud of smoke coming from the destroyer *Kang*. "Something hit the *Kang!*" the lookout shouted. Seconds later, another loud explosion rang out, and Yi watched in horror as a piece of the *Mao*'s Kilo-band fire-control radar for the SA-N-9 antiaircraft missile system crashed to the deck just aft of the bridge. Seconds later, another loud explosion rattled the ship. "Smoke coming from the *Kang!* Looks like he took a missile hit!"

"Never mind the *Kang!* Get me a damage report on *my* ship!"

The phone from Engineering rang just then, and the OOD took the damage report: "Kilo- and Ku-band fire-control radar array and X-band targeting radar for the Granit missiles hit, sir," the officer of the deck reported. "No casualties, no injuries. The flight deck is clear."

Thank the stars, Yi murmured to himself. Yi had never before been in combat—he had been based ashore during the Philippine and Vietnamese naval conflicts—and the speed of the attack, combined with the sudden realization that this big high-tech steel ship was vulnerable and they were very far from friendly shores, was beginning to invade his consciousness, replacing pure, abject fear with all other thoughts about his crew and his ship. "Very well." He slammed that phone down and picked up the one to his Combat Information Center. "Combat, bridge. Status report."

"SA-N-9 antiaircraft system is down to optronic guidance only," the combat officer responded. "Granit targeting system is degraded. We can tie it to the India- or Sierra-band navigation radars for target acquisition—as long as the target does not go outside the missile's sixty-degree seeker cone, it will track by itself."

Yi had to consciously straighten his shoulders and force himself to think to keep from panicking. "Very well. I want a full damage-control report, weapons stations first. Switch to backup fire-control sensors."

"Lookouts report missiles inbound!" the quartermaster shouted suddenly. "Small missiles, one hundred meters above the water, slow speed, numerous missiles! Should we engage?"

Yi felt his knees buckle and his heart pound in his chest. Enough, dammit, *enough*! "Signal the formation, secure all fire-control radars, *now*!" Yi shouted frantically. "Shut them down *now*! Order the entire battle group to switch to manual or optronic fire control." His instructions were carried out just in time, for a few seconds later Yi saw a small cruise missile streak overhead with a tiny whistling sound. It was performing a wide oval pattern about two hundred meters above the ship. "My God," he muttered as another missile whistled past, orbiting a bit lower and in the opposite direction—it felt as if they were large irritating mosquitoes buzzing just out of reach. "Use the AK-630s and shoot those damn things down, damn you—but *do not* use fire-control radars!"

"What should we do, sir?" the officer of the deck asked. "The *Kang* and *Changsha* cannot attack without using their radars."

"Be silent, damn you," Yi shouted. "Have Missile Attack Squadron One move forward in the group and attack the Nationalist frigate using optronic sensors. That should keep it busy so it cannot launch any more missiles against us, and maybe we will get lucky and destroy it. I want every ship in this fleet to go on the attack and destroy that rebel frigate immediately!"

Those small missiles must have been launched by a submarine or stealth aircraft, Admiral Yi thought. His long-range radars were not the best, but if there were any normal aircraft within a hundred kilometers or any subs within five kilometers, they would have detected them. That means that Taiwan was getting assistance—and with weapons that sophisticated, that assistance had to be from the United States.

"Any word from Beijing?" Yi asked.

"Beijing advises that a message is being relayed through the Army Air Force and Navy to provide support so that we may have some coverage in case Taiwan launches attack aircraft."

Yi swore again, then said, "I want whatever air support the PLA can provide out to support us *immediately*," Admiral Yi shouted. "Is that clear? Patrol aircraft, helicopters, gliders, I do not care! Tell Beijing in the strongest possible way to get us some air support! What about our fighters?"

"Interceptor One is ready to launch, sir." Yi looked out toward the flight deck. They had modified the takeoff positions on the carrier to allow up to three fighters to take off nearly simultaneously: the first fighter started at the holdback position farthest to port on the 195-meter launch point; another waited at the number two holdback launch position on the 210-meter spot at the port fantail; and a third fighter was being steered into position at the number three launch position at the starboard fantail position. The first Su-33 ran its engines up to full afterburner power, the steel wheel chocks retracted into the deck, and the fighter accelerated down the flight deck, then up onto the "ski jump" and into the sky. Once the first fighter cleared the bow, the second fighter began its takeoff run. The first fighter disappeared from view for a few moments as its momentum carried it down, but seconds later it could be seen gracefully arcing through the sky. Ten seconds later, the second Sukhoi-33 was airborne, chasing its leader.

"Get Interceptor Two up on deck and ready to go as soon as Interceptor One finds that American bomber," Yi ordered. "Find that American stealth bomber!"

ABOARD THE EB-52 MEGAFORTRESS
THAT SAME TIME

The NIRTSat radar satellite reconnaissance system used six low-orbiting satellites, with as many as three taking high-resolution "snapshots" of the desired target area simulataneously, then combining them electronically into a three-dimensional picture. But taking and processing these high-tech snapshots took time, sometimes as long as two minutes. McLanahan's supercockpit display system could predict the movement of ships and aircraft based on their previous position, heading, and speed, but in the heat of battle, two minutes was a very long time to be without up-to-date information.

As soon as the newest hi-res photo came in, McLanahan was on the interphone. "The carrier is launching fighters," he reported excitedly. "I'm picking up two heading north and climbing fast, passing five thousand feet. And I've got several small escorts overtaking the northern destroyer. Looks like they might be geting into launch position. Stand by, crew, radar coming on." He moved the cursor on the supercockpit display, designated all of the vessels closest to the Taiwanese frigate, then hit the computer command button: "Identify."

WARNING, ATTACK RADAR SWITCHING TO RADIATE . . . WARNING, ATTACK RADAR RADIATING . . . ATTACK RADAR SWITCHING TO STANDBY, the computer reported. In three seconds, the powerful Inverse Synthetic Aperture Radar on the EB-52 Megafortress measured each vessel in three dimensions with six-inch accuracy. It took another twenty seconds for the computer to compare each ship's measurements to the data in its memory files and identify each ship, along with its primary weapon and electronic fit.

The computer read off its search results: TARGET SIX IS JIANGWEI-CLASS FRIGATE, it announced in a very human-sounding female voice. ANTIAIR HQ-61 FOG LAMP, 100-MILLIMETER RICE LAMP DIRECTOR, 30-MILLIMETER ROUND BALL. ANTI-SHIP EIGHT EACH YJ-1 SQUARE TIE, 100-MILLIMETER SUN VISOR, 30-MILLIMETER SUN VISOR. TARGETS THREE, FOUR, SEVEN, NINE, HUANGFENG-CLASS GUIDED-MISSILE BOATS. ANTIAIR, 30-MILLIMETER, ROUND BALL FIRE-CONTROL RADAR. ANTI-SHIP FOUR EACH HY-1, 30-MILLIMETER. TARGET FIVE AND EIGHT, HOUKU-CLASS MISSILE BOATS. ANTIAIR 25-MILLIMETER. ANTI-SHIP, TWO EACH HY-1.

"That middle frigate is a real threat for us," McLanahan said. "We could easily be within range of that HQ-61."

"The range of a Hong Qian-61 is only six miles, sir," Vikram said.

"I heard of an improved version with triple that range," McLanahan offered. "That frigate might be carrying it."

"An improved HQ-61? I never heard about that."

"And what if it's really a Crotale SAM system?"

"Crotale has a max range of eight miles," Vikram said. "We're twenty-six miles from the PLAN fleet."

"Emitter, if you ever want to make captain someday," Cheshire suggested, "just nod and say, 'Yes, sir.' "

"Yes, sir," Vikram complied.

"Good boy," Cheshire said. McLanahan gave his DSO a thumbs-up.

"I don't think the Tacit Rainbow attack deterred them," Elliott said, with a smile. "I think we're still an item of interest. Let 'em have the Wolverines."

"Agreed," McLanahan said. "Stand by for pylon missile launch, crew." His fingers were flying over his touch-screen supercockpit display, designating nine vessels as targets. He then armed four of the attack-configured AGM-177 cruise missiles and programmed all four with all nine possible targets. The cruise missiles would attack the target list in order. If a target was not destroyed, it would attack; if missed, it would reattack; if destroyed, it would move to the next target in the list. "Stand by for pylon missile launch, crew. Wings level." McLanahan then hit the voice command button: "Launch commit Wolverines."

WARNING, LAUNCH COMMIT PYLON LAUNCH ATTACK WOLVERINE MISSILES, the computer responded on interphone, then entered an automatic launch hold.

"Launch," McLanahan ordered, canceling the launch hold. The Megafortress crew felt a slight shudder as the tiny bomb bays on the wing pylon weapons pods opened and four missiles were ejected into the slipstream. "Center up on the steering bug, pilot, heading zero-two-five to the refueling anchor point, and let's get out of here."

PEOPLE'S REPUBLIC OF CHINA PEOPLE'S
LIBERATION ARMY HEADQUARTERS,
BEIJING, CHINA
THAT SAME TIME

Admiral Sun Ji Guoming's executive officer did not wait for a reply before hastily knocking on his superior's office door and rushing in. The first deputy chief of staff was studying a large map of Taiwan and the east coast of China that had updated positions of several Chinese and Taiwanese military units depicted on it, including intelligence estimates of their size and strength. The aide bowed as Sun turned angrily toward him and said, "Sir!"

"I asked not to be disturbed!"

"Message sent here directly from East Fleet headquarters for the chief of staff," the aide went on. "The commander of the carrier *Mao* is requesting assistance."

"Assistance? Where is it? What's happening?"

"In the Formosa Strait, fifty kilometers south of Quemoy Island. The admiral informs us that the *Mao* and its escorts have been ordered to halt and submit to an inspection by a frigate of the Taiwanese navy . . ."

"*What?*" Sun shouted, leaping to his feet in absolute shock and surprise. The carrier battle group was still at least a day from its attack staging position near the Nationalist-held island of Quemoy—it should still be well inside *Chinese* waters. The attack on Quemoy was not supposed to start for another week at the earliest! "You say they are being confronted by the Nationalist navy?"

". . . and they are being supported by what they believe is an American *stealth bomber* firing cruise missiles!"

Sun's head snapped back to his aide as if he had heard a gunshot right behind him. "A *stealth bomber*? How do they know? Have they seen it?"

"Intermittent radar contacts, but shortly thereafter a series of devastating anti-radar missile attacks," the aide replied. "The weather is clear, their radars are operational, but they cannot detect the aircraft attacking them. The captain said he had no choice but to shut down all radar systems after he and one of his escorts, the *Kang*, were hit by anti-radar cruise missiles that came out of nowhere."

"Follow me," Sun ordered, and he and his aide ran out of the office and onto the private elevator that took them down to the chief of staff's underground command center. The command center was little more than a large radio shack, manned around the clock with communications specialists broken into four sections, representing the army, navy, air forces, and Second Artillery Corps, which controlled the land-based nuclear ballistic missiles. Except for exercises, it was rarely visited by anyone much above field grade rank, so it created quite a stir when Deputy Chief of Staff Admiral Sun Ji Guoming burst into the chamber and over to the chief of staff's seat. "Senior controller!" Sun shouted, as he put on his headset.

"Sir!" a voice responded. "This is Major Dai, senior duty controller."

"I want to speak with the commanding officer of the carrier *Mao Ze-dong* right now," Sun ordered. "And put up a chart with locations of naval air units in the Quemoy area and unit resource report data on our Sukhoi-27 wing."

"Yes, sir," Dai replied. In moments, a hastily sketched map of the Formosa Strait region went up on a rear-projection screen in front of Sun. "Sir, naval air units in current mission-ready status in the Quemoy region include the Nineteenth Air Wing at Quanzhou, with thirty J-6 fighter-attack planes, and the Seventh Air Wing at Juidongshan, with twenty-two J-6 fighters. In addition, the Fifty-first Air Wing at Fuzhou is operational with nineteen H-6 bombers."

"I want all three wings put on immediate combat alert," Sun said. "Any units on ready alert right now?"

Another long wait; then: "Negative, sir."

"Beginning today, those three air wings shall have one-third of their flyable planes on twenty-four-hour combat alert," Sun ordered. "I want as many J-6 fighters loaded with air-to-air weapons and cannon ammunition and launched as possible, and be sure they have functioning gun cameras. Their target is any unidentified aircraft in the vicinity of the *Mao* carrier group. What about the Sukhoi-27s?"

"The Second Air Wing at Haikou currently has twelve Su-27 fighters operational."

"Twelve?" Sun retorted. "It was reported all forty planes allotted for combat operations were operational! Damn you, Major, it is the command section's responsibility to see to it that the general staff has accurate information!" Dai stiffened and lowered his head in submission. It would be far too late to launch the Su-27s, Sun thought—the J-6s would have to do. "Get those J-6s airborne, and I want an Ilyushin-76 radar plane launched as well to assist in the search. Where is the chief of staff right now?"

"I will check, sir," the senior controller said. His staff was working more quickly now. "Sir, the chief of staff is in quarters. Shall I ring him?"

"Negative. Notify me at once when the chief of staff checks in with the command section."

"Yes, sir. . . . Sir, Admiral Yi on the carrier *Mao* is on channel two."

Sun switched his communications selector to the proper setting: "Admiral Yi, this is Admiral Sun. How do you copy?"

The transmission was heavy with static—obviously this was an HF shortwave radio patch, not a satellite hookup. "I read you, sir," replied the voice. "Do you wish a status report?"

"Go ahead with your status report, Admiral."

"We are in visual contact with a Taiwanese flagged warship, the *Kin Men*, a guided-missile frigate," Yi reported in a loud voice, as if he were shouting across the sky. "The frigate has opened fire on my group, hitting the destroyer *Kang* with missile fire. The *Kang* suffered minor damage and is still operational. The *Mao* destroyed several inbound missiles with terminal defenses but was hit by small anti-radar missiles launched by a suspected stealth aircraft operating in the vicinity in concert with the rebel ship. Minor damage only. We are still operational. We attempted to return fire but have encountered heavy jamming and anti-radar cruise missile attacks, and we are currently running silent and relying on passive sensors. I have launched two fighters in air defense configuration. We are still in contact with the Nationalist vessel."

"Have you made contact with the stealth aircraft?" Sun asked excitedly.

"Negative," Yi replied. "We get intermittent radar contacts, but nothing solid. We are currently attempting to make contact via optronics, and our fighters are airborne and beginning the search. Over."

"Admiral Yi, you will destroy that Nationalist frigate," Sun ordered. "Order a full-scale attack by every vessel in your battle group. You are permitted to use every weapon in your arsenal . . ." He paused for a moment, then emphasized, ". . . *every* weapon. Do not allow that rebel frigate to escape under any circumstances. Do you understand?"

"Yes, sir," Yi replied.

"Admiral Yi, you will then launch an immediate attack on Quemoy Island from long range," Sun said. "Again, you are ordered and authorized to use *every* weapon in your arsenal. Do you understand?"

There was a very long pause, during which Sun thought they had been cut off; but then: "Comrade Sun, I must have clarification," Admiral Yi radioed. "You are authorizing and ordering me to use *any* weapon in my battle group to attack and destroy the Nationalist military forces on Quemoy Tao. Is that correct?"

"Yes, that is correct," Sun said. "Any and every weapon in your arsenal is free to use. Your attack will commence immediately. And find that stealth bomber and blow it out of the sky!"

When Sun looked up after that interchange, he saw almost everyone in the command center staring at him. The senior controller's eyes were bulging. "Sir . . . I am sure you are aware that the *Mao* battle group carries nuclear attack weapons. Your order to the *Mao* could be interpreted that you ordered a *nuclear* attack against—"

"I ordered nothing of the kind, Comrade Dai," Sun said. "Only the minister of defense or the president can issue such an order, correct?" The senior controller nodded blankly. "Now, what I want is an immediate launch of those fighters. Crews should be responding to their planes by now."

"Yes, sir," the aide said. "The alert has been issued. I shall type up the order and submit it to the chief of staff for his approval."

Sun swung on his aide angrily and shouted, "Did I order you to type anything or submit anything to General Chin? I want those fighters in the air in less than thirty minutes—I will notify the general and get his approval. I want to be notified personally of every development immediately. Now, *move!*"

As the aide hurried off, Sun knew that he was never going to tell Chin or anyone else of this—until and unless the American stealth bomber was brought down. Then his hope was to personally deliver a gun camera tape of an American stealth bomber being shot down to President Jiang—and use it to begin his campaign to rid China's waters of the United States and its lackeys.

ABOARD THE EB-52 MEGAFORTRESS

In attack mode, AGM-177 Wolverine missiles moved too fast to be tracked by NIRTSat satellite snapshots, but the missile's datalink information allowed McLanahan to watch in absolute fascination as the missiles closed rapidly on their quarries.

All Wolverine missiles were programmed to execute a turn shortly after launch so the enemy could not simply trace the missile's flight path directly back to its launch point; missiles coming from many different directions also made it appear as if there were more attackers out there. Each Wolverine missile executed its "dogleg" as it glided down from launch altitude to sea-skimming altitude, between fifty and one hundred feet above the sea, guided by a pencil-thin radar beam that precisely measured the distance from the belly of the missile to the waves. During the glide, the missile automatically opened its turbojet engine air inlets and exhausts, warmed up the electronics for its radar and imaging infrared sensors, and activated its threat sensors, countermeasures system, and GPS satellite navigation system. With the GPS locked on to at least three satellites, it now had target circular error accuracy of less than thirty feet; once it locked onto eight satellites, its navigation precision was good to within *six inches* in both position and altitude. Just before reaching its cruise altitude, the computer commanded the turbojet engine to start, accelerating the missile to over four hundred miles an hour.

With a ripple of microhydraulically controlled skin, the Wolverine missile turned on a dime and headed for its first target. Once lined up on target, it activated its radar for just two seconds and compared the range to the target received from the radar to the range to target on its navigational flight plan—the two figures were within seven feet of each other. The missile sampled the GPS navigation information again, then took a longer radar fix of the target, getting bearing as well as range—now the two were within two feet of each other. Satisfied, the missile signaled back to the EB-52 Megafortress that it was on course and ready to attack.

Patrick McLanahan opened a new computer window on his large supercockpit display, then ordered the sensor feed from the missile displayed in the window. The radar image showed a bright white rectangle, with the missile's sensor's crosshairs centered on it. McLanahan switched to imaging infrared, and a small orange speck appeared; magnified, McLanahan could discern the long, gracefully swept bow, tall amidships superstructure, and huge bow-mounted 100-millimeter gun of the big Chinese Jiangwei-class guided-missile frigate. McLanahan ordered the missile to alter course to align itself with the longitudinal axis of the Chinese frigate for its attack.

Just then, a bright orange circle superimposed itself on the Chinese frigate's icon on the supercockpit display; simultaneously, Vikram called out, "Foxtrot-band air search radar up. . . ." Then, a few seconds later, along with a slow-paced *deedle . . . deedle . . . deedle!* warning tone: ". . . India-band target tracking radar . . ."

"Looks like they're locked onto all four Wolverine missiles," McLanahan said.

Suddenly they heard a fast-pitched *deedledeedledeedle!* warning tone in their headsets. "Missile launch!" Vikram shouted. "No uplink bearings in our direction . . . second missile launch . . . three, four missiles in the air, tracking the Wolverines . . . X-band gun control radars up on the patrol boats, looks like they got a lock-on too. Shit, looks like every Wolverine missile is an item of interest."

"Pick up my window numbers twenty and twenty-one," McLanahan suggested, "and watch the Wolverines in action."

The instant the first Hong Qian-61 antiaircraft missile left the Chinese frigate's rails, the Wolverine missile immediately matched bearings to the uplink signal's bearing, which meant that both missiles were heading nose-to-nose. Then, an instant before impact, the Wolverine missile accelerated to its top speed of 600 miles an hour, released bundles of radar-decoying chaff and infrared-decoy flares, and jinked away, using its mission-adaptive fuselage to turn twice as fast as the antiair missile could possibly turn. The HQ-61 missile still had a solid radar lock and hit— on the cloud of chaff.

As soon as it executed the first twenty-G turn, the Wolverine missile immediately dropped more chaff and flares and executed another turn toward its first target. It picked up the "Round Ball" fire-control radar trying to track it, and dropped more chaff and flares. The gunners aboard the Chinese Huangfeng-class patrol boat opened fire with their 30-millimeter guns, shredding the chaff cloud with hundreds of rounds of ammunition. Seconds later, the Wolverine missile, untouched, sped overhead and dropped its first bomb-bay load of thirty-six baseball-size bomblets. The Wolverine missile couldn't fully align with the vessel's longitudinal axis after evading the gunfire, so only about half of the bomblets hit the vessel—but it was enough to cause a fire in two of the patrol boat's Hong-Yang-1 anti-ship missile canisters. With the two port launch canisters on fire and the two starboard canisters damaged, the skipper of the patrol boat had no choice but to stop his attack run and jettison all four of his missiles overboard before they exploded and sank his ship. With nothing but his 30-millimeter gun remaining, he was effectively out of the fight.

The same Wolverine missile did better on the second and third PLAN patrol boats. Instead of crossing perpendicular to the target's path, the missile scattered its second load of bomblets directly down the second vessel's centerline. The two aft HY-1 missile canisters exploded, driving the vessel's stern down, then flipping the 175-ton patrol boat end-over-end through the air before crashing down into the sea. The Wolverine's third target, a lightly armed but faster sixty-eight-ton Houku-class patrol boat, managed to start a fast turn toward its stricken partner just as the Wolverine began dropping bomblets, so only a few of the one-pound bomblets hit the ship, causing minor damage. The Wolverine's final suicide-attack target, the lead Jiangwei-class frigate, finally stopped it with a double punch from two HQ-61 antiaircraft missiles and mur-derous fire from the frigate's two starboard 30-millimeter guns.

But even as advanced as the Jiangwei-class frigate was, its biggest fault was its downfall—its lack of antiaircraft armament. The Jiangwei had a single Hong Qian-61 sextuple missile launcher forward—only six mis-siles, and no magazine reloads. The frigate fired one missile at each Wolverine missile shortly after they got within range, then fired the last two at the first Wolverine missile to get close. It stopped that Wolver-ine—but two more Wolverines, attacking from different directions, struck the frigate with 250-pound warheads after successfully attacking their assigned primary targets with bomblets.

The fourth Wolverine missile used the success of its three brothers to score the biggest hits. With all of its previous targets already hit and disabled, the fourth Wolverine had the luxury of expending all of its weapons—three bomb bays full of cluster bombs, plus a 250-pound pen-etrating blast warhead—on the Jiangwei-class frigate alone. McLanahan switched his supercockpit window to the sensor view of the fourth Wolverine missile; the rest of the crew called up repeater views of the strike sensor on their multifunction displays and watched as the last Wolverine dropped its first load of cluster munition directly on center-line, circled around, dropped again, circled in the opposite direction, dodged some cannon fire, dropped its last load of cluster bombs in the stern area of the frigate, executed an impossibly sharp triangular course reversal, and plowed into the frigate just a few feet above the waterline, directly amidships on the starboard side.

"Shit! Did you see that?" Nancy Cheshire shouted. "That thing was alive! I saw at least a dozen fires on that ship before the last hit! Excel-lent!"

"Oh . . . my . . . ," was all Vikram could say.

"Let's get out of here, pilots," McLanahan said. "We're supposed to be on our way to the air refueling track."

"High-speed aircraft climbing rapidly, now at two o'clock, twenty-three miles, heading north," Emil Vikram reported. Vikram's threat scope was a duplicate of McLanahan's God's-eye view, but it displayed only airborne targets—the sudden appearance of two high-performance fighters less than thirty miles away were the main targets. "Nav radars fired up on the carrier, bearings locking on the *Kin Men*—I think they might be able to use their nav radars to target the Taiwanese frigate. That carrier might be ready to let go with a big salvo. Sun Visor fire-control radars from the second destroyer locking on the *Kin Men* too."

"I'm going within Scorpion missile range of the frigate," Brad Elliott said. "We'll back up the frigate's antiair weapons. Patrick, we've got to attack that carrier *now*. There's no way it'll get away unless we attack! And if it launches more fighters, we'll be sitting ducks!"

"Brad, we are already in deep shit by launching those Wolverines," McLanahan argued, looking over the top of his instrument panel to look at Elliott in the pilot's seat. "My nose is cold until we get—"

"Missile launch! I've got two missiles lifting off from the *Mao* . . . going supersonic!" Vikram shouted. "Two Granit missiles on the way!"

"Dammit!" McLanahan shouted. "Emitter, can you get them?"

"I've got them!" the defensive systems operator shouted. "I've got the missiles!" He touched the Granit missile's symbols, then touched the command trigger on his interphone panel and said, "Launch commit Scorpions one and two."

WARNING, WARNING, LAUNCH COMMIT SCORPION MISSILES. Then, after a few seconds: MISSILES AWAY. At that instant, one AIM-120 radar-guided missile leapt off a wing pylon from each wing and streaked toward the Chinese anti-ship missiles.

"The *Kin Men* is launching missiles!" McLanahan shouted. "Stand by for a second salvo from the—"

"I've got a second salvo from the carrier!" Vikram shouted. "Another two Granit missiles lifting off . . . Square Tie radar down, must've got hit by a Rainbow missile . . . looks like the Taiwanese frigate is firing more antiaircraft missiles . . . Sun Visor radar down . . ." Vikram immediately fired another two Scorpion missiles at the Chinese anti-ship missiles.

"Range to the lead destroyer is down to twenty miles," McLanahan warned. "Let's do a left turn to reposition. Left turn heading one-six-zero. We'll go out two minutes, then—"

Suddenly, Vikram shouted, "Another missile launching from the *Mao* . . . this one going ballistic! They're launching an M-11 missile! Missile heading toward the mainland . . . turning east, heading for Quemoy . . . another missile lifting off! Two M-11 missiles in the air!"

McLanahan shouted, "Brad!" but Elliott already had the EB-52 Megafortress in a hard right turn. "Lock 'em up, Emitter! You've only got a few seconds . . ."

"They're out of range!" Vikram shouted. The M-11 missiles were huge 13,000-pound solid-fuel rockets; they lifted off slowly but accelerated quickly and flew to much higher altitudes and speeds than anti-ship cruise missiles. "Dammit, I missed them!"

"Get ready in case they launch a second salvo!" McLanahan shouted. "We—"

"Shit, I've got that lead Chinese destroyer *in sight!*" copilot Nancy Cheshire shouted. While they were focusing on the Chinese M-11 missile launch, they had drifted to within twelve miles of the Chinese destroyer *Kang*—and there it was, right in front of them, way out on the horizon but close enough to see its enormous size. "Continue right turn, let's get out of here!"

"Missile launch!" Vikram shouted. "Second salvo of M-11 missiles in the air!" But he was ready for them this time—within two seconds of detecting the launch, two Scorpion missiles were in the air chasing them down. But seconds later, they heard a *deedledeedledeedle!* warning tone in their headsets. "Missile launch!" Vikram shouted. "That destroyer launched Crotale missiles on *us!*"

"Full countermeasures!" Elliott shouted. Vikram immediately activated the EB-52's AN/ALQ-199 MAWS (Missile Approach and Warning System), which used rear- and side-looking radars to search for the incoming missiles. Once the radars locked onto the incoming missiles, the computer system automatically ejected chaff and flare decoys to try to steer the incoming enemy missiles away. At the same time, tiny laser emitters popped up from the Megafortress's fuselage and fired beams of laser energy at the missiles, attempting to blind the missile's sensitive seeker heads.

The Chinese destroyer *Kang* had shut down its tracking radars because of the Tacit Rainbow anti-radar missiles buzzing around, so the only guidance left for the Crotale missiles was their own heat-seeking sensors, which were sensitive both to decoys and to the MAWS laser beams. One by one, the French-built Crotale missiles were diverted safely away from the Megafortress, and they crashed harmlessly into the sea.

"*Kang* reports launching Crotale missiles at extreme range on a large multi-engine aircraft that closed to within sixteen kilometers of their position," the officer of the deck reported to Admiral Yi on the bridge of the carrier *Mao.* "They also reported spotting anti-missile decoy flares on the horizon. They have lost contact."

Admiral Yi was already on the communications links, taking reports from squadron leaders in his fleet. "Hit? Hit by what? We detected no missile launches from the Nationalist frigate."

"They appeared out of nowhere, sir," the skipper of the Jiangwei-class frigate 542 reported. "Four large high-speed targets, all from different bearings, all around us. We fired -61s, but they all missed; we tracked them with fire-control systems, but they evaded our gunners. Patrol boat 1107 destroyed and lost with all hands. Patrol boats 1209 and 1136 on fire. Minor damage to patrol boat 1332. We have suffered major damage, one fire on deck three starboard not yet under control, one hole just above the waterline. We are being assisted by patrol 1108."

"Were they fighters? Maybe rebel F-16s dropping bombs?"

"Sir, I have never seen aircraft move like that," the skipper replied. "I swear to you, sir, they seemed to be able to move at *right angles,* as if they were on *rails*. They were subsonic, but we could not track them— our antennas could not move fast enough!"

It had to be some American secret weapon, Yi told himself as he blankly hung up the phone. Unless the Nationalists were getting help from cosmic sea gods, that was the only explanation—some kind of high-maneuverability air-launched missile fired by the American bomber. "Vector the fighters to the last bearing of those flares," Admiral Yi ordered.

"Bridge, Combat," the intercom blared. "Fighters have made visual contact! They report contact with an American B-52 bomber!"

Yi's mouth dropped open in surprise. A B-52, a nearly forty-year-old plane—and it had wreaked havoc throughout his battle group. "Shoot it down!" Yi shouted. "Tell those pilots to engage! I want to pick up that plane's wreckage and show it for all the world to see!" He then concentrated on his watch. "Missile flight time?" he shouted.

"Forty seconds to first detonation, sir," the quartermaster responded.

"Sound collision," Yi ordered. "Signal the battle group to sound collision." The alarm bells began ringing all across the ship; down below, men put the final clamps and cables on the helicopters up on deck and began clearing the flight decks.

ABOARD THE EB-52 MEGAFORTRESS

"Got 'em!" Vikram shouted. "Crotales no factor . . . Scorpions closing in on the M-11s!" He watched in fascination as the AIM-120 Scorpion missile's icons quickly and smoothly merged with the Chinese M-11 ballistic missile icons. What incredible power! Vikram thought gleefully. We're shooting down ballistic missiles, shutting down radars, turning away antiaircraft missiles, and getting ready to blow a carrier out—"

"Fighters!" Nancy Cheshire suddenly shouted out on interphone. "Two fighters at eleven o'clock high! They've got us in sight!" Just then, the threat receiver came to life with a fast, high-pitched *deedledee-dledeedle!* and a female aural "Missile launch . . . missile launch . . . missile launch!" warning. At the same time, streams of radar-decoying chaff and heat-seeking missile decoy flares began automatically ejecting from both internal tail ejectors. At the same time, Elliott grabbed the control stick and hauled it over hard left with his left hand, then jammed the throttles on the center throttle console to full military power.

Emil Vikram's fingers were flying over his defensive weapon controls, immediately activating the ALQ-199 HAVE GLANCE active countermeasures system. On the Megafortress's raised dorsal pod, tiny radar emitters popped up, slaved themselves to the enemy aircraft bearing from the threat receiver, and began tracking first the larger fighters and then the smaller, faster-moving Pen Lung-9 air-to-air missiles fired by the People's Republic of China People's Liberation Army Air Force Su-33 carrier-based fighters. As the missiles closed to within a mile, the ALQ-199 MAWS active countermeasures pods began firing laser beams at the missiles, blinding the sensitive radar sensors in the missile's nosecap. Any PL-9 missiles not decoyed by the chaff bundles or flares were hit by the lasers.

"Get on the horn, get some help up here!" Elliott shouted. "Clear on all weapons!"

Ignoring secure communications procedures, Cheshire activated the satellite transceiver and called, "Buster, this is Headbanger, we're under attack, two Sukhoi-33s!"

"Copy, Headbanger," Samson replied. "We're trying to contact the ROC Air Force for assistance. Use everything you got to get out of there. Stand by." The Megafortress crew got very quiet—they knew that help was very far away, and they were on their own.

"Stand by for AMRAAM launch!" Vikram shouted on interphone. The Sukhoi-33s began a lazy right turn right in front of the Megafortress— they were obviously not expecting a counterattack by such a large, lumbering target. Vikram quickly locked up both Su-33s on the EB-52's modified APG-73 attack radar from less than five miles away. "Roll wings level . . . birds leaving the rails, *now.*" In two-second intervals, the last two AIM-120 Scorpion AMRAAMs streaked off the left and right weapon pod launchers, and at less than six miles the medium-range active-guidance missiles were almost unstoppable. "Splash two!" Vikram shouted.

"How about that, Emitter—you're a damned ace!" Cheshire said.

"Don't start congratulating each other yet—I've got two more carrier fighters airborne," McLanahan said. "Emitter, do you have contact on—?"

Ccrraacckk!

Suddenly it seemed as if every molecule of air in the cabin were sizzling and popping like electrified popcorn. The interphone began to crack and sputter with loud static. Several aircraft systems popped offline, although all four engines continued to run perfectly.

"Hey, I just got some kind of spike in the electrical system," Nancy Cheshire reported. "Number two generator's off-line, essential bus B breakers popped. Check your systems, guys, before I reset."

"What was that?" Vikram asked nervously. "I never got any spike like that before."

"Just check your systems, D-so," Elliott responded. "Station check. Cabin altitude is eight thousand . . . fuel system . . ." Just then, a terrific rumbling reverberated through the Megafortress, followed by a tremendous buffeting. Unsecured charts and checklist booklets flew through the cabin, and anyone who didn't have their lap belts tightly snugged down felt the tops of their helmets bounce off the ceiling. "Jesus!" Elliott gasped as he tightened his grip on the control stick. "We running through a typhoon, or what? Anybody got anything?"

"I've got my stuff in standby," McLanahan reported. "I suggest a heading of dead east. Let's get some distance from that Chinese battle group until we get our gear back on-line. Emitter, get your switches in standby so Nancy can get that generator back on. Brad, let's ask the *Kin Men* if he's got anything."

"Rog," Elliott said, switching radios: "Gabriel, this is Headbanger, how copy? Gabriel, this is Headbanger on Fleet Two." Deciding that Captain Sung had dispensed with the code words by now, Elliott tried, "Captain Sung, this is Headbanger, you read?"

Just then, there was another sudden *snapp!* of energy that raced through the Megafortress—but this time, in a right turn toward the east, Elliott saw what caused it: "Holy shit, crew, I just saw a bright flash off to the northwest through the clouds! Jesus . . . oh man, I think it was a nuclear explosion!" He watched in horror as concentric rings of pure white clouds began to form far off on the horizon. The circular clouds raced across the sky, slowly dissipating as they got closer, until they disappeared—but moments later, another rumble and a hard shudder coursed through the big bomber. "I think that was the shock wave, crew. I think Quemoy got hit by a nuclear explosion!"

"That shock was much less than the first one," McLanahan said. "We're a good forty miles from Quemoy—but we were only about ten miles from the *Kin Men*. I'll be able to tell once my radar is back on-line, but the NIRTSat recon system isn't showing the *Kin Men* on the board, and we can't raise it by radio."

"The *Kin Men* got hit by a nuclear anti-ship missile," Cheshire stated flatly. The entire crew was stunned into silence, and no one argued with Nancy Cheshire on this point. A few years earlier, Nancy Cheshire had been flying in that very same seat in the very same EB-52 Megafortress (but before Jon Masters's new modifications), on a mission over Belarus during the Lithuania–Belarus conflict. They had used an AIM-120 Scorpion missile to shoot down an SS-21 surface-to-surface nuclear missile that had been launched by pro-Soviet forces against the Lithuanian capital of Vilnius—and, it turned out, against the Belarussian capital of Minsk, in an attempt to kill any anti-Soviet supporters and heat up the Cold War once again. Cheshire had been on board the EB-52 when the SS-21 had missile created a partial nuclear yield just twenty miles away, temporarily blinding her. Her crew had barely managed to fly the crippled bomber to safety in Norway. "We don't have anything to protect here anymore. Let's get the hell out of here."

"Let's get a piece of that carrier and the destroyer first," Elliott said angrily. "Son of a bitch, we should put that thing on the bottom of the ocean right *now* for what they've done!"

"Brad, forget about the carrier and give me a hard right turn to the east," McLanahan interjected. "We've got to get out of the area until we sort out our avionics problems and get some guidance on—"

"Fighters!" Cheshire shouted again. "Just above our altitude, nine o'clock, about five miles! You got 'em, Emitter?"

"I don't have anything!" Vikram shouted in a high-pitched voice filled with fear. "No radar, no Scorpion missiles . . ."

"Relax, Emitter," McLanahan said. "Get your stuff back on and let's see what we got. Check your tail cannon, see if you have control of the airmines."

Vikram turned all of his equipment to OFF, waited a few seconds instead of a few minutes, then turned them directly back to ON instead of waiting to warm them up in STBY. He then activated his helmet-mounted "virtual" steering controls for the Stinger tail defense airmine rockets. The B-52's old .50-caliber or 20-millimeter tail guns, which had been removed a few years earlier along with the gunner, had been replaced on the EB-52 Megafortress with an 80-millimeter launcher that fired radar- or radio-controlled rockets. The rockets, called "airmines," were detonated either automatically or by manual command out to nearly four miles; they contained dozens of tungsten steel cubes that could shred aircraft skin or shell out an engine if sucked into an engine inlet.

Vikram experimentally moved the airmine cannon by moving his head—wherever he "looked," the cannon pointed in that direction. Right now the display was blank, except for the azimuth and elevation readouts, the missiles-remaining counter at 50, and the status readouts, which all read ON with flashing red letters except for the cannon itself, which read OK in green letters. "Looks like the cannon is okay," he reported. "But the radars and datalink are still down. How can I track them if I can't see them?"

"They're coming around!" Elliott shouted. "Three o'clock, same altitude, about five miles."

"If that's all the information you got, Emitter, that's what you use," McLanahan said. "You've got to visualize where the fighters are, then lay the airmines out there and detonate them manually where you *think* the fighters will be."

"But I don't understand how—"

"There's nothing to understand, Emitter—just do it!" McLanahan shouted. *"Now!"*

Vikram focused his attention on the virtual gunnery display. He tried to imagine the fighters rolling in hard toward their target, arming missiles or guns, tightening the turn, decreasing the range . . . and then he pulled the trigger three times. A loud *bang bang bang!* and a brief, sharp shudder rocked the EB-52. In his virtual display, he saw three large circles moving away from him; the size of the circle represented the range from the bomber and decreased as the rocket got farther away . . . except the circle size did not decrease. Vikram moved his head to steer the first missile—nothing. He punched the DETONATE button with his right thumb—again, no indication that the missile had detonated.

"I think the radio link to the missile is down," Vikram said.

"Then don't try to manually steer or detonate the missiles," McLanahan said. "Prearm all the missiles to detonate at two miles—you'll just have to start pumping them out across the whole rear quadrant."

"But I won't know if I hit anything," Vikram protested as he punched in new arming instructions for all the remaining rockets. "Sounds like a waste of airmines."

"If you don't stop those fighters, Emitter, we'll waste a hell of a lot more than a few airmines," McLanahan said. "Start pumping them out." Quickly but methodically, Vikram started laying down lines of airmine rockets, describing a figure-eight pattern centered on the Megafortress's tail. The crew heard several loud *pops!* and a sharp, hard rumble through the plane as the cannon fired the rockets into the sky.

"Bandit, nine o'clock!" Elliott shouted on interphone. "He's firing guns!" The fourth Su-33 fighter had broken off his wingman's position when the leader had seen the exploding airmines and circled around, both Chinese fighters staying well away from the bomber's tail. Vikram swung the turret left, and fired. Elliott tried to help by breaking hard right to put the fighter back into the airmine cannon's lethal envelope, but not in time. Several 23-millimeter cannon shells hit the Megafortress's number four engine, causing it to disintegrate in the blink of an eye. The engine-monitoring computers immediately sensed the turbine overspeed and shut the engine down before it exploded. But the sudden loss of the right outboard engine, coupled with the steep right turn and full thrust on the left engines, threw the Megafortress into a steeper right break . . .

. . . too tight: the turn steepened, the airspeed decreased, the angle of attack increased, and the tight turn quickly wrapped into a 5G accelerated stall. The crew felt the rumble of the stall along the huge wings, felt the rumble deepen as the departed slipstream banged first on the spoilers, then the fuselage, then felt the neck-jarring jolts as the slipstream grabbed the V-tail assembly and rocked the bomber in both pitch and yaw simultaneously. No matter how much the pilots moved the control stick, the bomber would not respond—all of the control surfaces had been immobilized by a 300-knot blast of disrupted air, acting like a huge whirlpool slamming the bomber in every direction at once.

"Wings level! Wings level!" Cheshire shouted. The Megafortress was still in a one-hundred-degree right bank, and it felt as if it was tipping farther right, threatening to roll upside down.

"Controls won't respond!" Elliott shouted on interphone. "No response!"

"We got it, we got it!" Cheshire shouted cross-cockpit. She still did not have time to put on her oxygen mask. The FIRE #4 warning lights came on, but in the Megafortress that was only an advisory—the aircraft had already responded to the fire, shutting down the engine, activating the firefighting system, and rerouting fuel, hydraulic, bleed air, pneumatic, and electrical systems away from the stricken engine. "Damn, we lost number four!" Cheshire shouted. "Number four's already shut down! General, try airbrakes. Bring the power back to idle. Emitter, nail that fighter, for Christ's sake!"

"My gear's in reset, Nance!" Atkins shouted back on interphone. "I'm blind for the next ninety seconds!"

"Stand by," Elliott responded. "Airbrakes six, power coming back . . ." All of the crew members were thrown forward into their shoulder straps as the airspeed rapidly bled off. Elliott held the control stick full forward, easing it slightly left every few seconds to test if the controls were responding. At first it felt as if the nose was rising, threatening to send them into a tail-first spin right into the sea, but a few long, tense seconds later, the nose tucked under and the artificial horizon attitude indicator stopped its tumble. Elliott applied slight left rudder and left bank, and the left wing came down slightly. In very, very gradual increments, he fed in left bank, being extra careful not to bleed off any of the slowly increasing airspeed. He felt a slight rumble in the wings and fuselage and lowered the airbrakes. The rumble remained—they were still right at the initial buffet, right at the edge of the stall.

"Passing five thousand!" Cheshire shouted.

As the bank decreased below forty degrees, Elliott smoothly began reapplying power, and the airspeed increased faster. Now, with the wings almost level, the nose down below the horizon, and airspeed increasing, he slowly began feeding in back pressure to decrease the rate of descent. At first there was no response—their airspeed had decreased below flying speed, *way* below—so he held the stick forward and fed in a bit more power.

"Four thousand feet!"

Another try—this time, Elliott felt pressure on the stick as he pulled, and he kept the back pressure in until he felt it mush again, then released. The nose was ten degrees below the horizon now, and the stall buffeting was all but gone. A bit more back pressure . . . no, too much, forward again, nose moving down, airspeed increasing, good . . . a bit more back, wings level, good, no mushing, a bit more back pressure, pitch up to eight degrees, six degrees . . .

"Three thousand feet!"

Elliott slowly began moving the throttles forward. Power spooling up to one hundred percent, another try for more altitude . . . good, nose coming up to four degrees, almost level, airspeed still rising, descent rate decreasing . . . "Two thousand . . . one thousand . . . Jesus, Brad, you got it?"

There! Nose on the horizon, airspeed right at takeoff speed, wings level—they were flying again! Elliott looked up from his airspeed indicator and saw how close they got to the ocean . . . shit, the waves looked close enough to be spraying salt water on them! The radar altimeter read 200 feet, just barely out of the cushion of air known as ground effect. They were flying! "I got it, crew, I got it," Elliott said triumphantly. Airspeed was above 200 knots, so he lifted the nose above the horizon, and the radar altimeter started up . . . 250, 300, well out of ground effect now and we're still flying and airspeed's still incr—

The 23-millimeter shells from the Chinese Sukhoi-33's gun attack stitched a single line of inch-wide holes along the upper fuselage of the Megafortress beginning just aft of the trailing edge of the right wing, straight up and across the crew compartment. The steel shells punctured the avionics "canoe" on the fuselage just before tearing into the aft and center body fuel tanks, causing a terrific explosion. The shells continued through the crew compartment, piercing Emil Vikram's ejection seat and shredding his head, body, instrument panel, and left-side fuselage area, missing McLanahan and Elliott by only inches. A scream erupted from McLanahan's lips as he watched his partner get blown to pieces right before his eyes. Vikram's chest looked as ragged and raw as an old scarecrow—thankfully, the pieces of his helmet hid his decimated head. Blood spattered against the forward crew compartment and left-side cockpit windows just before the left windows disintegrated. The crew cabin explosively decompressed, creating a sudden solid fog in the cockpit, then a virtual hurricane of thundering wind and violent sound. Brad Elliott was thrown to the right as his head and upper torso took the entire brunt of the hurricane-force winds ripping through the blasted left cockpit windows.

Through her screams of terror and shock, copilot Major Nancy Cheshire's training took over. She was battered by the hurricane-force slipstream and shocked by the explosions ripping through her plane, but she managed to focus on her one and only priority: flying the airplane. Everything else had to wait. Still two hundred feet above the South China Sea, the EB-52 Megafortress was still flying and still accelerating, so she held on to those two facts with every ounce of her skill, experience, and strength. The wings were still attached, three of the plane's four engines were still running and still producing smash, and they hadn't hit the rock-solid ocean yet—and it was her job to keep it that way.

"Guard your throttles!" she heard a voice thunder. Just as she laid her hands on the throttle quadrant, Patrick McLanahan reached across the center console and began unbuckling Elliott's lap belt and parachute harness straps. "You okay, Nancy?" McLanahan shouted over the windblast.

"Yes!" she shouted back. She didn't dare take her eyes off her instruments, but out of the corner of her eyes she saw McLanahan detach Elliott from his ejection seat, drag him out of the pilot's seat, lay him down on the deck between the pilot's seats and instrument console, hook up his oxygen mask and interphone cord, turn his regulator to OXYGEN 100%, and begin checking his wounds.

"How is he, Patrick?" Cheshire asked.

"He looks okay," McLanahan replied. "A few cuts on the left side of his face and shoulders." He quickly wrapped bandages from a first-aid kit around the worst-looking wounds. Thankfully McLanahan had thought to detach the man from his seat rather than simply undo his shoulder straps, because now Elliott had a parachute on and at least had a fighting chance to eject or do a manual bailout if they got hit. "How are you doing up there?"

"I feel like I'm suddenly flying an ambulance plane rather than a bomber."

"Can the wisecracks, co," McLanahan snapped—but he was happy that Nancy Cheshire was still cracking wise. If she was too quiet or too serious, it was an indication they were in *serious* trouble! Satisfied that Elliott was breathing on his own and secured the best he could be, he crawled back into his seat and called up the aircraft systems status page on his supercockpit display. "Number four's shut down, no further fire indications," he announced, acting as copilot while his only other surviving crew member flew the plane. "Successful fuel system transfer, successful hydraulic and electrical shunts. Auto transferring fuel from the fuselage and mains to the wings, because I think we're leaking fuel."

"We're on the deck at mil power and four hundred knots, and I think that's all we're going to get out of her," Cheshire added. "We've lost the left-side windscreen and all of the left-side controls and indicators. At least it's warm out there."

"Defense is tits-up," McLanahan reported after doing a status check on the defensive suite. "All weapons went into emergency safety shutdown with the engine fire. I'm going to reset everything. Radar should be up in ninety seconds. If we still have weapons, they'll be up in two minutes. Nav systems successfully reset and reloaded. All weapons went into emergency safety shutdown."

"What about those fighters out there, Muck?" Cheshire asked.

"If we can see him and track him on the attack radar, there's a chance," McLanahan said as he started to check his own equipment. But a few seconds later: "I've got no-go lights on all internal and external weapons, Nance—they might've been hit by a bullet or damaged by the fire. Looks like we got squat. Left turn heading zero-four-five, co. We're heading right for Taiwan. If we got any help out there, that's where they'll be. I'll do another restart, but I think my stuff is dead."

"Any contact with the Taiwanese air force?" Cheshire asked on interphone.

McLanahan tried all the radios. "Negative," he responded. "The electromagnetic pulse from the nuclear explosions shut down all the radios. Nothing's getting through."

"We won't make it," Cheshire said. "That Chinese fighter is probably lining up on us right now. Without weapons or countermeasures, he can slice us up at his leisure."

"I'll jettison the wing weapons pods so we can get max performance," McLanahan said. Moments after punching off both wing pylons: "Hey, I've got a green light on the bomb-bay Striker missiles! The wing weapons pods must've been damaged from the explosion on the number four engine—jettisoning the bad missiles cleared the continuity faults on all the other missiles. But there's still no way we're going to hit a fighter with a three-thousand-pound Striker missile . . ." But that didn't stop him from repowering the Striker missile rotary launcher and getting the eight remaining missiles on-line.

"Radar's up!" McLanahan shouted over the screaming windblast coming through the Megafortress's shattered left windows. "Bandit six o'clock, five miles!"

"Nail him!" Cheshire shouted on interphone. "Launch the Strikers!"

"Got him!" McLanahan shouted. He touched the fighter symbol on his supercockpit display, which designated the target, then hit the control stud on his trackball pad and spoke, "Launch commit Striker."

CAUTION, NO AIR-TO-AIR WEAPONS AVAILABLE, the attack computer responded.

"Override that caution," McLanahan ordered the computer. "Launch commit Striker."

WARNING, WEAPON SELECTION OVERRIDE, WARNING, WEAPON PERFORMANCE HAZARDOUS, RECOMMEND LAUNCH ABORT . . . RECOMMEND LAUNCH ABORT . . .

Just then, they felt the Megafortress's tail slide to one side, followed by a heavy buffeting. "Jesus, I think we're hit!" Cheshire shouted.

"Launch," McLanahan ordered.

WARNING, LAUNCH COMMIT STRIKER, BOMB DOORS OPENING.

"Wings level!" McLanahan shouted. "Gimme a slight climb." Cheshire raised the nose and leveled the wings. As she did so, she felt the rumble of the aft set of bomb-bay doors swinging up into the bomb bay, and a Striker missile was ejected into the slipstream. The missile dropped two hundred feet, wobbly stabilized itself, then ignited its first-stage rocket motor. Just as the bomb doors slid closed, another electrical spike drove through the EB-52's electrical system, sending the good systems back into reset.

The Chinese Sukhoi-33 pilot had just released the trigger on his fighter's cannon after a three-second burst from the left rear quadrant at about a half-kilometer distance when he saw the big 2,900-pound missile ignite its rocket motor. The missile shot straight ahead, climbed almost straight up, then looped backward and down right toward him! He got off a quick one-second burst at the bomber before dropping decoy chaff and flares and breaking hard right away from the missile and plugging in full afterburner power.

Guided by the Striker's onboard radar, the Striker missile heeled sharply, ignoring the tiny clouds of chaff dropped by the fighter. With incredible precision, the Striker missile lined up on the Sukhoi-33's tail and cruised in. The Chinese pilot made a last-ditch dodge to the left, but even the high-performance jet was no match for the speed of the big Striker missile at full thrust. The explosion completely vaporized the fighter—nothing recognizable was left to hit the water.

"I'm blind again," McLanahan shouted on interphone. He started to roll the trackball across the screen to highlight the target—again, nothing. "I think I lost my system, Nancy," he said. "I'll try a reset. Let's hope this last asshole runs out of gas or—"

Suddenly, Cheshire screamed, *"Fighters!* Twelve o'clock! Right in front of us! Launching missiles! *My God!"* She could clearly see the twin trails of air-to-air missiles leaving the wing hardpoints of the plane in front of them, streaking directly toward them—it was as if the missiles were aiming directly for *her!* It was like watching a demonstration video of an air-to-air-missile launch. Nancy Cheshire closed her eyes and waited for the impact, waited for the explosion, waited for death . . .

. . . so she didn't see the missiles streak just a few dozen yards overhead, past the Megafortress, and hit the last Chinese Sukhoi-33 carrier fighter, seconds before it opened fire on the EB-52 from close range.

When she found herself still alive, Cheshire opened her eyes. There before her, making a graceful left turn to parallel her course, was another EB-52 Megafortress! The second Megafortress, paired with hers, had come off the refueling anchor when the shooting started and had just arrived in the area. "Oh my God, it's Kelvin and Diane's crew," Cheshire breathed. "When the shooting started, I forgot all about them coming on station. They must've just come off the tanker and headed right down here when they heard the shooting start."

"What a beautiful sight," McLanahan said to Cheshire. He was behind her again, checking on Elliott. "Get on their wing—it looks like they're headed back to the air refueling anchor."

"You got it," Cheshire agreed. "How's Brad?"

Elliott's oxygen blinker looked OK, so he was breathing; McLanahan checked for any signs of chest trauma or bleeding, and found nothing. Elliott's eyes were closed, but when McLanahan gently touched his eyelids, the veteran three-star aviator opened his eyes. "Quit fucking with me, nav," Elliott groused.

"Are you okay, sir?"

"I feel like I've got a two-thousand-pound bomb on my chest," he responded. "The windblast must've knocked the wind outta me."

"Any other pain? You're not having a heart attack on me, are you, sir? You took one hell of a slam by that windblast when the cockpit windscreen let go."

"Hey, I'll compare EKGs with you any day, Muck," Elliott grumbled, trying to sit up against the starboard bulkhead. "We okay?"

"Kelvin Carter showed up and saved our bacon right at the nick of time," McLanahan said. "We're on his wing, heading back to the anchor."

Elliott nodded. He looked a little pale, and his oxygen blinker showed a slightly shallow, labored breathing pattern. McLanahan removed a flight glove and tried to take Elliott's pulse, but he shook McLanahan's fingers off his wrist. "Get away from me and help Cheshire fly the beast," Elliott said. "I'm fine. It's her flying you need to keep an eye on now."

"Har har," Cheshire said.

"Brad . . ."

"Get out of my face, nav. I'm fine," Elliott said.

Deciding that there was nothing more he could do for his friend and aircraft commander now, McLanahan nodded. He retrieved both his and Elliott's flight jackets and covered the pilot up with them. "I'll check on you in a few," he said.

"You better not wake me up trying to play nurse," Elliott said, giving his young protégé a thumbs-up. "Get back to your seat. And Muck . . . I mean, Patrick?"

"Yeah, Brad?"

"We had to take on those Chinese warships, didn't we?" Elliott asked. "We had to help defend those ships, didn't we?" The pain in his eyes was obvious—but whether it was from his injuries or from having doubts about his actions, McLanahan couldn't tell.

"We had to do something, Brad—we're not out here flying around for nothing," McLanahan replied.

The smile in Elliott's eyes seemed to light up the cockpit, despite the windblast damage. "You're damned right, Muck," Elliott breathed behind his oxygen mask. "You're damned right."

"Mr. President, there is no one on Capitol Hill more aware of the need for extreme security than me," the new Senate Majority Leader, Barbara Finegold, said, as the group settled in for the meeting in the White House West Wing's Cabinet Room, "but eventually you *have* to release some information to the congressional leadership. Now might be the perfect time to do it."

"Senator, as I told you before this photo op began, there is nothing else I can tell you," the President said, with a forced smile. "I have procedures I need to follow too, and I have to wait on the results of the security review."

"I see," Senator Finegold said, letting out an audible exasperated breath. The seating had been rearranged after the press had departed, so now Finegold, the forty-eight-year-old former Los Angeles mayor and third-term senator from California, was seated across from the President, instead of two seats from him as in the official press photos. On her side of the table was House Minority Leader Joseph Crane and several other prominent House and Senate Democrats. Seated to President Martindale's right was Vice President Ellen Whiting, Secretary of Defense Chastain, House Majority Leader Nicholas Gant, Senate Minority Leader Michael Fortier, and White House Chief of Staff Jerrod Hale; on the President's left was Secretary of State Hartman, Joint Chiefs of Staff chairman Admiral George Balboa, National Security Advisor Philip Freeman, CIA director Layne W. Moore, and Attorney General Robert M. Procter.

"Great meeting, everyone, thank you," the President said. Chief of Staff Jerrod Hale stood, a signal for the rest of the President's advisors to start heading for the door, but the President said, "We have a few minutes more. Any other questions I can answer for anyone?" Hiding his impatience, Hale stood beside the door and listened intently to every word.

"Mr. President, I'm afraid this might require some Senate Arms Services Committee hearings to determine exactly what happened in the Persian Gulf," Finegold forged on, "and to respond to the question brought up by the media and by several well-known military experts as to exactly how the radar sites in Iran were destroyed. If it's true that the only way those sites could have been bombed was by an American stealth bomber secretly flying all the way across China and Afghanistan, as has been speculated, I think the congressional leadership needs and has a right to know."

"You certainly have the right and the authority to call such hearings," the President said. Although Kevin Martindale had been successful in regaining the White House by a slim margin, he had not been as successful in helping to keep a majority in the Senate, and Barbara Finegold was a powerful and worthy adversary. Tall, dark, immensely popular, with a fashion model's face and figure, she was already being touted as a shoo-in for her party's presidential nomination in the year 2000, outstripping the former administration's vice president and a host of other male candidates. "We will cooperate all we can—"

"But the White House would insist on closed-door hearings," Secretary of Defense Chastain interjected. "All records would be placed in the highest classification level possible."

"Given the current events concerning China," Secretary of State Hartman added, "we think that's the most prudent avenue to take."

"Fine—I agree," Finegold said. "Then you agree to cooperate in committee hearings?"

"I might remind the President that the Pentagon's security review on the events in the Persian Gulf hasn't even been completed yet," National Security Advisor Freeman said. "We don't even really know to what extent everything is classified yet. Our review could take several months."

"I see," Senator Finegold repeated stiffly. This was the face of the opposition, she thought—this White House was tough, experienced, and well organized under Kevin Martindale. It might take several months for hearings to begin if these political pros put on a full-court press to postpone them.

But the unwritten "three-month honeymoon" period after the inauguration was now over, and the Martindale administration was fair game to any inquiries she could concoct. "Well, I'll see to it that the SASC gets together with you and the Pentagon folks in drawing up a list of witnesses and agreeing on a format," Finegold said. "I'm counting on your full cooperation." The President nodded stiffly and gave her a cocky smile. It was obvious to Senator Finegold that the entire Cabinet had given the idea of Senate hearings very careful thought and had already begun to arrange its ground rules, all of which would be designed so the White House and Pentagon would reveal as little hard information as possible.

"The other matter I wanted to mention to you, Mr. President," Finegold said, leaning forward and interlacing her long fingers on the table, "was your proposal to repeal the 1979 Taiwan Relations Act, which would allow for full diplomatic recognition of Taiwan. Did you think it was wise to announce this proposal to the entire world before consulting with Congress? To my knowledge, you didn't even consult with leaders in your own party before announcing your intention to support Taiwan's independence from mainland China and to allow an exchange of ambassadors."

"Is there a problem?" the President asked. "Don't you feel we should support Taiwan's independence efforts?"

Finegold looked angry. "Frankly, Mr. President, I hadn't thought about it," she said testily, "just as I haven't considered what the proper response might be in Northern Ireland, or Cyprus, or dozens of conflicts anywhere else. The point is, we should be deciding these questions *together*. It would help the ratification process tremendously if the Senate Foreign Relations Committee and the leadership knew what you have in mind before announcing it to the world."

"My hand was forced by Taiwan's abrupt vote for independence—they chose not to consult with us, or anyone else for that matter," the President said. "I felt it was necessary to make a decision and take a stand quickly, before China decided it needed to give its errant province a spanking. I will be sure to consult with you closely the next time."

"The world still considers Taiwan a province of China, Mr. President," Finegold said. "We've isolated ourselves and put ourselves on a collision course with mainland China by recognizing the Republic of China."

"Do *you* think it's nothing but a rogue republic, Senator?" the President asked. Finegold shook her head in exasperation, and the President went on, "The question is important, Barbara. Read your history books. The Nationalists were our allies in World War Two, every bit as important in establishing a 'second front' in Asia as Britain and France were in Europe. Because of a Communist-sparked civil war, our allies were pushed off the mainland and onto a rock in the Pacific Ocean. They've endured artillery bombardment, constant military threats, global loss of diplomatic recognition, and economic isolation. Today, they're one of the richest industrial democracies in the world, and they still count the United States as a friend and ally despite what we've done to them over the past thirty years.

"Now they've taken a major step in deciding their fate as a nation by rejecting their Communist overlords and declaring independence, and they've asked for our support. I proudly gave it to them. I took a stand. Now you have to do so as well."

"The Congress has got to look at the overall effect on our economy and the military threat," Finegold argued, "before we vote to repeal the Taiwan Relations Act or ratify your recognition of an independent Taiwan."

"The net effect of the President's declaration is zero, Senator," Secretary of State Hartman said. "China might decide to retaliate by imposing strict tariffs or even banning our goods, but we feel that China cannot long continue such a measure. They need our markets just as much as we need their investments."

"So you tell American companies to be still and patient while they suffer because we've turned away thirty billion dollars' worth of markets in China in favor of three billion dollars' worth in Taiwan, all because we like supporting the underdog?" Joseph Crane asked. "If you had consulted with Congress instead of charging off, we would've advised further negotiations to help bring the two Chinas back together gently and peacefully, rather than rip them apart suddenly."

"Mr. Crane, Taiwan has been looking down the barrel of a Chinese artillery piece for the past forty years," Secretary of Defense Chastain argued. "China isn't interested in gentle reunification—they're insisting on total absorption, by force if necessary."

"China is ready to completely 'absorb' Hong Kong," Crane retorted, "and the process is going along smoothly and peacefully."

"Apples and oranges, Mr. Crane," Hartman said. "Hong Kong is Chinese property leased by Great Britain, and the lease is simply expiring. The Republic of China on Formosa represents a free and democratic society that we've supported for nearly one hundred years, a society and government that is one of the richest and fastest-growing economies in the world, modeled after our own. It's being threatened by a totalitarian Communist power that wishes nothing less than to eliminate it—not assimilation, not sharing, not coexistence, but complete elimination of its democratic, capitalist foundation. The President has chosen to act to support this Asian friend and ally. The question is, what is the Senate leadership going to do—support the President, or cut his legs out from under him?"

"You've put us in a very embarrassing position, Mr. President," Finegold said, addressing Martindale directly. "You are the leader in all foreign relations and matters of state. But those decisions affect the country, and so Congress is given powers of checks and balances over your decisions, in the form of ratifying treaties and passing laws. This relationship expects—no, *demands*—cooperation and compromise from all parties concerned. Your unilateral announcement of support cuts *our* legs out from under us. We should support our president, but what if his decision is the wrong one? We can't absolve ourselves of the blame if our own citizens are hurt by our decisions; we can't point fingers at the President. At the very least, Mr. President, you've forced us to delay any action on repealing the Taiwan Relations Act or recognizing the ROC until we've had a chance to study the idea."

"For how long?" Hartman asked.

"Impossible to say, Secretary Hartman," Finegold said. "The committee staffs are just now being organized. It could take weeks just to be able to sit down and decide what areas need to be studied."

"Very similar to the problems you said you'd encounter in deciding about what areas of the air attacks on Iran and the Persian Gulf could be included in Senate hearings," Crane added.

"You're not suggesting that we do any less due diligence in examining the risks to national security of revealing details of our military actions just so we can see reasonable progress from Congress in furthering our foreign policy agenda?" Hartman asked incredulously.

Representative Crane smiled mischievously. "If the foot-dragging fits, Mr. Secretary . . ."

"We *all* want progress, Secretary Hartman," Senator Finegold said, putting a hand on Crane's arm as if to calm him down. "If we all keep that in mind, I think we—"

Suddenly a man in a business suit and wearing a wireless communications earset opened the door, saw the chief of staff standing nearby, and whispered something in his ear. Most everybody in the room recognized the newcomer as Marine Corps Colonel William McNeely, the White House military liaison who worked in an office next to National Security Advisor Philip Freeman's. He was carrying a plain black briefcase, and Finegold realized with a faint shock what it was: McNeely was the man responsible for the "football," the briefcase containing a communications transceiver that put the President in contact with the National Military Command Center at the Pentagon and several other military command posts—so he could issue instructions to the nation's nuclear forces while on the move.

Jerrod Hale quickly stepped over and stooped between the President and Vice President; a moment later, all three shot to their feet. "Meeting adjourned," the President said quickly. The door to the Cabinet Room flung open, and Secret Service agents flooded in.

"What's going on, Mr. President?" Finegold asked excitedly as the senior Cabinet members and the President and Vice President were surrounded by Secret Service agents. Finegold and Crane tried to follow, but they were held back inside the Cabinet Room by the Secret Service. "What in hell do you think you're doing?" Finegold cried out at the agent holding her.

"You're instructed to remain here until the President's party departs," the agent replied.

"She's the Senate Majority Leader!" Congressman Crane shouted at the agent. "She's supposed to accompany the President."

"You're instructed to *stay*," the agent said in a firm voice, as if he were talking to his pet German shepherd.

The Democratic congressional leadership could do nothing but watch in amazement as three Marine Corps helicopters touched down on the south lawn of the White House and scooped up the President, Vice President, and his Cabinet advisors. "It must be an emergency evacuation," Finegold said, reaching for a cell phone in her purse. "Something's happening."

"Hey!" Congressman Joseph Crane shouted. "I see Gant and Fortier getting on the helicopter! Why the hell can the Republican leadership follow the President on his getaway choppers, but we Democrats can't? They got plenty of room on those things. . . ." But his outrage was drowned out by the rapid departure of Marine One. The three helicopters executed a position change shortly after takeoff, a sort of "shell game" in the sky with helicopters to confuse or complicate any terrorists' efforts to kill the President.

They were finally allowed to leave, long after the helicopters were out of sight, and Finegold and her colleagues, still hopping mad at their snub, made their way to the lower entrance to the West Wing. They were surprised to see Admiral George Balboa standing in the doorway leading to the driveway just outside the West Wing, talking on a handbag-size transportable cellular phone handled by an aide. He did not see the congressional Democratic leaders approach as he slammed the phone down into its holder in disgust. "Admiral Balboa, I'm surprised to see you here," Barbara Finegold said in true amazement. "I thought you'd be with the President."

"A little mix-up," Balboa offered in a low, rather contrite voice.

"I'll say. Those two butt-kissers Fortier and Gant hop aboard the chopper and leave you stranded," House Minority Leader Joe Crane said. "Since when do congressmen steal seats out from under important presidential advisors?"

"I . . . I was on my way to the Pentagon," Balboa said.

"Since when does the chairman of the Joint Chiefs of Staff not accompany the President, especially during an emergency White House evacuation?" Finegold asked. Balboa's eyes widened when he heard Finegold describe exactly what had happened—and only then did Finegold know she was correct. "I know Colonel McNeely's function as well as I know yours, Admiral. Can you answer my question? Why is the chairman of the JCS not accompanying the President during a military emergency?"

"I should probably not answer," Balboa said, "except to say that I have responsibilities at the Pentagon right now."

"I guess with the Secretary of Defense bugging out with the others, you'd be pretty much minding the store," Crane said. "Where's your chopper? Don't tell me you gotta drive?"

Balboa looked embarrassed, then hurt. "The . . . the airspace around the capital has been closed," he explained. "No aircraft can depart until . . ."

"Until NEACP departs," Finegold added—and, to her surprise, Balboa nodded. Another correct guess, she congratulated herself. Crane looked a little confused, so she explained, "NEACP, Joe, is the National

Emergency Airborne Command Post, the militarized version of Air Force One, designed so the President can be in touch with military and civilian leadership all over the world. It only flies when there's a danger of some vital command and control center being knocked out—say, Washington, knocked out by a nuclear attack."

"*What!*" Crane exploded. "A nuclear attack! You're saying someone is going to attack Washington . . . *right now?*"

"I don't know," Finegold said. She turned to Admiral Balboa and projected every bit of charm, influence, authority, glamour, and friendliness she could toward the embittered veteran Navy officer. "Can you tell us, Admiral? We have a right to know."

Obviously, George Balboa had been struggling with some dilemma for quite some time, well before this emergency, and now the pressure of all these events were coming to a head in his mind. He nodded, more to himself than anyone around him, then motioned for them to follow him back inside. Using his passcards, he escorted Finegold and Crane, without their aides, back into the West Wing, then downstairs by elevator to the White House Situation Room. Except for a staff of guards and communications officers, the rather small, unimposing room was empty. "I'm not going anywhere—it would take me an hour to get to the Pentagon in rush-hour traffic," Balboa said after he closed the door to the secure conference room. "I'm isolated. I can't talk with my command center or the national command authority."

"What's going on, Admiral?" Finegold asked again.

"This is *strictly* confidential."

"This conversation is not taking place," Finegold assured him as sincerely as she could. At the same time, part of her politically brilliant mind was already searching for ways to cover her tracks when—not *if*—she leaked any of what she was about to hear. "Don't worry, Admiral—we'll get a briefing on all this shortly anyway."

Balboa nodded. That was true—he would probably be giving the briefing in a couple hours anyway. He took a deep breath. "Two nuclear explosions have occurred near the Formosa Straits," Balboa said breathlessly, as if wanting to get it all out as fast as he could. Crane gasped in surprise again; Finegold remained impassive. "Both were low-yield devices. One occurred at high altitude near the island of Quemoy, which is a Taiwanese island near the coast of mainland China; the other occurred at sea level in the Formosa Strait, about sixty miles south of Quemoy."

"My God," Crane muttered. "Are we at war with China?"

"The detonations occurred during a naval skirmish between a Chinese carrier battle group and a couple of Taiwanese warships," Balboa went on. He fidgeted nervously, which told Finegold that he was concealing some other tidbit of information, probably something about American military units involved in the skirmish. "Both Taiwanese vessels were destroyed. No word yet on the Chinese ships."

"And what about the American forces?" Finegold asked. Balboa began to look like a fish out of water—he realized, as if waking up from a bad dream, that he had said too much. "What happened to the American subs?"

Finegold saw the hint of relief in Balboa's face—she had guessed wrong. "All four subs shadowing the Chinese fleet are safe," Balboa said.

"Thank God," she replied. Time to take a chance, roll the dice, Barbara Finegold told herself. She leaned toward Balboa, turning him away from Joe Crane so it felt as if they were talking alone and confidentially, and asked, "What about the stealth bombers? Did they make it out? Hopefully they were far enough away when the nukes went off."

Balboa looked into Finegold's eyes, searching to see whether or not she knew or was just guessing. In response, Finegold gave him her sternest, most confident expression, not breaking lock with his eyes even for a moment. Balboa asked himself the question, *Does she know about the bombers?* and his tortured mind answered, *Obviously so.*

"They're safe," Balboa said. "They weren't involved in the nuclear explosions—in fact, they probably shot down other Chinese missiles and may have even intercepted the missile that exploded over Quemoy, resulting in only a partial yield. They're safely on their way back."

"Good . . . that's damned good news, Admiral," Finegold said. Outside, she appeared relieved, but inside, her brain and her guts were leaping. The President sent stealth bombers over the Formosa Strait—bombers that could apparently fire anti-missile weapons? In the face of harsh congressional investigations that he might have illegally used stealth warplanes to bomb Iran, the President actually dared to use them *again,* just a few weeks later, in the middle of a China-Taiwan conflict? It was absolutely amazing, incredible, unbelievable! And now the "skirmish" was blowing up into possibly a full-scale nuclear war, one in which the United States was obviously going to get involved—and the President's hands were in deep, deep, deep shit, up to his armpits. The new President of the United States was possibly illegally involved in precipitating a *nuclear war.* "This information will go no farther than this room."

"Wait a minute, wait a minute," Crane gasped, finally getting up to speed with the others. "You're saying that . . . ?"

"Let's drop it, Joe—we're not here to pump the admiral for information," Barbara Finegold said, although she wanted nothing more than to do just that. "This conversation didn't take place. It *did not* take place. All we needed to know was that the evacuation was precautionary, and that no American forces have been mobilized."

"Yes, completely precautionary—definitely not a prelude to war, and no American forces are on alert," Balboa verified. "Our guys may have fired some weapons in self-defense . . ."

"The bombers?"

Balboa nodded as he continued, ". . . but no attack orders were ever issued by the President. None."

"We can support self-defense," Finegold said. "Even helping to protect innocent lives and property, especially if we knew the Chinese might use nuclear weapons. That action is acceptable."

"That's all that was used," Balboa added, looking as if a huge weight had been lifted from his chest. As long as he believed this conversation was off the record, Finegold thought, he felt confident in saying just a little bit more. Of course, she never *said* it was off the record, just that it never took place—which, of course, it obviously did. She took one more flyer: "You should be proud of your guys out there, Admiral."

His relieved expression hardened into a dark scowl, and Finegold was afraid she had said too much—or maybe she had hit the nerve that had been jangling in Balboa's brain all this time. He said fervently, as if pleading with her, "Don't look at the Navy, Senator. Not our ballgame."

"Jesus," Finegold gasped with as much sympathetic horror as she could summon. "You mean, the President shut your boys out again in favor of some other secret no-name sandlot pickup team?"

"You got it," Balboa responded bitterly, now convinced that the Senate Majority Leader really did know the entire score. "You got it."

That was all he had to say—but Barbara Finegold's heart was leaping in pure, abject joy. He had already said quite enough—and it might be enough to bring down a president.

"When men have minds set on victory, all they see is the enemy. When men have minds filled with fear, all they see is their fear."

—from *The Methods of the Minister of War,* Fourth-century-B.C. Chinese military textbook

CHAPTER

THREE

MINISTRY OF DEFENSE, BEIJING, PEOPLE'S REPUBLIC OF CHINA WEDNESDAY, 4 JUNE 1997, 0809 HOURS LOCAL (TUESDAY, 3 JUNE, 1909 HOURS ET)

"You have thirty seconds to explain," Chief of Staff General Chin Po Zihong thundered, "why you ordered this insane, monstrous attack. I have already ordered that you be dismissed as my chief deputy. Your response will determine whether or not you spend the rest of your *life* in prison for what you have done—or if you are executed as a traitor!" The Minister of National Defense, Chi Haotian, waited for the response as well, hands on the armrests of his chair, watching Chin's deputy—rather, *ex*-deputy—Admiral Sun Ji Guoming, with a sagging, tired grimace.

"Our carrier and its escort ships were under attack by rebel Nationalist naval forces, assisted by an unknown force launching anti-radar and anti-ship missiles, sir," Admiral Sun responded, his voice loud, steady, and assertive. "I suspected a stealth aircraft attack, based on the same type of reports during the recent United States–Iran conflict, and I immediately ordered a full-scale counterattack."

"*You* ordered? You are just a deputy, Sun, not a commander!" Chin thundered. "You have no authority to launch a strike mission or countermand my orders!"

"I beg your understanding, Comrade General," Sun said, with as much sincerity as he could muster, keeping his eyes averted, "but there was no time. Our forces were being decimated by the rebel warships and the American B-52 bomber. If I had gone through proper channels, the American aircraft would have wiped out our battle group."

"A B-52 bomber!" Minister of Defense Chi exclaimed. Chi knew well the power of the American B-52s—he had been in power during the abortive attack on the Philippines. "This is incredible! Are you sure, Sun?"

"The Nationalists used an American stealth aircraft to support an illegal intercept on the high seas against our warships, sir," Sun retorted. "The fighter pilots from the carrier *Mao* confirmed the sighting before they were shot down—another act of war. I used my judgment and ordered our battle group to commence their attack against Quemoy from long range—"

"With *nuclear weapons?*" Chin retorted. "You ordered Yi to launch a thermonuclear attack against the Nationalists?"

"I ordered Admiral Yi to do everything in his power to defend his battle group and carry out his attack orders," Sun replied. "I did not order him to launch a nuclear attack—but I support his decision to do so. His battle group is intact with only minor losses, the rebels have been severely wounded, and the world is paralyzed with fear. The mission was successful."

"You are absolutely *insane,* Sun!" Chin said, unable to believe what his subordinate was saying. "You actually think this action was proper? Do you think nuclear weapons are just another bullet to take from your belt and load into your pistol? Did you stop to think for one second about the consequences?"

"I have thought of little else, sir!" Sun responded. "Sun-tzu says that if an incendiary attack can be launched from outside without relying on inside assistance, it should be initiated."

"So now I suppose you think we should invade?"

"No, sir," Sun said. "We should desist."

"*What?* You approved a nuclear attack on Quemoy—don't try to deny it, Sun, you gave the order without specifically mentioning nuclear devices—then say we should not continue the invasion?" Chin shook his head in stunned disbelief. "I do not understand you, Sun! You orchestrated a nuclear attack against the Nationalists, an attack that may well isolate China for decades in the eyes of the world, and now you advise us to abandon the mission? Why? Explain yourself!"

"Because we initiated an incendiary attack against the Nationalist army on Quemoy, and they are quiet," Sun replied. "Sun-tzu teaches us that if the enemy is quiet after such an attack, wait and do not attack, for it means that the fires did not substantially weaken them."

"Explain in words other than this ancient drivel, Admiral!"

"The blast was not directly over Quemoy, and it appears it was not a full yield," Sun replied. "I think the rebel forces on Quemoy are mostly still intact, protected in underground command centers, garrisons, and marshaling areas. Besides, our fleet was substantially damaged, morale among the naval forces is low because of the ferocity of the stealth bomber attacks, our ground forces are not ready, and the Americans are on the alert. No, we cannot press the attack now. We have no choice but to withdraw."

Chin shook his head, totally confused. Minister Chi asked, "So what happens now, Admiral? We do not fight, we do not attack. The Paramount Leader's directive is no more. What are we left with, comrade?"

"Sir, we have proven that the United States committed an act of war upon the People's Republic of China by firing anti-ship missiles at our ships—this may be our most potent weapon against the influence of the Americans in our region," Sun said. "We have shown that the Americans are terrorists, that they will stop at nothing, break any law, to advance their agenda. This undeclared war, this illegal attack against our battle group, combined with their illegal overflight of our airspace without permission by an armed combat aircraft during the Iranian conflict, deserves immediate world condemnation! China has long been criticized, even ostracized, in the eyes of the world for our perceived human rights record—tell me, sir, how do you think the United States will be regarded in the eyes of the world when they are proven to be the greatest terrorist nation ever to exist in the history of the planet?"

To General Chin's surprise, Minister Chi was quiet—which was in effect an endorsement of Sun's actions. The tide was turning here, Chin thought—it might be best not to complain too loudly. But Sun Ji Guoming had clearly overstepped his authority and usurped the rank and office of the Chief of Staff of the Liberation Army, and he had to be removed from office as soon as possible. "You claim that a B-52 bomber shot down *three* Su-33 fighters, the best combat aircraft in our air army?" Chin asked derisively. "Impossible."

"That is the pilot's report, sir," Sun said excitedly. "The third pilot radioed details of the attacks just before he began his counterattack. The Sukhoi pilots are the best pilots in the air army; I believe their statement. It is too implausible to be anything but the truth."

"*That* is your criterion for judging the validity of this report—that it is too unbelievable to be a false or inaccurate report?" Chin exploded. "Have you gone insane, Sun?"

"Sir, Comrade Minister, we have seen intelligence reports on this aircraft from Russian sources," Sun said. "It was supposedly used in the conflict between Lithuania and Belarus. Our own analysts claim that these modified planes may have been used against us in our conflict in the Philippines—the planes we assumed to be standard B-52G or -H bombers could have been these planes—"

"Enough," Chin shouted. "You are too incompetent to wear those stars, Sun. You are a disgrace to the uniform and to your entire lineage."

"Wait, Comrade General," Minister of Defense Chi interjected in a low, gravelly voice. "I wish to hear more." Then, to Chin himself, he added, "And I wish to hear more from you about what you intend to offer as a response to the Central Military Commission."

"Very well, sir," Chin said. "Sun, you are dismissed—"

"I said, Sun shall stay!" Chi shouted.

Chin stood at attention and lowered his eyes as a sign of respect and obedience, but he was obviously seething over the fact that Chi Haotian was not giving him free rein in disciplining his subordinates. "Comrade Minister, there should be no discussion here over the fate of this insolent pup," General Chin said, keeping his voice respectful although he was fighting mad. "Sir, we could very well be facing nuclear war with the West because of this one unauthorized, ill-conceived, suicidal mission. It is only proper that Admiral Sun should not just be stripped of his position and rank and removed from the People's Liberation Army, but possibly imprisoned for life, for what he has done—"

"You seem to prefer doing battle with your subordinates rather than doing battle with the enemy, Comrade General," a voice said behind Chin. The chief of staff turned—and saw President Jiang Zemin himself enter the minister of defense's office, flanked by his bodyguards. General Chin shot to his feet in surprise; Chi and Sun snapped to attention and bowed respectfully. Chin Po Zihong was staring dumbfounded into the Paramount Leader's eyes. "So. Do you now wish to do battle with me, Comrade General?"

Chin quickly snapped out of his shock, realized what he was doing, and bowed deeply, keeping his eyes averted. "Forgive me, Comrade President," the general said. "I . . . I was not informed that you would be attending this meeting."

"No one appears to be informing you of anything these days, Comrade General," Jiang said with uncharacteristic sarcasm. He took a seat at Chi's desk and sat stiffly, regarding General Chin for several long moments. "The People's Liberation Army has suffered one of its most embarrassing, one of its most humiliating moments in its history today, General Chin Po Zihong. Wire services around the world are already reporting it; the presidents of most of the world's industrial nations have called me, demanding an explanation. Speak."

"Comrade President," Chin began, "my staff has just now informed me that there is evidence that an American stealth warplane was assisting the rebel craft, and that it was the Americans who attacked one of our destroyers and then shot down three of our fighter jets sent to monitor the—"

"Admiral Sun has already given me the details," Jiang said. Chin could not help but shoot a deadly glare at Sun for going over his head and reporting directly to the minister of defense and the president. "And do not think," Jiang added, "that Comrade Sun violated the chain of command—because I ordered him to take the initiative in case the Americans should try to interfere with our plans to occupy Quemoy Dao."

"You . . . you ordered him to act on his own, without my permission and without an approved plan from the General Staff?" Chin stammered.

"General, as Admiral Sun has so accurately pointed out, it has become apparent that the Americans are waging a war of terrorism against us," President Jiang said by way of response. "The Americans are choosing to use their stealth aircraft and guided standoff missiles to destroy our forces and keep our government off balance. They could have destroyed our ships and killed thousands of People's Liberation Army Navy soldiers and sailors, just as they did in their skirmish with the Islamic Republic of Iran.

"It is now obvious that the Americans hold the *Mao Zedong* carrier battle group at risk with their stealth bombers," Jiang went on. "This situation has become intolerable, and drastic action must be taken immediately. In keeping with my wishes and those of the people to rid our waters and our legacy of illegal and harmful foreign influences, Admiral Sun has developed a plan to do just that—first isolate, then cripple, then destroy the American air and naval forces operating off our shores."

General Chin's mind was spinning with confusion. Was he being replaced? Was his career in jeopardy from this young idealistic philosopher-quoting upstart? "Comrade President, I agree with everything you say," Chin said. "It is indeed the time to act. But are you proposing to place the forces of the world's largest military power in the hands of Admiral Sun Ji Guoming? He does not have the experience or the training. He possesses only rudimentary knowledge on how to deploy and command large naval forces, and very little knowledge or experience in commanding large ground and air forces."

"We will not place our military forces in Admiral Sun's hands, General—you will retain your command," Jiang said. "Admiral Sun will take command of certain . . . irregular forces."

"Irregular forces? What do you mean, sir?"

"In time, you will be briefed on the deployment of his forces," Jiang said, rising from his chair and heading for the door. "In the meantime, Admiral Sun has full authority from the Central Military Commission and my office to conduct whatever maneuvers or operations he sees necessary. He is obliged to notify you prior to the start of operations, and he is encouraged to seek your guidance and support, but he has no obligation to do either. Admiral?"

"Thank you, sir," Sun Ji Guoming said, bowing deeply to Jiang Zemin. He then bowed to General Chin and said, "General, you will order the *Mao* carrier battle group to withdraw from its attack on Quemoy and proceed at best speed to Xianggang."

"Xianggang? Xianggang?" Chin repeated in disbelief. Xianggang, formerly known as Victoria, was the capital and main port city on the island province of Hong Kong, which was set to return to Chinese control on the first of July. "Why should we sail it all the way to Hong Kong when it may be a critical weapon in the defense and occupation of Quemoy Dao?"

"The *Mao* and its escorts will be used to help celebrate our Reunification Day festivities," Admiral Sun said. "We shall stage fireworks demonstrations from its decks, invite guests and the international media aboard, even give cruises around Hong Kong on it."

"Use our aircraft carrier, our most powerful naval vessel . . . to give *rides?*"

"After that," Sun said calmly, "it will be deployed for an extended shakedown cruise to Lüshun."

"*Lüshun?* Why sail it to Lüshun, sir?" Chin protested again to Jiang. Lüshun, once known as Port Arthur, was an important international shipping and naval facility located on the tip of the Liaotung peninsula, between the Bohai, or Gulf of Chihli, and Korea Bay, 250 kilometers west of the North Korean capital of Pyongyang. "Do you plan to involve it in any attack operations in defense of North Korea, in case the Americans or South Koreans invade? If so, I think that is a foolhardy plan. The carrier will be more vulnerable to air attacks from South Korea, Japan, even Alaska. If anything, we should send it back to the Nansha Dao to defend our rights to access to the South China Sea."

"Comrade General, it is so ordered," Minister of Defense Chi Haotian interjected. "Withdraw the carrier battle group from Quemoy Dao and have them proceed to Xianggang at best possible speed."

Chin looked at Chi, then Jiang, with a stunned expression, but at the moment there was little he could do. He bowed and said, "Yes, Comrade Minister. Immediately. Any other demands?"

"No, sir," Sun replied, bowing respectfully. "My thanks to you."

General Chin Po Zihong ignored the gesture. He stood as the president and the defense minister departed, then stopped Admiral Sun as he headed for the door. "So," Chin said haughtily, "you now have the ear of the president. I see that spouting all that ancient military crap has paid off for you."

"Yes, sir," Sun responded simply.

"You may speak freely now, Admiral," Chin said. "We are practically colleagues, contemporaries." Sun's eyes narrowed at that very sarcastic remark. "Please. Tell me about your plan."

Sun Ji Guoming hesitated, not knowing whether or not to trust Chin's sudden friendliness; then he responded, "Sir, my staff has prepared a briefing for you and the general staff, outlining my ideas and suggestions. But this operation is not under my command, sir. I am merely advising the defense minister and Paramount Leader as to—"

"You are nothing more than a bold, loudmouth upstart," Chin said, "tossing about ancient maxims that no longer apply, to old men who were spoon-fed that crap since they were young boys and who long for a time when Maoist psycho-mystical garbage could conquer the world."

Admiral Sun smiled and actually appeared to relax when he saw the anger rising in Chin's words. "You do not believe in applying the teachings of Master Sun-tzu to today's challenges, General?" Sun asked. "We have spoken on this many times."

"Forget that *Art of War* shit, Sun," Chin interjected angrily. "What will you do against the Americans? I must know!"

"I am going to humiliate them, sir," Sun replied hotly. "I am going to show the Americans that they cannot roam freely over our waters and our region. I am going to make their allies turn against them, isolate them; then I am going to make the American people isolate and hate their own military forces."

"How? How will you do all this? What forces will you need? How many ships, planes, divisions?"

"This is not a mission for conventional military forces, sir," Sun said. "My forces will be everywhere, but nowhere; they will be as light as ghosts, but as powerful as the largest ships and the most powerful bombs in the world."

Chin saw he was going to get no more concrete information than that from Sun, so he shook his head and turned to leave. "It shall be a pleasure for me to see you collapsed and disgraced," he said over his shoulder at Sun Ji Guoming. "Quoting a bunch of dead philosophers will not help you when the American stealth bombers head over the horizon to decimate our cities and armies."

"They will not be able to launch anything against us, because they will have no targets on their radarscopes or sonars to attack," Sun said. "They will see nothing but empty ocean—and their own allies, out of control."

THE WHITE HOUSE OVAL OFFICE
TUESDAY, 3 JUNE 1997, 2105 HOURS ET

"My fellow Americans, good evening," President Kevin Martindale began his televised address to the nation. "I have some important news of a serious disaster that may have potentially serious implications for Americans both at home and overseas.

"At approximately six forty-five P.M. East Coast time, two large-scale explosions were reported in the vicinity of the southern portion of the Formosa Strait, between mainland China and the island of Formosa, the home of the newly independent, democratic Republic of China. Unconfirmed reports indicate that both explosions were nuclear, with yields measuring somewhere between one and seven kilotons.

"I want to assure the American people that we are completely safe, and the situation is under control," the President went on, deliberately slowing his delivery and speaking as sincerely and as firmly as he could. "First, no American military forces, except for some surveillance units, were in the area at the time of the blast, and the last reports I was given stated that there were no American casualties as a result of the explosions. Second, these explosions were not a prelude to a nuclear war between China and Taiwan or anyone else. It is not yet certain if the explosions were a result of an accident, a deliberate attack, or an act of terrorism. In fact, it is too early to tell precisely who launched the attack in the first place, although our suspicions rest with the naval forces of the People's Republic of China's Liberation Army, which have been threatening the Republic of China with attacks for many years. However, both sides in the conflict in the Formosa Strait suffered many casualties, and so we are still investigating. In any case, no one retaliated with similar weapons; no other attacks, nuclear or conventional, took place; and no nations have declared war upon anyone else. Third, there is no evidence so far of serious nuclear contamination or fallout. There are reports of Taiwanese and Japanese nationals fleeing their homes for fear of radioactive fallout, so as a precaution we are advising against travel into eastern China, Taiwan, or southern Japan until the panic has eased and we can assess the danger.

"Fourth, and most importantly, the United States is secure. The government is functioning, and we are carrying out the people's business, right here in Washington, same as ever. As commander in chief of our nation's military forces, I have not ordered any retaliatory strikes, and we have not mobilized any of our nuclear forces, nor do I intend to do so. I have ordered our overseas military bases around the world into a heightened state of alert, and I have ordered the Pentagon to hold meetings with high-ranking officers to determine the best course of action to take, but at this time none of our forces anywhere on earth are on a wartime footing. We are ready to respond if necessary, but so far all nations of the world are responding to this tragedy with patience and intelligent reasoning, and so I see no reason to elevate the level of tension by mobilizing any of our forces to a higher state.

"The United States stands ready to assist any countries who request aid, no matter who pushed the button. The nuclear genie has somehow sneaked out of the bottle after being safely sealed away for so many years, and the United States government pledges to do all it can to help see that the genie stays locked away again forever. I assure you, myself and all of my top advisors, civilian and military, are hard at work investigating this horrible tragedy. I will report back to you as soon as possible with more details.

"I'd like to leave you with one last thought, if I may," the President said. "When I was a kid, I remember a gag poster of an old crusty Navy guy, had to be a hundred years old, at the helm of an old weather-beaten wooden rowboat, with about a dozen more old sailors crowded into the little boat manning the oars, all lit up by a single lantern, and the caption on the poster said, 'Sleep tight tonight, the U.S. Navy is awake.' All joking aside, my fellow Americans, I can tell you that a good portion of the United States Navy, along with their comrades in arms in the Air Force, Army, Marines, Coast Guard, and all of the other paramilitary, Guard, Reserves, and civilian members of the best fighting force in the world, the United States armed forces, are awake tonight, watching and ready to defend our homeland, our freedom, and our way of life. Give them your support and trust, and sleep tight—we *are* awake. Thank you, good night, and God bless America."

The President knew enough to keep his eyes straight ahead, looking into the camera, until well after the red light was off and technicians started coming over to unplug the mikes from his suit jacket lapels. He shook hands and offered thanks to a few of the technicians, the director, and the all-important makeup person, then made his way to his private study while the cameras and sound equipment were removed from the Oval Office, where Chief of Staff Jerrod Hale had the bank of six regular-screen TVs and two big-screen TVs on in the President's study. Already in the study with Hale was National Security Advisor Philip Freeman and Secretary of State Jeffrey Hartman; Communications Director Charles Ricardo followed the President.

The study was where Martindale did his real office work—the Oval Office was usually reserved for important meetings and "photo opportunity"–type office work, like signing important legislation. The study had two curtained bulletproof windows, but unlike the Oval Office, the Kevlar-reinforced curtains were always kept closed. Along with the bank of televisions, the study had two computer systems, with which the President was thoroughly educated; it had an exercise treadmill, plenty of seats for secretaries and staffers, and wall-size electronic monitors to display computerized charts, diagrams, or images. It was a good place to watch and listen to the media's reaction to the President's address. Afterward, the President's "spin doctors" would prepare Q&A point papers for all of the top advisors, and within minutes of the address they would be sent out to talk with the press and put some finer finishing touches on the President's remarks.

"Good speech tonight, Mr. President," Ricardo offered.

"It sucked," the President said grumpily, retrieving a can of Tab from the little refrigerator near his desk. "Too skimpy on details—the press will be clamoring for more from anyone they see. The rumors are going to start flying. Let's get the point paper done and get the staff out there so we can head off the rumors as much as possible. First thing I want to know is, what about the screwup with the Democratic leadership getting on Air Force One? What in hell happened?"

"The Secret Service screwed up, Mr. President—there's no polite way to put it," White House Chief of Staff Jerrod Hale replied. "I'll talk to the Presidential Protection Detail chief myself. The PPD got confused because they were still escorting the press out of the building when the choppers showed up and they got word of an 'actual' evacuation. Anyone they didn't recognize or specifically not accompanying you were held back."

"They didn't recognize Finegold? She was on TV more than I was during the last five months of the campaign!"

"When the Secret Service realized it was an 'actual' evacuation rather than an 'exercise,' " Hale went on, "they went a little bonkers. They should have escorted everyone from the Cabinet Room into a chopper and taken them to Andrews with you. But once you were on board Marine One with an 'actual' evacuation warning order, they ordered all choppers to launch. If this continues to be an issue in the press, I'll get the chief of the PPD on the morning talk shows to explain the mix-up."

"No," the President snapped. "No one takes the heat for 'mix-ups' around here but me."

Hale was flipping through a small stack of messages that had come in since the President's address to the nation; he placed one on the desk in front of the President. "A thank-you note from President Lee of Taiwan," he said. "He heard about the death of a crew member and wants your permission to thank the EB-52 bomber crews personally."

"How in *hell* did the ROC find out about the Megafortresses?" the President asked incredulously. "That chance encounter outside the Oval Office? Had to be more than that."

"We'll find out, sir," Freeman said. "It was obviously more than a leak—it was a direct exchange of classified information, a serious breach."

"Just find out who did it and throw his ass in jail," the President snapped. "Next, I want to know—"

"You better take a look at this, Mr. President," Ricardo interrupted, pointing to one of the televisions. "It looks like Finegold's giving a press conference inside the Capitol."

The group listened with shocked expressions as Senator Majority Leader Barbara Finegold announced that the Senate Foreign Relations Committee and Senate Armed Services Committee would be holding joint hearings on the report that the President had sent long-range bombers to attack Chinese warships, and whether or not these attacks prompted the Chinese to launch and detonate nuclear weapons—or if the American bombers had been the ones that dropped the nuclear weapons. She quoted the official Chinese government news agency, Xinhua, as saying that B-52 Stratofortress bombers had been spotted in the area launching nuclear-tipped missiles just before the nuclear explosions occurred, and that they had gun camera video to support the claim. Sprinkled throughout the statements and Q&A afterward were words like "independent prosecutor," "violation of the War Powers Act," "breach of trust," and "terrorist."

"This is unbelievable! Who in hell does she think she is?" the President shouted. "How in hell did *she* find out?"

"It's a guess, Mr. President, nothing more," Ricardo said. "The Chinese news agency is putting their own spin on the skirmish, and Finegold is latching on to it. She's been on the stealth bomber warpath ever since the Iran conflict. She's slinging shit, looking to see what sticks, that's all."

"Terrorist," Hale muttered bitterly, when he heard the word a third time. He had moved over beside the President so only he could hear his comment. "Sounds like Admiral Balboa put a bug in her ear. I'll bet he's talked to Finegold."

"Don't even *think* about shit like that unless you've got evidence, and I mean *concrete* evidence, that he's done something wrong," the President said. "Not *one word,* not even an angry glance in his direction."

"Kevin, when are you going to stop coddling Balboa?" Hale asked the President in a low voice. Hale was probably the only man in America who could call the President by his first name, and even he rarely used the privilege—he was certainly mad enough to do so now. "He's a self-serving snake. Force the bastard to retire, or fire his ass. He talked to Finegold, I know it."

"Jerrod, you and your father taught me all I know about leadership," the President said. "You taught me how to come from nowhere, come from defeat and divorce and obscurity, how to pull together a disorganized party and almost take back the White House and Congress all at once. We didn't do it by eliminating anyone who ever disagreed with me."

"What about loyalty, Kevin?" Hale asked. "You always demand absolute loyalty from your people."

"Balboa is not just an appointee, Jerrod—he's a soldier," Martindale replied. "I'm the commander in chief. He either follows my orders, or he destroys his own reputation and honor."

"What if he doesn't give a shit about his reputation and honor, as long as he gets whatever the hell he wants?" Hale asked acidly. "Maybe Finegold promised him a job somewhere. What if he just decides, since he's on his way out soon anyway, to destroy your reputation along with his own?"

"If his false accusations stick, then maybe I don't deserve to be in the White House," the President said.

Hale clenched his jaw in response. "That's nonsense, and you know it, Kevin," Hale said. "The people can be manipulated into thinking anything. There's nothing noble in losing the White House because Balboa decided to betray your trust, or because the press latched on to a juicy story and let it blow all out of proportion."

"Hey, Jer, let me remind you, in case you forgot—I *did* send a B-52 bomber over the Formosa Strait, and it probably *did* precipitate the Chinese attack on Quemoy," the President said. "Balboa and Finegold aren't lying—they're just talking out of school."

"But Balboa works for you, sir," Hale said. "He knows better than to blab to anyone, especially the leadership of the opposition party. Balboa's got to be stopped."

"We can handle him, Jerrod, but not by cracking his skull open with a baseball bat," the President said. "Keep your eyes and ears open, but take no direct action. Got it?" Hale nodded, but he was seething nonetheless. "Get Chastain and Balboa on the videophone." The President turned to Philip Freeman. "What have you got for me, Philip?"

"Preliminary report from CINCPAC, Admiral Allen, says that either a Taiwanese SAM fired from one of their frigates, or an air-to-air missile fired by the EB-52 Megafortress stationed over the Formosa Strait, shot down a nuclear-tipped Chinese rocket or cruise missile, resulting in a partial nuclear yield," Freeman said. "Had it not been for the EB-52, Quemoy would've been toast—or glass, depending on how powerful a *full* yield would've been. The Taiwanese frigate, identified by the EB-52 crew as the *Kin Men,* was destroyed by a nuclear-tipped cruise missile."

"Looks like putting that EB-52 thing out there was a good idea after all," the President said.

"Maybe not, sir," Freeman said. "Good possibility that Taiwan could have fired first, followed closely by the Megafortress. Our side could've started the whole thing."

"Shit," the President muttered, shaking his head. "Who was flying the . . . ah, damn, never mind, don't tell me, I know. Brad Elliott was flying the Megafortress, right?" Freeman nodded. "They all right? Elliott, McLanahan—he always flies with Elliott—and the rest of the Megafortress crew? They must've been close when the nukes went off."

"Substantial damage, one casualty on Elliott's EB-52," Freeman said. "The electronic warfare officer, a young lieutenant. Elliott was slightly injured. The plane's on its way back, escorted by another Megafortress."

The President felt sorry for the dead crewman, but only because he had the bad luck of flying with Brad Elliott. "It was probably Elliott who spilled the beans to the ROC." No one in the room offered to refute that theory. "Any chance whatsoever that the nukes came from one of the Megafortresses?"

Freeman paused—and that pause, the realization that he didn't know, made little hairs on the back of the President's neck stand up. "I'll order the Defense Intelligence Agency to do a complete security audit and inspection of the Megafortress project office at Edwards, Sky Masters,

Inc., and their facilities on Saipan and on Guam," Freeman said grimly. "I would love to say that Brad Elliott would never do such a thing as launch a nuclear weapon without permission—and it hurts me to even *think* this—but I can't. In fact, I would assume he could get his hands on whatever weapon, nuclear or otherwise, he desired, in fairly short order."

"I'll lock his cell at Leavenworth permanently myself if he's to blame for all this," the President said angrily. "How about any of our ships? Could they have launched a nuclear weapon?"

"None of our surface forces in the Pacific theater have nuclear weapons deployed on them, sir," Freeman said. "We have three Ohio-class ballistic missile boats on patrol in the Pacific–Indian Ocean fleet; only one, the *West Virginia,* was in range at the time of the explosion. We're trying to get in contact with him."

"How often do they check in?"

"Varies, but it's much more often than during the Cold War," Freeman said. Nuclear-powered ballistic missile subs on patrol, even now years after the end of the Cold War, did everything they could to remain undetected for long periods of time, sometimes spending as long as a month sitting on the ocean bottom. These days, they spent less time in total seclusion, but it was still important for them to remain undetected and autonomous, so contacting one was never an easy job. "All of the Los Angeles- and Sturgeon-class attack subs had their nuclear weapons removed five years ago."

"Double- and triple-check everything, including all vessels that could have had nukes on board—I don't care how long it's been," the President ordered. "If there's even the wildest possibility that a ship could have loaded and fired a nuclear missile, I want it checked out. What about Taiwan? Do their ships carry nukes?"

"The *Hsiung Feng* anti-ship missile, which is a license-built version of the Israeli Gabriel, is reported to be able to carry a nuclear warhead, although the Israelis never deployed the missile with them," Freeman replied. "We believe one of the frigates involved in the skirmish carried these missiles. The larger frigate carried American-made Harpoons and Standard missiles and ASROC rocket-powered torpedoes, which all were at one point or another capable of being fitted with nuclear warheads. Although we never sold any nuclear-capable weapons to Taiwan, if it once had nuclear warheads, there's every possibility that Taiwan could have readapted their weapons with small nuclear warheads. But chances are very low the explosions were from Taiwanese weapons."

"Doesn't exactly fill me with confidence," the President said grimly. "I want to talk with President Lee of Taiwan as soon as possible, and I hope the hell he comes clean with me." He paused, deep in thought; then: "Let's talk about China going to nuclear war with Taiwan—or us," he said grimly. "Any thoughts?"

"Becoming more and more of a reality, sir, considering what's happened," Freeman replied. "Last year, despite their threats, I would've said it was virtually impossible. Last week, I'd have thought it was improbable. Now I think it's possible that we could see more low-yield attacks against Taiwan . . ." He paused, then added, ". . . and possibly Okinawa, Guam, South Korea, even Japan. Like you said, sir, the genie's out of the bottle."

The President slumped in his chair and put a weary hand on his forehead, shielding his eyes as if fighting off a massive headache. "Damn," he muttered. "Was it a mistake to send those bombers over the Strait? Would any of this be happening?"

"I think it would be ten times worse, Mr. President," Jerrod Hale said.

"I agree," Freeman added. "Quemoy might be a smoking hole in the ocean, and Formosa might be under attack as well. Those bombers—in fact, that *one* bomber—deterred the PLAN from continuing their attack."

"But we weren't talking about China destroying Okinawa, Guam, or Japan before," the President said. "Shit, maybe it would've been better if they succeeded in their invasion."

"Then we'd still be here, talking about our options—except China would have attacked and perhaps destroyed an independent, capitalist, pro-America democracy in Asia," Freeman said. "Sir, this isn't your fault—the People's Republic of China is driving events here, not you. The best we can do is anticipate, react, and hope we don't escalate the conflict any faster than it's already moving."

The President stopped and considered that point of view, then nodded his agreement. "Sometimes I don't know if it's my guilty conscience, or the press, that makes me think I'm responsible for every disaster in the world these days," the President said. "But I'm not going to sit on my ass and watch China or anyone else start World War Three."

He paused again, shaking his head as if scarcely believing the words that were forming in his head. Finally, he said, "Philip, contact Arthur and George Balboa—I want the commanders in place to prepare to put our nuclear forces back on alert." The President's study seemed to get very quiet, as if all of the air had suddenly been sucked out of the room; even the unflappable Jerrod Hale had a shocked expression on his face. "I want it done as quietly as possible. Just the commanders for now—no aircraft, no subs, no missiles. I want them formed up and ready to start accepting their weapons, but they don't get any weapons until I give the word." Hale looked at the President, silently asking, "What about Balboa?"—he knew that there was no way this could be kept quiet with Balboa chairing the Joint Chiefs of Staff. But the President remained resolute.

Freeman nodded. "I'll draft up an executive order for your review and signature," he said. "The order will stand up the Combined Task Forces inside U.S. Strategic Command. The CTFs will meet in Omaha and organize their staffs, but nothing else until you give the word." The President nodded absently—he could afford to forget that aspect of this growing threat for now. But Freeman pressed another problem into the foreground: "What about McLanahan and the Megafortresses? Keep them on patrol for now?"

The President recognized that Freeman had phrased the question carefully, interjecting his own opinion into the question—he wanted the EB-52s, with their powerful offensive and defensive weapons, to stay. The President nodded. "As long as they pass a security review, they stay on patrol."

"Balboa probably won't like that," Hale offered.

"Probably not," the President responded. "But the reason we sent those things out there—because we needed something out there right away, something that could keep an eye on the Chinese and respond in case the shooting started—has come to pass. We need them now more than ever."

"Admiral Balboa will call for sending in the carriers," Freeman said.

"No way I'm going to send them in now—they'd be sitting ducks for another nuclear attack," the President said immediately. "I'm not going to send any carriers into the region. We got one carrier in Japan and the other near Pearl Harbor?"

Freeman nodded. "Both are ready to get under way as soon as ordered. The *Independence* can be in the area in less than two days. *Washington* in about four days."

"Good," the President said. "If we need them, I'll send them in—until then, we put *diplomatic* pressure on China to back off, and we keep the Megafortresses on station. Now let's finish up what in hell we're going to tell the media, before someone else fires another shot at my backside."

U.S. PACIFIC COMMAND COMMAND CENTER,

PEARL HARBOR, HAWAII

TUESDAY, 3 JUNE 1997, 2031 HOURS LOCAL

(4 JUNE, 0131 HOURS ET)

NOW ENTERING THE VIDEOCONFERENCE, the computer-synthesized voice announced, LIEUTENANT GENERAL BRADLEY ELLIOTT, RETIRED; COLONEL PATRICK MCLANAHAN, RETIRED; MAJOR NANCY CHESHIRE, USAF, ANDERSEN AIR FORCE BASE, GUAM. CLASSIFICATION, TOP SECRET. VOICE AND DATA SERVICES TERMINATED; PLEASE CHECK OPERATIONAL SECURITY AND RE-ENTER SECURITY ACCESS CODES. A moment later: THANK YOU. FULL VIDEO-CONFERENCE SERVICES ACTIVATED.

When the large LCD flat-plate monitor came to life, what Lieutenant General Terrill Samson saw came as a welcome relief: Brad Elliott, Patrick McLanahan, and Air Force Major Nancy Cheshire, alive and well. The Sky Masters, Inc., satellite-based teleconference established a secure, real-time voice, video, and datalink between several different offices around the world: from U.S. Pacific Command headquarters at Pearl Harbor, Hawaii, where he and Admiral William Allen, commander of U.S. Pacific Command, waited; the Joint Chiefs' "Gold Room" Conference Center at the Pentagon in Washington, D.C.; all the way to the three aviators in a secure hangar at Andersen Air Force Base on the island of Guam.

Samson let a long, deep sigh of relief escape his lips. "Good to see you folks," he said.

"It's even better to be seeing *you,* sir," Cheshire responded. "Believe me."

"I believe you, Major," Samson said with a wry smile. "I'm very sorry about Lieutenant Vikram. My condolences to all of you."

He paused respectfully for a few moments, which gave him a chance to study the three on the videoconference monitor. They all looked exhausted, absolutely bone-tired . . . but Elliott looked worse. Samson knew that Elliott had been hit by pieces of windscreen and the windblast when the Chinese Sukhoi-33 fighters attacked; he could see a bit of evidence of injury, but lots of evidence of something else. Elliott looked whipped, almost ragged; his breathing appeared labored, his lips slightly parted as if he were forced to breathe through his mouth to get more air.

"What's happening now, Earthmover?" Elliott said. That voice had the same cockiness in it—it sounded like the old Brad Elliott. He didn't look so good, but the old fire and steel was still in his voice and definitely still in his mental attitude.

"We're waiting for the Pentagon to jump in on the videoconference," Samson said. "I'd like to ask a few questions before the CNO or JCS comes in."

"No one is responsible for Emil's death or for what happened on this mission but me, sir," Patrick McLanahan said immediately. It was very obvious that Patrick, as well as the others on camera from Andersen Air Force Base on Guam, had come right from the plane to the videoconference after landing their crippled bomber. All were wearing wrinkled flight suits, and had dark smudges under their eyes; the men had ragged, unshaved faces. "I take full responsibility."

"Stand by one, Patrick," Samson interjected. "I didn't think I'd need to remind you, since you've flown missions like this before, but the reality of the situation is that *no one* is responsible for what happened, because this incident *never happened,* do you understand? Lieutenant Vikram died in the course of his military duties—no other explanation is needed or will be offered. If it becomes necessary, the government will pick the most mundane, unexciting, plausible reason for Emil's death, but it won't be necessary, because everyone involved, from Vikram's family to the President of the United States, is legally and morally bound to keep their mouths shut in the name of national security. If they don't, they will find that the blame will fall on *them.*

"This is also a good time to remind you folks that you are volunteers in a completely black, highly classified government program," Samson went on. "If you screw up, your identities will be erased from all public or government records; if anyone digs to find said records, they'll find the dead themselves at fault. When you step on board that monster, you cease to exist, and any memories of you will be manipulated by the government that you sacrificed your life to serve. So it does no good to blame yourselves, because no one is going to accuse or indict you—they will either forget you or deny you. Everybody understand?"

No reply, not even nods, from the three aviators. They all knew that it was a screw job in the worst possible sense: they were going to risk their lives for their country, and the best they could ever hope for is that they would be completely forgotten by that same country, and that no one would ask any questions about their deaths because the reply would trash their reputations. "You also understand," Samson went on grimly, "that you can excuse yourself from this project at any time, without prejudice or harm to your careers?" Again no response. "I take it that you all understand your rights and all the realities here. Talk to me later if you like.

"We are going to be joined on this teleconference in a few moments by a few other parties, but first I wanted to find out how you guys are doing. I know it's hard on you because of the loss of Lieutenant Vikram. I'm very sorry. Please, speak up." There was no response. Samson gave them a few more moments, then urged them, "You were just involved in a nuclear exchange. You went head-to-head with over fifty armed Chinese warships. You saw hundreds of sailors get killed and injured, some by your hand. Are you guys doing okay?"

"What do you want us to say, sir?" Nancy Cheshire finally spoke out. "We got Emitter killed, and we got our butts shot up. We stopped the PLAN, I think, but I don't know if it was worth Emil getting killed. I have a feeling, when we hear from JCS and CINCPAC, that the answer to that will be 'no.' "

"I'll give you an answer, Earthmover—we were hung out to dry," Brad Elliott said angrily. "We were strung out by you, by the Navy, by the White House. You sent us into a no-win situation where the only way we could make a difference, the only way we could use the power we had at our command to do some good, was to disobey orders."

"Brad, c'mon," McLanahan said wearily. "We're not accusing anyone right now. We knew what we were doing."

"Patrick's right, Brad—you knew the game you were playing long before wheels-up in Blytheville, Arkansas," Samson said. "You knew you were going to be given a short leash. You knew the brass didn't support you. You knew the Navy didn't want you. But you launched anyway. Once over the cover area, you could've just obeyed orders and watched Quemoy get incinerated—but you acted. We're all going to pay for that decision."

"We had to do what we did, sir," Cheshire said. "We couldn't just sit back and watch."

"Guys, I think it was a good decision to defend the Taiwanese ships and attack those Chinese ships—Emil Vikram did not die in vain," Samson said. "But I think we're going to get hammered for making it. What's done is done. I think the Chinese were going to use those nukes over Quemoy anyway, so everything that happened was bound to happen anyway. As far as what happens to you . . . well, we suck it up and move on. Hell, I might be submitting *my* application to Jon Masters before the day's out."

"Wear a nice suit, Earthmover," Elliott said. "You're gonna need it."

"We're not done here until I know that Lieutenant Vikram didn't die for nothing," McLanahan said. "Support or not, we're not leaving the theater until we know the PLAN isn't going to keep on lobbing nukes at Taiwan or anyone else. There's still no other U.S. forces nearby that can oppose them—our five Megafortresses are the only heavy strike group that can take on that carrier battle group."

"That decision will be made soon, Patrick," Samson said. "I don't think you'll get what you want."

"Stop thinking like a staff puke and start thinking like a warrior again, Earthmover," Brad Elliott said. "You might learn something."

"Hey, Brad, you might want to cool your jets a little bit before the brass gets on the bird," Samson said. "An attitude like that won't win you any friends right now."

"We expect you to argue our case for us, sir," McLanahan said. "Keep us in the theater until the President decides what other forces he's going to send in."

"We're still operational, sir," Cheshire added. "Tell 'em to send us back in. We've proven we can do the job. If a war is going to start, if Quemoy is in danger of being invaded, Taiwan will still need our help."

Samson shook his head, silently marveling at this group's apparent cold-bloodedness. Young stupid heroes, he decided. Flying into combat was all part of a day's work for them. Hell, McLanahan was probably the most levelheaded one of the group, and he was ready to take another Megafortress back and twist the Chinese dragon's tail once again. "Your comments are noted, guys. Do what you need to do on the ground to get your damaged plane ready to fly, but CINCPAC wants patrols halted until they get the word from CINCPAC or the Joint Chiefs."

"Oh, goodie," Elliott said sarcastically. "Hmmm. I wonder what *they'll* say?"

"They'll ask, Brad, 'Who authorized the launch of those Wolverine missiles?' " Samson replied hotly. "They'll ask, 'How did Taiwan know our secure UHF synchronizer codes?' They'll ask, 'Was it was really necessary to launch attacks on almost a dozen Chinese warships when it would've been easier and safer for you to do as you were ordered to do, do a one-eighty, and get the hell out?'

"You guys did a really great job out there," Samson concluded, with a definite weariness in his voice. "You proved that the heavy bomber, properly loaded with the right high-tech weaponry, can do a variety of missions over vast distances with speed, precision, and stealthiness. But you all know the old maxim: one 'oh shit' will erase a hundred 'attaboys.' Sorry to say it, but I think you're going to see the truth in that old saying in just a few moments."

It stayed silent until an electronic tone warned the participants that new conferees were linking into the system: NOW ENTERING THE CONFERENCE, DR. CHI-YANG SHIH, SECRETARY GENERAL, NATIONAL SECURITY COUNCIL, OFFICE OF THE PRESIDENT, TAIPEI, REPUBLIC OF CHINA. NOW ENTERING THE CONFERENCE, ARTHUR CHASTAIN, SECRETARY OF DEFENSE, WASHINGTON. CLASSIFICATION, TOP SECRET. ALL CONFEREES NOTE, VOICE AND DATA IS NOW TERMINATED; CHECK OPERATIONAL SECURITY, THEN ENTER YOUR SECURITY CODE TO CONTINUE. There was a slight pause as videoconference administrators double-checked security for their rooms and reentered their security codes; then the computer acknowledged, THANK YOU. FULL VIDEOCONFERENCE FEATURES ACTIVATED.

"General Samson, folks, Dr. Chi-yang Shih asked to join us for a few moments on this videoconference," Secretary of Defense Chastain began. "Dr. Chi-yang, please go ahead."

"Thank you, Secretary Chastain," Chi-yang Shih said. Dr. Chi-yang was in his late fifties but looked considerably younger. He wore gold-rimmed round spectacles, making his round face appear even rounder, but his tailored suit gave him a definite air of authority. "General Elliott, Colonel McLanahan, Major Cheshire, it is indeed a pleasure to speak to all of you. On behalf of President Lee Teng-hui and my fellow citizens of the Republic of China, I wish to express my deepest heartfelt gratitude from my nation for your work, and our deepest sympathy for your loss of your fellow crew member. Your efforts resulted in saving hundreds of lives on Quemoy Tao. Because of you, the island's defenses are still viable. I promise you, the prayers of millions of my people, and especially the prayers of sixty thousand of your fellow soldiers on Quemoy Tao, will be with you and Lieutenant Vikram tonight and for all time."

"Viable? How is that possible, sir?" McLanahan asked. "The explosion . . . ?"

"Was at an altitude of approximately eight kilometers and at least fifteen kilometers south of the city of Shatou, thanks to you and your fellow airmen," Chi-yang replied. "It appears that the missiles fired from your aircraft destroyed the Chinese M-11 missiles while in flight, resulting in a partial-yield nuclear explosion, around the order of five to six kilotons. Damage was limited to overpressure and did not include thermal or blast damage, and we feel radiation deaths and casualties will be minimal as well. Unfortunately, the crew of the *Kin Men* was not as fortunate."

"My God," McLanahan muttered. All three airmen finally appeared to relax. They realized how very, very fortunate they and the people on Quemoy were.

"Communications have been disrupted in the area because of the blast, and there were some casualties, but there was only minor damage to the island's defense systems," Chi-yang went on. "In addition, our island garrisons are mostly underground, so our forces are safe. If the Communists attempt an invasion, they will still find a most formidable force opposing them."

"With all due respect, sir, that carrier battle group is still dangerous," Elliott said. "They sank two of your best warships, and they can still mount a deadly invasion force against Quemoy."

"Thanks to your brave efforts, it appears that the Communist fleet has stopped its northward progress and may even be withdrawing from the area," Chi-yang replied. "It is true, Quemoy has been crippled, but the Communists will not test our resolve. It even appears that the carrier battle group is being recalled all the way to Hong Kong, and that the ground and rocket forces along the Formosa Strait have been stood down. A major catastrophe has been averted because of you, and I again wish to thank you most sincerely."

"Dr. Chi-yang, was the captain of the *Kin Men* ordered to go out there and take on that carrier battle group all by itself?" McLanahan asked.

Chi-yang paused for a long moment, then sighed, lifted his shoulders, and responded, "Captain Sung's orders were to make contact with the Communists' battle group and warn them not to approach Quemoy Tao. We do not know why he opened fire on the battle group—and unfortunately, we may never know. He may have believed that the firepower provided by your aircraft could protect him. It matters little now, because we believe that it was the PLAN's intention to attack with nuclear weapons in any case—in which case, Captain Sung and his crew will be hailed as national heroes for saving Quemoy Tao. As you will be.

"Before I terminate this conference, my friends, I must tell you," Chi-yang went on, his voice choked by emotion now, "that my father was a deputy liaison to General Claire Lee Chennault and the American Volunteer Group, whom you call the Flying Tigers, during the Great War of Liberation with imperial Japan. He assisted many brave American Flying Tiger fighter pilots to survive and fight to keep the Burma Road open in our struggle against the Nipponese empire, before America entered the Great War of Liberation.

"I am struck by the similarities between that time, sixty years ago, and now. We Nationalists are no longer in control of the mainland, as before, but the aggressors are our own brothers, their minds tainted by the ugly stain of communism. But we and you, our American friends, are still comrades in arms now, just as we were then—even in secret, as it was then. General Samson, General Elliott, Colonel McLanahan, Major Cheshire, you and your fellow aviators are America's new Flying Tigers, protecting the weak against the menace of imperialism and Communist dictatorship. I am proud to continue my father's great mission. Thank you again, my young American friends. Call on me whenever you need assistance, and it shall be yours. I am your servant." The connection from Taiwan terminated with the computerized voice announcing, NOW DEPARTING, DR. CHI-YANG SHIH, TAIPEI, REPUBLIC OF CHINA.

The videoconference screen was blank as Dr. Chi-yang departed; when security was restored in Washington, Joint Chiefs of Staff chairman Admiral George Balboa was on the hookup from the Pentagon, along with Admiral Frederick Cowen, the chief of naval operations. "Very, very touching," Balboa began acidly. "You did it again, Brad, you old son of a bitch. You screw up in the worst possible way, ignore orders, start firing missiles all over the damn sky, and you precipitate a damned *nu-*

clear attack, and somehow you have world leaders kissing your boots and comparing you to the Flying Tigers. Incredible."

"Kinda makes you want to slit your own wrists right now, doesn't it, George?" Elliott said with his irritating little grin.

"You will *shut your mouth* right now, Elliott," Balboa shouted angrily, pointing at the videoconference camera. "What the ROC government thinks of you right now doesn't carry one ounce of water with me! You deliberately violated direct orders from me, the National Command Authority, and CINCPAC to hold fire and withdraw. You are more than just a menace, Elliott, you are a *disgrace* to any American who has ever worn a uniform."

"General Elliott had nothing to do with what we did over there, Admiral Balboa," McLanahan said. "I was the mission commander on that flight, I gave the orders to launch, and I'm responsible for the death of Emil Vikram."

"Don't forget the deaths of five hundred Taiwanese sailors, an estimated three hundred Taiwanese civilians on Quemoy, and dozens of deaths and injuries aboard the Chinese warships," Balboa interjected. "You're responsible for all of them!" McLanahan's shoulders sank, as if he had just been reminded of a painful event in his life. "You're going to have to live with all that, Mr. McLanahan. Even though I can absolve myself by reminding myself that I never sanctioned this mission and never thought you should be involved, I too will have to live with the horror of all those lives lost."

"Why don't you just be a total asshole and completely wash your hands of the whole thing, George?" Elliott retorted. "Nobody's stopping you."

"What I would like even better is to shut you down, have those planes cut up into little pieces, and throw you in prison," Balboa said. "There is a question of how the Taiwanese found out so much about this operation, and I have a feeling you were responsible for that. As for this operation, it looks as if the President wants to continue this foolhardy plan. If the loss of one of your airframes and Lieutenant Vikram poses a problem, Mr. McLanahan, I expect you to report promptly to Admiral Allen so we can make alternate arrangements."

"A replacement crew and plane is being ferried from Blytheville as we speak," McLanahan said. "It'll arrive in about twenty hours. But we can maintain a normal schedule right now."

"Then do it," Balboa said. "But you are not authorized to speak with anyone else, especially foreign nationals, at any time. The only persons you are authorized to communicate with are units or command posts briefed to you prior to takeoff. Failure to comply with this order will subject you and your co-workers to the most severe penalties allowable. Is that clear?"

"Yes, sir," McLanahan said. Elliott shook his head and rolled his eyes at his partner acceding to Balboa's lame threat so passively, but McLanahan ignored him. "Sir, I need permission to contact Lieutenant Vikram's family."

"Denied," Balboa said. "My staff will decide how to handle notification. You worry about your patrol missions and keeping out of trouble. Dismissed." The videoconference link was abruptly terminated.

"What a butthead," Elliott fumed. He got up and found himself a cup of coffee. "I'll bet he wanted so badly to shit-can us that he probably considered ignoring the President's orders. That asshole, blaming *you* for all those deaths. Ignore all that, Muck. The PLAN's at fault for attacking the ROC and for killing Emitter, not you."

McLanahan got up. His muscles were aching, a by-product of long hours in the Megafortress's cockpit, nearly an hour of sheer terror while under attack by the People's Republic of China's People's Liberation Army Navy, a dead crew member, two hours of nursing a crippled bomber back home to an emergency landing in marginal weather—and then, after all that, a tongue-lashing by the chairman of the Joint Chiefs. All in all, a pretty shitty twelve hours. He wasn't ready to hear Round Two from Brad Elliott. "Let's give it a rest now, Brad, all right?" McLanahan asked. "We've got a lot to do—get repairs going on our damaged bird, get the patrols back in the air." He wanted to call Emil's family, whom he had met several times, but decided against it.

"The first thing I'm going to do is make a few phone calls back to Washington," Elliott said resolutely. "I've got plenty of markers to call in. Balboa doesn't have the authority to cancel our contract. If we put a little pressure on him, he'll be forced to back off. We should—"

"Do nothing," McLanahan said angrily. "Nothing. No phone calls, no markers. Just back off, okay?"

"What in hell's the matter with you?" Elliott asked. "You can't let jerks like Balboa run our lives. He's the chairman of the Joint Chiefs, not commander in chief or the damned emperor."

"Brad, he's running this operation."

"Balboa and Allen are pissed because we launched a couple Rainbows and Wolverines and protected that frigate," Elliott went on. "They would've done the same if they were flying that mission, but because *we* did it, they're mad. I'll tell you the truth, son—if it was *their* plane, or if they had a ship of their own in position, theyd've blasted that carrier and destroyer and as many of the other ships back there to hell in the blink of an eye! You know it, and I know it."

"I hear you, Brad, and I agree one hundred percent," McLanahan said. "But *they* are calling the shots, not *us*. That's the difference. We weren't given the go-ahead to make our own attack decisions. It may be hurt pride, or embarrassment, or professional jealously, whatever—it doesn't matter. They say 'jump,' we ask 'how high?' "

"What about Sung? What about those Taiwanese sailors? They died right before our eyes, waiting for our help."

"Brad, if that had been an American ship down there, I'd have stayed until all our weapons were exhausted, and then I would've helped the other Megafortresses roll in on target, and then I'd go back and reload and come back out again," McLanahan said. "But it wasn't one of ours."

"So you *don't care* what happens to them?" Elliott asked incredulously. "Man, this doesn't sound like you at all."

"What I care about is how this weapon system integrates with our other military forces," McLanahan said, "not how we can kick ass and sink ships all over the Pacific. We're not mercenaries, and we're not avenging angels."

"What is this? I don't believe what I'm hearing," Elliott shouted, shaking his head. "Did you think you had a chance of 'integrating' the Megafortresses with any project coming out of the Pentagon? Did you really think Balboa was going to embrace you and the Megafortresses, whether or not you did as you were ordered to do?"

McLanahan was silent—he knew Brad Elliott was right. The Megafortresses got to fly over the Formosa Strait only because he and Terrill Samson had earned the Presdent's attention and respect as a result of the secret Iran bombing missions. Patrick had deluded himself into believing that he could reintegrate the modified B-52s into the American aerial strike force—but that was not going to happen. The current Pentagon brain trust did not care for large land-based bombers. They weren't going to pay any money to keep any around, no matter how high-tech they were. The Quemoy mission was dead right from the start.

Emil Vikram may indeed have died for nothing.

"Screw it, Brad, just screw it," McLanahan said irritably. "I'm tired of your military services bigotry, I'm tired of the political games, and I'm tired of risking my neck for nothing. Just shut up and—"

"Whoa, whoa, listen to yourself, Muck," Elliott said. "You sound like a quitter, like a spoiled brat who just wants to take back his bat and ball and go home. What is with you? This doesn't have anything to do with Wendy being pregnant, does it? You're not trying to keep us out of harm's way because you got one in the oven, are you?"

"Wendy's *pregnant?*" Cheshire exclaimed. "Is it true? You didn't tell us this, Muck!"

"Tell 'em, Muck," Elliott said, that cocksure grin on his face again. He guessed, McLanahan knew, and he was smug and happy that he guessed right.

"Yes, it's true," McLanahan said. "We didn't say anything because we're only going on our third month." McLanahan jammed a finger in Elliott's face. "General, it has nothing to do with Wendy—it has to do with *you,*" he shot back angrily.

"What about me? I'm doing my job, the job I was hired to do!"

"Hired by whom? Jon Masters, the U.S. government—or the Taiwanese government?" McLanahan asked.

"What in hell are you talking about?" Elliott retorted, perhaps a little too vehemently.

"I'm wondering how that Captain Sung synchronized onto our comm channel during our surveillance," McLanahan said hotly. "The chances of him finding our initial frequency, channel-hopping along with us, then calling in the blind and reaching us at the exact moment we were in the area—I'd say that was a thousand-to-one shot."

"A kid with a Radio Shack scanner and some brains can do it," Elliott said. "You know that."

"So how did he know we were flying a bomber?"

"He must've guessed," Elliott said. "That Taiwanese ambassador saw us in the White House; he knows we're bomber guys, and he passed the info along to his navy. Hell, stealth bombers have been in the news for months now."

"So I suppose you guessed the captain's name, then?"

"What?"

"You mentioned the captain's name, Sung, even before he called us on the secure channel," McLanahan said. "You also admonished Sung for launching the attack when he did. You didn't bother getting an authentication—even though you got one from Samson, talking to him over an even more secure satellite freq—because you knew Sung *couldn't* authenticate. And you were quick to blame the Navy for lousy communications security, when it was *you* all along."

"You're nuts, Muck."

"Nuts, huh? Why don't I call back to Blytheville and get Wendy to pull the phone records from the day before our launch?" McLanahan asked angrily. "We can get the caller's name and number for any call in or out of headquarters, and Security might even be able to get a transcript. You must've been in contact with someone right before launch—we can find out who it was."

Elliott was about to protest again, but he looked at McLanahan's stone-angry face and cracked a smile. "Jesus, I can't believe I guessed right: you *are* going to have a baby," the old ex–three-star general said. "I think of you as a son, Patrick. I feel like I'm going to be a granddad."

"Stick to the point here, 'grandpa.' "

"All right, all right—yes, I was in contact with the Taiwanese—with Kuo, the new ambassador to the U.S. that we ran into in the West Wing," Elliott said resignedly. *"He* called *me,* and that's the goddamn truth. He knew, or guessed, everything we were about to do. He told me about Taiwan's plans to block the Chinese fleet. He told me about the intelligence they received about China putting nuclear warheads on its land attack and anti-ship missiles. And then he asked for my help. What in hell was I supposed to do?"

"You were supposed to hang up and report the foreign contact to the security department at Sky Masters, Inc.," McLanahan said, "and sure as hell, you weren't supposed to confirm any information or reveal any information to him, like the synchronizer codes! Jesus, Brad, if Balboa ever finds out—no, I should say, *when* Balboa finds out!—he's going to throw all of us in prison for twenty years! It's a clear violation."

"Balboa's too stupid to find out, and besides, I think the ROCs will cover their trail and explain away the rest," Elliott said confidently. "Don't worry about it."

It was no use arguing with Elliott over this, McLanahan decided—

as usual, he felt he was invincible, not just above the law but somehow blessed by God and given full authority to stretch the law and the truth with impunity. He continued to study his friend and mentor, watching him sip coffee; then: "You okay, Brad?"

Elliott seemed startled, then annoyed, that anyone was watching him. He scowled over the rim of his coffee mug. "I'm fine, Muck. Why?"

"How's the chest pains?"

"Chest pains? What chest pains?"

"You complained of chest pains on the plane."

"I just got blasted half out of my seat by an imploding one-hundred-pound sheet of Lexan," Elliott responded. "You'd be in pain too."

"Nothing else? Shortness of breath, numbness in the arms, blurred vision, feelings like indigestion, headaches?"

"Hey, Dr. Pat, I did not, nor am I now, having a heart attack or stroke," Elliott retorted. "Sure, I got rattled when that windscreen blew out in my face. Yeah, I could use about twenty-four hours of sleep—in fact, that's where I'm headed right now. You want to waste time hooking me up to monitors and making me walk a treadmill, go ahead—I challenge *you* to keep up with me! In the meantime, Balboa will be chopping up your planes right there in the hangar and trying like hell to toss *our* company into the crapper. You make the decision, mission commander. I'm going to hit the rack."

On his way out, Elliott bumped into none other than Wendy McLanahan. Without one bit of surprise at her being on Guam, he gave her a kiss on the forehead. "Congratulations, gorgeous," he said simply, then walked away toward the exit.

"Brad? Hey, General, how about . . . ?" But he was off, leaving Wendy confused.

"Wendy!" Patrick exclaimed, taking his wife into his arms. They kissed tenderly, enjoying a long, warm embrace. "What on earth are you doing here?" he asked, still in her embrace.

"Jon needed help, and I volunteered," she said. "I was en route when I found out about the mission, about Emil. I'm so sorry, Patrick."

"Thanks, sweetie, but I'm worried about you, about the baby."

"I'm working on the computer and the phone, nothing else," Wendy said. "I flew first-class commercial on United and Cathay Pacific, not on the NIRTSat booster launch plane or the tankers. I'll be fine." Wendy accepted a hug and another round of congratulations, first from Nancy Cheshire, then from a few of the other crew members and specialists in the hangar. "It looks like the cat's out of the bag."

"Brad guessed," Patrick said. "Of course, he threw it in my face."

"He did what?"

"I'll explain everything, sweetie," McLanahan said, "but it's not a fun story."

* * * * "CINCPAC, are you still up?" Admiral Balboa called.

"CINCPAC's up, along with General Samson," Admiral William Allen responded. The videoconference between Hawaii and the Pentagon was still active.

"I've got orders for you too, General," Balboa said. "Apparently the President still thinks highly of your judgment. You will report immediately to Admiral Henry Danforth at STRATCOM to stand up CTF Three."

"Yes, sir," Samson responded. He wasn't stunned at the news that STRATCOM was standing up, or forming, the CTFs, considering all that had just happened in the Formosa Strait—he was stunned at being chosen to command one of them, after the day's debacle.

STRATCOM, or U.S. Strategic Command, was a combination of the old Air Force Strategic Air Command, the Navy's Fleet Ballistic Missile Submarine Force, and the Air Force–Navy Joint Strategic Target Planning Staff. Based at Offutt Air Force Base near Omaha, Nebraska, the command of STRATCOM changed periodically between Air Force generals and Navy admirals; now, it so happened (not so coincidentally, with a Navy admiral taking charge of the Joint Chiefs of Staff) the organization was commanded by a Navy four-star admiral, Henry Danforth. USSTRATCOM had an unusual makeup. In peacetime, STRATCOM played "war games" and drew up contingency plans for major conflicts with other nations—conflicts usually involving nuclear weapons. It had no aircraft, no ships, no weapons, no troops other than its small group of planners, and no bases.

But in times of military crisis or war, STRATCOM transformed into the world's most powerful fighting force. STRATCOM could quickly "gain" all the aircraft, submarines, bases, and soldiers it required from the various U.S. armed services to fight a full spectrum of conflicts, from show of force and nuclear deterrence alert to a full-blown intercontinental thermonuclear war. STRATCOM geared up its warfighting capabilities in stages by forming Combined Task Forces, or CTFs, representing the three legs of the United States' nuclear triad—submarine-launched ballistic missiles, land-based intercontinental missiles, and long-range land-based bombers, plus their major support services. STRATCOM would "gain" land-based intercontinental ballistic missile forces from Air Force Space Command, sea-launch ballistic missile forces from the Navy's COMSUBFLT, bombers from Air Force Air Combat Command, and aerial refueling tanker planes from Air Force Air Mobility Command. Samson, as commander of all the Air Force's intercontinental heavy bombers and the highest-ranking expert on long-range bombers, was being given command of CTF Three, the strategic nuclear bomber leg of the triad.

"Admiral Allen, you will retain direct command of the EB-52 bombers on Guam," Balboa went on. "They've caused enough trouble, but the National Command Authority still wants them over the Strait for now. I'm going to snatch Ken Wayne for CTF One." CTF One was the task force in charge of the submarine-launched intercontinental ballistic missiles; Vice Admiral Kenneth E. Wayne was COMBALSUBFLT, the man in charge of the Navy's ballistic missile submarine fleet.

"Aye, aye, sir," Allen responded.

"Is STRATCOM gaining any weapon systems, sir?" Samson asked.

"None have been requested," Balboa replied. "The President wants the CTFs together just in case the shit hits the fan. But I think he's over-reacting—I think Martindale got a little scared with those nukes going off. Taking an unexpected no-shit, this-is-not-a-drill ride in the E-4 NEACP 'Doomsday Plane' probably put the fear of God into him too." Samson saw Allen chuckle, and he felt like hitting him in the mouth. There was nothing funny about it—there was plenty of reason for the President of the United States to be scared when something as horrifying as a nuclear explosion occured.

"But nothing will happen," Balboa went on confidently. "It'll be a good exercise for STRATCOM, and then we'll all go home."

> "In general, in battle one gains victory through the unorthodox. . . . One who excels at sending forth the unorthodox is as inexhaustible as Heaven, as unlimited as the Yangtze and Yellow rivers . . ."
>
> —SUN-TZU,
> *The Art of War*

CHAPTER FOUR

IN THE FORMOSA STRAIT, FIVE KILOMETERS
SOUTH OF HONG KONG
THURSDAY, 19 JUNE 1997, 0811 HOURS LOCAL
(WEDNESDAY, 18 JUNE, 1911 HOURS ET)

"Contact!" the undersea sensor operator reported. "Slow screws, cavitating, bearing . . . bearing zero-eight-zero, range . . . range eight thousand meters and closing, speed eight knots, depth unknown."

The combat action officer aboard the Chinese aircraft carrier *Mao Zedong* nodded, then passed along the information to the bridge. The commanding officer of the *Mao,* Admiral Yi Kyu-pin, picked up the intercom phone himself. "Combat, bridge. Identification?"

"Sea Dragon–class submarine, sir," the combat action officer responded. "It is the same one that has been shadowing us since we entered the area."

"You are positive of the identification?"

"Yes, sir," the combat officer replied. "We are positive. We can even identify the exact vessel—it is number 795, the *Hai Hu.* This rebel vessel has a distinctive rudder flutter, and the Holec alternators have a distinctive waveform pattern as well. Its identification was confirmed by

ASW aircraft before we arrived at Hong Kong, and we have maintained steady contact on it since. Identification confirmed."

Admiral Yi Kyu-pin swiveled in his seat and noted the sub's position on the large glass wall chart in front of him. The Chinese carrier was riding at anchor just five kilometers south of Hong Kong; that put the Taiwanese sub well inside Hong Kong territorial waters, which, as far as Yi was concerned, were Communist Chinese waters, and always had been. Since the attack on Quemoy less than two weeks before, Taiwanese subs had been brazenly approaching Chinese warships, trying to sneak as closely as they could without being detected. They were not very good at it. In trying to arrest a rapid closure rate, the Taiwanese sub captain had actually reversed the pitch on his propellers, causing cavitation—air bubbles trapped in the prop wash and sliced apart, causing extreme undersea noise that could be heard for many kilometers (however, if the Taiwanese sub had *not* cavitated its screw, the Chinese destroyer's sonar operators probably would not have detected the sub until it moved much closer).

It was all part of the game—except today, the game was about to change. "Very good," Admiral Yi said. "Maintain passive contact and report when it closes within five thousand meters or opens any outer doors."

"Yes, sir. I estimate it will close to within five thousand meters in twenty-three minutes on its present course and speed."

"Very well." The commander of the *Mao* hung up the phone, then rose and exited the bridge without issuing any other orders. He made his way quickly to the communications center, dismissed all but the senior officer on duty, sent a single coded message, then made his way back up on deck.

The early-morning air was cold, but Admiral Yi could detect the first scents of summertime warmth on the sea. The air was fresh and clean, not like the putrid air surrounding the port city of Guangzhou, the large industrial city north of Hong Kong. Life on the sea could be exciting, but all but a few of his years in the brown- or green-water People's Liberation Army Navy had been spent within helicopter range of shore, and most of those had been spent in the thickly polluted inland waterways leading to China's naval ports.

The admiral walked to the port rail and looked forward, sorry to be missing the fresh air blowing in from the east but wanting to take a look at his charge. He saw its curving "ski jump" bow and the open doors to the twelve missile launch tubes embedded in the flight deck just aft of the ski jump—and he felt sick to his stomach.

Mao, its four escort destroyers, and several smaller escort, support, and resupply vessels had returned to Victoria, Hong Kong, to participate in Reunification Day celebrations leading up to July 1, less than two weeks away, when Hong Kong would officially become part of the People's Republic of China once again after one hundred years as a British leasee. The carrier's superstructure and gunwales were covered with festive flags and bunting, and every night they staged brilliant fireworks demonstrations from the carrier's aft deck. Almost all of the carrier's combat crews and half of the ship's complement had been taken off, replaced by nearly a thousand civilians from all over the world, anxious to see what it was like to live aboard an aircraft carrier—especially one that had just seen combat. Instead of performing anti-submarine sweeps, the *Mao's* helicopters were being used to shuttle civilians from Hong Kong out to the carrier for rides and tours on the huge warship.

The Chinese government, of course, denied that it had done anything wrong at all during the skirmish near Quemoy, and Admiral Yi had sworn to hundreds of reporters and government officials that he did not launch any attacks against the outlaw rebel Nationalists except to defend his ship and others in his group—the Nationalists and the Americans were to blame. The Taiwanese frigates had attacked the peaceful Chinese group of ships in international waters without warning. It was the rebel frigates and the American B-52 bomber that had launched the nuclear missiles, after unsuccessfully attacking the Chinese ships with conventional weapons. One missile had been destroyed by Chinese antiaircraft fire; the other missile, fired by the American stealth bomber toward the Chinese port city of Xiamen, near Quemoy Island, had detonated early. In the interest of peace, President Jiang Zemin had announced, China would move the peaceful group of ships back south to Hong Kong.

The sudden, swift, ignominious withdrawal from the Quemoy Island attack plan really hurt Yi's pride. He felt as if his entire crew, his entire battle group, felt he had betrayed and abandoned them. True, the American stealth bomber had taken a swift, heavy toll on the battle group, but the attack plan itself was still alive, and chances for success had been good. But no more.

Now the carrier *Mao Zedong,* China's greatest warship, was little more than a pony for children to ride—and the rebels on the island of Formosa were thumbing their noses and baring their asses toward mainland China. The thought really upset Yi and his fellow commanders. The world believed the Republic of China was the bright and promising young star, and that the People's Republic of China was the cruel governess seeking to stunt the younger nation's growth and aspirations. Everyone believed unification would eventually happen, but the world now mandated that it be subject to Taiwan's timetable, not the People's Republic of China's. China would have to disavow communism and somehow "catch up" to Taiwan's fast-growing capitalist economy before unification could become a reality.

This could not, would *never*, be tolerated. Lee Teng-hui and his bastard government on Taiwan had to come back into the Communist fold. It was ludicrous, ridiculous, to ask over a billion Chinese Communists to change their form of government over the desires of twenty-one million money-grubbing Taiwanese capitalist rebels. They would be surrendering their way of life simply because of *money,* and no true friend of the workers of the world would ever tolerate that.

The captain's walkie-talkie beeped, and he raised it to his lips. "Speak."

"Message from headquarters," the watch officer on the bridge reported.

"Read it."

"Message reads, 'Starbright.' End of message."

"Very well," Yi said. "Out."

The walkie-talkie beeped again: "Target one has moved within specified range, sir," the combat action officer reported, referring of course to the Taiwanese submarine trying to sneak in close to the *Mao Zedong*.

"Very well," the captain replied. "Continue to monitor." He picked up the binoculars on the leather strap slung around his neck and scanned the horizon to the south. He saw nothing but a few large fishing vessels far out on the horizon, their net booms extended, hauling huge nets out of the South China Sea. He often wondered about the hard but peaceful lives those men experienced, and wondered if destiny would ever allow him the luxury of choosing such a life for himself and his family. Yi loved the sea and had always wanted to be near it, part of it, but it seemed as if his desires and dreams had never been a factor in what sort of life he led.

If Yi had continued to watch, he would have seen the crew of the two fishing boats use their fishing net tackle to hoist four huge steel canisters off their decks and into the sea; seconds later, both boats were departing the area in considerable haste. The four canisters they had tossed overboard were American-made surplus Mk 60 CAPTORs (enCAPsulated TORpedoes), which were Mk 46 acoustic-homing torpedoes enclosed in a launch tube. The Mk 60s were remotely activated ten minutes after being dropped overboard. The torpedoes' sonars locked onto the largest vessel in its sensor field—the carrier *Mao Zedong,* less than ten miles away—and then automatically launched themselves at the target.

The captain saw the need to force the Taiwanese Nationalists to submit to rightful Chinese government rule; he understood the need first to break down this cult of protectionism that had formed around Taiwan since they had claimed independence, that Taiwan was in the right and should be permitted to ignore and contradict Chinese authority simply because it was smaller or richer or more Western-like. But he would never understand all of it, all the politics and ideologies involved, all the various dynamics in the government and in the military that seemed to threaten to tear apart the very fabric of Chinese life.

The tours had just started. Today was "Our Children, Our Future Day" on the carrier *Mao.* The decks were crawling with hundreds of children of important Chinese Communist Party officials, foreign businessmen and politicians, and special invited guests. The kids could sit inside a Sukhoi-33 fighter that had been set up on one of the one-hundred-meter launch points, crawl around the anti-submarine helicopters, pretend they were launching off the deck or shooting antiaircraft missiles and guns, play with signal lights, and generally invade almost every square centimeter of the huge vessel. A large group of children had walked up the steep twelve-degree ski-jump incline and were peering nervously over the edge as a crewman explained how fighters launched from the carrier. A few brave boys even stepped right up to the rounded lip of the ski jump and looked down over sixty meters to the sea below.

The image made Yi smile. He was proud of those brave children, he thought—he didn't know them, did not know their families, but he was proud of how brave they were. Too bad . . .

Yi's walkie-talkie beeped several times—the ship-wide alerting system. "All hands, all hands, this is the bridge, stand by for emergency action stations. Captain to the bridge."

The captain keyed the mike on the walkie-talkie: "Captain here. Report."

"High-speed screws detected by passive sonar, sir," the officer of the deck responded excitedly. "Torpedoes in the water, bearing one-niner-five, range four thousand two hundred meters and closing. Additional torpedoes detected at bearing three-zero-zero."

The captain closed his eyes. It had begun. Although not as he would have envisioned the Battle For Chinese Reunification to commence, it had finally happened. "Sound general quarters," he ordered. The ship-wide mechanical alarm bells began ringing immediately. "Clear the flight deck, launch the ASW helicopters, prepare to retaliate against the rebel submarine. Haul anchor and prepare to get under way. Warn the rest of the fleet that we will be maneuvering for ASW air combat operations and ready all submarine countermeasures. Send a flash satellite emergency message to Eastern and South China Sea Fleet headquarters and advise them that the *Mao* carrier group is under attack by Taiwanese submarine forces."

The first explosion occurred less than six minutes later, on the port side forward. Yi was surprised to feel how much the deck shook and rolled. His big, beautiful, 6,000-ton ship heeled and shuddered like a wooden toy boat wallowing in a summer monsoon thunderstorm.

The civilians crowding the flight deck thought that the alarm bells were part of some demonstration or drill staged for their amusement, and so it seemed that no one was reacting to his orders. Crewmen tried to herd the civilians to stairwells, but they all stood around or moved closer to the helicopters, gun mounts, and access hatches, waiting to watch the new demonstration they thought was about to begin. He looked on with absolute horror as several children on the ski jump, bowled over by the force of the explosion, fell overboard—the deck-edge safety nets had been retracted into their stowed positions. He could not hear the children's screams over the clanging of the emergency alarm, but in his mind he could hear them all too plainly. Clouds of smoke began to billow out from the port side, completely obscuring the forward flight deck. Civilians were running everywhere in a panic, hampering the damage control party's response. A second explosion erupted, just a few dozen meters aft of the first, also on the port side.

It had finally begun, the captain thought again as he raced for the bridge. It seemed a rather ignoble way to start such a glorious war of liberation and reunification, but nonetheless it was finally under way. . . .

As soon as the crowds of confused civilians could be cleared away, four ex–Soviet Kamov-25 helicopters on the deck of the *Mao* began turning rotors and preparing to get under way; each helicopter was armed with two E40-79 air-dropped torpedoes. Also launching from the fantail of the carrier *Mao* was a Zhi-8 heavy shipboard helicopter, carrying a dipping sonar array for searching for submarines.

The five helicopters flew a precise course eastward in a tight formation. The crowd of civilians watched in fascination as the formation hovered less than five miles away. The large helicopter hovered close to the surface of the South China Sea and reeled out its sonar transducer at the end of a cable; it let it dangle in the ocean for several seconds before reeling it back in, flying several hundred yards away, then hovering and dunking again. After the second dunk, one Ka-25 helicopter zipped south a few hundred yards, and the crowd of onlookers could see the splashes as it released both its torpedoes.

Not every detail of the attack could be seen from the decks of the *Mao,* but as if they were hosting some kind of sporting event, a radio operator was giving a running commentary on the chase: "Search One has detected an unknown target, bearing one-niner-zero . . . Attack Two, transition south five hundred meters and stand by . . . Search One, target one bearing two-eight-three, Attack Two, do you copy . . . ? Attack Two copies new target fix, stand by for weapons release . . . torpedoes away, torpedoes away, all units be advised, remain clear . . . torpedoes running, both torpedoes running . . . torpedoes going active, all units, new target bearing, mark, target data transmitting . . ." Moments later, the crowd screamed and shouted in surprise when two terrific explosions and huge geysers of water erupted from the ocean near where the helicopter had dropped its deadly load.

The attacks continued for nearly an hour, until all of the torpedoes had been exhausted. In the meantime, the carrier *Mao* had lifted anchor and had begun maneuvering toward where the helicopters were operating. The carrier was creeping toward them at minimum steerageway power until they received the news—the enemy submarine had been hit, and it was on its way up to the surface. Several minutes later, the crowd of civilians still on board the *Mao* was treated to an unusual sight: a crippled and smoking submarine bobbing on the surface. It was announced to all that it was a Dutch-designed Zwaardvis-class attack submarine, with a crew of 67 and a combat load of 28 wire-guided U.S.-made Mk 37 torpedoes.

It was also announced that the submarine was identified as the *Hai Hu*—an attack submarine owned and operated by the rebel Nationalist government on the island of Formosa.

It was without a doubt one of the most beautiful, yet one of the most dangerous outposts in all the world, Chung-Kuo KungChuan (Republic of China Air Force) C-130T transport pilot Captain Shen Hung-Ta thought. Once they got below the clouds, the islands looked so warm and inviting from the air—one might easily forget the dangers hidden nearby.

Air Force Captain Shen was just twenty miles out from Matsu Air Base, the northernmost military base belonging to the Republic of China. Matsu Air Base was on Pei-Kan-T'ang Tao, one of a cluster of eight islands lying just ten miles off the coast of mainland China. Just forty miles to the west was the city of Fu-Chou, a city of one million residents, plus its air force, army, and naval coastal defense bases with another six to twelve thousand troops. The Matsu Islands had a grand total of fifteen thousand Taiwanese troops stationed here, mostly in underground bunkers and air and coastal defense sites—and that number probably included a few goats, Shen thought.

Whatever it was, the number didn't matter. Matsu was officially a Taiwanese "coastal defense" outpost, with Taiwanese-made Hsiung Feng (Male Bee) anti-ship cruise missiles and U.S.-made Improved-HAWK antiaircraft missiles stationed there, along with one special forces group and a light infantry division. Unofficially, Taiwan had several sophisticated intelligence-gathering listening posts in the Matsu Islands, along with special communications systems, the National Security Bureau of Taiwan could tap into China's telephone, telegraph, and telex network from the Matsu Islands, and a string of undersea sensors in the East China Sea were monitored from Matsu so Taiwan could remotely monitor the movement of Chinese ships north of Taiwan. Matsu also stationed a few S-2T Tracker submarine hunters there on occasion to search for Chinese and

North Korean submarines cruising the Formosa Strait and East China Sea, and the main long-range radar array atop Matsu Mountain monitored the movement of Chinese ships and aircraft between the South and East Fleet headquarters.

"Matsu Approach, Transport One-Five, approaching intersection Bravo . . . now," Shen reported as he flew his cargo plane inbound to Matsu North. Each phase of the approach into Matsu had to be carefully and exactly executed; any deviation could trigger an air defense alert from Matsu and also from Yixu Air Base in mainland China. Shen knew that almost one hundred Chinese fighters, mostly Chinese copies of Russian MiG-17, -19, and -21 interceptors, were based there, along with HQ-2 surface-to-air missiles and numerous antiaircraft artillery units. Shen's approach into Matsu North Air Base put him only thirty miles east of Yixu Air Base in mainland China, well within radar and antiaircraft missile range.

"Transport One-Five, Matsu Approach, you are cleared to point Charlie."

"Cleared to Charlie, One-Five, wilco," Shen replied, using the American phrase "wilco" for "will comply"; American aviation slang was considered acceptable terminology to all ROC controllers, even in this very sensitive area so close to the mainland.

Along with electronic encoders and precise control of flight time and navigation, security checkpoints were established all along the approaches to the two airfields in the Matsu Islands; the checkpoint coordinates were changed with every inbound flight and issued to the crew prior to departure. Each checkpoint had to be reached within a quarter-mile and reported plus-or-minus one-tenth of a mile or the aircraft might be considered hostile. The final checkpoint was within visual range of ground spotters so positive visual identification could be made before final landing clearance was issued. Many times, Shen and his crew had to break off a picture-perfect approach because they forgot to report over a checkpoint.

But such serious errors were fortunately rare, and in general flying so close to the mainland, so close to the enormous military might of the People's Republic of China, was very routine, almost mundane. The key was in a careful cross-check. Captain Shen double-checked that the proper tower control frequency was set—it was. Double-check the ILS (Instrument Landing System) frequency, get a good Morse code ident—

got it. Double-check the inbound course set—got it. Double-check the NDB (Non-Directional Beacon) frequency set, get a good ident, then check that the marker beacon lights were working—got it. Gyro heading indicators checked with the "whiskey" compass—done, both within five degrees, which was a lot but acceptable. Double-check the ILS with the VOR (Very-high-frequency Omnidirectional Receiver) on the copilot's side, in case the glideslope went out—done. If there was any big deviation, the copilot would call it out and they'd decide as a crew which approach to use. In this weather, losing the ILS might mean returning back to Taipei because the VOR was never as accurate as the ILS, but both appeared to be working fine. Shen wished he had a GPS (Global Positioning System) satellite navigation receiver, but this old transport wasn't slated to get one for several weeks.

Now the business of shooting a "no shit" instrument approach got under way. For any pilot, even one with as many hours as Shen, flying totally on instruments, without one single reference outside the cockpit, was always tension-filled. The C-130's autopilot was a simple heading-hold system, not coupled to the ILS, so Shen was hand-flying it on this approach. It was like playing a video game, maneuvering the sixty-thousand-pound plane in order to keep two needles on the HSI (Horizontal Situation Indicator) forming a perfect cross in the center of the instrument. The needles' movement got more sensitive as they got closer to the field, so Shen's inputs had to be more careful, more delicate. But if he kept those needles centered perfectly, at just the right airspeed, he would be lined up perfectly on the runway, in position to execute a landing without any gross turns or dives.

"Coming up on point Charlie," the copilot announced.

"Approach flaps," Shen ordered, and the copilot put in twenty degrees of flaps, which slowed the big transport down nicely to just below approach speed, they'd get back up to approach speed as they started down the glideslope, the invisible electronic "ramp" that would take them to the runway. Shen now focused all his attention on the instruments, performing a careful scan of the four primary flight instruments—the copilot would look after the engine instruments and other indicators. The HSI in the center of the instrument panel in front of the pilot was a combination gyro compass, omni bearing indicator, and ILS indicator, so that was the central instrument to watch; next was the artificial horizon, back to the HSI, then out to the airspeed indicator, back to the HSI, out to the altimeter, back to the HSI, out to the vertical velocity indicator, back to the HSI, then perhaps a quick scan of the engine instruments and a peek out the cockpit windscreen before starting the scan all over again.

"Point Charlie . . . now," the copilot said, resting his hand on the gear handle. "Glideslope alive." When the glideslope needle on the HSI reached five degrees above center, Shen ordered the copilot to lower the landing gear. "Gear down," the copilot repeated, as he put the handle down. A red light in the handle illuminated, meaning the gear was unlocked, and the three gear-position indicators moved from UP to black and white stripes, indicating the gear was in an intermediate position. "Gear moving . . ." One by one the gear indicators showed DOWN, and seconds later the red light in the gear handle went out. "Three down and locked, red light out," the copilot said. He reached over and moved an indicator bug on the altimeter. "Decision height, two-forty."

"Roger," Shen said. He lowered the nose, reduced power, and transitioned smoothly onto the glideslope. There was a pretty good crosswind from the west, and Shen banked left to center the localizer needle.

"Transport One-Five, contact tower," they heard on the radio. Right on time. The transmission was a bit scratchy—a storm was brewing, Shen thought, a big thunderstorm. Hopefully they'd be on the ground well before it reached the airfield.

"One-Five going to tower," the copilot acknowledged, then switched channels and announced, "Matsu Tower, Transport One-Five point Charlie inbound on the ILS."

There was a scratchy, barely readable "Roger, One-Five," then a garbled "Clear to land," and the copilot acknowledged the clearance and reported the clearance to Shen as he set up the ground control frequency. The ground spotters had issued the landing clearance early, considering the cloud cover—maybe it wasn't as thick as it looked from up here, Shen thought.

Needles centered perfectly, airspeed right on the dot—this approach was going well. A bit more crosswind correction, left wing down . . . "Two thousand to go," the copilot said.

"Engines look good," the engineer, sitting behind the copilot, said. He looked at the forward instrument panel, triple-checking the indications prior to landing. "Gear, flaps, lights, all check." He made a quick announcement on intercom to the passengers in the back, ordering them to check that their seat belts were on. "Before-landing check complete."

Bit more left—there, needles centered again, right on the glideslope. The Doppler was not locked on—it commonly did not lock on over water—but even without it he knew he had some pretty hellacious west winds. No sweat, he could handle it.

"One thousand above," the copilot said.

"Doppler's OTL," the flight engineer said, meaning "out to lunch," "mag compass . . . it's OTL too." The flight engineer quickly checked the engine and flight systems, looking for any sign of trouble.

"Looking good, a little hot," the copilot said. Shen was right on the glideslope, so he pulled the throttles back slightly to get back on the proper airspeed. That should be his last correction, he reminded himself—any more corrections this close to the airfield and he'd be "chasing" the ILS needles, which would porpoise him all over the sky. Nice, easy, small corrections from here on out. "Five hundred to decision height."

Shen completed another scan, ran his eyes over the engine instruments—all OK, all needles pointing in roughly the same direction—then back to the HSI—right on the glidepath—then quickly up to the mag compass above the center of the windscreen . . .

. . . and it read sixty degrees differently than the inbound course to Matsu Airport. A sharp thrill of panic clutched at Shen's throat. The ILS needles were perfectly centered, the DME (Distance Measuring Equipment) put them at the proper position on the approach—but they were sixty degrees off course! If the ILS was wrong and the gyro and mag compasses were correct, they were far, far off course—into Red China's airspace. "What in hell's going on with the heading?" Shen shouted. "I'm centered up, but the compass says we're way west."

"My VOR's centered up, too," the copilot said. He quickly punched the buttons on the audio panel. "I've got good idents on the ILS, VOR, and NDB. DME's okay . . ."

"Electrical and vacuum systems okay," the engineer said.

"The tower's got us, they cleared us for landing—if we were off course, they'd have said something," the copilot said. "The gyros must be screwed up."

"But the gyro compass and mag compasses are both reading the same," Shen shouted, the fear rising in his voice. He suddenly jammed the throttles to full power and raised the nose, trying to stop the descent on the "glideslope." "Damn it, we've been MIJIed!" MIJI stood for Meaconing, Interference, Jamming, and Intrusion, a common enemy tactic to disrupt communications or air traffic by playing havoc with radios and radar signals; oftentimes it was done just to confuse, but sometimes it was done to force a pilot into unintentionally violating enemy airspace. On the radio, Shen said excitedly, "Matsu Tower, Transport One-Five, executing missed approach procedures, proceeding to holding point Tango, acknowledge." No response. "Matsu Tower, Transport One-Five, how do you copy? We are executing missed approach. We suspect enemy MIJIing in effect. Acknowledge!"

"Transport One-Five, Matsu Tower, cancel missed approach, we have you on the glidepath. You are cleared to land, winds three-three-zero at seven knots, if you can hear me, ident, please."

The copilot automatically hit his IDENT button, which would electronically draw a highlight box around the data block for his aircraft on the tower controller's radarscope. "Matsu Tower, Transport One-Five is executing a security missed approach, we are in the turn, acknowledge, over!" The radio was still scratchy, as if they were still a long distance away from the base . . .

. . . and seconds later, the C-130 popped through the clouds—and the windscreen was filled with the lights of the city of Lang-Ch'i, just a few miles ahead, and farther ahead on the horizon was the mass of lights of the city of Fu-Chou, less than twenty miles away. Shen realized they were well within Chinese airspace—they were practically over Chinese soil!

"Transport One-Five, ident received," the voice said. "Continue inbound, do not turn. Be advised, still clear to land. Acknowledge with an ident."

The copilot was about to automatically hit the IDENT button again, but Shen hit his hand away. "Don't touch that! Something is not right," he said. "Set EMER in the IFF, get on GUARD channel, and notify someone that we are being MIJIed. We're flying over Chinese airspace!"

"What in God's name is happening?" the copilot breathed, as Shen started a steep right bank turn to the east.

"I do not know," Shen said. "We can do nothing but the proper procedures. We shall go to point Tango and attempt to—"

Suddenly the entire aircraft shuddered and dropped several feet, as if it had hit a sudden wave of turbulence, sharp and hard enough to disengage the autopilot. "I have the aircraft!" Shen shouted, grasping the control yoke and rolling wings-level. "Check instruments!"

The engineer quickly scanned the engine instruments. "All systems okay," he responded.

"Everything looks okay," the copilot agreed. "Clear to reengage the autopilot."

"I will hand-fly it," Shen said, "until we get everything straightened out. I will fly the mag compass until we get everything sorted out. Get on squadron common channel and—"

"Hey!" the copilot shouted. He pointed out the windscreen in horror, then looked at his pilot. "Is that . . . is that Matsu?"

Shen stopped and stared out the window; his copilot followed his gaze, then gaped in amazement as well. Half of the island seemed to be on fire. Smoke billowed from hundreds of burning buildings, the northern half of the island was completely obscured in black smoke—even the ocean seemed to be on fire. "What is it? What's happened?"

"They are attacking," Shen said woodenly. "The Communists . . . this entire thing was a diversion. The Communists must've launched a rocket attack on the island, thinking that we were attacking them! Gear up! Let's head back to Sungshan, fast!"

The radios were a completely indecipherable babble of voices, so the crew forgot about reporting their position and prayed that their coded transponder would still be showing to Taiwanese air defense forces while they turned away from Matsu. Everyone on the flight deck was riveted to the left-side cockpit windows as they turned eastbound away from the air base. "Fighters are airborne," Shen said. "At least we have fighter coverage. We should . . ." And then he froze, his mouth turning dust-dry: "Those are not Taiwanese fighters! Those are Communist fighter planes!" Soon, those fighters were swarming over the C-130, and moments later it was sent crashing down into the sea.

It turned out to be a very well-coordinated attack—a missile bombardment from shore-based batteries from Lang-Ch'i Army Base on the mainland, followed moments later by a wave of fighter-bombers from Yixu Air Base. Captain Shen, his crew, and his aircraft were only a small part of the casualties of the Chinese attack on the entire Matsu island chain. Within hours, the Matsu Islands were completely defenseless.

"Headbanger Two reporting on station," Nancy Cheshire radioed on the secure satellite net.

"James Daniel copies, Headbanger," came the reply. Just ten miles north of the EB-52 Megafortress, flying 15,000 feet above the Formosa Strait, was a small task force of two American Oliver Hazard Perry–class guided missile frigates, the *Duncan,* a Naval Reserve Fleet ship with eighty Naval Reservists on board, and the lead vessel in this task force, the *James Daniel;* they had been moved into the area of the recent skirmish between the Chinese People's Liberation Army Navy and the Quemoy flotilla of the Republic of China's navy. The American task force's nominal orders was to stand by and render any possible assistance if requested by both China and Taiwan, as salvage and recovery vessels from their respective countries tried to recover whatever was left of their stricken vessels; their actual mission was to show the American flag and try to prevent a re-eruption of hostilities between the two Chinas. But even though there was very little rescue or recovery work being done by anyone, the frigates—and now the EB-52 Megafortress—were on patrol, ready for action.

The crew of the Megafortress was very quiet, except for the intense but hushed coaching going on in the back of the crew cabin. Extra seats had been bolted into the deck beside the offensive and defensive operator's consoles, and Patrick McLanahan and the crew DSO, Megafortress veteran Air Force officer Major Robert Atkins, were seated in the jump seats giving instruction on using the sophisticated electronic attack, surveillance, and defensive systems to newcomers Air Force Captain Jeff Denton in the OSO's seat, and Navy Lieutenant Ashley Bruno in the DSO's seat.

"There—is that Xiamen's long-range surveillance radar?" Bruno asked, pointing at the large threat display.

"Don't ask me—ask the computer," Atkins said, acting his part as the patient but demanding instructor. "You've got a full-up system, so use it." Atkins had joined the Megafortress program almost at its inception, recruited from the handful of 4.0-grade-point-average-or-better Air Force Academy graduates who had also graduated high in their Undergraduate Pilot Training classes. Atkins was the best of the best—a straight-A student in electrical engineering from the Zoo, in the top 20 percent of his UPT class, who had managed to earn a master's degree in business administration while a FAIP (First Assignment Instructor Pilot). He had been recruited personally by Wendy Tork McLanahan, the director of the Megafortress's advanced electronic warfare suite design team at HAWC, and he had remained there for several years, refining the high-tech electronic detection, analysis, countermeasure, and counterattack systems on the Megafortress "flying battleship."

And, like Nancy Cheshire flying in the copilot's seat, he had seen combat before in the Megafortress: over the Philippines, over Lithuania, and over the United States. Back then, actually flying the beast hadn't been his strong point—he could design systems built perfectly for a crewdog, but he didn't enjoy flying itself. But flying was part of the job, and besides, no one said "no" to the boss, Lieutenant-General Bradley James Elliott. Even after HAWC disbanded and Atkins set off to get his doctorate at the Massachusetts Institute of Technology as part of a joint industry–Air Force program, he could not escape, or resist, Brad Elliott's call to glory.

"Right, right," Ashley Bruno responded. Bruno, a former Navy engineer from the China Lake Naval Weapons Center, touched the threat display and keyed the computer voice interface button with her left foot and said, "Computer, identify."

SIERRA-BAND BEAN STICKS EARLY-WARNING RADAR, the computer responded.

"It's not necessary to preface your commands with 'computer' or anything else," Atkins said.

"I know," Bruno said, wearing a playful grin. "But I guess I'm still a Trekkie at heart. Mr. Spock always started a voice command with 'computer.' " She keyed the voice command switch again: "Computer, are we in detection range of the Bean Sticks radar?"

NEGATIVE.

"Computer, what is the estimated detection range of the Bean Stick radar?"

ESTIMATED EFFECTIVE DETECTION RANGE IN CURRENT CONFIGURATION, FIFTEEN MILES, the computer responded. EFFECTIVE DETECTION

RANGE WITH BAY DOORS OPEN, TWENTY-SEVEN MILES. EFFECTIVE DETECTION RANGE IN CLEAN CONFIGURATION . . .

Bruno keyed the voice command button twice to cancel the report. "Thank you, computer," she said.

"I think, I *hope,* what Atkins is saying, Lieutenant Bruno," Brad Elliott cut in on interphone, "was that it would be faster and more efficient in a combat situation to just say what you want and *can the fucking bullshit!*" He spat the last four words like heavy-caliber gunshots. "This is not a starship *Enterprise* reunion, and it's not a computer game. Now, do it right or I'll beam your Trekkie ass into the goddamn ocean—with my boot, not a transporter."

"Yes, sir," Bruno responded contritely.

McLanahan said to Denton, "Read up on the emergency electrical attack procedures for a few." While the student OSO called up the hypertext tech order flight manual on the supercockpit display and began reading, McLanahan leaned back in his jump seat and clicked the interphone button twice. He and Elliott had used that command many times in their ten-year relationship to signal one another to "go private" on the interphone panel, which would allow the two to talk to each other without the rest of the crew listening in.

Sure enough, Elliott was on private to meet him. "What?"

"Ease up a bit, Brad," McLanahan said.

"The newbies need to keep their minds on the job and stop fucking around."

"Bruno's doing okay," McLanahan said. "So is Denton. We can all use a little comic relief."

"If Bruno does her *Star Trek* routine in training, she'll do it in combat," Elliott said. "You know it, I know it."

"Okay, Brad, okay," McLanahan said. "Yes, you're right, we're supposed to be training like we're going to fight. But you're being a little hard on Bruno. Wouldn't be because she's sitting in Vikram's seat, is it?"

"Screw you and your amateur psychoanalysis, Muck," Elliott snapped. "I know how to train newbies." McLanahan heard the click that meant Elliott had switched back to normal interphone.

McLanahan fell silent as he followed Elliott back to normal interphone. In the past two weeks since the skirmish near Quemoy Island, Brad Elliott had been quiet, moody almost to the point of irritation, and demanding of everyone with whom he came into contact. He flew the

EB-52 with practiced, methodical precision, strictly by the book—which he should know, because he had personally written most of it and reviewed all of it for many years—but he did it more with dogged impatience, without his usual sense of happiness and purpose.

Well, there was certainly nothing going on to get too excited about right now. The worldwide hue and cry over the nuclear detonations near mainland China had quieted all participants down considerably. Only about a third of the world media believed the People's Republic of China's Liberation Army was responsible for the dreaded nuclear explosions; the rest of the blame was equally divided between the United States and Taiwan. This was considered a major propaganda victory for China and a complete propaganda disaster for Taiwan and the United States.

As a result of the heavy media and governmental scrutiny, however, the Formosa Strait was relatively free from heavy military presence—a fact that McLanahan was able to verify by looking at the EB-52 Megafortress's God's-eye display on the supercockpit monitor, which was now being operated by Captain Denton. The fifty-plus-vessel People's Liberation Army Navy carrier battle group was gone, dispersed to various bases or sent south toward Hong Kong to participate in Reunification Day festivities. As far as McLanahan could tell, the PLAN had only one ship of any size in the region; it had just appeared on the latest NIRTSat inverse synthetic aperture radar sweep.

"Okay, did you get IDs on the ships closest to the frigates?" McLanahan asked.

"Yep," Denton responded. "Coastal trawlers and fishing vessels, both less than fifty tons. Neither moving faster than nine knots."

"Good," McLanahan said. "Remember, the system can squelch out small vessels like that if necessary, based on size or speed, but it's always best to check out everything. Also remember that the ISAR system isn't infallible, so even if those ships show as not hostile, even if you recheck six times, don't ignore them. But right now they're far enough away from the frigates to be safe, so you can mark those ships as noncombatants."

That action turned out to be a mistake, because precisely at that time, crew members aboard the two Chinese "noncombatants" were dropping the last of a dozen large SS-N-16 missile canisters overboard. The SS-N-16, code-named "Stallion," was an air- or submarine-launched rocket-powered torpedo, except these weren't going flying before releasing their deadly cargoes. Once sailing clear of all torpedoes, they were activated by radio command. Simultaneously, the canisters activated their sensors, detected the distinctive high-speed, high-powered screws of the U.S. Navy warships, and turned toward them. Once perfectly aligned with their targets, they powered up their payloads—each canister carried a E45-75A torpedo with a 200-pound penetrating-blast high-explosive warhead, sitting atop a solid-fueled rocket booster—and the countdown commenced . . .

• • • • New NIRTSat satellite radar data was being downloaded every eight minutes; in less than a minute, the supercockpit God's-eye view was automatically updated, and the map of the surveillance area had to be reexamined as if for the first time. "Okay, we see the 'noncombatants' are still poking along—in fact, it looks like they're heading away from the frigates, cruising at ten knots," McLanahan said to Denton. "What else you got?" When Oakley didn't answer in a few moments, McLanahan pointed to the screen. "Looks like we got a newcomer, probably pulled out of Xiamen a couple sweeps ago. Remember, the NIRTSat data isn't really God's-eye—it's better than turning on a radar and letting the bad guys know we're up here, but it's not perfect . . . yet. Let's get an ID on that ship there, Jeff."

"Rog," Denton responded, expertly rolling the trackball cursor over the stored NIRTSat radar image. Jeff Denton, a former F-16 Fighting Falcon pilot, Gulf War vet, and F-15E Strike Eagle backseater, had had the bad luck of joining HAWC just weeks before it closed last year. Unable to get another fighter-bomber assignment anywhere, he had been forced to accept an early-out bonus and found himself unemployed right near the holiday season of 1996. Fortunately, just as the bonus money had started running low, he'd gotten the call from General Samson to do some flying for a private defense firm he had never heard of, Sky Masters, Inc., in Blytheville, Arkansas, which was working on some former HAWC projects.

Denton had jumped at the opportunity—never expecting to be suddenly flying a hybrid B-52/B-1B/B-2 monster over the Formosa Strait in Asia, near where a nuclear war had almost broken out just a few days earlier.

"Identify this return," Denton ordered the computer, being careful to make the command short and sweet, lest he bring down the wrath of the legendary General Brad Elliott on *himself.*

IDENTIFICATION UNKNOWN, the computer responded. SEARCHING . . . TARGET IDENTIFIED AS SLAVA-CLASS CRUISER . . . TARGET IDENTIFIED AS KIROV-CLASS CRUISER . . . TARGET IDENTIFIED AS FEARLESS-CLASS ASSAULT SHIP . . . TARGET IDENTIFIED AS TYPE 82-CLASS ACCOMMODATIONS SHIP . . .

"You got a cruiser, Muck?" Nancy Cheshire, flying as copilot, asked. A warship of that size always got a lot of attention from every member of the crew, especially the ones who had once faced those fearsome vessels. "Where is it?"

"Cancel the report," McLanahan said. Denton double-clicked the voice command switch. "Looks like the computer's a little confused— either there's not enough radar data, or the data quality isn't good enough. It's a big sucker, though, and it's moving pretty good—over twenty knots, and crossing in front of the frigates' course. After what's happened in this area recently, I might not call that a friendly move. So what do you do now?"

"Ask the DSO if they got any idea what it is, based on electronic emissions," Denton replied.

"Excellent," McLanahan said. "The attack computer system is supposed to get that information from the defensive computer suite automatically, but sometimes it won't make the connection. Try it."

"Way ahead of you," Bruno responded. She had briefly looked at the God's-eye view and matched the signals received by her system with the computerized charts. "Nothing but a commercial nav radar from that contact—looks like a Furuno or Oki system—and wide-spectrum radio transmissions, everything from HF single sideband to UHF. I get an occasional IFF interrogator, too, maybe a Square Head." The old Soviet IFF interrogator code-named "Square Head" sent radio triggering signals out to another vessel or aircraft, asking for a coded radio response to help identification—of course, the EB-52 Megafortress or the U.S. Navy ships in the area would never respond to a foreign IFF, so all they would get would be silence.

"Not much help there," McLanahan said. "What else, Jeff?"

"Test the system, see if it's working okay?"

McLanahan shrugged. "In a combat situation, I wouldn't waste time on that. But now, with things quiet, press on." Denton rolled the cursor onto one of the nearby U.S. Navy frigates, and the system quickly and correctly identified it as a Perry-class frigate; he tried IDing one of the previously classified "noncombatants"—it again reported as a trawler. "What else, Jeff? Time's running out."

"Call the Navy and ask if they can get an eyeball on it," Denton suggested.

"Excellent suggestion," McLanahan said. "Never forget to ask someone else in your formation or task force to help out."

"Fat lot of good asking the Navy for anything does," Elliott grumbled.

McLanahan ignored him. "Do it. Think about what you need to give the Navy pukes first, get the data together, then call."

"Rog," Denton nodded, pleased at himself for keeping up with the almost legendary Patrick McLanahan. He measured out a quick range and bearing from the prebriefed target reference point, called the "bull's-eye," then keyed the mike: "Crew, OSO is going out over Fleet SATCOM." He waited for any negative replies, then switched over to the secure satellite frequency. *"James Daniel,* this is Headbanger."

A sailor with a very impatient voice that sounded as if he were sixteen years old responded, "Calling *James Daniel* on FLTSATCOM, go ahead." The voice sounded as if it didn't recognize the call sign "Headbanger," although it was the one briefed to all participants and the one they had been using since the beginning.

"Headbanger requesting a visual or optical ID on radar target bearing two-four-three at fifty-seven bull's-eye, over."

The answer came back almost immediately from a different and far more annoyed operator: "Headbanger, unable at this time due to weather." The weather was marginal, but it certainly wouldn't keep a Navy helicopter from its patrol under normal circumstances, McLanahan thought. "Keep this channel clear. Out."

"Told you," Elliott said. "The squids hardly know we exist, and they sure as hell don't care."

McLanahan ignored that remark, too, but he was starting to get a little exasperated. "Okay," he said, turning his attention back to Denton. "Anything else you can try?"

"We could launch a Striker or Wolverine at it and take a look on the datalink," Denton deadpanned.

"That sounds like an expensive suggestion," McLanahan said, "not to mention the fact that it could cause an international incident—or worse. You might have to just go with incomplete information. If you had time, you could go through all of the computer's guesses and try to get a feel for the analysis; in less hostile or non-stealth situations, you could turn on the attack radar and get an ID from the inverse synthetic aperture radar."

"But I'd assume at this point that it was hostile," Denton interjected. "The computer guessed at two Russian cruisers; that sounded like the worst-case analysis, so I'd go with that—either the Russians decided in the past couple days to send a cruiser down the Strait to see what all the excitement was about, or the Chinese have a really big destroyer or cruiser patrolling the area."

"I'd buy that," McLanahan said. "So give us the rundown on your worst-case scenario. Remember, you're the surveillance and intelligence officer on the Megafortress, along with the DSO, as well as the weapons officer—you've got to be ready to sing out with important information the rest of the crew might need to make decisions on how to press the attack."

"Rog." He opened a small window on his supercockpit display and hit the voice command switch: "Display and read order of battle on Slava-class cruiser."

SLAVA-CLASS CRUISER, VERTICAL LAUNCH SA-N-6 ANTIAIRCRAFT MISSILES, MAX RANGE 60 MILES, X-BAND TOP DOME DIRECTOR, the computer began, reading the information as well as diagramming the weapons and radar information on the supercockpit display. TWO TWIN SA-N-4 ANTIAIRCRAFT MISSILES, MAX RANGE FIVE MILES, FOXTROT, HOTEL, AND INDIA-BAND POP GROUP TARGET TRACKING WITH OPTRONIC BACKUP; ONE TWIN 130-MILLIMETER DUAL-PURPOSE GUN, MAX RANGE FIFTEEN MILES, X-BAND FIRE CONTROL WITH OPTRONIC AND MANUAL BACKUP; SIX 30-MILLIMETER ANTIAIRCRAFT GUNS, MAX RANGE THREE MILES, X-BAND BASS TILT FIRE CONTROL WITH OPTRONIC BACKUP; SIXTEEN SS-N-12 ANTI-SHIP MISSILES, MAX RANGE THREE HUNDRED MILES, JULIETT-BAND TARGET TRACKING . . ."

"That's good enough," McLanahan said, and Denton stopped the computerized report. "The computer always reads the antiaircraft order of battle first, and now you know the reason—that SA-N-6 system can eat our lunch right now, if they ever got a lock on us. You should also know that the SA-N-6 is a very devastating anti-ship weapon, too. You might want to scan through the ship's radar fit, too—it's unlikely that a cruiser has a commercial Furuno or Oki nav radar, but sometimes the military radars will look like commercial or civilian sets at long range or low power—"

Suddenly, an alarm rang out in all their headsets, and a blinking icon appeared on the supercockpit display. "What is that?" Elliott asked.

McLanahan urged Denton to start talking as they both studied the display: "High-speed low-altitude missile," Denton said. "Looks like it came from the Chinese cruiser . . . second missile launch, same azimuth . . . shit, it looks like they're headed for the *Duncan* and *James Daniel!* The Chinese are firing missiles at our frigates! More missiles . . . I've got at least four, no, five . . . six missiles in the air!"

"Brad, let's try to get within Scorpion range," McLanahan shouted. The Megafortress immediately banked right and began a fast descent in response. "DSO, you got those inbounds?"

"No—no uplink signal, no terminal radar detected," Bruno reported.

"We need the attack radar," McLanahan said.

"Rog. Crew, attack radar coming on," Denton announced.

"What do you got, Muck?" Elliott shouted on interphone.

"Six supersonic ballistic missiles," McLanahan said. "Not sure, but I think they were fired from the large ship cruising west of the Navy frigates."

"What do you mean, you 'think' they were fired from that cruiser?"

"Because we didn't get an exact ID on the ship and they didn't come exactly from that ship's azimuth," McLanahan explained.

"But it's the only warship around, right?"

"I'm not sure if it *is* a warship, Brad."

"I think we can assume six supersonic anti-ship missiles were fired from a ship that big," Elliott said. "Spin up the Strikers and let's take that sucker down."

"Missiles will impact in less than one minute," Denton reported. "We should be in range to intercept with Scorpion missiles."

"I'll get on the horn with the Navy and warn them of the inbounds," Nancy Cheshire, the crew copilot, said.

"What kind of ship is that out there?" Elliott asked.

"It's a cruiser," Denton responded.

"We don't have an exact ID on it, I said," McLanahan corrected him. "Computer couldn't match it, and we couldn't get an eyeball."

Elliott was on the secure satellite channel in an instant: "Atlas, this is Headbanger," he radioed. "Are you getting the picture here? We've got six inbounds heading for our frigates."

"Headbanger, this is Atlas," the operator at the U.S. Pacific Command headquarters responded. "We copy. Stand by."

"Stand by?" Elliott retorted. "Where the hell is Allen—having dinner with the Chinese ambassador? We need a decision up here, Atlas!"

"The *James Daniel* reports they have contact on the inbounds," Cheshire reported.

"Checks—both frigates opening fire," Denton shouted as he watched missile icons speeding away from the frigates toward the incoming Chinese missiles. "Looks like they got a clear—"

"Fighters!" Bruno shouted. "Large formation at four o'clock, five-zero miles, high . . . another large formation at one o'clock, four-seven miles and closing, high."

"This is starting to smell like a trap," Elliott said. "Secure the attack radar and let's—"

"More fighters!" Atkins reported for Bruno, who appeared to be getting a little overwhelmed by this sudden attack. "Three o'clock, five-zero miles and closing . . . first formation is breaking into two, we've got four formations of fighters inbound on us!"

"Attack radar down," McLanahan said, as Denton deactivated the Megafortress's radar.

"The inbound Chinese missiles disappeared!" Denton interjected. "Just before the frigate's missiles hit, they vanished!"

"Stallions," Atkins said. "Russian-made rocket-powered torpedoes. They're sea-skimmers until they get within SAM range of a target, then dive underwater."

"More fighters inbound!" Bruno shouted. "Two fighters, very high speed, two o'clock, four-five miles and closing *fast!* Range forty miles . . . they might have a radar lock on us!"

"Might be a Foxbat or Foxhound," Elliott said. The Russian-made MiG-25 Foxbat and MiG-31 Foxhound fighters, designed to intercept the American B-70, B-56, FB-111, and B-1 supersonic strategic bombers, were all-titanium built Russian superfighters, the fastest fighters in the world, capable of high-altitude supersonic dashes well over three times the speed of sound; they had been on the international export market for many years. "Get those damn things!"

"C'mon, Ashley, get on 'em . . . stand by for pylon launch, crew! All countermeasures systems active!" Atkins shouted over interphone, reaching over Bruno's shoulder and activating the Scorpion antiaircraft missiles. Seconds later, he had designated two missiles apiece against the incoming fighters, and the AIM-120 missiles were on the way . . .

. . . but Bruno's delay in launching the antiaircraft missiles proved decisive. The incoming fighters started a descent at thirty miles that accelerated to well over three times the speed of sound, heading directly at the Megafortress. The Scorpion missiles expended all of their thrust in powering toward the attackers, so by the time the missiles closed in on their targets, they had no energy to maneuver and exploded several dozen yards aft of the high-speed attackers.

"Clean misses," Atkins said. "Stand by for pylon . . ." But just then, they heard a fast-pitched *deedledeedledeedle!* warning tone. "Missile launch!" Atkins shouted.

"Break!" Bruno shouted.

Just as Elliott was going to ask which way to break, Atkins interjected, "Hold heading, pilot! They're trying a nose-to-nose launch—very low percentage, especially against us. I've got the uplink shut down!" The Megafortress's powerful jammers shut down the fighters' attack radar and the steering signal between the missile and the launch aircraft; when the missiles' own terminal homing radar activated, the jammers shut them down too. At the same time, the HAVE GLANCE active countermeasures system destroyed the missiles' seekers with laser beam blasts. But the Megafortress's own attack radar automatically shut down so the enemy missiles couldn't home in on it, so they were temporarily blind again. "You see them out there, pilot?"

"Negative . . . wait, I got them!" Cheshire shouted. "They're headed right for us! Twelve o'clock, about five miles, coming down fast! Ready to break!"

"Go nose to nose with them, pilot!" Atkins shouted. "Nose to nose! Pylon launch!" Atkins powered up two AIM-120 Scorpion missiles and uncaged their infrared seekers instead of launching on radar guidance. Both missiles locked onto the red-hot superheated fuselages of the enemy fighters immediately, and seconds later, both missiles streaked out of the weapons pods on the wings right at their quarries. But by the time the Scorpions launched, the two Foxbat fighters had flown right over the Megafortress, missing it by just a few hundred yards. The incredible blast of the supersonic shock wave passing over the EB-52 felt like another nuclear explosion. Elliott and Cheshire looked on with amazement as the front cockpit windscreen buckled and wavered as if it was ready to implode again.

The Scorpion missiles switched from infrared to radar guidance, picked up steering signals from the side- and rear-looking radars, and streaked up and backward to pursue the fighters. They almost did not have enough energy to tail-chase the fighters—the Foxbats were flying three hundred miles per hour *faster* than the most sophisticated air-to-air missile in the world!—until both Chinese superfighters came out of full afterburner and began a hard turn back to the west to pursue the Megafortress. The sharp turn quickly sapped the big fighters of all their energy, enough for the Scorpion missiles to catch up to them, activate their own onboard terminal homing radars, and lock onto the fighters. One Scorpion missile failed to fuze properly and missed; the other made a direct hit, shelling out one engine and causing a massive fire. The pilot ejected seconds before his superfighter exploded in a terrific orange fireball.

"Attack radar up—I've got a lock on the last fighter," Bruno said. "Stand by for—"

"Better save it," Atkins interjected. "We've got only two Scorpions remaining, and it looks like the last fighter is bugging out. They were both going full blower on the attack, and if they do that they only have enough fuel for thirty minutes of flying time. He's on his way home. The closest of those fighter patrols are at eleven o'clock, forty miles and closing."

"We've got to get out of here, Brad," McLanahan said. "Those Foxbats got a pretty good fix on us, and they're probably vectoring in the other fighters. The U.S. frigates are at three o'clock, eighteen miles. Right turn to heading zero-eight-zero should get us back on coverage. We need some help from those frigates or from Taiwan air defense, if they're up."

"Sons of bitches!" Elliott cursed. He got a good look at the speeding Foxbat fighters too, and that was the closest he ever wanted to get to those big, deadly jets. His heart was pounding, his forehead sweating like crazy—he had never felt so close to death before in all his life. "They better be up here!" He switched to the secure satellite channel: "*James Daniel*, this is Headbanger, what's your status?"

"Vessel calling *James Daniel*, keep this channel clear and do not approach this task force," the operator responded.

"What in hell are you talking about?" Elliott retorted. "We're up here on patrol with you, you squid idiot! We saw the Chinese cruiser launch Stallion rocket torpedoes at you. What's your status?" There was no response. Furious, Elliott switched to the secondary channel and keyed the mike: "Atlas, this is Headbanger. How do you copy?"

"Loud and clear, Headbanger," the operator responded. "What is your status? Over."

"Our goddamn status is that we were under attack by Foxbat fighters and we've got four more formations of fighters closing on us," Elliott replied hotly. "Both frigates are also under torpedo attack. We need fighter coverage up here and we want permission to attack the Chinese warship that is trying to blow your frigates out of the water."

"Headbanger, this is Atlas," Admiral William Allen responded himself seconds later. "We copy you were under attack by Foxbats and have more fighters in the vicinity. The ROC is vectoring fighters at this time, ETA zero-eight minutes, flight of two F-16s. Second flight of four F-16s is scrambling from Makung, ETA one-five minutes. We recommend you depart the area and head towards the Pescadores." The Pescadores was a group of Taiwanese islands, located forty miles west of Formosa and sixty miles southeast of the EB-52's present position, where several Taiwanese air and naval bases were located.

"Heading one-two-zero, direct Makung," Denton immediately interjected.

"No, we're not leaving!" McLanahan shouted. "If we leave the frigates, they'll be defenseless—and we can use their help against those fighters. We're staying overhead the frigates until the Taiwan air force arrives. Nancy, get on the horn and send in Carter in the other Megafortress."

"You got it, Muck."

"Sounds like a shit-hot plan to me," Elliott responded. On the satellite channel, he radioed: "Atlas, this is Headbanger, negative, we're holding our position. There's a big ass ship, a cruiser or destroyer, about twenty miles northwest of your frigates." He could hardly believe he was having an argument with CINCPAC—*again*. "We've got it locked up, and we saw it launch those torpedoes. They were rocket-powered torpedoes, and we *watched* that cruiser launch them."

"The frigates are conducting anti-torpedo countermeasures at this time," Allen said, "but they did not report contact with any Chinese warships or submarines. We have had that entire region under surveillance for several days, and we noted no large warship movements . . . stand by."

"Jesus, there they go again—'stand by,' " Elliott said angrily. "Stand by and watch the Chinese blast us to hell."

"The *Duncan* has stopped dead in the water," Denton reported, as he zoomed in on the American frigate task force. He called up more information, then added, "Something's wrong—the ISAR's not IDing properly anymore."

"That might mean it's hit and may be sinking," McLanahan said. "If part of its structure is underwater, the inverse synthetic aperture radar won't scan it completely."

The interphone got very quiet after that—but only for a few moments, until Brad Elliott shouted, "Destroy that damned Chinese cruiser *now!* You're clear on the bomb doors! Launch the Strikers, dammit!"

"Brad, we wait until we get the word from CINCPAC," McLanahan said. Here it comes again, he thought—another long, drawn-out argument with Elliott on whether or not they should . . .

McLanahan stopped as he felt a familiar rumble and heard the sound of windblast, and the words "Strikers away." Jeff Denton, still in the offensive systems officer's seat, had obeyed Elliott's command and launched two Striker missiles at the still-unidentified vessel! He had quickly and efficiently designated the unidentified vessel, using touch-screen commands, and prosecuted a double Striker missile attack! Seconds after launch, the Striker missiles had ignited their powerful first-stage motors and blasted out over the Formosa Strait toward their target. They were supersonic just a few seconds later, climbing on a ballistic flight path to almost forty thousand feet.

"Jesus, Denton!" McLanahan exclaimed. "Steer those missiles clear!"

"Why? We're attacking, for Christ's sake!" Denton shouted.

"We don't have *permission* to launch!" McLanahan said. "Steer those missiles away from that target!"

Denton looked confused, stunned, and horrified all at once. "But the AC said—"

McLanahan didn't blame Denton; he was doing as his aircraft commander ordered: destroy the Chinese ship. Unfortunately, Elliott had jumped the gun. Again. McLanahan frantically checked to be sure that Denton hadn't locked up one of the Navy frigates—he hadn't. "Get manual control of the missiles, steer them towards the southwest, away from land!"

"Stay on the target, OSO," Elliott said. "Continue the attack."

From his jump-seat position, McLanahan didn't have voice command of the attack computer. When he tried to reach across, push Denton out of the way, and command the Striker missiles to steer away from the vessel, Denton pushed him back. "Hey, Colonel McLanahan, the missiles are on the way," Denton said. "That was the ship that hit the *Duncan* with torpedoes. The AC said to *attack,* dammit—why are you pushing me?"

"Because I'm the mission commander, Denton, and I say we don't attack until we get a valid order from CINCPAC to attack!" McLanahan said. "Break the sensor lock, Denton. Give me manual control!"

But it was too late. Just then, the TV image from the Striker missile's imaging infrared scanner appeared on Denton's supercockpit display, just seconds from impact. The first radar-only image was of a massive ship, very tall, riding very high out of the water. McLanahan hit a touch-screen button to switch to imaging infrared view—and then they saw it.

It was not a cruiser, or a large destroyer, or even a warship of any kind—it was a passenger and vehicle ferry. They caught a glimpse of some kind of barge or service tender being towed on a very short hawser behind the larger ship, which could have explained the ISAR's confusion over the proper identification of the target—but there was no doubt over the identification now! The ferry had a tall vehicle access amidships and three decks above that, and it looked as if it was choked with automobiles and delivery trucks. "Oh my God, it's a passenger ship, a ferry!" McLanahan shouted. "C'mon, Denton, break auto lock, steer those missiles away!"

Denton immediately deselected the AUTO LOCK touch-screen button on the supercockpit monitor, which gave him manual control of the missiles. McLanahan immediately reached over and rolled the trackball left . . .

. . . but it was too late. McLanahan and Denton watched in horror as both Striker missiles plowed into the port side amidships of the passenger ferry; they even clearly saw passengers standing on the port rail near the bow just before the missiles hit. Five seconds later, the second Striker missile registered a direct hit as well.

"Oh, my God," Denton muttered. "What did I do? What in hell did I do?"

"Forget it, Jeff—Jeff, dammit, snap out of it!" McLanahan shouted. "Your responsibility now is with your crew and your aircraft. Get on the radar and find out who we're up against." But it was no use—Denton was frozen, stunned by confusion, fear, and a dozen other emotions. McLanahan had no other choice. He reached across Denton's shoulder, unfastened his shoulder straps and seat belt, and one-handedly hauled Denton out of the OSO's seat. Denton did not resist this time. "Jeff, go downstairs, strap into a seat and parachute, and monitor the flight instruments. Make sure your seat is unpinned and ready. Go!" Denton was lucid enough to offer a silent apology to McLanahan before climbing down the ladder to the lower-deck spare ejection seats. McLanahan activated the Megafortress's attack radar, which scanned the skies in all directions; he shut it down as soon as the system had recorded all air, sea, and land targets.

In the meantime, Bob Atkins had swapped seats with Bruno and was now in command of the defensive weaponry. "Okay, crew, nearest fighter formation is now ten o'clock, thirty-three miles and closing," Atkins began. "I don't think they have a radar lock on us, but they got a good solid vector from the Foxbats, and they're headed this way. I've got a second formation low, twelve o'clock, fifty-three miles and closing."

"A low CAP, Bob?"

He studied his threat display for a moment; then: "Don't think they're fighters, Colonel. I'm showing surface search radars only—no air search or target-tracking radars. They're looking for the frigates. I think we've got anti-ship attack planes inbound. Colonel, call the *James Daniel,* see if they got the inbounds and find out if they can coordinate with us."

"Rog," McLanahan said. He switched his radio to the fleet common frequency: *"James Daniel,* this is Headbanger, how copy?"

"Headbanger, this is *James Daniel* on fleet common tactical one. Suggest you clear the area and head east. Stay out of this area. We are responding to inbound bandits at this time. Clear this frequency."

"Second flight of bandits, low altitude, eleven o'clock, forty-eight miles," Atkins reported. "I've counted eight inbounds so far in two formations. There's probably more. I need another radar sweep."

"JD, this is Headbanger. You have at least eight inbounds on an anti-ship missile attack profile, and we've got more than twice that number after us," McLanahan said. "Let's make a deal—you get the fighters, we'll take the attack planes. Deal?"

There was an excruciatingly long pause; then a different voice responded: "Okay, Headbanger, it's a deal. This is the TAO on the JD. Stay north of us, and we'll keep your tail clear."

"Copy that, JD," McLanahan said with relief. "Give us your search and track bands to avoid."

"Stop buzzer on India-three through Juliet-ten to keep our scopes clear," the tactical action officer on the *James Daniel* replied. "You're clear to jam all other freqs—and I hope you're not a bad guy, or else we've just screwed ourselves. You got a wingman?"

"Affirm," McLanahan said. "He'll be coming in from the north."

"Keep him north. Good hunting."

"Center up on the heading bug, heading three-zero-five to intercept," Atkins called out.

In the meantime, Nancy Cheshire was on the secure satellite frequency to Headbanger Two: "Two, this is lead, how copy?"

"Loud and clear, Nance," Colonel Kelvin Carter responded from the second EB-52 Megafortress.

"Authenticate echo-echo."

"Poppa."

"Loud and clear," Cheshire said. "Stand by."

"I got 'em," McLanahan said. He centered his cursor on the trailing formation of Chinese fighters, the ones closest to Carter. As he did so, the information from his attack computers was being shared with the second Megafortress, which meant Carter's crew did not even have to activate its attack radar. "Two, this lead, there's your bandits."

"Tied on radar," Major Alicia Kellerman, the OSO on Headbanger Two, replied. "I show you've only got two Scorpions remaining, lead. Maybe you better bug out."

"Let's see what kind of havoc we can cause first," McLanahan replied.

"Have fun. Two's in hot."

It took only the last two of Atkins's Scorpion missiles to break up the first formation. The formation consisted of eight Q-5 Nanchang fighter-bombers, copies of the Soviet Sukhoi-17 fighter-bomber, armed with four AS-10 electro-optical attack missiles each. The fighters broke up into four groups of two, spread apart and in trail by several miles—Atkins merely locked up the two lead formations. The Q-5 fighter, with variable-geometry wings, was fast and agile, but the AS-10 missile had a maximum range of only six miles and required the pilot to acquire the target using the TV sensor on the missile itself. Atkins jammed the Q-5's mapping radar, which meant the Chinese pilots had to climb so they could visually acquire the two Navy frigates—and that made them sitting ducks for Atkins and his Scorpion missiles. Both missiles hit dead on target, destroying two Q-5s, and their wingmen promptly did a one-eighty and headed for home.

"Pilot, mil power, heading two-zero-zero," Atkins ordered. "I've got two formations of two still inbound. They split up, but we know who they're going after—they gotta converge soon. We gotta be there ahead of them." The Megafortress banked hard in response, speeding southward toward the two Navy frigates. "Okay, I've got the closest bandits at our seven o'clock, ten miles—they're only a few miles from their launch points. Stand by for Stinger launch. Give me a hard turn to one-five-zero."

As Elliott threw the Megafortress into a hard left turn, Atkins activated the tail-mounted Stinger self-defense rockets, locked up the formation of Q-5 bombers to the west, and began laying down a string of Stinger airmines in the path of the Q-5 fighters. The airmines exploded far ahead of the fighter-bombers, probably too far to be seen, but Atkins was hoping that he might catch one or both of the fighters with the large cloud of flak pellets generated by the exploding rockets. When the Megafortress was just a few miles from the northernmost formation, Atkins shouted, "Hard right, heading two-five-oh!" and as the bomber turned, Atkins started pumping out rockets in front of the second formation.

This time, they were closer to the Chinese fighters—one direct hit. The pilot of the single-engine Q-5 fighter, his engine shelled out by hundreds of steel pellets from the Stinger rockets, bailed out seconds before his Q-5 fighter exploded when the engine tore itself apart. His wingman stayed on the attack run and launched all four of his AS-10 missiles, copies of the American-made Maverick attack missiles, at the *James Daniel.* The Chinese pilot locked all four missiles on target, then started a hard right turn away from the frigate—directly into the lethal attack cone of the Megafortress's Stinger tail cannon. At least six of the Megafortress's Stinger rockets hit home, shredding the Q-5's canopy, engine, forward fuselage—and pilot.

"JD, this is Headbanger One, one fighter launched on you!"

McLanahan shouted on the satellite fleet common frequency. "We show four inbounds!" But the warning came too late. The frigate's Phalanx close-in weapon system, a 30-millimeter radar-guided Gatling gun, destroyed two of the AS-10 missiles that had auto-locked onto the frigate, but the other two hit home. Their forty-pound high-explosive warheads struck the helicopter hangar and the forecastle. The nearly one-inch-thick Kevlar armor around the command spaces protected the bridge and forecastle, but the other missile destroyed the *James Daniel*'s starboard-side helicopter hangar, the 75-millimeter gun, and the amidships Mk 92 fire-control radar antenna, and an explosion in one of the starboard Mk 32 anti-submarine torpedo tubes created a fire and extensive damage.

Fully loaded and hungry for vengeance, Kelvin Carter and his crew aboard Headbanger Two attacked the second large formation of Chinese attackers from maximum range. The second formation of Chinese aircraft was four H-6 bombers, copies of the thirty-year-old Soviet Tupolev-16 Badger heavy bomber; each bomber carried two huge Hai Ying-4 Sea Eagle anti-ship missiles. Two H-6 bombers were hit by Scorpion missiles and were forced to break off their attacks, but the other two got within range of the Navy frigates, fired their cruise missiles, and turned for home. Carter's crew launched their last six Scorpion missiles at the Sea Eagle missiles, destroying two of them. The *Duncan* managed to destroy one with its 76-millimeter gun and damage the last one with its Phalanx close-in weapon system, but even damaged, the three-quarter-ton cruise missile devastated the *Duncan*. The missile hit the aft starboard quarter, tearing a huge hole in the stern.

It took several more minutes for Atkins and McLanahan both to declare the area secure. At least eight Taiwanese F-16 and F-5 fighters were nearby, patrolling the airspace from sea level to forty thousand feet. "JD, this is Headbanger, how copy?" McLanahan called.

"Loud and clear," the *James Daniel*'s tactical action officer responded. "We show clear to the north. The Taiwan air force showed up and kicked ass to the south."

"What's your status?"

"We both got hit pretty bad," the TAO reported. "We're still under way, but fires up on deck are still not under control. *Duncan* is heavily damaged—we're setting up to receive survivors. She probably won't make it."

"Crap," McLanahan cursed aloud. "JD, Headbanger One is going to clear off north and hit the tanker. Headbanger Two will stay on station, in case the PLAN shows up. We'll be rotating our coverage as long as you need us. We're fully anti-ship capable. We'll still need the Taiwan Air Force in the area to help with antiair coverage."

"Copy, Headbanger," the TAO replied. "We sure would appreciate all the help we can get. I sure as hell won't bad-mouth you zoomies anymore."

"Sorry we couldn't be more help," McLanahan said. "We'll be watching your backside. Headbanger One clear."

THE PRESIDENT'S STUDY, WHITE HOUSE
OVAL OFFICE, WASHINGTON, D.C.
WEDNESDAY, 18 JUNE, 2151 HOURS ET

It was right there, on a CNN "Breaking News Special Report"—live video of a sinking Chinese ferry, about twenty miles from Quemoy Island. Again and again, CNN also replayed the videotape that had been turned over to them at their Beijing bureau by the Chinese government—a video showing two missiles slamming into the ferry, the explosions, the fire . . . CNN was also showing videotape of a similar attack on the Chinese aircraft carrier *Mao Zedong,* during Reunification Day celebrations. First they showed the fireworks, the children, the flags, the awestruck civilians on tour—and then they showed the devastation just seconds after torpedoes from an unknown attacker slammed into the carrier. The videotape clearly showed the damage, showed the injured and dead civilians . . .

. . . and it showed what caused all that death and destruction, a captured Taiwanese attack submarine, forced to the surface, captured, then sunk by Chinese shore- and carrier-based naval forces.

"My God," someone muttered. "This is the most incredible tape I've ever seen. We've got to respond right away."

"The first damn thing I want everyone to do is to *calm down,*" the President of the United States, Kevin Martindale, said as he swiveled uncomfortably in his chair. The members of his staff and the military representatives were on their feet watching the TV monitors in absolute shock and horror. "I'm not taking any more phone calls from the media for the rest of the evening, especially from CNN. I don't care if Jane Fonda herself calls asking for more information." With the President in his study adjacent to the Oval Office was Philip Freeman, the President's National Security Advisor; Robert Plank, Director of Central Intelligence; and chairman of the Joint Chiefs of Staff Admiral George Balboa, representing the uniformed services.

Entering last and standing beside and slightly behind the President was his chief of staff, Jerrod Hale. "Secretaries Chastain and Hartman are not available," Hale told the President. "The Vice President and Mr. Ricardo are en route, ETA ten minutes."

"I need to talk to Jeffrey and Arthur ASAP," the President told Hale. Turning to his assembled advisors, the President began, "Phil, get us started."

"Yes, sir," Freeman said, opening a red-jacketed folder with the words "TOP SECRET" emblazoned on the cover. "About an hour ago, approximately seven P.M. Washington time, eight A.M. Hong Kong time, several very unusual and deadly events occurred in the Formosa Strait region almost simultaneously. We're seeing the press reports of what happened, but I have the preliminary field reports, and they paint a much different picture.

"First, several missiles were fired at two U.S. Navy frigates operating near Quemoy Island," Freeman said. "One frigate, a Naval Reserve Fleet ship named the *Duncan,* was hit by two torpedoes and slightly damaged. The EB-52 Megafortress was in the vicinity at the time of the attack, and the crew reported that it detected the missile launch and pinpointed the ship that launched the missiles. Without permission, the Megafortress attacked."

"Ol' Brad Elliott hit his intended target, too—except it turns out it was a Chinese *passenger ship,*" Admiral Balboa interjected hotly. "Brad Elliott disregarded orders and blew the shit out of a *passenger ferry.*"

"Casualties?"

"The Chinese report sixty-eight civilians dead, over two hundred injured," Freeman said somberly. "Unable to verify it yet, but judging by the videotape, that's an accurate number. Rescue efforts are under way, as we can see."

"Oh, God," the President murmured; then, in a much louder, angrier tone: "What possible explanation did Elliott give?"

"The crew claims that the ferry was towing a barge that made it look like a cruiser or destroyer on radar, and that the rocket-powered torpedoes launched at the *Duncan* and *James Daniel* did come from the direction of that ferry," Freeman said. "They said they were just protecting the frigates."

"General Freeman, I wish you'd stop being a mama's boy to Brad Elliott," Admiral Balboa exploded. "Technical glitches, wolf in sheep's clothing, saving the day, spooks and goblins—forget the damned excuses, because he's got a million of them. The bottom line is that Elliott attacked *again* without permission. He didn't do a complete target assessment and fired two heavy missiles at a noncombatant."

"But the Megafortresses redeemed themselves," Freeman went on. "They stayed with the frigates and helped to fight off a Chinese air attack on the frigates. According to reports from the *James Daniel* and the Megafortress's crew, China launched several formations of fighters and attack planes, including four heavy bombers with large anti-ship cruise missiles. Elliott and his wingman in the Megafortresses used their anti-aircraft weapons to shoot down a number of the attackers; Taiwan Air Force fighters helped to fight off several formations of Chinese fighters."

"None of this would have happened," Balboa argued, "if Elliott hadn't put those two missiles into that ferry."

"I disagree, Admiral," Freeman said. "Those fighters and attack planes were on the scene within minutes of the attack on the ferry. This was a planned attack, made to look like retaliation for our attack."

"That's bullshit, Freeman."

"All right, all right," the President said. He turned to Freeman and said, "Looks like Brad Elliott screwed up big-time, Philip. Is he on his way back to Guam?"

"No, sir," Freeman replied. "Both Megafortresses are on station with the *James Daniel* and *Duncan,* in case any Chinese naval vessels try to approach. The Taiwanese air force is also overhead, in case there are any more air attacks."

"Sir, we've got to stop fucking around with these damned B-52 monstrosities and take command of the region," Admiral Balboa said, completely abandoning all courtesy toward his commander in chief. "We need the *Independence* to move into the Strait to assist the frigates in recovery and withdrawal, right *now.* And we've got to initiate an investigation of that missile attack—Elliott and whoever else screwed up has to be held liable. Congress, our allies, and the American people are going to scream bloody murder over this. Elliott needs to have his nuts chopped off!"

"Admiral, I warned you, watch your damned mouth when you're speaking to the President," Jerrod Hale snapped.

"Jerrod, easy—I'm upset, too," the President said. "All right. Terminate all the EB-52 patrols, recall those bombers back to wherever the hell they came from—hide them away someplace where the press can't find them, until we have the spin under control. When they get back to Guam, I want a full investigation of the incident . . ." he paused, then added, ". . . with the intention of filing criminal charges against Elliott, McLanahan, whoever was in command of the aircraft that fired the missiles against the ferry. This is going to be serious." He paused again, then added, "And get the *Independence* group under way to take up patrol positions in the Strait. We can use commercial or allied salvage services to assist the frigates, but the reason we're moving the *Independence* into the Strait is to help the frigates."

"Yes, *sir.*" Balboa nodded and was on the phone immediately, issuing the orders. "In the meantime, sir, what do you suggest we tell the press about the attack on the ferry?" Balboa asked. There was a definite edge in his voice this time, as if he was rubbing the President's nose in the filth caused by his decision to send in the EB-52 Megafortresses. "We will *not* blame this attack on my frigates—*they* obeyed orders and did not open fire, unlike *your* damned thingamajigs."

"Admiral . . ." Jerrod Hale warned him, picking up on his disrespectful tone of voice. Balboa glared at Hale, but kept silent by taking an unrepentant sip of coffee.

The President did not show any anger at the chairman of the Joint Chiefs of Staff. "We tell them . . . that we had armed military patrol aircraft in the area that mistakenly fired on the ferry," he said. "No elaboration beyond that. We can report the rest in closed-door briefings if necessary, but no details about the Megafortresses to the press." Freeman and Hale nodded; Balboa showed little reaction. "All right. What else happened out there?"

"At almost the exact same time, sir, the Chinese carrier *Mao Zedong* was hit by three torpedoes as it lay at anchor near Hong Kong," Freeman replied. The President's jaw sagged, and he muttered a barely audible "Ah, shit." "It was part of Reunification Day celebrations; it carried a skeleton crew of about a thousand, and approximately a thousand civilians, most of whom had slept aboard the ship. The carrier reportedly sustained major damage. Casualties are reported to be heavy.

"The carrier responded with an attack by several helicopters, at which time they attacked and damaged a Taiwanese Sea Dragon–class submarine, forcing it to the surface. The crew was taken off the sub, and then it was blown to bits and sunk by gunfire from the carrier *Mao.*"

"Jesus," the President muttered. "What does the ROC say about it?"

"Taiwan hasn't issued any statements so far," DCI Robert Plank responded woodenly. The President looked surprised, then frustrated, then angry at the news. "We know that a couple Taiwanese subs have been shadowing the *Mao* since it returned to Hong Kong after the attack on Quemoy—we've got two subs in the vicinity as well, although we were careful to stay out of Hong Kong waters. Apparently the Taiwanese navy decided the *Mao* was too inviting a target and decided to be heroes and sink the son of a bitch. Their plan backfired."

"Simultaneously, it appears that a Taiwanese C-130 transport plane was detected near Lang-Ch'i Army Base, twenty miles west of Matsu Island—over the Chinese coast," Freeman went on, shaking his head in disbelief. "China claims that Taiwan was attempting either to drop a bomb on the base or insert spies or commandos into the area. The transport plane was shot down. Mainland China retaliated by launching rocket attacks on the Matsu Islands, the Taiwanese island chain located just off the Chinese mainland northwest of Taipei."

"What in hell is Taiwan up to?" the President asked. "Have they gone crazy? This is a damned nightmare! I want . . . Holy shit, look at that!"

They looked—and they were stunned beyond belief. There on CNN was a fuzzy, grainy black-and-white photograph—of the EB-52 Megafortress! The announcer said that the photograph had just been received by the Chinese News Agency, who had gotten it from the People's Liberation Army Air Force. It was a head-on shot, so it was difficult to make out details or get any solid identification—but for the men in the room, the identification was painfully easy. The B-52 fuselage, the unusual tail surfaces, the pointed nose, the weapons pod—it was the EB-52 Megafortress, all right.

"Very nice gun camera picture—of a top-secret stealth attack plane!" Balboa said sarcastically. "I guess the cat's out of the bag now, isn't it?"

"Save it, Admiral," the President said irritably. He noticed Jerrod Hale answering the phone on his desk—shit, he thought, it's starting already! Thirty seconds after the pictures were shown on CNN, the phone calls were coming in hot and heavy. "The official response about those photos is going to be 'no comment.' Is that clear?" Hale caught the President's attention. "What?"

"State Department is getting flooded with calls from the foreign ministries of Japan, Russia, North Korea, Iran, about a dozen others—they all want to know if we're at war with China and if we have a fleet of those Megafortresses deployed around the world ready to strike," Hale said. "They all want an explanation."

"We can expect calls to start coming in from Congress, too," the President said wearily. "All right, Jerrod, I'll start making calls—the Japanese prime minster first, then the Leadership, then Russia, then any other Asian allies that want a call. North Korea can go screw itself in the corner. What about Taiwan? What's Lee's explanation, dammit?"

"As best as we can figure without talking to President Lee," Freeman said, "Taiwan wanted to knock that carrier out of commission, then cripple Lang-Ch'i Army Base, which is the main staging point for China's invasion force for the Matsu Island chain."

"One plane? One bomb dropped by a transport plane? What kind of damage can one transport plane do?" the President asked.

"The transport was a C-130 Hercules," Freeman replied, "and Taiwan has the BLU-82 bomb in its inventory—that's a 15,000-pound fuel-air explosive bomb. It's enough to level anything aboveground for a radius of two miles. We don't have any verification that Taiwan employed a Big Blue, but it would be a logical weapon to use against Lang-Ch'i Army Base."

"Hold it, hold it—we're getting ahead of ourselves," the President said irritably, getting more and more confused. "Why hit this Lang-Ch'i base? Were the Chinese getting ready to invade Matsu? Was it supposed to be a preemptive strike to avert an invasion?"

"The PRC attacks on Matsu and Quemoy have been expected for many months, ever since the Chinese war games in 1996," Freeman replied. He searched his notes, then added, "China had deployed the 117th and 134th Marine Divisions, both reserve units, to Lang-Ch'i last year; they deployed the 54th Group Army, including the 165th Airborne Regiment, as well—nearly two hundred thousand troops in that area alone."

"Under the circumstances, I wouldn't blame Taiwan for lashing out in these two areas, if in fact they did," the President said. "So did China take Matsu?"

"Latest word is that no PRC troops have been landed on Matsu," Freeman replied, "but China has a very limited amphibious landing ship fleet, so a massive marine invasion was not anticipated right away. Matsu Air Base was bombarded and heavily damaged. But overall it appears that China is showing a bit of restraint."

That was a bit of welcome relief, however little. "What in hell is going on around here?" the President repeated. "Is Taiwan trying to goad China into attacking? If so, it's a suicidal plan."

"Mr. President, the first thing I'm noticing here is the coincidental placement of these video cameras on both the carrier and the ferry," Plank said. "They're obviously not civilian models—they look almost broadcast quality. Both cameras recorded the weapons impacts as if they knew exactly where they'd hit—they weren't photographing persons or events on deck, but pointed out over the side. China also got those tapes to the CNN bureau in Beijing in an awful damned hurry—they didn't even bother to review the tapes themselves, as if they *knew* what would be on them. And the observation that General Freeman made earlier—that those Chinese attack planes showed up within a half hour of the strike on the ferry—well, it looks suspicious."

"Bob, are you suggesting that China *staged* these attacks?" the President asked. "How is that possible? How could they know a Taiwanese sub was approaching the carrier? How would they know we had a bomber near that ferry, and how would they know when or if they'd launch missiles? It's a real stretch."

"I know it is, sir—I'm making an observation based on what I'm seeing on the news, with Chinese-supplied video," Plank said. "But it wouldn't be hard to set up. The attack on the carrier would be easy—simply lay some torpedoes in the water, shoot 'em off, and take pictures as they hit the carrier. The ferry attack would be harder to stage, but not impossible—lay the torpedoes in the water, send the ferry out when our Navy ships approach, set off the torpedoes by remote control, and hope the frigates fire back. I don't think they anticipated the Megafortress attacking, but they knew we had stealth aircraft in the vicinity."

"It's crazy, Bob," the President said. "Let's concentrate on what we know, instead of what we don't. I want—"

He was interrupted by Jerrod Hale's hand on his shoulder. "Prime Minister Nagai of Japan, on the 'hot line' for you."

"Oh, shit," the President muttered. Kazumi Nagai was fluent in English, so the President needed no translator—no reason to postpone taking this call. He picked up the phone: "Mr. Prime Minister, this is President Martindale. How are you today, sir?"

"I am fine, Mr. President, and I hope I find you well," Nagai responded. His speech was clipped and sharp, yet still respectful enough.

"You are calling concerning the news reports about the attacks against Chinese property, supposedly by American and Taiwanese forces."

"Yes, Mr. President," Nagai said sharply. "I was surprised and dismayed by the photographs—we knew nothing of such aircraft, and are very concerned that it was employed by you in this monstrous attack. Is it true that the aircraft photographed by Chinese reconnaissance planes that have been shown on CNN belongs to the United States, and was it involved in the attack on the passenger ferry in the Formosa Strait?"

"It's true, Mr. Prime Minister," Martindale replied. "I can explain further, as long as we are guaranteed full confidentiality of all the information during this call."

"I agree, Mr. President," Nagai said. "Please continue."

"It's an experimental long-range reconnaissance and attack plane, derived from the B-52 bomber," the President explained. "The same plane was involved in the skirmish that resulted in the Chinese nuclear missile attack, but our plane did not not have anything to do with the nuclear attack, except to intercept at least one of the Chinese missiles while in flight."

"Intercept? How?"

"That's not important right now, Mr. Prime Minister," the President said. "Revealing all the capabilities of the plane has nothing to do with the two incidents."

"It would be better if you allowed *us* to make that determination, sir," Nagai said acidly. "But please continue."

"In the most recent incident, the plane was on patrol when it detected a multiple missile launch from a nearby vessel. The aircrew incorrectly identified the vessel as a Chinese warship. One of our surface vessels was hit by a rocket-powered torpedo and was disabled. Fearing a second attack would destroy the crippled vessel, the armed reconnaissance aircraft returned fire."

"But if it was not a warship that initiated the attack, how could the aircrew launch an attack on an unarmed passenger ferry?" Nagai asked.

"This is as monstrous a mistake as your accidental downing of the Iranian Airbus over the Persian Gulf!"

"Mr. Prime Minister, this was an accident precipitated by China by making the ferry look like a warship on electronic sensors, and by launching some kind of missile attack from the direction of the ferry, perhaps by submarine," Martindale said. "I assure you, this accident will not happen again. The aircraft have been recalled, and an investigation has been launched."

"Will the results of this investigation be kept secret, as the existence and use of this aircraft has been?"

"I'll see to it that you get a copy of the results of the investigation as soon as it is prepared," Martindale said. "I only ask that this matter remain totally confidential. I hope I've answered all your questions. Thank you for—"

"Mr. President, I must convey the thoughts of many in my party concerning American military activities recently," Nagai interjected, his voice much sterner now. "It appears that you are very quick to initiate military actions, especially covert, stealthy actions, versus negotiations and consultations with your allies. Many members of my government, including members of all political parties, have expressed outrage over your activities. First, you attacked Iran without consultations and without a declaration of war; now you are embroiled in a conflict with China. In neither case were any of your friends or allies notified or consulted."

"All I can say now, Mr. Prime Minister," Martindale said, "is that my actions were necessary and vital to protect our national security interests. Your government was notified of our plans to initiate military action against Iran because of its attacks on Persian Gulf states—I'm sorry, but I did not feel it necessary to explain our plans in detail at the time. The important thing was that a wider conflict was avoided and peace was restored."

"Restored? Not when oil has nearly doubled in price over the past four months; not when oil shipments to Japan have been cut by almost ten percent!" Nagai argued hotly.

"If Iran had been successful in closing off the Persian Gulf and destroying the oil-producing capabilities of the Persian Gulf coast states, what do you think you'd be paying for whatever oil you got from there, Mr. Nagai?"

"My government is also outraged over your decision to support the independence of Chinese Taipei," Nagai said, rapidly switching to a different topic. "That was an ill-advised thing to do, Mr. President. Declaring your support for a rebel Chinese province, one that is in conflict with many of your Asian allies, including Japan, was a very unwise course of action."

"Again, Mr. Prime Minister, I thought it was best to act quickly in the best interests of our national security," Martindale said. "Taiwan's declaration of independence was a total surprise to me, as was China's swift action to form a naval carrier task force to threaten or destroy Taiwan or its territories."

"Your decision to take Chinese Taipei's side," Nagai said, again using the term "Chinese Taipei" instead of "Taiwan" or "the Republic of China"—that usage spoke volumes about the depth of Japan's resentment toward Taiwan—"has inflamed the anger of many in my country and my government. They feel America no longer supports Japan's vital national interests. It would be difficult for my country to support America's vital interests in Asia if you no longer support ours."

"What are you saying, Mr. Prime Minister?" the President asked. "America will always be a strong and loyal ally of Japan."

"I am conveying a warning to you, Mr. President, that America could be made to feel most unwelcome at its bases located on Japanese soil if it is ever perceived that Japan's national interests are not being served," Nagai said in carefully measured words.

"You're threatening American bases in Japan if we continue to support the Republic of China or defend it against mainland China?" Martindale said, trying hard not to get angry or excited. "Is that what you're telling me, Mr. Prime Minister?"

"China is a valuable trading partner with Japan—we have put aside our historical differences in favor of growth and prosperity for the future," Nagai responded. "Any actions, either against China or on behalf of Chinese Taipei, that might provoke further economic or military retaliation against Japan would be considered a hostile act against us. The people of Japan would become infuriated if it was learned that American warplanes or warships staging out of bases in Japan were responsible for an economic, political, diplomatic, or military calamity befalling Japan. In such a case, for example, access to those bases might be restricted to the supply of fuel and provisions only, not the supply of weapons."

"You're saying that if we continue our actions, Japan will prohibit American military forces from on-loading weapons for our ships and planes? That's what I'm hearing from you, Mr. Prime Minister."

"That is all I have to say on the subject, Mr. President. I hope that we, your true friends in Asia, are consulted before any other situations arise. What will your response be to the attack on your warships, Mr. President?"

"We will be sending the aircraft carrier *Independence* and its escorts from Yokosuka to the Formosa Strait to assist in recovery efforts."

"The aircraft carrier? Do you think that is wise, Mr. President?" Nagai asked, with a tone of voice that revealed his obvious displeasure at the news. "It will be considered a threatening act against China, a retaliatory action."

"We have a right and a duty to protect our vessels on the high seas, Mr. Prime Minister," Martindale said. "The frigates were attacked by Chinese fighters and attack planes, including bombers."

"Obviously reacting to the attack on their passenger ferry—a purely defensive move," Nagai interjected. "Sending your aircraft carrier now will only be considered a hostile act and a serious escalation of hostilities. May I suggest sending a support or rescue ship that does not have a strike capability? It will take your carrier several days to travel to the scene of the incident—other vessels can be dispatched much quicker."

"We will send whatever vessels or equipment we feel necessary to save lives and preserve our property and rights of travel on the high seas," the President said flatly. "If it takes a carrier, we'll send one—or two, or three if necessary. But we will not be chased out of any international waterways."

"That, sir, sounds like the words of an angry and desperate man," Nagai said bitterly. "Again, you flaunt your military power without regard to whom it might affect. Sir, with all due respect, I suggest you leave the *Independence* in port and assist your stricken warships by some other means. Japan will be pleased to assist you—we have salvage ships powerful enough to take your frigate in tow and keep it afloat, and we can provide them to you immediately. We even know that Chinese Taipei has salvage and rescue ships that can assist, and they can be on the scene within hours instead of days. But sending in the carrier *Independence* will only be seen as a hostile act, perhaps even an act of war. My government cannot support such a decision."

"I'm sorry we can't count on your support, Mr. Prime Minister," the President said. "But we will do whatever we feel is right and necessary."

"Can you at least assure me that you will not consider retaliatory or preemptive military actions against the People's Republic of China?"

"It never was my intention to initiate any offensive military actions against China, sir," Martindale responded. "All of the events in the past two weeks have occurred because of China's aggressive actions against the Republic of China and against America. Our moves have been in reaction to Chinese threats and intimidation. If it becomes necessary to act, we will. But I am not sending any warships into the Formosa Strait to intimidate, aggravate, threaten, or attack anyone. The carrier *Independence* will assist in recovery efforts only, and we will not seek retaliation. We will attack only if we come under attack."

"I hope not, Mr. President—I hope not," Nagai said. "I have one last question, Mr. President."

"What's that?"

"Sir, we have been notified by our intelligence services that you have convened your Strategic Command's Combined Task Forces battle staff," Nagai said. The President's jaw dropped open in absolute surprise. "We know that this battle staff is convened to organize and equip your country's strategic nuclear forces."

"Mr. Prime Minister, I cannot confirm such a thing."

"I understand, Mr. President," Nagai said. "I only hope that if this was true, that it does not mean that the United States is traveling down the slippery slope to a nuclear confrontation with the People's Republic of China. The movement of the *Independence* carrier battle group into the Formosa Strait will certainly elevate hostilities to a dangerous level already—if it became known that America was also considering reactivating its nuclear deterrent forces, the level of tensions worldwide would increase tremendously. Even worse, if it became known that the *Independence* or any of its escorts carried tactical nuclear attack weapons—"

"Mr. Nagai, I don't like what you're insinuating," Martindale interjected angrily. "I will not discuss the disposition of any of our strategic systems, and I will not tolerate veiled threats from you to pass along incorrect or misleading information designed to enbarrass the United States or further your own political agenda. I advise *you* to reconsider your actions very carefully. Thank you, and good night." The President slammed the phone back on its cradle. "No more calls from that rat bastard Nagai, got it, Jerrod? How dare he deliver ultimatums to me!" The President sat fuming for several long moments; then: "I want to talk with President Lee and President Jiang as soon as possible, President Lee first."

"The ambassador from the PRC, Hou Qingze, is standing by for you, sir, calling from New York," Jerrod Hale said. "Line two. He's been on hold since you took the call from Nagai."

The President nodded, impressed—and even less impressed now by Taiwan's silence. He took several deep breaths to wash the anger out of his head, then hit the button and picked up the phone: "Ambassador Hou, this is Kevin Martindale. Sorry to have kept you waiting."

"Not at all, Mr. President," Ambassador Hou Qingze responded in very good English, with a hint of a British accent. "I am honored to speak with you tonight. I first wish to convey the deep sadness and regret of President Jiang and the government and people of the People's Republic of China over the recent conflict between the Nationalists and our country."

"Does your country have an explanation, Ambassador?"

"I am sorry to say, Mr. President, that the People's Liberation Army Navy forces overreacted to certain actions by the rebel Nationalist terrorist forces," Hou said. "My government deeply regrets our actions and is very embarrassed."

"Overreacted? You fired *nuclear missiles* at Quemoy, sir."

"My government strenuously denies that we launched any nuclear weapons at anyone, Mr. President," Hou said sincerely.

"We've heard your denials several times a day for the past two weeks, sir," the President said. "It doesn't change the facts—we *know* the missiles were fired by your ships."

"We must respectfully disagree, sir," Ambassador Hou said. "But the purpose of my call, Mr. President, if I may, was not about the past conflict, but to explain our actions in this recent string of attacks.

"The torpedo attacks by the Taiwanese submarine shadowing the *Mao Zedong* carrier group could have been an accidental firing, or an insolated rogue attack. The sudden appearance of a Taiwanese submarine so close to our ships, after our nations had agreed not to sail any submarines in the Strait during the carrier group's transit, caused our naval forces to sound an attack alarm," Hou said rather contritely. "We were totally caught unawares, and our forces reacted.

"Further, it now appears that the so-called bombing attack by the Taiwanese transport plane was merely a navigational error. The pilot apparently had instrument problems caused by a nearby electrical storm that caused him to cross into our airspace, which alerted our air defenses, who then perceived the incursion as a prelude to an attack, to which we responded by launching a counterattack," Hou continued. "Again, our forces were caught unaware and surprised, which, combined with the announced attack on the carrier group just minutes earlier, caused confusion and fear, and so we overreacted. On behalf of my country, I am deeply sorry for this unwarranted action against the people of Matsu, and beg forgiveness."

The President was silent for several long moments. It appeared as if the Chinese had come clean—they were admitting that they screwed up! Their explanation seemed totally plausible: two isolated incidents, both sparked by Taiwan, occurring only moments apart, caused the Chinese military to surge forward. "I see," the President said on the phone, believing Hou but not yet willing to admit it. "What are your country's intentions now?"

"My government informs me that all further troop movements have been halted against Matsu, and no further attacks will be initiated," Ambassador Hou replied. "We regret the loss of life and the destruction of property, but under the circumstances I believe our reaction, dishonorable and unfortunate as it was, was fully justified. We shall transmit our apology to the Nationalist government immediately. And, in the interest of peace, we assure you and the rest of the world that the crew of the Taiwanese sub will be treated fairly. We are not in a state of war, but the sailors of the submarine that attacked our carrier will be treated as if they are prisoners of war—with respect and fairness. My government will also agree to submit the matter to an international tribunal."

The President was impressed and heartened at these proposals; it definitely appeared as if China was ready and willing to compromise and not isolate themselves. Were they being perhaps too willing? the President thought. "May we get a copy of your withdrawal orders and a written account of China's actions in this conflict?" he asked.

"I shall have it delivered to Secretary of State Hartman's office and to the White House within the hour, Mr. President," Hou replied.

The President was taken aback by the openness and cooperation Hou showed—of course, it all remained to be seen, but he was still surprised by China's apparent forthrightness. "Very well, Mr. Ambassador," the President said. "We look forward to your continuing cooperation in this very serious matter."

"I pledge my country's sincere cooperation," Hou said. He paused for a moment, as if embarrassed to bring up the point; then: "I have been instructed to ask you, Mr. President, for some sort of explanation for the horrible and tragic event that occurred near Quemoy a short while ago." He heard Martindale pause at the question, then hastily added, "If you wish not to speak of it now, sir, I understand. There are delicate and critical factors to be analyzed."

"There is still a lot of confusion over exactly what happened, Mr. Ambassador, in the incidents near Hong Kong and Matsu as well as the one near Quemoy," the President replied. "But since you've been honest with us, Mr. Ambassador, we'll be honest with you, as long as this information is held in the strictest confidence."

"Of course, Mr. President," Hou responded.

"The attack on the passenger ferry was prompted by a missile attack on two U.S. Navy frigates," the President said. "An armed patrol plane flying in the same area detected the attack on our ships and, mistakingly believing the missiles came from the ferry, returned fire. Our sensors reported that the ferry was a warship, and it was on a convergent course with our patrol ships, so when the missile attacks occurred, our patrol plane commenced an immediate counterattack."

"The EB-52 Megafortress bomber, it has the capability of distinguishing between different vessels from such long distances?" Hou asked.

The President's head jerked up at the mention of the Megafortress—they knew! The Chinese government knew about the Megafortress! This was the second conflict against the Chinese in which the bomber had been used, so it was not totally unexplainable—but to hear the aircraft's nickname used so casually was a great shock to the President, who had been involved with the weapon system since its inception and had managed to keep it a closely guarded secret, even from most of the rest of the U.S. government. "I cannot discuss types of aircraft or the capabilities they may or may not have," President Martindale responded, trying to keep his voice level and moderated. "All I can say is that the attack was accidental, and these patrol planes are being removed from the area to avoid any further accidents, in the interest of peace. We were hoping that you might have some explanation for the attack on the American frigates."

"We removed all warships and submarines from the Quemoy Island area, Mr. President, also in the interest of peace," Ambassador Hou said. "We do not have any explanation for this so-called torpedo attack. I can of course confirm that some naval air and air force units responded to the alert of an American invasion, and in their zeal overstepped their authority and attacked your frigates. On behalf of my country, I sincerely apologize for that attack. I have been advised that your Megafortress engaged some of our aircraft as well. A very formidable aircraft, I must admit."

"I trust the People's Republic of China will not seek any retaliation for this incident or any others that occurred today, and that we can work together to restore peace and stability to the region," the President said, ignoring the remark about the Megafortress. The amount of information Hou and the Chinese had gathered during the last engagement was incredible, he thought. There was probably no way they could ever keep the Megafortress secret again.

"The People's Republic of China shares and echoes those thoughts, Mr. President," Ambassador Hou said warmly. "I must tell you that my country's reconnaissance planes did make contact with the Megafortress patrol plane, but were under orders not to fire upon it after it withdrew from the area, even though it attacked the civilian ferry, attacked our defensive aircraft, and thereby caused so many deaths." The President of the United States gave a silent laugh—only the Chinese could call an H-6 bomber loaded with two huge anti-ship missiles "defensive." "We will not prevent any other armed patrol planes from entering international airspace anywhere in the region, but we do ask that these modified B-52 bombers be excluded from the region, in the interest of peace. The power of these combat aircraft is a significant threat to the People's Republic of China."

The President was again reeling from Hou's words. They knew about the Megafortress, all right! He was sure that soon the rest of the world would know, despite Hou's promise to keep all this confidential. "We agree, Ambassador," the President said. "As long as a state of war does not exist between our two countries, we will refrain from sending any heavy strike aircraft near Chinese airspace."

"Your words are wise and strong, Mr. President," Hou said warmly. "On behalf of my country, I thank you. In the search for peace, Mr. President, China still seeks reunification of its territories split apart from her by imperialists and rebels. The United States can play a critical role in that reunification.

"I have been authorized by my government to extend this invitation and request: Would the United States consider mediating talks between my government and the Nationalist government on Formosa, seeking complete reunification of the two Chinas by the year 2005? Like the successful talks between Britain, Portugal, and my country for return of Hong Kong and Macau, the United States could act as honest broker for the glorious reunification of China, while still preserving the economic strength and ideological diversity of the Nationalist movement. Will you do it, Mr. President? Will you consider President Jiang's request?"

"I'm honored, Mr. Ambassador, but as you know, I have already announced our intention of recognizing the Republic of China as an independent and sovereign nation," President Martindale said. "In our view, the Republic of China has established a strong and viable democratic government and society, equal to that of any nation in Asia, and therefore has earned the chance to grow and develop as an independent nation. I don't wish to offend the People's Republic of China, but I am prepared to support Taiwan's right to become independent. I hope that your country would recognize the reality of this situation and peacefully come to terms with President Lee."

"With the support of the United States, we are prepared to do just that, sir," Hou said. "We understand that you must still repeal the Taiwan Relations Act of 1979 and seek ratification of the proposal by your senate. The government of the People's Republic of China humbly asks that you simply attach an addendum to your proposal, agreeing *in principle only* to the notion of the people of Chinese Taipei seeking autonomy until the laws of the People's Republic of China can be liberalized, but fully endorsing the goal of reuniting the two Chinas by the year 2005. You would then have no need to expend political capital in repealing an existing law, and you ensure the support of your senate by seeking a worthy and satisfying goal, one that has already been endorsed by most of the world's national leaders."

"I will take that idea under advisement, Mr. Ambassador," the President said. "Thank you for your time and assistance. Good night, Mr. Ambassador." Hou was still thanking Martindale profusely for his time and patience when the President hung up. The President took a deep breath, then a sip of coffee. "Well, either Hou was a very convincing bullshitter or one sincere Chinese. They admitted they screwed the pooch."

"They admitted they overreacted, but they didn't admit they were wrong or not responsible," Freeman pointed out. "I still think they're too easygoing about all this. Hundreds of Chinese citizens and soldiers were just killed, supposedly by Taiwanese and American sneak attacks, and their ambassador is *apologizing?* Doesn't feel right to me."

"Still think it's a setup, Phil?" the President asked. "Still think China started it all, hoping to start an invasion?"

"As far as would the PRC risk attacking their own ships just to force a showdown with Taiwan?" He paused for a moment, then said, "I won't speculate. I suppose it's possible . . ."

Admiral Balboa shook his head and gave a sound of disagreement that sounded like an exasperated snort. Balboa was shorter and not as lean or athletic as Freeman, but he compensated for a lack of stature with an animated, expressive, restless demeanor that could not be ignored. He said, "Ex-*cuse* me, General Freeman, but in my opinion, it's ridiculous to suggest that the Chinese would shoot four torpedoes at its own warships just to *hope* to provoke Taiwan into starting a war. I think we can rule that idea out."

"I'm not ruling anything out, Admiral," Freeman said, "but I'll agree, it's pretty unlikely. But this incident is only ninety minutes old. It's just too early to know anything. Everything that Mr. Plank said rings true with me, tells me that perhaps the Chinese set this whole thing up."

"Like you said, General," Balboa interjected, "the invasion plans on Matsu were in place and well known for over a year. Taiwan's been threatening to sink that carrier if it ever entered the Formosa Strait. None of this is a big surprise."

"Well, the press has latched on to this incident like it's the beginning of World War Three," the President said irritably. He glanced at his watch, then looked at Jerrod Hale, his chief of staff. "Jer, have Chuck work up a media point paper for me for tonight. I want it made clear that I view these incidents with great concern, and I make myself available at any time to assist in negotiations for peace. I'm calling for a cessation of all hostilities in the Formosa Strait immediately."

"You may want to consider a line acknowledging our culpability in the escalation of this conflict, sir," Hale said. "We can't kill a hundred civilians and then say, 'Everyone, back off or else.' "

"I don't want it to look like I'm the one that started it all, either, Jerrod."

"I'd consider mentioning the call from Ambassador Hou, the pledge of cooperation, and your pledge to remove all armed patrol aircraft from the region," Hale said. "You're going to come under tough scrutiny anyway—now's not the time to be evasive."

"You're right. Let's set up a press conference for tomorrow morning." The President turned to Robert Plank and asked, "What's China's military up to these days, Bob? They've been pretty quiet over the past few weeks, haven't they?"

"Quiet, except of course for this carrier group that they claim just got attacked by Taiwan," Plank replied. "It's incredible to me how much the balance of power shifts when that carrier relocates—it's the biggest warship and most powerful battle group in the South China Sea region. Its escorts are considered third-rate, but the carrier group represents a significant threat to the entire region. The South China Sea belongs to China now."

"I think that's a little premature, Bob," Freeman interjected. Director of Central Intelligence Robert Plank was another one of President Martindale's political supporters, a partner in a prestigious Atlanta law firm before cochairing the President's election committee and running the campaign in the strategically important southeastern states. Plank knew little about politics and nothing about running an intelligence bureau. To his credit, he knew people, he knew international law, and he knew how to manage a team and manage a crisis. But in Philip Freeman's eyes, Plank was pretty much disengaged from the everyday business of the intelligence game and really put his skills to work only in tight situations.

"The Agency has their best team on the case," Plank said to the President, ignoring Freeman. "I can have someone brief you on China's specific military standing."

"What's China's next move, Bob?" the President asked.

"I think they'll sit and wait, hope this blows over, keep the pressure on Taiwan and us, and see what we'll do about it," Plank replied. "I see no reason whatsoever to get excited over yet another shoving match between the two Chinas."

"This is not a damned 'shoving match,' Bob—the Chinese brought nukes into the region and used them against Quemoy!" Freeman retorted.

"I think there's a power play going on in the Central Military Commission, and the nukes were not Jiang's idea," Plank said earnestly. "The dispersal of the Chinese carrier battle force, after spending so much time and money in assembling it, is proof that whoever came up with the nuke idea has been discredited. It would be a mistake, in my estimation, to escalate this thing any further by any overt actions on our part. We should definitely exclude the modified B-52 things from the area. B-52s have always had a very negative connotation—as in 'doomsday,' as in 'global thermonuclear war.' "

"I agree," Balboa interjected. "Things have been messed up pretty good with the Megafortress fiasco. But we need a presence in the Strait—we needed it two weeks ago, but now we need it more than ever. The *Independence* is fired up and ready to depart Yokosuka—I suggest we let it head down the Strait to assist the *Duncan* and *James Daniel*. It was supposed to be in Hong Kong for Reunification Day ceremonies, but I don't think that's a good idea now, for obvious reasons. The Vice President was supposed to be in Hong Kong for Reunification Day—is she still planning on attending the carrier rendezvous?"

"As far as I'm aware, she's still on," the President said. He turned to his national security advisor. "Phil? You agree with the plan to send the carrier into the Strait now?"

Freeman hesitated—which angered Balboa, although he kept silent. Finally: "Sir, the only problem in this whole thing is that I feel we're being led around by the nose by the PRC," Freeman said. "I smell a setup. Perhaps we should wait until Director Plank has a chance to investigate the incidents further before we send *Independence* into the area."

"Always gotta be the odd man out, don't you, General?" Balboa asked with undisguised exasperation. "With all due respect, General, I think it's *you* that's being led around by the nose—not by the PRC, but by Elliott, McLanahan, and Samson. We gave them a shot, and they couldn't come through, thanks to Elliott. If things get really hairy for the *Independence,* we can triple-team China with all three carriers—the *Washington* will be on station in a few days, and *Carl Vinson* will be right behind it."

"We should continue air patrols over the Strait—"

"We can send the P-3s out of Misawa or the S-2s shore-based at Atsugi," Balboa said. "If things get out of hand, we can send in F/A-18 Hornet fighter-bombers out of Okinawa. I think we can count on the Navy guys to simply observe, and not *start,* World War Three over there. U.S. presence should be a major stabilizing influence in Asia, not a destabilizing one."

Balboa was the definition of interservice bigotry, the President decided, but now was not the time to argue about any lack of objectivity he might be displaying. "Philip, anything else?" the President asked. When Freeman had no reply, he continued, "Have Defense draw up a plan of action; I want the *Independence* moving as soon as possible. Don't delay getting whatever help is needed for the frigates, but I want it known that *Independence* is going there to assist in recovery efforts only." He paused for a moment, then added, "Just for my own peace of mind, Admiral—none of our carriers carry any nuclear weapons, right?"

"Absolutely not, Mr. President," Balboa said. "All special weapons—nuclear, biological, and chemical—were removed from all Navy warships except ballistic missile submarines at least five years ago. None exist in the surface fleet."

"Not even pieces of one? No nuclear components?" the President asked. It was a well-known fact that the U.S. government "fudged" information on nuclear weapons aboard Navy vessels to bypass a country's "nuclear-free" policy by simply dismantling the weapons on board, so technically there were only "nuclear components" on board, not "nuclear weapons."

"No nuclear components either, sir," Balboa said. "Of course, we still have nuclear delivery components in the field—aircraft, missiles, et cetera—but I can certify to you that we have no nuclear weapons or nuclear weapon components in the field at this time."

"Good—because you *will* have to certify it, in writing," the President said. "Make your commanders do it, too."

"The security review that you ordered was completed on both Sky Masters, Inc., and the Megafortress project office at Edwards Air Force Base—all clean," Freeman interjected. "No special weapons have been detected, no special-weapon delivery subsystems have been installed or ordered or designed."

"Good—I want that report in writing as well, Philip," the President said. "Next, Admiral Balboa, get together with the Chiefs and Secretary Chastain and put the Megafortresses back in mothballs. Get them off Guam and back in the States soonest. We gave them a try, and it didn't work. Then get together with Naval Investigative Services and the Justice Department and start an investigation on those missile launches and the attack on the Chinese ferry. We might have to sacrifice some heads to show the world we're not on the warpath."

Admiral Balboa's smile was unabashedly broad and self-satisfying. "Yes, *sir*," he said with undisguised enthusiasm. "I'll take care of that embarrassing mess right away."

Balboa's anxiousness to start tearing at Elliott was a little unnerving, but the President let it go—it was time for Balboa to retake charge of his military forces, and time for the President to back off and stop micromanaging the military. He asked, "Status of the Strategic Command stand-up?"

"All of the Combined Task Forces are fully manned and ready to move when you give the word, sir," Balboa said. "Of course, the CTFs agree that we see no reason right now to gain any nuclear assets whatsoever. CINCPAC is still in command of the Pacific-China theater. If we identify a target in Asia, CINCPAC should gain whatever resources he wants to handle it."

"Fine," the President said. "I agree with them—we don't need any nuclear forces unless China tries to make another move using nuclear weapons. But I don't think we'll see any more of that. Give me a report from CINCPAC tomorrow afternoon."

Jerrod Hale had picked up the phone again to answer another call. The President noticed Hale's silent, almost expressionless signal. "Anything else for me, Admiral?"

Balboa was in mid-sip. He swallowed, looking expectantly at the President, then at Hale, then back again. "No, sir."

"Thank you, and good night," the President said, curtly dismissing him. Hale bent over to talk quietly with the President, effectively isolating the chairman of the Joint Chiefs of Staff. Balboa blinked in surprise, put down his cup of coffee with an irritated clatter of china, and departed. After Balboa departed, the President sighed aloud. "Senator Finegold— already? She couldn't even wait until morning?"

"You don't need to take this call, Kevin," Hale said. "You're busy handling the crisis. I'll tell Finegold that we'll brief the leadership before we issue any statements to the press."

President Martindale sighed heavily, rubbing the dull ache developing in his temples. He knew he should talk with Finegold; he knew that, if he didn't, the first thing she was going to do in the morning was get on the network morning shows, complain about not getting briefed in a timely manner by the White House, then put her own ridiculous spin on the developments. Without hesitating any longer, he hit the button on the phone: "Hello, Senator."

"Thank you so much for taking my call, Mr. President," Senator Barbara Finegold responded. "I'm sorry for interrupting you—I know how busy you must be right now."

"I'm afraid there's not much I can tell you right now, Senator," the President said cautiously. "The facts are that two Navy frigates were hit by Chinese submarine and air attacks in the Formosa Strait, and one of our patrol planes accidentally attacked a Chinese ferry. I don't have any independent confirmation on any other incidents over there."

"What kind of patrol plane was that on the news, Mr. President?" Finegold asked. "On the news, it looked like a B-52 bomber."

"It was a new, experimental class of long-range patrol and attack aircraft, based on the B-52 but with some modern enhancements," the President replied. "Its actions were totally defensive in nature, occurring only after one of our frigates was hit."

"Have you spoken with China yet, Mr. President? What are they saying about all this?"

"I have, and the Chinese are apologizing for their rash actions," the President replied. "Of course, they're blaming everything on preemptive attacks by Taiwan, an allegation that we have not yet confirmed."

"A Chinese aircraft carrier and a military base were attacked—if we didn't do it, then who else could have done it except Taiwan?" Finegold asked. "They got the submarine that attacked the carrier, and they shot down a bomber overflying their military site. I think that's pretty compelling evidence, don't you, Mr. President?"

"Do you want to take China's word for all that's happened, or would you like some independent confirmation first, Senator?" the President asked heatedly. Jerrod waved his hands palm-down at the President, reminding him to "take it easy."

"I see lots of innocent civilians killed and hurt on CNN, Mr. President," Finegold said testily. "Are you saying that all this is a fake, a fabrication by China? If it is, it's pretty good work."

"What I'm saying is, we don't have independent confirmation of anything right now."

"I'd like a joint congressional task force to go out there to look for themselves," Finegold said. "Can we count on Pentagon travel support?"

"Of course. Military, common carrier, whatever's available."

"We'd like to see that patrol plane first," Finegold said. "We'd like to talk to the crews, interview the commander, get some details."

The President hesitated, and he could feel the tension building. "That may not be possible, Senator," he responded. "They're still on patrol, assisting in recovery efforts. I've ordered the plane brought back to the States after they finish their patrol—that might be the best place to look at it and talk to the crews."

"I was hoping to do it sooner rather than later, Mr. President," Finegold said. "My staff tells me the bombers are based out of Guam—if that's correct, perhaps we could see them on our way out to talk with representatives of the Japanese, Taiwanese, and Chinese governments."

The President subdued an exasperated sigh. Finegold knew too much detailed information, details she could only get through direct communication with very high-ranking sources. He had hoped that Hale would be wrong about George Balboa squawking to Finegold, but it seemed more and more likely now.

"Very well, Senator. I'll see to it they're made available to you or your staffers," the President said. "But I caution you that the President is still the nation's diplomat. Although I certainly grant that members of Congress can visit and meet with any foreign leaders they choose, it is the President who makes foreign policy, negotiates treaties, and deals with matters of state. You carry much influence around the world, Senator Finegold, and your visit might be confused by foreign leaders as an official government communication."

"We will make our intentions and the purpose of our visit crystal clear, Mr. President," Finegold said testily, adding, "but I thank you for the civics lesson." The temperature of the Oval Office turned decidedly cooler just then. "May I ask what response you intend to initiate in the wake of these so-called Chinese attacks, made to look like Taiwanese attacks? Will you retaliate against China?"

"I intend to rescue as many survivors as I can from the disaster in the Formosa Strait," the President said, "and then I intend to bring our ships and soldiers safely home. After that, I haven't decided. But I do not intend to break diplomatic relations with China or mount any sort of retaliation."

"That's good to hear, Mr. President," Finegold said. "And I hope you'd be so kind as to consult with Congress before initiating any economic or military sanctions against China."

"Of course, if the opportunity presents itself," the President replied. "Thank you for calling, Senator. Good night." He hung up the phone before she could ask another question. "The nerve of that witch!" he said half aloud. "Instructing *me* on my duties and responsibilities to Congress!"

"You've got to be careful, Kevin," Jerrod Hale said. "Don't go to the mat with her over the phone—you don't know who's listening. If you want to chew her out or tell her where to stuff her suggestions, get her out here to the White House and then let her have it. Make *her* get dressed and haul her tight narrow Nob Hill butt outside. You can then bring several members of the House leadership over so you have a nice big audience to watch her squirm."

"Thanks, Jer. I know all this—I just need reminding, when the pressure's on," the President said. "All right. I want a shot-up, stripped-down Megafortress on Guam to show the senator—and I want all the rest of them off the island and into hiding or chopped up into confetti as soon as possible. Get on it."

OFFICE OF THE PRESIDENT, BEIJING, PEOPLE'S REPUBLIC OF CHINA FRIDAY, 20 JUNE 1997, 0917 HOURS LOCAL (THURSDAY, 19 JUNE 1997, 1817 HOURS ET)

"Under ordinary circumstances, Admiral Sun Ji Guoming, I would be most inclined to offer you congratulations for a job well done," Chinese president Jiang Zemin said coldly. Standing beside him was chief of staff of the People's Liberation Army, General Chin Po Zihong. "But I cannot do so. Admiral, you told me that you could bring down the entire pro-Western alliance, enabling us to merely walk onto the Nationalist-held islands without resistance. I have not seen this happen yet. What I have seen is dozens of deaths of our comrades near Hong Kong and our new carrier severely damaged *by our own hands,* nearly a hundred deaths from the ferry attack near Quemoy, nearly a dozen of our fighters shot down by the Nationalists without one loss of their own—and, worst of all, our ambassador in Washington *apologizing* to the President of the United

States and to the world on the floor of the United Nations for our actions!"

"You must have patience, Comrade President," Admiral Sun replied. "Allow me to summarize our recent achievements." Jiang nodded, and Sun went on: "The United States has removed two of its four warships from the Formosa Strait, and its submarines have been pulled back even farther from our ships and bases. The stealth bombers that the Americans sent to spy on us and assist the rebels to attack us have been discredited, exposed as aggressors, and soon will be completely removed from the region. The President of the United States has been exposed and labeled an aggressor, almost on a par with Saddam Hussein or Mohammar Quaddafi. He is being investigated for ordering the stealth bombers to attack Iran, and now he will be investigated for his secret undeclared warlike actions against us in the Formosa Strait, using the formerly secret modified B-52 bombers. His own people fear and distrust him—soon, his allies all over the world will fear and distrust him as well.

"More importantly, now the United States and the Nationalists have been isolated by the world community—the world sees them both as warmongers, willing to do anything to further their own aims," Sun went on. "President Martindale will find considerable difficulty in getting support from his congress for his plans to support the Nationalists' drive for independence. If we maintain the pressure and continue to open up in front of the world media, the momentum will swing to our side. Then Martindale may be forced to support our idea for reunification with Taiwan by 2005. With Taiwan once again isolated, even from the United States, it will be ready for annexation at any time."

"That all sounds fine, Admiral," General Chin said. "But we must still deal with the military realities here. The United States is withdrawing two frigates, but with two frigates and four submarines still in the area, they are still a very strong military force in the Strait—and we lost a good percentage of our fighters and bombers in that engagement."

"It is as I have said, General," Admiral Sun said. "Our J-series fighters must not engage Nationalist F-16 fighters unless they have full radar coverage and enjoy at least a six-to-one numerical advantage. In that fight, we had a three-to-one advantage and fared poorly. We also did not count on the American stealth bombers launching air-to-air missiles. The H-6 bombers would have had better success if they had only flown against the frigates' surface-to-air missiles or if the Nationalists had been forced to divide their fighters to chase after our bombers."

"Nonetheless, our losses were severe and swift," General Chin said. "I find it impossible to imagine that this plan of yours can still be accomplished when we lose forces to the Americans like this."

"In fact, this proves the truth of my plan, General," Sun argued. "Again we have shown that the Americans are difficult to defeat in a direct naval engagement, whether by air or sea. But the unorthodox attack on the Americans proved successful—we claimed two American Navy frigates, and we leave the Nationalists and the Americans confused and reluctant fighters in the Strait. The tide is beginning to turn for us, Comrade General."

"You claimed that you could draw the American carriers into the Strait, where they would be vulnerable—yet the closest American carrier, the *Independence*, is apparently ready to depart Japan, possibly to rendezvous with two other carriers somewhere near Formosa, possibly in the Strait itself," Chin observed. "They can still strike our coastal bases from their carriers, and still enjoy air protection from the rebel air forces on Taiwan."

"The *Independence* will never depart Japan, comrade," Admiral Sun said grimly. "Its death is already being planned—and with it, the death of the pro–Western Asian alliance as well."

"I think it is about time you informed us of what you intend to do, Admiral Sun," Chin said angrily. "It is obvious that the level of aggression has greatly escalated. If you intend on throwing China into general war with the West, be so kind as to let me know so I can alert our regular military forces and defend the motherland."

"It will not be necessary to mobilize the army, Comrade General," Sun said with a smile. "The biggest naval disaster since the Great War will occur, by our hands—and the world will be rushing to China's aid, to protect us against the great satan, the United States of America."

ANDERSEN AIR FORCE BASE, GUAM
THURSDAY, 19 JUNE 1997, 1444 HOURS LOCAL
(WEDNESDAY, 18 JUNE, 2344 HOURS ET)

"Do you realize what's happening?" Admiral George Balboa exploded. "Do you have any idea what you've done?" The chairman of the Joint Chiefs of Staff was seated at the conference table in the Joint Chiefs Conference Center at the Pentagon, but his voice was as sharp and as clear as if he were right there in the base command post's battle staff room on Guam. "Have you seen the news? That plane of yours is being shown on TV all over the damned world, along with pictures of your attack on that passenger ferry."

"We've seen it, Admiral," Patrick McLanahan said. He, Brad Elliott, and the rest of the crew of the EB-52 Megafortress involved in the recent skirmish in the Formosa Strait near Quemoy Island were participating in the secure videoconference between the Pentagon and Andersen Air Force Base on Guam. The base command post's battle staff room had been sealed and curtained off, with guards posted outside. To Patrick McLanahan, it was a little like closing the barn door after all the horses had run away. The world now knew of the EB-52 Megafortress— why all the security *now*? "The pictures of us were obviously taken by the MiG-25 Foxbats that intercepted us."

"What possible explanation can you offer the President for what you've done?" Balboa asked.

"The Chinese set us up," McLanahan said confidently. "We've compared notes with the crew aboard the *James Daniel,* and we agree—that ferry was altered to make it look like a warship."

"How in hell could they do that?"

"By towing that barge behind them," McLanahan replied, "they made themselves look another one hundred and fifty feet longer."

"They were towing a garbage barge, for Christ's sake!" Balboa retorted. "Thousands of those barges are being towed around the Strait every week, and no one's mistaken them for warships before!"

"A garbage barge with steel radar-reflective walls, being towed on a short rope very close to the ferry—and the barge was fitted with an IFF interrogator," McLanahan reminded him. "It was sending out identification interrogation signals just like a warship. Why would a civilian vessel have a Square Head IFF on board?"

"That's such a lame excuse, McLanahan, that I'm embarrassed for you for making it," Balboa said. "An aviator with your reputation making wild accusations like that to cover up your own mistakes—it's pretty sad. You obviously picked up a signal from someone else, or you mistook a standard marine nav radar for an IFF."

"But even if it was an IFF, as you claim, why in hell did you attack that ferry?" Balboa asked. "Even if that ferry really was a Chinese cruiser—and you geniuses should know China doesn't *own* any cruisers—you didn't have permission for any weapon releases, let alone those Striker rocket bombs. Why did you open fire?"

"As we explained in our report, Admiral, the Navy frigates were under attack by rocket-powered torpedoes," McLanahan said. "We have no defenses against torpedoes—our decoys or jammers wouldn't have done any good. All our sensors indicated that a Chinese warship had launched numerous Stallion torpedoes at the frigates. The *Duncan* was a sitting duck for another salvo. We had no choice but to return fire."

"Even though you didn't have permission, even though you were not given a command."

"I had permission to launch," Jeff Denton interjected.

"What was that?" Balboa asked. McLanahan turned away from the videoconference camera and glared at Denton to remain quiet. "What did you say, Captain Denton?"

"Nothing."

"Repeat what you said, Captain, or I'll have you arrested and thrown in the brig right now."

Denton looked at Elliott, then at McLanahan, who wore expressionless faces now—the bell could not be unrung. "Sir, the frigates were under attack."

"Who ordered you to launch, Captain?"

Denton paused, then lowered his eyes. "General Elliott," he said in a low voice.

"Repeat that last?"

"General Elliott," Denton blurted out. "Sir, we were under attack by what we thought was a Chinese cruiser, by four formations of Chinese fighters, and then by Foxbat fighters. I was in the OSO's seat—I controlled the Strikers."

"But it was Elliott who ordered you to launch, correct?"

"The *Duncan* was dead in the water, and the other frigate was coming about to help it," Denton said excitedly. "Our guys were going to get plastered. I knew we had to do something. So when General Elliott ordered me to attack the cruiser, I did. The computer said it was a cruiser, Admiral. The computer was running good."

"That's enough, Captain," Balboa said. "That's enough—to file charges in federal court against General Elliott for criminal misconduct. Maybe even murder in the second degree."

"*What?*" McLanahan shouted. "You've got to be joking, Admiral!"

"You think that's funny, Mr. McLanahan? This is even better—I'm going to file charges against *you* for the same thing. You were the mission commander, and even though you had Denton in the seat, you were responsible for his actions. And because Cheshire, Atkins, Bruno, and Denton are all active-duty officers, I'm preferring charges against them under the Uniform Code of Military Justice for disobeying a direct order, for conduct unbecoming an officer, and for dereliction of duty."

"George, I was expecting you'd try to get me thrown into jail," Brad Elliott said with amazing calm, "but to threaten any of these other outstanding individuals with a crime is beyond ridiculous—it's psychotic. If you carry through with this stupid idea, you're the worst example of a leader that has ever worn a uniform."

"I believe *that* honor has already fallen to *you*, Elliott," Balboa said. "And I'm not through yet. Because of your illegal, criminal actions, the entire Sky Masters, Inc.'s, Megafortress project has been compromised, and it now falls upon the government to clean up the mess. As employees, officers, directors, and shareholders of the company, yours and Mr. McLanahan's actions have implicated Sky Masters, Inc., in your criminal activities as well. You can kiss any idea of a military service contract good-bye, I'll see to that. How would it look to reward a company that started a nuclear exchange and killed hundreds of civilians with a multimillion-dollar defense contract?"

"George, the only persons you're going to harm are those who believe in things like performance, value, integrity, and honesty," Elliott said. "Obviously, you don't believe in anything like that. Our hardware and our people did a good job. You shouldn't punish a good company because you want to make *my* life miserable."

"Fortunately, it's all tied together, Elliott," Balboa said. "I get to shit-can you and your friends all at once—and you brought it all on yourself. All you had to do was obey orders and stay out of the fighting, but you didn't, and now I've been ordered to make sure that you don't screw up again. Here are your new orders, folks, and if you disobey them, you will find yourself in prison and your company shut down, buried in tax liens so deep you'll need a bulldozer to get out from under them:

"Unfortunately, since you are the only ones who know how to fly those things you've been screwing with, I can't confine you in the custody of federal marshals until you return to the States. Within three days, you are to make repairs to your aircraft sufficient to make them airworthy, and then you will return all of the aircraft leased from the government directly to the Aerospace Maintenance and Regeneration Center at Davis-Monthan Air Force Base, Tucson, Arizona—the Boneyard."

"You can't do that, sir," McLanahan said quickly. "Those planes are out on a long-term lease with Sky Masters, Inc. The money's been paid."

"Well, that explains a lot, McLanahan—you only care about your contracts, your money, not about obeying orders, or preserving national security, or selling out the commander in chief," Balboa said. "Forget the money, McLanahan—your company will never see it, and anything already paid will be seized by the government. The lease will be canceled. The money we'll seize will be used to pay for the federal marshals I've assigned to guard the aircraft and to keep you and the folks from Sky Masters, Inc., under surveillance."

"But those planes belong to Eighth Air Force and Air Combat Command," McLanahan said. "I signed for them myself from General Samson and ACC. They're not fragged for the Boneyard. They still have assigned hangar space and a project office at Edwards."

"Not anymore they don't," Balboa said. "I recommended they be dismantled and the program canceled, and the Chiefs will agree.

"If the aircraft are not flyable, the aircraft will be destroyed in place, wherever they are, and the costs of the destruction and cleanup will be charged to Sky Masters, Inc., in the lawsuit that will be filed that same day. Written orders will be transmitted to you shortly. That is all." The computer announced that it had cut off Guam from the videoconference.

"Shit, I can't believe it," Elliott swore. He got up slowly, massaging his left arm and shoulder. He popped a couple of antacid tablets and washed them down with a cup of coffee. "Balboa's an asshole. He always was. He's probably still carrying a grudge from our days at the National War College. He can't stand to lose face. He'll blame everybody else for the smallest failure and take away anyone else's accomplishments."

Patrick McLanahan opened the door to the command post battle staff room, which signaled Jon Masters and Wendy McLanahan that they were permitted to enter. He saw the looks on their faces, and knew that they had been listening in to the entire communication—after all, Jon Masters had designed the satellite-based communications system they were using, so he would know how to bypass the Pentagon security encryption routines. "I can't believe this—it's like a nightmare," Wendy said, as she came over and put her arms around her husband. "They can't do this! You risked your lives for this project, and now he wants to throw you in *jail?*"

"I believe he can do it," Patrick said. "He's got my attention. Jon?"

"Already called home plate, and the legal beagles are on their way—plus they're filing injunctions in D.C. and in Arkansas federal court, trying to prevent Balboa from canceling the contract without a performance review," Jon Masters said. "But Balboa moved even quicker—he's already got Navy SPs from Agana Naval Base guarding the planes. They've got the ramp shut down—nothing's moving.

"The lawyers say we can probably keep ourselves out of court, maybe even get the contract money, but they think Balboa can throw us in jail just by uttering the magic words 'national security,' and they're positive he can have those planes chopped up into little pieces anytime he wants. He's got my attention too."

"Let me call in my markers, Muck," Elliott said earnestly. He had found a seat and was leaning forward, elbows on his knees, hands holding his head. "Balboa's got plenty of skeletons in his closet, and I know the boys who can take 'em out and put 'em on display. He'll back off pronto, I guarantee it. If it doesn't work, we'll go right to the White House—heck, Muck, you and me, we got dirt on Martindale that I know will make him squirm."

"Brad, I told you already, I'm not interested in fighting the Pentagon over this," McLanahan said. He studied Elliott for a moment, and decided that he felt much worse than Elliott looked right now. "We've lost. We've invested millions in the project, but it just won't get on track with brass like Balboa fighting us from the top. We just can't do it. It's not fair to ourselves, it's not fair to our loved ones, and it sure as hell isn't fair to the shareholders."

"Why in hell are you so concerned about shareholders, Patrick?" Elliott said angrily. "Jeez, have you completely lost your entire spine?"

"My damned priorities are different, Brad," McLanahan said. "I work for Jon now, not the U.S. government. I've sold everything I own to invest in Sky Masters, Inc., and help this company, and I don't want to see Balboa and the federal courts drain our capital and our life savings fighting lawsuits. If we cooperate and let the government hide us, we can walk away with our company intact, ready to develop more technology and compete for more contracts. But if we fight them, they'll sic federal marshals and lawyers and judges on us for the next ten years—

and we can still lose. I don't want my child to have a father in a federal penitentiary."

"Listen to yourself!" Elliott shouted, jumping to his feet. "We did good out there, Patrick. You're letting bozos like Balboa make you think that you screwed up. Nobody screwed up here—not you, not Denton, not me. We did what we *knew* was right. Balboa is trying to make us believe we did the wrong thing and that we deserve to be punished—next, he'll be telling us that we're not going to jail because *he* interceded on our behalf. It's bullshit, Patrick! Don't fall for it! If you give up, if you let assholes like Balboa chop up nearly ten years of hard work, we lose— just as surely as if we lost a one-hundred-million-dollar lawsuit."

"Forget it, Brad," McLanahan insisted. "It's not worth the fight, not worth the aggravation. We did some good jobs in the Megafortresses, but the Pentagon doesn't want them. We can't fight them all."

"At least we'll give it a fighting chance," Elliott said. McLanahan shook his head and headed for the door to the battle staff room. "Dammit, McLanahan, I already lost one organization because I let the pencil-pushers and brown-nosers tell me that I couldn't cut it. Now it's happening again—except *you're* letting it happen."

"Brad, I'm tired. I've been shot at and yelled at and kicked around all day," McLanahan said. "I'm getting out of here."

Elliott blocked his path. He was almost a head taller than McLanahan, but in size and physical strength, he was no match for his young protégé—but that didn't stop Elliott from getting into his longtime colleague's face. "What's the matter, Muck? You ready to hang up your spurs and turn your back on your friends just because you're too scared or too tired to stand up to someone? You want to just sit back on your ass at your desk and push papers and collect your salary and pension, while jerkoffs like Balboa screw Jon and everyone else in this project?"

"Brad, give it a rest."

"I want to know exactly what you plan on doing about this, Mr. Mission Commander, Mr. Corporate Executive," Elliott shouted, sweat popping out on his forehead in large glistening drops. "Answer me!"

"Brad, c'mon," Wendy tried.

"No, wait just a sec, Doc," Elliott said. "Let the corporate big shot here tell us what he intends to do. How are you gonna sell us out? You gonna hide behind Masters's lawyers?"

McLanahan was glaring at his old mentor and friend, his jaw tight, his blue eyes blazing. Wendy saw the building rage in his eyes and tried to hurry him to the door. "Brad . . ."

"You forgetting about Cheshire, and Atkins, Denton and Bruno, the ones who volunteered for the project?" Elliott said. He was almost nose to nose with McLanahan now, his breath ragged and excited, his eyes blinking from the tension, veins pulsing in his neck from the anger. "Are your lawyers going to help them out? Or are they going to be chewed up and spit out by Balboa and his JAGs?"

"Brad, let's table this discussion for later," Wendy said resolutely, taking Patrick's hand and leading him to the door.

"Talk some sense into your old man, Doc—hey, don't you walk away from me! You show me some respect, mister!" Elliott shouted—and then he made the mistake of trying to pull McLanahan around to face him. Instead, he shoved Wendy in the back, and she lost her balance and crashed facefirst into the door that Patrick had just half opened.

Patrick McLanahan caught Wendy before she sagged to the floor, stood her back up on her feet, made sure she was going to stand on her own, saw that she wasn't hurt—and then turned on Elliott. With never-before seen quickness, Patrick had Brad Elliott's neck in his hands and slammed him back to the wall. "You old son of a *bitch!*" he snarled in a low, menacing voice. "You ever touch Wendy again, I'll break your neck!"

"I'm all right, Patrick!" Wendy said. "Let him go!"

Patrick felt hands on his arms right away—Cheshire and Atkins, ready to pull him away from Elliott—and the anger dissipated immediately when he heard Wendy's voice. He loosened his grip on Elliott's neck—but Brad still seemed to be choking. When he released him, he immediately collapsed. Patrick was able to lower him gently to the floor and noticed his shortness of breath, the panicked look in his eyes, and the contortions and spasms in his left arm.

"Christ, I think he's having a heart attack!" he shouted. "Get an ambulance—*now!*" Nancy Cheshire was already on the phone, dialing the paramedics at the base hospital. McLanahan unzipped Elliott's flight suit, exposing his chest, preparing to give CPR if necessary. "Hang in there, Brad, goddamn it," Patrick McLanahan said. He felt crushed inside, thinking that the last words his best friend might have heard from his lips were words of anger and hate. "C'mon, Brad, you old warhorse, hang in there. . . ."

"Can't the damned harbor police do anything about this?" U.S. Navy Captain Davis Manaus complained. "Where the hell are they?"

"They're out there already, skipper," U.S. Navy Captain Sam Anse replied, scanning the area with his binoculars. "Every harbor patrol, prefecture police, and Maritime Self-Defense Force unit stationed in the Bay is out there."

It was not hard to understand why it was impossible to believe that fact. Admiral Manaus's ship, the American aircraft carrier USS *Independence,* was surrounded by what one lookout estimated as two thousand boats of every shape, size, and description, all decked out in white sheets and flying white flags. Most of the people on each ship were dressed in white, with white bandannas with the red "rising sun" of Japan over their foreheads. Interspersed among the white-clad protesters had to be another several dozen boats with camera crews from all over the world. The police and Navy security units had been circulating around the *Independence* all night and all morning, keeping protesters away from the carrier's hull; many of the protesters were carrying buckets of red paint, obviously destined to decorate the ship's hull.

It took several more hours and much restrained but angry appeals all the way to the office of the prime minister, but eventually the tugs were allowed to be brought into position, and the *Independence* was moved away from the wharf and into the bay. Protesters on loudspeakers and bullhorns tried to convince the tugboat captains and harbor pilots not to assist the carrier out, and for a brief moment it appeared as if their appeals might take hold, but seemingly by inches the great warship was under way and heading out into the Gulf of Sagami.

The *Independence,* now with its escort group assembled and in formation—three anti-submarine warfare frigates, two Aegis guided-missile cruisers, and a replenishment ship—was about twenty miles south of the tip of the Miura Peninsula, roughly in the middle of the Gulf of Sagami, when it was safe for fixed-wing flight operations to get under way again. There were still a few protesters shadowing the carrier group, but they were not allowed closer than three miles from the carrier, well outside the perimeter established by the escort frigates. The battle group had accelerated now to flight ops formation speed of twenty-seven knots, so very few of the smaller protester's vessels could keep up.

The first aircraft to launch were the rescue helicopters, two huge Sikorsky SH-3H Sea Kings with two pilots and two rescue swimmers on board. Next were the E-2 Hawkeye radar planes, which could extend the radar "eyes" of the battle group out almost 400 miles. The Hawkeye's crew would act as the long-range air traffic controllers for the carrier, vectoring incoming aircraft toward the carrier until the final approach controllers on board the carrier itself took over. One KA-6D aerial refueling tanker then launched, followed by four F-14A Tomcat fighters on outer perimeter air defense patrol, with two more Tomcats positioned on the number three and four catapults on alert five status, ready to launch and help defend the carrier group.

The first aircraft to arrive was the least attractive but most appreciated aircraft of all—the twin turboprop C-2A Greyhound, known as the "COD," for Carrier Onboard Delivery. The COD ferried crewmembers, passengers, supplies, spare parts—and most importantly, the mail—on and off the ship several times a day. Ungainly and slow when "dirtied up" and ready for the "trap," or landing on the carrier, the COD was cleared to land, reporting its landing weight as 48,000 pounds, just two thousand shy of max landing weight—it was loaded to the gills with crew members who hadn't made the departure, extra crew members, a few civilian passengers participating on a "Tiger Cruise" for a few days, and a pallet of mail sacks.

The approach was a little high, and that spelled trouble right away. Nailing the airspeed, nailing the initial approach and rolling in on final at the right altitude to capture a centered Fresnel glide path landing indicator, called the "ball," then nailing the desired angle of attack, making very slight corrections to stay on centerline and stay on glide path—that was the key to a successful "trap." Corrections in a heavyweight COD had to be made very, very carefully—crew members describe it as "thinking" throttle movements rather than actually applying huge inputs and then having to take them back out again. Many pilots liked to carry a little extra airspeed, knowing that a plane configured to land, with gear, flaps, slats, and hook extended, was going to slow down fast with the slightest reduction in airspeed; also, it took several seconds after any throttle advancement for the turbine engines to spool up to desired power, so being on the positive side of the power curve was important. But high and fast was a bad combination.

Altitude was corrected with power, airspeed corrected with angle of attack—just the opposite of cruise. The pilot pulled off a fraction of an inch of power, and immediately felt the sink rate increase. He had to ignore the sensation of sinking too rapidly and concentrate on his scan—ball, airspeed, ball, AOA, ball, centerline, ball. Enough of a power correction: the LSO, or landing system officer, ordered more power just as the pilot was pushing the throttles forward. The tiny speck of a carrier deck was quickly becoming bigger and bigger. Enough power; recheck and correct pitch angle to get the AOA indexers centered again.

OK, OK, the pilot told himself, this was not going to be a pretty landing, but it was the first of about three he'd make today. He was now at the reins of a bucking bronco. If everything starts smoothly and inputs are gentle, the ride down the chute is smooth and easy—relatively speaking for carrier landings. But very often, if one parameter is off, then it'll be hands and feet dancing on the controls, throttles, and pedals all the way—and that's the way it was on this one. The ball was staying centered, but it was like controlling a marionette dance routine.

On touchdown, he was still on the backside of the power curve, nose very high, power coming up but way late. All carrier landings were characterized as "controlled crashes," and landings in a heavyweight COD were even more so. This was going to be a doozy—a two-wire trap, just fifty feet from the edge of the fantail, slow and wobbly. He was not going to earn any Brownie points for that one. The nose was going to come down like a felled tree if he didn't fly it down carefully before the arresting wires stopped him short. The pilot felt the jerk of the arresting wire, saw the deck director signal a good catch, pushed the throttles to full power in preparation for a bolter in case of a broken wire, saw the edge of the landing deck coming up to meet him but at the same time saw the airspeed rapidly decreasing, felt his body squished harder and harder against the shoulder straps, jammed the throttles to idle . . .

. . . and then his aircraft, his carrier, his world disappeared in a flash of white light.

"The most important lesson
learned from the Persian Gulf
War of 1991 is this: if you are
ever to go to war against the
United States of America,
be sure to bring a
nuclear weapon."

—Republic of India's
military chief of staff

CHAPTER
FIVE

**ELLSWORTH AIR FORCE BASE, RAPID CITY,
SOUTH DAKOTA
FRIDAY, 20 JUNE 1997, 2232 HOURS LOCAL
(SATURDAY, 21 JUNE, 0032 HOURS ET)**

With flashes of lightning from an early-summer thunderstorm illuminating the night sky to the west, the first aircrew bus rolled out onto the aircraft parking ramp. The ramp was brown and dusty with disuse, with tall weeds poking up through the cracks in the reinforced concrete. The bus rolled along in between two long lines of airplanes, finally turning in and parking between two of them. All of the planes were surrounded by maintenance men and vehicles; all except the ones toward the back of the line were encircled with red ropes supported by orange rubber cones, with the cones toward the nose of each aircraft marked "ECP," or "Entry Control Point." The aircrew stepped off the bus, unloaded their gear, and shuffled toward the armed security guard at the gap in the rope marked "ECP" as if they were in a dream—or perhaps caught in a nightmare. Although it was much easier and quicker to just step over the red rope surrounding the plane, the crew members knew what dire consequences awaited them if they dared to do so—security police terms like "kiss concrete" and "jacked up" came immediately to mind.

The guard checked each crewman's line badge against his access list, then waved them inside the roped-off area. They met with the airplane's crew chief and assistant crew chief, where they reviewed the aircraft Form 781 maintenance logbooks, accomplished a short crew briefing covering restricted area access and preflight actions, then ran through the first few steps of their "Before Boarding" and "Before Power-Off Preflight" checklists.

Two of the crewmen, each carrying one of the steel CMF containers and their helmet bag, began climbing up the long, steep ladder into the belly of the plane, followed by the other two crewmen carrying the canvas pubs bags. After a quick check to make sure both of the aft ejection seats were safetied, they piled their gear onto the upper deck, then used "monkey bars" to pull themselves up into their seats both left and right. Once they were in their seats, the second two crewmen could climb past them, crawl down a short tunnel, over the chemical toilet, and into the cockpit.

While the pilots were performing their "Power-Off Preflight" checklist, the two crewmen behind them slid one steel canister each into slots behind and beside their seats, then secured the canisters to the aircraft with steel cables and padlocks. Each CMF container had two compartments: the smaller top compartment was closed and sealed with a steel numbered trucker's container seal, secure but easy to open and access; the bottom compartment was sealed with the same cable and padlock that secured the canister to the plane as well as a trucker's seal—a little more difficult to open than the top compartment.

The top compartment of the CMF, or Classified Mission Folder, container held the launch authenticators, the decoding documents necessary to authenticate a launch order under the SIOP, or Single Integrated Operations Plan—the plan to fight an intercontinental nuclear war. The lower compartment, secured by a padlock as well as a steel seal to better protect the contents, held the decoding documents needed to authenticate a nuclear attack order and to prearm the nuclear weapons, the attack timing sheets, and the charts and computer data cassettes they needed to fly their attack route. The green canvas bags contained more decoding documents and the charts and computerized flight plan cassettes to fly the escape and refueling routes on the way to the Positive Control Turn-Around Point, known as the "fail-safe" point—the point where they could not pass without a valid attack execution order broadcast by the President of the United States himself.

They opened the green canvas bags and took out several red vinyl binders, paper-bound booklets, and a couple of grease pencils, stuffing each booklet into a slot or cranny around their workspace so they could have quick and easy access to it, even in the dark. They then completed their own checklists, making sure all of their equipment's power switches were off, and plugged their oxygen masks and interphone cords into the aircraft outlets and placed the helmets over the headrests of their ejection seats, ready to go. When they were finished, they all climbed out of the crew compartment and met back outside on the ground.

They performed the walkaround inspection together, beginning at the nose gear strut and working clockwise past the nose, right side, right engine nacelles, right wing, and then into the forward bomb bay. Even though the crew had practiced this procedure regularly over the years, this was the first time all but one of them, the crew OSO, or offensive systems operator, had ever done it for real: preflight a B-1B Lancer bomber in preparation for nuclear war.

"Cripes," Air Force Lieutenant Colonel Joseph Roma, the crew OSO muttered aloud. "We're back in the big glowing smoking hole business again." The other crew members just stood and stared. For Roma, this was like some kind of nasty dream, like the world's worst case of déjà vu. It was the middle of the Cold War all over again.

Joe Roma was an eighteen-year veteran of the U.S. Air Force, not including three years in the Civil Air Patrol in high school in Corfu, New York, and four years as a full-scholarship ROTC cadet at Syracuse University—he had worn some version of an Air Force uniform for over half his life. Proudly, most of that time was not spent in a blue uniform, but in a green one—an Air Force flight suit. He had attended two years of undergraduate, advanced, and B-52 bomber combat crew training, then been assigned to a B-52 bomb wing in northern Maine. Because there was not much to do up in Loring Air Force Base, Maine, most of the time, Roma—tall, slim, dark, and athletic, but too boyish and gangly-looking to be taken seriously by the really good-looking ladies in Aroostook County, Maine—had busied himself with the intricacies of the venerable B-52 bomber.

His dedication had been rewarded with rapid advancement from R (Ready) crew status to E (Exceptional) status, then simulator operator, instructor nav, S (Select) crew status, Standardization-Evaluation Crew, then back to Castle Air Force Base for upgrade to radar navigator; then quickly through R-, E-, and S-crew status, instructor radar nav, then Stan-Eval again. In the meantime, he transferred to Andersen Air Force Base on Guam, another remote assignment, and he immersed himself in career-building projects: a master's degree in business administration, a half-dozen military schools by correspondence. He was selected for a variety of Wing and Air Division–level assignments, such as target study officer, weapons officer, command post controller, and Wing bomb-nav officer, in charge of training and outfitting the B-52 squadron navigators. Roma loved every new assignment, and the Air Force rewarded his enthusiasm and dedication with rapid promotion to major.

But nothing he'd ever done compared with his newest assignment: to be part of the initial cadre of instructors for the B-1B bomber at McConnell Air Force Base in Kansas. The B-1B was everything he'd wished the B-52 could be: fast, sleek, stealthy, powerful, accurate, and reliable. The "Bone" became Roma's new obsession. Roma, still unmarried, was promoted to lieutenant colonel in short order and eventually became chief of Stan-Eval for the B-1 Combat Crew Training squadron, the first navigator ever selected to that position—before or since. Roma was then reassigned to Ellsworth Air Force Base as bomb-nav operations officer of the Strategic Warfare School, the "graduate school" for long-range bombing planners and commanders. While at the SWC, Roma studied and worked with the commander of the SWC, then–Brigadier General Terrill Samson, becoming one of Samson's strategic bomber experts, developing strategies and tactics for employing bombers in any kind of conflict anywhere in the world. Roma was "getting great face time," as his fellow crewdogs put it, and he was considered a shoo-in for a choice Pentagon assignment, for Air War College, perhaps even a bomber squadron of his own.

That never happened, but not because of Joe Roma. The heavy bomber in general and the B-1B bomber in particular was the new albatross around the military budget's neck. Although the "Bone" was a far more deadly bombing platform than any other attack plane in the world, many of the bomber's specialized systems, especially the electronic warfare system, had never been perfected; and because of high gross weight due to refitting the plane to carry cruise missiles, there were lots of restrictions on B-1 flight parameters. Congress was ready to cancel the B-1, and only passing an intensive six-month operational readiness assessment saved it.

Disappointed but not dejected, Joe Roma went back to the Seventh Wing at Ellsworth Air Force Base as the Wing's chief of Standardization-Evaluation, spending as much time doing flight and simulator check rides as he did at his desk. Flying meant more to him than promotion or command, and he had a huge warehouse of information to pass on to the young crewpuppies. By the end of the year, all of the B-1Bs were going to be in the Air National Guard and Air Force Reserves, and probably so would Joe Roma. With all of the B-52s going into retirement, the B-1Bs accepted more of the long-range bombing responsibilities, including the nuclear mission, without exceeding treaty nuclear delivery vehicle restrictions.   ˉ

Now, when the Wing was called to war, evaluators and instructors were no longer required—but aerial warriors were in great demand. Joe Roma asked to go back to the only place he ever really wanted to be—in the cockpit of the B-1B Lancer bomber. As a tribute to his expertise and knowledge, he was assigned the greenest E-status crew—top-notch flyers, but totally inexperienced in pulling alert—to be the first Ellsworth crew to begin generating a plane to get ready to go to war.

"Ted, we need a lifter, flashlight, and dental mirror," Roma asked his crew chief. The lifter was a maintenance platform that was wheeled inside the bomb bay that lifted the crew up twelve feet in the air so they could reach the weapons. Roma opened his "plastic brains"—crewdog slang for his checklist—and reviewed the weapon settings written on the proper page in grease pencil. "Here's what we're looking for, guys," Roma said. "We were briefed these settings during target study. They're easy to remember—the weapon designers were smart and made all the normal settings with green *S*'s, so that's what we look for. All *S*'s mean the weapons are safe and they're set correctly—retarded laydown burst, low yield, two-minute delay, no contact backup. I want each of you to use the mirrors to check the settings."

This supersonic B-1B Lancer was rather lightly loaded. The aft end of the forward bomb bay contained a Common Strategic Rotary Launcher with eight AGM-89 Advanced Cruise Missiles, each with a 1,000-mile range and 100-kiloton nuclear warheads, five times more powerful than the weapon that exploded over Hiroshima, Japan; with terrain-comparison and satellite navigation, the cruise missiles had twenty-foot accuracy even after a three-hour low-level attack flight. The aft bomb bay contained a 3,000-gallon auxiliary fuel tank.

Once the weapons were inspected, the crew continued their walka-round inspection of the aircraft, then climbed up the boarding ladder and assumed their stations on the flight deck. A few moments later the interphone came alive as the pilots turned on battery power, followed by the interior lights when external power was applied, and the crew began their "Power-on Before Engine Start" checklists. Roma powered up his equipment, started a full cardinal heading gyro alignment on his Offensive Avionics System, loaded the mission cartridges into his navigation computers, then checked in with the Ellsworth command post: "Rushmore Control, Rushmore Zero-One, radio check."

"Loud and clear, Zero-One," the command post senior controller responded. "Authenticate Oscar-Mike."

Roma knew the senior controller and smiled at the "Oscar-Mike" challenge code—OM, or Old Man, was usually reserved as a radio tribute to him. "Zero-One authenticates Charlie."

"Loud and clear, Zero-One." They repeated the procedure with the other UHF radio, with the secure UHF, and finally with the satellite teletype terminal.

The next step: checking the weapons. With the weapons monitoring system off, Roma checked each weapon station to be sure each weapon and each weapon release circuit was indeed off. He then turned the system on and flipped through each weapon station again, watching for green SAFE lights indicating each weapon was safed and had passed its continuity and connectivity self-tests with the B-1B's weapon computers. Checklist complete, he shut down the weapons-monitoring system.

Next he checked the PAL, or Permissive Action Link, the computer that would allow him to prearm the weapons. He entered a test code and received a good SAFE and READY indication. Once programmed with the correct prearming code transmitted to the crew by the National Command Authority—the President of the United States, along with the Secretary of Defense—the PAL would allow the crew to prearm the nuclear weapons. The PAL would allow only five incorrect prearming attempts, then automatically safe the weapons permanently. The PAL was mounted on the forward instrument panel between the OSO and DSO, and Roma got his DSO's attention so he could visually double-check that the PAL was good. "Paul, PAL check."

The DSO, Paul Wiegand, leaned over and checked the light indications on the PAL. "SAFE and READY checks."

"Push to test," Roma said, hitting the TEST button. All of the lights on the panel illuminated, with the SAFE light flashing.

"Checks."

"PAL off," Roma said, shutting off the system. "Arming switch lock lever safety wire."

Wiegand looked over and saw that the safety wire to the mode switch lock lever was installed and secure. "Secure," he responded. Because the PAL was a nuclear weapon component, protected just like a nuclear weapon itself, access to the PAL was strictly two-person control—no fewer than two persons had to be present whenever handling the PAL or any nuclear weapon or component. Additional safety was added by providing a single, physical, positive action to any attempt to prearm any nuclear weapon, such as breaking the thin steel safety wire off the lock lever before moving the lock lever over so the arming switch could be moved from SAFE to ARM.

By this time, the navigation gyros had fully aligned, and he set the mode switch to NAV. "Chris, I'm in NAV, ready for engine start."

"Defense is ready for engine start."

"Rog," the copilot replied. A few minutes later, the pilots started all four engines, then began their electrical, hydraulic, fuel, environmental, flight control, terrain-following computer, and autopilot checks, swept the wings back and forward, and cycled the bomb doors and rotary launcher. One of the flight-control computers flunked a mode check, so the crew chiefs were scrambling to find a spare computer to swap. It took an hour and a half before a spare was found, and another half hour to finish the checks and shut down the engines. The crew then performed the "cocking" checklist, which configured all switches and systems so the aircraft could be ready for taxi and takeoff just minutes after hitting one button.

"Control, Sortie Zero-One, code one, cocked on alert," the copilot reported after the crew finished their checklists.

"Zero-One, control copies, cocked on alert. Assume normal alert, time two-one-zero-eight-zero-seven, authentication Oscar. Control out."

Roma looked up the date-time group and checked the authentication code; it was correct. "Authentication checks, crew," Roma announced. The only response was the interior lights switching off as the pilots turned off the battery switch, and they were left in the dark. As the crew climbed out of the big bomber, motored the entry hatch closed, and walked toward the squadron headquarters building, Joe Roma thought that he was being left in the dark in more ways than one.

It was after one-thirty in the morning, but Roma's day was just beginning. The Wing's goal was to generate four of its twenty B-1B Lancer bombers and six of its eighteen KC-135R Stratotanker aerial refueling tankers for nuclear alert within the first twelve hours, ten bombers within thirty-six hours, and sixteen planes within forty-eight hours. Crews that had just finished placing one plane on alert were immediately cycled back to begin preflighting another plane while its crews were being briefed. Roma was assigned the task of giving refresher briefings to oncoming crews on nuclear weapon preflight and handling procedures, and he also filled in giving route and target study and inventorying the CMF, or Classified Mission Folder, boxes for the crews placing aircraft on alert.

At the twelve-hour point, nine A.M. local time, Roma was in the Wing Battle Staff Room, attending the hourly battle staff meeting and the first major progress briefing of the alert force generation. The news was not good: Sortie Zero-Four was still at least thirty minutes to an hour from being ready, and it might even require an engine swap or a completely new airplane. It was no secret that the morale of the B-1B community was at an all-time low after flying hours were cut and after learning that all of the B-1s would be going to the Air National Guard or Air Force Reserves starting in October—crew members, officers, and enlisted troops alike were spending more time looking for new assignments or applying for Guard or Reserve slots.

"Aircrew response has been marginal to good overall," Roma said when asked about how the aircrews were reacting to the recall and late-night generation. "About thirty percent response in the first hour, seventy percent in three hours—not bad when you consider the average commute time is forty minutes for the crew members that live off-base, which is about two-thirds of the force."

"It's unacceptable," the group commander interjected angrily. "The crews were dogging it."

"I don't think anyone was dogging it, sir," Roma said. "It's Friday night. We just finished a wing deployment exercise and an Air Battle

Force exercise. People were out of town for the weekend, going to graduation parties, getting ready for summer vacation—this was a bolt-from-the-blue nuclear generation."

"All right, all right," the wing commander interrupted. "The bottom line is we have more crews than planes right now. What's the problem?"

"The training on the SIOP-required gear and availability of spare parts for the number of planes required for alert, sir," the chief of logistics interjected, referring to the specialized equipment needed to generate a plane for war under the Single Integrated Operations Plan. "We're having to break into prepositioned deployment packs for spare parts and equipment. Going from zero planes available for nuclear generation to fifteen ready in just thirty-six more hours is eating up our supplies and overloading the avionics shops."

"Besides, it's been almost a year since we've moved nukes for real, sir," the munitions maintenance chief added. "We've got a whole generation of troops that only have basic education and virtually no experience in special weapons."

The strain was showing on the wing commander's face. "No excuses, dammit," he said, rubbing a hand over his weary face. "Our job around here is to generate planes and get ready for combat operations, and I'll shit-can anyone who doesn't understand that. How well we do on our generation schedule depends on the leadership abilities of the men and women in this room. I want us back on schedule before the next battle staff meeting—I hold the senior staff officers and group commanders responsible. Cancel the intelligence briefing—we've got a job to do out on the ramp. Dismissed."

Things had been somewhat disorganized during the first several hours of a the full nighttime nuclear alert generation—that was situation-normal in any unit Roma had ever been in—but by midmorning things appeared to be humming along pretty well. By the time Roma returned to his office in the squadron building, his entire staff—including everyone recalled from leave—was busy. Everyone had been assigned an alert sortie. Most were not scheduled to start generating their alert line for several hours, so they were busy running simulator sessions, running mobility line duties, running errands for the Wing staff, or helping the maintenance crews to bring a plane up to preload status.

Roma's E-mail mailbox had more than two dozen new messages in it in just the last thirty minutes, so he turned on the TV in his office to get the latest news and sat down to start reading and returning messages. The news seemed to be a jumble of confusion, very much like the situation at Ellsworth Air Force Base as five thousand men and women were trying to get twenty planes ready to fly off and unleash nuclear devastation on the People's Republic of China.

Little else was known about the nuclear disaster in Japan except what had been reported hours ago: the American aircraft carrier USS *Independence,* all eighty thousand tons of it, including approximately 5,200 officers and enlisted men and women, had disappeared when what eyewitnesses called a small nuclear explosion erupted in the late-morning hours in the Gulf of Sagami, about sixty miles south of Tokyo.

Roma couldn't believe what he was hearing.

The disastrous news didn't stop there. Two escort frigates and a 50,000-ton replenishment ship carrying 150,000 barrels of fuel oil cruising near the carrier had capsized in the explosion, and all hands were feared lost—460 more men and women presumed dead. Two guided-missile cruiser escorts had been substantially damaged in the explosion, with hundreds more dead or injured. Several other vessels, civilian and commercial, in the vicinity of the explosion had also been lost. The force of the blast was estimated to be equivalent to 10,000 tons of TNT.

The Japanese prime minister, Kazumi Nagai, immediately blamed the accident on the United States, saying that the *Independence* had been carrying nuclear weapons and that one of the warheads had gone off when a C-2 Greyhound cargo aircraft made a crash landing. U.S. President Kevin Martindale went on national radio and TV immediately, reporting the accident and denying that the *Independence* or any U.S. warships near Japan were carrying nuclear weapons, but his denials seemed to be falling on deaf ears throughout the world.

The Japanese Diet, under heavy pressure by Nagai, immediately ordered all American military bases in Japan sealed and all U.S. vessels, military or civilian military contract, to remain in port until they could be inspected by Japanese nuclear officials and Japanese Self-Defense Force soldiers. Again, Japan was the site of a nuclear explosion, and accusing eyes were on America. South Korea, Singapore, Malaysia, Indonesia, Australia, and New Zealand immediately followed Japan's precautionary move—no U.S. warships or civilian ships contracted by the U.S. military could enter their territorial waters, and they could not leave, until they were inspected and certified that they carried no nuclear weapons.

The People's Republic of China went one step further, restricting all U.S. warships from coming within a hundred miles of its shores or they would consider it an act of war. They knew that the *Independence* had been bound for the Formosa Strait, and they surmised that the United States was using the attacks on the two frigates *Duncan* and *James Daniel* as a pretext to launch a preemptive nuclear strike on China. All U.S. warships already within the one-hundred-mile buffer zone had twenty-four hours to get out, or they would be attacked without warning. China then revealed the position and even the identification of four U.S. submarines in the Formosa Strait and South China Sea, including two ballistic missile attack subs, and estimated that perhaps as many as ten more were in the vicinity, ready to wage war on the People's Republic of China.

In hours, virtually the entire Pacific Ocean was off-limits to the U.S. Navy.

Joe Roma knew all of this was bullshit. First, he knew from intelligence reports that all nuclear weapons had been removed from all Navy warships except some ballistic missile subs, just as they had been removed from American bombers, since 1991—and nothing that he had been briefed lately caused him to believe that the recent incidents with China had altered that policy. It was possible that the President had changed his mind and rearmed hundreds of capital warships around the world in less than a month, but Roma thought it very unlikely.

Second, nuclear warheads do not go off by themselves, no matter how badly they are abused. Roma knew enough about the inner workings of a modern-day nuclear warhead to know that it would take much more than a crash landing to set it off, even one that had been prearmed and was ready to be released or launched—they had dozens of safety devices and delivery parameters that had to be met before a full nuclear yield could result. If one parameter or interlock was not satisfied, or if there was the slightest bit of damage to a weapon, it simply would not function. It was possible that an accident or internal failure could cause a large non-nuclear explosion, scattering radioactive debris, but a full yield from a damaged weapon, even if it had been prearmed, was virtually impossible.

Bottom line: the nuclear device had to have been set. The protests in Yokusuka Harbor before the *Independence* set sail would have provided the perfect opportunity for a terrorist to plant a device somewhere on the hull.

But for some reason no one was suggesting this might be the work of a terrorist. There were plenty of so-called experts on all of the networks, and almost all of them were blaming the United States for sloppy handling of nuclear weapons during a time of crisis caused by the United States flying stealth bombers all over Asia. The United States government, and President Kevin Martindale and his administration in particular, were being blamed for the deaths of nearly six thousand American soldiers, the loss of fifteen billion dollars' worth of military hardware, the astronomical environmental disaster that was likely to occur in northeastern Japan and the northern Pacific Ocean, and for threatening the world with thermonuclear war.

While Roma had a "compose new message" window open on his computer answering other messages, he decided to drop a line to his old teacher and mentor, Lieutenant General Terrill Samson, commander of Eighth Air Force. No doubt Samson was at U.S. Strategic Command headquarters right now, in the huge underground command center that had formerly been the nucleus of the Strategic Air Command. It was a simple message, not demanding a reply: "What's happening, boss?" along with his phone number and E-mail address. He then forged ahead with the pile of E-mail messages waiting for his response.

Roma was halfway through his list of E-mail messages when he was interrupted by a page. When he tried to return it, he was notified by an electronic voice that he needed a secure telephone to dial it. The only STU phone he knew of was in the command post, so he went over to the command post communications center and dialed the number.

"Samson. Go."

Roma's mouth went instantly dry. "General Samson? This is Joe Roma, returning your page."

"*Paisan!* How the hell are you?" Terrill Samson asked excitedly. Their times together at the Strategic Warfare Center had always been relaxed and informal, more like a college campus or pro sports team rather than a strict military unit. And Terrill Samson had been like a pro football coach—unrelenting and harsh at practices, demanding and disciplined during the missions, but not afraid to share a cigar and a pitcher of beer or two after a successful game.

"I'm doing fine, sir."

"Got your message," Samson said. "I'm sure you've got to be knee-deep in the generation out there, right?"

"That's an understatement, sir," Roma said.

"You pulling a line?"

"Sortie one," Roma replied. "The other lines are coming up slow but sure."

"I thought you were the S-01 crew IOSO." The S-01 crew Instructor Offensive Systems Officer was the number one bombardier of the best, most experienced crew on the base—that slot belonged to Joe Roma.

"They put me with E-05," Roma said. "Great crew, but they got no experience with SIOP stuff. Hardly anyone does around here—the maintainers, logistics, crewdogs, even some of the commanders."

"That's why we got you old warhorses pulling crews, *paisan,*" Samson said. "Something else on your mind, Joe? I'm a little busy."

"Yeah," Roma said, his mind reeling after what had to be the understatement of the century. He hesitated a moment, unsure whether or not he should bring this up, then decided, what the hell: "General, what in hell are we doing loading nukes? I'm not criticizing you or my orders, and you know I'll do the job, but what's out there that we can't blow up with a GATS/GAM or conventional cruise missile?"

"Do I have to explain the whole concept of nuclear deterrence to you, *paisan?*" Samson asked, with only a hint of humor in his voice. "Just do everything by the book and you guys will be fine."

"Sure, we'll be fine, sir," Roma said. "But the whole concept of using forty kilotons to destroy an entire city is silly, when all we need to do to stop the enemy is blow up a command post or comm center or runway. If the nukes did something that conventional bombs couldn't do, I could understand what's going on, but the nukes . . . well, hell, sir, you know what I'm talking about. We discussed this lots of times at the SWC."

"You're preaching to the choir here, my friend," Samson said. "Tell me something I don't know."

"Give me a few hours and I'll put together a few B-1 sorties that'll stop the Chinese dead in their tracks," Roma said confidently. "Load us up with some GBUs and some real defense-suppression stuff and tell us what the targets are, General—me and the boys will take them out for you. We don't need the nukes."

"The word came down from CINCSTRATCOM, not me," Samson said, referring to Admiral Henry T. Danforth, commander in chief of U.S.

Strategic Command. "The admiral said he wanted the bombers to go formal to the big dance."

"Does he really intend to use the nukes, sir?" Roma asked.

"Hell, Joe, you know that all we need to do is *prove* to the bad guys that we *might* use them, demonstrate our resolve, and we've won," Samson said. "The boss thinks that generating the bombers and sticking them back on alert will show the Chinese and everyone else that we mean business."

It was the old Cold War schtick, Roma thought, and frankly, he thought he'd never hear the "party line" from Terrill Samson. Samson's basic philosophy was very simple: give him an objective, and he'll find a way to do it. Even if the White House had given Samson a vague order like "Stop China," Samson would have found a way to do it—and without using nuclear weapons, which Roma knew Samson thought were barbaric at best and murderous at worst. "Loading nukes on the Beaks and Bones isn't going to convince anyone of anything, sir, and you know it," Roma argued.

"The word came from on high, *paisan,*" Samson said. "Too late to argue about it. They tell me 'jump'—yada, yada, yada, you know the rest."

"Pardon me for speaking out, sir, but if you want to send the Chinese a message—if you think, like I do, that the Chinese or some radical Japanese planted a backpack nuke on the *Independence*—then blasting through Chinese air defenses and destroying a couple missile bases will do the trick. They know full well that we won't start a nuclear war, and we know that the Chinese don't have the force structure to wage a nuclear war or stage a massive invasion."

"Joe, I agree with you, but you've got to remember that the *Independence* and three other ships were blown up by a nuclear weapon, and we lost *six thousand troops,*" Samson said pointedly. "The Joint Chiefs think it was the Chinese, and if it was, it'll be the second time in a month they've attacked American forces and the second time they used nuclear weapons. They're obviously trying to force the U.S. out of Asia, and the President is not going to allow that. We're lining up other options, but the President and Secretary of Defense definitely wanted the nuclear forces back on alert until we find out what bases we have available to us overseas and whether or not we can use the carriers."

"Sir, I understand that the President wants revenge," Roma said, "but no one out here on the line thinks he's going to use nukes on anybody. It's an exercise in futility." He paused, then: "General Samson, the recent skirmish against Iran, the attacks on the targets inside Iran and on that carrier—that was a stealth bomber attack, wasn't it? You planned those attacks, didn't you?" Samson didn't answer right away, so Roma went on: "If so, sir, let's do it again. Pick the targets in China that are the greatest threat to us or our allies, then send in the B-1s and B-2s. We'll loudly kick ass for you, I guarantee it."

There was what felt like a long, uncomfortable pause; then Samson said distractedly, "Stand by one, Joe," and the line went quiet. Roma wished this conversation had never taken place—he was embarrassing himself in front of his mentor and superior officer. It sounded as if Joe Roma was squeamish about the possibility of using nuclear weapons, or going to war, which he definitely wasn't. He also felt that perhaps he was being perceived as taking advantage of his access and friendship with Terrill Samson to voice his opinion, which he certainly didn't need right now.

Suddenly, the line opened up again: *"Paisan,* you're on the line right now with another fellow bomber puke. Joe Roma, say hello to Colonel Tony Jamieson, pilot type and ops group commander at Whiteman. Tiger Jamieson, meet Phone Colonel Joe Roma, navigator type, Stan-Eval chief at Ellsworth." The two aviators exchanged confused "hellos."

"You are not going to believe this, guys, but you both called me out of the clear blue sky, with no invitation or prompting from me or anyone, within five minutes of one another—and you both suggested the exact same damn thing," Samson said, with obvious pride in his voice. "We're busy loading nukes on both the Bones and Beaks, and two of the best heavy drivers in the business call to tell me I'm making a big mistake. Maybe I am.

"You asked about the attacks on Iran, Joe—Tony Jamieson was the AC on all of them, including the five-thousand-mile trek across Chinese, Indian, and Pakistani airspace."

"You flew those missions, Colonel?" Roma asked incredulously. "I want to hear about all of the missions, sir. It's exactly the kind of thing we've been preaching for years—the power of the long-range bombers, especially the B-2."

"The Bone would have no problem doing exactly what I did, Roma," Jamieson said. "We can cruise through Chinese airspace in anything we want—they don't have the gear to detect us, let alone shoot us down. We damn well proved we can hit any target anywhere in the world, son— only problem is, the mission was classified, and when some little snippet of information leaks out, the President gets hammered for it. But yes, we sure as shit did it."

"Who was your mission commander, sir?" Roma asked. "I'd like to talk with him, too."

"You better ask the general about *him*," Jamieson said, with a definite edge of sarcastic humor in his voice. "I don't think I'm at liberty to discuss him. He was a good stick, knew his shit cold, but he scared the bejeezus out of me every time I stepped into the Beak with him."

"Jamieson's MC was a guy named McLanahan, Joe."

"I knew a guy named McLanahan who won all those Fairchild Trophies in Bomb Comp a few years ago," Roma said. "Kinda hard to forget that name. He won two Bomb Comps while flying B-52s, back when B-1s were the hot new jets to beat."

"He's the one," Samson said. "He's been working with me on another project, since the White House started getting all the heat about the B-2 raids over Iran. He flies a modified B-52 bomber that is unlike anything you have ever seen. When they grounded the B-2s, I talked the White House into sending a few of these modified B-52s over the Formosa Strait to keep an eye on the Chinese. The plan blew up in my face, although McLanahan's BUFFs did okay."

"Sounds to me like the brass effectively grounded all the heavy bombers, sir," Jamieson observed. "Loading the fleet up with nukes means they won't be flying if war breaks out with the PRC."

"Looks that way, Tiger," Samson said.

"So now the brass doesn't believe anything you say, and so if you went back to them and tried to convince them to quit using nukes and plan some long-range strikes with conventional munitions, they probably won't listen to you," Jamieson added bluntly. "So where does that leave us?"

"I don't know if my opinion means squat in the Pentagon or the White House anymore," Samson said resolutely, "but I'm going to try to put a halt to this nuclear nonsense and get back to the business we've been in for forty years now—carrying big-time heavy iron to the enemy. I want you two to put together some attack sorties for us so I can go back to the Pentagon and give them some alternatives."

"Now you're talking, General," Jamieson said happily. "We can get on the network and have some Bone and Beak sorties drawn up right away."

"Absolutely," Roma said excitedly. "I'll pull some preplanned packages off the shelf and update them with the current intel—and I know, if the plans are approved, that we can generate some non-nuclear planes a hell of a lot faster than the nuclear ones."

"That's for damned sure," Jamieson agreed.

"Then get to it, boys," Samson said. "Make us proud!"

OVER THE FORMOSA STRAIT, NEAR JUIDONGSHAN, FUJIAN PROVINCE, PEOPLE'S REPUBLIC OF CHINA SUNDAY, 22 JUNE 1997, 0245 HOURS LOCAL (SATURDAY, 21 JUNE, 1345 HOURS ET)

The Chinese People's Liberation Army Air Force radar controllers aboard the Ilyushin-76 Candid, an ex-Russian airborne radar plane, spotted the first rebel attack formation just minutes after the aircraft launched from bases at Taichung and Tainan on the island of Formosa. "Attention, attention," the controller called out excitedly, "enemy aircraft attack formation detected, one hundred twenty miles east of Juidongshan."

The operations officer stepped back to the radar controller's console and studied the display. Unfortunately, it was not a sophisticated display like what the American E-2 or E-3 Airborne Warning and Control System plane had—the targets appeared as raw radar data blips with simple numeric electronic identification tags attached, with no altitude readouts; speed, bearing, and distance were computed by centering a cursor over the target using mechanical X- and Y-axis cranks and reading the information off the meters. As the formation got closer to the mainland, however, the blips started to break into pieces—now there were at least four blips, which meant anywhere from four to sixteen attackers.

"Comm, report enemy aircraft contact to Eastern Fleet headquarters," the ops officer ordered.

"Yes, sir," the communications officer responded. They had no satellite communications link; all long-range communications had to be done by shortwave, so it took a lot of time. Finally: "Eastern Fleet headquarters acknowledges contact and replies, 'continue patrol as ordered.' End of message."

"Very well," the operations officer said.

There was a slight pause, during which the ops officer could see several heads turn in his direction in some confusion. Finally, the senior controller asked, "Sir, would you like us to vector in air defense units on the attackers? We have units of the 112th Air Army, two flights of J-8 fighters, four planes per flight, within intercept range." There was a very long, uncomfortable pause. The senior controller repeated, "Sir, the rebel attackers will be over our airspace in less than five minutes. What are your orders?"

"Have one flight of J-8s stay behind to guard this aircraft," the ops officer finally responded. "You may send any available J-6 fighter units to intercept."

"But the J-6s are not certified for night intercepts."

"That is why they have *you* to guide them," the ops officer responded. "The J-8s stay with us. Send any J-6s you feel have the nerve to fight the Nationalists."

"Yes, sir," the controller replied. He assigned the task of guarding the Il-76 to one of his best intercept officers, then ordered another controller to call up two flights of J-6 fighters from Fuzhou to intercept the attackers. "Sir, we count at least four flights of attackers," the senior controller reported. "If the rebels follow their standard attack plan, that means at least sixteen hostiles. Shall we call for more defenders?"

"Negative," the ops officer replied. "You will protect this radar plane with all air assets available to you. Do not let any rebel fighters near this plane."

"But, sir, if this is a complete attack formation—uh, sir, sixteen bombers would cripple Juidongshan."

"You have your orders, senior controller," the operations officer said. "Not one enemy fighter gets within fifty miles of this plane, or I will have your stars. See to it." The senior controller had no choice but to comply.

Without a threat from Chinese air defense fighters, the Taiwanese attack went off without a hitch. It was a full strike package, with all sixteen Republic of China Air Force F-16s equipped with Falcon Eye imaging infrared targeting and attack sensors and loaded with attack munitions. First to go in were four F-16s carrying four CBU-87 cluster bombs each, targeting the Chinese CSS-N-2 Silkworm coastal anti-ship missile installations and air defense missile and artillery sites—these were easy prey for the cluster bombs. The Mk 7 cluster bomb dispensers carried a variety of anti-personnel, anti-armor, and anti-vehicle bomblets, scattering destruction over a very wide area of the naval base with good precision and devastating results.

While the first wave of F-16s pulled off to assume a combat air patrol over the target area, using their wingtip-mounted Sidewinder missiles and internal 20-millimeter cannon, the second wave of eight F-16s moved in with four Mk 84 high-drag general-purpose bombs, targeting the submarine maintenance pens, headquarters buildings, fuel storage, and communications facilities. Coming in at low altitude—some pilots shoved their prized F-16 Fighting Falcons right down to two hundred feet, almost grazing the tops of antennas and trees—the attacks were very effective. Some pilots even spotted several ES3B-class diesel-electric attack subs at the piers and secured beside sub tenders and attacked them with great success, using their 20-millimeter cannons in strafing mode. With freedom to roam the skies and the base's air defenses all but neutralized, any F-16 that missed a target could circle around and come in again, so every assigned target was hit, along with a few important targets of opportunity.

The third wave of F-16 fighters never crossed the shoreline, but their attacks were just as successful. These attackers carried four Mk 55 bottom mines per plane, scattering them in precise patterns near the submarine pens and in nearby Dongshan Harbor, covering most of the sea approaches to the naval base. The Mk 55 mine moored itself to the bottom of the harbor and waited. When it detected a large magnetic presence, such as a ship or submarine, it would detach itself from the bottom and start for the surface, then explode when it sensed itself near its target.

As the Nationalist fighters started their withdrawal, twelve J-6 fighters from Fuzhou Army Air Base to the north moved into attack formation and tried to jump them. The fight was over in a matter of seconds. Without even dropping their external fuel tanks, the Taiwanese F-16 fighter-bombers were able to maneuver clear of the Chinese fighters' lethal cone of fire, and in an instant the hunted would become the hunters. The Chinese PL-2 air-to-air missiles could only lock onto a target from the rear, where it had a clear look at the "hot dot" of a fighter's jet exhaust, which meant every move a Chinese pilot was going to make was already known by every Taiwanese pilot. It was a simple exercise to wait for a Chinese pilot to commit to a rear attack, then jump him from above or from the side, where the American-made Sidewinder missiles were still effective. In less than two minutes, nine Chinese J-6 fighters had been shot down; the other three merely launched missiles at the slightest detection indication—they didn't even know if it was friend or foe—then did a fast one-eighty and bugged out.

The senior controller aboard the Il-76 radar plane watched the attack on his radar screen in sheer horror. Juidongshan Naval Base had just been attacked by rebel Nationalist fighter-bombers, and they had just sat back and watched without doing a thing! In a fit of rage, he whipped off his headphones and dashed over to the operations officer's console in the front curtained-off section of the cabin. A young marine guard tried to block the officer's path, but the controller pushed him aside. "What in blazes do you think you are doing?" the senior controller shouted angrily. "Juidongshan has been hit hard by the Nationalists, and you sit here doing nothing!"

"I am following orders, Captain," the operations officer replied calmly. He paused, then waved for the marine guard to step into the rear cabin, out of earshot. "The Nationalists' attack was expected."

"Expected? What do you mean?"

"Our subs were evacuated hours ago," the ops officer said. "Only a few decoy ships remained, enough to whet the rebel bomber's appetites and waste their bombs. Base personnel were sent into air raid shelters. The only ones still aboveground on that base are TV reporters."

"TV reporters? We allowed our base to be bombed simply for a propaganda ploy? What is going on here?"

"That is none of your concern, nor mine," the operations officer responded. "It is all part of some strange plan coming from Beijing. Return to your post and continue monitoring for other attacks in our sector. This is supposedly part of a large attack plan by the Nationalists, so we can expect more attacks tonight."

The next wave of Taiwanese fighter-bomber attacks occurred just minutes after the senior controller returned to his console. "Attention, attention, enemy fighters detected, crossing into restricted airspace seven-zero miles east of Xiamen Air Base, heading west," one of his controllers reported. "Two large formations, estimating sixteen to thirty enemy aircraft."

The senior controller gasped inwardly as he called up the radar plot on his display. If it was two cells of sixteen aircraft attacking Xiamen, this meant that the Nationalists had committed their entire fleet of F-16 Fighting Falcons to this attack. "Comm, notify Fuzhou, scramble every plane they have," the senior controller ordered. He knew Fuzhou had almost one hundred fighters based there, perhaps one-third of them armed, fueled, and on ready five alert, with another ten or twenty capable of launching and escaping before the rebel fighters arrived overhead; that force might be able to hold off the rebels until the remaining force could be launched or moved and the base personnel evacuated. Unlike Juidongshan, the senior controller knew that Xiamen had not been evacuated. "Get me a report on how many fighters can launch. I want—"

"Nothing," said a voice behind him. It was the operations officer himself, standing over his shoulder. "No fighters will launch from Fuzhou. Vector the three surviving fighters from the Juidongshan engagement to Shantou, get them on the ground as soon as possible."

"What?"

"*Do it,*" the ops officer snapped. "No more arguments from you—lives depend on it. *Move.*"

Land-based radars at Xiamen confirmed what the Il-76 crew feared—it was an all-out assault, with more than thirty F-16 fighter-bombers in eight formations coming in at different altitudes and from different directions. No fighters challenged them.

The F-16 pilots knew that the Hong Qian-2 surface-to-air missiles based at Xiamen, just five miles west of the Taiwanese island of Quemoy, had a maximum range of 34 miles and an optimum range of only 20 miles. The HQ-2s were old copies of ex–Russian SA-2 "flying telephone pole" missiles, huge lumbering two-stage missiles designed to attack 1950s—and 1960s-era bombers, missiles with big warheads but with unreliable, slow, and easily jammable radio remote-control command guidance—hardly a match for the swift and nimble F-16s.

The Taiwanese satellite intelligence was excellent, and the F-16's APG-66 attack radars locked onto the navigation and bombing aimpoints with ease; once the radars were locked on and a navigation update taken, the Falcon Eye imaging infrared sensors were activated and slaved to the four possible targets at each target waypoint. At forty miles, little could be seen on Falcon Eye or radar except for larger buildings; most of the F-16s were going hunting for the more vital buildings in the complex—headquarters, air- and coastal-defense weapon sites, communications, barracks, weapon-storage facilities, aboveground fuel storage, and . . .

Threat receivers blared to life seconds after the F-16s sped inside max HQ-2 missile range, as the search and height-finder radars switched to target-tracking and missile-guidance modes and several surface-to-air missiles leapt into the sky from Xiamen. The F-16 pilots activated their electronic countermeasure pods and dropped chaff to decoy the enemy radars. At night, it was easy to spot the HQ-2 missiles as they lifted off their launchers, trailing a long bright yellow plume of fire. All of the HQ-2s went ballistic, powering up to very high altitude, thousands of feet above the F-16s. Their second-stage boosters ignited, powering them up even higher, some 30,000 feet above the Taiwanese attackers, before starting their terminal dive toward the F-16s.

The F-16s' ECM pods effectively jammed the Chinese target-tracking radars, so the Chinese missile technicians had to continually relock their radars onto another target—but they had no way of knowing that they had locked onto a cloud of radar-decoying chaff until several seconds after lock-on, when they would notice that the target was hanging in the sky at zero airspeed. They had only seconds to reacquire another legitimate target, because the HQ-2 missiles were on their way down toward the rebel F-16s.

The F-16 pilots had detected only perhaps six or eight HQ-2 SAM launches, with one or two missiles targeted on each inbound attack formation. Even if all of them hit an F-16, which was extremely unlikely, the strike package would still be intact. The Chinese defenders might have one more shot at the F-16s if they were lucky, but more likely the F-16s would blow through a second wave and be over the base, and then the fun would start. Another turkey shoot, just like their successful brothers down over Juidongshan. Quemoy Tao, the Taiwanese-controlled islands east of Xiamen, would be safe from attack and finally avenged for the Chinese nuclear attack that had almost destroyed . . .

In the blink of an eye, all thirty-two Taiwanese F-16 fighter-bombers disappeared.

The special emergency underground command center in Beijing had been used only a few times in its forty-year history. The bunker had been used for long periods of time during conflicts between China and the Soviet Union in 1961 and 1979 that threatened to go nuclear; the other time was during the last major Chinese invasion of Taiwan, in 1955, when the United States had threatened to use nuclear weapons to stop the Communists from overrunning Taiwan. Built by engineers from the Soviet Union, the bunker was a perfect, albeit slightly smaller, replica of the Kremlin underground emergency bunker in Moscow, used when there was no time to evacuate the political and Party leadership from the city.

The 8,000-square-foot steel and concrete facility, set six stories under the Chinese Ministry of Defense on forty huge spring shock absorbers to cushion the shock of nearby nuclear explosions, was designed and provisioned to accommodate an operations, support, and security staff of thirty-eight—many of whom were women, the implications obvious— plus fifty high government officials. Now it contained the proper amount of staff and technicians, but perhaps three times the maximum number of government officials. President Jiang Zemin and his closest civilian and military advisors were seated around a simple rectangular table in the center of the bunker. Surrounding them were the other high officials and their aides, then a ring of communications, intelligence, and planning officers at their consoles and workstations that fed the president and his advisors a constant stream of information. Finally, the remainder of the government officials that had threatened, bribed, forced, or cajoled their way inside were jammed into every remaining nook and cranny of the bunker.

President Jiang scowled as he surveyed his surroundings. They had been in the bunker since midnight, when intelligence had reported that the rebel Nationalist air attack was under way. Eighty persons stuffed into the small enclosure was bad enough—180 was almost intolerable. But it was too late to open the blast doors. The worst part was that the one man he wanted to talk to was not present. This was an outrage! he thought. Sun Ji Guoming was going to suffer for this.

"Excuse me, Comrade President," the defense minister, Chi Haotian, said. "Admiral Sun is on the line via satellite."

"Where is he? I ordered him to be here before the attack began!"

"Sir . . . comrade, he is *airborne,* calling from a bomber aircraft over Jiangxi province!"

"What? Give me that!" Jiang snatched the receiver from Chi. "Admiral Sun, this is the president. I want an explanation, and I want it *now!*"

"Yes, sir," Sun Ji Guoming responded. "I am aboard an H-7 Gangfang bomber. I am using it as my airborne command post to monitor the attack on the rebel Nationalists on Taiwan. We are ready to begin our attack on Makung, Taichung, Hsinchu, Tainan, and Tsoying. I request permission to begin our attacks. Over."

Jiang was so angry that his words were coming out in confused sputters. "I ordered you to report here, to me, before these attacks began!" he shouted. "Why have you disobeyed me?"

"Because I do not think I could have squeezed into your command center there, sir," Sun responded. Jiang couldn't help but look around himself again and cursed the cowardice and failure of discipline that filled this bunker up like this. "Besides, sir, not every flag officer of the People's Liberation Army can be in an underground shelter—someone must lead our troops to victory. I therefore decided to lead the bombing raid on the rebels myself."

"This is insubordination at the highest level!" military chief of staff General Chin Po Zihong thundered. "He has insulted every man in this room! Admiral Sun must be stripped of his rank and imprisoned immediately for this!"

President Jiang looked around the impossibly overcrowded bunker and was embarrassed and shamed. He could not censure a commander who was out flying with his troops, ready to take on the high-tech, well-trained Nationalist air force. "I think it would be difficult for any of us to arrest Comrade Sun, since he is free and is struggling on behalf of the People's Republic of China, while we are in this concrete sardine can!" Jiang said in a loud voice. "We are safe, and we dare accuse Comrade Admiral Sun of insubordination while he risks his life to be seen by his fellow soldiers?" Chin fell silent. Jiang returned to the receiver: "Comrade Sun, can you report on the status of the operation?"

"Yes, sir," Sun responded. "As expected, the Nationalists attacked Juidongshan with conventional bombs and air-dropped mines. The base was moderately damaged, but we suffered no casualties. Four of our J-6 air defense fighters were shot down, with four presumed casualties. The Nationalist attack on Xiamen was stopped completely, with an estimated thirty-two Nationalist F-16 fighters obliterated. No estimates on Nationalist casualties on Quemoy Dao, but observed aboveground damage was extensive. No damage, no casualties at Xiamen. All of our invasion forces are intact and awaiting your orders for the second phase of our attack."

President Jiang hesitated. This was easily the most monumental decision of his life. Up until now, he had almost completely escaped criticism for the People's Liberation Army's activities in the Formosa Strait or South China Sea region since these conflicts had begun about a month ago. He had been roundly criticized for bringing the former Russian, former Iranian aircraft carrier into the western Pacific; he had been criticized for amassing an attack fleet against Quemoy; he had been criticized for his policies against allowing more home rule of Hong Kong. But ever since Admiral Sun had begun his unconventional-warfare campaign against Taiwan, very little criticism had been directed against him—it had all been directed against the United States and against the rebels on Formosa, even though Admiral Sun and the People's Liberation Army under his command had precipitated everything that had occurred!

But from here on, China's true designs would become evident—there would be no more feigned innocence, no more pointing fingers at the Nationalists and the Americans for their aggressive acts. Although some of what had occurred could be explained away as acts of self-defense, it would be much harder to cry "Foul!" in the future if he gave the order that Admiral Sun Ji Guoming was seeking.

"I want reports on American, Japanese, Korean, and ASEAN member reactions to the attacks on Juidongshan and Xiamen," President Jiang ordered his staff. "I want a media statement prepared, explaining that our activities were purely defensive in nature and provoked by the Nationalists' aggression. I want reports from our ground forces commanders near Xiamen, asking about the readiness of our forces. I want an intelligence report on the Nationalists' troop situation on Quemoy and Matsu Dao." Jiang turned to the radio: "Admiral Sun, I have ordered reports from Xiamen and from our embassies and information offices in the Pacific to get reaction on the attacks. I will issue my orders when these reports are transmitted to me and I have had a chance to evaluate them."

"With all due respect, Comrade President, you cannot wait—you must give the order now, or abandon the invasion plans," Admiral Sun replied. "This decision must be made immediately. Our bombers must strike while the rebels are confused and stunned by the aftermath of the attack on Xiamen, and before they disperse their aircraft or hide them in reinforced underground storage facilities. We can cripple the rebels' air forces in one night if we strike right now, comrade. We must not hesitate. Our bombers are airborne and can only remain in this orbit, below the Nationalists' long-range radar coverage, for a few minutes longer before our fuel status will render us non–mission effective. We can midair refuel the H-6 bombers, but the other bombers must return to base to refuel, which will upset our strike timing and prevent success. I need an order right now, sir."

The overcrowded, stuffy, noisy, smelly underground bunker suddenly became as quiet as a grave, as if everyone could somehow hear the conversation between their Paramount Leader and the enigmatic, almost legendary navy admiral who had turned their tranquil, blissfully isolated lives upside down these past few weeks. They all knew that the conflict between the People's Republic of China and the rebel Nationalists on Formosa was about to move to a whole new level—and they were glad to be sixty feet underground right now, too.

ABOARD AN H-7 GANGFANG BOMBER, OVER THE
WUYI MOUNTAINS, EASTERN CHINA
MOMENTS LATER

Sun Ji Guoming was a career navy man, but he had to admit that the power and the speed of the heavy bomber was something to behold, something that could easily make a sailor trade in his slickers and sea bag for a flight suit.

Admiral Sun was strapped into the instructor pilot's seat of an H-7 Gangfang H-7 supersonic bomber, one of six ex–Soviet Tupolev-26 "Backfire" bombers the Chinese People's Liberation Army Air Force purchased from Russia in 1993. Sun was leading an attack formation of thirty Xian H-6 bombers, Chinese-built copies of the Soviet Tupolev-16 bomber, which launched from Wuhan People's Liberation Army Air

Force Base, three hundred miles west of Shanghai, about an hour before sunset. Along with the bombers were six HT-6 Xian tankers, which were H-6 bombers configured to act as aerial refueling tankers.

Once reaching the air refueling orbit areas, each bomber took on a token on-load of fuel, around thirty thousand pounds each. The HT-6 tanker unreeled a long, six-inch-diameter hose with a large three-foot-diameter basketlike drogue at the end from each wingtip, and the H-6 bombers engaged the drogue with a probe protruding from their wingtips. Even with an observer guiding the two planes to the contact position from observation blisters near the tail of the HT-6s, Admiral Sun was astounded by the precision of the bomber pilots, able to stick the six-inch probe into the drogue in the semidarkness and then stay in formation long enough to successfully transfer the fuel, even in a turn—it took almost ten minutes, with the two planes flying less than thirty feet apart at over three hundred miles an hour, to transfer a relatively small amount of fuel. Sun's H-7 bomber used a long refueling probe that extended far ahead of the nose, so they did not need an observer—they simply flew right up into the basket and plugged in. How the pilot could maneuver a 250,000-pound aircraft inflight to within three feet of a moving point in space was amazing.

After refueling, the gaggle of bombers broke up into three cells of ten planes and proceeded to orbit points on the west side of the Wuyi Mountains, about two hundred miles from the Formosa Strait, staying at 5,000 feet to keep below the top of the Wuyi range. The reason: Le Shan, or Happy Mountain. The Taiwanese Le Shan air defense system was one of the most sophisticated in the world. Radar information from three long-range radar arrays based in the Chungyang Mountains of central Taiwan, along with radar data from radar planes, ships, civilian air-traffic-control radar systems, and even some fighter radars, were combined in the Happy Mountain underground air defense center located south of Taipei. One hundred military controllers scanned over a million and a half cubic miles of airspace, from the surface to 60,000 feet, and directed almost one hundred American-made F-5E Tiger II air defense fighters, ten Taiwanese-made Ching Kuo fighters, more than fifty Hawk air defense missile sites, twenty Tien Kung I and II surface-to-air missile sites, fifty Chaparral short-range antiaircraft missile sites, and more than two hundred antiaircraft artillery sites located throughout the Republic of China's islands. Le Shan's mountaintop radars could see deep into mainland China, and its air defense weapons were first-class. The Tien Kung II antiaircraft missile system, based on the American Patriot antiaircraft system, had a kill range so great that the missile battery located at Makung on the Pescadores Island thirty miles west of Formosa could shoot down Chinese aircraft launching from three major coastal bases in eastern China shortly after takeoff!

After the order was received from Beijing, Admiral Sun ordered the bombers to start moving eastward out of their staging orbits and begin their attack runs, and he radioed for the first phase of the attack to begin. More than three hundred fighters, mostly J-6 fighters led by radar-equipped J-7 or J-8 fighters, lifted off from Shantou and Fuzhou Air Bases and streamed eastward—launching two or three planes at a time, it took nearly twenty minutes for each base to launch its full complement of planes. In that time, the H-6 bombers accelerated to attack speed of 360 miles per hour, streaming over the Wuyi Mountains in three different tracks. One hundred Chinese fighters therefore became the "spearhead" for each ten-plane bomber formation, with the three spears headed right for the heart of Taiwan. With the fighters three to five minutes ahead of the bombers, the six large formations rendezvoused over the coastline and move en masse toward Taiwan.

The first target was the Pescadores Islands, about three-fourths of the way across the Formosa Strait. The first Chinese attack formation, directed by a Ilyushin-76 Candid radar plane, occupied the high- and mid-CAPs, or Combat Air Patrols, and were met by five formations of four F-5E Tiger fighters at their same altitude. Although the Taiwanese F-5s were outnumbered five to one, the Chinese Il-76 radar planes could give only an accurate range and bearing to the Taiwanese fighters, not altitude, so an accurate fix on the Taiwanese fighters' position was hard to establish. Also, because the formations of Chinese fighters was so large and they were inexperienced in night intercepts, it was difficult for the Chinese fighters to maneuver in position to attack. The Taiwanese fighters were able to use their speed and maneuverability to get in an ideal counterattack position, and the fight was on.

The massive formations of Chinese fighter planes fired their Pen-Lung-2 air-to-air missiles at extreme range, whether they had a radar or heat-seeking lock-on or not. The sky was soon filled with Chinese air-to-air missiles screaming toward the Taiwanese defenders, but most were simply unguided projectiles, more distractions than threats. One by one, the Chinese attackers fired, closed range, fired more missiles, then turned and headed back to the mainland just before reaching optimum AIM-9 Sidewinder missile range. When the Taiwanese fighters pursued the retreating Chinese fighters, the Chinese fighters occupying the mid-CAP started a climb, hoping to get behind the Taiwanese fighters and into the PL-2's lethal cone, but this attack was broken up by Taiwanese fighters coming in lower and chasing the newcomers away.

There were some brief "dogfights," with Chinese and Taiwanese fighters turning and dodging one another trying to get into attack position, but the Taiwanese pilots and their superior air defense radar system had the upper hand. Seventeen Chinese fighters were shot down, versus one Taiwanese F-5E. The Taiwanese defenders easily pursued the Chinese fighters across the Formosa Strait nearly all the way back to the Asian coastline, picking off J-6 and J-7 fighters one by one, then darting away before getting in range of Chinese long-range air defense sites that dotted the coast.

But while the Chinese fighters engaged and diverted the bulk of the Taiwanese fighter force, the first formation of ten Xian H-6 bombers was able to stream in just a few dozen feet above the dark waters of the Formosa Strait in toward the Pescadores Islands. The air defense radar controllers were concentrating on the huge numbers of fighters and gave all their attention to them, and so they didn't see the bombers until it was too late. Taiwanese Tien Kung II surface-to-air missile sites at Makung and Paisha in the Pescadores attacked the incoming bombers at over forty miles, but the H-6 bombers attacked first.

The lead bomber in each ten-plane formation carried two Hai-Yang-3 cruise missiles on external fuselage hardpoints. The HY-3 was a massive 6,600-pound missile powered by a rocket engine. Once programmed with the target coordinates and navigation and flight information dumped into the missile's onboard computers, the missiles were released. Seconds after launch, a solid-fuel rocket engine propelled the missile past the speed of sound; then a ramjet engine deployed from the missile and automatically ignited. The HY-3 missile climbed to 40,000 feet and accelerated to almost four times the speed of sound in just a few seconds. At over 2,000 miles per hour, the missile covered sixty miles in less than twelve seconds . . .

. . . and each HY-3 missile carried a small low-yield nuclear warhead.

The first missile worked perfectly, exploding five miles over Penghu

Island, the main island in the Pescadores Island archipelago, and creating a bright nuclear flash that blinded dozens of unwary, unprotected Taiwanese pilots and flattened most aboveground structures on Penghu Island. The nuclear burst also released an electromagnetic wave that disrupted communications and damaged unprotected electronic circuits for almost a hundred miles in all directions. The second HY-3 missile had been programmed the same as the first to be used as a backup, so it was merely destroyed by the blast of its brother.

Three of the follow-on Chinese H-6 bombers were damaged by the nuclear blast and had to turn back for home, but seven of its wingmen survived the shock wave, intense flash, and electromagnetic pulse and raced in to their target. The lead bomber that had carried the HY-3 missiles carried 12,000 pounds of gravity weapons in its bomb bay; the others who had not been carrying cruise missiles held 19,000 pounds of bombs. The fires on Penghu and Yuweng Islands, the two main fortified islands in the Pescadores, made initial target location easy, and the H-6's bombardiers picked out the crucial military targets with ease. The lead bomber began the attack with four 2,000-pound high-explosive bombs, cratering the naval yard, headquarters buildings, radar sites, and fixed coastal air and ship defense sites. Two of the follow-on bombers also used large high-explosive bombs, while the rest followed with eighteen 1,000-pound cluster bombs, which scattered thousands of antipersonnel bomblets and anti-vehicle mines throughout the islands.

With the outer air defense structure collapsed, the attack on the Taiwanese home island of Formosa itself could begin. The northern attack group launched nuclear-armed Hai-Ying-3 missiles at the Republic of China's air force base at Hsinchu, just forty miles southwest of the Taiwanese capital of Taipei, and at the air force base at Taichung; the southern strike package launched nuclear HY-3 missiles at the air force base at Tainan and another missile at the Taiwanese naval facility at Tsoying, just a few miles north of the large industrial city of Kaohsiung. All of the attacks were devastating. Even after suffering heavy losses when the bombers flew close to surviving air defense sites, more than two-thirds of the Chinese H-6 bombers survived and successfully attacked their targets with bombs and cluster munitions.

The Chinese bomber pilots were not nearly as well-trained as their Western counterparts, and they flew even fewer hours than American crews even in an age of deep cutbacks in flying time, so their bombing accuracy was poor—less than 50 percent of their bombs hit their assigned targets. But the high-altitude nuclear airbursts had done most of the devastation already—four Taiwanese military bases destroyed or substantially damaged; one small, two medium, and one large city were ravaged. Most of the Taiwanese fighters that had launched to chase down the Chinese J-6 and J-7 fighters suddenly found themselves without a base to return home to; some did not have the fuel to return to alternate landing sites, and their pilots were forced to eject over uninhabited areas of the Taiwanese countryside as their fuel-starved planes flamed out.

Admiral Sun followed the H-6 strike package in his H-7 Gangfang bomber, arriving over his orbit point northwest of the Pescadores just as the second and third H-6 bombers started their attacks. Wearing his gold-lined goggles to avoid any flashblindness damage by the nuclear bursts on the horizon, Admiral Sun Ji Guoming surveyed the results of his sneak attack. He could see every nuclear explosion clearly: a bright ball of light like a mini-sun illuminated every cloud in the sky, lighting up the island of Formosa and making it appear like a huge photograph lying on the surface of the ocean. Every detail of the tall eastern mountains, every river valley, every aberration of the vast western coastal plains could be seen for a brief instant in spectacular, frightening relief before being swallowed up by the darkness again. Although not nearly as big as their nuclear cousins, the big non-nuclear high-explosive bomb attacks looked like large, bright red and yellow flashbulbs, followed by the glow of ground fires; and the cluster bomb attacks on Taichung and Tainan could be seen as a line of tiny pinpoint flashes of light that streaked across the darkness far below.

"Radar reports rebel fighters launching from Taipei, Admiral," the copilot aboard Sun's H-7 bomber reported. "One or two at a time, disorganized flights."

"Probably escaping, not coming after us unless one wants to be a hero looking to try to ram one of our bombers in the darkness," Sun commented. He never even considered that his aircraft might be in danger—with those nuclear explosions ripping into the arms and legs of the Nationalist dragon, the rebels seemed completely defeated already. "In any event, our bombers will escape. Where are the returning flights of rebel fighters heading?"

"North, towards Taipei," the copilot responded.

"Excellent," Sun said. The rebel air forces obviously didn't feel like fighting after learning that several Chinese bombers had slipped through their fingers and that their homeland had just been ripped apart by nuclear and high-explosive bombs. Chiang Kai-shek International Airport and Sung Shan Air Base near Taipei were probably the only large air bases surviving west of the Chungyang Mountains.

They would make easy targets for follow-on strikes. The third wave of Sun's attack on Taiwan should be launching now—M-9 mobile ballistic missile attacks from secret presurveyed launch sites in Jiangxi and Zhejiang Provinces. The M-9 missile had a range of about three hundred miles, and Sun had targeted at least six missiles on each of the surviving major civilian and military airfields in Taiwan. The missiles were not as accurate as bombers, but they did not need to be—the first two missiles targeted against all but the airfields around Taipei had nuclear warheads, again programmed for high-altitude airbursts so as to spread out the blast effects of the warheads and minimize radioactive fallout and residue at ground zero.

The volleys of missiles aimed at Chiang Kai-shek International, all non-nuclear, should ensure that the airport could not be used to launch military strikes against the mainland. Sun was very careful not to explode any nuclear weapons over Taipei. The Nationalist capital was still the capital of the province of T'aiwan, the twenty-third province of the People's Republic of China, and it would not do to kill any loyal Communist Chinese. He would need the support of the people to complete his task of reuniting the island with its mainland motherland.

In the meantime, an armada of two hundred Q-5 Nanchang fighters, copies of the Soviet Mikoyan-Gurevich-19 attack plane, would be arriving from Guangzhou, Nanjing, Wuhu, and Wuhan Air Bases to Fuzhou. At daybreak they would conduct non-nuclear mopping-up strikes against all the Taiwanese military bases, loaded with a long-range drop tank and two 2,000-pound bombs or cluster munitions. One by one, they would attack any major surviving targets.

Sun wanted more Xian H-6 bombers for these attacks, but he had been allotted only the H-6s used by the People's Liberation Army Navy for this raid—the air force's H-6s were still held in reserve, committed to long-range nuclear attacks against targets in Russia, India, and Vietnam. Perhaps after President Jiang and the Central Military Committee learned of his success over the rebel Nationalists, Sun thought, it might be possible to convince them to let him have the rest of the H-6s so he could continue the air offensive against Taiwan. With most of the rebel's long-range air defense radar system down, the H-6 bombers would stand a better chance against the surviving Taiwanese air defenses.

Then, he thought happily, perhaps the Paramount Leader would allow him the honor of destroying China's other regional enemies and adversaries. Defeat was unthinkable at this moment.

The nuclear-armed M-9 ballistic missiles easily reached the military bases on the east side of the island, hitting Lotung, Hualien, and Taitung. Sun could see the bright flashes of light far on the horizon as the missiles hit their targets. The accuracy of the M-9 missile was poor, perhaps one-half to one mile miss distance after a three-hundred-mile flight—poor by most standards, but perfectly acceptable with nuclear warheads.

Sun never once thought about the devastation he was creating down there. The rebel Nationalists were bugs to be squashed, nothing more. Sun truly believed that the vast majority of citizens on the island of Formosa wanted to rejoin their long-lost friends and families on the mainland, and that the subversive Nationalist government, supported by the terrorist rebel military, was preventing reunification by declaring their so-called "independence," as if that were possible or even thinkable. Although most would probably prefer the less intrusive, capitalist society that existed there now, Sun believed that they would accept a Communist government as long as all the Chinese people were reunited. Sun was killing only filthy rebels, not fellow Chinese. If it took a nuclear weapon to reunite his motherland, so be it.

Sun Ji Guoming did not delude himself—he knew that it was very unlikely that rocket or bombing raids alone would destroy even a substantial portion of the rebels' military force. He knew that the rebels had perfected the art of building vast underground shelters and hiding huge numbers of troops, equipment, and supplies within the eastern mountains. Quemoy Dao had turned many of their 1950s- and 1960s-era underground shelters into tourist museums, so it was possible to see the quality construction of some of these complexes—they were certainly strong enough to withstand any kind of shelling or bombing, except perhaps for a direct groundburst hit with a nuclear weapon. Sun had no plans to use nuclear groundbursts in any attack. If they had any desire at all to occupy the land they took back from the Nationalists, it was not a good idea to make that ground radioactive.

Rumors had been flying for years about huge army bases underground, where two entire generations of citizens and soldiers had grown up and trained. Sun had even heard about caves cut into the rock big enough to hide a cruiser, or massive underwater caves turned into submarine pens where the only access in or out of the base was underwater, as in Sweden. He dismissed most of these rumors. Anything big enough to house a capital warship, several submarines, or more than a few hundred men had to be carefully engineered, and that took time, money, and vast amounts of equipment and manpower—and that meant security leaks and evidence. In all of Sun's years in the People's Liberation Army, with all the spies they employed all over Asia and the world, no exact proof had ever been produced of any legendary rebel underground military bases.

Admiral Sun switched to his interphone and keyed the mike: "Continue on course," he ordered. "Notify me when your attack checklists are complete." He received an acknowledgment from his crew. The H-7 bomber started northward toward Fuzhou, staying close to the mainland coast in case any surviving rebel fighters tried to take a pass at them. It was accompanied by a single HT-6 Xian tanker aircraft. After passing near Fuzhou, Sun's H-7 and the HT-6 took up a northbound course, out over the East China Sea.

The attack on Taiwan's major military bases was a great success, but Sun knew that the real threat to China didn't come from Taiwan, but from the United States of America. Sun had managed to keep the area around Taiwan clear of American aircraft carriers by planting a "backpack" nuclear device on the USS *Independence* and detonating it just after it had left its Japanese port of Yokosuka—and to his immense surprise, the United States had not retaliated against anyone, not China, not Japan, not Iran. The nearest American carrier was nearly a thousand miles away, and intelligence reported that it might take up stations in the Sea of Japan to defend Japan and South Korea, instead of moving toward the Formosa Strait to assist the rebel Nationalists.

America had to be stopped, Sun knew. The United States had to learn to respect the waters and airspace around China, as the United States expected other nations to do around its waters.

But the political leaders around the world, even in China, did not have the stomach to do what was necessary to ensure their sovereignty in their own territory when faced with the threat of domination by the United States. Sun Ji Guoming knew what must be done, and he knew that he must force his own political leadership to accept what was right and what was necessary. There was no choice, no other way.

Admiral Sun switched his radio panel to the Great Wall satellite communications system again, linking directly into the Beijing emergency military command center, and asked to speak with the Paramount Leader again.

"The wrath of the entire planet will be upon the people of China for what has been done today," President Jiang Zemin intoned, when he came on the line a few moments later. He had obviously been informed of the extensive and deadly nuclear attack on Taiwan, and the doubt and worry crushing his every thought was evident in his tired, wavering voice. "Our lives, our future will never again be the same."

"The future is now, Comrade President," Admiral Sun said. "You have seen to that. You have opened the way for us to reunite our shattered country from the destruction of foreign imperialism. But there is one more step to be done. Give the order, and it will be done."

"I cannot do it. It is insanity."

"Comrade, you may rely on me to be the instrument of your vision," Sun said in a firm, confident voice. Jiang did not order him to abort the mission or return to base, so he was *positive* that Jiang was going to give the order. He was a little hesitant—but who wouldn't be? "I will be the sword of your promise to the Chinese people. Give me the order, and I shall accomplish the deed. Afterwards, you may tell the world that I was an insane man who stole a jet and nuclear weapon at gunpoint—if you must betray me, so be it. I will always be loyal to you, to the motherland, and to the Chinese Communist Party. But this must be done. You know it to be true. We cannot succeed if the final step is not taken."

"You have done enough, Admiral," Jiang said.

Again, the Paramount Leader was expressing doubts, but he still did not give the order to abort. "You must tell me to abort the mission and return to base, Comrade President," Sun said. "If you do, I will obey. But you will also lose the opportunity to all but eliminate the Western imperialist–dominated threat to China's existence. I urge you, sir—no, I demand it. Save Zhongguo. Save China. Give the command."

There was no response—not even a "wait." A few moments later, a command post operator relayed an order from the president to stand by.

Sun continued northward over the East China Sea and, almost an hour later, they were just a hundred miles east of Shanghai. Sun ordered the final refueling to commence, and thirty minutes later the HT-6 Xian tanker was left with just enough fuel to return to base at Wuhan. Sun's H-7 Gangfang bomber turned slightly west and continued into the Yellow Sea, beginning a descent from 30,000 feet to 5,000 feet, sneaking in under the long-range radar coverage from Kunsan and Mokpo in South Korea, now less than three hundred miles to the east. After the attack on the rebel Nationalists, the Americans and South Koreans would surely be on their highest states of alert, and any unidentified aircraft flying anywhere near their shoreline or bases on the Korean Peninsula would quickly be intercepted.

Although a fully fueled H-7 had an endurance of about seven hours, Sun could not wait that long to get a response from Beijing. He would simply fly to his next checkpoint—if he did not receive approval for the final phase of his plan, he would head westbound and land at Wuhan People's Liberation Army Air Force Base, then begin planning another night of attacks on the Nationalists. It was important that—

"Attack One, this is Dark Night, respond, please."

"Dark Night, I am listening. Go ahead, please."

"Attack One, you are ordered to proceed. Repeat, you are ordered to proceed. Do you understand?"

Admiral Sun Ji Guoming wore a smile like a young child's at his first circus. "Attack One understands," he responded. "Attack One out." Sun then switched to the interphone and instructed the stunned bomber crew to carry out the attack orders.

The attack was simple and completely without threat from anywhere. From an altitude of 5,000 feet and an airspeed of 240 knots, the H-7 Gangfang bomber flew toward a preprogrammed point in the north-central part of the Yellow Sea, about one hundred miles east of the North Sea Fleet headquarters base at Qingdao, and then two long, slender shapes dropped from their semirecessed spaces in the H-7 bomber's belly. Three large parachutes deployed immediately from each object, and by the time the objects were 1,000 feet above the water, they were both hanging almost exactly vertical in their chutes, almost all rocking motions stopped. The H-7 bomber turned westward and accelerated to its maximum speed of nearly the speed of sound . . .

. . . so it was well clear of the area when the rocket motors of the two M-9 ballistic missiles ignited. The stabilizer parachutes released seconds after the flight computer detected full power chamber pressure in the rocket motors, and the M-9 missiles climbed rapidly in the night sky. One missile headed eastward, while the other headed northeast—both over the Korean Peninsula.

The Republic of Korea AN/EPS-117 air defense radar station at Seoul was the first to detect the missile launches, just seconds after the M-9s crossed the radar horizon, and the U.S.-made Patriot and I-Hawk surface-to-air-missile sites at Inchon and Seoul were instantly alerted. By the time missile-launch detection was confirmed, the second missile was out of range as it headed farther north over the demilitarized zone. The first missile was tracked and engaged by eight Patriot batteries—one by one they opened fire with double Patriot anti-missile missile launches.

The first two Patriot missiles hit their target, breaking the M-9 missile into several pieces. The other Patriot batteries continued to fire at the larger pieces of the Chinese missile—in all, eight Patriot missiles were launched, effectively chopping the thirty-foot-long, eighteen-inch-diameter M-9 missile into pieces no larger than a suitcase. The M-9's nuclear warhead was hit directly by one Patriot, detonating the high-explosive fusion initiator portion of the warhead and scattering radioactive debris over Inchon and the west-central coastline, but there was no nuclear yield.

The Korean People's Army Air Force of North Korea did not detect the second M-9 missile until after it had crossed the coast and was headed down over the center of the Korean Peninsula. The KPAAF's SA-2 and SA-3 fixed missile sites at Kaesong and one SA-5 mobile missile site at Dosan were the only units capable of attempting to intercept the M-9 missile, but all of these missiles were older, larger, less reliable strategic air defense missiles and were not designed to shoot down something as small and as fast as a ballistic missile. Untouched and unimpeded, the Chinese M-9 missile streaked out of the sky . . . and detonated its nuclear warhead about 20,000 feet above the large military city of Wonsan, on North Korea's east-central coastline.

The warhead had the explosive power of 20,000 *tons* of TNT, so although the missile missed its preprogrammed target coordinates by over a mile and a half, the effect of the blast was devastating. The nuclear explosion leveled the southeast portion of the city, completely destroying half of the aboveground buildings and facilities of the Korean People's Army's Southern Defense Sector headquarters, and substantially damaging the KPA Navy's Eastern Fleet headquarters and the surface and submarine naval bases located on Yonghung Bay. Although the city of Wonsan itself was spared from much of the nuclear blast because of the miss distance, almost twenty thousand civilians were killed or wounded in the blink of an eye that night, along with thousands of military men and women and their dependents on the military installations.

Sun Ji Guoming scanned all the possible radio frequencies for any signs of the death and destruction he had caused that night, but the atmosphere for hundreds of miles around had been charged by the nuclear detonations and all the bands were jumbles of static—he could not communicate with anyone until he was almost all the way across the Gulf of Chihli and over the coast near Tianjin, just sixty miles from Beijing. No matter, he thought. The war was on.

Soon, Sun knew, China would be handed the keys to its twenty-third province, Taipei, by a world praying for the bombing and missile attacks and the nuclear devastation to cease. The world would soon know that China would not be denied complete reunification.

U.S. STRATEGIC COMMAND COMMAND CENTER, OFFUTT AIR FORCE BASE, BELLEVUE, NEBRASKA SATURDAY, 21 JUNE 1997, 1601 HOURS LOCAL (1701 HOURS ET)

"The invasion of Taiwan appears to be under way," the intelligence officer said casually. If it were not such a serious matter, many of the men assembled before him might be laughing at the understated irony of that statement. It was not just Taiwan that was under attack—it seemed the stability of the entire planet was crumbling.

"The Chinese are on the move everywhere," the intelligence officer continued. He was standing at the podium on the stage in the U.S. Strategic Command command center, three stories underground in the middle of Offutt Air Force Base in central Nebraska. "At least three divisions massing along Xiamen Bay at Amoy, Liuwadian, Shijing, Dongshi, and Weitou. At these and several other locations, PLA artillery and rocket units have begun shelling the northern shoreline of Quemoy in an obvious 'softening-up' attack. We're looking at three hundred multiple rocket launcher units, two hundred and twenty artillery batteries, and at least sixty short-range ballistic rocket units arrayed along the bay. Resupply is coming in mostly by rail and by truck."

"What about amphibious landing capability?" one member of the STRATCOM staff asked. "We've been briefed that the Chinese don't have much of an amphibious assault capability. How are they going to move three divisions to Quemoy?"

"The reports of the People's Liberation Army's lack of amphibious capability was apparently grossly underestimated," the briefer responded. "Most forces needed for an amphibious invasion were not based with active-duty units, but sent instead to reserve and militia units that kept them separate and inactive. Now that the reserves and militia have been called up to support the invasion, we have a better picture of the PLA's amphibious assault capability, and it is quite substantial:

"The Taiwanese government has already reported airborne assaults in the early-morning hours by several cargo aircraft, with as many as a thousand commandos dropped on Quemoy in the past couple hours. They also report several forty-five- and thirty-five-meter air-cushion landing craft spotted along the western shores of Quemoy, including three on the beach. Each of these can carry as many as fifty troops and two fast armored assault vehicles, armored trucks, mobile antiaircraft artillery units, or small tanks. The Taiwanese have not reported where these commandos may be massing; they speculate that it may be part of a large reconnaissance or artillery-targeting patrol, or perhaps a plan to insert a great number of spies on the island. China was reported to have only a few of these air-cushion landing craft, but we're seeing reports of as many as a dozen.

"Several classes of amphibious assault ships have been spotted on shore, including some never classified previously and many thought to have been discarded or not in service," the briefer continued. "It's very difficult to determine exact numbers, but one estimate said that the PLAN has enough ships for a twenty-thousand-man assault on Quemoy anytime. They could possibly lift an entire brigade onto Quemoy in two to three days if unopposed."

"How many troops does Taiwan have on Quemoy?" one of the staff officers asked.

"Estimated at between sixty and seventy thousand," the briefer replied. "But we have not been given any casualty reports from the attack earlier today. Any troops stationed in unprotected areas might have been injured enough to make them combat-ineffective."

"Estimate of that number?"

There was a slight pause, as the enormity of the number he was about to give caught up with him; then he responded in a hard-edged monotone: "Half. As many as thirty-five thousand casualties possible on Quemoy."

The STRATCOM members listening were stunned into silence. They could hardly believe what had happened: in repelling a Taiwanese air invasion of Chinese invasion forces arrayed around Quemoy, the People's Republic of China had launched several surface-to-air missiles armed with nuclear warheads. The entire Taiwanese air invasion armada, estimated at thirty-two frontline U.S.-made F-16 Fighting Falcon fighter-bombers—two-thirds of its F-16 fleet and 10 percent of its entire active military air inventory—had been destroyed instantly.

"The five massive nuclear explosions occurred almost directly over Quemoy Island at an altitude of about thirty thousand feet, high enough so the fireballs did not touch the ground, but near enough to cause extensive damage from the heat and overpressure," the briefer went on. "Danger of radioactive fallout is low; the southern portion of Taiwan and northern Philippines might be affected. The aircraft carrier *George Washington* has been diverted to keep it out of the danger area."

"In apparent retaliation for the attacks on the mainland, China staged a massive counterattack, beginning with a feint by large fighter formations that drew away Taiwan's air defense fighters, followed by three large formations of heavy bombers attacking with short-range nuclear cruise missiles and conventional gravity bombs that almost completely destroyed four major air bases in the western portion of Taiwan," the intelligence officer continued. "The Chinese then followed up with medium-range nuclear ballistic missile attacks on three eastern Taiwan air and naval bases. The nuclear warheads were small high-altitude airbursts, less than forty-kiloton yields, but they were very effective. Half of Taiwan's air defense system, including substantially all its air forces and a third of its ground-based air defense weapons and radars, were destroyed."

"Any reports about Taiwan's defense posture?"

"Virtually nothing from Taipei at all, sir," the briefer replied. "Lots of reports of Chinese troop movements, but nothing regarding their own forces. No sign of the sixteen F-16 fighter-bombers that hit Juidongshan earlier. AWACS radar planes report formations of fighters, believed to be F-5s, over northern Taiwan, but Air Combat Command and the Navy want to get a better picture of the situation over Taiwan before moving radar planes closer.

"Now, over to the east, something else broke out between North and South Korea about an hour after the attacks over Taiwan began," the briefer went on. "The ROK air force detected a ballistic missile inbound from the west-northwest, possibly from the North Korean naval base at Haeju or from a surface ship off the coast. Air defense missile units at Inchon and Seoul successfully engaged and destroyed the inbound. The ROK then reported a second missile headed north over the border. Moments later, a hot nuclear detonation was detected over Wonsan, the army and navy headquarters base in the eastern DPRK. The ROK denies it fired any missiles, although it does admit they returned artillery and rocket fire with the North at many different locations along the DMZ after the nuclear explosion.

"The ROK is on full military alert, as is the North." The intelligence officer ran down a summary of the military deployments on both sides— almost two million troops and thousands of tanks, military vehicles, artillery pieces, and rockets were staring at each other all along the 140-mile-long frontier, with about a dozen clashes already breaking out in various parts of the DMZ. "Of course," the briefer summarized, "all nations in the region are on a high state of alert."

"No shit," Admiral Henry Danforth, the commander in chief of U.S. Strategic Command, gasped aloud. "Any idea at all who launched against the Koreans?"

"Both sides are denying it, as are the Chinese," the briefer responded. "We have polled our naval and air forces in the Yellow Sea and western Korean Peninsula region, and no one fired anything—the Navy is conducting an audit of all its forces, but that will be hampered by the alert. We've ruled out the Chinese ballistic missile subs—one has been in dry dock for some time, and the other two Chinese boomers are being shadowed by American attack subs, and they report no activity. The only possible explanation is one or two Chinese missiles that were supposed to hit Taiwan somehow veered six hundred miles off course and accidentally hit Korea, but that's unlikely. We're still investigating."

"Sweet Jesus, I can't believe it," Danforth muttered. "China actually went ahead and pushed the button." Admiral Danforth swiveled around in his seat until he could see General Samson, sitting behind him in the second row of the Battle Staff Room. "Still think we should recommend to the President that we take the bombers off nuclear alert, General Samson?" he asked.

"Admiral, the invasion of Quemoy, Taiwan, and perhaps even South Korea was going to occur no matter how many nuclear weapons we put back on alert," Samson said. "The Chinese destroyed an American aircraft carrier, launched a nuclear bombing raid on Taiwan, and I believe tried to instigate a second Korean War by shooting missiles over both North and South Korea—but are we any closer to declaring war on China, let alone a nuclear war?"

"I think we are, and the National Command Authority apparently agrees," Danforth said. "I'm recommending to the NCA that we go to DEFCON Three, deploy the ballistic missile sub fleet, put the bombers on restricted alert, and MIRV up all of the Peacekeeper and Minuteman ICBMs." The fifty LGM-118A Peacekeeper missiles were America's largest and most powerful nuclear weapon. Headquartered in Wyoming but based in underground silos in Colorado and Nebraska as well, the huge 195,000-pound missiles, when fully "MIRVed up," could carry as many as ten Mk 21 nuclear Multiple Independent Reentry Vehicles to targets as far as ten thousand miles away. The five hundred LGM-30G Minuteman III missiles now on alert at bases in North Dakota, Wyoming, and Montana carried up to three Mk 12 nuclear warheads.

"Sir, I believe that would be a mistake," Terrill Samson said earnestly. "I've got to restate my position for the staff."

Danforth looked very perturbed—Samson could see a jaw muscle flexing in the dim light of the Battle Staff Room. But CINCSTRATCOM motioned for Samson to step down. "Let's hear it, Terrill," he said. Samson gathered up a folder of notes and stepped down to the podium in front of the auditorium-like seats of the Battle Staff Room.

"Admiral, I'll be as blunt as I can—the Chinese won't believe we will use nuclear weapons against them because *I* don't believe we would," Samson said, "and if you can't make *me* believe it, they certainly won't."

"The President, the Secretary of Defense, the chairman of the Joint Chiefs, and *me* say you're wrong," Danforth said irritably. "Part of the problem is, General, is that the bombers aren't coming up fast enough to make the Chinese think we're serious about putting a nuclear strike force on alert. That's *your* responsibility."

"With all due respect, Admiral, I think you're wrong," Samson said. "The bombers are taking twice as long to come up as we planned because the crews practice all year for *conventional* bombing missions, but almost never for nuclear missions. The Chinese know this. We are just *now* discussing moving up the generation schedule for the bombers, several hours after we lose six thousand troops in a nuclear attack—if we were serious about using nuclear weapons, our counterattack would have been launched long ago."

"I don't appreciate your talking in absolutes about things we have no way of knowing, General," Danforth said. "Make your point."

"Sir, my staff and I have prepared a target list and strike plan for central and eastern China that I would like approval for issuance of a warning order," Samson said. "I want four B-2s, twenty B-1B bombers, and eight KC-135 or two KC-10 tankers, plus a list of non-nuclear weapons. The target list includes Chinese long-, intermediate-, and short-range nuclear missile sites, known nuclear weapon storage and maintenance bases, air defense sites, and communications centers . . . virtually the same targets we have at risk under the SIOP, sir, but targeted with bombers carrying conventionally armed cruise missiles, precision-guided cruise missiles, and satellite-guided gravity bombs.

"We can halt the SIOP generation of the bombers I need and reconfigure them easily for the conventional mission," Samson continued. "I plan to launch all twenty-four aircraft, pick the best twelve and have them continue to their targets, and recover the remaining twelve on Guam for refueling and launch them as a follow-on attack. Within twenty-four hours, we can have the bombers launched; within eighteen hours, the bombers will be striking targets in China and recovering at Guam, ready to begin round-the-clock attack operations. Commit the remainder of the bombers, and we can begin surge operations that can hold China's entire military at risk and even assist in air operations over North Korea at the same time if needed. I can guarantee—"

"Frankly, General Samson, your management of the Air Force bomber fleet up to this point has been something far less than adequate," Danforth interrupted, with a definite note of exasperation in his voice, "and I don't think you're in a position to guarantee anything."

"Sir, I feel that *your* current deployment of the bomber force is a waste of time, money, and manpower, and will do nothing to resolve the situation." Samson could see Danforth bristling with anger, but decided to quickly press on and say what he thought. "I urge you in the strongest terms to recommend to the NCA and the Joint Chiefs to abandon the nuclear generation and adopt this non-nuclear attack strategy my staff and I have drawn up. More lives and more time will be wasted if you don't."

The Battle Staff Room was quiet, deathly quiet. Danforth sat motionless, a finger on his lips, expressionless. After a few long moments, he sat up and waved to Samson with the back of his hand. "Thank you, General Samson," Danforth said. "That will be all."

"Yes, sir." Samson picked up his papers, left the podium, and headed back to his seat in the Battle Staff Room.

"I said, that will be *all,* General," Danforth repeated. Samson stopped, confused. "What I mean, General," Danforth said angrily, "is that you are relieved of duty."

"What!" Samson exclaimed; then, quickly regaining his composure, he asked, "I beg your pardon, Admiral?"

"You have failed to carry out your orders to generate the bomber fleet to wartime readiness as directed by the National Command Authority and this command; instead, you have wasted our time by advocating a posture that runs completely counter to orders that originate from the commander in chief himself," Danforth said. "Further, you don't seem to have any desire to follow my orders, and you have insulted and disgraced your fellow commanders in this room by your flagrant disregard for your superior officers and their lawful directives. You are relieved of command of CTF Three and are ordered to report back to Barksdale Air Force Base immediately to await further disciplinary action. Have your deputy report to me ASAP. Get out of my command center."

Stunned, Terrill Samson turned and headed for the door. He had to wait several long moments for the safelike blast door to be opened by security guards, and he could feel the stares of his colleagues on the back of his head—it was a very uncomfortable period of time until he could be escorted out. He had been fired. For the first time in his long and distinguished military career, he had been fired. Even worse, his commanding officer had said he had "failed"—and that was the worst slap in the face of all.

It was no great surprise when Patrick McLanahan entered Brad Elliott's hospital room fifteen minutes before official visiting hours began and found his friend and former commanding officer on the phone. He looked a little embarrassed when he saw McLanahan's disapproval. "Get back to me on that right away," he told his caller, his voice slightly nasal from the oxygen cannula. "Don't worry about the time—call me back as soon as you get the info." He hung up.

"You're obviously doing much better, Brad," Patrick said disapprovingly. "The nurses said you ordered the phone turned on ten minutes after you woke up last night."

"Don't start nagging me," Elliott said with a scowl. "I'm feeling just fine."

"You need rest, Brad, not more work," Patrick said. "You have a secretary and a staff back in Eaker, remember that. Have them take some of the jobs you want done. Or just call me or Wendy—she'll do whatever you want done."

"Okay."

Obviously, he hadn't heard a word Patrick said. He gave him a knowing, sarcastic smile and added, "The nurse said you're doing good. The clot-busting medication is working—no surgery, not even angioplasty. But she said you're up at all hours of the day and night making phone calls and watching the news on TV. This has got to stop or you'll never heal."

"All right, all right, I will," Elliott said.

"What are you up to, anyway, Brad?"

"I'm trying to get hold of Samson and Vic Hayes, see what in hell the fleet is doing." He nodded toward the two TV sets installed in his room, one tuned to CNN and the other to the Armed Forces News Service, which broadcast news and directives to all military units worldwide. "The news said Taiwan attacked the mainland, but then all hell seemed to break loose and there hasn't been a damn thing since. What do you got?"

"The attack's been verified," Patrick responded. "The Chinese got it on video again and showed it on several international news networks—

Taiwanese F-16 Falcons, bombing and strafing the shit out of Juidong-shan Naval Base. Successful hit, from what the news said. Maybe a couple subs, headquarters building, a POL farm, air defense sites. They report lots of casualties, but we haven't seen any on TV."

"Shit hot," Elliott exclaimed happily. "The ROCs have the right idea. Now I just wish we'd get into the game." He noticed Patrick's downcast expression. "You heard something else? What?"

"There was another ROC attack last night on the amphibious attack staging bases near Xiamen," McLanahan replied. "Much larger strike package—perhaps the remainder of Taiwan's F-16 fleet."

"Great! I didn't hear anything about it in the news. They kick ass too?"

"Not exactly," Patrick said. "Satellite radiation sensors indicate the attack formations were hit by surface-to-air missiles with nuclear warheads. Five detonations were detected, all in the twenty- to fifty-kiloton range, about twenty miles east of Xiamen over Quemoy Island. No survivors."

"*What!*" Elliott exploded. "The Chinese used SAMs with *nuclear warheads?*"

" 'Fraid so," McLanahan said. "No statement yet from the Chinese government."

"They'll probably say that the Taiwanese fighters were carrying nuclear weapons and they accidentally went off," Elliott said disgustedly. "If that doesn't work, they'll admit that their SAMs had nuclear warheads on them but they were provoked into using nuclear weapons because a thousand crazed Taiwanese attack planes were bearing down on them, assisted by an American stealth bomber, or some crap like that. The damned thing is, the world press will believe them." Elliott fell silent for a moment; then: "I wonder what in hell Samson and the Chiefs are doing now? We should at least be lining up some strikes against Chinese ICBM or medium-range ballistic missile sites, especially the nuclear sites."

"Might be too late," McLanahan said. "China retaliated against the Taiwan attack—they attacked with nuclear-armed air-launched cruise missiles and medium-range ballistic missiles. Taiwan got blasted all to hell. They're not a smoking hole in the Pacific, but their big air bases got creamed."

"I don't believe it!" Elliott exclaimed. A cold chill ran up and down his spine. He remembered the nuclear scares of the past thirty years, but it had never come to an all-out nuclear exchange . . . until now. "No wonder I can't get anything out of anybody. What else, Muck? What else happened?"

"Looks like someone popped off a couple ballistic missiles over North and South Korea," McLanahan went on. "Wonsan in the North got hit."

"With a goddamn *nuke?*"

"Yep," McLanahan said. "Looks like we're one radio call from starting a new war in Korea—and this one might go nuclear or biochemical right away."

"Oh, shit, this is incredible!" Elliott cursed. "We've got to get in the ball game, Muck! We've got to talk with Hayes or Samson. All I see is this stuff on the news about ballistic missile subs put out to sea—I haven't heard squat about the bombers."

"Samson put them on alert," Patrick said.

"Well, no shit," Elliott said. "But why in hell hasn't he deployed them here?"

"They're on SIOP ground alert, Brad," Patrick replied. "Samson's not at Barksdale—the President ordered STRATCOM to stand up the Combined Task Forces. Samson's at Offutt."

"SIOP alert? What beanbrain activated the SIOP?" Elliott thundered. "The Chinese know we're not going to use nuclear weapons on anyone, especially not a third world country like the People's Republic of China! We should have launched non-nuclear strikes against the Chinese sub and missile bases by now, knocked out their nuclear warfighting capability. The bombers should have been over their targets hours ago. We don't need nukes to send the Chinese to the bargaining table. What in hell is Earthmover doing at Offutt, anyway? We could have this thing over with by now."

"Brad, relax," Patrick said. "Things are quiet right now. Everybody's backed off to neutral corners."

"Oh, sure—after they nuke Taiwan into another dimension!" Elliott retorted. "How long do you think that'll last? Not long—probably just long enough for everybody to load up their artillery shells and gravity bombs with nuclear or chemical warheads."

"I'll call Samson at Offutt and get him to stop with the nukes, put conventional cruise missiles on the bombers, and start laying down the law to the Chinese before someone starts another nuclear exchange.

With the Megafortresses already here, we can take care of the radar sites and long-range strategic defenses, if Balboa or Allen haven't already sent the EA-6 Prowlers in." The EA-6 Prowlers were the combined Navy and Air Force medium-range and carrier-based anti-radar planes, able to jam and attack enemy radar and air defense sites. "Maybe I can get some charts and draw up a flight plan so you can have it in the computers ready to go in case we get the word to—"

"We're grounded, if you remember, Brad," Patrick said. "We've been doing nothing but getting the damaged bird ready to go and packing up all our equipment before the Navy or the federal marshals seize it. We'll be ready to depart in a couple days."

"No one is going to seize anything, Muck," Elliott said. "Balboa was just blowing gas."

"They've got marshals surrounding the hangars and our headquarters, backed up by Navy SPs," Wendy McLanahan said, as she entered the room just then. She gave Elliott a welcoming kiss. "Nice to see you up and around . . . but the nurse says—"

"Who said you two could talk to my blabbermouth nurse, anyway?"

"Never mind that—you need the rest, not more work," Wendy admonished him.

"What about the Megafortresses?"

"Balboa's for real, Brad," Patrick said. "We'd probably have been flown back to Washington to appear in federal court already, except for the *Independence* disaster—air traffic has been shut down completely over the Pacific."

Elliott sighed wearily, looking as if all the moisture had been sucked out of his body. Stuck in bed, grounded, facing legal action, and having his prized Megafortresses shut down and one step out of the Boneyard was almost too much for him to handle. He had been calling everyone he knew back in the States, gathering information, asking for favors, trying to find some avenue he could pursue to get the chairman of the Joint Chiefs of Staff off his back and get the Megafortresses flying again, but no one returned his calls. With this new disaster in the Pacific, George Balboa had all the power and influence now. "Dammit, I need to talk with Samson soonest."

"I brought bad news, then," Wendy McLanahan said. "Terrill Samson called from Offutt. He's been relieved of duty as commander of Combined Task Force Three."

"Oh, shit," Patrick exclaimed. "How did that happen?"

"One word—CINCSTRATCOM. Henry Danforth," Elliott said. "He's a younger but stupider clone of George Balboa. He doesn't know how to handle the heavy bomber fleet and doesn't trust Samson or anyone else to run the fleet for him, because he's afraid the Air Force would kick ass and overshadow the carriers and Navy air."

"He got into an argument with CINCSTRATCOM over releasing some of the B-1s and B-2s for conventional missions," Wendy said. "I guess the argument got too personal."

"He probably asked for Major-General Collier to replace him, Samson's vice at Barksdale," Elliott guessed. "Collier's a good guy, but he hasn't run a wing in almost ten years. Samson's the bomber guy. I think we're aced out completely."

"At least Earthmover was in there trying to get STRATCOM steered in the right direction," Patrick McLanahan said. "The bombers don't belong in the nuclear mission now—probably not ever. If the shit really hits the fan and we have to go nuclear, the subs and ICBMs are the best weapons then—we should be using the bombers for non-nuclear strikes deep into China. But with the B-52s retired and the B-1s and B-2s stuck on nuclear alert, there's no long-range aircraft to be used for non-nuclear strikes."

"So we're out of it," Elliott summarized with an exasperated sigh. "We busted our nuts and risked our necks out here for nothing. Man, what else could go wrong today?"

Just then, a gentleman with a dark suit and tie—definitely the last outfit one would expect to see on the tropical island of Guam in late June—walked into Elliott's room. "Mr. and Mrs. McLanahan? General Elliott?"

"Wrong room," Elliott said immediately. "Get out."

"I'm McLanahan," Patrick said.

The man immediately placed an envelope into his hands, then walked over and did the same to Wendy and Brad Elliott. "Order to appear," the man said.

"What in hell is this?"

"Federal court in Washington, five days from now," the guy said. "Have a nice evening." He walked out.

"Balboa's for real, all right," Patrick McLanahan said as he opened the summons. "The list of charges against us is two friggin' pages long."

"I'll get these over to the Sky Masters attorneys and get the paper-work started on this," Wendy said, taking the summons and giving El-liott a kiss on the cheek and her husband a kiss on the lips. "Don't you boys worry about this. Brad, get some sleep, please."

"I will, babe," Elliott said, giving her a reassuring smile. She left McLanahan and Elliott alone. The ex–three-star general nodded toward the door. "Shit. I always thought I'd buy the farm in the cockpit of a B-52 after just saving the world from thermonuclear meltdown. Instead, I'll go down in a fucking federal courtroom with a bunch of lawyers suck-ing my guts out through my ass with a straw."

"I know how you feel, Brad," McLanahan said. He took a chair be-side his friend's bed, folded his hands on his knees, and stared at the floor, looking as if he were at confession or praying. "I'm sorry about what I said the other day, Brad. . . ."

"Forget it, Muck."

"I'm serious. I'm really sorry." He paused, then went on in a quiet voice. "You know, all I wanted to do was fly. All I ever wanted to be was a flyer. Jon Masters is great, and he's fun and exciting to work with, and the money is great, and it's good to be working with Wendy in a low-stress environment, but the truth is, I don't want to be a corporate executive weenie. Wendy likes that stuff, but I'm strangling to death. Jon fixates on the bottom line, the profits and the publicity and the prestige he gets when he goes for another big defense contract. I don't look at it that way."

"I know you don't," Elliott said with a satisfied smile. "I know you, Patrick. Ever since the day I first met you, I was inside your head. I had you pegged." He chuckled as he remembered the day, so long ago and so far away. "You with your flight suit unzipped, no scarf, your boots looking like you polished them with a Brillo pad. You'd just won your second Fairchild Trophy. You were hell on wheels, the hottest hand in the Air Force, Top Bomb. Any other crewdog would have traded the name and the trophies for a choice assignment. You could have worked for a dozen CINCs all over the world. You could have had a staff of twenty at the Pentagon. Two- and three-star generals were fighting each other to get to endorse your officer effectiveness reports. But you, stand-ing in the hallway with your beer and your give-a-shit attitude—all you wanted was to climb aboard the B-52 and drop some more shack bombs. You told me so, and you've proved it a dozen times since. Why would I think you'd ever change?"

Patrick laughed as his thoughts interlinked with Elliott's, through time and space, from the present to the past and back again over dozens of battles, through tragedy and triumph. "Hell, I think I've got to change, General. I'm afraid I'll get left behind—" And then he stopped abruptly, his cheeks flushing red under his longish blond hair.

"You were going to say 'left behind like you,' like *me,* right, Muck?" Elliott said. Patrick raised a pair of sad, apologetic blue eyes at his friend and mentor, to the man he had just betrayed with his thoughts. Elliott smiled reassuringly back. "Hey, Muck, it's okay. I see myself in you, Patrick, but sure as shit, you're not like me. I get things done by blasting ahead, by kicking ass and doing things my way and to hell with anyone that thinks they know better than me. You don't do it that way. You plan, you train, you build, and you let the smart commanders and the smart decision-makers come to you. You're smart, working with guys like Jon Masters—I can only stand the skinny dweeb for a few minutes a day and that's it. We're different, Muck. You're the future of the Air Force, bud."

"Some future," McLanahan said. "In five days, we'll be entering a plea in front of a federal judge on about twenty different charges. We could go to prison for ten years."

"In five days, you'll be a commanding officer in charge of the greatest strike force the planet has ever seen, snatching victory from the jaws of defeat," Elliott corrected him proudly. "And after that, you'll take your rightful place in the world. It won't be behind a desk, and it won't be in a federal prison. That's my prediction."

McLanahan smiled a cautious, hopeful smile, but Elliott extended a confident, reassuring hand, and the young bombardier took it warmly. "I like the way you think, sir," he told him.

At that moment the door to the room opened, and a gentleman in a dark suit and tie, similar to the federal marshal's, came in. McLanahan quickly stood, blocking the man's path, and motioned for the man to step outside. "Excuse me, sir, but the general needs his rest and can't be disturbed right now."

"Hold on, Muck," Elliott said. "You don't remember this gent, do you? Ambassador Kuo Han-min, meet Colonel Patrick McLanahan, my friend and colleague." The Asian gentleman smiled a very pleased and excited smile, bowed, and extended a hand. "Muck, meet Ambassador

Kuo Han-min, ambassador to the United States from the newly independent Republic of China. You ran into each other outside the White House Oval Office, remember?" McLanahan's expression told Kuo that he remembered, which pleased him even more.

"What are you doing here, Ambassador?" McLanahan asked as the ambassador took his hand and shook it. "How did you get on base? How did you know to find us here?"

"I told him, of course," Elliott said. McLanahan turned a shocked grimace toward his ex-boss. "Hell, Muck, don't act so damned shocked—you knew it all the time. I talked to Kuo before our patrols began over the Formosa Strait; I've talked to him almost every day since. We've co-ordinated our moves as much as we could over the past month." McLanahan could do nothing but nod—yes, he knew, or at least strongly suspected, that Brad Elliott was sharing information with Taiwan all the time, not just before the initial patrol but ever since then.

"Very pleased to meet you, Colonel," Kuo said with a warm, admiring smile. "You are a very great hero in my country. Many members of my government and my military wish to meet you and extend to you every courtesy and honor."

"I appreciate it, Mr. Ambassador," McLanahan said, trying to stay polite despite his uneasy feeling that Brad Elliott was tiptoeing on the very thin line between cooperation between allies and treason. "Someday I'd like to visit Taiwan. I've never been there before." His tired voice, however, signaled that it might be a very long time before he got the opportunity to visit anywhere but a rec room in a minimum-security prison facility.

"I have heard of your legal troubles, my friend," Kuo said. "It is very unfortunate that your bravery is not rewarded by your own government. I wish there was some way we could help."

"Perhaps you could tell us about the attacks you staged against China, sir," McLanahan suggested.

"Of course," Kuo said. "The attacks were planned as preemptive strikes against the communications, headquarters, and fuel-storage facilities that might be used in an attack against Quemoy Tao, which our intelligence said would be the Communists' first target."

"Did you know the PRC had nuclear-armed surface-to-air missiles?"

Kuo shrugged. "Yes, Colonel, we knew," he replied. "We know of many Communist nuclear weapon deployments, both tactical and strategic. Part of he strike against Xiamen was against their suspected nuclear-armed Hai Ying-2 and Ying Ji-6 land-based anti-ship missiles."

"Nuclear anti-ship missiles?"

"The Communists have an extensive menu of tactical nuclear weapons, Colonel, similar to the American arsenal in the 1960s and 1970s," Kuo said. "Their ships carry short- and intermediate-range ballistic missiles with nuclear warheads, and their subs use nuclear-tipped torpedoes and can lay nuclear-armed mines, similar to the Mk 57. They employed nuclear cruise missiles from their long-range bombers on their attacks on my country, and we believe they can launch medium-range ballistic missiles from their heavy bombers as well. The world has looked the other way for many decades, but we on Taiwan have lived under the shadow of a powerful nuclear adversary."

"Shit," McLanahan swore. "No one ever suspected they had a nuclear arsenal like that. Have you ever shared this information with the American government?"

"Always, but our information was disregarded as unreliable, biased, and unverifiable," Kuo said. "I believe your government simply chose not to believe our information, that starting a war with China over its military hardware would mean financial and economic disaster to your country. Many other pieces of information were discarded by your government. We reported the actual size of the Communists' amphibious assault fleet to your chairman of the Joint Chiefs of Staff directly, but your official published estimates did not reflect this. We reported the Communists' advanced ballistic missile capabilities, including air- and sea-launched M-9 nuclear ballistic missiles, but that went unheeded as well. The Republic of Iran has far less military hardware than Communist China, and you sent your stealth bombers over there secretly to bomb their bases—but for some odd reason, your government refuses to punish China for its aggression.

"Our information is reliable," Kuo went on, "and we expected the Communists to begin using these weapons against us at any time. We believed the *Mao* battle group and their attempted attack on Quemoy to be the first step. The attack on Quemoy by nuclear missiles fired by the carrier *Mao Zedong* that you stopped with your amazing EB-52 Megafortress was typical of the People's Liberation Army. Since then, however, their tactics have become very confusing, very unconventional—not at all like the People's Liberation Army and its leadership. The attack on the *Mao* was obviously a complicated and well-orchestrated ruse."

"Your sub was caught in the immediate vicinity, and reports said the PLAN recovered pieces of torpedoes used by your navy," McLanahan pointed out. "It could be a well-planned ruse—or it could have been an attack by your submarine."

"Our submarine did not fire on the carrier," Kuo insisted. "Yes, we were shadowing the carrier, but we did not attack."

"Can you prove it?"

"The Communists covered their tracks very effectively by sinking the submarine instead of capturing it," Kuo said. "We cannot prove our contention—just as it is difficult for you to prove that your frigates were fired upon by underwater-launched rocket torpedoes. The faked attack against your frigates, in which you were involved? Pure genius, if I may say so. Setting off the underwater-launched rocket torpedoes at the same time a passenger ferry cruises near the area, a ferry equipped with radio emitters to make it appear like a warship? The sheer imagination of the plan must be applauded, do you not agree?"

"I agree," McLanahan said. It was the only possible explanation, and one that he had suspected right from the start. "So this leaves us alone, isolated, and with China holding all the cards. They've got the world believing both Taiwan and the United States are trying to provoke a war—and in trying to defend themselves, they seem to be given tacit permission to use nuclear weapons."

"After Taiwan, the South China Sea and Spratly Islands will fall to the Communists—as you have stated, Colonel, they will be allowed to defend their new conquests with nuclear weapons," Kuo said grimly. "The entire world will be in danger if the Communists are allowed to control access to the South China Sea." He paused, looking first at Elliott, then McLanahan. "We were praying for a miracle, that your amazing EB-52 Megafortresses might be able to come to our defense once again."

"There isn't a snowball's chance in hell of us getting those planes back into action," Elliott said. "It would take a small army to move those Navy security policemen. And even then, we'd have no place to take them."

McLanahan had been quiet for several long moments, but now he was looking at Kuo and Elliott, a glimmer of an idea in his eyes. "We can get them off Guam," he said.

"You and what army, Muck?" Elliott asked.

"Getting past the marshals and Navy security is the easy part," McLanahan said with a sly smile. "But if we fly the Megafortresses back to the States, they'll be ground up into asphalt filler in a matter of days, and we'll be in front of a federal court judge fighting for own freedom and the survival of our company. We need a base of operations. Sky Masters, Inc., has a support base on Saipan, and he has pretty good connections with the sultan of Brunei, who would probably be happier than hell to have the Megafortresses based in his country."

"If you are able to get your aircraft off Guam with weapons and support personnel, I have a base you can use," Ambassador Kuo said proudly. "We have skilled aircraft technicians, a good supply of fuel and ordnance, and very good security."

"A base on Taiwan?" McLanahan asked. Kuo bowed in assent with great enthusiasm. "With all due respect, sir, Taiwan has been hit pretty hard. It might be too dangerous."

"It would be, as you might say, the last place anyone would look for your EB-52 Megafortresses," Ambassador Kuo said with an unabashed grin. "Please, Colonel McLanahan, let me explain. . . ."

ANDERSEN AIR FORCE BASE, AGANA, GUAM
MONDAY, 23 JUNE 1997, 1901 HOURS LOCAL
(SUNDAY, 22 JUNE, 0401 HOURS ET)

The "six-pack" crew truck pulled up to the first hangar on the north side of the aircraft parking apron, and was immediately surrounded by U.S. Marines in green-and-black battle dress uniforms carrying M-16 rifles slung over their shoulders. As Patrick and Wendy McLanahan, Brad Elliott, Nancy Cheshire, and Jon Masters stepped out of the big pickup truck and began unloading their gear, a Navy officer in a clean, neatly pressed white tropical uniform met up with them, accompanied by a security guard wearing black fatigues with "U.S. MARSHAL" in yellow across his chest.

"A little late to be out working, isn't it, Mr. McLanahan?" the Navy officer asked. He glared at Brad Elliott, obviously surprised to see him up and about. Elliott gave him his best mischievous grin in return.

"Not if we want to depart by tomorrow night," Patrick replied. The rest of his crew tried to carry their gear past the Marine guards, but were stopped by a raised hand from the Navy officer. Patrick put his bags down at his side. "Is there a problem, Commander Willis?"

U.S. Navy Commander Eldon Willis pointed at the bags of flight gear, and the federal marshal and a Marine guard began searching them. Willis was the commander of security forces at Agana Naval Base on Guam, sent up to Andersen Air Force Base to personally supervise the security on the EB-52 Megafortresses ordered by Admiral George Balboa, chairman of the Joint Chiefs of Staff. Willis took this assignment very seriously and knew that it might be a path to getting an assignment for the Chief of Naval Operations or even for Balboa. "I didn't expect you out here tonight, Mr. McLanahan." He turned to Elliott. "And I certainly did not expect you either, General. I hope you're feeling better, sir." He used the words "sir" and "General," but it was obvious that Willis offered no sign of respect to the retired Air Force three-star.

"Peachy, Willis, just peachy," Elliott said, with his maddening grin.

Willis gave him a sneer along with a slight bow. In the meantime, the guards finished their inspections. "Tech orders and checklists, Commander," the marshal reported. "No flying gear."

The Navy security officer nodded, disappointed that they hadn't found anything a little more incriminating. "I hope you weren't planning on running engines tonight," Willis said.

"That's precisely what we had in mind," Patrick said. "We're going to tow all the planes over to the north apron, then run 'em one by one."

"The DC-10 tanker too," Jon Masters said. "We'll do the final checkout on it tonight, then start loading up tomorrow."

"I wasn't advised about any of the planes being towed outside," Willis said pointedly. "My orders are to not allow any activities that were not approved in advance."

"What do you think we're going to do out here, Commander—steal our own planes?" McLanahan asked with a boyish disarming smile. "Look, Commander, either we depart on schedule tomorrow night or my company loses millions when you guys chop up these planes. We're running a little behind with maintenance glitches. All we need is to run engines for a few minutes. It's too much of a hassle to clear out the hangars to run engines inside, so it would be better if we could—"

"Denied, Mr. McLanahan," Willis said sternly. "No clearance, no activity."

McLanahan stepped a bit closer to Willis and said in a low, somewhat emotional voice, "Hey, Commander, would it kill you to extend a little professional courtesy to me? I am officially retired from the service, despite what you might have heard about me. How long have you been in the Navy?"

"That is hardly the topic of conversation here."

"I was in for sixteen years," McLanahan said. "Yes, I took the early out—actually, I was strongly induced to accept it, or else I would have stayed in. I was on the O-6 list, and I was just a couple months from pinning on. I understand you've been selected for O-6, and you pin on next week?" No reaction from Willis. "That's great. I wish the Air Force had that frocking policy, pinning on your new rank as soon as you're selected for promotion. You Navy guys get the best of everything."

"Mr. McLanahan . . . *Colonel* McLanahan," Willis relented, "I cannot allow these planes to be towed out onto the apron without prior approval."

"It's *very* important that we tow them out, Commander," Nancy Cheshire said. Willis turned to look at the Air Force pilot. Willis had seen Cheshire out around the planes several times before, and although she was pretty enough, he had always thought of her as a tomboy, probably a lesbian, and dismissed her.

Not this time. Her flight suit had been altered to accentuate her figure, and her flight suit's top zipper had been unzipped to mid-chest, revealing a more than ample bosom, firm and round. Her hair had been pinned up, revealing a long, slender neck. Her eyes were shining green, round and inviting, and he saw those eyes dip down to check him out, her lips opening up slightly as if she was impressed and perhaps a little excited about the dashing figure he thought he cut in his tropical whites.

"Can't you give us clearance, just this once?" Cheshire implored him. "We'll be done in less than two hours, and we'll have them back in the hangars by midnight." She hesitated, then added, "I'll notify you in person when we're finished."

Willis puffed up his chest, excited at that prospect but not ready to concede one bit. But that thought was quickly canceled by a slight girlish grin on Cheshire's lips that spoke huge volumes to the Navy officer. Willis said, "I'm sorry, but I cannot allow the planes to leave the hangar without prior clearance." But he paused, then added, "But you may open both sides of the hangars and run engines inside."

"We really need to do this outside."

"Denied," Willis said. "Run engines inside the hangar, or not at all."

McLanahan shook his head, muttered something to himself, lowered his head in defeat, then nodded. "Very well, Commander. Inside the hangars only. It'll have to do. Thank you."

"Notify me in my office when you are complete and closed up," Willis added, glancing again at Nancy Cheshire. She arched her eyebrows, silently asking the question, and he answered with an almost imperceptible nod. He stepped away, issued instructions to the federal marshal and his NCO in charge of the security detail, gave one last glance at Cheshire, who still had her eyes locked on him—on his butt, he guessed—and stepped away to his waiting Humvee.

"Thank you, Commander," Patrick shouted after him—his thanks were not acknowledged. He turned to the others with him: "Okay, gang, we can't do this outside, so the noise levels are going to be bad, but we'll have to make do. Let's run the 'Before Starting Engines' checklist for ground engine-running maintenance first, then climb on board. We're all going to have to help out. Let's go."

It took just a few minutes for the flight and maintenance crews to clear out the hangars and open up the double-ended hangar doors, and within half an hour the deafening sound of the Megafortress's huge jet engines could be heard. The Navy security guards put on noise protectors, but were still forced to retreat to their Humvees to escape the noise.

Fortunately, shift change was coming up soon, so the guards wouldn't have to contend with the noise for too long. Sure enough, a radio report announced that relief crews were on the way, and the security guards packed up their equipment and got ready to depart when the oncoming crews reported in. At the same time, a long convoy of canvas-covered trailers moved from one of the hangars on the other side of the twin runways to the west, accompanied by the standard four armored vehicles, moving toward them. The guards were curious, but the relief crews were arriving, so it was *their* problem now.

The relief-crew Humvee for the front of Hangar No. 1 stopped directly in front of the offgoing crew's Humvee, shining their headlights directly into the offgoing crew's eyes. Six men stepped out, all wearing Navy-style integrated helmet–noise protectors; the oncoming detail chief carried the detail duty log and the weapon inventory sheets, as required. The Marine detail chief was going to get out and start the weapon inventory, but the oncoming detail chief was already at the door, holding the logs and inventory sheets out. His crew opened the doors in back and began to step out . . .

. . . and then all hell seemed to break loose.

Doors flew open. Guys were yelling something. Confusion. Gas began to fill the interior of the Humvee. Doors were closed, then wedged shut. The headlights on the other Humvee snapped off. The sweet odor of the gas, a slight choking sensation . . . then nothing.

The doors were opened to ventilate the gas, and a guard wearing a gas mask pushed the unconscious offgoing detail crew chief over against the huge engine hump in the middle of the Humvee, jumped in behind the wheel, and drove off. Outside, Marine Gunnery Sergeant Chris Wohl raised a walkie-talkie to his lips. "Bravo check."

"Bravo secure."

"Copy. Break. Charlie check." One by one, Chris Wohl checked in all the members of his fifty-man commando team. In less than a minute, Chris Wohl and the members of his Intelligence Support Agency special operations commando team, nicknamed Madcap Magician, had completely subdued the four entire Marine Corps security rifle platoons that had been guarding the five Megafortress hangars.

"Break. Leopard. All secure."

"Copy," Air Force Major Harold Briggs, the commander of Madcap Magician, responded. Briggs, an ex–Air Force security police commander at the HAWC, was in the lead Humvee escorting the convoy of trailers from the secure hangar that held the Megafortress's weapons—his team had subdued the Marines guarding the weapons while Wohl's team had taken down the guards surrounding the planes. The convoy was ushered into the hangars, while another long convoy emerged from the weapons hangar on its way to the planes.

Several Humvees converged on Hangar No. 1 as its engines were shut down. As each crew member climbed out of the planes, they did a very unmilitary-like thing—they gave each Madcap Magician commando a hug. "Damn it all, it's good to see you, Hal," Elliott said. Neither had seen the other since the High Technology Aerospace Weapons Center had been closed.

"Same here, General," Briggs said. "You look like a million freakin' bucks, sir."

"Don't bullshit a bullshitter, Hal," Elliott said. "I feel like shit. But I'm sure glad you're here."

"We weren't going to miss this party for all the nukes in China, boss," Briggs said. He motioned to Chris Wohl. "Chris, you remember General Elliott, right?"

"Of course. How are you, sir?" Wohl said, shaking hands with the retired three-star general. Wohl and Elliott first met while preparing for a secret rescue mission to Lithuania, when Wohl had been asked to train McLanahan, Briggs, and another HAWC commander, now dead, in enough commando-style tactics so they could safely accompany a Marine Force Recon team. Wohl had been against the entire plan, but had been convinced to carry on by Brad Elliott himself.

"Peachy, Gunny, peachy," Elliott responded. "Glad to have you along. Thanks for the help."

"Nothing to it," Wohl said matter-of-factly. "This entire detachment needed a good ass-kicking. They were way too complacent. I was happy to give it to them."

"I brought along a guy who said he knew a little about B-52s," Briggs said. Out of the Humvee came a gentleman a little younger than Elliott. "You remember Paul White, don't you, sir?"

"Damn right I do," Elliott said happily, and they exchanged handshakes, then embraces.

"Good to see you again, General," White said. Paul White was a retired Air Force colonel, an electronics engineering expert who'd been assigned to Patrick McLanahan's bomber base years earlier. Upon retirement from active military duty, White had become the original commander of the Central Intelligence Agency–sponsored unit called Madcap Magician. White's unit had been involved in the Iranian conflict earlier that year; White himself had been captured by the Iranians. Although he had been rescued unharmed by Briggs, Wohl, and the other surviving members of Madcap Magician, White had been decertified from intelligence work and forced to retire. "I hear we're going to kick some Chinese butt. Can't wait to fire up those turbofans."

The real reunion came when Patrick and Wendy McLanahan emerged and greeted Hal Briggs. These three had first been together years earlier in the original Megafortress project started by Brad Elliott, when Patrick and Wendy had been selected by Elliott to help design and test-fly the first Megafortress, a modified B-52 nicknamed "Old Dog." That test program started ten years earlier had suddenly become an operational mission when Elliott and his crew of engineers and flyers had flown the Old Dog over the Soviet Union to destroy a ground-based laser site that had been shooting down American satellites, and threatening an inter-continental nuclear war between the superpowers. The bastardized mission had been a success, and the ragtag test crew had become the centerpiece of the Air Force's most highly classified installation, the High Technology Aerospace Weapons Center, nicknamed Dreamland.

"I never thanked you for helping my ass over Iran, Patrick," Hal Briggs said. "I knew you were up there doing shit, I knew it! I heard the Iranians launching every SAM and triple-A projectile they had, and I knew it was either a raid by every bomber in the fleet, or a couple Scream-ers launched by Patrick McLanahan. Thank you for saving my narrow ass, brother."

"My distinct pleasure," Patrick said. He shook hands with Wohl. "Good to see you, Gunny. Great work taking over this airfield. I don't think the Marines will ever know what hit them."

"It was no problem, sir," Wohl responded. He motioned to his Humvee, and two of Wohl's commandos brought out Commander Willis. "I thought you should explain things to the commander." Wohl ripped the piece of duct tape off the Navy commander's face, leaving a cherry-red mark on either side of the angry officer's face.

"I will see you thrown in prison for the rest of your life, McLanahan!" Willis shouted. "This is a complete outrage! You are nothing but a crim-inal and a traitor!"

"I'm taking what belongs to me, Eldon," Patrick said. "We're going to keep you and your men nice and safe and out of the way. I'm sure you'll be found shortly after we've departed."

"Where the hell do you think you're going to go, McLanahan?" Willis spat angrily. "Where do you think you're going to hide five fuck-ing B-52 bombers? You might as well give yourselves up now. Or maybe you can just defect to Russia or China or wherever the hell you're headed, you lousy stinking traitors!"

"I'm not going to defect, Eldon—we're going to fight," Patrick said. He nodded to Wohl, who nodded to his men, who wrapped another long piece of duct tape over Willis's mouth. "Get him out of here, Gunny," McLanahan said.

"With pleasure, sir," Wohl said humorlessly.

Patrick turned to Hal Briggs. "The rest of the flight crews were taken off the island and sent back to the States," Patrick said, "so we've only got enough flight crews for one plane. We're going to load all the weapons we can on Jon Masters's DC-10 launch plane, and upload all the defensive weaponry we can on the bombers themselves. We're short on maintenance crews too, so we've got to do a lot of the loading and preflight stuff ourselves, so we can use all the help your guys can give us. After the Redtail Hawk mission, I figured your troops are somewhat familiar with loading air-to-mud stuff on bombers."

"You got it, Patrick," Briggs said, rubbing his hands together with sheer excitement. "Man, this is great! Do I get to go flying this time?"

"We're way short on crew members, so we can use all the help we can get."

"In that case, I brought along someone who might help," Briggs said. He motioned to his Humvee, and a single man stepped out. It was hard to see his face in the glare of the headlights . . .

. . . but Patrick McLanahan knew who it was the minute he stepped out of the vehicle, even without seeing his face, and the brotherly embrace they shared in the glare of the Humvee's headlights was genuine and tearful. "My God, Dave, it's really you, it's really fucking *you,*" Patrick breathed, his voice choked with emotion. Wendy, Briggs, and Brad Elliott joined the two, and they all clustered around one another like a close-knit family reunited after many painful years.

David Luger and Patrick McLanahan had once formed the Air Force's most effective bombing team ever. Because of their skill, knowledge, expertise, and seamless teamwork, they had both been selected by Brad Elliott for the secret "Old Dog" project. When the test project had suddenly turned into an operational mission, together Patrick, Luger, Wendy, Brad Elliott, and two more crew members, now dead, had successfully attacked and destroyed the Soviet anti-satellite laser site.

But the crew had been forced to land their battle-damaged plane on an abandoned Soviet airfield in eastern Siberia. The crew had managed to steal enough fuel to depart the base, but in the battle that ensued after they refueled the EB-52, Dave Luger had left the bomber to draw fire from the Red Army soldiers that had arrived. His heroic actions had allowed the Megafortress and the rest of the crew to escape, but he had been severely wounded and left behind in the frozen wastes.

Luger had been feared dead and was nearly forgotten until Paul White and members of Madcap Magician, performing a daring rescue inside a secret Soviet research facility in the Baltic republic of Lithuania, had discovered Luger inside the same facility—White had been a simulator instructor and designer with David and Patrick McLanahan at Ford Air Force Base in California, and he'd recognized Luger instantly. White had contacted Brad Elliott, who'd combined forces with Madcap Magician and Marine Corps Gunnery Sergeant Chris Wohl and mounted a covert rescue mission. David Luger had been returned safely to the United States, but had had to be placed in security isolation because he had been declared dead, and his sudden reappearance would have caused questions about the then-classified "Old Dog" project.

Patrick McLanahan's longtime partner David Luger returned the embrace, crying like a child and pounding Patrick's back with joy. "Hal told me you were going flying, and that it might be illegal, so we decided to go all the way and spring me out of security isolation," Luger said in his familiar Texas drawl. "He filled me in on the way. I guess we're not so classified after all, are we?"

Patrick was still not believing his partner and best friend was standing in front of him. "God, Dave, I still can't believe this," Patrick gasped. "Man, a whole lot of shit has happened since I saw you last. I never thought either one of us would make it."

"Well, we made it, and I'm ready to do some flying and serve up a heapin' helpin' of whup-ass," Luger said excitedly. "And I've been studying, too."

"Studying? The Megafortress?"

"Damn right, bro," Luger said. "Ever since the Redtail Hawk rescue, and after finding out you guys were still together and still flying Megafortresses, I've been studying up on everything you've been doing. Hal and Paul and John Ormack and Angelina Pereira, before they died, were secretly giving me EB-52 tech orders for months, the latest stuff. I haven't seen a Screamer or a JSOW or a Wolverine, but I know how to load, program, and launch them and all the weapons we can carry on a Megafortress. I can sit in any seat and run the systems, and I could even fly the beast with a little help. So just tell me where in the hell we're going and I'll help you get us there!"

Patrick McLanahan looked at his assembled circle of friends and comrades-in-arms, and felt the pride and happiness well up in his heart. They were all together once again: the crew of the original EB-52 Megafortress, the "Old Dog," minus its copilot John Ormack and its gunner Angelina Pereira; Hal Briggs, his friend and fellow warrior; Paul White, his former instructor turned high-tech rescue expert; Jon Masters, the boy genius whom Patrick had dragged out of the laboratories and corporate boardrooms to show him what defending your country and risking your life in combat was *really* about; Nancy Cheshire, the smart-mouth hard-as-nails test pilot who had been in combat in the Megafortress even more times than Patrick McLanahan himself; and newcomer Chris Wohl, the brooding, powerful Marine who suffered himself to be around all these Air Force techno-soldiers and who had shown them all what it was like to kill while looking directly into the eyes of the enemy instead of from the sky.

And, last but not least, they were all together with the beast that had started the whole thing ten years earlier—the modified B-52 strategic escort "battleship" they called the Old Dog. Over the past ten-plus years, they had done some incredible, mystifying, unheard-of things in the strange pointed-nose, V-tailed, fibersteel-skinned demon.

Now they were faced with their greatest challenge—to leave the protection and support of the United States military, fly to a strange new land, and attempt to turn the tables on a giant military superpower that was willing to risk a global thermonuclear holocaust to assert its domination. The odds seemed enormous.

"Guys, listen up for a minute, all of you," Patrick McLanahan said. "I don't mean to insult any of you, but I'm going to remind you that what we have done and what we are about to do are probably among the most dangerous things you will ever do or ever contemplate doing. If we succeed, you will not be rewarded for a job well done—in fact, you might find yourself in federal prison for a long, long time. My child . . ."

"Your . . . *what*, Muck?" David Luger asked incredulously. "Your *child?*"

"Yes, my child—*our* child," Patrick said, reaching over to take Wendy's hand. "My child could grow up fatherless, or he could be born with his father in prison—in fact, he or she could be *born* in prison. And of course, we could all die successfully defending our country, and no one will thank us, or we could die in total obscurity, and it will be as if we never existed at all. I know we're not in this business to get thanks from anyone, but I do know that we fly for our country and to preserve our freedom. Well, our country's leaders don't want us to do what we're about to do.

"On the other hand, if we don't do this mission and if we turn ourselves in to Sky Masters, Inc.'s, lawyers in Washington, we could have a pretty good chance of surviving lawsuits and court-martials and returning to our former lives with our fortunes and careers intact," Patrick went on. "I think Jon Masters and I have enough friends in high places, including the White House, to go to bat for us. Between our political pals and our lawyers, I feel pretty confident that if we stop now, our careers and our company can survive all that we've done up until now, even including taking this airfield. So you see, you've got nothing to gain and everything to lose if we go on."

"So what else is new, Patrick?" Hal Briggs deadpanned.

"If you're done talking, Colonel," Nancy Cheshire said, "I think we better get off this airpatch before someone happens by. Let's go."

Patrick McLanahan searched the faces of all those surrounding him—there was not one downturned eye, not one uncertain fidget, not one shred of doubt evident in any nuance or expression. They were all ready to fight. "Very well, folks," Patrick said. He turned to Brad Elliott and asked, "You feel up to doing some flying again, sir?"

"You try to stop me, Muck," Elliott responded. The retired three-star looked at his young colleague and protégé with great admiration, but said nothing else as he headed back to the hangar to get ready to load and launch his bomber.

"Good speech, boss," Nancy Cheshire said as she followed. "Corny as hell, but very inspirational. Made me weepy all over the damn place."

"Thanks, Nancy. High praise coming from you," he deadpanned. "And I'm not your boss."

"Maybe you will be," Cheshire said. "You sure sound like a commander giving a pep talk to the troops before stepping."

"It'll be all I can do to keep us out of prison, Nance," Patrick said. "Try to keep the general straight."

"No problem, Colonel," Nancy Cheshire said eagerly. "See you on the other side." She trotted off after Elliott.

"Dave, it's you and me in the back," Patrick said. "We'll do a little on-the-job training on the equipment." The eagerness and excitement in

Luger's eyes immediately took Patrick back to their heyday, winning trophies and building an unmatched reputation for themselves. Plus, they had a lot of damn fun—and, despite the danger they faced, it felt like it was going to be fun again. "Everyone else evacuates with Jon's DC-10."

"You still haven't told us where we're evacuating *to*, Patrick," Jon Masters pointed out.

Patrick McLanahan smiled a mischievous grin that could have been directly cloned from Brad Elliott himself. "I'll brief you just before we shoot the approach, Jon," he said. "You'd probably want to stay right here and take your chances with Commander Willis and the federal marshals if you knew where we were going or how we were going to get there."

OVER THE PACIFIC OCEAN, TWENTY MILES
SOUTHWEST OF HUALIEN,
REPUBLIC OF CHINA (TAIWAN)
JUST BEFORE DAYBREAK

"Hualien approach, Military Flight One-One," Nancy Cheshire radioed. "Requesting GPS approach runway zero-three right."

"Military One-One, Hualien approach, do not fly in the vicinity of the Republic of Taiwan or you may be fired on without further warning," the precise but heavily Chinese-accented English-speaking voice responded. "All airspace in and around the Republic of China is restricted due to the air defense emergency. Say your PPR number."

"Stand by." Cheshire referred to a Post-it note stuck on the center multifunction display on the forward instrument console. "One-One has victor-alpha-one-seven-alpha-two-lima." A PPR, or Prior Permission Required, number was standard operating procedure for most military installations, even halfway around the world on the island of Formosa, just ninety miles east of the Asian mainland. Any aircraft attempting to land at a base without a PPR would certainly be detained and its crew arrested—or worse.

"Hualien Approach understands," the Taiwanese approach controller replied after a long pause, repeating the code warily, as if there was something very wrong. Hualien Air Base in east-central Taiwan was the largest Taiwanese military base on the east side of the island, the home of several Taiwanese Navy air and surface units as well as two Taiwan Air

Force fighter-interceptor and fighter-bomber squadrons—at least it had been, until a nuclear-tipped Communist Chinese M-9 ballistic missile destroyed most of the base. Now it was a flattened collection of burned-out foundations and scorched aircraft revetments, with large blackened piles of metal here and there the only evidence that several dozen aircraft once were based there. Just three miles to the west, the Chung Yang Shang mountain range rose precipitously right up to 10,000 feet above sea level in just a few miles.

"Military Flight One-One, cancel GPS approach clearance," the approach controller said.

Nancy Cheshire and Brad Elliott looked at one another in astonishment. "Say again, control?" Cheshire radioed. "Have we been cleared to land? Is there a problem?"

"Cancel approach clearance," the controller repeated angrily. "Contact the controller on security frequency channel one-one immediately or you will be considered a hostile intruder. Comply immediately!"

Cheshire acknowledged the transmission and switched channels, but she was totally confused. The weather was pretty good right now—scattered clouds, good visibility, some swirling winds because of the mountains but not too bad. The runway was in sight in the growing dawn. In the military world, the GPS, or Global Positioning System satellite navigation system, was far more accurate than any other kind of instrument approach. GPS signals in the civilian world were downgraded by the U.S. Department of Defense to prevent America's enemies from using the system against America—not so on the EB-52 Megafortress. The EB-52's Global Positioning System was accurate to within *six inches* in both position and altitude, which made it hundreds of times more accurate than any other navigation instrument in existence.

Cheshire quickly set up the primary radio for the next controller, who was on a special military frequency accessible only by planes using the HAVE QUICK secure radio system, which shifted frequencies for both air and ground units simultaneously based on a computerized timing sequence. "Button one-one on radio one," the copilot announced. "Hualien approach on backup, Hualien ground on radio two with their command post on backup. I've got the GPS approach dialed in as a backup."

"Thanks," Brad Elliott responded. "I got the radios." He keyed the mike: "Hualien radar, Military Flight One-One with you, level five thousand, thirteen out for runway zero-three right."

"Military Flight One-One, this is Hualien final controller," a voice responded sternly, "execute *all* of my instructions *immediately*." The Megafortress pilots noted the extreme emphasis on the words "all" and "immediately." "In case of loss of communications, immediately execute missed approach procedures. You must not delay any missed approach procedures. Do you copy?"

"One-One copies."

"Roger. Do not acknowledge further transmissions. Descend to two thousand, turn left heading zero-eight-one. This will be a PAR approach to runway zero three right." Elliott and Cheshire dialed in the new heading and altitude, and the autopilot complied. "Five miles to final approach fix." The controller made the same reports—altitude, heading, and position—every five seconds. For the EB-52's pilots, it was a complete no-brainer—simply dial in the numbers in the autopilot and watch as they got closer to the runway. The approach looked like a mirror image approach to what the GPS was showing them, so the backup was working, too.

"Maybe it's a local procedure—PAR approaches only, as a security measure," Cheshire offered. The PAR, or Precision Approach Radar, was a controller-operated instrument landing procedure where a radar controller guided the plane down to the runway by the use of two high-speed, high-resolution radars—very accurate, but not as accurate as GPS and not necessary because they could see the runway. Elliott shrugged—it didn't matter now, because they were lined up for landing and they hadn't been shot down yet. They could see the runway, the GPS was giving them good info along with the PAR controller—everything was humming along OK.

At the final approach fix, the beginning of the final segment to landing, Elliott called for the "Before Landing" checklist and lowered the landing gear. "Three green, no red," Cheshire announced, checking the gear-down lights. Elliott checked them as well. Everything going smoothly—PARs were so simple, a monkey could do it, given enough bananas.

"Passing final approach fix," the controller reported. "Check gear down, heading zero-four-two, altitude one thousand two hundred, slow to final approach speed."

"Military Flight One-One gear down," Elliott radioed—that was the only allowable radio call, done as a safety measure. Cheshire began reading the portions of the "Before Landing" checklist not already accomplished—flaps, lights, starters, weapons stowed, radar standby, seat belts, shoulder harnesses, crew notified . . .

"Heading zero-three-one, five-hundred-feet-per-minute rate of descent, altitude seven hundred feet, three miles from touchdown," the controller intoned. "Heading zero-three-one, six hundred feet altitude, two miles from touchdown. Report runway in sight."

"Runway in sight," the pilot responded—he had had it in sight for the past five minutes. He expected instructions to take over visually about half a mile from touchdown, when the PAR radar could not update fast enough to provide accurate course and glideslope data. One last check around the cockpit, check the gear, check . . .

"One-One, lights off," they heard the controller say. "Two miles to touchdown, heading zero-three-zero, altitude four hundred."

"What did he say?" Elliott asked aloud.

"He said turn the lights off," Cheshire replied. She reached up to the overhead switch panel. "Want 'em off?"

Well, this was stupid, Elliott thought. But he had the runway made and most of the rest of the airfield in sight. "Okay, lights off, but I don't know why the hell—"

Just as Cheshire flicked the breaker switches, they heard, "Military One-One, turn left *immediately*, heading three-zero-zero, descend to three hundred feet, maintain final approach speed!"

"What!" Elliott exclaimed. That was a ninety-degree turn to the west—*directly toward the mountains*! He crushed the mike switch: "Hualien, repeat that last!"

"Military One-One, turn immediately!" the controller shouted. "Turn now or execute missed approach instructions!"

Elliott grabbed the control stick and power controller, paddled off the autopilot, and swung the EB-52 Megafortress hard onto the new heading. "Where the hell is the terrain? Lower the radome." Cheshire hit a switch on the overhead panel, and the long, pointed SST-style nose of the Megafortress lowered several degrees to improve forward visibility.

"Heading two-niner-eight, altitude two hundred feet, three miles to touchdown," the controller intoned. The vectors were coming in faster: "Heading three-zero-niner, altitude one-fifty, two point five miles to touchdown . . . *now* heading three-four-nine, altitude two-twenty, two point two miles to touchdown . . ."

"The son of a bitch!" Elliott shouted, making the sudden right turn with fifty degrees of bank, "He's vectored us right into the side of a mountain! What in hell is going on?"

"Brad, stay on the vectors," Patrick McLanahan shouted on interphone. "Kuo told us it was going to be a hairy approach."

" 'Hairy?' We're headed right into the side of a fucking mountain!"

"One-One, I show you well above glide path, fly heading three-five-zero, altitude two hundred feet . . ."

"General, this is nuts!" Cheshire shouted. "I see mountains all around us!"

"Shut up, everyone, *shut up!*" Elliott shouted. "This doesn't look good. I'm going missed. Radome in flight position." He keyed the mike trigger as he pushed the throttles forward: "Hualien, I'm executing missed . . . wait, stand by! Wait on the radome!"

Just before Elliott began pushing in power to execute a go-around, he saw what looked like a long, tall cleft in the mountainside. It looked like a depression at first, but as they got closer, it was obvious that it was far deeper than a depression, more like a hollow, or even a huge cave . . .

"One-One, start a right turn, heading zero-two-zero, altitude one-fifty, touchdown point in two miles, advise when you have the runway in sight."

"Runway?" Cheshire exclaimed. "I don't see no freakin' runway!"

Elliott started his tight right turn. The mountains were everywhere—they were in a deep river valley, with sharply rising mountainous terrain in every direction except behind them, toward the sea. Straight ahead, the mountains were less than four miles away—it would take every bit of power, and a lot of prayers, if they had to climb out of this defile right now. He couldn't afford to make careful, cautious turns now—every turn had to be at forty degrees of bank, crisp and positive, so he could line up on the center of the cave.

The glow from the cave got brighter, and wider, and taller . . . and then, suddenly, the entire outline of the hollow in the mountain was outlined in dull yellow. It was enormous, more than 600 feet across and 200 feet high. Now, a bit closer in, the outline of the edge of a *runway* could be seen, *inside the cave!* "Co, you . . . you see what I see?"

"I see it," Cheshire breathed, "but I don't freakin' believe it."

"One-One, Hualien final controller," the radar controller radioed, "proceed visually. If unable, execute missed approach instructions immediately. You have ten seconds until your missed approach point."

"No . . . no, we got the field . . . uh, we got *it* in sight," Elliott responded. "Proceeding visually."

"Roger," the controller said—the EB-52's pilots could practically hear a huge sigh of relief from the controller. "Remain this frequency for ground controller. Max runway length one thousand eight hundred meters, approximately six thousand feet, favor the right side of the runway. Welcome."

The controller's voice sounded so relieved and casual, almost ecstatic, that Brad Elliott felt as if he were in a dream—because he was still far from home free right now. He felt as if the Megafortress's pointed SST nose was the end of a piece of thread, and the cave mouth was the eye of a needle, and the Megafortress was barely small enough to squeeze inside! "Flaps full, airbrakes six!" Elliott ordered. "My God, I don't believe it!"

It was way, way too late to go around at this point—even the power of the Megafortress's CF6 turbofans couldn't fly it clear of the mountain now. Even a ninety-degree bank turn with maximum back pressure and clinging to the edge of the stall wouldn't save them. They either landed now, or they would die in the blink of an eye. The right wingtip dipped, pushed down by a gust of wind right at the mouth of the cave, and for an instant Elliott thought he wouldn't be able to raise the wingtip fast enough before it crashed into the side of the cave and spun them around inside. He forced the image of death out of his mind's eye.

The Megafortress touched down several hundred feet from the edge of the cliff—Elliott landed way long, a poor touchdown even on a normal runway in perfect conditions. He didn't wait until the front trucks were on the ground; he pulled the throttles to idle, jammed the thrust reverser levers full down, waited as long as he possibly could stand for the reversers to deploy, then started to shove the throttles forward. There was a huge black aircraft barrier net at the end of the concrete, and it was *right there*, right in front of them! Elliott kept on shoving the throttles forward, almost into military power. The Megafortress began to shake as if they were in an earthquake.

"Ninety knots!" Cheshire shouted. Elliott tapped the brakes and felt the pressure on his shoulder harness—good, they had brakes! He pressed the toe brakes farther, and the Megafortress responded. Thrust reversers still on, he pressed the brakes farther, right up to where he could feel the anti-skid system begin to cycle the hydraulic power in the brakes on and off. He depressed the toe brakes all the way, no more time to tap or save the brakes.

Full brake power, full reverse thrust, and the barrier was still rushing up to meet them. A little more than a hundred feet beyond the barrier was a steel jet exhaust blast fence, and then the back of the cave wall itself—complete darkness, cold deadly granite. It was very much like the end of the line in a subway tunnel.

But they did stop in time—the retracted nose of the EB-52 missed the barrier net by less than half the length of the aircraft. Except for test flights, it was the shortest landing any of them had ever made in an EB-52 bomber—less than 6,000 feet. They used 50 percent less runway than they had ever used before. A "follow-me" truck appeared off their right wingtip, and a ground crewman on the back of the truck beckoned to them with a yellow-lensed flashlight and a hearty wave. Elliott deactivated the thrust reversers, grabbed the steering knob, and gently eased the throttles forward.

Taxiing inside the cave was like driving through a low-ceiling indoor parking garage with a high-profile vehicle. Everywhere they looked, they saw cheering soldiers, some jumping up and down in happiness as they held their ears against the bone-jarring noise and echo—Elliott and Cheshire mercifully shut down two engines to cut down on the noise. They were directed to a parking spot just off the edge of the runway, just a few hundred feet behind Jon Masters's DC-10 tanker and satellite launch plane.

The four bomber crewmen were instantly mobbed the moment they opened the lower hatch and climbed out. The first to greet them were Wendy McLanahan, Jon Masters, Paul White, and Hal Briggs. Wendy hugged her husband so tightly he thought he heard some neck vertebrae snap, but he hugged her just as closely and as tightly. "Patrick, oh God, you should have seen you fly into the cave!" Wendy exclaimed through tears of relief and joy. "I swear, it was like watching a bat fly into a tiny hole in the wall! I saw the wingtip down, and I thought you weren't going to make it!"

After everyone climbed out of the Megafortress, they had a moment to look at the incredible structure. It was an immense underground airfield, with a single 200-foot-wide, 6,000-foot-long runway in the middle of the gigantic structure! On the other side of the runway were a line of about a dozen Taiwanese F-16 fighters—the Taiwanese had actually managed to land F-16 Fighting Falcons in the cave!—along with a few S-70 helicopters and S-2 Tracker turboprop maritime surveillance planes. Patrick McLanahan and Brad Elliott had a grim feeling that those planes represented what was left of the entire Republic of China air force.

After shutdown, the stunned American crew members were met by several officers and several more armed guards. The senior officer stepped forward, shook their hands excitedly with a broad smile, and said in very practiced English, "Welcome to Kai-Shan, my Flying Tiger friends, welcome. I am Brigadier General Hsiao Jason, commander of this installation. You must be General Elliott, and you are Colonel McLanahan." Both of them were still too stunned to respond, which pleased Hsiao immensely. "You and your men are suffering from Kai-Shan Psychosis, the inability to do anything but stare up at the ceiling, the instant abandonment of all military courtesies and even coherent speech," Hsiao said with a smile. "The disease will affect you long after you leave this place, I assure you. Please follow."

Indeed, it was hard to keep from staring at the detail of the huge underground facility. The ceiling was geodetic reinforced steel honeycomb, with segments three inches thick widening to six inches toward the ceiling and ventilator openings interspersed throughout—it was like a huge modern subway terminal, only several times larger. Several steel support columns, spaced every thousand feet on either side of the runway, soared into the sky from floor to ceiling, set just a few feet from the edge of the runway. The runway itself was concrete, with arresting wires a few hundred feet from the approach end to stop aircraft equipped with tail hooks—and, Briggs noted, all of the Taiwanese F-16 fighters and S-2 Trackers had tail hooks. Looking out the open mouth of the cave, all they could see were mountains—a straight-in approach to Kai-Shan was not possible.

"We've heard rumors about this place for years," Wendy McLanahan remarked, "but we never thought it truly existed!"

"Kai-Shan has been in operation for about six years," Hsiao said. "It was originally intended as the underground command center for the Le Shan air defense network system, but an alternate mountain location closer to Taipei was located and used instead. This was then used as an emergency shelter for troops and politicians until the new caverns deeper inside the mountain were excavated. When we realized we had enough space inside for an airfield, the decision was made to convert it. Our first fixed-wing aircraft, an S-2 Tracker, landed inside the mountain three years ago; the first F-16 landed here just a few months ago."

Walking across the runway to the south side of the facility was like walking across Grand Central Station or the Toronto Skydome. "We completed this facility late last year, after ten years of construction and ten years of design and development work," General Hsiao was saying. "The main airbase chamber is almost eight hundred *million* cubic feet in volume, about half of it natural granite and limestone reinforced with steel and concrete. It is actually a combination of about one hundred smaller caverns, hollowed out and reinforced to make several large caverns. There are approximately two hundred thousand square feet of additional support, housing, and storage space on two levels above and below the airbase chamber. Above your heads is approximately six thousand feet of solid rock.

"We are capable of accommodating up to twenty F-16–size fighters on this level along the side of the runway, plus another twenty or so belowground, accessible via those elevators there and there," Hsiao went on. "The complex includes weapon, fuel, and spare parts storage, enough to keep two medium attack squadrons supplied during around-the-clock combat operations for about one week. We can house as many as two thousand air base personnel down here, plus a command and control facility of one hundred, plus barrack two thousand additional troops. We have a twenty-bed hospital, four dining facilities, two laundries, even a movie theater."

"Sir, how in the world . . . I mean, how was it possible to keep this facility a secret?" Patrick McLanahan asked as they reached the other side of the chamber, behind the huge steel blast deflectors and into the rock wall itself, to where administrative and mission planning rooms had been set up. "The number of construction crews must've been immense. The money, the equipment, the manpower—all of it must have created attention. How was it possible to avoid all scrutiny?"

"Same way we do it, Patrick—by keeping our mouths shut and kicking anyone's ass who dares to open theirs," Brad Elliott said.

"Precisely," General Hsiao replied. "The strictest security measures possible were employed. But this side of the island is very sparsely populated, and it attracts little attention. Once the engineers and workers were safely inside, work could be done in total secrecy."

"How did you make out during the Chinese attack on Hualien?" Paul White asked.

"We were safe—Kai-Shan is shielded by the mountains, and our cave shield was in place and is thick enough to withstand a bomb strike, so we received no damage from the nuclear blast," Hsiao replied. "Our facilities are full of the injured and dying, though. We have cremated nearly a thousand men, women, and children since the attack here at Kai-Shan alone—we know of over eight thousand casualties in Hualien alone, and there are undoubtedly many more that were simply incinerated in the blast. Our revenge will be sweet, my friends."

They heard the sound of a start cart outside on the airfield, and General Hsiao ordered the door closed behind them, which muffled the noise considerably. "One of our air patrols is preparing to depart. Shall we watch?"

The sight was unbelievable. A Taiwanese F-16 fighter, armed with four Sidewinder missiles and a centerline fuel tank, taxied to the very back of the runway. The barrier net had been removed, and the blast fence was diverting the F-16's engine exhaust almost straight up into a cluster of ventilators. "The engine exhaust is vented outside through several steel plenums and sideways out across the mountains, where it is less likely to be detected by infrared imaging satellites," Hsiao explained.

The F-16 ran its engine up to full power, then full afterburner power, and released brakes. It looked very much like an aircraft carrier takeoff—the fighter stayed on the deck until reaching the mouth of the cave, then shot off into space. A few minutes later, the barrier net was lowered and an F-16 came in for landing from a patrol. Again it resembled an aircraft carrier landing—the F-16 suddenly appeared at the cave mouth at slow speed, with its nose high in the air; it hit the runway, caught one of the arresting wires, the nose came down hard on the runway, and the fighter screeched to a halt at the end of the arresting wire. Ground crewmen came running out to disconnect the wire from the hook and marshal the fighter to the elevator to take it down to the belowdecks aircraft hangar for servicing.

"My God," Nancy Cheshire exclaimed. "What if a plane has to bolter? What if they miss a wire? What if a wire or arresting hook breaks?"

"Then, if the barrier does not catch them, we will probably all die," Hsiao Jason said matter-of-factly. He smiled broadly and said, "Actually, my friends, *your* two planes have been the first fixed-wing aircraft to land at Kai-Shan without using an arresting wire. We were all in fire shelters for the landing of the DC-10. But the landing of the bomber—well, I think we were all up on deck to watch. It was most spectacular, worth dying in a fireball to see." The American newcomers were all too stunned to respond. "You must be very tired. We have prepared meals and rooms for you and all your troops."

"With all due respect, sir, we'd like to get to work and launch our first sortie at dusk," Patrick McLanahan said.

"Dusk? You mean, *tonight*?" General Hsiao exclaimed. "You will be ready to fly *tonight*?"

"With any luck, yes," Patrick said. "We need assistance from your aircraft maintenance troops to help turn the bomber and to upload the weapons. Can we count on assistance from your flight crews to help in mission planning?"

"You may count on us for anything you desire," Hsiao said happily. "You truly are the new Flying Tigers, my friends. In fact, my F-16 flight crews request the honor of accompanying you on your first raid."

"That would be excellent, sir," Patrick said. "We'll be lightly loaded taking off from here, so we can use some extra firepower. Have your pilots ever done any aerial refueling?"

"Only in simulators, Colonel McLanahan," Hsiao said.

"Well, I've heard that doing it for real is easier than the simulator, so your crews will be refueling tonight," Patrick said. "Our transport jet is configured as a tanker. We have the latest intelligence data—it's a few hours old, but I think it'll be useful for tonight. We'll see about getting our own Sky Masters recon and targeting satellite up in the next day or so. Let's get to work, everybody. We'll be launching in about twelve hours."

"The general who advances
without coveting fame and
retreats without fearing
disgrace, whose only thought
is to protect his country
and do good service for
his sovereign, is the jewel of
the kingdom."

—SUN-TZU,
The Art of War

CHAPTER
SIX

**BANDAR-ABBASS NAVAL BASE, ISLAMIC
REPUBLIC OF IRAN
TUESDAY, 24 JUNE 1997, 2121 HOURS LOCAL
(1251 HOURS ET)**

"Here it comes," the sonar operator aboard the Los Angeles–class nuclear-powered attack submarine USS *Miami* reported. He flipped open the intercom channel: "Bridge, sonar, target alpha is in the channel, bearing three-one-four, range six thousand yards, speed six knots."

The first officer acknowledged the call, then rang the captain in his quarters. "Skipper, the *Taregh*'s moving." The captain joined his first officer on the twelve-year-old, 7,000-ton submarine's bridge a few moments later.

"Sonar, what d'ya have?" the captain ordered.

"Positive contact, sir," the sensor operator said. The WLR-9/12 acoustic emission receiver/processor suite was an extensive computerized system that in effect "pointed" the sensor operator to a particular sound picked up from the myriad of noises from the sea, allowed the sensor operator to scan the suspect, fine-tuned the sound, and attempted to identify it. "Target alpha's coming out of Bandar-Abbass, heading south. She's making noise, probably getting ready to blow her tanks."

The captain took a deep breath in anticipation. For the past several weeks, their only assigned target had been staying close to home—but now it was on the move, and that probably spelled trouble. "Target alpha" was the *Taregh*, which meant "Morning Star"—the Islamic Republic of Iran's first attack submarine. Purchased from Russia in September 1992, the *Taregh* had sent the world into a tailspin by introducing yet another advanced weapon system into the hands of an aggressive, fundamentalist Islamic nation in the Persian Gulf.

Although the Iranians had purchased a second Kilo-class sub from Russia and were threatening to buy more, the threat of Iran filling the Persian Gulf with attack subs, and thereby threatening nearly half of the world's oil supply, had never come to pass. The *Taregh* had never ventured far from Bandar-Abbass and had spent most of its time cruising the Strait of Hormuz and the Gulf of Oman between Bandar-Abbass and its as-yet-uncompleted home port of Chah Bahar.

Since the recent conflict between the United States and Iran, the United States had assigned one nuclear-powered attack sub to monitor the *Taregh*'s whereabouts. Fortunately, the *Taregh* had proven to be an easy shadowing assignment—while Iran's aircraft carrier *Ayatollah Ruhollah Khomeini* had been busy attacking other Gulf states during the brief naval and air skirmishes in the area, Iran's attack subs had played no part. The *Miami* had simply stationed itself in the Strait of Hormuz just outside Bandar-Abbass, concealed by the noise of the hundreds of ships crowding the channel, and waited. While stationed in the Strait, the crew of the *Miami* had been able to extend its antennas and collect vast amounts of information on the Iranian fleet's deployment, and occasionally intercept important communications from fleet headquarters. But their primary assignment, the *Taregh*, had always been a nonplayer, stuck in port except for brief cruises and exercises. During the U.S.-Iran crisis, the United States and its Persian Gulf allies had not been flying anti-submarine patrols over the Strait of Hormuz, Persian Gulf, or Gulf of Oman, which meant that, if it was not shadowed as soon as it left port, the *Taregh* could sneak out of the Strait and make its way into the Persian Gulf itself, where it would be much harder to detect and track, and it could lay waste to all commercial shipping traffic heading in or out of the Persian Gulf.

"Looks like we're going sailing," the captain announced. He ordered that the ship be made ready to answer bells immediately. Thirty minutes later, the *Miami* pulled out into the Strait for the first time in almost four weeks.

Tailing the *Taregh* was easy as long as it was on the surface. Other vessels got out of its way, so it traveled a straight course, and its large, blunt nose and wide hull meant that it had to churn out a lot of rpms from its big six-bladed propeller just to maintain steerageway. The *Taregh* was escorted by two tugboats as it left the crowded naval base and headed south toward the center of the Strait of Hormuz; one tugboat eventually dropped away as the channel traffic cleared. The tugboat would also help mask the *Miami*'s noise. The captain of the *Miami* ordered the distance increased to 12,000 yards, almost seven miles—the maximum useful range of his passive sonar system.

The *Taregh* finally made its dive at the absolute worst place its skipper could pick—at the narrowest and shallowest part of the Strait, between Bandar-Abbass and the eastern tip of Qeshm Island. The shallower water restricted the *Miami* to less than periscope depth. The *Taregh* was making minimum steerageway even while submerged, and now it was getting more difficult for the *Miami* to maintain course at the slower speed. Channel traffic was increasing as well. Qeshm Island was a busy petroleum drilling and refining area, and commercial-vessel traffic was heavy all day and all night in this area. The *Miami* maintained 12,000 yards' distance from the *Taregh*, even when the Iranian attack sub seemed as if it was barely moving.

It suddenly seemed as if the *Taregh* was getting a lot of visitors—large, slow-moving vessels flitting nearby, centered generally over the sub. It was unlikely that the Iranian navy would allow onlookers to get within a mile of one of its subs. "What in hell are those things?" the captain muttered. "Service vessels? Supply vessels?"

"Shit, it's going to turn around," the first officer said, as they waited. "Something on the tub broke, they can't fix it, and they're going to turn around and head back to the barn."

"We're not that lucky," the skipper said. "That'll cut our patrol time down, that's for sure. Who the hell knows? We'll maintain our distance until he starts motoring."

They did not have to wait long—soon, the *Taregh* started to pick up speed, now reaching twelve knots, and the skipper ordered the *Miami* back on the pursuit. With the steam turbines running at a more comfortable speed, the *Miami* felt steadier and more seaworthy in the shallow waters, and the skipper even began to relax a bit, although he wouldn't relax completely until they were safely out of Iranian waters, out of the Strait of Hormuz, and out of this weird, unfriendly water. The warm, dirt-laden, polluted salt water of the Strait of Hormuz always played havoc with sensors, and it was harder to maintain depth and control roll and yaw. But the *Taregh* was starting to move faster, now above fifteen knots, and the faster they went, the steadier the ol' *Miami*—

"Bridge, helm."

The skipper clicked open the intercom: "Bridge, go."

"We've got a problem. Recommend emergency stop."

"All stop," the skipper said immediately—when the quartermaster at the helm suggests an emergency maneuver, you make it and sort out the problem later. "I hope it's your imagination. On my way." He arrived at the sub's helm station as fast as he could. Both diving plane helmsmen had their arms extended full out, and they appeared to be struggling with the airplane-like control wheels; the quartermaster standing between them was watching the navigation and performance instruments, while technicians were checking the hydraulic, pneumatic, and electrical panels. "What in hell's going on?"

"I think we snagged something," the quartermaster said, in a quiet, exasperated voice. "Lots of pressure on the controls, and we're losing response."

"Shit," the skipper said. "Back two-thirds." The skipper waited until their speed through the water had decreased to zero, then ordered, "All stop. Rudder amidships."

"All stop. Rudder amidships, aye . . . sir, my rudder is amidships," the helmsmen responded.

The *Miami* had a closed-circuit zoom TV camera in a pressure vessel on the top of the sail, and the captain and quartermaster studied the picture. Sure enough, a large black net had completely enveloped the nose of the submarine. The net was huge—it engulfed the entire front of the sub all the way from the nose up to the sail. Swiveling the camera athwartship, they saw the net covering the sailplanes; aiming the camera aft, the net was angled upward away from the rudder and propeller, but was even now starting to drift down toward the stern. The top of the net could not be seen, but it appeared to extend far beyond camera range, even possibly to the surface.

"I think we're caught in a damned drift net," the quartermaster muttered. "It's got to be a thousand feet long and two hundred feet high, at least. Japanese drift nets are dozens of miles long sometimes."

"That's impossible—you can't stop a seven-thousand-ton submarine with a nylon net," the captain remarked. "Besides, what's a damned drift net doing in a big ship channel? Who would . . . ?" The skipper answered his own question: the Iranians were hunting for American submarines. "Let's get a diving team suited up and ready to assist if needed. It looks like the stern's still clear—let's see if we can back out of this thing. Helm, all back slow."

But it was too late. As they began to try to extract themselves from the drift net, the top of the net began to sink even faster, and minutes later, the rudder and propeller appeared to be covered by the net. "Damn, the net's in the prop," the captain muttered.

"That'll be the end of the net, then, sir," the quartermaster said. "Our prop would break even a steel cable net." But he was wrong. Instead of slicing the net up into pieces, the net simply began winding itself around the propeller blades.

"What in hell . . . all stop, *all stop!*" the captain ordered. "Christ, what in hell is that net made of? Helm, all ahead slow, let's see if we can kick that net clear." But it was no use—the net was completely fouling the propeller. "Dammit, *dammit* . . . all right, looks like we've got to put the divers over the side," the captain said. "Once we cut the prop free, we'll go as close to the bottom as we can and try to turn north and sail out the side of the net." He flipped on the ship-wide intercom: "Attention all hands, this is the captain. Looks like we're caught in a big drift net. Chief of the boat, report to the helm, stand by to deploy diver salvage team."

"Bridge, sonar, heavy high-speed screws bearing three-two-zero, range eight thousand yards and closing fast. Large patrol vessel or small corvette or frigate. I'm picking up a patrol helicopter flying low over the water, too." Moments later, they heard the first active pings of a sonobuoy dropped just a few hundred yards away—the search for the trapped sub had begun. The next several sonobuoys were much closer—they had been pinpointed. The patrol vessel was soon joined by several more, all converging on their location.

The captain's jaw dropped open in surprise. Not only was this *not* a random, unlucky accident—it now appeared to be an intentionally set trap. The Iranians had deployed some kind of unbreakable net in the ship channel right behind their attack submarine *Taregh*, and they had snagged themselves an American attack submarine.

"I think the fuckers found us," the captain said. He hit an intercom button: "Comm, this is the captain. Deploy the satellite antenna buoy, send a distress signal immediately."

The antenna buoy had reached the surface and was transmitting for about three minutes when the first depth charge was launched from the Iranian frigate and splashed into the water over the trapped American sub.

GOVERNMENT HOUSE, BEIJING,
PEOPLE'S REPUBLIC OF CHINA
WEDNESDAY, 25 JUNE 1997, 0301 HOURS LOCAL
(TUESDAY, 24 JUNE, 1401 HOURS ET)

The Central Military Commission meeting broke into loud cheers and uncharacteristically hearty applause as the members watched their TV monitors. The CNN "Early Prime" news broadcast from the United States—practically all TV sets in Government House had been tuned to CNN twenty-four hours a day since the conflict with Taiwan had begun—opened with video taken from Iranian navy sailors in the Strait of Hormuz south of Bandar-Abbass. They showed an American nuclear-powered attack submarine on the surface, covered with an immense net in which they had become entangled while spying on the naval facilities near Bandar-Abbass. Iranian warships surrounded the sub, with dozens of guns of all sizes trained on the helpless American warship and its crew, who had been forced to surrender after a massive depth-charge barrage, and who were now kneeling up on the sub's deck, hands on top of their heads. The video was being transmitted directly from Iranian vessels to the Islamic Republic News Agency offices in Tehran, where CNN had a news bureau, and from there the Iranians allowed the live video uplinked directly to the United States for rebroadcast in the middle of the afternoon in the United States and in "prime time" in Europe.

Proudest of all in the room was Admiral Sun Ji Guoming himself. After leading the successful bombing raids against Chinese Taipei—and performing the secret missile attack against North and South Korea, which only a few members of President Jiang's command post staff knew about—he had returned like a conquering hero to Beijing to receive the praise and gratitude of Paramount Leader Jiang Zemin and the entire Politburo of the Chinese Communist Party. But this latest action was icing on the cake—the ignoble capture of an American attack sub well within Iranian territorial waters.

Sun was proud because *he* had suggested the trap. He had devised a plan years ago to use huge drift nets made of Kevlar, as light as nylon but stronger than steel, to try to trap enemy submarines. Each net cost millions of *yuan* to make, but Iran, North Korea, and several other nations were happy to make the investment. It was simply a matter of patience: creating an inviting target for enemy spy subs, then laying out the net and hoping that an unwary, complacent sub captain sailed into it.

A louder volley of laughter erupted when the American news showed three old fishermen in their dilapidated old boat, which the Iranian Navy had allowed into the patrol area, their dirty canvas trousers pulled down around their ankles and their bare asses hanging over the side of the junk, defecating into the Strait of Hormuz next to the American submarine. CNN also showed people of all ages throwing buckets of trash and sewage onto the captured sub, burning American flags and then tossing them into the Strait. A piece of video even captured a brief glimpse of an antenna buoy that had broken loose from the American sub when the depth-charge attack had begun, and retrieved by a small motorboat with young children at the helm. The children circled the area, scanning the water with flashlights and torches to try to find more souvenirs.

"Excellent, excellent!" President Jiang shouted, clapping and smiling like a schoolboy at a football match. "I am almost embarrassed *for* the American president and his submarine sailors! He must be the laughingstock of the entire world!" He received congratulations and acknowledgments from several Politburo and CMC members, then stepped over to Admiral Sun. "What do you think the Iranians will do with their American captives, Admiral?"

"I have already been in contact with the Iranian military's chief of staff," Sun replied, rather wistfully. "The crew will be tried as spies, and their vessel held. It is quite a catch for them, and it is perfect payback for what the United States did to the aircraft carrier *Khomeini* when it was in their hands. In time, the crew and the vessel will probably be released, but not until the Iranians have examined and photographed every square centimeter of that submarine."

"You seem disappointed, comrade," Jiang said. "Their violation of international law is obvious to all. Should they not be made to pay for their crime?"

"I believe they are paying more severely now than anything the Iranians could possibly do to them," Sun said. "Destroying a helpless, hapless submarine and its crew would be cruel, and the Iranians would lose face in the eyes of the world. Sun-tzu tells us that to attack the enemy's *tao* is more hurtful than attacking his armies. I respectfully suggested that the Americans be released, but I do not think the Iranians will listen to my suggestion. Perhaps if you could call the Ayatollah Khamenei directly, he might listen to you." China and Iran had forged a strong new military alliance in the past few months, and the level of cooperation between the two nations had grown rapidly despite the severe damage the aircraft carrier *Khomeini,* now the *Mao Zedong,* had sustained while in Iranian hands.

"Very well—I shall do as you suggest, Comrade Admiral," Jiang said, with a smile. "I will of course issue a communiqué demanding an explanation from President Martindale as to why his submarine was so far into Iranian waters."

"May I suggest you follow up the communiqué with a live televised address on CNN or the British international news network, demanding an apology?" Sun added. "Nothing galls the American people more than to be forced to offer an apology, especially to an Asian or to one from the Middle East—both are seen as far inferior races. It will help to solidify the opposition to President Martindale's military and foreign affairs policies."

"Very good—I shall instruct my staff to do as you suggested," Jiang said happily. He turned to accept the congratulations of more high-level Party members, then turned back to Sun and asked, "So. What is the next step, Admiral?"

"My task is nearly complete, Comrade President," Sun said. "My objective was to eliminate the United States as a threat to Zhongguo and to pave the way for us to retake Formosa. My task is done."

President Jiang looked startled. "Your task . . . is *finished?*" he asked incredulously. "But we have not retaken any territory, and the armies of the world are on heightened alert against us."

"General Chin and the People's Liberation Army may retake any of the rebel-held islands at his leisure," Admiral Sun said casually. "There is none to oppose him now. But I suggest we do nothing but offer overtures of peace, friendship, and reunification to everyone—I predict our loyal brothers on Formosa will choose to be reunited with us very soon. The elimination of the rebel Nationalists' major weapons of war, and the erosion of the Western alliance structure in Asia, means that the Nationalists are defenseless. They can choose reunification . . . or death."

"But what about the Americans, Comrade Admiral?" Jiang asked. "Will we not soon face the wrath of the American military? Certainly the threat from them has not yet diminished?"

"The United States dares not attack us now—they are in the wrong, and will be forever chastised throughtout the world if they attack," Sun said confidently. "The North Korean People's Army is massing on the demilitarized zone and will probably attack, and now the Iranians have captured proof of additional American aggression against them, so the conflict in the Persian Gulf may threaten to reignite. These conflicts will occupy all of America's attention—Taiwan is not as serious a concern to the United States compared to Korea or the Persian Gulf."

"You are obviously correct," a Politburo member commented, "because the United States does not directly threaten China as yet. They have their nuclear missiles and bombers on alert, but even their lawmakers are opposed to their deployment and urge negotiations. They may even sponsor legislation to kill President Martindale's attempt to recognize the rebel Nationalist government's independence, and support reunification."

"We do not know what will happen in Washington, comrade," Sun Ji Guoming said. "But all in all, it does not matter. America is confused and splintered, and it has confused and fractured its Asian alliances as well. It can no longer oppose us."

"But what about the invasion of Quemoy?" Jiang asked. "Our troops are restless as medieval warhorses, biting at the bit and ready to honor themselves in battle. Why not begin the attack now?"

"Is there still a danger of radiation or fallout from the surface-to-air missile attack?" one of the Politburo members asked. "Is this why you do not begin the invasion?"

"It is not because of radiation, comrade," Sun replied. "We do not invade because we do not *need* to invade."

"What . . . ?"

"Sun-tzu teaches us that victory is best achieved by attacking an enemy's *tao* instead of its armies or cities," Sun explained. "We have three hundred thousand troops stationed around Quemoy Bay, ready to begin the assault. We may take the island and capture nearly fifty thousand rebel troops anytime we wish. So we have already won the battle, comrades. With the tip of our sword touching the rebels' chest, we do not need to thrust it into their heart to prove our domination or power. The rebels have been defeated, but it would be better for them to surrender to us. I expect to receive terms of surrender at any moment."

OVER THE FORMOSA STRAIT, NEAR XIAMEN, FUJIAN PROVINCE, PEOPLE'S REPUBLIC OF CHINA THAT SAME TIME

The attack began with a single AIM-120 Scorpion missile launch, but it was the deadliest—because it downed the Chinese Ilyushin-76 airborne radar plane stationed over the Formosa Strait near Quanzhou, which was monitoring all air traffic between Fuzhou and Shantou, the vital Chinese military bases opposite Formosa. The EB-52 Megafortress was thirty miles away, flying just a hundred feet above the sea, tracking the Il-76 with its 360-degree radar array on the dorsal fuselage fairing; the Scorpion air-to-air missile hit the fuselage of the Il-76 squarely at the right wing root, shearing off the wing and sending the Russian-built plane and its twenty-two crew members spiraling into the Formosa Strait. Within seconds, almost all of the Chinese military's long-range surveillance capability had been eliminated.

It was David Luger's first kill after returning to the Megafortress's crew; and if he hadn't been so busy finding and lining up more targets, he would have stood up and whooped for joy. But the mission, and the killing, had just begun.

Because of the completely unknown performance capabilities taking off from the Republic of China's Kai-Shan underground airfield complex, the Megafortress was lightly loaded for this mission. Each of the two rotary launchers in the bomb bay contained four Wolverine cruise missiles and two Striker attack missiles, the configuration mixed so the attacks could continue even if one launcher was damaged or had malfunctioned. The Megafortress also carried one Striker attack missile on each wing weapon pod, along with four AIM-120 Scorpion air-to-air missiles in each pod—there were no Stinger airmine rockets in the tail cannon. The weapon load was a full 12,000 pounds under normal mission capacity. To save even more weight, no fuel was carried in the fuselage tanks, except the lowest amount necessary to stay within the weight and balance center-of-gravity envelope, which saved an additional 50,000 pounds.

"Crew, stand by for bomb-bay missile launch," Patrick McLanahan announced. "Quadruple Wolverine missile launch. Radar coming on . . . radar stand by." McLanahan took a thirty-second satellite update for the navigation computers, in order to tighten down the accuracy of the system as much as possible prior to launch. Then he checked the accuracy of the nav computers by taking a three-second attack radar fix and then comparing where the aiming crosshairs lay on the stored radar image. When McLanahan moved the crosshairs onto the exact preprogrammed spot, the difference between the radar fix and the nav computers was only fifty-seven feet. He decided to accept the satellite fix.

"Launch point fix in, bomb doors coming open." He clicked on the voice command switch: "Commit Wolverine attack."

WARNING, MISSILE ATTACK INITIATED, the computer replied, and automatically entered a launch hold until the order could be verified.

"Commit Wolverine attack," McLanahan repeated to verify the order.

LAUNCH COMMIT, WARNING, BOMB DOORS OPEN, the computer's female voice responded. The Megafortress's bomb doors slid inside the fuselage, and the forward rotary launcher in the bomb bay released the first AGM-177 Wolverine cruise missile. In eight-second volleys, three more Wolverine missiles dropped clear of the bomb bay, two total from each of the forward and aft rotary launchers. The missiles glided in a shallow descent as their flight computers sampled the air mass and did a microsecond flight-control check, exercising hundreds of tiny microhydraulic actuators built into the skin, then ignited their turbojet engines, throttled up to full power, and sped off toward their targets. As they began their 500-mile-per-hour flight, they downloaded navigation data from the GPS navigation satellite constellation and adjusted course, following the flight plan transferred to their computers from the Megafortress.

All four Wolverine missiles carried SEAD, or Suppression of Enemy Air Defense, packages in its sensor bay and three internal munitions bays. The missiles' sensor section contained combination infrared and radar-homing sensors, which would lock onto an enemy radar, then slave an infrared sensor onto the vehicle or building carrying the radar, and send targeting data to the missile's navigation computer. Two munitions compartments contained a total of eighteen anti-vehicle "skeets," and one weapon bay contained twelve Sky Masters ADM-151 decoy devices. The Wolverines had a preprogrammed flight plan based on Jon Masters's NIRTSat satellite data showing where some known garrisoned road-mobile SA-5 surface-to-air missile (SAM) sites, Honggi-2 SAM sites, and heavy antiaircraft artillery sites were located.

When the missiles flew within the estimated lethal range of the mobile SAM sites, the Wolverine missiles ejected a decoy glider. The decoys were tiny gliders with a specially designed shape, and contained tiny transmitters that made each glider appear as big as a full-size fighter—to a Chinese SAM radar operator scanning the skies for enemy aircraft, the decoys made it appear as if an enemy attacker had suddenly appeared out of nowhere right on top of them. When the SAM site operators activated their target-tracking radars to try to shoot down the "attacker," the seeker head in the Wolverine missile detected the signal and locked onto the location of the emitter, then used that new position plus its satellite navigation system fix to update its flight plan.

The Wolverine cruised over the target location and seeded the area with anti-vehicle skeets. Each skeet had a canister that contained infrared sensors and several copper rods. The canister would spin as it was ejected from the Wolverine missile. When the infrared sensors detected a vehicle-size target below, it would detonate a small explosive charge that would instantly melt the copper rod and shoot it at the target. The high-speed slug of molten copper was powerful enough to penetrate the thin steel of heavy trucks or light tanks. Each skeet could fire several slugs at once in all directions, sometimes shooting several slugs into one vehicle.

The Wolverine missile would fly its preprogrammed flight plan, cruising over the area, dropping decoys, and then dropping skeets over any SAM sites detected. Each Wolverine missile had the capability of destroying dozens of targets on its flight, so with four Wolverine cruise missiles operating in a thirty-by-thirty-mile target box, almost a thousand targets were instantly at risk. The skeets worked their devastating magic with gruesome efficiency. Not only were surface-to-air missile sites at risk, but any hot vehicles within a hundred yards of the skeets were likely targets—troop carriers, transports, supply trucks, even small buildings, anything with a warm core. Once a copper slug burned through the outer layer of its target, it had cooled sufficiently so that the second hard surface it hit caused the slug to break apart instead of burning through. For most targets, this meant that the copper slug first penetrated inside a passenger or crew compartment of a vehicle, ricocheted off a second hard surface, then instantly turned into thousands of bits of bulletlike projectiles that bounced around inside, shredding anything in its path.

The results of the Wolverine missile's deadly flight was evident to the crew of the Megafortress as they approached the Chinese coastline. Off in the darkened distance, they could see numerous patches of bright red flashes as the skeets went off, followed seconds later by bright yellow or white flashes as a truck, tank, or other vehicle was hit and destroyed. Many times they saw spectacular secondary explosions, as a skeet activated over a missile or antiaircraft artillery site, causing missiles to explode or entire ammunition magazines to cook off. After each Wolverine missile's deadly cargo was expended, the missile would do a kamikaze crash into the next SAM site it detected.

The net result: by the time the Megafortress was "feet dry" over the Chinese coast, more than fifty mobile antiaircraft weapon sites had been destroyed or put out of commission in the area, another three hundred vehicles of all shapes and sizes had been hit—plus over a thousand soldiers and sailors had been killed or injured.

But the Megafortress wasn't the heavy hitter in this attack. Following the EB-52 and coming in from several directions at once was a twelve-plane attack formation of Taiwanese F-16 Fighting Falcons. The Republic of China's F-16s—all but four of their surviving fleet of sixteen—had lagged several minutes behind the EB-52, waiting until the long-range Ilyushin-76 radar plane and the ground-based air defenses had been destroyed before making their move. Spread out over forty miles in six flights of two, the F-16s dashed in at 300 feet above the Formosa Strait, the waves acting as their only terrain-masking feature. But although the air defense sites along the coast had detected the F-16s a full six minutes before they attacked, they could do nothing about it—because the Wolverine missiles were knocking out the missile-control and target-tracking radars long before the Chinese defenders could launch a counterattack.

The EB-52's Wolverine cruise missiles had destroyed the air defense units and many of the larger vehicles arrayed around Quemoy Bay preparing to invade Taiwan's Quemoy Island—the F-16 Fighting Falcons' mission was to destroy or disrupt the estimated three hundred thousand troops getting ready to cross the bay and retake Quemoy for mainland China. Each F-16 carried six 800-pound CBU-59 APAM (Anti-Personnel, Anti-Materiel) cluster bomb units, which scattered 670 one-pound bomblets over a football field–size area. When the CBU-59 releases were computer-sequenced, laying the dispersal footprints end-to-end, the swath of destruction for each F-16 equaled over 350,000 square feet, the size of a suburban shopping mall. Some of the bomblets were fuzed to detonate on impact; others used tiny trip wires that would cause the bomblet to explode if disturbed or if a vehicle passed nearby. All unexploded bomblets would self-detonate after a period of time, anywhere from five minutes to twenty-four hours after being sown. One baseball-size bomblet could destroy a small vehicle, damage a large wheeled vehicle—or kill anyone standing within thirty feet.

Since the majority of Chinese amphibious and infantry forces ready to invade Quemoy were either traveling in trucks or bivouacked in tents along Quemoy Bay, awaiting orders to begin the main assault, they were caught mostly in the open and fully exposed to the cluster bomb attack. Except for sporadic, unguided antiaircraft cannon and small-caliber fire, the F-16s began their egress from the target area completely unopposed. One Taiwanese F-16 Fighting Falcon was hit by cannon fire and was forced to eject, but not until he flew his stricken fighter east of Quemoy Island, practically into the arms of waiting Taiwanese patrols.

"Center up on the steering bug, heading two-eight-three, five minutes thirty seconds to the next turnpoint," McLanahan reported to the Megafortress crew. They had crossed the Chinese coastline forty miles south of Xiamen, over Futou Bay; the new heading would take them south and west of the city of Zhangzhou and along the southern edges of the Boping and Wuyi Mountains. "Minimum safe clearance altitude, five thousand five hundred feet. High terrain twelve o'clock, twenty miles." They were flying at treetop level using the EB-52's COLA (COmputer-generated Lowest Altitude), in which the satellite-based navigation system compared its present and projected position, along with airspeed and heading, with a huge database of terrain elevations to compute the lowest possible altitude the Megafortress could fly without hitting any terrain or known man-made obstructions, and without using any radar emissions that might give their location away.

"Bandits, twelve o'clock, no range, no altitude yet," Luger called out. "Just popped up . . . got a range estimate now, about forty-one miles and closing fast . . . speed five hundred knots. I think we got a couple Chinese Sukhoi-27s in the area, guys—and the son of a bitch might have gotten a look at us."

GOVERNMENT HOUSE, BEIJING,
PEOPLE'S REPUBLIC OF CHINA
THAT SAME TIME

A group of Chinese Communist Party Politburo members had joined Jiang in congratulating Sun Ji Guoming for his service. Jiang continued his praise for Sun, saying to all of his colleagues, "A stroke of genius, igniting a conflict on the Korean Peninsula at the same time as your attacks against the Nationalists. The Chinese Taipei issue certainly does pale in comparison to the prospect of a new Korean War."

"In your address to the world, Comrade President, may I also suggest that you offer to mediate a resolution of the conflict between North and South Korea, and perhaps go as far as to refuse to commit any of our troops to assist President Kim Jong-il if he refuses to participate in negotiations," Sun suggested. "That might prevent the South from beginning its own offensive. Of course, if the South or the United States attacks the North first, we should threaten to use all of our resources to assist President Kim. The same for the Iranian conflict, if one should develop— we can offer to convince the Iranians to halt any aggression, in exchange for a greater presence in that region."

President Jiang was obviously impressed by Sun's ideas. "I still find it hard to believe," the Paramount Leader said, "that we have used *nuclear weapons* against the rebel Nationalists and even against the United States, and we still apparently face no threat of retaliation. What has happened to the vaunted American military machine?"

"The machine is still there, Comrade President, and it is still powerful," Sun warned. "That American submarine was probably sitting near Bandar-Abbass for weeks, and no doubt there are American submarines near most of our coastal military bases and ports as well that we have failed to detect—perhaps even with nuclear attack missiles. And if the Americans ever get proof that we planted the nuclear explosive on the *Independence,* we may indeed find ourselves at war with the United States. But as long as Martindale and his generals do not have a clear target, they cannot strike without being labeled as 'warmongers,' which is a hated name in America. We must not act rashly, but we must continue to keep the American president unbalanced and uncertain."

"Excellent advice, comrade Sun," Jiang said warmly. At that moment, an aide came up to Sun, bowed to the president, and handed Sun a message. "You have been a trusted and most valuable adviser to me. Your hard work and loyalty have been favorably noted by the Party."

"Thank you, Comrade President," Sun said. He glanced at the note, then went on, "It is my honor as well as my duty to carry out the wishes of the—" And then he froze in complete surprise and muttered, "What in blazes?"

"What is it, comrade Sun?"

"The Quemoy invasion forces at Xiamen Bay are under air attack!" Admiral Sun Ji Guoming exclaimed. "Air defense sites, missile emplacements, amphibious assault staging areas . . . it is a massive attack force! But where? Where did it come from?"

"What about casualties?" President Jiang asked breathlessly. "Did we stop them? Did we sustain any losses?"

Sun Ji Guoming read the message carefully, his eyes widening and his jaw slackening further and further as he read. Finally, he responded in a quivering voice, "The air defense sites . . . they were hit by precision weapons, some kind of armor-piercing weapon that homed in on our antiaircraft radars. Then more aircraft, believed to be Nationalist F-16 fighter-bombers, flew over and dropped cluster munitions on the infantry staging areas. Casualties are . . . believed to be high."

"High? How high? How many casualties?"

"There is no report, sir," Sun explained. "This is obviously a preliminary report—"

"What do you mean, Admiral?" Jiang exploded. "There have been high casualties, but you do not know how many? Where did this attack come from? I thought you told me the rebel Nationalist air force had been destroyed!"

"It *has* been destroyed, sir," Sun said, his mind swirling in confusion. "I am sure of it! We hit every major rebel air base with a nuclear missile, and we have attacked every known alternate rebel air base with gravity weapons. The attack must have come from another base in the region, perhaps South Korea or Japan, perhaps even the Philippines."

"But all of those countries pledged not to support the rebels or the United States in any offensive military missions," Defense Minister Chi Haotian interjected. "They promised that the United States would not be permitted to stage attacks against us from their soil."

"Then the attackers must have come from Formosa," Sun said. "I do not know how they managed to sneak past our radar planes and elude our air defenses, but they cannot destroy all our air forces. My Tupolev-16 heavy bombers are standing by—I shall order another heavy bombing attack against the rebels, this time attacking their civilian airfields and alternate bases—any field capable of staging F-16 fighter-bomber attacks against us."

"It is so ordered," President Jiang said. "You must execute this mission immediately. We must retaliate against the Nationalists right away."

"Yes, sir," Sun said, relieved that the president and Politburo members weren't turning this bad news against *him*. "I also ask permission to use the entire fleet of Tupolev-26 supersonic bombers to spearhead the attack. If some of the rebels' F-16 fighters survived our air raids, we must use the high-speed bombers to penetrate their fighter screen and attack the targets."

Jiang Zemin hesitated. He did not approve of Sun using the newly acquired Russian-made supersonic bombers—at one and a half billion *yuan* each, the six Tupolev-26 supersonic bombers and the other weaponry, spare parts, test equipment, and support items necessary to maintain the high-tech machines, purchased from Russia amid great international fear and outrage, represented one of China's biggest single defense outlays. But Jiang also did not want to appear too reluctant in front of the Chinese Communist Party Politburo members to do all that was necessary to defend the country and subdue all its enemies. If he asked the Politburo for permission to use the Tu-26s, he would probably be refused—but now, with an apparent disaster confronting them, each Politburo member was wondering why Jiang was taking so long to give Sun Ji Guoming the weapons he needed to win. "Permission granted," Jiang said finally.

"Thank you, Comrade President," Sun said. "The rebels will be put back in their place, I guarantee it. This was the Nationalists' 'Battle of the Bulge'—it does not represent a change in fortunes for them." Sun turned and strode purposely out of the chamber, feeling the concerned and dubious stares of Jiang Zemin and the CCP Politburo on the back of his neck.

President Jiang was immediately joined by General Chin Po Zihong, the chief of staff of the People's Liberation Army, who looked at the retreating form of Admiral Sun Ji Guoming with obvious distaste. Jiang motioned for Chin, his foreign minister Qian, and his defense minister Chi to join him in a private office. "I want a full report on this attack, Comrade General," President Jiang ordered. "This is unthinkable and totally unacceptable!"

"Yes, Comrade President," Chin said. "The admiral has clearly lost control of the situation. He thinks that the Americans will simply retreat like scared rabbits. This situation proves how wrong he is."

"But his plan seemed to have been working so well."

"How so, Comrade President?" General Chin retorted angrily. "Your original orders were for the People's Liberation Army to return Zhonggua to its rightful position in the world, with all of the lands taken from us returned and our country unified once again. Despite all our losses, civilian and military, and despite the loss of face we have suffered by using nuclear weapons, have we actually taken any territory away from our enemies anywhere? Our thirteenth province, Formosa, has been blasted into a charred rock. We spent billions of *yuan* mobilizing our invasion forces, but Sun has not even landed one battalion on either Quemoy or Matsu—he sends his little 'probes' out, but he has not mustered the courage to lead the People's Liberation Army on a true mission, only these long-range aerial bombardments. Now, with hundreds of thousands of our best troops exposed and vulnerable, the rebel Nationalists and their capitalist masters have struck hard against us. We may not have the forces available to accomplish an invasion now. No one is to blame except Sun Ji Guoming."

President Jiang was clearly horrified by Chin's argument. "What can we do?" he asked.

"The American-led attack on our forces near Xiamen could have come from one place only—Andersen Air Force Base on the American-occupied island of Guam," Chin said. "Our intelligence clearly showed that several of the stealth-modified B-52 bombers were secretly sent there—no doubt more of them, and other long-range bombers as well, had been dispatched since Sun's indiscriminate bombardment of For-mosa." He paused, drawing Jiang's full attention to him; then: "We must destroy Andersen Air Force Base. We must destroy the American bomber base that threatens us."

"Destroy an American air base?" Jiang repeated in a horrified voice. "A direct attack against one of America's most important bases in the Pa-cific theater? We cannot!"

"We *must*, Comrade President," General Chin said urgently. "Oth-erwise we will be open to attack at any time by American bombers. We must strike quickly and decisively." Jiang hesitated, clearly fearful of even *thinking* of making such a decision. "This is not an act of aggres-sion, Comrade President," Chin went on. "This is retaliation for their at-tack against our ground forces. We have the right to defend ourselves against American stealth bomber attacks."

"But destroying this base will not stop the American long-range bombers," Minister of Defense Chi Haotian, who had joined the dis-cussion after Sun had departed in such a hurry, interjected. "We now know that the Americans were able to fly stealth bomber attacks into Iran from their North American bases."

"With Andersen Air Force Base shut down, the Americans will have to use far more resources to attack us," Chin argued. "We are far stronger than Iran—where one stealth bomber nearly decimated the Iranian mil-itary, it would take many more even to begin to affect the People's Lib-eration Army. This will only serve to bring all the parties involved to the bargaining table sooner."

"I wish I could believe this to be true, General," Jiang said. "I want to believe that we can accomplish peace by using force."

"We have already started on this path, Comrade President," Chin said in a flat, matter-of-fact tone. "Admiral Sun made a compelling ar-gument, and the decision was made to support his unorthodox plan. He was successful in convincing America's allies to cease their support. But now his plan has stalled, and the attacks are coming from a colonial base near China that is wholly occupied by the Americans—Sun's plan did not affect American military operations out of Guam. We must show the Americans that we will not tolerate their slaughter from the skies. We must attack and neutralize Andersen immediately."

"How do you propose to do it, Comrade General?" Minister Chi asked.

"The best way possible—a missile attack using our Dong Feng-4 intermediate-range ballistic missiles," Chin said. "We have ten such missiles on alert, headquartered at Yinchuan and deployed throughout Ningxia Huizu and Nei Monggol provinces. I would propose launching all ten missiles at Guam—because of the poor accuracy of our missiles and the strong anti-missile defenses erected on Guam, we may need all of them to neutralize the American military installations on the island. The missiles carry different warheads, depending on the serviceability of the missile itself: most missiles carry a single sixty-kiloton warhead, although some carry a single two-megaton warhead, and the most advanced missiles carry three sixty-kiloton warheads."

Jiang Zemin was astounded by the power at his command—he had never, ever considered using these weapons in all his years of service to China. "You must find out exactly what we have ready to attack," President Jiang said, his voice heavy and shaking with emotion. "I want to limit the number of launches so it will not appear to America's long-range sensors that we are starting a large-scale intercontinental war. The missiles with three warheads is my first choice, followed by the low-yield single-warhead weapon, and finally the large-yield missile. What other strategic forces will we have in reserve that hold the United States at risk?"

"This will leave us all twenty of our DF-5 missiles in reserve," Chin replied. "Ten of these reserve missiles have small, multiple warheads; five of the remaining ten have single one-megaton warheads, and the other five have single five-megaton warheads. The Dong Feng-5 missiles are our largest, most accurate, and deadliest weapons—we can target American intercontinental ballistic missile sites and ninety percent of the population of North America with them. Of course, we still have approximately one hundred H-6 bombers that could possibly reach Alaska or the West Coast of the United States; they can carry nuclear bombs or nuclear-tipped cruise missiles. We also have a number of road-mobile Dong Feng-3 missiles and Q-5 attack planes deployed, but these are only capable against targets in Asia, such as South Korea, Singapore, or Japan."

Jiang nodded, understanding but not quite believing the awesome power that lay at his fingertips, waiting for his word to send them on their deadly way. "This is incredible," Jiang said breathlessly, shaking his head. "The Party has promised we would never be the first to use nuclear weapons. We have already broken our pledge by using these horrid weapons against Taipei, but we reasoned that we were using these weapons against a rebel government within our own territory, not against a foreign power. But I ordered a nuclear attack against a Nationalist warship, then an American warship, and then a nuclear attack against an ally, simply to try to distract the Americans from attacking us. Now I must consider a full-scale nuclear attack against an American military base. I do not know if I can make this decision, Comrade General. It is too much."

"You have almost the entire Politburo and Central Military Committee assembled here this morning, Comrade President," Chin reminded him. "Call an emergency meeting with them right now. I will speak to them; together, without all the philosophical ramblings from Sun, we shall get their full support before issuing your orders."

Jiang relented and gave a faint nod. In three minutes General Chin Po Zihong had called an emergency meeting to order on behalf of the president to present his plan to stop the Americans—and twenty minutes later, he had his orders.

ABOARD THE EB-52 MEGAFORTRESS

THAT SAME TIME

"I've got an L-band Phazatron pulse-Doppler radar beating us up," David Luger called out. "It's a Sukhoi-27, all right. Clear me for maneuvers and all countermeasures."

"Clear!" Brad Elliott shouted, tightening his grip on the side-mounted control stick. "You're clear for all maneuvers as long as you nail that bastard! Just keep us out of the rocks!"

Patrick McLanahan called up a God's-eye view of the area surrounding their bomber. "Very high terrain northeast," McLanahan said. "River valley west and northwest, almost sea level."

"Then let's start with northeast and take this son of a bitch into the rocks," Luger said. He put his fingers on the manual decoy dispenser button. "Stand by for maneuvers, crew. Pilot, break right!"

Elliott jammed the Megafortress hard to the right, feeling his butt press into the seat as the EB-52 started a hard climb to start cresting the rapidly rising terrain of the Boping Mountains. When he reached sixty degrees of bank, Elliott pulled on the control stick until he heard a stall warning tone, then released the back pressure but maintained the turn right at the edge of the stall. As Elliott started the hard turn, Luger punched out one small tactical decoy. The glider decoy, similar to the ones used in the Wolverine SEAD cruise missiles, had radar cross-sections dozens of times larger than the Megafortress itself. "Roll out, pilot," Luger ordered, when they reached ninety degrees heading change, and Elliott quickly rolled the big bomber left.

The jink worked—but for only a few seconds. The Chinese Sukhoi-27's Phazatron N001 pulse-Doppler radar was a "look-down, shoot-down"–capable radar—it could stay at high altitude and look down to find enemy aircraft because the pulse-Doppler radar could reject radar clutter caused by terrain. One way to beat a pulse-Doppler radar system was to reduce the closure rate between aircraft, so in effect the aircraft looked like a piece of terrain on radar. By dropping a cloud of chaff and then turning ninety degrees to the Su-27's flight path, the closure rate between the Megafortress and the Su-27 equaled the airspeed of the Su-27, which caused the system to reject the Megafortress as a possible target. And since the decoy glider proved to be a much more inviting target and still carried a good closure rate on the Su-27, the fighter's attack radar programmed the decoy as the new target.

The Chinese Su-27 fighter pilot selected a Pen Lung-2 radar- and infrared-guided missile, received a lock-on tone, and got ready to press the LAUNCH button—until he realized his target was rapidly slowing down. The unpowered glider decoy made an inviting, easy-to-kill target, but it could not maintain the same airspeed as the Megafortress. The Chinese pilot canceled the attack when the target's airspeed began to decrease below 300 knots—no military attack plane was going to fly that slow unless it was getting ready to land. He verified his decision by closing within five miles of the target, then attempted to lock onto the target with his Infrared Search and Track System. It would not appear on the IRSTS—the pilot knew it had to be a decoy, then. Any military attack plane would show clearly in the large supercooled eye of the IRSTS. He broke radar lock and commanded another wide-area search.

That delay gave Luger an opportunity: "Stand by for Scorpion launch, crew!" he shouted. He hit the voice command button: "Launch one Scorpion missile at target number one."

WARNING, LAUNCH COMMAND INITIATED, the computer responded in a soft, calm, female voice.

"Launch," Luger ordered.

SCORPION MISSILE PYLON LAUNCH, the computer announced, and a single AIM-120 AMRAAM collected target azimuth from the threat warning receiver, streaked out of the right wing weapon pod, climbed a few hundred feet, then arced left toward the Sukhoi-27. A few seconds after launch, the computer said, WARNING, ATTACK RADAR TO TRANSMIT, and the omnidirectional attack radar activated for four seconds, enough to lock onto the fighter and feed updated target range and bearing to the Scorpion missile. ATTACK RADAR STAND BY, the computer said as it shut the radar down itself. With a fresh target update, the AIM-120 missile activated its own on-board radar seeker, instantly locked onto one of the Su-27 fighters, made a slight correction as its pilot detected the brief Megafortress radar lock-on and tried to make a last-ditch evasive break, then exploded just as it detected that it had closed to well within lethal range of its forty-four-pound high-explosive warhead.

The attack worked. The explosion occurred just a few feet behind the Su-27's right wing near the fuselage, sending shrapnel through the fighter's right engine and piercing right wing fuel tanks. The Chinese pilot was quick, and managed to save his prized jet by immediately shutting down the right engine before it seized or tore itself apart, but this jet was out of the fight—he had just enough fuel and control of his plane to keep himself upright and limp home. Even more important, his wingman, another Sukhoi-27, was ordered to lead his stricken comrade back to base—a Su-27 was too valuable and too expensive a weapon to be allowed to make an emergency single-engine landing at night in rugged terrain without assistance.

"Threat scope's clear, gang," Luger reported, with a sigh of relief. "Clear to center up."

"Left turn heading three-three-two to the next turnpoint," McLanahan said. "High terrain twelve miles, commanding on it. Minimum safe altitude in this sector, six thousand one hundred feet."

"Good going, Major Luger," Nancy Cheshire offered. "Sounds like you've been doing your homework."

"I've never left this thing, Nancy," Dave Luger said, wearing a broad smile under his oxygen mask. "Even after all these years, it's as if I've never left. I've . . ." He hesitated, studying the new threat signals, then reported, "Looks like bandits at ten to eleven o'clock, well below detection threshold, closing in on us but not locked on. Now I got fighters at five o'clock, not locked on but heading this way. We got fighters all around us."

THE WHITE HOUSE OVAL OFFICE,
WASHINGTON, D.C.
TUESDAY, 24 JUNE 1997, 1419 ET

"One of our subs is caught in a *fishing net* in the Strait of Hormuz?" Senate Majority Leader Barbara Finegold asked incredulously, the surprise and exasperation etched in her elegant features. "How in the world did that happen?"

As Senator Finegold spoke, the President of the United States moved from the high wingbacked chair near the fireplace, where he and leaders from both the House and the Senate—which the media were calling the "President's crisis team"—had had their most recent "crisis team photo opportunity," and back onto his more comfortable leather chair at the head of the coffee table in the formal meeting area of the Oval Office. He made a show of loosening his tie and taking a sip of orange juice, as if he were ready to settle down and get comfortable while talking to the Senate Majority Leader.

Seated beside him was Vice President Ellen Whiting; and seated around them were members of the President's national security team—Secretary of Defense Chastain, Secretary of State Hartman, and National Security Advisor Freeman, along with chairman of the Joint Chiefs of Staff Admiral Balboa and Chief of Staff Jerrod Hale. Seated next to Senator Finegold was the Senate's chief political counsel, Edward Pankow, then House Majority Leader Nicholas Gant, and House Minority Leader, Joseph Crane.

"It was obviously not a normal fishing net—the crew characterized it as a large drift net made of Kevlar, a synthetic material used in protective armor, as light as nylon but stronger than steel," Philip Freeman replied. "It was obviously a trap."

"Where was the sub trapped, General Freeman?" Finegold asked.

Freeman hesitated, but the President nodded, and he responded, "About three miles south of Bandar-Abbass, in the Strait of Hormuz. It's a busy channel, used by hundreds of deepwater ships a day. The *Miami* was shadowing the Kilo-class attack missile submarine *Taregh* when it was—"

"Was it in international waters?" Finegold asked warily, as if afraid of the answer.

"That is in some dispute," Philip Freeman said. "The Iranians claim all waters up to the center of the Strait of Hormuz, plus three miles around its islands. The International Maritime Court gives Iran three miles from the mean high-water line."

"Then I'll rephrase the question, General Freeman—*was* the *Miami* in Iranian waters at all? Did we provoke the Iranians in any way?" Finegold asked.

"Senator, we seem to provoke the Iranians simply by our very *existence*," Freeman responded. "Yes, our submarine was on patrol in Iranian waters, but I don't think it's fair to say we provoked any kind of action against our submarine or its crew."

Finegold shook her head and gasped in amazement. "We had a nuclear attack submarine that actually sailed up to an Iranian naval base, in Iranian waters? That's like an Iranian attack sub sailing up into the Mississippi River all the way to New Orleans, isn't it?"

"Senator Finegold, we've briefed the Senate on our intelligence procedures before," Secretary of Defense Chastain said. "Our mission is to monitor the whereabouts of the Iranian missile submarines. Normally, that can be done by satellite or patrol planes flying out of Saudi Arabia or Bahrain. The current emergency situation between China and Taiwan, and the recent events between us and Iran, prevent us from flying patrol planes in the area, so we need attack subs to shadow the Iranian subs. To prevent the *Taregh* from sneaking past us, as well as to monitor the Iranian fleet at Bandar-Abbass and in the Persian Gulf, we made the decision to send our patrol subs right near the Iranian naval bases. Normally, the mission is relatively safe. The channel is deep and wide, and the subs can roam around fairly freely."

"But they're *inside Iranian waters*, Mr. Chastain!" Finegold said incredulously. "We've committed an act of *war*!"

"We do missions like this all the time, Senator," the President interjected. "You're reacting as if you've never heard of such a thing before. It's a cat-and-mouse game. Once in a while, one side gets caught. The information we gather about Iranian naval forces is valuable enough to take the risk."

"What if the Iranians decided to sink the *Miami,* Mr. President?" Representative Joseph Crane interjected. "Would the deaths of one hundred and thirty more sailors still be worth it?" The President seemed to wince at that remark. The loss of the aircraft carrier *Independence* to a nuclear blast was still obviously very painful to him. "I'm very sorry, Mr. President," Crane added, without any real conviction, as he saw the ashen expression on the Chief Executive's face.

"But they didn't sink it," Chastain said. "The crew was under attack and, unable to maneuver, the captain made the correct decision and surfaced. The captain is guilty of nothing more than trespassing, and we expect our crew and our sub to be returned to us in short order."

"But not before the entire *world* gets a look at our nuclear attack sub on CNN, caught in a fish net well within Iranian territorial waters!" Crane retorted. "One of our best Los Angeles–class nuclear attack subs, flopping around in a fish net like a big steel mackerel, while a hundred Iranian boats drop garbage and sewage on it—they even showed one old fart taking a shit over it! And the Iranian sub still managed to get away. We look like incompetent assholes."

"Iran knows better than to provoke us," National Security Advisor Freeman said. "They know—"

"That if they piss you off, you'll fly another B-2 stealth bomber over their cities and bomb the hell out of them—or drop glue bombs on their air bases and ships?" Crane interjected derisively. "Is that what you did to them earlier this year, General Freeman?"

"Yes, that's what we did, Mr. Crane," the President said sternly. Both Crane and Finegold were shocked at the sudden revelation. "Yes, I flew B-2 stealth bombers over China and Afghanistan to strike targets in Iran, including dropping special nonlethal weapons on that ex–Iranian aircraft carrier. Satisfied?"

Crane nodded in triumph. "I will be, after a few more questions, Mr. President."

"They will have to wait, Mr. Crane," President Martindale said. "And I want that information held in strictest confidence, top-secret classification."

"And I respectfully decline, sir," Crane said defiantly. "I will call for House special hearings on the attacks, closed-door if necessary, to investigate whether it was necessary and appropriate for you to conduct such attacks."

"Hearings now, when Iran and China are on the warpath, won't help the situation one bit, Mr. Crane."

"Mr. Martindale, perhaps now that we understand that it *was* an American bomber responsible for attacking those targets in Iran and crippling its carrier, we have to look at other suspects, such as Iran, rather than focusing on Chinese or reactionary Japanese saboteurs."

"Congressional investigations will only show a divided government and feed the foreign propaganda machine," Jerrod Hale said. "It won't keep China or Iran off the warpath."

"Then maybe it will get *you* off the warpath, Mr. President!" Crane shot back.

"With all due respect, Mr. President," Senator Barbara Finegold interjected, holding up a hand to silence her overheated congressional colleague, "we do not understand your position regarding your use of military forces overseas. Your current actions are confusing and completely indefensible, and your intentions are not clear, especially with regard to Iran, China, and Chinese Taipei. My colleagues in the Senate need some guidance from you as to your intentions before we can even begin to formulate a support strategy."

The President noted with distaste that Finegold had fallen into the new convention, popular in the media since the conflicts had started about a month ago, of calling the Republic of China "Chinese Taipei" instead of the ROC or Taiwan. It demonstrated to Kevin Martindale exactly how far a lot of persons, especially the opposition, had gone in believing anything that might help stop the nightmarish conflict brewing between mainland China, Taiwan, and now the United States. Chinese president Jiang Zemin and the government of the People's Republic of China had engineered a major publicity campaign, to criticize the Martindale administration's reactivation of America's nuclear forces, especially the actions that violated the Strategic Arms Reduction Treaty warhead limits.

After China used nuclear weapons against Taiwan, the President of the United States announced that he was putting ten nuclear Multiple Independently targeted Reentry Vehicles (MIRVs) on each of the fifty Peacekeeper land-based intercontinental ballistic missiles, and ten nuclear MIRVs on the Trident D5 sea-launched ballistic missiles. But the angriest response came when the media announced that all of America's sixteen B-2A Spirit stealth bombers were now on nuclear alert, loaded with sixteen B83 thermonuclear gravity bombs, and twenty B-1B Lancer bombers were loaded with eight AGM-89 nuclear-tipped cruise missiles and four B83 nuclear gravity bombs.

America was back in the Cold War game, and almost no one, either in the United States or elsewhere, liked the idea.

"My intentions are simple, Senator," the President responded. "I'm going to support President Lee and the Republic of China against President Jiang and mainland China's military aggression. The reactivation of the Triad nuclear forces remains in effect, as well, especially given the cowardly attack on the *Independence,* the Chinese nuclear attacks against the Republic of China, and the sudden nuclear attack in North Korea and the volatile situation there. The capture of our sub by Iran doesn't change things one bit—in fact, it makes me even angrier and more positive that I'm doing the right thing."

"By what treaty or force of law can you do this, Mr. President?" Finegold asked. "The Taiwan Relations Act does not authorize you to defend Chinese Taipei; it is not a member of ASEAN or any other alliance of which America is an ally."

"Senator, I don't need a treaty or membership in an alliance to make a commitment to a friendly, peaceful, democratic nation," the President said. "I've pledged my support, because I don't think that China or anyone else has a right to impose its will by force on another country."

"Mr. President, my legal experts, as well as several think tanks we've commissioned, not to mention the Congressional General Accounting Office itself, have all taken a position that in a legal sense, Chinese Taipei is not a separate nation but in fact a province of China, as Beijing has asserted since 1949," Finegold said. "As I see it, that's the only logical conclusion that can be made. The Nationalist government fled the mainland and established a rebel government on the island of Formosa, which was Chinese territory recently returned to China from Japanese occupation. The Nationalists were nothing more than a deposed government.

"The fact that the United States supported the Nationalists' goal of someday retaking control of the mainland government, or that the Nationalists occupied the seat in the United Nations, doesn't alter the facts," Finegold went on. "The government in Beijing is the lawful and legitimate government of all the Chinese people, a fact which has been recognized by the United States since 1972 and by most of the rest of the world; and the Nationalist government is not the legitimate government, and therefore has no right to declare independence or ask for assistance from anyone, especially the United States of America. The conflict between China and Taipei is an internal matter, and therefore we have no responsibility to risk American lives or threaten the peace of the world by getting involved militarily in that conflict."

"Do you really believe this nonsense, Senator?" the President asked scornfully. "Can you seriously look at those two countries and then tell me that you truly believe that the Republic of China is nothing more than a deposed government living on an isolated province?"

"Mr. President, what I believe is that Chinese Taipei is running out kicking mainland China in the shins, then running behind the United States' skirts—and *we* get the bloody nose from it," Finegold said. "Taipei is not an innocent victim here. As long as they continue to illegally declare independence and try to instigate nuclear conflicts, they are dangerous. What purpose do you have for backing them?"

"The Republic of China meets the traditional benchmarks that the United States has applied to any nation seeking assistance in the last sixty years," Secretary of State Jeffrey Hartman interjected. "We require the new nation to have formed a pluralistic, democratic government with a written constitution, based on free, open, and regular elections with universal suffrage; we require a formal exchange of credentialed ambassadors; we require the new nation to provide for the common good, the common defense, and provide free and open access to its markets and communication between its people and the rest of the world; we require that the new nation apply for membership in the United Nations; and we require that the new nation openly and publicly ask for our assistance. The Republic of China has met each and every one of these criteria, Senator."

"In fact, Senator," Vice President Ellen Whiting interjected, "Taiwan has met more of these five traditional criteria than other nations that you have supported in the past have done, such as Bosnia, Kurdistan, and East Timor. Taiwan has proven to be a strong and true friend to the United States."

"One that apparently is taking advantage of this friendship to attack mainland China, oblivious to threat of global nuclear war," House Minority Leader Crane argued. He now saw his role in this debate as Barbara Finegold's defender.

"I seriously doubt that Taiwan is oblivious to the nuclear threat, Mr.

Crane," Secretary of Defense Arthur Chastain pointed out, "since it has just recently been devastated with nuclear attacks three times as severe as Japan ever endured."

"I didn't mean that Chinese Taipei hasn't been hurt by recent attacks by China, and I certainly don't mean to blame the dead," Crane said. "But it was Taipei's aggression that started this entire series of conflicts."

"My intelligence information suggests otherwise, Mr. Crane," the President said. "China was, and still is, in position to invade the island of Quemoy—there's no doubt about this. Taiwan was acting in self-defense when the attack first started on the Chinese aircraft carrier. The other incidents involved a carefully calculated string of actions by China to make it appear that Taiwan was the aggressor, when in fact it was China all along."

"Of course, I've heard this one from your advisor's press briefs—China attacked its own carrier with torpedoes, China put transmitters on its own ferryboat to make us think it was a warship, China planted a nuclear device on the *Independence,* and China even shot a nuclear missile at its own ally, North Korea, to make us think that the United States or South Korea or some other boogeyman was diverting attention away from China by starting another war."

"Those are the facts, Mr. Crane," National Security Advisor Freeman cut in.

"There's plenty of doubt about your so-called facts, General Freeman," Crane argued hotly. "But I have plenty of questions about the role that secret B-52 bomber played in igniting the conflict! I think that's the question facing us this afternoon, Mr. Martindale!"

"I suggest you calm down and be careful how you address the President, Mr. Crane," Jerrod Hale cut in.

"Relax, everyone, relax," Finegold said, holding up her long, slender fingers to both Crane and Hale. "We're not here to accuse or make demands." She allowed a few moments of silence in the room; then: "Mr. President, we in the Congress want to get behind you in this—"

"The House is one hundred percent behind the President already," House Majority Leader Nicholas Gant interjected, "and there seems to be a floor fight brewing concerning your blatant, public criticism of the President. Whatever disharmony is present on the Hill is from *your* media tirades, Senator Finegold!"

"We realize the tremendous pressure you're under, and we want nothing more than to show a united front to China and the rest of the world," Finegold went on, ignoring Gant's comments. "You are the nation's chief diplomat, but you should not operate in a foreign-affairs vacuum. Give me something positive I can take back to the Hill, something that shows we have room to compromise, something that shows we're not being intractable and demanding."

"I made a decision, and I'm sticking with it, Senator," the President said. "It might not be comfortable or popular, but I've got no choice. I'm counting on Congress's support, but I'm prepared to continue on without it."

"Mr. President, the financial markets are collapsing, the price of oil is nearly at a record high, and our allies are in a panic about whether or not you're leading them to the brink of World War Three," Crane said. "You've suddenly got nuclear missiles and stealth bombers all over the place, threatening a nuclear showdown with China. With Hong Kong and Macau rejoining the PRC, China is one of the world's richest countries and America's largest trading partner by far. You may have already destroyed any chance we had of normalizing relations and expanding trade with China. If there is any chance of salvaging some ties with China, you've got to reverse this deadly course you've set us on."

"You're suggesting we sell out Taiwan, Mr. Crane?" the President asked. "Do you think it would be a good idea to simply abandon them now?"

"You don't have any choice, Mr. President—unless you're ready and willing to fight China, economically and militarily, and risk a nuclear war," Crane responded. "According to the news reports, China is apparently ready to start the occupation of Nationalist Taipei by invading Quemoy and Matsu Islands with *four hundred thousand troops*. We can't stop that many Chinese troops from moving forward.

"Face reality, Mr. President—the island of Formosa and the Nationalist army have been blasted to hell, South Korea is on alert for its own invasion from the north and is under its own nuclear threat, Iran is threatening to close the Strait of Hormuz again because they caught us with our hands in the cookie jar, and Japan, South Korea, Singapore, and the Philippines won't let U.S. troops stage combat operations from their islands," Crane went on hotly. "And even if they did, it would take months to put together an invasion force, and they'd be under constant threat from Chinese air and rocket assaults. The death toll would be enormous. And then if China decided to mobilize its entire army? That's nearly *two million* active-duty soldiers, and almost *two hundred million* reservists, paramilitary, border guards, militia, and national police.

"You have *got* to think of something else, Mr. President! There's no way you can win! You've lost any tactical advantage we ever had. The only way to dislodge China's troops and stop them from reoccupying Taiwan is to use nuclear weapons, and we in Congress, on both sides of the aisle, will not support such a move. And we're willing to make that a public statement."

"The President of the United States does not respond to threats or blackmail, Mr. Crane," Vice President Whiting said angrily. "Not from the Chinese, not from the Iranians, not from the North Koreans—and not from a U.S. congressman."

"No one is threatening anyone here, Madame Vice President," Barbara Finegold said. She decided to use a bit gentler approach in trying to reach the President: "Mr. President, the Chinese government's suggestion is rational and logical, and it's in the best interests of the United States of America." Martindale made an exasperated "here we go again" expression, but Finegold went on quickly: "Mr. President, if China unites with Taiwan, the industrial and financial nation that results will be the largest potential marketplace ever conceived on this planet. Nearly a billion customers, many of whom are still living in turn-of-the-century conditions. Think of the investment needed to bring those people up to Western living standards."

"So you're concerned about the money aspect of a conflict with China," the President said.

"Of course I'm concerned about the financial aspect, and so are you," Finegold said, stepping a bit closer to Martindale as she spoke, letting the language of her body speak to the most powerful man on planet Earth as much as her words. "We're concerned with whatever it takes to make America grow and prosper, and one of the largest untapped resources in the world that we need to exploit is China, especially a strong, capitalist-leaning China united with Hong Kong, Macau, and Taiwan.

"Mr. President, you know, and I know, that China will become the next United States of America in terms of its economic and industrial strength," Finegold went on. "China is where America was three generations ago—mostly agrarian but becoming more urban, isolationalist, suspicious of all foreigners, but expanding rapidly and embracing change, as innovation and new ideas sweep across the frontier. China will not be ruled by warlords forever. We must stake our position to steer China in a direction that's right for them *and* right for *America*. *You* want to be instrumental in shaping China to meet America's needs. We cannot allow China to become isolated."

"Barbara, I agree with your sentiment . . ." the President began.

"Then stop this saber-rattling," Finegold said, her bright eyes locking tightly onto his. "Be the peacemaker, be the visionary. Let us join forces, Kevin. You and me. We can take control of this situation *together*." She knew she had far overstepped her bounds by calling the President by his first name, but her powers of personal seduction were one of her formidable strengths, and she was determined to use them—even here, in the Oval Office, with her adversary surrounded by his generals and chiefs, a place where she had almost no leverage at all.

"First, keep the carriers and the fighters away from China," Finegold went on. "Their very presence is destabilizing and a direct threat to China. Besides, we've proven that we can't keep our carriers safe from saboteurs. If the carriers aren't within striking distance, China won't feel as if they need to use nuclear weapons to counterbalance the threat."

"I've already ordered that the *George Washington* and the *Carl Vinson* stay in the Pacific for the time being," the President said. "Our fighters based in South Korea, Japan, and Alaska are committed to the defense of South Korea right now. They're not a threat to China."

"Very good," Finegold said. "Second, keep the long-range bombers out of the fight. Admiral Balboa has explained to me that the bombers are all on nuclear ground alert. I don't agree with the decision to put nuclear weapons on them, but keeping them on the ground in the United States is the best option." The President merely nodded, casting an irritated glance at Balboa. So he *had* continued to talk with Finegold, he thought.

"Thirdly, agree to make a statement saying that we support *eventual* reunification. You don't have to mention or reverse your statement supporting Chinese Taipei's independence—the press reports say that Lee Teng-hui's government won't survive for long anyway, that they've all fled the country. If the Nationalists can't survive, how can you be expected to support them?"

"The facts don't agree with your sentiment, Senator," the President said firmly. "First of all, we have no independent confirmation that President Lee has fled the country and his government has collapsed, and I am not going to abandon him at his greatest hour of need." Finegold heard how Martindale said the word "Senator" instead of "Barbara," and she could feel their intimate connection breaking down—she realized that the President was made of sterner stuff than she had ever given him credit for. He stepped back from her, reincluding the others in their conversation as he went on: "Second, it's obvious that China is not willing to peaceably wait a hundred years for Taiwan to join them—they are not willing to wait a hundred *days*, or even a hundred *hours*. Their uninhibited use of nuclear weapons proves that."

"China pledges to cease all military attacks and withdraw its troops from disputed territory."

"That's *not* what Foreign Minister Qian said, Senator," Secretary of State Hartman said. "China promised to stop all *nuclear* attacks and withdraw troops as soon as it is safe to do so. That's not the same as a military withdrawal."

"You're mincing words, Mr. Secretary," Finegold said. She watched the President relax, allowing his advisor's words to surround him like a stone wall. The spell was now broken, Finegold realized—they were back to being adversaries again. So be it. "What it means to me is that we'll stop the nuclear threat, and that's what's important here." She turned to the President again. She had tried to use reason and logic, tried to use a little vainglory, and tried a little sweetness—and failed. Now she had to try the direct approach, in none-too-subtle earnest: "It is *very* important that you *carefully* consider this opportunity to make peace with the Chinese, Mr. President."

The President turned toward Finegold, both curled locks of silver hair suddenly, angrily visible now on his forehead. Jerrod Hale uncrossed his arms, his body stiff with anticipation; at that same instant, Philip Freeman shut off and checked his pen-size pager in his jacket pocket, cleared his throat, and stood to use the phone on the President's desk. Both men's actions did nothing to relieve the thick tension that had just invaded the Oval Office. "Excuse me, Senator, but that sounded like a threat to me," he said.

"It's not a threat, Mr. President," Barbara Finegold said. "But there have been . . . rumblings, from certain important government quarters, that cast some doubt on your legal and ethical motivations in this crisis, beginning with the Persian Gulf conflict—"

"No doubt bolstered by your Senate hearings and your statements in the press," Nicholas Gant interjected.

"We are not going to tolerate intimidation or political blackmail, Senator," Vice President Whiting said angrily. "Your attacks on the President are nothing more than partisan politics, taking advantage of the crisis in Asia to further your own political agenda. The American people don't buy it."

"My political agenda is not the topic of discussion, Mrs. Whiting—it's the President's I'm worried about," Finegold said bitterly. "I'm worried that the President will sacrifice the lives of more brave soldiers and sailors just to try to show who's the cock of the roost!"

"That is *enough*, Senator!" Jerrod Hale exploded. "You are way out of line!"

"Hold on, Jerrod, hold on," the President said after listening to the message Philip Freeman had just whispered in his ear. "I've just been informed that an attack is under way against mainland China. An air raid has severely crippled the Chinese armies that were poised to invade Quemoy Island."

"An attack? Air raids?" Finegold sputtered. "Excuse me, Mr. President, but we've been sitting here listening to you explain how you've got things under control, that you're not trying to stir up a military free-for-all in three different regions of the world, that the capture of our sub by Iran was nothing more than a cat-and-mouse game gone awry—and now you tell us that you've staged a sneak attack on the Chinese army?"

"You don't understand, Senator—this attack doesn't involve any American military forces," the President said. "I haven't authorized any air attacks against China."

"But whoever's done it really did a good job," Freeman added. "Initial estimates say that up to one-tenth of the Chinese invasion force that had amassed in southern Fujian province near Xiamen was destroyed or crippled—that could be as much as fifteen, twenty thousand troops and thousands of vehicles. Components of four infantry divisions have been badly hit."

"*Four* divisions?" Secretary of Defense Chastain remarked. "It must've taken three or four heavy bomb wings to do that kind of damage."

"You're joking, right?" Senator Barbara Finegold asked, searching the President's and each of his advisors' faces carefully for any signs of playacting. "You're telling me that someone—you don't know who—has just killed as many as *twenty thousand men,* and you don't know who it was?"

"That's right, Senator," the President replied with a sly smile. "But whoever it is, they probably deserve a medal . . . unless they plunge us into global thermonuclear war in the next few minutes."

"Jesus Christ . . ." Joseph Crane gasped. "You seem pretty damn casual about this, Mr. Martindale!"

"There's not a damn thing I can do about what's happening out there, Mr. Crane," the President said, with his sly grin again. The only sign of concern on his face were the two silver locks of hair curling down over his forehead, but both Crane and Finegold were too stunned to notice. "If you'll excuse us, we're going to start monitoring this situation." The President and his advisors did not wait until the members of Congress recovered from their surprise before he stepped quickly out of the Oval Office to his private study.

OVER SOUTH-CENTRAL CHINA
THAT SAME TIME

David Luger counted no fewer than twenty Chinese fighters buzzing in their area—it was a miracle the EB-52 Megafortress did not collide with them.

Luger and the crew of the Megafortress were skimming less than 200 feet above the southwest side of the high, steep Tienmu Mountains. The area was dotted with dozens of small mining towns, and it took a lot of course changes to stay away from them as they headed northbound. McLanahan and Elliott would have liked their overall cruising altitude to be much lower—some of the Chinese fighter patrols were going down as low as 10,000 feet to look for the Megafortress—but that was impossible in this area. The valley floors were 500 to 1,000 feet above sea level, but would rise to 5,000, 6,000, even 7,000 feet in less than ten miles. The EB-52 was operating at peak efficiency, but even lightly loaded it could not climb more than 3,000 feet per minute without ballooning over a ridge.

Finally, even after all their aggressive maneuvering, there was no place for them to hide. Northeast of the city of Jingdezhen were ten small- to medium-size mining towns; to the west was the Poyang Lake floodplain, along with a Chinese fighter base at Anqing, just fifty miles to the northwest. "Crew, I'm going to take us between two of those mining towns to the north," Patrick McLanahan said. "We can't go any farther west. High terrain is east and northeast; min safe altitude is five thousand feet on this leg, then six thousand one hundred on the next leg. We're five minutes to the release point. I'm setting five-hundred-foot clearance plane for this leg so we don't balloon over these upcoming ridges."

It was a good plan of action, but the odds were turning against them.

As soon as the Megafortress climbed to establish the new clearance plane settings, a large S symbol appeared on Luger's threat display, which immediately went from blue to yellow and then briefly to red. Luger activated the Megafortress's trackbreakers, designed to "walk" a target-tracking or height-finder radar away from a solid lock with the bomber, but not before the radar got a good two- or three-second track on the bomber. "Search radar, eleven o'clock, momentary height-finder lock-on—ah, shit, that's why, they got a repeater radar off at one o'clock, up on a mountain peak," Luger shouted. "I think they got us. Trackbreakers are active. They'll keep the height-finder shut down, but we can expect company."

"Looks like we might have to attack a target of opportunity here," McLanahan said. He quickly expanded his God's-eye picture on his supercockpit display, then touched the icon for the Anqing fighter base. Anqing North was a small but active airfield that sat almost directly on a marshy tributary of the Chang Jiang River and right at the base of a 2,500-foot peak. The base had two medium-length runways, forming a T, and was laid out in typical fashion: the main base was located on the west, the housing area to the south, and the flight operations area to the northeast. McLanahan zoomed into the flight operations area of the base, which automatically called up recent NIRTSat photoradar satellite reconnaissance data from the EB-52's downloaded satellite data memory banks.

Although the raw reconnaissance images did not identify each particular building, Patrick McLanahan knew enough about the layout of a military air base to identify what he needed to know: the mass aircraft parking area, where over fifty J-6, J-7, and J-8 fighters were parked and fueled in preparation for a mission, was concentrated in one spot, in front of a very large building in the north-central portion of the flight operations sector of the base; and the big building housed the fighter wing headquarters, flying squadron headquarters, and the wing command post and communication center. McLanahan immediately programmed one Striker missile for the center of the mass parking ramp, and one missile for the center of the headquarters building.

"Stand by for pylon Striker launch, crew," he called out. He hit the voice-command switch: "Launch one pylon Striker missile on new target zulu."

WARNING, STRIKER LAUNCH COMMIT ORDER.

"Commit Striker launch," McLanahan repeated.

WARNING, STRIKER MISSILE LAUNCH, the attack computer responded, and the Striker missile in the left-wing weapons pod ignited its first-stage rocket motor and blasted skyward. It unfolded its large fins seconds after launch, reaching 10,000 feet in just a few seconds. It glided efficiently for about fifteen miles, dropping down to about 6,000 feet, before firing its second-stage rocket motor and climbing back up to 15,000 feet, when it began its powered ballistic dive onto its target. "Second Striker pylon missile launch coming up, crew," McLanahan said. "Pilot, give me a slight climb up to six thousand feet so we can get a good datalink signal."

The first Striker missile's terminal guidance sensor activated just eleven seconds prior to impact, and McLanahan switched to low-light TV mode. It showed the lights of the city of Anqing to the south and the smaller blotches of light a few miles north. As the missile closed in, McLanahan could start to make out the air base itself—the missile was guiding in perfectly. He could then see sparkles of light around the base—antiaircraft artillery fire. The missile continued its deadly plunge. McLanahan's fingers nestled on the steering-control trackball, but he never had to touch it—because the Striker missile plowed directly on target, right in the middle of the parking ramp. He could barely make out the outlines of a half-dozen blunt-nosed jets and a fuel truck just seconds before the 2,000 pound high-explosive missile hit. McLanahan switched to the second Striker missile just as its terminal guidance sensor activated. Good, the second missile appeared to be going right on target.

"Bandits, close in, nine o'clock!" Luger shouted. At the same instant, a loud, fast-pitched deedledeedledeedle tone and a verbal "MISSILE LAUNCH!" warning sounded in their headsets. "Break left!" A Chinese Sukhoi-27 fighter leading a flight of two J-8 fighters had used the information from Anqing's brief search radar lock on the EB-52 Megafortress to guide themselves within range of its Infrared Search and Track sensor, so it could close within missile range without using its attack radar—only the Megafortress's passive infrared threat warning system had seen them coming. The Chinese fighters launched their heat-seeking missiles at optimum range, less than four miles away.

Brad Elliott yanked the Megafortress's control stick hard left until the bomber rolled right into a full ninety-degree bank, then he pulled until he heard fibersteel screeching in protest. Luger was pumping decoys and flares out the right-side ejectors. Elliott ignored the stall warning horn, ignored Nancy Cheshire's screams that they were going to stall, ignored the initial buffet, the point at which disturbed airflow over the wings starts pounding on the trailing edges of the wings.

The Megafortress could lose 300 knots of airspeed and be for all intents out of control—but Elliott knew, from over ten years' experience in this creation of his, exactly what the point of no return was. It was the departure break, the point at which the turbulent airflow over the wing that was causing all the pounding and shaking suddenly starts to break free of the wing completely, and lift rapidly bleeds off. The Megafortress's crew were crushed down into their ejection seats as Elliott pulled to tighten the turn, but seconds later they felt light in their seats as the bomber started to drop out from under them. The Megafortress would stop flying in less than two seconds—time to roll wings level. At that point, the Megafortress was turning at four Gs, sixty degrees *per second*, as fast as or even faster than the Chinese fighters could ever turn. The Megafortress flew out of the lethal cone of five PL-2 missiles . . .

. . . but not away from the sixth deadly missile. One of the six Pen Lung-2 missiles was fooled by the hot, noisy decoy gliders, missed by several dozen yards, and exploded as its fuzing timer battery ran out—but the fast-turning EB-52 flew right into the exploding missile's lethal radius. Its shaped-charge high-explosive warhead blew a continuous rod of steel into the left rear side of the cockpit, decompressing the cabin and hitting Dave Luger with small pieces of shrapnel and fibersteel.

The cabin was already partially depressurized, but the sudden breach of the cabin seemed to have sucked the air out of every one of the crew members. But Dave Luger still found enough air in his lungs to scream aloud. *"Shit!"* he swore, holding his head with his left hand. A piece of shrapnel had ripped through the bulkhead and ricocheted off his instrument console before cutting painfully into his left thigh and left forearm and pinging off his helmet near his left temple. Luger looked down in surprise at the dark bloody gashes that had appeared as suddenly as a stroke of lightning. He felt no pain—yet. It was almost humorous for him to think that he had just been injured—again—flying a Megafortress mission. "Cripes, Muck," he said to McLanahan, as his partner turned to him in horror. "I think I just got nailed again."

McLanahan was out of his seat in a second, leaving the second Striker missile on its own. The second Striker, with no guidance inputs, relied solely on its own GPS satellite updates and its onboard nav computers and flew itself to its preprogrammed target coordinates, hitting sixty-eight feet north of the center of the Anqing fighter base's headquarters building. The 2,000-pound high-explosive missile leveled half of the three-story concrete building in a blinding flash of fire and a powerful earth-shattering blast.

"This is bull, Muck," Luger was saying. "How come I always get injured on one of these things? When is it going to be your turn? I always . . ." But then he looked down and saw that three long, angry red rips like huge tiger's claws arced across McLanahan's left shoulder and side across his back. "Jeez, Muck, you got hit too, dammit." A surge of energy coursed through Luger, and he helped his longtime friend and partner back into his own seat and helped him strap back in. McLanahan was already looking woozy, and Luger helped him reattach his oxygen mask, secured up to his face, and made sure he was on 100-percent oxygen.

"Stay with me, Patrick," Luger said, cross-cockpit. McLanahan nodded wearily, as Luger strapped himself back in and made sure his oxygen was on and 100 percent too.

"Where are the fighters, guys?" Nancy Cheshire shouted on interphone. The Megafortress was still mushy, right at the edge of the stall. Elliott and Cheshire could do nothing but keep the wings level, the nose below the horizon, and wait for the airspeed to come back—they hoped that would happen before they ran out of altitude. Cheshire shouted, "How are we on the cumulogranite, Muck?" No immediately reply. "You guys okay back there?"

"We're both hit, dammit," Luger responded.

"*What?*" Both Elliott and Cheshire snapped their heads around to look. "You guys okay?"

"Clear of terrain ahead, head westbound only—very high terrain north, south, and east," McLanahan shouted by way of response, his voice strained. "You're cleared down to three thousand feet in this area if you need it. When you can, give me a heading of three-four-zero. We're okay."

"Turns are a no-no right now," Cheshire said. "They don't sound very good. I'll go check them over. You got it, General?"

"I got the plane, Nance," Elliott acknowledged. They transferred controls with a positive shake of the control stick. Cheshire stepped out of her seat and crawled under the aft instrument console to check on both navigators.

"You're both bleeding like stuck pigs," Cheshire said as she examined their wounds. She looked across and saw small, jagged shrapnel holes in the fuselage. "Pilot, better check the instruments—we might have taken some damage."

"I got my hands full as it is, co," Elliott said.

"Dave took a crack in his head and a couple in the leg and arm," Cheshire reported on interphone. "Muck got a bunch in the back, left side, and left shoulder. You guys are going to have some cool scars to show your grandkids. Your seat-attachment shoulder harness is cut, Patrick— if we get in trouble, and if you get the time, think about using one of the downward-ejecting seats."

"Thanks, Nance," McLanahan said. "I'll keep it in mind. But as long as we're sucking dirt here, I'll stay in this seat."

"Okay." Cheshire found the first-aid kit and slapped as many large bandages and compresses on the biggest gashes as she could. "You GIBs will live," she said to the "Guys In Back." McLanahan's wounds looked the worst, but the blow to Luger's head worried her the most—he would have to be checked carefully for signs of a concussion or other head trauma. "Just please advise us before you pass out, okay, Dave?"

"Anything for you, Nancy," Luger replied. Cheshire gave Luger a wink and went quickly back to her seat and strapped in tightly.

"Where are those fighters?" Elliott asked.

"I'm going to do a radar sweep," Luger said, fighting off a wave of dizziness and nausea every time he moved his head. "Radar coming on." He activated the omnidirectional radar for a few seconds, then turned it back to STANDBY. "Fighters are turning right to pursue, at five o'clock high, eight miles."

"We're coming to the river floodplain area," McLanahan said. "Set for COLA altitude again. We've got four minutes until we get into any high terrain again."

"The search radar is down," Luger announced, "so they'll have a tougher time finding us. We'll—" Just then, the threat warning receiver bleeped again: "Fighters at six o'clock, coming inside six miles, I think they got a lock on us! Give me a hard turn to the right."

"Can't turn yet!" Cheshire shouted. "We're still not above three hundred knots!"

"I need a right turn fast!"

"Where are they?"

"Radar coming on . . ." Luger activated the attack radar, and immediately the warning tones sounded again: "Bandits, six o'clock, five miles!" he shouted. He instinctively activated the Stinger tail airmine cannon . . . before realizing with shock, "Shit! No tail cannon rounds! Activating Scorpion missiles!" But before he could command a AIM-120 launch, the crew heard, "MISSILE LAUNCH, MISSILE LAUNCH!"

"Break right!" Luger shouted.

"We can't!" Cheshire shouted back. "We got no airspeed! No airspeed!"

Luger ejected flares and decoy gliders again—but it was too late. The missiles were in the air, headed right for them . . .

. . . no, *not* for them! Seconds before they launched from four miles behind the EB-52 Megafortress, the two Chinese J-8 fighters were hit by Sidewinder air-to-air missiles, fired by two Taiwanese F-16 fighters. The F-16s had broken off from the returning bombing pack to escort the EB-52 Megafortress on its separate strike route. The F-16s could receive datalink information from the EB-52's radar, so it knew where to look for the Chinese fighters; then, using their Falcon Eye infrared sensors, similar to the Sukhoi-27's Infrared Search and Track sensor, the F-16s were able to sneak up on the Chinese fighters without being detected themselves.

The Chinese Sukhoi-27 was still alive, however, and now he was fighting mad. He broke off the attack on the Megafortress, wheeled, immediately pounced on the two F-16s, and fired two PL-2 missiles into one of the F-16s. The second F-16 was alone, trapped right in the crosshairs of the faster and equally nimble Su-27 . . .

No, not quite alone. "Attack radar on . . . commit Scorpion launch on air target X ray," Luger ordered, and he fired two over-the-shoulder AIM-120 missiles at the Su-27. Moments before the Su-27 closed in for the kill, he was blasted apart by a double hit of Scorpion radar-guided missiles. "Splash one -27," he announced.

"Thank you, Headbanger," the Megafortress crew heard over the emergency UHF channel in heavily accented English. "Good luck, good hunting."

"The F-16 is heading home," Luger said, as he studied his threat display. "But he's three hundred miles off his flight plan. I don't know if he'll have the fuel to make it all the way back to Kai-Shan."

"Yes, he will," McLanahan said. He quickly composed a satellite transceiver message on his terminal. "I'll send in Jon Masters's tanker aircraft. They can do a low-level pickup emergency refueling over the coast."

"Jon's tanker ever do an emergency refueling before?" Elliott asked.

"Hell no," McLanahan said. "I don't think Jon's tanker has ever refueled any other plane except a Megafortress and a couple others, and I know for sure that none of the Taiwanese pilots have refueled from Jon's DC-10. But now's a damned good time to learn. We don't need the fuel right now—the Taiwanese F-16 does."

In less than four minutes, the Megafortress sped across the wide, flat Chang Jiang River valley and across to the protective sanctuary of the Ta-Pieh Mountain range, just as another wave of fighters arrived from the neighboring Changsha fighter base to search for the mysterious attacker. The Megafortress continued northwest bound through the mountains for a few minutes, then cut northeast until they were at the extreme northeast end of the Ta-Pieh Mountains. From there, they launched their next attack: two Wolverine antiair defense cruise missiles against the surface-to-air missiles and antiaircraft artillery units defending the bomber base at Wuhan, followed by two Striker missiles.

As the Striker missiles sped inbound, McLanahan suddenly whooped for joy: "Hey, crew, I think we hit the jackpot!" He could clearly see two separate parking areas at the huge bomber base at Wuhan—both filled with heavy bombers. One area was reserved for at least forty H-6 bombers, lined up almost wingtip to wingtip; the other parking area had four H-7 bombers, former Russian Tupolev-26 supersonic heavy bombers. "I'm going to program the last two Striker missiles for the base, too—might as well nail the targets as we get 'em. The navy base at Shanghai will have to wait for our next attack opportunity." McLanahan steered the two Striker missiles already in flight at the H-7 supersonic bombers, planting one Striker in between two bombers so the tremendous blast knocked out both bombers at once, then launched the two remaining Strikers at the H-6 parking ramp. All four H-7 bombers went up in huge clouds of fire, and the Strikers destroyed eight more H-6 bombers and damaged several more.

As a parting gesture, McLanahan quickly programmed the last two Wolverine missiles to orbit over Wuhan bomber base and attack any targets of opportunity with the anti-vehicle skeets—any H-6 bomber that tried to start engines and taxi clear of the devastated parking ramp for the next forty minutes would be treated to a personalized demonstration of the power of an anti-vehicle skeet shooting molten copper slugs into it from out of the darkness. Another thirteen H-6 bombers, plus a number of fuel, security, and maintenance vehicles, were damaged or destroyed by the skeets launched from the Wolverine cruise missiles.

As the Chinese air defense fighters from Nanjing and Wuhu air bases converged first on Anqing, then Wuhan, to try to find and destroy the unidentified attacker, the crew of the Megafortress turned southeast through sparsely settled Zhejiang province, going feet-wet directly between the two Chinese naval bases at Wenzhou and Dinghai. Chinese air defense sites were in an uproar over the invasion on the garrisons at Xiamen, which meant that all available naval air fighter units had been sent on patrol to the south to try to stop any more Taiwanese invaders. Like a ghost riding the rising coastal fog, the Megafortress quietly slipped out of Chinese airspace and disappeared over the East China Sea.

The first detection was from the U.S. Space Command's Pacific Satellite Early Warning System, or SEWS, a large heat-sensing satellite that detected the bright flash of fire from the first 65,000-pound Dong Feng-4 ballistic missile lifting off from its fixed launching pad in east-central China. Since the launch detection was immediately correlated with a known DF-4 launch site, an automatic ICBM launch warning was issued by Space Command to all American, Canadian, and NATO military units throughout the world through the North American Aerospace Defense Command at Cheyenne Mountain. The entire Space Command complex, known as Team 21—the Space Operations missile detection wings, the worldwide communications network, and the crisis management team of the Cheyenne Mountain Strategic Defense Combat Operations Center— were on full alert when the next seven DF-4 missiles were detected moments later.

The commander of U.S. Space Command was called out of a lunch meeting with some of his visiting wing commanders, and he was quickly escorted to the Air Force Missile Warning and Space Operations Command Center. General Joseph G. Wyle was the new commander of "the Mountain." A father of three daughters, a former F-4 Phantom fighter WSO (weapons systems officer) turned computer engineer, Wyle was one of the U.S. military's few "triple hats," a commander of three major military commands: U.S. Air Force Space Command, in charge of all of the Air Force's satellites, boosters, land-based missiles, and launch facilities; U.S. Space Command, in charge of all of America's strategic defense systems, such as surveillance satellites and radars; and the North American Aerospace Defense (NORAD) Command, the joint U.S. and Canadian military team dedicated to detecting, tracking, and identifying all incoming threats against the North American continent. The four-star general had been the deputy "triple hat" commander under General Mike Talbot during the last major international crisis in Asia, when China had first started flexing its blue-water muscles against its neighbors.

"Still waiting for SEWS confirmation of a Chinese IRBM launch," the senior controller reported on the commander's net in the command center.

"Let's hear what you *do* know," Wyle ordered.

"SEWS Pacific detected a total of ten missile launches in east-central China," the senior controller reported. "Subsequent sensor hits showing large rocket plumes rising through the atmosphere, heading east. We have course and speed and approximate missile weight and performance data correlated through SEWS."

"So we're positive that we're looking at Chinese ballistic missiles?"

"The latest intelligence data says the Chinese still had DF-4 missiles at all of the ten known launch sites in the area of the current launches— not the longer-range DF-5, not any of the experimental long-range ICBMs, nor any civil or commercial Long March boosters," one of the intelligence officers reported. "So we can rule out with very good probability that the Chinese are not launching satellites, and that the attack is not against any targets in North America."

That basic information saved a lot of time and wasted efforts—and a lot of officers and technicians who were holding their breath finally could breathe. It was well-known to everyone that Peterson Air Force Base would be a likely target for any enemy seeking to wipe out America's defense network—but these missiles were not heading for the continental United States. "Good," Wyle said. "Let's notify the Pentagon and the NCA, but put it out over the non-emergency priority net."

"We've got a BMEWS confirmation of ten, repeat ten, inbounds powering up through the atmosphere," another controller reported. Space surveillance radar sites in Alaska, South Korea, and the Philippines called BMEWSs, or Ballistic Missile Early Warning Systems, now started tracking the inbound missiles, and trajectory projections appeared on the large full-color monitors in the operations center; they were backed up by radar satellites called DSSSs, or Defense Surveillance Satellite Systems. The probable target was pinpointed less than a minute from first detection: "Impact area, Guam," the controller said.

"Ah, shit—the Chinese launched an attack on Guam," Wyle muttered. "Get it out on the network—target Guam. Time to impact?"

"Twelve minutes," the controller responded.

"Dammit. I hope the Army toads are on their toes this afternoon."

"Sir, now we have a track update via BMEWS and DSSS," the controller reported. "We're showing three of the missiles taking a different trajectory—"

"Where?" Wyle asked. "South Korea? Japan? Alaska?"

"No, sir—it's a flatter trajectory, possibly a satellite insertion profile," the controller responded. "The three missiles are using power to maintain a two-hundred-and-ninety-mile altitude. They could be ready to insert satellites into orbit."

"FOB warheads?" Wyle speculated. He knew the Chinese had FOB, or Fractional Orbital Bombardment technology—the ability to put a nuclear warhead into low Earth orbit, then deorbit it anytime it circled the Earth. The warheads could stay aloft for weeks, virtually untouchable, and could threaten targets all over the globe.

"Unknown, sir," the controller said. "We should be able to get an eyeball on the payloads when they separate." Space Command maintained space surveillance telescopes all over the world, which would allow technicians to visually observe and identify a satellite in orbit—the telescopes were powerful enough to read a newspaper fifty miles away!

As the Chinese missiles reached apogee, their highest point in their ballistic trajectory at almost 400 miles up, the long-range Space Command radars detected the warheads separating from the boosters and beginning their reentry. "We have one missile making an erratic track—looks like it's breaking up in reentry," the controller said. Wyle muttered a silent prayer, hoping more would follow suit. "Three boosters are inserting payloads into low Earth orbit, repeat, three payloads entering orbit. We have three boosters MIRVing, repeat, three MIRVing . . . DSSS now reporting a total of twelve reentry vehicles, repeat, twelve MIRVs inbound, target Guam. BMEWS confirms that track, twelve reentry vehicles inbound, target Guam."

"Confirm for me that an air attack alert has been issued to all installations and on civil defense nets on Guam," General Wyle asked in a low, somber voice.

"We've confirmed it, sir," a communications officer said. "Full military and civil EBS notification." Wyle thought about all the times he had heard the Emergency Broadcast System tests on TV and radio and simply ignored the nuisance interruption. Of course, he had been in many places where people paid attention to EBS—during the floods near Beale Air Force Base in Marysville, California; the tornadoes near Omaha, Nebraska; and even on Guam during frequent typhoon warnings in the summer. But civil defense was a thing of the past, and suitable hardened, underground shelters outside of the military bases were rare on Guam. The population of that tiny, sleepy tropical island in the middle of the Pacific Ocean was going to take the full force of the Chinese missile attack . . . unless the Patriot missiles could stop them.

As fast as the information could be beamed out by satellite, the air defense units on the island of Guam were scrambled and activated. Two U.S. Army Patriot surface-to-air missile batteries were stationed on Guam, one on Andersen Air Force Base in the northern part of the island, and one at Agana Naval Air Station in the central part. Each Patriot battery consisted of a command trailer, three large flat "drive-in-theater screen" radar arrays, and twelve transporter-erector-launcher trailers, with four missiles per trailer, plus associated electrical power and communications relay trucks. The radars did not mechanically sweep the skies, but they electronically scanned huge sections of airspace up to fifty miles in all directions, so between the two sites the entire island of Guam was covered.

The phone at his console buzzed, and he picked it up—he knew exactly who it would be. "Wyle."

"General Wyle, this is Admiral Balboa," the chairman of the Joint Chiefs of Staff said. "I'm at the White House. The President and the SECDEF are here with me. What's the situation?"

"We detected ten missile launches from central China," Wyle reported. "We're tracking a total of twelve inbound ballistic vehicles, all heading for Guam. All tracks confirmed. We believe with high confidence that the missiles are Chinese East Wind-4 intermediate-range nuclear ballistic weapons. The reentry warheads are believed to be everything from sixty-kiloton to two-megaton yield."

"Sweet Jesus," Balboa muttered. "Any other launch detections anywhere?"

"None, sir."

"Anything headed for us at all?"

"Three missiles launched from China inserted small payloads into two-hundred-and-ninety-mile orbits, inclined approximately thirty degrees from the equator, sir," Wyle said, reading information off the large monitors in the command center. "We haven't identified them yet. Their orbits will take them over the Pacific, within about two hundred miles of the Hawaiian islands, but not over the CONUS. They fly over central China on the backside of their orbits, so they might be weather or communications satellites, or just decoys."

"I want those payloads positively identified as soon as possible, General," Balboa said sternly. "Status of the air defense sites on Guam?"

"Two Patriot batteries on Guam. Both are on full alert and will be directly tracking the inbounds in about five to six minutes," Wyle responded.

"The NCA wants an immediate notification on any other launches," Balboa ordered.

"Yes, sir, I'll do it personally," Wyle said. "Is the NCA going airborne?"

"Negative, but we've got Marine One and Two standing by."

"Might be a good idea to get them airborne until we sort this out," Wyle said. "If any of the inbounds hit, we'll lose the 720th Space Group on Guam—that cuts out a lot of missile and satellite tracking and control functions in the Pacific. The warning net might go down, or suffer a bottleneck."

"I'll pass along your recommendation, General," Balboa said. "We'll keep you advised." And the line went dead.

Everything that could be done was being done. Along with providing land-based nuclear intercontinental missiles to Strategic Command in case of a crisis, Space Command's primary function was surveillance, detection, tracking, and notification of an attack from space on the United States, its territories, and allies. That function was completed—now it was up to the last line of defense to minimize the damage.

The Patriot air defense missile batteries first detected the inbound warheads at ninety seconds time-to-impact, but they could not begin firing the first two-missile volleys until thirty seconds time-to-impact. The launches were done completely by computer control, sequencing the launches from both batteries so each salvo would not interfere with another. Every battery fired all of its missiles—that meant that every incoming nuclear warhead had *eight* Patriot missiles flying up to attack it, launched in four different volleys of two missiles each.

But despite software and hardware upgrades on the system since its debut as a ballistic-missile killer during the 1991 Persian Gulf War, the Patriot antiair missile system had never been designed to be an anti–ballistic missile weapon. The Patriot had the advantage of its own onboard terminal guidance radar, which meant it was much more responsive and agile and was more capable against fast-moving targets such as inbound ballistic missiles or warheads, and the new Tier 3 PUG (Patriot Upgrade Group) gave the missile a larger warhead and a new high-pressure hydraulic actuator system, so it could move its control surfaces faster to chase higher-speed targets. Nonetheless, it was still a matter of "bullet-on-bullet," nose-to-nose precision aiming that was still several years from perfection.

Out of twelve inbound warheads, three survived the onslaught of Patriot missiles. One sixty-kiloton warhead exploded two miles west of Orote Peninsula, a total of eight miles southwest of Agana, just 5,000 feet above the ocean, leveling most of the high-rise oceanfront hotels and condominiums and creating an instant killer typhoon. Another sixty-kiloton warhead was blasted off course by a nearby exploding Patriot missile and was harmlessly fratricided by the preceding nuclear detonation near

Agana. Although the blast damage, heat, and overpressure effects were enormous, casualties in the central part of the island would be termed minimal.

But one two-megaton warhead exploded just one and a half miles north of Andersen Air Force Base at an altitude of less than 3,000 feet—and every aboveground building on the base was wiped away in a blast that was greater than the power of five hundred typhoons. The nearby village of Fafalog completely disappeared in the fireball. Mount Santa Rosa, the verdant green hill overlooking the military airfield, was instantly denuded of all vegetation and then sliced nearly in half. The entire northern one-fifth of the island was immediately set ablaze, which was extinguished only by the 200- foot nuclear-spawned tsunami and typhoon-force winds that ripped into the scarred tropical island.

CHAPTER
SEVEN

SKYBIRD, SKYBIRD, message follows: kilo, three, seven, niner, eight, fox-trot, one . . ." the U.S. Strategic Command senior controller said over the command net, reading off a long string of phonetic letters and numbers, then repeating the coded message with the phrase "I say again . . ."

In the Eighth Air Force command center, two teams of two controllers were copying the message down, then beginning to decode the message separately, then comparing their results with each other; satisfied, they began running the associated checklist. The checklist would instruct them what message to transmit to the bomber forces under their command. Both sets of controllers composed the new message, then quickly verified it with each other.

Then, while the first set of controllers began reading the new coded message on the command post's UHF and VHF frequency, the second set of controllers copied the message and passed it along to the battle staff operations officer. He in turn decoded the message with another officer, checked their results with the first two sets of controllers—it checked once again. At least four sets of eyes always checked every message and every response to be sure they were accomplishing the proper action. If there was any error anywhere along the line—a nervous or cracking voice, a hesitation, anything—the other controller would slap a piece of paper over the codebook, and the controller reading the message would read, "Stand by," then start all over again. The stakes were too enormous to leave any ambiguities.

"Latest EAM verified, sir," the ops officer reported to the Eighth Air Force battle staff. "DEFCON Two emergency action message." The entire staff opened up their checklists to the appropriate page, as the ops officer began writing updated date-time groups up on the command timing board. DEFCON, or Defense Condition, Two was a higher state of readiness for all U.S. military forces; for the bomber forces, it placed them at the very highest stages of ground alert, just short of taking off. "Message establishes an 'A' hour only, directing force timing for one hundred percent of the force on cockpit alert status, plus fifty percent of available forces as of A plus six hours to go to dispersal locations," the ops officer went on. "Bases with missile flight times less than twelve minutes go to repositioned alert; bases with MFTs less than eight minutes go to engines-running repositioned alert. The message directs full Reserve and Guard mobilizations."

Every member of the battle staff reached for telephones as soon as the minibriefing was over. Lieutenant-General Terrill Samson, commander of Eighth Air Force, was on the phone to his boss, the commander of Air Force Air Combat Command, General Steven Shaw. He was put on hold.

Samson sighed but did not let himself become angry. He knew he was already effectively out of the picture—in more ways than one. Steve Shaw didn't need to talk to Terrill Samson for any important reason right now.

Barksdale's sortie board was filled with tail numbers and parking areas, but all the sortie numbers and crew numbers were blank. That's because they were all for B-52H bombers, and the B-52s had all been retired, deactivated. By October, all of them would be flown to Davis-Monthan Air Force Base near Tucson, Arizona, there to be cut up and put on display so that Russian, Chinese, and whoever else's spy satellites could photograph the birds and be sure their wings had been clipped for good. Not that Barksdale's ramps were vacant. Some of the B-1Bs from the Seventh Bomb Wing out of Dyess Air Force Base, Abilene, Texas, who were going to become Air Force Reserve bombers in October, had dispersed to Barksdale—they would probably be assigned here full-time when Dyess turned into a B-1B training base.

But all of the heavy bombers that had once been under Terrill Samson's command were now in the hands of U.S. Strategic Command and Admiral Henry Danforth—and since Samson had opened his mouth and dared to contradict Danforth's blind preparation for a nuclear war that was not wanted and probably would never come except by some horrible accident, Samson was not even entrusted with commanding his bombers under CINCSTRATCOM. He was a three-star general without a command, without any responsibilities. He still monitored the status of each and every bomber that was formerly under his supervision, but he was not in the chain of command anymore—he was not even in the advice and consultation loop.

The bomber SIOP generation, the preparation for all the land-based B-1B Lancer and B-2A Spirit bombers for nuclear war, was still not going very well. About three-quarters of the force was on alert now—but under DEFCON Three, 100 percent of the bombers had to be on alert. In addition, 25 percent of the force had to be dispersed to alternate operating locations—Barksdale was one, along with Fairchild AFB in Spokane, Washington, Grand Forks AFB in North Dakota, and Castle AFB near Merced, California—but just a few bombers had arrived, and it would take days for them to get on alert with nuclear weapons aboard. All of the alternate fields were former bomber bases, but it had been months, even years, since any of them had any big bombers land there, let alone any bombers with nuclear weapons aboard.

Terrill Samson could offer words of encouragement, or dispense advice, or rant and rave and threaten to kick ass if they didn't get moving faster. But it meant nothing. His words did not have any authority behind them anymore. Although his stand-down wasn't officially set until October, it was as if Terrill Samson had already been relieved of command, and retired.

"Terrill, Steve here," General Shaw said, as he came on the line a few moments later. "STRATCOM wants to put the B-2s on airborne alert. You got something on the shelf that we can give them in the next couple hours?"

"Yes, sir," Samson responded woodenly, disguising his shock and disbelief. Airborne alert, nicknamed "Chrome Dome" and immortalized in films like *Dr. Strangelove,* hadn't been done in more than twenty-five years because it was so dangerous to have nuclear-loaded bombers flying around for hours or even days on end—the old Strategic Air Command had lost two bombers and four nuclear gravity bombs during Chrome Dome missions. Now Danforth and Balboa, two Navy pukes, somehow thought it would be a good idea to do it again.

"I expected a slightly stronger reaction from you, Earthmover," Shaw remarked.

"Would it do any good, coming from me—or you?"

"Probably not, but I'd like to hear it anyway," Shaw said. "First answer the question so I can give STRATCOM their answer, then talk to me."

"We don't have any Beak-specific airborne alert tracks laid out," Samson responded, "but we can modify a few old B-52 racetracks and give them out to the B-2 crews. We can mate them to B-1B tracks, but we want to be sure we spread them out in case China decides to use nuclear warheads on air-to-air missiles." Samson wondered why his deputy, General Michael Collier, who was the bomber chief for Strategic Command after Samson had been relieved, hadn't called in the request directly from STRATCOM headquarters at Offutt. The only explanation was that Danforth, commander in chief of Strategic Command, was disregarding Collier's recommendations, as he disregarded Samson's.

"Sounds good. I knew I could count on you. Pass them along to Offutt soonest," Shaw ordered. "Now, lay it on me. Give me your thoughts. Quickly, please."

"Yes, sir," Samson said. "I want to make another pitch to the Chief and the National Command Authority about the bomber force. We have got to take them off SIOP alert. I've got a series of plans we can present to the NCA—"

"I don't have time to make the same pitch we tried yesterday, Terrill," Shaw said. "I'm up to my eyeballs. STRATCOM wants to put nukes on the Strike Eagles now."

"What?"

"You heard me," Shaw said. "We're going to have all four F-15E Strike Eagle wings—the 3rd at Elmendorf, the 4th at Seymour-Johnson, the 366th at Mountain Home, and the 48th at Lakenheath—loaded for the SIOP and deployed to Elmendorf for operations against North Korea or China. CINCSTRATCOM is looking at North Korea starting a nuclear exchange within a few hours."

"That's nuts, sir," Samson said. "That'll suck a fourth of your tankers away. Losing Guam was bad enough for the tankers—putting nukes on F-15s for possible missions against North Korea will drain even more tankers away."

"You're exactly correct, Earthmover, and that's the argument I made—but the JCS and STRATCOM are on autopilot for Armaggedon. They think that if we put more nukes on more planes, the Chinese and North Koreans will back off," Shaw said. "Anyway, I'm still waiting on a cocked-on-alert call from your Bones. Pass along a good word for me to the boys and girls at Whiteman for a good job in getting the B-2s loaded up so fast."

They were loaded up and put on alert just so Danforth and Balboa could start dinking around with them, such as putting them on airborne alert, Samson thought bitterly. "I will, sir," he responded; then, quickly, Samson went on: "Sir, I'd like a chance to meet with you and General Hayes on my plan to neutralize the Chinese strategic forces. We have missions on the shelf right now, ready to go, where we can take out every one of the Chinese long-range-missile silos without using nuclear weapons. I'd like to—"

"Sorry, Earthmover, but I can't," Shaw interrupted. "I went to STRATCOM with your suggestions without any luck, and I've got a second message in with the chief. They want to keep all the bombers on nuclear alert—they think it gives them the most leverage to have the bombers, especially the B-2s, loaded with nukes and threatening to destroy targets in China."

"It's obviously not working, sir, because China went ahead and destroyed Andersen and nearly wiped out the capital city of Guam," Samson interjected, "and we still haven't retaliated. *Someone* did, but it wasn't us."

"Sorry, Earthmover," Shaw repeated. "To a certain extent, I happen to agree with the JCS. We can't risk losing the B-2s on a deep strike mission inside China."

"The B-1Bs can soften up China's air defense well enough for the B-2s to go in."

"But then they're up against thousands of fighters and triple-A sites,"

Shaw argued. "We can't destroy all of them. Eventually, the B-2s would be fully exposed. If we lost even ten percent of the B-2 fleet on this attack, it would be a staggeringly demoralizing loss—and it would seem even worse if we didn't do commensurate damage to the Chinese military. We might then be forced to use ICBMs or nuclear cruise missiles to destroy Chinese targets, and then we'd be on the very slippery slope we want to stay off. We'd be sending nuclear warheads over the pole, over Russia. That would make the Russkies very nervous, and we don't want them involved in this fight, on either side."

"Sir, we've got a plan that would practically ensure destruction of the Chinese long- and intermediate-range strategic offensive arsenal, without a devastating loss on our side—and without using nukes," Samson said. "But I need the B-1 and B-2 bombers. All of them. They're not doing any good loaded with nukes. With you, me, and General Hayes talking to the SECDEF or maybe even the President, we might be able to convince him to let us try my plan before it's too late."

There was a slight pause on the other end, followed by an exasperated but resigned sigh; then: "Okay, Terrill, I'll make the request once more. But it's not going to work."

"Thank you, sir," Samson said. "I can fly out to Washington at any time to meet with the Chief or the NCA."

"You just stay at Barksdale, and I'll tell you when to show to give your dog-and-pony show," Shaw said. "Keep quiet till then, okay?"

"Yes, sir," Samson replied—but Shaw had hung up before Samson gave his response. It was not a friendly suggestion to keep quiet—it was an order.

Sometime during the conversation with Shaw, Samson was handed a note. He asked a question of the briefer, then half-listened to the reply as he glanced at the messageform—and then his heart skipped a beat. He threw a "Continue on" order to his battle staff and dashed out of the battle staff room to the comm center. "What did you pick up?" he asked the command post senior controller.

"A message on that special SATCOM terminal you had installed here, sir," the senior controller said. He handed Samson a printout. "Auto decryption on this end." The message read: "HEADBANGER SENDS. URGENT REQUEST EMER AR RNDZVZ W/ SINGLE DRAGON16 25N117E 10K ONLOAD. USE RED7 ARFREQ. ADVISE ASAP. OUT." A later message read: "HEADBANGER FINDS

FOUR H-7 MANY H-6 AT TDELTA SKIPPING TFOXTROT AND TGOLF. THX FOR EMERAR WITH DRAGON16. NAV27 ARCP OK. OUT."

"Wasn't Headbanger the call sign of that modified B-52 that broke out of Andersen past the Navy and U.S. marshals and then disappeared, sir?" the senior controller asked.

"It sure as hell is," Samson replied excitedly. "Shit. This means that not only is Elliott, McLanahan, and the rest of that motley crew alive, but they're flying a damned mission—over fucking *China*!"

"That attack on the PRC garrison at Xiamen?"

"A SEAD Wolverine cruise missile attack," Samson surmised. "A couple of those cruise missiles could wipe out dozens of SAM and triple-A sites. Then they get someone to follow up with cluster-bomb attacks."

"The 'Dragon-16'? You don't suppose they mean Taiwanese F-16s? That EB-52 is flying SEAD missions for Taiwanese F-16s?"

"Yep, and then continuing on deep inside China to do more bombing missions," Samson said proudly. "I'll bet the next intelligence message we get says that Wuhan has been attacked by unidentified bombers—maybe a couple other targets between Xiamen and Wuhan, or between Wuhan and the East China Sea."

"But I thought all the Taiwanese F-16s were destroyed, along with their bases."

"Obviously some survived—along with one Megafortress and Jon Masters's tanker and a few of his gadgets," Samson said. He searched a map of China: "The Chinese H-6 bomber base is at Wuhan, west of Shanghai," he said. "It sounds like McLanahan found some H-7s—those are Tupolev-26 supersonic bombers—and decided to expend their remaining weapons there, instead of a couple other preplanned targets. But where are they flying out of? Who is running that operation?"

"We could find out," the senior controller said. "If I can still receive their SATCOM transmissions, I suppose we can send *them* a message just as easy."

General Samson broke out into a broad grin, the first one in many, many hours. "Move over, son," he said excitedly. "I've got to call me up some renegades so we can get to work cleaning up this war—before it gets completely out of hand."

As Terrill Samson sat down to start typing out messages, he called for his executive officer. "Get the C-21 fueled up and ready to depart for

Andrews. I want every preplanned strike package we've got to attack the Chinese ICBM complexes, bomber bases, and radar sites—and I want it all ready to go within the hour. Then contact Lieutenant Colonel Joseph Roma at Ellsworth and Colonel Anthony Jamieson at Whiteman, drag them off alert or wherever they are, and have them standing by with their conventional strike packages. Tell them I'm taking some of their bombers off nuclear alert—and then we're going to work the way we were *meant* to go to work!"

KAI-SHAN MILITARY COMPLEX, NEAR HUALIEN,
REPUBLIC OF CHINA
WEDNESDAY, 25 JUNE 1997, 0651 HOURS LOCAL
(TUESDAY, 24 JUNE, 1751 HOURS ET)

The roar of jet engines could be heard far below, creating a constant rumbling and vibration throughout the medical facility. The Taiwanese staff appeared not to notice. They worked with silent efficiency, quickly and quietly loading up medical supplies for the evacuation.

David Luger had just been wheeled into an examination room from the X-ray lab. He was lying on a gurney, a thin sheet concealing all the other bandages on his left leg and arm. The left side of his body looked as if he had been spray-painted with a mixture of black, yellow, and brown paint—it looked like one continuous bruise from his head to ankle, and his left eye was swollen almost completely shut. "I tell ya, I'm okay," Luger was protesting to the doctor accompanying him. Patrick and Wendy McLanahan, Brad Elliott, and Jon Masters were waiting for him; Patrick's injuries, not nearly as serious as Luger's, had already been treated.

"What's the scoop, Doctor?" McLanahan asked the attending physician, who was carrying Luger's X rays.

"Severe concussion, as we suspected," the Taiwanese doctor replied, holding up each pertinent X ray as he spoke. "Slight cranial fracture. Partial hearing loss in the left ear, slight fracture in the left orbit. Cuts and bruises all along the left side of his body where he took the brunt of the explosion. Broken left knee, swollen left ankle and left foot. If I did not know he was hit by an exploding missile, I would say he had been hit by a bus."

"I'm okay, I said," Luger protested. "Damn, we kicked some ass, didn't we?"

"We sure did," Brad Elliott said, a broad smile on his face. "It was just like the first Old Dog flight. They threw everything but another Kavaznya laser at us, and we fought through it all and bombed the crap out of them!"

"So let's gas up and get ready to fly another sortie," Luger said.

"Not you, Dave," Patrick said. "You're grounded. We'll take the next run ourselves. I can handle both the OSO and DSO's stuff."

"This damned headache won't keep me from at least helping mission-plan for you guys," Luger said. "We still have to knock out the air de-fense sites around Shanghai."

"What I'd like to do is bomb the crap out of the Chinese ICBM silos and launch sites," Patrick McLanahan said, a definite tone of anger in his voice—very uncharacteristic for his buddy, Luger thought.

"We know where they are—we just need to get in there and nail 'em," Jon Masters said, his voice as bitter as Patrick's. "Our guys back at Blytheville launched two more satellite tracks over central China, and we think we've pinpointed all the DF-5 and DF-3 silos and launch sites. One more NIRTSat launch and I can have each and every one targeted, along with a good number of mobile missile launchers."

"But we're low on weapons," Patrick went on. "We're down to only two Strikers, two Wolverine missiles, and two Scorpion missiles. The ROC has plenty of fuel, air-to-air missiles, and cluster munitions left over, but our rotary launchers can't carry the cluster bombs."

"Shit, maybe we can send Hal, Chris Wohl, and Madcap Magician back to Andersen to steal us the rest of our Megafortresses," Luger said with a grin—and then he noticed that the others did not share in his quip. In fact, everyone looked real funereal all of a sudden. "But why all the focus on the Chinese ICBM sites all of a sudden? I thought we were going after air defense sites."

"Oh, that's right—you were being checked out up here when we heard," Wendy said. "Dave . . . the Chinese launched a nuclear ICBM attack against Guam."

"*What?*"

"Andersen has been destroyed—it was attacked with a *two-megaton* warhead," Wendy went on sadly. "Agana and most of the northern half of the island have been severely damaged."

"Oh, my God," Luger said in a low, completely horrified tone. "Was it a retaliation against *our* attack? Did we cause the Chinese to attack with nuclear missiles?"

"The Chinese were committed to using nuclear weapons to attack their enemies long before you came to our assistance, Major Luger," Brigadier-General Hsiao Jason, commander of the Kai-Shan Military Complex, said as he entered the examination room. He extended a hand to David Luger. "I wanted to thank you for your sacrifice and good work, Major. I am very proud of all of you, and very grateful."

"We're not done yet, General," Elliott said. "We're going to load up each and every weapon we can and shove them right down China's damned *throat*!"

"We will—when we get the right opportunity and the right targets, Brad," McLanahan said. "Right now, we've got to finish repairs, then see if we can mount any of the ROC's cluster munitions on our rotary launchers. Wendy, Brad, can you help General Hsiao's techs finish the repairs on the DSO's stuff?" Wendy nodded, gave Dave Luger a kiss to help speed his recovery, and hurried off back to the EB-52.

Patrick turned back to Luger. "Bedrest for you, chum." He noticed Dave Luger wearing the archetypical "shit-eating grin" on his face, which looked even more funny with half of his face swollen and purple. "What are you grinning at?"

"You, Muck," Luger said. "Look at you—tossing orders around, and everyone's jumping, even Brad Elliott. Pretty cool. You've taken over this team, whether you know it or not."

"So I'm like some modern Asian Robin Hood with his merry band of outlaws, huh?" Patrick remarked. "Sticking it to the Chinese and defending Taiwan."

"I don't mean just the mystical Zen bombardier, Patrick—you're turning into the boss man around here," Luger said seriously. "When we first started flying together, you didn't want to have anything to do with commanders, not even aircraft commanders. You'd been offered dozens of command positions even before you made the major's list, and you turned them all down. I don't know how many more positions you were offered since the Old Dog mission—probably another couple dozen. Everybody knew you and respected your talents, but you weren't a leader, and you never wanted any leadership positions. Now everybody's waiting for you to give the word, even Brad."

"If you're done busting my chops, Dave, I'm gonna head downstairs and check on our plane."

"I'm serious, Muck, I really am," Luger said. "I'm not busting your chops. You've really changed. You're not just a crewdog anymore—you're a leader, a commander." He smiled again. "Who woulda thunk it?"

"Not me," Patrick said. He gave Luger a thumbs-up and left him in the company of a nurse and a security guard.

Nancy Cheshire met McLanahan on the tarmac. The Taiwanese were busy launching frequent air patrols over Formosa, and the air inside the cavern was thick and heavy with jet exhaust that the ventilators were having trouble keeping clear. "How are we doing on mating the CBUs to the Megafortress, Nance?" Patrick asked.

"We might be able to do something if we can mount a few racks onto the lower three beams of the rotary launcher," Cheshire replied. "If we can, that'll give us at least six CBUs per launcher. Unfortunately, there's not enough room to mount racks and bombs on the entire launcher, only the bottom three stations. We're pretty certain we can do a 'straight six' arrangement and put six CBUs on the lower and inboard stations of the wing weapon pods—that's another twelve. With both launchers full, we can carry as many CBUs as six Taiwanese F-16s."

"Great news," Patrick said.

"This is even better news, I think," Cheshire said. "We downloaded this off the satellite communications terminal—an *incoming* message, addressed to *you*."

"Incoming?" Patrick remarked with surprise. "Is it from Sky Masters? They're the only ones that we've been talking to."

"Nope, it's not from Arkansas . . . it's from Louisiana," Cheshire said, wearing her broad, Cheshire cat smile. Patrick stopped short as he read . . . and he too began to put on a broad smile.

"Nancy, I want power on the airplane, and—"

"You got power and the SATCOM terminal's fired up," Cheshire said, but Patrick didn't hear her—he was trotting, now running, toward the EB-52 Megafortress, to reply to the incredible message he'd just received.

"This madness must stop, Mr. President," Foreign Minister Qian Quichen said via an interpreter on the hot-line phone from Beijing. The foreign minister's voice in the background betrayed his agitation and anger. "The people of China are clamoring for war, sir! They want revenge for the bloodthirsty sneak attack on our cities. President Jiang is going to make a personal appeal for calm on national television this morning, but he is under tremendous pressure from the military, the Congress, and the Politburo to retaliate against your naked aggression."

"I'm sorry, Minister Qian, but I've told you twice already—the United States had nothing to do with any of those alleged attacks against your cities," President Kevin Martindale said. With him in the Oval Office were his closest advisors: Ellen Whiting, Arthur Chastain, Jeffrey Hartman, Jerrod Hale, Philip Freeman, and Admiral George Balboa. An Army military intelligence officer fluent in Mandarin Chinese was interpreting and making notes for the President. "None of our bombers or attack planes were involved. Do you understand me, Minister Qian? No bombers of any kind under my command were involved in any attacks."

"Then you . . . you are not being truthful," the halting response came from Beijing.

"He said you are a liar," the Army-Chinese language specialist interjected. "He said you are a 'damnable liar.' His exact words, sir."

"That son of a *bitch*," the President swore half aloud, taking his fingers off the phone's "dead-man switch" so Qian could not hear his curses. "Who the hell does he think he's talking to?" He reactivated the handset once again, "Minister Qian, let's all compose ourselves and act like civilized men," he said, forcing every bit of calm he could into his voice. "You can call me a liar, you can believe me or not believe me, I don't care. But here are the facts as we know them, sir: you launched ten intermediate-range ballistic missiles on an American military installation and destroyed it with a nuclear warhead. Do you dispute those facts, Minister Qian?"

"We do not dispute the fact that we launched rockets," Qian said through his interpreter, "but the rockets were not attack rockets, and they contained no nuclear warheads, only meteorological data packages."

"Minister Qian, our satellites and radar stations tracked those missiles from the moment they were launched to the instant they hit Guam," the President said angrily. "The ten missiles that you launched from your launch sites in Ningsia and Inner Mongolia Provinces were the ones that were tracked heading for Guam. We detected the warhead separation and tracked each individual warhead as it reentered the atmosphere—we even tracked the one missile that destabilized and crashed into the Pacific Ocean, and with luck we'll recover pieces of it and prove to the world that it was a Dong Feng-4 ballistic missile with a nuclear warhead, as we believe it is. We have incontrovertible evidence of a Chinese nuclear attack on Guam, Minister Qian. The question now is, what is China going to do next?"

"Mr. President, the weather satellite rockets launched a few hours ago that you say you tracked were not responsible for the unconscionable devastation on your colonial island," Qian said. "We have data to show the exact trajectory of our weather satellites that were inserted into low Earth orbit by those rockets, and we will be most happy to send that data to you. The satellites are still in orbit, a fact that any capable government can check on its own. As for the warheads that you say separated from our rockets, we cannot say. Your equipment or your analysis was obviously faulty. We had no reentry vehicles on our rockets, especially not nuclear warheads."

Unfortunately, Qian was partly telling the truth, the President reminded himself. Three of the rockets launched among the ten inserted had later been identified by space surveillance cameras as visual- and infrared-spectrum photo weather satellites. As far as anyone could determine, these three satellites were harmless—and their presence afforded a weak but defensible explanation for the multiple Chinese rocket launch. It still could not erase all of the other evidence that China had attacked Guam with nuclear weapons, but now the possibility, however slim, that China had *not* shot rockets with nuclear weapons on board had to be carefully investigated. And that would take time.

"Minister Qian, I would like you to pass along a message to President Jiang and to the other members of your government," President Martindale said firmly. "Tell him that I am going to speak to the leaders of both houses of Congress about going to the full Congress and the American people and asking for a declaration of war against China."

Even the interpreter, trained not to react emotionally to anything he heard or said, gasped at the announcement and had trouble providing a translation both of the President's message and of Qian's response: "You . . . you must not, sir!" Qian's translator said in a quivering voice. "Mr. President, we are at odds only with the Nationalists on Taiwan, not with the United States of America. Please, sir, stop your support of this illegal and disruptive society, and assist the world community with re-uniting all of China, and we promise that China will work tirelessly to strengthen the ties between our two nations."

"Please pass along my message to President Jiang, Minister Qian," the President said stonily. "I will be ready any time of the day and night to receive his reply. Good day to you, sir." The President handed over the phone to Jerrod Hale with a grim expression on his face.

"You want a drink, Mr. President?" Hale asked. "I could sure go for one."

"Not now, Jerrod," the President said testily. He ran a tired hand over his eyes. "Christ, I feel like a cornered animal, with no other option but to lash out at anyone and everyone in front of me."

Secretary of Defense Arthur Chastain got off the phone near the cof-fee table in the informal conference area of the Oval Office. "Pentagon reporting a firefight across the DMZ, near Changdan. A North Korean special forces team blew up a tank maintenance facility. No reports yet on casualties or damage. Several artillery rounds were also fired towards Seoul, probably a probe. The USAF reports one F-16 anti-radar patrol fighter shot down five miles south of the DMZ by a surface-to-air mis-sile; North Korea claims it was flying in the north. Pilot's believed to be a casualty."

"I want to find a way to send some assistance to South Korea," the President demanded. "What's the best way? Arthur? Admiral? Let's hear it."

"Sir, we've got the *George Washington* in the Pacific, just a day or two from its operations area in the Philippine Sea," Balboa said. "If we can get the Japanese to allow our supply ships to move out of their har-bors, we can bring in the *Washington* to begin air ops against North Korea."

"But that's the problem, Admiral—Japan won't allow us to move any ammunition supply ships out of their harbors," Chastain said. "We've got food and fuel from Japan, but just a trickle of ammunition and spare parts. The *Washington* would be good for combat operations for about two weeks, and then it runs short." He turned to the President: "The best option would be to bring in more carriers, sir. With three carriers in the Philippine Sea and East China Sea area, we could conduct reduced-level offensive air ops against North Korea, and perhaps have a limited holding force should China decide to attack. With four carriers, we could conduct full-scale air ops against North Korea or China, and do a holding force against anyone else trying to hit us from the side."

"*Four* carriers," the President muttered. "As many as we had in the Persian Gulf War, but without the nearby supply bases."

"We run the risk of having too few carriers available in case things blow up in the Middle East," Philip Freeman interjected.

"We've got plenty of assets, General Freeman," Balboa argued.

"*Lincoln* would have to stay in the Arabian Sea to keep her eye on whatever the Iranians might do, now that they've captured one of our subs and might not give it back—and it might be better to bring another carrier out of the Med to reinforce her, or send more land-based planes from the States to Saudi," Freeman explained. "So we cancel *Lincoln's* planned rotation and send *Carl Vinson* in to work with *Washington*. That's two. We'd then have to send *Kitty Hawk* out of the Indian Ocean to reinforce *Vinson* and *Washington* until we can get *Nimitz* under way from Alameda. A fourth carrier would have to come from the Atlantic Fleet."

"I count two carriers that we can place on North Korea's front doorstep in two days, three within a week, and four in a month—so far, I don't see a big problem here," Balboa said. "The carrier crews are ready to get into action—they want revenge for the attack on *Lincoln* earlier this year by Iran, the death of the *Independence,* and now for the attack on Guam. This is shaping up to be a carrier war, sir," Balboa said with a touch of barely disguised glee in his voice and eyes. "Let the boys go out and kick some butt."

"It's a lot of carriers within range of China's missiles," Freeman pointed out.

"We can take care of China and her missiles," Balboa said confidently. At that moment, one of Balboa's military aides entered the Oval Office, stepped over to the admiral, whispered in his ear, then departed again.

"Seems like you have visitors, Mr. President," Balboa said. "Air Force chief of staff Hayes, Shaw from Air Combat Command, and Samson from Eighth Air Force. They probably want to pitch another hackneyed bomber idea to you. I heard rumblings from General Hayes that Samson was kicked off the Combined Task Force in Strategic Command because he was resisting putting 'his' bombers on nuclear alert."

"I'm not thrilled about keeping them on alert either," the President said bitterly. "But I don't want to talk with them. Those three screwed up big-time with how they handled the Megafortress project. Elliott, McLanahan, Masters, all their weapons, and one of the Megafortresses are missing after they apparently *steal* the planes, ignoring my orders, and now Finegold and her committees are on my ass because they think I was hiding them." The anger was evident on the President's face—but Philip Freeman detected something else. A twinge of sadness, perhaps? "Now we've lost all the Megafortresses with the rest of Andersen Air Force Base. You handle them the way you see fit, George. That's your chain of command."

"Yes, sir," Balboa said happily. He shot a smug, satisfied glance to Philip Freeman, who had engineered the whole bomber thing behind his back all these past months, but he had stepped out of the Oval Office. Freeman had been shot down just as surely as Samson and his precious bombers had been.

"Get the carriers moving towards the Philippine Sea, and we'll see what Jiang has to say to me," the President ordered. "Jeffrey, stay in contact with Qian, keep the pressure on."

"Yes, Mr. President," Secretary of State Hartman replied.

"Jerrod, call the Leadership, set up a meeting for us later tonight so we can discuss what to do about China," the President said. "I might have to compromise with Finegold on Taiwan, but Taiwan can take a backseat for now—I want a united front beside me when I go on TV and tell the American people about what the hell happened to Guam."

At that moment, Philip Freeman walked into the Oval Office, strode right up to the President, and handed him a note. President Martindale gulped, swallowing hard, then dropped the note on his desk in surprise. "Get them in here, *now*," the President said to Freeman.

"*What?*" Balboa retorted. "You mean Hayes, Shaw, and Samson? You're going to talk to those three? Why? I thought you were going to leave them to me, sir?"

"McLanahan, Elliott, his crew, his plane—they're alive," the President said. "They were the ones who staged the attacks against China, against the coastal air defense bases and the bomber base. They led the last remaining Taiwanese fighter-bombers in to attack China's invasion force."

"That's impossible!" Balboa shouted. "Where are they? How could they possibly still be operating?"

"They're flying out of an *underground base* on Taiwan," the President said. "An underground air base!"

"That's bullshit . . . er, I'm sorry, Mr. President, but I've never heard of any such thing," Balboa said.

"Admiral, McLanahan and Elliott flew their Megafortress bomber right up into central China," Philip Freeman said. "If what General Samson says is true—and we'll confirm it with satellite imagery—they may have knocked out a third of China's long-range-bomber fleet *in one night*. We shouldn't be questioning this development—we should be discussing how to turn this unexpected windfall to our best advantage."

"I told you about Elliott, Mr. President," Balboa said angrily. "I told you he was a loose cannon. It was this unauthorized attack that prompted China to launch their ICBM attack on Guam. Elliott's responsible for this disaster!"

"What Elliott and McLanahan are responsible for is getting our asses moving and *making* things happen, rather than sitting around and *waiting* for things to happen," the President said. The President was now ignoring his Joint Chiefs chairman. "Get them in here," he told Freeman with a broad, hopeful smile on his face. "They survived, dammit—they *survived*!"

OVER THE EAST CHINA SEA, NORTH OF TAIWAN
FRIDAY, 27 JUNE 1997, 2012 HOURS LOCAL
(THURSDAY, 26 JUNE, 0912 HOURS ET)

The 221st People's Maritime Patrol of the People's Republic of China, based on Yuhuan Island thirty miles east of Wenzhou, Zhejiang Province, had been formed in 1955, flying rag-wing biplanes off the coast every hour of every day for forty-two years except in the most extreme weather conditions. The group's mission was to patrol the coastline, operating roughly from Shanghai to the north all the way to Hong Kong to the south, although the group's aircraft mostly patrolled the Formosa Strait.

The 221st was like an exclusive club. There were only one hundred members in the unit, and there would only ever *be* one hundred members—no more, no less. Prospective members had to be recommended by three other members, screened by a selection committee, and approved by the commander. Members served for life, and the only vacancies were the ones caused by death or court-martial, never by resignation. The group had several members over the age of ninety who still strapped into the back of their patrol planes and stared out the observation windows looking for enemy ships or ships in distress—the same as they had done for the past forty-plus years.

In 1985, the 221st was given a new class of aircraft, its first metal-wing plane: three Hanzhong Y-8 maritime patrol aircraft, a copy of the old Soviet An-12 "Cub" transport. The plane was over twenty years old then, but it represented a significant upgrading of the group's patrol capabilities. Along with numerous observation windows, the Y-8 carried electronic radio direction finders, which could scan for radio transmissions and provide a bearing to the transmitter. With two or more bearings, the operator could fix the location of the transmitter with surprising accuracy. The Y-8 was a four-turboprop smoke-belching monster that could barely fly above 10,000 feet, but it could stay aloft for as long as twelve hours and fly in almost any kind of weather. The members of the 221st, old and young alike, loved it.

One of the 221st's planes was on patrol one evening over the East China Sea, north of Taipei, when the radio DF operator caught the first bearing to an unidentified aircraft. A second bearing fix established the target's course and speed—out away from the Chinese coast, heading to the north of the island of Formosa. The operators were also able to identify the VHF radio frequency of the target and eavesdrop on their uncoded conversations—they were speaking not Mandarin Chinese, not even Taiwanese or Hakka, but English! The Y-8 crew decided to pursue the targets out as far as they could to the east to find out where they were headed.

Several DF bearings on several frequencies told the Y-8 crew members that there was more than one target in the area—they counted six so far, all heading east-northeast—but not toward Taipei, as the crew would've guessed. The targets all flew well north of the northern tip of Formosa. Because there were no fighter patrols up over the Nationalist capital—the airfields had been very effectively bombed out by Chinese missile and bomber attacks—the Y-8 crew decided to fly low, only 1,000 feet above the East China Sea, and cut east, close to Taipei. That way, they could track the targets no matter which way they headed.

Their strategy worked. The targets gradually turned south, down into the Philippine Sea, and the Chinese Y-8 crew was able to follow them. The VHF radio transmissions became more frequent. They also started receiving VHF bearings from Formosa—near the military base at Hualien. Was that possible? Hualien had been hit and destroyed by Chinese nuclear-tipped M-9 missiles days ago—that had been confirmed. Could it be possible that the Nationalists had rebuilt the base so quickly?

There was only one way to find out—go take a look. The Y-8 crew started to fly south along the eastern Formosa coastline. Slowly, careful to avoid any ships or clusters of lights on shore, throttled back with minimum propeller pitch to cut down on noise, they inched their way along the coast toward Hualien. Soon, the target bearings were turning . . . turning westbound, right in front of the Y-8! Westbound? Hualien's runways were oriented generally north-south—the coastal mountains in this area to the west rose steeply out of the sea . . .

. . . and suddenly, the Y-8's observers on the starboard side spotted the military base at Hualien. It was as flat as a pancake. Not much detail could be seen, but the crumbled foundations, the large pieces of debris scattered everywhere, and the fires still burning in many places told them that the base was completely unusable.

So where in blazes were the Taiwanese targets going?

The Y-8 crew continued southbound until the radio DF bearings started to shift toward the north. According to their charts, the high terrain in this vicinity was over 12,000 feet, just fifteen miles to the northwest, but the alluvial plain southwest of Hualien was almost ten miles wide and would allow them to stay low while turning around. They started a starboard turn over the coast, looping around back to the northeast. If they kept the town of Hualien just off the starboard wingtip, they would be clear of the transmission lines along the highway to the west and well clear of the—

The Y-8 crew heard a sudden rushing sound, which quickly grew into an ear-shattering roar. A jet fighter had just missed them! It had flown *underneath* them, about 200 feet *lower* than the big Y-8, heading northwest! That was insane, impossible! There was nothing to the northwest except 10,000- and 11,000-foot mountains. . . .

But then they saw the glow of light from a wide chasm cut into the rocks, and the Y-8 pilot instinctively banked to port to head toward it—as long as he could see light, there were no mountains in the way. The light grew, expanded . . . and then, to the crew's amazement, they saw *sequenced flashing landing lights*! There was an *airfield* down there! It was unbelievable! Impossible! The Y-8 banked hard to port and descended—and then they could clearly see inside the huge cave, and sure enough, there was an entire airstrip inside that monstrous cave! It was a secret rebel Nationalist airfield, actually built *inside the mountain*!

This was too important a discovery—they had to break radio silence. The Y-8's communications officer immediately sent out an emergency position report on the shortwave—the UHF radio would certainly not get out this deep in the mountains. He did not listen for a reply—he just continued to transmit the position as best he could estimate, adding that they had discovered a secret rebel airfield.

Suddenly, a flash of light and a streak of fire erupted from the north part of the cave. In the blink of an eye, the streak of fire reached out across the sky and struck the number four engine. The engine exploded in a burst of fire, shearing off seven feet of the starboard wingtip along with it. The rebels had obviously detected the Y-8 crew's HF transmissions and had instantly homed in on them, and the base was obviously very well defended. They added that bit of information to their continuous radio reports—and now it was time to get out of there as fast as they could!

Full power on the other three good engines, full pitch, and the Y-8 started a slow climb. The pilots were flying on a prayer now—thank the stars the Y-8 was a tough bird. Only the quick work of the copilot to shut down the engine and cut off fuel from the right wing kept them from crashing in a ball of flame. As best they could estimate, they were heading for the Mei River valley, which cut westward up through the Chung Yang Mountains. They were at 3,000 feet and climbing at 1,500 feet per minute. On either side of the valley, the mountains rose very steeply—within five miles north and south of the river, the peaks were as high as 11,000 feet! It was completely pitch-black outside. He would have to trust his compass and his navigator to keep them in the valley long enough to climb to a safe altitude. The Chung Yang range was not very wide—in twenty miles, less than six or seven minutes, they would be at the summit. Once on the western side, they could hug the mountains until they were sure they could not be tracked, then pick their way west until they could get back over the Formosa Strait, then—

The two Sidewinder missiles fired from the pursuing Taiwanese F-16 fighter each hit and destroyed an engine, tearing them off the wings in a huge ball of fire. The Y-8 burst into flames and veered sharply right, and it hit the granite wall of the mountains seconds later.

But the Y-8's radio operator had made over a dozen position and contact reports in that short period of time, and almost every one of his transmissions had been received by military listening posts in mainland China.

The secret Taiwanese underground airfield at Kai-Shan was a secret no longer.

OFFICE OF THE PRESIDENT, GOVERNMENT HOUSE, BEIJING, CHINA
A SHORT TIME LATER

"We have them, Comrade Admiral!" Jiang Zemin said joyously as Admiral Sun Ji Guoming was ushered into the president's office. "General Chin has just briefed me. A secret air base! Do you believe it? A secret underground air base in eastern Formosa, just a few miles west of Hualien, cut into the mountain itself. We have its exact location." Admiral Sun did not react to the news. "Now is your chance, Comrade Admiral. You can attack and destroy the rebel Nationalists' remaining air forces with ease."

Sun bowed to President Jiang and the chief of staff, General Chin, but remained silent for several long, uncomfortable moments. Finally: "Comrade President, I request permission to be relieved of duty."

General Chin rolled his eyes in complete exasperation. Jiang laughed and said, "Relieved of duty? You are a national treasure, comrade! And victory is within your grasp, the victory you told me we could achieve before Reunification Day! One of our maritime patrols tracked a group of rebel F-16s back to their secret lair, an underground air base near Hualien. We sent in commandos, who verified their location. We must draw up a strike plan and destroy that facility immediately!"

"Comrade General Chin's forces are more than capable of destroying that facility, sir," Sun said. "You do not need me any longer. I am of no use to you now."

"Why do you say such things, comrade?" Jiang asked. "Are you ill? Did you suffer some family misfortune?"

"I am unable to continue my duties because I feel we have lost our *tao*," Sun replied solemnly.

"What in blazes are you talking about, Sun?" Chin exploded.

"We have lost our way, our reason for going to war in the first place," Sun said, keeping his eyes averted. "We may achieve a victory over the rebels, but we cannot win this conflict now. The *tao* we follow will not lead to a true and honorable victory."

"That is nonsense, comrade," Jiang said. "You have done well. It is your right, your destiny, to deliver the final blow to the Nationalists. This is a great honor we bestow on you. You deserve it."

"But this cannot be my victory because it is not my *tao*—it is the *tao* of Comrade General Chin," Sun said. "The nuclear attack on Guam was his way, his road to victory. It is not mine. I cannot lead the People's Liberation Army forces along this path."

"The Paramount Leader has conferred a great honor upon you, Sun," Chin said impatiently. "Take it. Plan a strike mission using any air, rocket, or naval assets you desire. We expect this underground airfield complex to be destroyed or occupied by the People's Liberation Army within forty-eight hours."

"I humbly request to be relieved of duty," Sun intoned.

"Request denied, Admiral," Chin responded. "Carry out your orders. Present a strike plan to the Paramount Leader and myself within eight hours, and prepare to execute the plan within forty-eight hours."

"Sir, I humbly request you to accept my resignation from your service," Sun Ji Guoming said, bowing deeply in total obeisance. "A man cannot follow other than his own *tao*. Mine is lost. I am of no usefulness to you any longer."

"That is not true, Comrade Admiral," Jiang said. "What are you trying to tell us?"

"I am saying that to return to the *tao* that will ensure victory, we must now strive to make peace just as ferociously as we strove to destroy," Sun said. "We must gather our forces to our center and protect it, and in doing so show the world that we are no longer a threat. We should configure all our air and naval forces for defensive operations only. We should destroy all our remaining offensive ballistic missiles, and openly pledge never again to employ thermonuclear weapons—"

"Are you insane, Sun?" Chin Po Zihong exploded. "Stop now? Obviously the rebels are far stronger than we anticipated. We need to destroy them quickly and utterly. And we need our nuclear-deterrent forces now more than ever to ensure that the United States will not attempt a massive attack against us."

"Sir, Sun-tzu teaches us that if faced with superior forces, do not fight. We may feel we have gained the upper hand, but Sun-tzu's words are a warning to us. Our forces are not superior to the United States. The American forces are massing over the horizon. I can sense it. I can feel it. They have not been destroyed. I urge the Paramount Leader to immediately contact the American president and pray—no, I urge him to *beg* for peace."

"*What?*" Chin retorted angrily. "*Beg? We* should beg the Americans?"

"Yes, sir," Sun said. "Now. Immediately. Before it is too late."

"Admiral Sun, you are dishonoring yourself by this flagrant display of pompous indignation and insubordination," Chin said angrily. "Your request is *denied*. You are *ordered* to prepare a strike plan against the rebel Nationalist underground airfield complex and present it, in person, to me and the president's staff within eight hours. Is that clear?"

"Yes, sir," Sun replied.

Chin looked at the president, who was looking at Sun Ji Guoming as if he had grown a second head on his shoulders. With no additional comments, Chin snapped, "Then get out of here." Sun bowed again, turned, and departed. Once Sun had left, Chin said, "All that Sun-tzu crap has addled his brain, I think."

"Unfortunate," Jiang Zemin said. "He appeared to be such a promising young officer. Perhaps we should reconsider this attack plan, Comrade General?"

"Because Sun thinks it is not his 'way' to do this attack?" Chin retorted. "He is upset because his plan of waiting for the Nationalists to capitulate did not work. He is upset because in the end we had to use brute strength to shove the Americans out of Asia. He thought he could do it with unorthodox methods and trickery, and his lack of vision allowed the Nationalist air force and the Americans to counterattack. We cannot allow that to happen again. We are on the threshold of a great victory over the rebels on Formosa, comrade, and this attack will break the backs of the Nationalists once and for all. Every missile, every attack plane, every bomb we have available should be used against this mountain hideout. We shall pound the Nationalists' mountain fortress into sand!"

"But what if the Americans do stage a counteroffensive?" Jiang asked. "Perhaps we should be watchful, gather our forces, and prepare to repel an American attack. We can deter the Americans by sheer force of numbers. Surely they will not try a nuclear attack if we ask to begin peace negotiations now."

"And then where will the rebels be? Rebuilding their forces, getting more assistance from the Americans, and conducting more hit-and-run air attacks on our forces," Chin said. "No. We should attack the rebel mountain complex immediately. If Sun will not do it, I have many more competent generals who will."

OVER TAIWAN, REPUBLIC OF CHINA
SUNDAY, 29 JUNE 1997, 0319 HOURS LOCAL
(SATURDAY, 28 JUNE, 1419 HOURS ET)

The attack began with a heavy missile bombardment with conventionally armed Dong Feng-9 and -11 missiles from the mainland. Their accuracy was not great, but it didn't need to be—because more than three hundred missiles launched from sixteen different locations, with warheads ranging from 500 pounds to more than 1,700 pounds of high explosive, peppered the area around Kai-Shan for over an hour. Every square inch of a twenty-five-square-mile area around Kai-Shan was blasted away. Along with the effect of the nearby nuclear explosions at Hualien, the area resembled the surface of the moon in very short order.

The second phase of the attack was by a completely new weapon system: China's Type-031 attack submarine. In the day preceding the attack, the Type-031 sub, named the *Yudao,* had left its port at Shanghai and had cruised without incident right up to the mouth of the Mei River, less than five miles from the cave entrance to the Kai-Shan airfield complex, and waited. At the preplanned time, the *Yudao* surfaced, took a final targeting fix using its Golf-band targeting radar—aiming at a tiny radar reflector placed near the cave entrance by the Chinese commandos—and began firing Yinji-6 "Hawk Attack" guided missiles at the cave. The first four Yinji-6 missiles blasted open the movable armored doors to the cave entrance, finally exposing the interior of the complex to attack. Two of the remaining four Yinji-6 missiles flew inside the cave itself, creating spectacular gushes of fire and exploding rock from within.

The third phase of the attack was the most impressive, and was certainly the largest Asian aerial attack force since Japan's naval air forces in World War II. Led by thirty H-6 bombers, watched by an Ilyushin-76 radar plane, and guarded by ten Sukhoi-27 and thirty Xian J-8 air-superiority interceptors, an attack force of two hundred Nanchang Q-5 fighter-bombers, each carrying two 1,000-pound bombs plus a long-range fuel tank, swept over the island of Formosa to begin the attack on Kai-Shan.

The H-6 bombers went first. From ten miles out, they launched huge Hai-Ying-4 missiles at the complex. These missiles merely flew straight to a set of coordinates, and were meant to knock down or destroy any rock outcroppings that might still be obstructing the cave entrance. Although the HY-4 missiles were not designed for land attack and some did not perform well in this hastily planned role, the destruction they caused left the attack path wide open for the waves of Q-5 bombers to follow.

As if they were doing a standard traffic pattern entry to land on Kai-Shan's underground runway, the Q-5 fighter-bombers flew eastbound over the Chung Yang Mountains at 1,000 feet above ground until they were about ten miles offshore, then turned southbound for three miles, then northwestbound, descending to 500 feet and lining up on the cave entrance. The planned procedure was a "toss" delivery, where the pilots would pull up sharply about two miles in front of the cave, then pickle off the bombs, which would fly on a ballistic path right into the cave. There could be no delay on the pull-up—the Chung Yang Mountains rose from 500 feet to nearly 10,000 feet within five miles, so there was only a six-second margin of error. The best bombardiers from all over China were picked for this important mission.

The first flight of ten Q-5 bombers started their runs, and the plan was working better than anticipated. The lead bombers announced that pilots could fly a hundred feet higher to get a flatter toss into the cave, because parts of the ceiling of the cave had collapsed and they couldn't arc the bombs in quite as high anymore. As the first flight of Q-5 bombers cleared the target area, the second flight started their turn inbound on the attack course . . .

. . . just in time to hear the warning screams over the command frequency: "Warning, warning, all aircraft . . ." and then the loud, incessant hiss of static. Pilots all over the sky over Taiwan were switching to alternate frequencies, but all they found there, after a few seconds of trying to speak, was more static. The Il-76 Candid radar plane orbiting over Formosa might as well have been back on the ground, because no one could hear or talk with its all-important radar controllers.

It was up to the Sukhoi-27s and radar-equipped Shenyang J-8 fighters now—but it was soon apparent that they were mostly out of the fight as well—the jamming was intruding on their attack radars. The J-8's older radars were easily jammed; the Su-27's modern pulse-Doppler radars and advanced counterjamming functions worked better. "Enemy planes, heading westbound!" the Su-27 pilots shouted on the attack frequency—but that did no good, because all of the VHF and UHF frequencies were jammed. No warnings and no formation orders could be sent or received. Two electronic-warfare EA-6B Prowlers from the USS *George Washington,* and two more EA-6Bs from the USS *Carl Vinson* had set up an effective electromagnetic net around the island of Formosa, denying the Chinese air force the use of any radio or radar frequencies except those in use by the U.S. Navy attack planes bearing down on the Chinese air armada.

The first target was the Ilyushin-76 radar plane—and that task was left to the nine surviving flyable Taiwanese F-16s, which had launched out of Kai-Shan just after sunset, along with Jon Masters's DC-10 tanker-transport. Four Su-27s guarded the Il-76, but in the confusion caused by the EA-6B Prowlers jamming their radios and disrupting their radars, they were no match for the wave of F-16s. All four Su-27s were shot down by the F-16s, against the loss of one F-16—and then each F-16 took a shot at the Il-76 radar plane. At least a dozen AIM-9 Sidewinder missiles plowed into the Chinese radar plane, sending huge burning pieces spinning into the Formosa Strait. The eight Taiwanese F-16s then withdrew from the area and linked up with Jon Masters's DC-10 tanker-transport orbiting over the Pacific, where they all refueled and headed to Kadena Air Base in Okinawa.

The confusion between the Chinese planes allowed the Navy fighters to get into missile range. A total of twenty-four F-14 Tomcats and twenty F/A-18 Hornets from the two carriers in the Philippine Sea began launching missiles. The Tomcats could open fire from over seventy miles away with their huge AIM-54C Phoenix long-range antiair missiles, while the Hornets attacked from as far as twenty miles away with medium-range AIM-7 Sparrow and AIM-120 radar-guided missiles. Nearly half of the Su-27s and J-8 fighters covering the attack force were destroyed before the Navy fighters closed in within range of their short-range AIM-9 Sidewinder heat-seeking antiair missiles, and another eight Su-27s and J-8s fell to AIM-9 missile attacks. The surviving Chinese fighters fled before the American fighters got a chance to close within cannon range. The Chinese fighter-bombers that had not dropped their weapons simply punched off the bombs and fuel tanks wherever they were and turned westward to get away from the unseen predators closing in on them.

But the Chinese bombers retreating from the area were just being herded into another trap—ten four-ship formations of U.S. Air Force F-15C Eagle fighters from the Eighteenth Wing at Kadena Air Base on Okinawa and the Third Wing from Elmendorf Air Force Base in Anchorage, Alaska, all loaded with six AIM-120 AMRAAMs and two AIM-9 Sidewinders apiece. The F-15s spread out over the Formosa Strait and simply waited for the Chinese aircraft to fly right into their laps before opening fire. Twenty-three F-15 pilots claimed kills that night, and three more claimed multiple kills. Any Chinese HQ-2 surface-to-air missile sites that tried to lock onto the F-15s over the Strait were destroyed by U.S. Navy A-6E Intruders launching AGM-88 High speed Anti-Radiation Missiles.

The attack lasted just minutes; as fast as it had begun, it was over. The radios were clear, and attack radars were as effective as they ever were. But in that few minutes, the damage was horrifying: the Il-76 radar plane, eleven H-6 bombers, four Su-27s, eighteen J-8 fighters, and forty-one Q-5 fighter-bombers had been shot down, with no losses to American aircraft. Each and every Navy and Air Force plane made it back to its carrier or base, then began rearming and setting up for local-area air defense in case the Chinese tried a counterattack.

The Chinese fighters and bombers lucky enough to escape the American hit-and-run attack from the darkness soon found other problems. Twelve B-1B Lancer bombers from Ellsworth and Dyess Air Force Bases had been sent over eastern China, loaded with eight AGM-86C cruise missiles with non-nuclear high-explosive warheads, and eight AGM-177

Wolverine antiair defense cruise missiles, to attack air bases and air defense sites throughout southeast China. The military landing strips at Fuzhou, Ningbo, Hangzhou, Jingdezhen, Nanchang, and even Shanghai were cratered by cruise missiles, and the Chinese approach and ground-control radars and some air defense missile and artillery emplacements had been destroyed by the Wolverine missiles. All of the fighters scheduled to land at these bases had to be diverted . . .

. . . except there were no military fields within range to send them. The number of planes destroyed or damaged simply by running out of fuel or attempting to make a forced landing at a civil airstrip or highway quickly exceeded the number of planes shot down by American fighters.

But the B-1Bs' mission was not to deny landing strips to Chinese fighters low on fuel, but to open a gaping hole in China's multilayered air defense and surveillance radar network to allow yet another attacker to slip in unnoticed—six B-2A Spirit stealth bombers from Whiteman Air Force Base. The B-2 bombers went feet-dry over several points along the Chinese coastline from Shanghai to Qingdao, taking separate low-level attack routes inbound to their targets—the intercontinental ballistic missile bases in north-central China.

The twelve Dong Feng-5 missile silos and twenty Dong Feng-3 launch sites, with two DF-3 missiles assigned per site, were spread out over 10,000 square miles in two Chinese provinces, and heavily defended by HQ-2 surface-to-air missile sites and antiaircraft artillery sites—but the B-2s swarmed over the missile fields near Yinchuan in Inner Mongolia province and, one by one, attacked.

Each B-2A carried sixteen AGM-84E Standoff Land Attack Missile (SLAM) guided weapons on two internal rotary launchers. Each SLAM was a Harpoon turbojet-powered anti-ship cruise missile fitted with an imaging infrared television sensor in the nose and a GPS satellite navigation guidance system. The coordinates of the targets were all loaded into the missile's memory by the B-2's attack computer; each B-2 bomber merely had to fly to a predetermined launch point and release the missiles. Once released from low altitude—300 and 500 feet above ground—and as far as fifty miles from the target, the missiles would get a final navigation update by its GPS receiver and guide itself to the target, skimming less than a hundred feet above the ground at 250 miles an hour. The missile was even programmed with turnpoints so they would not reveal the location of the B-2 launch aircraft. Once the missiles were launched, the B-2 bombers turned eastbound and began the treacherous 1,500-mile trek back across hostile airspace to their first post-strike refueling anchor.

Sixty seconds prior to impact, the AGM-84E SLAMs began to transmit images of their assigned target area—but they did not transmit the pictures back to the B-2s that launched them. Instead, the images were picked up by a lone aircraft flying over the Chinese ICBM missile fields at 20,000 feet.

The EB-52 Megafortress had launched from Kai-Shan with the remaining nine flyable Taiwanese F-16s and Jon Masters's DC-10 just after sunset. The Megafortress was armed with every drop of fuel and every remaining weapon it could possibly carry: two Wolverine cruise missiles and two Striker rocket bombs on the forward bomb-bay rotary launcher; six CBU-59 cluster bomb units on the aft bomb bay; and one AIM-120 Scorpion air-to-air missile and four AIM-9 Sidewinder air-to-air missiles on each wing weapon pod. After an aerial refueling, the EB-52 flew north over the East China Sea and waited for the B-1 and B-2 bombers to arrive from the United States. Once the B-1 bombers laid down the cruise missile barrage along the Chinese coastline, the B-2 and the Megafortress cruised in toward the Chinese ICBM fields. With the attention of the entire Chinese air defense system focused on the Formosa Strait, it was a simple exercise for the six B-2s and the lone EB-52 to penetrate disrupted Chinese airspace and head for their assigned targets.

The EB-52 arrived in the Chinese ICBM field several minutes before the B-2 Spirit stealth bombers got to their launch points. Flying in the defensive systems officer's seat, Wendy McLanahan started the attack by launching the Wolverine missiles over the ICBM missile fields. The two Wolverines used their decoys and radar seekers to hunt down any antiaircraft radars, then attacked them with antiarmor skeets.

"The Wolverines are working," Brad Elliott said. "I can see the place starting to light up." Several antiaircraft artillery sites opened fire, some very close by but locked onto the decoy gliders, not the Megafortress. Streams of heavy antiaircraft artillery tracers arced into the sky—followed a few moments later by a bright flash on the ground and secondary explosions rippling across the expanse of darkness.

"Very cool," Nancy Cheshire remarked, as more missile and triple-A sites were hit. "The Wolverines are working great."

"You spoke too soon," Wendy said. "I've lost contact with both Wolverines. Both of them got shot down."

"I've got missile video starting to come in," Patrick McLanahan announced. As each SLAM got within range, a window would open up on his supercockpit display, and he could watch as the missile approached the target. A wide white rectangle in the center of the video indicated the missile's preprogrammed target area. As the SLAM got closer, Patrick could make out more and more detail of the exact target spot, and he resized the target rectangle until it enclosed only the spot he wanted to hit. A small white dot represented the missile's impact point, and Patrick resized the rectangle so the dot could stay inside the rectangle without too many gross flight-control corrections.

"I've got fighter radar activity at three o'clock, range unknown," Wendy announced. "We're running out of time."

Patrick could hear the tension in her voice. He had been against having her on this mission at all—her wounds from the last time she had flown on an EB-52 Megafortress had only recently healed, not to mention the danger to the child she carried. But Wendy had been the first to demand that she go along, and hers was the loudest voice arguing against her husband. No one else knew the Megafortress's defensive suite and weapons better than Wendy Tork McLanahan. Patrick might be able to operate the systems by himself if the bomber was not under attack, but if it ever became an item of interest and came under active attack, it would take one crew member's full attention to defend the Megafortress. If there was going to be any chance of success on this raid, Wendy had to go along.

"Got a range now, three o'clock, forty miles and closing," Wendy reported. "I've got multiple bandits—four, maybe six. One of them looks like a Su-27. Signal threshold is low, but they've got several sweeps on us. They could get a lock on us in three to four minutes."

Two SLAM missiles would be targeted against the DF-5 silos—the first SLAM would crack open the silo, and the second would dive inside and destroy the missile. The first 1,400-pound Standoff Land Attack Missile would execute a pop-up maneuver a few seconds before impact, then dive directly down onto the silo cover to crack open the silo; the second SLAM would follow a few seconds later, execute the same pop-up and dive maneuver, and destroy the missile inside. The DF-3 missiles were stored on erector trailers inside storage sheds near each launch site, and it was a simple task to target each storage shed and destroy the missile inside.

The SLAM launches had been coordinated so that the Megafortress could fly eastbound out of the target area and he would be within effective datalink range of each SLAM, working west to east. As soon as one SLAM would hit, another window popped open, and Patrick would start steering another SLAM in to its target. Some SLAMs did not transmit their TV images, so it was unknown if they ever hit their targets, but each SLAM was guided by a precise inertial navigation system updated by GPS satellite navigation signals, accurate to at least ten feet in altitude and position, so even without a TV datalink they were very accurate weapons. Out of seventy-two SLAMs successfully launched from the B-2s, fifty-one reached their assigned targets and transmitted a good enough TV picture so Patrick could assess the damage and call the target destroyed or knocked out of commission.

"But we got three DF-3 and two DF-5 sites where we don't know if they got hit," Patrick announced to his crew.

"Perfect—we got two Strikers and six CBUs left," Brad Elliott said. "Let's go back there and finish the job."

"Two o'clock, thirty-two miles and closing," Wendy announced. She then looked over at her husband and saw him intently watching her. "I agree," she said. "Let's go get 'em."

"The odds are that the SLAMs got the last missile sites," Patrick said. "They've been running great, all of them."

"But we can't be sure, can we?" Nancy Cheshire asked.

"We can wait and get a satellite downlink from Jon's NIRTSats," Elliott said. "Those can tell us if they got hit. How long until we get a picture?"

"We won't—we didn't get a new constellation up in time," Patrick said. "The best info we'll get is from our synthetic aperture radar or from a Striker video link."

"Then let's do it," Wendy said. Patrick turned toward her, and she saw something that she'd rarely seen before—the fear in his eyes. "Patrick, we've *got* to go back," Wendy said on interphone. "We don't have a choice. We didn't come all this way to leave any targets left." Patrick knew she was right. They had risked everything to fly deep into the heart of the People's Republic of China and attack these important targets—as long as they had weapons left, they had to use them.

Patrick touched his supercockpit display and called up the five surviving targets. The closest one was only ten miles away; the farthest, a DF-5 long-range ICBM site, was nearly forty miles farther west.

"Gimme a left turn heading two-five-seven, center the bug, stand by for bomb-bay Striker launch," Patrick ordered.

"No." The words came from none other than Brad Elliott. "We're not turning back. We're going to use the gas and the weapons we have left to fight our way out of here."

"Brad . . ."

"I'm overruling you this time, Muck," Elliott said determinedly. "You may be the mission commander, but I'm the aircraft commander, and I'm responsible for the lives on board this plane. We're six hundred miles inside China, alone, with only ten defensive missiles and three hours' worth of gas left. We did our job. Two DF-5s and six DF-3s are not going to threaten anyone."

"Brad, we can do it," Wendy said. "We can take out those last sites."

"Forget about it, Wendy," Elliott said. "Let someone else worry about them. You and Patrick and Nancy have a life that's more important than blowing up a couple missile sites in the middle of nowhere. Patrick, call up the exit point and pick the best way to get us out of here."

Patrick looked as if a huge weight had been lifted off his shoulders— he even smiled. "Okay, Brad," Patrick said. "We've got one DF-5 site that'll be within range just a couple minutes to the north, and all of the DF-3 sites are east and southeast. We'll leave the last DF-5 site for some other time." He entered commands on the supercockpit display, then said, "Give me a left turn to zero-three-seven and center up. Bomb-bay Striker launch coming up . . . in one hundred seconds." Elliott responded by turning the Megafortress to the northeast.

"Bandits are at five o'clock, twenty-five miles and closing," Wendy reported. "I'm targeting the lead Su-27 for one Scorpion launch. Looks like we might have two Su-27s leading a total of eight J-7s or J-8s. The second formation of fighters is moving to eight o'clock, thirty-three miles."

"They're going back to defend the western surviving DF-5 site," Cheshire guessed. "It must still be active."

"Bomb doors coming open . . . missile away!" Patrick said as he processed a Striker missile launch. Elliott immediately rolled right and centered up on the first DF-3 launch site.

"Bandits got a good look at that missile launch!" Wendy cried. "Bandits at six o'clock, eighteen miles and closing . . . stand by for pylon missile launch . . . radar lock, they got a radar lock . . . no, radar's down, they're closing in to heater range . . . missile away, missile away!" An AIM-120 Scorpion missile streaked out of the left weapon pod, arced up and over the Megafortress, and plummeted down on its quarry. "Splash one!" Wendy shouted. "Splash . . . *no*, the Su-27's still up! I hit one of the other fighters! The Su-27's still coming!"

"Good terminal video," Patrick called out. Sure enough, the Dong Feng-5 missile silo they had just launched on had not been touched by any of the SLAMs. Patrick centered the targeting crosshairs directly on the movable concrete silo cover, and hit it directly in the center. "Got it!" he shouted.

"Stand by for second pylon launch!" Wendy shouted. "Missile away!" The last Scorpion missile flew out of the right weapon pod, and this time it did not miss. "Splash two!" she shouted. "Got the -27! The other fighters are breaking formation. . . . I've got two formations of J-8s now, closest at three o'clock, seven miles and closing. The second formation's at six o'clock, twelve miles."

"First DF-3 site twelve o'clock, twenty miles," Patrick called out.

"I need a turn!" Wendy shouted.

"Do it!"

"Right forty degrees!" Wendy cried, and Elliott hauled the Megafortress into a tight turn. "I'm jamming their ranging radars! I've got a lock! Pylon launch, *now*!" The AIM-9L Sidewinders mounted in the weapons pods were not directly mated to the Megafortress's attack system—they had to be pointed at a target and allowed to find their own target. But once Wendy had turned the Megafortress at the oncoming Chinese fighters, the Sidewinders quickly detected the fighter's hot-wing leading edges and sent a MISSILE LOCK signal. As soon as Wendy got the signal, she punched off one Sidewinder. It homed perfectly on its target and exploded right in the path of the J-8, sending it spiraling to the ground.

"Splash two!" Cheshire crowed when she saw the explosion and saw the burning plane plummet to earth. Wendy immediately selected another Sidewinder that had locked on to a fighter and let it fly. This one disappeared from sight with no explosions—clean miss.

"Hold this heading—we're going nose to nose with them!" Wendy shouted.

"Shit—they're right on us!" Elliott shouted. Both he and Cheshire saw numerous winks of light in the darkness as the J-8 fighters opened fire

on the Megafortress with their 23-millimeter cannons, then peeled off.

The Megafortress's crew heard what seemed like hundreds of hammerlike blows all over the aircraft, then the rumble and roar of the Chinese jets flying just a few hundred feet away from them. "Check the instruments!" Elliott shouted to Cheshire. "Patrick!"

"Right turn and center up!" Patrick responded.

Elliott started a hard right turn—and immediately decreased the turn when they felt a hard, sharp rumbling on the right wing. "We got something hanging on the right," he said. "Nance, you see anything?"

"No," Cheshire responded. "But I've got fluctuating number four hydraulic pressure. It feels like we might have lost a spoiler."

The DF-3 missile sites were situated along the same access road, roughly in a line about five miles apart. "Radar coming on . . . radar stand by," McLanahan said as he took the release fix. The synthetic aperture radar image showed the Dong Feng-3 launch complex in stark detail: the launch pad, gantry, and the two railroad lines leading from the launch pad to the two missile-storage sheds, spaced about 200 yards apart. The Megafortress rolled in on the first site. "Doors coming open . . . bombs away!" McLanahan shouted. He sequenced the releases so that the bomblet scatter pattern of one CBU-59 cluster-bomb unit was centered directly on the missile sheds.

The tactic worked. Each DF-3 storage shed was blasted apart by hundreds of one-pound bomblets, and the scatter pattern was large enough to encompass the launch pad and a nearby electrical transformer farm, which shut down power to the complex's air defense artillery site located to the north. The second missile was only damaged in the attack, but the first 59,000-pound liquid-fueled DF-3 missile caught fire and created a massive explosion that wiped out the second missile very effectively.

But the sudden destruction of the DF-3 site alerted the air defense units protecting the other two remaining sites, and seconds later the horizon was illuminated with six antiaircraft artillery guns opening up. Wendy had used her jammers to shut down the triple-A site's tracking radars, so the Chinese gunners were blindly sweeping the sky with their guns. The airspace over the two remaining DF-3 sites was shimmering with thousands of rounds of artillery shells.

"I got no choice, guys," Elliott said, and he broke off the bomb run by turning hard right. "We can't go through that mess."

"Continue your right turn fifty more degrees," Wendy said. "Let's get a few of these J-8s off our tail while we wait for those gunners to run out of ammo." As soon as Elliott rolled out of his hard right turn, Wendy let one, then two Sidewinders fly, and both shots were rewarded with bright flashes and flickering streaks of light across the night sky.

"I'm centering up," Elliott shouted, and he yanked the Megafortress over into a hard right turn back toward the DF-3 sites. The blobs of tracers were still slicing through the sky, forming an impenetrable curtain of deadly bullets all across the target area. "C'mon, you bastards," Elliott cursed. "You don't have that much ammo . . . you're going to run out any second—"

As if on cue, one stream of tracers abruptly stopped. It was only one ZSU-37-2 site, but it was enough. Patrick centered his crosshairs on the second two DF-3 storage sheds, made sure the rotary launcher had positioned two more CBU-59 units in the bottom drop position, and made the release. The terrific explosion that rocked the Megafortress told them the second attack had been a success.

The two triple-A sites guarding the last DF-3 site swung west toward them and began raking the sky around them, and for a moment it seemed as if every antiaircraft artillery site in front of them got a direct bead on them—but then the shooting stopped. The triple-A sites had either run out of ammo, or they had damaged their gun barrels by several minutes of almost continuous shooting. Elliott centered the computer steering bug on the last target . . . just twenty more seconds, and they'd be heading home.

The last twenty seconds seemed like twenty hours—but soon the bomb doors rolled open, and McLanahan shouted, "Bombs away! Doors coming!"

Brad Elliott saw a flash of white light off to his left, and then his vision exploded into a blaze of stars and his body felt as if he had hit a brick wall.

"*Brad's hit!*" Nancy Cheshire screamed. The entire left side of the cockpit appeared as if it had been shredded apart by a giant tiger's claw. Cheshire grabbed the control stick, then experimentally juggled the throttles. But the flight-control computer had already determined that the number one engine had been destroyed, and the computer immediately had shut off fuel to the engine, activated the fire-extinguishing system, and isolated electrical and hydraulic power. "I lost number one—it's shut down!" she called out. "I still got the airplane! Sing out back there!"

"Offense is okay!" Patrick responded. He looked over through the thin haze of smoke and saw Wendy leaning over in her seat. Her console looked as if a grenade had exploded inside it, and the windblast from the shattered left cockpit windows was blowing a vortex of smoke and debris back over Wendy McLanahan. *"Jesus! Wendy!"*

"I'm all right, I'm all right," they heard over interphone. "I . . . I just got a face full of smoke."

"Hang on, Wendy!"

"No! Patrick, stay strapped in!" Wendy cried out. "I'm going to stay down here to stay out of the smoke."

"What do you got back there, guys?" Cheshire asked, the panic rising in her voice.

"It looks like we got squat," Patrick responded. "The DSO's station is toast, and my stuff is in reset." He concentrated on the red flashing indications on his right-side instrument panel: "The last Striker missile is showing an overtemp condition, but I can't shut it down and I can't jettison it until my equipment comes back up. I'll try to restart it."

"We got a major problem up here, kids," Nancy Cheshire said, quickly scanning the instruments. Most of the electronic instruments were blank; she concentrated on the auxiliary and backup gauges. "We lost number one, we're on emergency hydraulic power, and we got one generator left. All I got right now is the damned whiskey compass. Brad . . . Brad looks real bad. I think he's . . ."

"Go ahead and say it . . . you thought I was dead," Brad Elliott said. Slowly, painfully, with help from Nancy Cheshire, he hauled himself upright in his seat, and Cheshire locked his inertial reel in place.

"Brad!" Patrick shouted. "Are you all right?"

"Hell no," Elliott said, coughing to clear his throat of a mass of blood. "But they can't kill me that easy." His voice was barely a whisper over the thunderous roar of the jet blast coming through the shredded fuselage.

"We're gonna make it, Brad," Cheshire said on interphone. "Hang on."

Elliott scanned the nearly blank instrument panel and chuckled, the laughter quickly changing into a full-body convulsion. "I highly doubt it," he gasped, after the convulsions stopped.

"Nance, give me a right turn back to the east," Patrick said. "We'll try to get as close to the Yellow Sea or the Bo Hai as we can get. Hal and Chris are standing by on Okinawa with Madcap Magician and the Taiwanese air force—they might be able to pick us up."

"Muck, we're six hundred goddamn miles from the Yellow Sea, we're surrounded by fighters, and we're all shot to hell," Brad Elliott said. "I got a better idea—we jump out."

"No way," Cheshire said.

"You're a sweetie, and I've always had the hots for you, co," Elliott said, "but you all know this is the only option. When those fighters come back, they'll blow us to pieces. I'd rather not be on board when that happens, thank you very much."

"We made it before, Brad," Patrick said. "We can make it again."

"We're in the middle of Inner Mongolia, hundreds of miles from help, and we're down to emergency everything," Elliott said. "We got no choi—"

Suddenly, the Megafortress buckled under them and slew nearly sideways. Cheshire straightened the plane out only by using both hands on the control stick. "We got hit, number four's on fire!" she shouted. This time, the computer did not shut down the engine automatically. Cheshire jammed the number four throttle to idle, then to CUTOFF, then pulled the yellow fire T handle to cut off fuel to the engine and activate its fire extinguisher. "Still got a fire on number four!" Cheshire shouted. "It won't go out! It won't go out!" There was a bright flash of light and another violent explosion jerked the bomber nearly upside down. "Fire! Fire!" Cheshire shouted.

"Eject! Eject! Eject!" Brad Elliott shouted.

Patrick looked over at Wendy. She returned his glance—but that was all the hesitation she allowed herself. She jammed her fanny back into the seat, straightened her back, pushed the back of her helmet into the sculpted headrest, tucked her chin down, crossed her hands, and pulled the ejection ring between her legs. Her shoulder harness automatically tightened, snapping her shoulders and spine back into the proper position; the overhead hatch blew off, and she was gone in a blinding cloud of white smoke. Patrick pulled his handle as soon as he saw she was gone.

Cheshire looked over at Brad Elliott—and hesitated. "Go!" she shouted at him. She grabbed the control stick. "I got the plane! *Go! Eject!*"

To Nancy Cheshire's complete astonishment, Brad Elliott reached down beside his ejection seat—and pulled the red manual man-seat sep-arator knob, then reached up and twisted the center of his five-point har-ness clasp on his chest. His parachute shoulder straps and lap belt fell away with a clatter. He had detached his parachute from his ejection seat and then opened up the clasp to his parachute harness! He would never survive an ejection now! *"Brad, what in hell . . . ?"*

Brad Elliott reached over and grasped his control stick and the throt-tles. "I got the plane now, Nancy," he said. "Get out of here."

"Brad, goddammit, don't do this!"

"I said, *eject*!" Elliott shouted.

Nancy Cheshire's eyes were wide with fear, locked onto his with a questioning stare . . . but somewhere in Brad Elliott's reassuring eyes, she found the answer. She touched his right hand in thanks, nodded, then assumed the proper ejection position in her seat and fired her ejection-seat catapult.

"Finally, I get some peace and quiet around here," Brad Elliott said half aloud.

He didn't need an attack computer or even a compass to do what he needed to do now. Off in the distance, he could see flashes of light from another heavy barrage of antiaircraft fire—it was coming from the last Dong Feng-5 intercontinental nuclear ballistic missile site, the one that hadn't yet been destroyed. He steered his beautiful creation, his EB-52 Megafortress, right at the tracers.

The fire was still burning brightly on the right wing; he had no in-struments, no weapons, no jammers or countermeasures. But the Megafortress was still flying. In Brad Elliott's mind, it would always be still flying.

Ten minutes and two fighter attacks later, it was still flying. It was still flying, as fast and as deadly as the day, more than ten years ago, he'd rolled onto his first bomb run over Dreamland in the Nevada desert, when he nosed the giant bird over and down, aiming it directly for the door of the last Chinese DF-5 ICBM missile silo. The Megafortress did not protest, did not try to fly out of the crash dive, did not give any ground proxim-ity warning. It was as if it knew that this is what it was supposed to do, what was finally expected of it.

. . . . "Patrick! Wendy!"

"Here!" Patrick shouted. Nancy Cheshire limped over to the voice, and soon found Patrick and Wendy McLanahan. Thankfully, both appeared unhurt. "You okay, Nance?" Patrick asked.

"I think I broke my damned ankle," Cheshire replied. "Wendy? You okay?"

"I'm fine," she replied. Patrick had her lying flat on her back, using their parachutes as a sleeping bag to keep her comfortable. They both had plastic hip flasks of water out and were sipping from them. "My back's sore, but I'm okay." She touched her belly. "I think we're all fine."

"Did you find Brad?" Patrick asked Cheshire. No reply. "Nance? Did Brad make it out?"

As if in reply, they all looked to the west as a bright flash of light and a huge column of fire rose into the night sky. It was not a nuclear mushroom cloud, but the geyser of fire and the billowing cloud of smoke reflecting the flames of the exploding DF-5 ICBM sure resembled one. "My God!" Wendy exclaimed. "That's where the DF-5 is, isn't it? Is Terrill Samson still flying bombers out here? How did . . . ?"

"Brad," Patrick breathed. He looked from the exploding DF-5 to Nancy Cheshire. "He didn't make it out, did he?"

"He made it," Cheshire replied with a smile. "He made it . . . exactly where he wanted to go."

"In general, in battle one
endures through strength and
gains victory through spirit
. . . When the heart's
foundation is solid, a new
surge of *ch'i* will
bring victory."
—from *The Methods of
the Ssu-Ma,*
Fourth century B.C.
Chinese military text

EPILOGUE

BRUNEI INTERNATIONAL AIRPORT, BANDAR SERI
BEGAWAN, THE SULTANATE OF BRUNEI
TUESDAY, 1 JULY 1997, 1200 HOURS LOCAL
(MONDAY, 30 JUNE, 2300 HOURS ET)

Oddly enough, the jets that pulled off to an isolated part of Brunei International Airport and maneuvered beside each other nose-to-tail were both Gulfstream IV long-range business jets—but one was in the red and white livery of the Chinese Civil Aeronautical Administration, and the other was in the plain white with blue trim of the United States Air Force. Guards of the Sultan of Brunei's Gurkha Reserve Unit, the elite paramilitary palace guard, ringed the parking ramp, while armored personnel carriers and heavily armed Humvees roamed the area beyond.

The inner guards seemed oblivious to the noise of the Chinese Gulfstream as it pulled into its assigned parking spot. It did not shut down its engines. A set of stairs had been rolled out and placed near the exit door on the port side of the Chinese Gulfstream; the USAF Gulfstream had used an integral airstair that extended from the plane itself, and the exit door was already open and ready. Two lines of GRU commandos quickly formed between both sets of stairs, and one guard carrying an infantry rifle was stationed at the top of the stairs of each plane.

The door of the Chinese Gulfstream opened, and a lone man wearing a plain gray tunic appeared and stepped down the stairs. At the same time, a lone individual in a plain dark business suit walked down the USAF Gulfstream's airstair. They walked across the ramp between the two lines of armed GRU commandos and met in the center of the tarmac. They regarded each other for a moment; then the American made a slight, polite bow. The Chinese man smiled, made an even slighter nod, then extended a hand. The American shook it hesitantly. No words were exchanged. Both men turned, walked a few paces away, turned sideways in front of the GRU commandos, then looked toward their respective aircraft.

At that, several individuals began emerging from both the USAF and CAA jets and stepped down the airstairs. Ten men wearing blue and white polyester jogging suits and white running shoes emerged from the USAF jet; two women and one man, wearing white baggy peasant's outfits and sandals, stepped off the Chinese jet. In single file, the two columns of individuals walked across the tarmac between the GRU commandos. The men who came off the USAF jet walked more and more quickly until they were virtually running up the airstairs into the Chinese jet, but the American man and two women prisoners strode deliberately, proudly, toward the USAF plane.

All except the last man of each side. As if by some unspoken signal, the two men slowed, then paused as they passed each other. The Chinese man straightened his shoulders, then bowed to the other prisoner and said in English, "Good fortune to you, Colonel Patrick Shane McLanahan. Happy Reunification Day."

"Same to you, Admiral Sun Ji Guoming," Patrick McLanahan said. They bowed to each other again. McLanahan glared at Chinese Minister of Defense Chi Haotian, gave him a smile, then said in a loud voice, "Happy Reunification Day, Minister Chi." Chi Haotian's face was an expressionless, stony mask as he turned and headed quickly back to his waiting aircraft.

"Welcome home, Colonel McLanahan," the American in the dark business suit, Secretary of Defense Arthur Chastain, said. He clasped McLanahan on the shoulder and steered him toward the waiting Gulfstream.

"Whatever," McLanahan said tonelessly as he boarded the Air Force C-20H Gulfstream for the long ride home. Gunnery Sergeant Chris Wohl, on guard at the top of the airstairs with an M-16 rifle with a M-206 grenade launcher attached, gave Patrick a "way to go" smile and nod as they passed one another. McLanahan did not return the sentiment.

Only when the wheels were up and they were heading east on their way back to the United States did Patrick McLanahan finally shed the tears of joy, and tears of sorrow, that had been welling up in him for the past ten years.

• • • • "Admiral Sun Ji Guoming flew a Sukhoi-27 fighter right onto Kadena Air Base and surrendered to the U.S. Air Force," Secretary of Defense Chastain told him. "He then asked to make a public statement on the international news. He said who he was and said that he would reveal the government of China's entire plan for the destruction and re-capture of Taiwan unless China agreed to a cease-fire and a prisoner ex-change was arranged. Jiang Zemin agreed immediately."

They had done a brief stopover in Hawaii, where the three ex-prisoners were examined by doctors and found medically fit—there was no injury to Wendy and Patrick's child. Now they were somewhere over the southwest United States, almost home.

"Everyone has pretty much backed off after your attack," Chastain explained. "Of course, almost all of China's strategic forces had been knocked out by you and General Samson's bombers—all they had left were a few H-6 bombers and some mobile medium-range missiles, noth-ing that could threaten the United States and virtually nothing that could threaten its neighbors. Even North and South Korea seemed to have backed away from the DMZ, although things there and in the Middle East are still pretty tense." He paused, then added for about the sixth time since leaving the prisoner swap in Brunei, "I'm sorry about General El-liott. He was a genuine American hero."

Patrick wasn't thinking about where they were headed—he assumed to a federal prison somewhere—but he was shocked when the C-20H zoomed into a desert airfield. Although there were no signs and no visi-ble landmarks on the hazy late-afternoon horizon, Patrick knew exactly where they were: the high desert of south-central Nevada, beside the dry lake turned camouflaged airstrip at Groom Lake, at the secret U.S. Air

Force research base known as the High Technology Aerospace Weapons Center, nicknamed Dreamland.

Well, Patrick thought, he should have known. HAWC was not a military base anymore—it certainly made a good federal prison, especially for suspects who broke the law as badly as they did.

But when the C-20H pulled up to its parking spot next to the old base operations building, he noticed that the buildings had a fresh coat of paint on them, there was a new mobile control tower deployed on the dry lake bed, and the guards waiting on the tarmac were not waiting to take him into custody—they were guarding Marine One and Marine Two, the military VIP transport helicopters belonging to the President of the United States.

President Kevin Martindale was waiting for Patrick, Wendy, and Nancy Cheshire as they stepped off the airstair onto the carpet covering the hot concrete parking ramp at Dreamland. "Welcome home, Patrick, welcome home," the President said warmly. They were all there: National Security Advisor Philip Freeman, Air Force chief of staff General Victor Hayes, Air Combat Command commander Steve Shaw, and Eighth Air Force commander Terrill Samson. With them were Dave Luger, Jon Masters, Hal Briggs, Chris Wohl, and Paul White. They all went inside the new base operations building to escape the still-broiling heat of Nevada's desert summer sun.

"Patrick, you've done a great service to me and to the nation, and I just wanted to greet you and tell you myself," the President said. "You and your fellow crew members have almost single-handedly averted a world war by your heroic actions."

"Sorry, but I don't feel very heroic, sir," Patrick said.

"Because of General Elliott. I'm sorry for your loss, Patrick," the President said solemnly. "Brad Elliott was one helluva warrior. He was stubborn, determined, and headstrong—and he was one of the best I've ever met. He'd probably hate what I'm about to do—and I feel damn good thinking about him cursing my name for all eternity." The President steered Patrick toward a large covered sign on the wall, and he pulled it off himself. The sign read: WELCOME TO ELLIOTT AIR FORCE BASE, GROOM LAKE, NEVADA, HOME OF THE HIGH TECHNOLOGY AEROSPACE WEAPONS CENTER (USAF OPERATIONAL TEST AND EVALUATION CENTER DET. 1).

"Elliott Air Force Base?" Patrick exclaimed. "But . . . how? I thought . . ."

"Yeah, my predecessor closed down HAWC—I just opened it back up again," the President said. "Meet HAWC's first new commander—Lieutenant General Terrill Samson. We're still closing down Eighth Air Force, but Terrill has the same fire in his belly that you and Brad Elliott have, so he's the new boss here—and heaven help us. I have a feeling that the ghost of Brad Elliott will be walking this place for many years to come."

The President withdrew something from a pocket. "I've got to get going—I'm going to spend a weekend of relaxation in Las Vegas before going back to Washington to continue the fight against Senator Finegold and her attack dogs. But I have one last request for you first before I go."

The President of the United States shook Patrick's hand, pressing something into his palm. "Let me know soonest, okay? Be good, and congratulations on your new baby. A boy, I believe, am I right?" He gave Wendy and Nancy Cheshire a kiss, turned, and departed, followed by his national security advisors. The roar of the engines on the Marine transport helicopters could be heard seconds later.

Patrick opened his hand and found a pair of silver stars nestled in his palm.

"I need a director of operations here at HAWC, Patrick," Terrill Samson said proudly. "I could think of no one else suited for the job but you. You get brigadier-general's stars and a command of your own, and you get to work with the hottest jets and the hottest weapons coming off the drawing boards. Dave Luger—*Lieutenant Colonel* Dave Luger, I should add—has agreed to sign on as a senior engineer and senior project officer here. What do you say?"

Wendy slipped her arm around Patrick's waist and hugged him close. He looked into her shining, proud eyes, but could not find an answer to the question he was silently asking—only the continued promise of love and support for whatever he chose to do.

Patrick's eyes then unconsciously searched out and found Jon Masters. The young scientist and businessman-of-sorts was drinking his ever-present squeeze bottle of Pepsi. He gave him a wink and a smile.

"Patrick?" General Samson urged him. "What do you say? Be my second in command. In three years, this will be your base, your command."

Patrick McLanahan caught a glimpse of Hal Briggs. The young commando motioned outside, where his Humvee was waiting.

"I'll let you know, sir," Patrick said with a broad smile. "I'll let you know." He took Wendy by the hand, led her out into the warm Nevada evening into the waiting Humvee, and they drove toward the crimson sunset—out into the future.